BOOK ONE OF THE

NOSS🐺SAGA

WOLF OF WITHERVALE

JOAQUÍN BALDWIN

Library of Congress Control Number: 2023903512
ISBN: 978-1-961076-00-6 (e-book)
ISBN: 978-1-961076-01-3 (paperback)
ISBN: 978-1-961076-02-0 (hardcover)

First Edition, 2023.
NS1.H1

PAPERBEAR

To the queer adventurers,
who venture to wonder
and wander beyond.

Unthawing Ocean
Elanubril
Khaar Du Tribes
Teslurkath
Fjordsulf
Serac Slopes
Fjordlands
Koroberg
Isdinnklad Sea
Needlecove
Zovaria
Moordusk
Zovarian Union
Nebush
Old Karst
New Karst
Klemes
Varanus
Free Tribelands
Quiescent Ocean
Allathanathar
Dunewaak
Unclaimed Territories
Yenwu
Yenmai
Yenwu State
Esduss Sea
Azurean
Kingdom of Bauram
Kizad
Gulf of Erjilm
Taring
Ashen
Republic of Lerev
Nisos
Normouth
Capricious
NOSS
Jerjan Continent

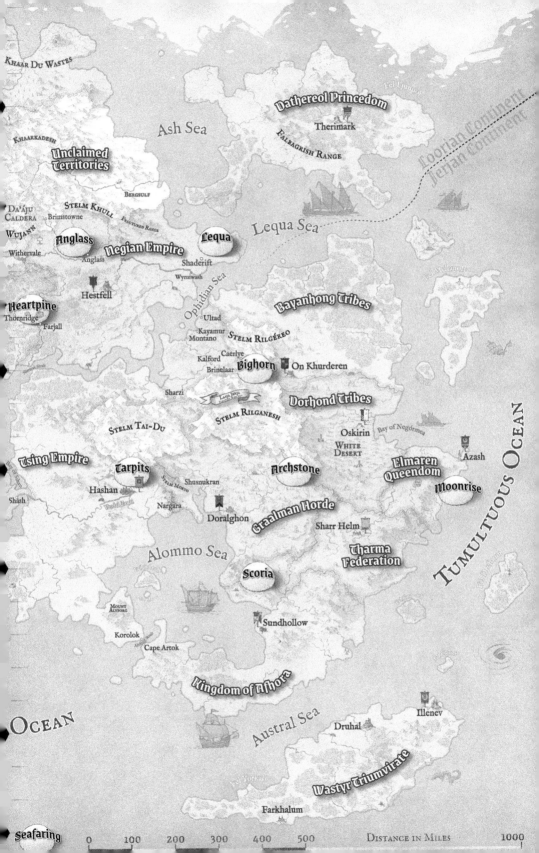

TABLE OF CONTENTS

Author's Note

Hello reader, Joaquín here. Before you get started, I have a short trigger warning and a few recommendations.

Content warning

This is an adult fantasy series that depicts explicit sex (oftentimes of unconventional natures, a few times of dubious consent), animal cruelty, drug use, violence and war, parental abuse, slavery, racism, suicide, and genocide. With that said, I do not mean to scare anyone away—this is not a grimdark fantasy, yet mature themes are present through all six books.

Maps and illustrations

To properly read all the detail on the maps, I recommend you see them at full resolution and in color. You don't need to read with a map by your side, but seeing the complexity of the world and the promise of the greater story to come will enhance your experience, I guarantee it. Visit the link below to find all the maps, illustrations, and other goodies.

Pronunciations & glossary

I developed an entire language called *Miscamish* for the world of Noss, phonetics and all. You don't need to know it, but if you learn the pronunciations, it'll help you figure out the sounds of this world. There is a pronunciation guide in the appendices at the end of this book (also on the link below), as well as a glossary, list of characters, locations, and more. Fear not, I made sure to have no spoilers there.

Supplemental Materials

Follow this link to access all the Supplemental Materials, including the color illustrations, maps, glossaries, lists of characters, locations, and more.

JoaquinBaldwin.com/book1/extras

WOLF OF WITHERVALE

WOUNDED FOX

The gray fox fled through the forest, her paws quiet as an owl's shadow, her whiskers bending like grasses fighting a storm. She glided beneath ferns and wriggled her tired body into a hollow log.

Thwump. Thwump. Thwack! Three arrows narrowly missed their target, lodging themselves into the dirt and the splintered wood.

The fox snaked out and sprinted away. Downhill she sped toward the oak groves, hearing the howl of the foxhounds behind her and the *tchtchtchwick* of the crossbows reloading. The smell of glacier waters from a nearby creek flooded her with determination. With her heart in her throat, she unflinchingly pressed on.

Fwip. Fwip. Thud! Two arrows missed, but the third hit the skin above her shoulder blades, sliced through it, and exited on the opposite side in a spray of blood. Despite the tearing pain, she did not slow.

The smell of iron permeated the air, rendering the cries of the hounds more ecstatic. Unless the fox found a place to hide, she would run out of breath, out of muscle. Out of sense.

Whap! Another arrow scraped by her abdomen, tearing a clean cut on her belly. She cried out a whimpering wail, yet still, she did not falter. She had seen her tribe murdered and enslaved, had cried in despair as she witnessed the light extinguished from her daughter's eyes. Her task was too important for her to fail. She would push through to the very end and protect the ancient artifact.

She felt the energy of the forest around her, like electricity tingling her gray, orange, and white fur. Her eyes were heavy with exhaustion, but she could see without seeing. The path ahead was clear to her, as if the connections to every organism in the forest—from the smallest mite to the tallest tree—shared her pain and urged her forward.

Down a loose pebble trail lay a ramshackle old cabin. The gray fox sensed a sympathetic presence in front of it. A boy. She rushed toward him, leaving a red trail behind her.

The hounds howled.

PART ONE
WITHERVALE

CHAPTER ONE

LAGO VAARI

Lago's curly hair was caked with mud, his blue shirt now brown with splattered dirt and blood—but he knew most of the blood wasn't his own, so he kept his proud, cocky smirk. He seemed unfazed that he'd gotten in trouble at school. Again.

Professor Crysta Holt wiped a wet rag on Lago's forearm, revealing tender, pink skin. "Just why in Takh's two names do you need to go so rough on them?" she asked.

Lago flinched, gritting his teeth. "They started it! I was just defending myself. They got what—what they deserved!" he said, a bit too righteously. "If I don't do nothing about it, then I end up in the mud anyway. Might as well have them taste some of it."

Crysta tilted her head in a motherly gesture. With a muddy finger she pushed a strand of auburn hair away from her eyes; it had been let loose again, instead of tied in the customary bun the female scholars wore.

"I know you didn't start it. All I'm saying is that you get a bit too carried away." She deflated in a sigh. "I'll talk to Borris's and Wailen's parents after class, but I won't be able to defend your actions unless you manage *some* level of self-control." She wrapped a gauze around his elbow and pulled the filthy sleeve over it. "I cleaned up what I can, but there's nothing I can do about your muddy rags. Why don't you go home and wash up?"

"But it's not even lunch time yet."

"You are not dragging that mud into the classroom. I'll see you back in class next week." She reached for his oversized leather bag to hand it to him.

Lago abruptly pulled the bag from her hands, not wanting her peeking into his private business. "Thank you, Crysta," he said. Most students called her Professor Holt, but Lago felt he could be a bit more personal with her, at least when his classmates weren't around.

Crysta tweaked the corner of her lips into a forced smile. She was somewhere in her late thirties, and aside from her biting and judging stares, she did not look exactly professorial; the coat over her blouse was of the wrong size and matched neither the color of her skirt nor her chaotically disorganized satchel.

"I'll go clean up," Lago said, "and I promise I'll bring the book back on Moonday, or Khuday at the latest. I'm almost done."

"Take your time with it. And enjoy your weekend." She ruffled Lago's dark curls and pulled back a dirty hand. She wiped the mud on the one clean spot on his blue shirt. "Here, I believe this is yours."

Lago swung the bag over his shoulder, slid off the stone wall, and rushed from the school grounds, waving goodbye without looking back.

Lago had lived all of his twelve years in the Withervale Mesa, a quaint city built on a sandstone outcrop that extended northward from the granitic Stelm Ca'éli, stretching in an uphill slant like the prow of a proud ship. He thought the Withervale Mesa looked much better than Withervale proper, not only because of the impressive formation of the mesa itself, but because the city was built over the foundations of a civilization from before the Downfall. The treacherous bridges, gloomy passageways, and rune-carved archways reeked of ghost stories and the promise of ancient treasures. The old treasures were all gone by now, but that couldn't stop a child's imagination.

Lago's school was on the East Flank, hundreds of feet below the main grounds of the mesa. He took the stairs carved directly into the sandstone prominence, running his curious fingertips over the textured sediments and feeling them change, layer by layer, exploring the time compressed within them as if flipping through the pages of a most ancient book. His hands were the same color as the sandstone after a light Summer rain.

To avoid the stomping traffic of muskoxen, caribou, and bison on Runestone Lane, Lago balanced himself on a drainage canal, then climbed to a stone bridge that gave him a bird's-eye view of the East Flank and a clear line of sight to the distant Anglass Dome, stretching greener and taller than any of the mountains around him. Lago hopped onto a retaining wall, tiptoeing around planters, scaring off somnolent doves and prowling cats.

"Hey Lago!" a merchant yelled, driving his cart toward the marketplace. "Could you ask Theo to stop by the tent in the morrow? Got all them silks he asked for months ago!"

"I'll let Dad know. Thanks, Lorr Tuam," Lago politely replied, then hurried home.

He knew he would get in deep trouble—maybe even get a fresh beating—if his father found him in such filthy clothes. Luckily, it was only midmorning, so he had time to wash his garments, hang them to dry, and maybe find a way to cover up a few of his bruises before his father returned. Lago preferred to avoid any sort of confrontation with his volatile father, so he did what any kid in his place would do and lied—or hid the truth—often.

He turned the corner of Ashlar Street and saw a caribou-pulled cart tied to the old, crooked maple in front of his rust-colored home. *He's home early,* he thought, as he creeped to the sandstone wall. *He must've gotten a new delivery.* He carefully peeked through the open window.

Arr rooff, rrowff! Bear said.

Bear was Lago's mostly mutt, barely shepherd dog. The three-month-old pup popped his head up to the window, sensing Lago was home. Bear was energetic and as easily excitable as, well, a pup. His coat was brown, with uneven white splotches that gave his fur a textured, coarse look, like fresh graupel on a muddy road. Lago had never seen a real bear. He heard they only lived in the Stelm Wujann, or farther in the northern wastes, but he knew they were sizable and ferocious. He hoped *his* Bear would grow up to be that way.

"Bear, down!" came the voice of Theo Vaari, Lago's father.

Bear tried to claw his way out, but Theo snatched him by the tail, dragged him in, and slammed the shutters. Lago flattened to the wall, his heart kicking like a trapped animal. When the next wagon passed by, he snuck behind it, escaping without being seen.

Well, at least it's still early, he thought. He knew exactly where he could go to clean himself and his clothes: he would go to his Diamond Cave. It was a bit of a hike to his secret hideout, but Lago could be back by eventide and pretend he had just returned from a long day at school—his father would be none the wiser.

As he waited for his chance to cross Runestone Lane, Lago looked north, toward the highest point of the mesa, where the octagonal tower of the Mesa Observatory rose. This was where Crysta worked after school every day, often late into the night.

"Ye crossing or what?!" a gaunt-faced woman squawked, bumping Lago's shoulder. He had been lost in thought and was holding up traffic. He hastened across.

He reached the edge of the mesa and began his descent, hopping down three steps at a time. He peered toward the western face of the mesa: the steep cliffside looked as if it had been slashed by a giant sword. The bottom strata had formed from compressed volcanic ash, carved by wind and rain into hundreds of pockets over millions of years. This neighborhood was known as the Hollows, where miners made their crude homes inside any large-enough holes, accessing them by precarious rope ladders and eroded sandstone platforms.

Trails of black soot smeared upward from the holes, built up from centuries of cooking and heating smoke. The whole formation looked like the hives of an alien wasp with an exquisitely perturbed sense of geometry. Lago thought it looked magical, particularly at night, when the holes glowed like a fiery constellation. In one of these holes lived Lago's best friend, Alaia. He considered stopping by, but it was only Onguday, so she would be working at the mines.

Lago continued through the shantytown west of the mesa, where the coal mines were located, spilling mounds of tailings that dirtied up Ore Creek. He couldn't wash his clothes in those ochre-colored waters; he was just passing by. He sauntered farther west beyond the coal mines, hopped over the perimeter fence, and strolled toward the mountain footpath.

The loose pebble trail ascended toward the oak groves, a mountain path that was always picturesque, no matter the season. It was mid-Autumn, only the fifth day of the month of Fireleaf, yet the oak forest was already littered with acorns, and the leaves were fully changing colors. Though it was a bit chilly out, the biting sun burst through the orange leaves and warmed up the heart and soul just enough, with a promise of a deeper Autumn to come.

Lago reached a field of scattered remains of ancient cabins, most of them nothing more than a few slabs of wood marooned on flimsy foundations. This was the site of a logging town, abandoned generations before Lago was born, where skeletons of dilapidated buildings protected themselves from mischievous children by flashing their splinters and rusty nails.

A bit off the pebble path, past a heavily flowing glacial creek, were a few more derelict shacks. Lago skipped on the usual rocks to cross the clear stream and approached the remains of a forsaken cabin hiding under an old oak tree. The structure had no roof other than the browning oak leaves, a scant memory of window frames, and a door that served no purpose other than to indicate where the entrance used to be, given that the walls on either side of it had toppled down long ago. Only the back wall of the shack was still mostly intact, supported by an enormous boulder.

This was where, two years ago, Lago and Alaia found their Diamond Cave.

Chapter Two

The Diamond Cave

Two years earlier…

"This one's not so splintery," Alaia said, dragging a tree stump into their 'living quarters,' to serve as a table, or chair, or whatever it needed to be. They both liked the old shack way up by the creek, because the oak's canopy gave it a semblance of a roof, and the nearby boulders an air of privacy.

They built their fortress there, hanging torn rags as banners of their imagined coats of arms, decorating the broken foundations with multi-colored pebbles rescued from the creek, painting the still-standing walls with mud, and hanging glittering shards of glass from the oak's branches.

"There's a heavy one by the creek," Alaia said, dropping her stump with a thump. "Care to help me with it, Gwoli?" *Gwoli* was the word for *younger brother* in Alaia's Oldrin tongue. She was two years older than Lago, and two fingerbreadths taller, and liked to tease him a bit.

The Oldrin were a race from the far east of the Jerjan Continent, in lands where the White Desert flowed into the shores of the Tumultuous Ocean. They had the unfortunate trait of growing bony protuberances on their bodies, which they called *spurs*. Sometimes spurs grew out of their elbows, sometimes their knuckle bones poked outward, or they would sprout horn-like bumps on their skulls, knees, ankles, or shoulders. It was just the way they were, but other races felt uncomfortable with their uniqueness, thinking the spurs might be contagious, cursed, or worse.

Alaia had two spurs. The first was a ridge of thirteen bones protruding from her spine, starting between her shoulder blades and extending to the small of her back; she called them her 'thirteen sisters.' The second was a rounded, horn-like spur only two fingerbreadths high, poking out from the right side of her forehead, just below her hairline; she called that one her 'nub.' Most Oldrin did everything possible to hide their external bones, and although Alaia kept the ridge at her back beneath her overalls, the spur on her head she displayed in a way that made it unquestionably beautiful: she would braid her hair in complex patterns radiating from it, adorning her braids with flecks of mica or iridescent feathers, as if an explosion of sparkles was spreading from her little nub.

Unlike the bronze and olive complexions of most Oldrin who worked at the coal mines, Alaia's skin was gorgeously dark, often darkened even more after she was done with her shifts. Nearly all the mine workers were Oldrin, who started to work as soon as they were old enough to lift a lamp, a pick, or carry bundles of coal on their backs. They weren't exactly slaves in the Zovarian Union, but with how underpaid and overworked they were, they might as well have been.

Alaia had arrived with a refugee caravan when she was only two years old. Not remembering her parents nor homeland, all she knew was the life at the mines and the adventures of being a kid growing in freedom and poverty. She was optimistic, opportunistic, and could make the best out of any situation.

She put her working gloves back on, fixed the straps on her miner's overalls and said, "Grab it from that branch, fewer splinters." Together, they lifted the bulky log. "From your legs! Don't lift from your back, you nubhead!" she corrected Lago, using the insult he had once used on her, one she was still jokingly mad about.

Lago fixed his posture and picked up his end of the log. It was an exhausting struggle uphill, but they managed to carry the chunk of wood into their fortress.

"Where do we put it?" he asked.

"On top of the stump, like a pedestal?" she suggested, leading the way. She directed her side of the log down and helped Lago push his end up until the log was vertical. "Outstanding construction skills! We'll be done building this palace before the mists of Umbra arrive." And with that said, the precariously balanced log tipped over, smashing loudly against the back wall of the shack.

A square portion of the wall suddenly swung inward, taunting with an intriguing creak. The wooden panel was mounted on hidden hinges, as if there was a shutter leading right into the face of the granitic boulder.

"Why would they put a window against a rock?" Lago asked. He reached forward and pulled at the panel. The old hinges protested, but the panel swung open in full.

Carved into the face of the rock was a perfectly round tunnel, just wide enough for a child to crawl in on their knees, or for an adult to squeeze in on their belly. Four feet into the tunnel was a round, stained cedar door.

"Gwoli, what is that...?" Alaia muttered nearly soundlessly.

"It's like a secret tunnel."

"Maybe forest sprites live there."

"Or a giant snake."

"How would a snake turn a doorknob?"

"Dunno. Go in and ask your sprites."

"Hey, you found it, you go in first," she said, pushing Lago toward the hole.

"You let the log drop—"

"It fell on your side, I was—"

"—don't push—"

Alaia pushed harder and Lago practically fell into the hole.

"Okay, fine, give me a hand then." He brushed aside a dusty spiderweb and climbed in, inching forward on his knees until he reached the corroded, copper doorknob; it was round, cold as ice, and had a sharp, electric smell. He turned it carefully, feeling the teal patina flake off beneath his fingertips. He was afraid the doorknob would break, but with a satisfying click the door unlocked, and inward it squeaked open.

"It's unlocked!" he said.

A musky scent wafted out, ancient, dry, forgotten.

"What's in there?" Alaia asked, unable to contain her curiosity any longer.

Lago squinted as he let his eyes adjust. "Hold on," he said, "I think I see the floor. Stay put, I'll go in." That was harder to do than he had expected, going head first. He lowered his arms until they touched the sandy ground, then pulled his legs through like a frog, then stood proudly.

"Shit!" he cried, scraping his head on the low ceiling.

"What is it?"

"Bumped my head, all fine."

The cave suddenly darkened. Alaia was crawling in, blocking the scarce light. She dropped in a bit too hastily and toppled in a clumsy roll. She stood fast to compensate, also hitting her head in the process. "Shit!" she blurted, but she was too intrigued to be embarrassed. "It's really cold in here," she observed.

It was more than cold, it was frigid.

Lago wrapped his arms around himself and peered above him. "Look at the ceiling. It curves. Maybe it's like one of the homes at the Hollows?"

Their eyes were adjusting, but they still couldn't see much. At this time in the afternoon, Sunnokh's rays weren't falling directly on their fortress, so they found themselves in shadow.

"Get your lamp," Lago urged Alaia.

She wormed out like a graceless ferret, then came creeping back in with a metal lamp in front of her—part of her everyday mining tools. Lago took it and lifted it up to reveal the most wonderful sight his eyes had ever seen.

We found the night sky trapped inside a rock, he thought. He was staring up at a dome of shining stars, at sparkling constellations just beyond the reach of his hands. The stars were simple calcium-rich crystals built up over the ages. They wouldn't look like anything more than grains of light-colored sand in normal circumstances, but when Lago held the lamp exactly in front of him, the crystals reflected the light in a shimmering, nearly supernatural sparkle. As long as he held the lamp in the same relative position to his head, the reflective light effect followed.

"Are you alright?" Alaia whispered. "You look more empty-headed than usual."

"Can't you see this?" he replied in a nearly reverential tone.

"It's nice but I—" and then the light angled just right for her to catch the effect. "Whoa, it all lit up!"

"It's like diamonds! We found a diamond cave!" Lago exulted.

The cave wasn't made of diamonds, but that didn't matter. It was an ancient dwelling, carved by a civilization from before the Downfall. Thousands of years later, the dwelling was found by the people who built the now defunct logging town, who repurposed the dome-shaped space into a cellar. Debris left by the previous owners littered the ground: planks of wood that must've been a shelf in a previous life, iron utensils rusted beyond recognition, thick shards of shattered glass, and one half-buried jar stuffed with what at some point might've passed for pickled root vegetables, but by now was closer to an amniotic fluid gestating an ominous specimen.

"It looks like a dead baby," Lago pointed out, letting the lamplight shine through the turbid liquid. "We should make a bread roll with it and give it to Borris. He'll eat anything."

"What do you think they did here?" Alaia asked, dabbing a finger at the salty crystals on the ceiling, then tasting them.

"It's like a cellar? I think?" Lago guessed. "To keep food fresh. Must be the water from the creek that keeps it so cold."

"Well, it's *our* cellar now," Alaia said, waving her arms in an inelegant spin. "And it sure could use some decorating."

Every weekend, the two of them brought in rocks, bottles, and whatever they could find to embellish their secret hideout. Lago took the left side, where he built a miniature fort with sandstone bricks and slabs of wood. He littered the ground with protective pinecones and painted his name on the wall in bold, white letters: *Lago Vaari*.

Alaia pitched a tent with a moth-eaten blanket suspended in an armature of pine branches and decorated her side with the bones of squirrels, foxes, and hares she'd found drying around the forest. The two of them made up games, shared the town's gossip, and even lit a bonfire once, though the smoke got so dense that they never tried that again.

It was perfection. In their Diamond Cave, they could be as loud and obnoxious as any kid ever dreamed of being, alone in their private cosmos.

CHAPTER THREE

SONTAI AND THE MASK

Those were the best of times, Lago reminisced. Two years seemed like ages ago, and who could blame him? Two years amounted to a substantial portion of his life.

He was panting like a dog when he arrived at the shack. He had come alone this time, but that was alright; he sometimes came on his own when Alaia was busy, and he had some work to do anyway. He walked around the freestanding door next to no walls and hopped across a toppled beam toward the back of the cabin. After peeking around distrustfully in case spies lurked nearby, he swung open the secret panel, then crawled in, pushing his leather bag in front of him.

The bag dropped with a muffled thud. Lago didn't go inside. Instead, he crawled out again and ambled toward the creek, where he took his muddied clothes off.

During Summer, Lago and Alaia would bathe in this creek. Despite being very self-conscious of his naked body, Lago did not feel uncomfortable being naked around Alaia; they had long ago satisfied their curiosities about anatomical differences, as children do, and would often spend time together unclothed inside their Diamond Cave, pretending to be barbaric cave dwellers.

Lago washed his clothes as well as he could, plopped them wet and flat over a sunlit boulder radiating warmth, then approached the crystal-clear pool. He loved this time of year, when the fallen leaves drew fiery spirals in the round pond. Their hypnotic circling made him so relaxed—he could watch them for hours.

After sinking his brown feet into the pool, he decided this would be the quickest possible bath: the glacial meltwater was way too cold, and even the biting light of Sunnokh would not be enough to fight the mid-Autumn breeze. He washed in haste, taking special care of his muddy curls, then shook himself dry as he imagined Bear would have. He sprawled on a hot rock, butt cheeks up and spread to let the breeze dry all his crevices. Once dry, he pissed downstream, shook it off, then headed naked into the Diamond Cave.

He sat his fully warmed ass on a hole-riddled bucket, then pulled his school lunch from his leather bag: a pear and a rice patty wrapped in morseleaf. The boy devoured it all eagerly—the fight at school, the hike, the cold water had all left him ravenous. After tucking the trash away, he pulled out a leather pouch. He loosened the drawstrings and removed a delicate wooden box that when opened revealed a series of square compartments with colorful, dried pastes in them. He scraped off a bit of paste—the blue one, his favorite—and in an empty compartment mixed it with a few drops of a sharp-smelling solvent he dripped from a tiny bottle. With a minute brush he stirred the solution and soon had just the right amount of fingernail lacquer ready to be applied. This was what had gotten him beaten up earlier at school: his classmates had peeked in his bag, found his box of fingernail lacquers, and smelled easy prey.

"You are all just jealous," he half-thought, half-muttered. "You are the sissy, Borris. I bet your boyfriend Wailen likes to kiss your fat titties."

Lago didn't know why he liked to paint his nails; he just did. He looked prettier that way, and it was nobody's business anyhow. He had gotten in big trouble the first time he did it: when his father saw his hands, he gave Lago quite a beating. Nowadays, he only painted his nails when in total privacy.

Before the blue lacquer dried up, Lago crushed and sprinkled tiny flecks of mica over his nails, which stuck like constellations of gold. Alaia had taught him how to do that.

He blew on his nails, waiting for the sparkling lacquer to dry.

He was getting cold, sitting naked in the gloomy cellar. The Diamond Cave always sucked the heat straight out of his marrow. He crawled back out, peeled his wonderfully warm clothes off the sunny boulder, and got dressed. As he walked back to the shack, he heard a distant howling.

Wolves? he thought, then turned his head to listen more intently. *No, those are hounds.*

He stood by the shack's freestanding door, looking up the pebble path in the direction of the howls, and there he saw the strangest of things: a gray fox was running directly toward him.

Weird kind of fox for these mountains, he thought. *Is that blood?*

The gray fox halted a mere five feet in front of him, dripping red over the pebbles that adorned the shack's perimeter. The fox checked behind her, shaking in fear and exhaustion, then looked up at Lago, as if she knew he understood her peril.

"Do you need help?" Lago said out loud, surprised that he didn't find it odd to be talking to a wild animal.

The fox trembled, whimpered, and bled from her shoulder blades and belly. Lago felt pity for her.

The howling of the hounds sounded closer.

"Over here, I'll hide you, quickly!" he cried out and hurried to the secret doorway. As if the fox could understand his words, she followed and jumped in, leaving drips of blood on her way over. Lago hastily closed the hinged panel over the hole, then stumbled back to the front of the shack. *Shit, there's blood on the pebbles,* he realized. Without thinking too much about it, he grabbed all the tainted pebbles and hurled them toward the creek. Some fell in, some splashed blood around the shore. Lago's heart was about to beat out of his chest. He wasn't sure why this moment was important, but he felt an urge to follow through with his instincts.

The pack of foxhounds had just turned around the path, coming directly toward him. Five soldiers held their leashes while also holding crossbows and recurve bows. A tall woman with long, silver-blonde hair led the group; her left temple was shaved and tattooed with a ranking insignia—evidence of previous honors and victories.

Those are marking from the Negian Empire, Lago thought. Since he was very young, he had been taught not to trust Negians, who were enemies of the Zovarian Union.

"Over there!" he blurted out. "The fox ran toward the creek!"

The soldiers turned in the direction Lago pointed to without questioning him nor slowing. At the creek, the hounds easily picked up the scent of the bloodied pebbles. Their blonde leader signaled to spread out: three followed the creek downstream, while the rest crossed it in search of a trail.

Once the soldiers were out of sight, Lago took a deep breath and bolted toward the Diamond Cave. He crawled in, and as his eyes adjusted to the darkness, what he saw was not a gray fox, but a much larger form slowly becoming solid to his eyes.

On the cold ground was a pool of blood, and on it lay a wrinkled old woman. The back of her neck was dripping; her hand clutched her red belly. She seemed to be wearing a skin-tight laced dress that covered her body with black, geometric patterns.

"How did you get—" Lago started, then stopped, confused. "Where is th-the fox? Where did—"

The old woman pushed herself up to her knees while protectively holding something to her chest. With crazed, desperate eyes, she wailed, "*Jienn ëath elmath khe Silv, baalith khelefat ampalv! Baakiag! Baak... ia... g...*"

"I-I don't understand... I'll go get help, I'll—"

"*Grest!* No! Stay!" she gasped. "*Miscamish*, speak little Common..." She struggled to find the words, speaking them in a raspy, gurgling-wet voice. "Please, not let find. *Agnargsilv*... Please, keep safe."

"I w-won't let them find you. But you need help, you are *bleeding*. I... I need to—"

"Safe!" she snapped, red spittle dangling from her mouth. She inched closer, dragging her knees over her coagulating blood. Lago saw now that she wasn't wearing a lace dress but was completely naked: her terracotta-colored skin was covered in tattoos. She reached toward Lago and pressed a large, black object to his chest. "*Agnargsilv, ampalv,* keep safe."

"What is it?" he inquired. Whatever she was handing to him was too dark to see in the void of the cave.

"Agnargsilv..." was her simple reply.

"I... I'm Lago. Where did the fox... Was it... What's your name?"

"Sontai," she replied, with a hand over her sagging, inked breasts. "Agnargsilv, you take. Dangerous, you hide, keep safe. *Walmalmem*. Only give for my grandson, *please*. Secret."

"Where is your grandson? I can take you to—"

"Bonmei, son of daughter. Bonmei. Please, promise. Agnargsilv safe, give only for Bonmei. Secret to others." She smiled at him with bloodied teeth and gums. Lago could tell she was using all her strength to hide the pain, to hold that lamentable, pleading grin.

"I promise, I'll keep it safe. I'll give it to your grandson, Bonmei."

"*Voss unnith jienn*, Lago, *unnith*. Grateful. Grateful..." And then her eyes went white with fear. "Safe, hide!" she whimpered, as the howling of the hounds echoed nearby.

"Sontai, stay here. Stay, I'll be back." He handed the dark object back to her.

"Promise!" she lamented.

"Yes, I promise! Stay quiet, please!" He hurried out, closing the round door first and the wooden panel after. He peeked around the edge of the cabin and saw all the hounds and soldiers gathered by the creek again. Their blonde leader calmly approached, scanning the road and even up the trees.

Lago was composing himself when he noticed one grave mistake: there was a trail of blood over the splintered boards of the cabin. He tried to wipe the blood off but only managed to smear his right hand in it. He hastily flipped some loose planks over the smears, then stood firmly by the front of the shack.

The soldier approached confidently, with a powerful, dominant stride. She wore a thin suit of the finest leather, which made not the slightest noise. Hanging at her back was a quiver along with a beautiful crossbow of red sandalwood, finely inlaid with bone and copper.

She stopped uncomfortably close to Lago, measuring him. Her eyes were the color of brushed steel. "Boy, what is your name?"

"Lago. I am-I'm Lago," Lago stammered, concealing his blood-covered fingertips behind his back.

"Lago, our trail is running cold. I need you to tell me exactly what you saw. Do not skip any details. Think hard and remember clearly."

"Yes, Lurr." Lago swallowed the lump in his throat and nervously spouted, "She was a gray fox, we don't have gray foxes on this side of the Pilgrim Sierras, so my guess is that she was from the south? Cream paws, gray back, black stripe on the tail. She had a cut on the back, like, like around her neck or shoulders, and a—and another on the belly. Seemed badly hurt. Went over that way"— he pointed with his chin—"where your dogs are sniffing about. She tried to jump the creek but fell in."

"She?" the woman inquired.

"You can tell the girls from the boys by their size," Lago quickly replied, digging himself out of the hole.

"Thank you, Lago. That is unfortunate, but it is as I suspected." She squatted down so her cold, gray eyes met Lago's. "Now let me see your hands."

Lago's terror was double: for the blood on his hands, for his lacquered fingernails. "I don't know anything else, Lurr, I—"

"Just show me your hands, please."

Lago kept his bloodied hand behind his back and raised the other one forward, palm up to hide his nails. He felt the woman covering his palm with a strong hand, placing something cold in it, and closing it tight, all without losing eye contact.

"You are very observant, Lago. Thank you for your help," she said, then pulled forward her beautiful crossbow. "When you are older"—she caressed the sinew drawstring—"if you ever find yourself near Hestfell, look for the Arbalisters' Commons. Tell them Fjorna Daro sent you, and mention your own name. I *never* forget a name. You'd make a great recruit, boy. I'll make sure you get proper training. You'd be better off fighting for the Empire."

"Thank you, Lurr Daro, I will."

Fjorna smiled, for the first time; a formidable and tempestuous smile. As she stood, she ruffled Lago's curls—he hated it when people did that, and hoped he managed to hide his displeasure.

The woman checked her surroundings, letting Lago clearly see the ranking tattoos on her shaved, left temple: they were so numerous that they ran all the way behind her ear. They looked important. *She* looked important.

Fjorna turned away and walked toward the creek, waving hand signals. Her squad swiftly reacted and continued their chase downstream.

Once Fjorna was out of sight, Lago finally dared to open his hand; in it was a sixteen-sided silver coin. The face of Emperor Uvon dus Grei was stamped on one side and the laurels of the Negian sigil on the other. *A silver Krujel, from the Negian Empire,* Lago thought. *That's so far. Fjorna must've traveled a long way in pursuit of… Sontai!* he remembered, then rushed back to the cave.

Sontai was dead.

Lago had never seen a dead person before. It was not scary; it was simply gruesome and sad and miserable. The nutty, iron-heavy smell of blood made him nauseated. He swallowed painfully, feeling lightheaded.

He suddenly realized he had closed the door behind him earlier, leaving Sontai in complete darkness. Alone. To die.

He knew there was no helping it, but still tried pushing on the old woman's shoulder, whispering her name. "Sontai… I'm so sorry…" he mumbled, lips quivering. Tears welled up in his eyes. "I wish I could've done more." He saw the dark object Sontai had wanted him to take tucked beneath her. He respectfully moved her arm away and took the object—it was impossibly light, as if made of solid air. He carried it toward the opening to shine light on it.

What he saw was a fox mask, or maybe a wolf mask, or some sort of dog; he wasn't sure. It was heavily stylized, uncannily black, with the most intricate details carved onto it. The mask was beautiful, severe; it exuded power and invoked reverence. It had an ominous streak of blood running over the flattened brow.

Lago looked at Sontai once more, still unable to comprehend how there had been a fox there before, and now all that remained was the corpse of an old woman. "I promised you I'd keep it safe. I will. I'm sorry I couldn't do more for you… I—" he began to weep. "I will give it to your grandson. I don't know h-how I'll find him, but I w-won't let anyone else know about it."

He slumped against the cold wall and openly wept.

It must have been an hour later when Lago pulled himself up. He avoided looking at the dead body, but still caught a glimpse of the black-dried blood on the ground.

He carried the mask to the creek, where he washed off the blood and examined the details up close. It was wet and glistening, pure black with sparkles of sunlight dripping all over it, like the deepest starry sky. He ran his fingers over it, feeling the pointed ears, the piercing eyeholes, the hollow muzzle. The patterns on the mask flowed in the direction the fur would on a real animal but split in knotted motifs to merge back in elaborate, calligraphic filigrees. Even the tiniest surfaces described compounded forms, weaving multiple images into one, changing depending on the angle of the light.

The mask didn't have a headband, so it was not clear how it should attach to someone's face—Lago's head was too small for it either way, but the concavity felt inviting, alluring. He looked through the eyeholes and briefly hesitated; but then, with an inexplicable conviction, he pressed the mask to his face.

What he experienced then was indescribable agony. He felt as if the mask fused onto his face, becoming one with it, and crunched down into his skull and spine, making his brain explode in aching torment. It was as if he could feel the anguish of everything around him: the pain in his heart, the pain of Sontai dying, the pain of the forest, of the earthworms in the soil, of the tiny crayfish hiding under rocks in the creek, of every cell in every orange leaf that fell to be washed into the stream. He felt it all, unable to stop it.

Lago was not aware that he was screaming. He wailed on the ground, scratching his head until the mask detached, and he found himself collapsing out of breath. The experience had been so intense that he wasn't sure if it had lasted a heartbeat, or an entire day. Cheek flat on the dirt, he stared at the mask, and the voids of its eyeholes stared back, unblinking.

Once his body recovered from the shock, Lago stumbled to his feet, carefully picked up the cursed artifact, went back to the cave, and hid the mask inside his bag. "I don't know what to do," he told himself, or Sontai, or the world. *I don't understand what just happened,* he thought, finding tears in his eyes once more.

He looked down at the corpse, truly looked at it, as if trying to convince himself that this was all real. It was still there, undeniably still there.

"I can't leave you like this," he told the dead woman. "I'm sorry. I'll come back tomorrow, but I will keep—I'll keep this thing safe."

He wiped the snot off his nose and slung the bag over his shoulder.

"I'm so sorry," he said once more, then left.

CHAPTER FOUR

THE CONFESSION

Lago's clothes were dirty again, this time from rolling on the ground. It was getting dark, and he had a long walk home. Luckily, Sceres was nearly full, tinting the whole landscape with the purple light of her Amethyst season; he walked in a daze beneath her amaranthine moonlight.

He had promised Sontai he'd keep the mask a secret. He thought about telling his father about it, about her, but even entertaining the idea made guilt bubble up in his chest. *But her family will be looking for her,* he thought as he shuffled his feet homeward. *And she deserves a proper funeral. And how am I to find her grandson all on my own? Someone must know Bonmei, but if I ask around, I might get in trouble.*

He furtively peeked inside his bag. The dark mask stared back at him from within, as if judging his very thoughts. *I can't tell him. Maybe Alaia, but not him.*

The lamps were alight in his house. He sauntered in, trying his best to pretend it was perfectly normal to be back so late. Bear rushed to greet him with yips and slobber.

Lago kept the pup at arm's length. "Shh, down Bear, stay."

His father was fixing garments at the sewing table, facing away from him.

"You are late," Theo Vaari said without turning to face him. "Too much schoolwork?"

Lago had been almost ready to tell him about his earlier fight with his classmates, but he saw a way out in the way his father phrased the question, so he took it. "Yes. Sorry Dad, class ran late."

Theo sat in silence.

Lago began to glide quietly toward his bedroom.

"I saw Professor Holt earlier," Theo said. "She was on her way to the observatory."

Lago froze.

"She asked me how you were doing. Told me those boys beat you up real good again. She seemed to think you were home."

"I went to the creek, I lost track of time—"

"Uh-huh…" Theo resumed working.

Lago could not measure his father this way. *Is he mad? Is he over it already? Why won't he turn around?* He waited for a signal, but none came, so he decided to make his escape.

"Lago," his father said, making him stop again. Theo lowered his tools and straightened his back. He stood, turned his chair around, and sat back down, facing his son. Lago knew this meant one of *those* conversations was about to happen, and much as he wanted to flee, he did not dare.

"Son, you can't keep doing this," Theo said, trying to remain composed but with the strain in his tone betraying him. "And look at you—you didn't even bother to wash yourself."

"I did, I washed my clothes at the creek and—"

"Stop. I didn't raise you to be a liar. You are filthy as an Oldrin. Were you playing at the mines again? I told you not to associate yourself with that spur."

"Don't talk about Alaia like that!" Lago exploded.

"Watch your tone, boy," Theo said, standing up and placing a thick-knuckled fist over the metal buckle of his belt. "Now tell your father the truth, before I force myself to get it out of you. Where were you, if not at the coal mines?"

Lago averted his eyes. Bear jumped at him, uncertain of how to behave with the tension he felt boiling in the room.

"Bear, stop," Lago said, trying to keep the mutt away.

"Where were you?" Theo insisted.

"Stop, Bear, no," Lago said. As he pushed the dog off, he noticed his colorful nails and quickly pulled his hands away, hiding them behind his back.

"What…" Theo croaked. He snatched Lago's arm and pulled it forcefully up, nearly dangling the child from it. He stared at the lacquered nails, for a moment seeming more sad than angry. He let out a seething reprimand. "You… How dare you? You stole these lacquers from your mother's box! I told you to never touch her things."

"No! I mean… They… No… I, I found them at, at…"

"Not one more fucking lie, boy." He pulled harder on the arm, bringing Lago's face closer to his. His reddening eyes glared at Lago's soiled clothes, scraped cheeks, and lying eyes before focusing on his nails. "Is this your little

secret, then? Don't think I didn't know… You've always been a filthy lorrkin."
He began to scrape at the lacquers with his own nails, making Lago squirm.

Lago wriggled as he yelled, "Stop, stop!"

Theo let go, making Lago drop on top of his bag. Bear barked, jumping on Lago while thinking it was all just a game.

"Wash those paints off, sissy!" Theo ordered, then reached for Lago's bag. "I'm going to put those lacquers back with her belongings, and Takh help me if you ever—"

Lago had for a moment forgotten all about the mask, but as his father pulled on his bag, he felt a compulsion to protect it. "No! Don't touch it!" he cried, snatching the bag away and backing himself into a corner of the room.

Bear yelped and whined next to them.

"Give me that," Theo quietly said, taking a measured step forward.

"Dad, stop, I don't have them with me, I—"

"Give me what you stole, or I swear by the Shield of Creation that I'll—"

Lago bolted, diving under his father's legs.

Theo turned in a daze, then blindly reached down and seized Lago's bag while the kid scrambled away. "What is this?" he asked, feeling the strangely solid presence inside the bag, yet confused as to why it felt so light.

Lago stopped, turning sharply while feeling his heart ripping through his ribs. He could not even utter a word as he watched his father untie his bag's flap.

"There is more you are hiding," Theo said. "What else did you steal?"

Lago jumped at him in a shriek, pulling at the bag so violently that the strap burned through Theo's fingers. The bag flew across the room, but before Lago could rush to get it, Theo grabbed him by the collar, choking him to a stop.

"L-let me… G-go!"

"You lying pile of dung, no wonder those boys beat you up. Why did you turn out like this? I wish your mother had never—"

Lago wailed and thrashed so wildly that his tunic's collar ripped. He pushed his father away and stood defiantly in the middle of the living room, placing himself between Theo and the bag. "I'm not, not l-letting you," he mumbled. "Why do you always—"

Slap! Theo struck Lago's face, sending him to the ground.

"Maybe those boys know best. Maybe a good beating is what you need." Theo stood over him and raised a fist.

Bear jumped on the man, pulling him backward by his waistcoat. Theo briefly lost his balance, then kicked hard at Bear's side. The dog flew against a chair and collapsed in whimpers.

"Bear!" Lago yelped. He rushed madly toward his father and pushed him with all the strength he could muster; it was not much, but Theo slid on the carpet and toppled backward, smashing his head on the sewing table. Lago shrieked as he jumped on top of his father, punching incoherently. "I fucking hate you!" he cried as he jabbed and clobbered. "I hate you, I hate you, I—"

Theo came back to his senses and shoved the child off him. He tried to stand but could barely keep his legs straight. "Lago, get over here! I'll kill you, little cocksucker. It's your fault, it's always been your fault… I'm gonna—" His legs failed him, sending him down on his face.

Lago grabbed his bag, then struggled to pick up his injured dog. "Come, Bear, stand up," he pleaded. "Come on, boy, come with me."

Theo stumbled to his feet and lowered himself onto the couch. "The very first day you showed up, you killed your mother. And now… now you try to kill your own father. You bring Takhamún's Spear into my house, you un-grateful—" Theo touched something wet behind his head; his fingers emerged coated in blood. He stared at his red fingertips, growing even angrier for having stained his favorite couch. "See what you've done?! Come over here, now!"

"No, I won't," Lago said in tears.

"Don't you dare question your father, you prick. Get your ass—"

"No! I don't want… I don't want to…" He cradled Bear with one arm while holding firmly to his bag's strap. "I'm leaving," he said with uncertainty.

"Put that bag down and come help your father up," Theo said, pretending to be calm.

"No. I won't. I'm not…"

"Don't you dare walk away, boy."

Lago locked eyes with his father, seeing nothing but a blur.

He slowly backed toward the door.

"Not one more step!" Theo warned.

As Lago closed the door behind him, he heard Theo's voice one last time.

"I don't *ever* want to see you again! You hear me? Do you hear me?"

CHAPTER FIVE

PROFESSOR CRYSTA HOLT

Crysta was working late, as she usually did on Ongudays and Sunndays. She paced around the observatory, double-checking her numerical charts, then took the spiraling steps down to the extensive library, which once had been the nave of a pre-Downfall temple.

The observatory was part of the Mesa Monastery. Chest-high walls of igneous rocks surrounded the expansive grounds, which also housed the orchard, temple, cemetery, and the monks' residences. The Havengall Congregation owned the observatory and kindly loaned it to scholars who came all the way from Zovaria to use the telescope, browse the library, or work on their research. But there were no scholars there other than Crysta, not so late at night.

She brewed a new pot of emberwood tea and took it with her back up the steps. The top of the tower was an octagonal room with eight arched windows, allowing the telescope to be aimed at almost any angle, except for directly above. It was an odd irony that Crysta mostly used the telescope to stare not up at the stars, but down, toward the Anglass Dome, which extended its viny tendrils less than a hundred miles east of Withervale.

She peered through the eyepiece and stared at the interwoven vines that made up the dome's surface, focusing on a tenuous point of light that seeped from somewhere deep inside.

There were sixteen domes in the lands of Noss; fifteen of them spread across the two great continents, while an odd one loomed far away in the Capricious Ocean. The domes were massive tangles of vines, eighty miles in diameter, and so tall that scholars had calculated their summits reached as high as seven miles up. Crysta had spent her career studying these mysterious lifeforms. Her specialty was analyzing the fluctuations of the point-light phenomena known as wisps, which almost exclusively appeared at higher elevations—something glowed deep within the vines, something unknown, but not unknowable.

No one could tell for sure how the domes had originated, or what their purpose was. Some legends said they grew out of the ground to swallow the Miscam tribes of old; some said they had always been there, since before the Gestation Epoch; some even claimed they were constellations fallen from the skies, like spiderwebs of light, which later grew solid and green. The domes were just there, eating up vast swaths of land: impenetrable, exhaustively monumental, inscrutable. They were made of leafless, thorny vines of a scale so extreme that some branches were tiny like needles, while others were twisting pillars with diameters greater than entire city blocks. This thicket of vines formed a tight outer wall with roots that dug down for miles, straight into soil, rock, or water.

The domes had a waxy, teal-green sheen to them. The largest vines had a grayish tint, that, from a distance, gave the domes a textured surface, like the skin of a green melon. They were the highest structures in all of Noss, and as such, they piled up snow at their curved summits, yet somehow built up a lot less than the mountain ranges around them. The snowcaps gave them a coarser layering on top, with the snow accumulating more evenly on the thicker vines, while falling down through the smaller gaps. Where the snow fell to was anyone's guess.

Crysta opened an old book to compare her observations to those left generations before her. As she flipped through the pages, she skipped through observations of other domes as well, most of which she had never seen with her own eyes.

All sixteen domes looked quite similar, with slight differences in the length and curve of their thorns, subtle hue shifts related to temperature and soil, and pattern variations at their bases due to mosses, lichens, and other plants that grew on them. The two outliers were the Ashen Dome on the southern end of the Tsing Empire, which smoked from its gray-snowed top like a volcano, and the Varanus Dome in the far west, which was still mostly dome-shaped but behaved more like an out-of-control thicket and had spread out of Fel Varanus like a tentacled creature, sinking threateningly into the Esduss and Isdinnklad seas.

No one could see very far inside the dome's dense walls, but Crysta could at least glimpse those mysterious points of light that every now and then made themselves apparent. To her, the scattering and intensity of the wisps' light indicated that the domes must be hollow, and that the walls of vines must be around half a mile thick at the base, and thinning as they crested up, though that was after adding too many assumptions to her data.

Daring explorers had cut into the wall before but could get no deeper than a few hundred feet. When cut, the vines oozed a white, milky sap that was corrosive to most metals, sticky, and produced painful allergic reactions known as the white hives. The remaining vines would then bend down to close the gaps, so fast that one could see them move.

Over the centuries, many attempts had been made to pierce through the vine walls, using war machines, digging underground, and even trying to burn them. Although the white sap was flammable, burning with a weak, green flame, the domes would not catch on fire, and their sap would scab and seal up any damage. Horror stories—perhaps true, perhaps not—told of careless adventurers who cut deep into the vines only to be trapped between the sap and thorns, their screams muffled as the vines closed darkness around them forever.

The domes appeared in legends that dated as far back as sixteen hundred years, over a century before the Downfall. It was now the year 1448 A.D. During the past millennium and a half, human civilization had rebuilt itself from the ruins of the great calamity. In the first year of the Downfall Epoch, something set the lands of Noss afire, killing most of humankind, decimating the flora and fauna of the two continents. Land and sea then rebounded into a glacial period that lasted for two centuries. The Reconstitution Epoch began once the cold abated, followed by the Conquest Epoch. Humans multiplied, recolonized, and rebuilt, using the technology abandoned by the dead civilizations, guessing at and relearning the purpose of the old artifacts, but not remembering much about their own past—somehow all the historical writings that had survived seemed purposely contradictory, particularly when they discussed the origin of the domes.

There was an inherent anachronism to the technology of post-Downfall Noss. The resurrected machines were not always understood, and knowledge in certain basic fields was lacking, while it thrived in more complex ones. The world of Noss had found a new balance, even if a somewhat disjointed one; but it was not only in humans and their endeavors that the balance had regained its grasp, for nature too had reclaimed the scarred lands. Although most of the megafauna had gone extinct, the species that survived the cataclysm had spread with lustful eagerness and were once again thriving.

Scholars from the northern wastes of the Khaar Du, to the southernmost archipelagos of Wastyr, from the cold shores of the Quiescent Ocean to the ravaged ones of the Tumultuous Ocean, could not agree on what had caused the Downfall. But all clues pointed to the domes.

There were two major secular ways of thought regarding the domes. One camp suspected the domes were the source of the Downfall, the point of origin for the fire and ice that had killed so many millions, now lingering as scabs, or blisters, unhealing throughout eternity. The other camp proclaimed that the domes were a force of good created to contain the Downfall, locking inside them a cancer that must never be released. Both of those ideas—and a few less-popular ones—were somewhat compatible with the religious interpretations of the Doctrine of Takh, the prevalent religion in both the Zovarian Union and the Negian Empire. The Takheists had disagreements with the secular in-terpretations, as they did not mention the Twin Gods, but as long as the core tenets of the Takh Codex were not directly contradicted, the Doctrine was tolerant of scholars postulating their profane theories.

Crysta had her own hypotheses, influenced by studies from the much more technologically advanced Tsing Empire: she thought that perhaps the answer resided in the heavens. The Downfall could have been caused by a meteor, a comet, or maybe a star that got too close and brought forth all the destruction. She'd place her bets on a comet. It was an unpopular idea, particularly since it failed to explain how the domes related to the Downfall, but that's why she was studying them.

Crysta dipped her quill into the inkwell, then delicately scribbled notes; the intensity of the southwest quadrant wisp was fluctuating again, at the same magnitude as observations taken at this time last year. It was going to be a long night of careful monitoring, followed by crunching numbers.

She finished a stale fried fig pastry and tried to take a sip of her emberwood tea. The cup was empty, and so was the teapot. *Didn't I just brew a new pot?* she thought. Down she went again, for another refill.

A knock at the front door startled her.

Who could it be at this hour? she wondered. She peeked through the key-hole and gasped, quickly unlocking the heavy oak doors.

"Lago! What happened to you?"

Lago's eye was purple and swollen. Bear was next to him, limping, but able to walk on his own.

"Can I come in?" he shyly pleaded.

Chapter Six

The Telescope

They sat around a lamp-lit table.

The expansive room was dark, with the books disappearing into vertical phantoms at the upper shelves. Lago didn't tell Crysta about Sontai, or the mask. He was already feeling guilty about wanting to tell his father earlier and seeing what that had gotten him made him feel like he had deserved it. He said nothing about that, but told Crysta everything about the fight, how his father had hit him, how he'd kicked poor Bear.

"But why?" Crysta asked, sprinkling more leaves in the pot, then pouring boiling water into it. "I don't understand. Just because you got home late? Or did he see your new bruises?"

With a mix of fear and shame, Lago pulled his hands over the table and showed her his lacquered nails.

Crysta covered her mouth and felt her heart break. "It's... the same reason Borris and Wailen picked on you earlier, isn't it?"

"They... How did you know?"

"I have two kids. Eddena, the oldest, she's like you. She went through the same struggles. Well, not just her, *we* went through our struggles, together. It took some time, but my husband finally came to accept her the way she is."

Lago did not understand what he and some girl named Eddena had in common, but he nodded as if comprehending.

Crysta took one of Lago's hands in hers. "You will find a lot of people who will hate you, or fear you, just because you are different, but you have to remain true to yourself, no matter what."

"That's what my friend Alaia always says."

"The Oldrin girl with the little horn?"

"Yeah. Though she's much braver than I am."

"Maybe, but that doesn't mean feelings don't affect her the same way they affect you." She paused. "Perhaps I could talk to your father and see if—"

"No, I can't go back there. It's not the first time—he's always had it against me, since I was a kid," he said, as if he was no longer a kid. "Not all the bruises you see at school are from Borris and... and... Dad blames me for Mom, and he never... He'll beat me even worse if I go back... He'll kill me."

"Take it easy. I won't get in the way. You can stay here tonight, and maybe Sunnday, but I'll have to talk to the monks about it. Once Moonday arrives, there will be other scholars working here."

"Don't worry, I have somewhere I can go."

"You mean with that gal? What's her name again?"

"Alaia."

"Alaia. But isn't she a mine worker? She probably lives in one of those holes in the Hollows."

"She does. Those holes look exciting, actually. It's like our..."—he almost mentioned their Diamond Cave—"I mean, I don't think she'd mind."

Crysta's tea finished steeping. She brought an extra cup. "Would you like some?"

"Yes, please."

She poured some emberwood for Lago, added a bit of honey, and stirred it for him. "Well, your situation is a bit more complicated than finding a place to sleep," she said, handing him the cup. "You'll need to buy food, blankets, clothes, that sort of thing. And I wouldn't want you to stop going to school."

Lago took a sip from his tea, then spat it out on the saucer. "It's... burned. How do you even burn tea?"

Crysta chuckled. "It's just a smoky varietal. Tastes like sitting in front of a campfire, doesn't it?"

"It's more like chewing on the ashes the next morning."

"Fine. I'll add some milk for you. It'll smoothen it out." She did, but it still tasted like ashes. "Well, here's what I propose. My youngest kid, Corben—well, he's young but still a few years older than you—he was helping me here up until last month, but he got a job at the shipyard. I think his heart is at sea, not in the stars. That's all he talks about anyhow. What I mean is, I could use some help here. It's nothing fancy, but it's honest money. I noticed you doing deliveries for your father down in the city. There are errands for the observatory that need doing, and you know your way around."

"That'd be amazing. Dad makes me do all these chores but never pays me. That's why I always carry such a large bag to school—it's filled with his textiles."

"I gathered as much. So, if you help me here in the evenings, and on Sunndays you carry out deliveries, I can offer you, say... a hundred Qupi per week? Does that sound fair?"

"A whole Quggon? That's a lot!" Lago said, then thought for a moment. "I mean, that won't cover school, but I can save up, and go back when I have enough again."

"Oh, don't worry about school. We have a program for students with good grades. You've done well enough to qualify, so I can sign you up for that. Your costs will be covered, but you'll have to buy your own supplies. Do we have a deal?"

"Of course!" Lago said.

In truth, there was no program at the Birth-Light School for students with good grades; the professor planned on paying for Lago's expenses out of her own pocket. Crysta was wealthier than she let show, and she liked to keep that private, because her money came not from the meager wages of academia, but from the Zovarian army. The observatory was located at a strategic border between the Zovarian Union and the Negian Empire, and more often than not, she kept her telescope aimed down to track the Negian forces in the east. She had clever mathematical models to estimate the sizes of armies and their movements, and a secret way of sending this information almost instantly to Zovaria.

Crysta had more work to finish, so she cleaned the dishes and looked for blankets and a pillow for Lago. "Here you go. You can sleep on the couch. Bear already took one half of it, so the other half will have to do for you."

"Can I see what you are working on?" Lago nearly begged.

"If you want, but it's awfully boring."

"Then it'll put me to sleep—win-win."

"Very well, but only for a bit," she said, then led him up the spiraling steps.

Lago's only prior visit to the octagonal tower had been three years ago, when delivering a bundle of silks to a scribe. He couldn't remember the name of the scribe; he couldn't even remember their face. All he recalled was the sublime octagonal room, the mystifying artifacts, the walls lined with ancient volumes, the deep-red rug with an ironwood table over it. The charts, rulers, notebooks, the delicate sconces, the inlaid woodwork of the handrails—they all filled the room with an air of mystery and secrecy. The telescope had also been there but hidden beneath a white sheet. He recalled the smell of pinewood from the iron fireplace, mixed with the camphor fumes of the inks drying on the scribe's book, and the oily musk of the leather bindings.

He smelled the exact same aromas as he climbed the stone steps. He stepped onto the landing and walked beneath the arched threshold. It looked exactly like he remembered it, except that this time the light came from lamps and candles, and the room was messier, with papers and notebooks piling in every corner.

"Disregard the mess," Crysta said, feet pushing a stack of notebooks aside to make a path for Lago. "Maybe you could organize things a bit once you start? I could really use some help."

The telescope was uncovered this time, wide end sticking out the eastern window. It was made of brass, bigger than Lago's entire body if he were to lie on his side, and probably much heavier. It had dozens of knobs and smaller tubes with ornamental carvings sticking out from the sides; he could not guess at their purpose. A heavy brass tripod held the telescope up, with bulky feet that curved around in a floral design. Lago approached it, reverently.

"You never brought us up here during school trips," he mentioned.

"Of course not, this is extremely delicate equipment. The last thing I want is dirty children touching everything," she said, glaring at Lago, who was fumbling with a knob. He didn't take the hint. "Keep your hands off, but you can look through the eyepiece. Over here. That's right. What do you see?"

"I… I don't know? It's too dark. It looks like tree trunks woven together."

"That's the Anglass Dome under purple moonlight. You are looking at the northwestern quadrant, about three miles above ground level. See that branch that curves like a horseshoe, right in the center?

"The thicker one?"

"That one. It looks tiny from here, but it's thicker than this tower. Thicker than this whole building and the entire grounds of the monastery. It's about eight hundred feet wide."

"That's wild! How do they grow so big?"

"Nobody knows," Crysta answered, "that's one of the things I'm trying to find out. Most scholars study the weather patterns around the domes. Rain shadows, convergence zones, that kind of thing. But my focus is on the wisps, tracking how they fluctuate through time. During the Winter Solstice, wisps glow for about nine hours through the night, and during the Summer Solstice, they glow for about sixteen hours, from the early evening into the morning, matching our cycles almost exactly but offset by half a day."

"I have no idea what that means," Lago confessed.

"Let me show you. The one in this quadrant is already too dim to see." She pushed Lago away to turn a few knobs, aiming the telescope in a slightly different direction. "Take a look here, right in the center."

"Looks like a star stuck on the vines," Lago said with a wide smile.

"Doesn't it? The thick vines are stationary, but the smaller ones slowly shift over time, very, very slowly. Every once in a while, the tangle of millions of small vines shifts in just such a way that one can glimpse into the domes. That's what we are seeing here. Oftentimes they show at the same spot every year, lasting a few weeks, so they are a convenient way to measure light variations."

"I mean, I see the light, but can't really see what's inside."

"It would be very hard, because the dome is far away. However, we might soon get a chance to truly peek inside one of the domes. I heard rumors that the roof of the Heartpine Dome—the one south of us—just collapsed in one spot, and this happened not long after all its wisps went dark. Have you ever seen that dome?"

"Once, years ago, when Fedi, Shela, and I went hiking to the Ninn Tago Viewpoint. But the dome looked solid to me."

"Apparently, a huge hole opened up, right where there used to be a discoloration in the vines. It's on the south side, so you wouldn't see it from the Ninn Tago. I don't know if the rumors are true, but I sent a scout to find out. Peering inside the domes has been one of my wildest dreams since I was very young. Maybe we will finally figure out the secrets they hold."

Crysta turned a few more knobs. "But back to wisps. There's a dome far west, in Fel Varanus, which is *full* of them. Every night you can see them. It's a strange dome, not smooth and round like all the others, but gnarly and knotted and full of burls, extending into the sea like a spiderweb. A magnificent sight, and quite scary. And so many wisps! You can spot several of them in the same night, but they vanish much more quickly, so they are hard to measure. You should see them during a hazy night. They look like lighthouses, shooting white beams straight out."

"I'd like to see that!"

"I bet you would. But they say sharp-toothed dragons roam those islands, with spiky tails paddling the cold seas."

"I'd like to see those too!"

"Maybe once you are older, if you travel west. In the meantime, you can spend time looking at these wisps, though they rarely show up—at most one or two at a time. I could teach you more about them, and about the domes. And I could also teach you about stars and planets if you'd like."

"That'd be—um... thank you. It's a lot. I just have to—"

"Sorry, I didn't mean to overwhelm you."

"It's been a long day," Lago admitted, letting his shoulders slump. "But it does sound interesting."

"Well, I still have several hours of observation to do tonight, the boring kind. How about this—next time we can look at Sceres, together, and we can go from there."

"That'd be wonderful. Thank you, Crysta."

Lago wanted to see more, but so much had happened in such a short time, and his head was drowning in fatigue.

Crysta noticed his heavy lids. "Let's get you to bed, okay?" she said and led Lago back downstairs. "I'll be going home in a few hours. I'll be quiet, you won't hear me. I'll ask you to please leave in the morning and close up behind you, since I won't have a chance to warn Chaplain Gwil of our arrangement, and he's not going to believe a little boy he finds sneaking inside his library. But I'll be back here in the evening. If you feel ready, we can get you started with work then."

"I'll be here." Lago looked at the floor, shuffling his feet. "Thank you again, for everything," he said, then quickly embraced Crysta's side and sat on the couch next to Bear, who was already snoring.

"You are welcome. May the moon light your path," she said.

"May the stars guide your heart," Lago replied, finishing the traditional greeting.

Crysta extinguished the lamp and quietly returned upstairs.

CHAPTER SEVEN

SONTAI'S FUNERAL

Lago rose early from a deep but restless sleep. He felt the weightless mask shift inside his bag as he slung it over his shoulder and headed out to the coal mines. Bear followed him, limping only slightly, mostly for attention.

Alaia wouldn't be working today, so he figured he'd find her by the pit fires, where the miners ate their communal breakfast on Sunndays. The Oldrin loved to share, despite how little they had for themselves, and Lago was starving. Bear, too, could use some scraps.

Hundreds of mine workers paced about the fires, plucking chickens, peeling potatoes, boiling water, chopping vegetables, working in unison even though no one was locked to a designated job. Alaia was skinning a lamb, which was already beheaded and hanging from its back legs. As Lago approached, she handed him a knife. It was wet and sticky.

"You do the left leg, then we pull the skin down together. What happened to your eye?" she inquired, without stopping her work.

Lago shrugged, fidgeting with the knife.

"It's early. You doing a delivery?" she asked, as she expertly sliced the skin of the lamb's right leg.

"Just... visiting. There are some things I need to tell you about."

"Do tell!" She grabbed his hand and directed it toward where he was supposed to make the cut.

"This is gross..." he said. "I really don't know how to—Bear! Stop that!"

Bear was lapping at the coagulating blood by their feet. Lago could smell it, and it brought back a gruesome image, making his stomach churn. He dropped the knife, leaning on the tree the lamb hung from.

"Gwoli, what is wrong?" Alaia asked.

"I don't feel so well. There's stuff we need… we need to talk about."

"Say no more. Hey Mellorie, could you take care of this?" She passed her knife to a teenager who was carrying firewood. She wiped her hands, helped Lago up, and walked with him, picking up hard-boiled eggs, salted crackers, and milk on their way, leading him away from the bustle, toward her hole in the Hollows.

Alaia's cliffside dwelling was accessible through stairs carved on the sandstone, which led to an unhinged wooden panel that acted as a door. Two round holes served as windows on either side of the entrance, and a ventilation hole opened over the doorway, for when she lit fires to keep warm, or to cook.

Alaia moved the wooden panel to the side, then took Lago's hands to help him step through the raised threshold.

The naturally carved pocket was only ten feet across, with walls stratified in a vibrant mix of sandstone colors that held a thick layer of pebbles protruding at the center. For a bed there was a bundle of wool blankets, separated from the cold ground by a meshed framework of sticks. Cozy, minimal, just how Alaia liked it.

Lago sat on the wool blankets with Bear, while Alaia sat on the curved threshold, silhouetted by the overcast morning light.

After Lago had a chance to eat and drink, Alaia finally said, "Now you tell me what's wrong."

"It's a long story. I don't even know where to start," Lago said, looking up at the soot-blackened dome above him—it was scraped with playful patterns and child-like drawings. It reminded Lago of their Diamond Cave, which he knew would never feel the same way again.

"You can start with how you got that bruised eye."

Lago spilled out the whole story, beginning with his fight at school. He told her about that surreal moment when he'd seen the gray fox, and how he'd managed to divert the foxhounds toward the creek. He mentioned the blonde soldier, Fjorna, and showed Alaia the silver Krujel she had given him. He then spoke of Sontai and how she had died in a pool of blood and shadows. He dared not mention the dark mask, uncertain whether he should be telling anyone else about it.

Alaia had to interrupt before Lago could continue. "Wait, wait, this old woman, how did she get in our cave?"

"I told you, the fox! When I came back in, the fox was the woman."

"That makes no sense. She was a fox?"

"Or she turned into a fox, and back...? I don't know."

"Old women don't just suddenly turn into foxes. Not the other way around, either."

"I know! Anyway, she spoke very little Common, and didn't say much before she died."

"Maybe she was a Nu'irg from the old myths."

"What's a Nu'irg?"

"The spirits of different kinds of animals. They say they used to roam Noss, but went to sleep after the Downfall and have remained asleep since. They could shapeshift into other creatures. That's what they say, at least."

"I don't think she was a spirit, she looked very much human to me. I don't think those stories are literally true."

"I'm just throwing out some ideas... Your story is weird enough on its own already."

"I'm not making it up, I'm serious. I don't know what happened... there was a fox, then there was this lady, it was all so confusing. But that's not all that happened..." Lago pushed himself to continue, telling Alaia about the fight with his father, about leaving his home, and his night at the observatory with Crysta. It took a while for him to get it all out, and he had to stop a few times, holding back tears. Alaia was a good listener; if she interrupted, it was for important clarifications, or to allow him to keep the story moving, never to go off on tangents.

"And I left the observatory this morning and came straight here. I didn't know where else to go," he finished.

"Lodestar guide us. That is some fucked up day, Lago." Alaia said. She quieted; a bit dumbstruck. She studied Lago's face, then scratched her nub, keeping her eyebrows raised. "You know, you don't even need to ask. There's enough room here if you want to be roommates—Camilla moved to Northlock months ago, so I've had this huge place all to myself. It's not as fancy as what you are used to, but the rent is zero Qupi per month. You can cover half of it if you feel like it, or don't."

"Thank you, that's kind of what I wanted to ask about, just didn't know how. I can't go back to my dad's place. Except, I'll have to sneak in to get my clothes, but that's it, I don't want to see him again. And Crysta has a family, it wouldn't be fair to ask more from her after all she's done. And I'm not about to go live with the monks—they'd turn me into a bald, chanting ghoul."

"That settles it, then, you're staying here. Which side of this luxuriant dwelling would please you most?"

Lago let a sad but relieved smile escape. He pointed to his right, toward the north side of the hole. "If I don't sleep with my head pointing north, I wake up without any sense of direction, so that end will work better."

"You are mental."

"It's true!"

They shared an awkward pause. Lago caressed Bear and kept his eyes on the silty floor. After a long sigh, he said, "I don't think I want to go back in our Diamond Cave anymore. But I want to give Sontai a proper funeral."

"I can ask Headmaster Nameeri, he can help us with—"

"No!" Lago interjected. "We can't tell anyone about Sontai."

"Why not? What about her family? Someone needs to tell them."

"There's something else I haven't told you yet, about what happened there." Lago clenched his jaw and tightened the grip on his bag's strap. "Before Sontai died, she gave me something. But I'm not supposed to tell anyone. I promised her."

"But now you *have* to tell me. What did she give you?"

Lago slowly uncinched his bag, then removed the mask. "Sontai said to keep this secret. To give it to her grandson, Bonmei. I think Fjorna was after this. She's from the Negian Empire, they aren't supposed to be here in our lands. If she finds out I lied to help Sontai, and then took this, I'm as good as dead."

Alaia stretched her hands out to grab the mask.

"No!" Lago pulled the mask to his chest. "It's too dangerous."

"Dangerous? But it looks beautiful. Just look at all that detail."

"It's... I don't know how to explain it. I was stupid and put the mask on. It was like the mask clenched to my skull. It was so painful, like it was making me feel all kinds of pain all at once. I don't know how to describe it."

"I won't put it on, I promise. Just a look?"

"But... Be careful, please."

Lago handed over the mask. Alaia rotated it and scrutinized all the gorgeous, overlapping filaments. "It's so light!" she exclaimed. "Like it's made of feathers! Is it a coyote? No, more like a jackal. I'm not sure."

"I think it's a fox," Lago guessed. "Maybe Sontai used it to turn into the fox. It must have some sort of magical power, or some curse."

"That makes as much sense as anything else you've told me so far." Alaia tapped her knuckles hard on the mask's brow.

"Don't break it!"

"Relax! It's harder than rock. So light, and so strong..."

"But *anyway*, we can't let anyone know about this. No mentioning Sontai, or the mask. And we can't bury Sontai, 'cause the hole is so small. It makes me sick just thinking about having to pull her out like that."

Alaia pondered. "I have an idea. We can give Sontai a funeral, a proper one, and let our Diamond Cave be her holy mausoleum. I don't feel like we'd want to go play in there anymore, not after this, anyway."

"Yeah, I had that same feeling. But we'll have to carry a lot of sand in there to bury her."

"There's no need to bury anyone. You Zovarians have the strangest customs. I'll show you how *we* do it, the Oldrin way."

Once on the pebble path, Alaia kept herself busy picking wild berries and flowers. "For the ceremony," she said, though she ended up eating most of the berries.

They crossed the creek, checking their surroundings in case the Negian soldiers had been sneaking around, and respectfully entered the cave. Lago handed Alaia a bucket of water, then stood to the side to watch.

Alaia dipped a white cloth in the water and washed Sontai's hair, feet, and hands. She braided Sontai's gray hairs into exquisite forms, then set down a circle of flowers around her head. She carefully opened Sontai's jaw and placed sixteen berries in her mouth. *"Two pairs twice doubled*, like the silly Takheists say. This way Sontai's path will be clean ahead of her, and she won't be hungry on her way to her next life," she explained in a whisper. Two stones she placed over Sontai's eyes, one white to allow her to see the Tunnel of Omo'ulére, one black to allow her to see her own shadow, so that she knew where her feet stood inside the fiery light.

Lago peered shyly, trying to watch Alaia's workings while at the same time averting his eyes from Sontai's body. He watched her place a wooden figurine on the ground, of an Oldrin goddess curled tight into a ball, with three horns wrapping around her back like a triple crescent—Pliwe, Alaia had once told him the goddess was named.

She lit a tallow candle in front of the carving, inhaled the smoke, and said a prayer in the Oldrin tongue.

"What does the prayer say?" Lago whispered as quietly as he could, not wanting to disturb the spirits.

"I don't know. I memorized the sounds, but I don't know what they mean. But I think that's better than nothing."

With the ceremony finished, Alaia blew the candle out, picked up her Pliwe statue, and signaled Lago to exit the cave. He did, feeling relief, but also feeling as if he was running away from a responsibility. They filled the tunnel entirely with rocks big and small, then placed a final, larger boulder to seal the entrance.

I won't break my promise to you, Lago spoke in his thoughts. *Farewell, Sontai. I wish I could've done more.*

They swung the wooden panel over the sealed tunnel and leaned a dozen splintery planks of wood over it, making it as unappealing and inaccessible as possible.

They would never again return to this place.

CHAPTER EIGHT

SEASONS OF THE MOON

It was late in the afternoon by the time Lago and Alaia returned to the Withervale Mesa. Lago had nothing to wear other than the muddied clothes he had worn to school the previous day, so he wanted to get that taken care of right away. After turning right on Ashlar Street, Lago spotted a gaggle of urchins digging through the trash, right across the street from his home. "What are those kids doing?" he asked Alaia, moments before he realized the answer to his own question. "Hey, those are my clothes!" he yelled as he chased after them. Alaia pursued Lago and stopped him before he hurt the young children.

"Lago! Stop that! They were just—"

"They are taking my stuff!"

"Easy! Let it go! They're gone!"

He looked at his clothes and toys, all spilled on the ground. What the kids hadn't taken was packed tight with rotting food.

"Watch it. There's broken glass in there," Alaia said, helping him recover what was salvageable. She stood up to keep watch. "At least your father doesn't seem to be home."

Lago clenched his jaw. "I need to go inside, there's other stuff I should grab." He gazed up at his home, if he could call it that any longer.

Alaia nodded. "I'll guard the streets with Bear. Grab all you can, you don't want to be doing this again."

"Okay, okay, I'm going." Lago crossed the street and hugged the wall as he snuck to the back of his old home. His father wasn't there, at least that much was obvious. He pushed a stick under the shutters of the back window and pulled it quickly back; the shutter swung open with the friction. He clambered up and dropped inside.

Molding dishes were piled in the kitchen sink. The small dining table was streaked with blood. Scissors weighed down a strip of white cloth and a blood-soaked kitchen rag. *I hope it hurt*, he thought.

He walked through a narrow sandstone hallway, ignoring the door to his father's room, and turned left into his own bedroom. The place was trashed. His bedframe was split, clothes littering the ground. A vase lay shattered in the corner beneath uselessly dangling shelves. Theo had discarded his son's belongings in a hurry, neglecting a few useful items in the trash heap he had left behind.

Lago began to toss all he would need into his bag: the few straggling pieces of clothing, a book about insects he had borrowed from Crysta, an old pair of sandals, an oilskin tarp he sometimes used as an umbrella. He forced a blanket into his bag, but his pillow would not fit, so he carried it under his arm.

He then kneeled down and slid aside a loose floorboard under which he had hidden an additional bottle of fingernail lacquer solvent, a sewing kit, shiny glass marbles, a sheathed knife, and his life's savings of twenty Qupi.

Lago realized he'd need some things from the kitchen too, so he went back and threw the most obvious utensils into a pot, as well as dried meats and nuts, feeling nervous about the loud sounds he was making.

He probably has money stashed in the sewing table's drawer, Lago thought, heading toward the living room. He thought he heard Alaia's voice calling from beyond the kitchen window, but as he was about to turn, he saw the front door open.

His father stood there like a framed statue. He took a step in, then slammed the door behind him.

"You little thief… You thought you could just come back and—"

"Don't you—" Lago said, stepping back toward the kitchen. He heard Bear barking outside.

"Don't you what? You are in *my* house. I told you I never want to see you again. Drop that, you are done taking from me."

"These are my things."

"*These are my things,*" Theo mocked. "Who do you think bought all that? Drop it, or I'll make—"

Lago tossed the pillow to his father's face. Theo pushed it away and began to remove his belt, wrapping it around his knuckles.

"Stop!" Lago said, backing up against the sink. "Stop or I'll…" he reached into the sink and pulled out a butter knife. He aimed it toward his father, hands shaking with fear. "I'm tired of you always—"

"What are you going to do with that, huh? Stab your father with a dull knife? I'll show you—"

Lago weakly hurled the knife. It hit his father on the hip, bouncing off harmlessly.

Theo shook his head, then lunged. Lago ducked under the kitchen table.

"You will pay for that, sissy," Theo said, kicking the table away. "You are not getting away this time. I could snap your neck with just one—"

Crash! A brick flew through the kitchen window. Theo twisted around and saw a dark shape ducking behind the shattered glass.

"What in Khest, who—" Theo turned back around, but Lago was no longer there. He looked behind the toppled table, finding nothing, then looked to his side and saw Lago bolting toward the front door.

Lago knew he could not outrun his father, not with all that he was carrying. He grabbed the key on the living room table, opened the door, and slammed it behind him. He fumbled with the key, hearing stomping boots coming for him. The key went in, but the doorknob was already swiveling. The key turned just as the door was about to open.

Shit... shit... Lago held tight to his belongings and ran away while the door shook the frame. He saw Alaia rushing to meet him. "Help me with it," he exhaled, handing her the pot filled with kitchen utensils.

"Are you alright?"

"Let's get out of here," Lago yapped. They turned around a corner and scurried under a bridge to take a shortcut into a busy area of town.

The cacophonous marketplace of the mesa was lively with the weekend traffic, smelling of simmering shrimp skewers, foreign spices, and unwashed muskoxen. They carried the conspicuous bundles to the west side, down the switchback steps, across the rickety bridges, and at last into Alaia's hole.

Lago dropped down, panting like a dog.

"It's fine," he said, noticing her concern. "He didn't get to me. Thank you for... for the brick."

"You can't be taking Runestone Lane no more, or you'll end up crossing paths with him."

"He's a coward. He'd never hit me in public. I'll try to avoid it, but I'm not concerned."

Lago set up his little nook on the north side of the hole, feeling a bit embarrassed at how, despite only grabbing a small sampling of all that he had owned, he still had about four times more possessions than Alaia did. But they'd share, and it would feel good to share.

He finished making his bed, which was nothing more than a blanket over his clothes. He wrapped the dark mask in a dirty towel and socks, and hid it in a splintery crate, which became his nightstand.

"Shit, it's past sunset," he said. "I'm already late. I don't want to mess up my first night working for Crysta. Can you take care of Bear?"

Alaia glanced at Bear, who was dozing in a pool of drool. "I don't think he needs any taking care of. He'll learn to navigate the Hollows by talking to the other dogs."

"Please, you don't believe in those spritetales, do you?"

"Spritetales? It's just common knowledge! Dogs can talk to dogs, cats to cats, birds to birds. All in their heads, without having to say any words out loud. I've seen Bear doing it, he stops next to other dogs and they just... chat about dog things."

"He stops to smell their asses."

"Which is a polite conversation starter, for their kind."

"Just... keep an eye on him, will you?"

Alaia shrugged and began to light a fire to cook by.

"I might be back late," Lago warned her. "I don't know exactly what Crysta will be needing help with."

"I sleep like a rock, don't worry. May the moon light your path," she said.

"May the stars guide your heart," he replied.

Sceres was just beginning to rise over the Anglass Dome, purple as the night before, but slightly tinted toward magenta due to the atmosphere. The Ilaadrid Shard beamed brightly that evening, making it hard to see the moon's cratered, purple face.

Lago took the side streets instead of Runestone Lane, rushed through the monastery grounds' exterior gate, then knocked on the heavy doors of the observatory. He was greeted by an amiable monk, who was old but carried his years well. His dark-blue robes were embroidered with copper-colored threads that interwove in knots shaped like flowers, vines, and branches. His sleeves were long, so long that if he had not been keeping his hands clasped by his chest, they would have dragged on the ground.

"You must be Lago," the bald monk said. "Professor Holt told me you'd come by. I am Chaplain Gwil, a servant of the Havengall Congregation. I'm sure you will be a wonderful help to our order—I am truly grateful you are here."

"I'm here to see Crysta, actually."

"Of course, of course. She should be up in the tower. Watch your step, son."

Lago tried not to show his discomfort at hearing the word *son*.

Chaplain Gwil continued, "That eye of yours looks as purple as Sceres. There is an unguent I could—"

"It's fine, really."

Gwil nodded. "I will be down here in the library for a wick or two, maybe an hour more if you need me. After that, I'll take my leave to the dormitories, to rest with my fellow monks."

"Thank you, Lorr Gwil."

"Chaplain, or just Gwil, if you please."

"Sure," Lago said and rushed upstairs.

Crysta was unloading notebooks from her untidy satchel. "Lago, just in time," she said. "How are you feeling today?"

"Much better, thank you."

She checked on his bruised eye and forced her cheeks up into a sympathetic smile. "I'm hoping maybe you had a chance to talk to your father? I know it's complicated, but I thought—"

"No!" Lago snapped, then squeezed his lips into a tight line. "I mean, no, I went back, and..."

"You did? Did you get to—"

"He said he never wants to see me again. That he'd snap my neck. I threw a knife at him."

"Shit." Professor Holt straightened her coat, to show a semblance of composure.

"It's better this way," Lago said. "Maybe he'll leave town, like he always said he would. He never wanted to live in my mom's old home, even the whole textiles business was hers. He always hated it here."

"I'm sorry, Lago. I won't push it, but you'll have to keep me informed as things progress. Don't worry, I won't talk to your father unless you tell me to. So, what have you decided?"

Lago brightened up a bit. "I'm staying with Alaia. Already made my bed in there, got my clothes and stuff. She's very excited about it. And Bear doesn't mind."

Crysta beamed with relief. "If you need anything, let me know," she said. "And you can ask Chaplain Gwil as well. I'm sure you two will get along."

"About that," Lago said, "he mentioned I'd be of help to the Heaven... Heavenguild..."

"Havengall Congregation."

"Yes, that. What did he mean?"

"Well, when I asked if you could run bigger errands on Sunndays... How do I put it? The monks are the ones who really own this observatory. It's all part of their monastery, and they are the ones who would need the help. I'm more of a guest, borrowing their facilities while I work on my research. Other than the assistance I'll need on weekdays, the rest of your work would be dictated by the monks."

"Oh…"

"Don't panic, they are fine people. You'll see once you get to know them. But to start with, I have some things you could help me with here in the tower, if you are ready."

"Yes, of course!" he said, downright thrilled to have something to put his mind to rest with.

Crysta gave Lago basic chores, from cleaning the drafting table, to alphabetizing books, to sorting her notes by date. It was something to get started until they found their rhythm. She told him that ever since Corben—her younger son—went to work at the shipyard, more of her stuff had been piling up, and it wasn't usually this messy.

Once Lago was done with his tasks, Crysta waved at him from the eastern window. "Lago, come look."

The telescope was aimed at the moon's Ilaadrid Shard: a fragile yet sharp point of pure white. Lago looked through the eyepiece at the piercing beacon on the moon's northern hemisphere.

"Whoa! Is that? That's really Sceres?"

"Yes, take a close look at her shard. With just your eyes, it looks like a little triangle of bright light. But with the telescope you can see it's more like a mountain of glass, stuck right in the center of the Segnar Crater. During her waning gibbous phase, the shard lines up just right and reflects Sunnokh's light straight back at us, that's why it glows so fiercely. It's the same during her first quarter, but then Sceres rises at noon, so we see her shard glowing as the Daystar."

"Dad says that as the moon moves through the sky, she sometimes bumps into stars, and they get stuck on her. I asked him why the stars always get stuck on the same spot, and he just didn't care to explain it."

"There are a lot of myths that try to explain what the shard is, or the 'beacon,' as they call it in the Jerjan Continent. By using telescopes like this one, cosmologists can tell a more accurate story. See how there's a circle around the shard? And lines almost like the spokes of a wheel? That's the Segnar Crater. We think the shard is an asteroid that crashed on the moon billions of years ago, causing an explosion so big that it dug that huge hole and sent debris out into those lines."

"It's so beautiful," Lago said, eye still glued to the eyepiece. "It's like a diamond growing on a field of lupins."

"Are we getting poetic? But speaking of that purple color, you might not be so far off. We don't know whether there are flowers on the moon, but it does seem as though her six seasons are caused by some sort of life form. That thin, aquamarine-green edge that goes all around her edges, that's Sceres's atmosphere. It means there is some sort of air there, and that might mean there is life, too."

Lago could see the thin atmosphere clearly now, like a luminescent shield, but he also noticed a hazy smear across the shadowed side of Sceres, a stretchy whiteness thin as gossamer.

"Is that... smoke?" he asked.

"Good eyes!" Crysta said. "But no, they are clouds. Thin clouds, nothing like the ones we get here on Noss. You normally can't see them because Sceres is too colorful, but they reveal themselves more clearly during Obsidian."

"I've seen that before," Lago said. "Her black face gets odd patches."

"Exactly. Do you remember the six seasons of the moon we learned at school?"

"Hmm, let's see. Sulphur when she's yellow, that's during our Summer. That one is easy to remember. Amethyst when she's purple, in Autumn, like now. Then in Umbra she turns to Jade... Umm, then she's pink in Winter, and we call it Tarmalin... Tarmo, Tar—"

"Tourmaline. Go on."

"Tourmaline, right. Then during Thawing she turns all kinds of bright colors, and it's her Pearl season."

"And there's one more..." Crysta encouraged him. "Which we mentioned earlier."

"Oh, of course! And when she's black, during our Spring, that's her Obsidian season."

"Very good! You even got them in the right order, though we normally start counting in Winter, or Tourmaline. If you look through the telescope again, what colors do you see?"

"Purple. Other than the shard, I mean."

"But take a look deep in the shadow of the Segnar Crater. It's hard to pick out, because the shard is a bit blinding, but see if you can spot something."

"There's a bit of green in there!"

"That's right. Just around the edges of it. That green will begin to expand in about a month, once Autumn ends and Umbra begins, and then Sceres will be in Jade. When that happens, to everyone else it will look like a soft burst of green expanding from the crater. But we who can peek closer will see little specks of colors growing until they cover all her mountains and valleys. Like mold growing all around a rotting orange."

"That wasn't so poetic."

Crysta chuckled. "It was to me! Fungi are exciting, and beautiful."

"Gross. So... the moon is alive, then?"

"We don't know for sure," Professor Holt answered truthfully. "It does look like her colors are caused by some type of plant, but our telescopes aren't yet powerful enough to see as much detail as we need. We gave the six seasons the names of minerals and rocks because that's what they look like when we gaze upon them from down here, and people like to describe things in terms they are familiar with. We'll be covering all these topics next year in school, but I thought you'd enjoy a little preview. Since you'll be helping me in here, it'll be easier if you are familiar with the terminology."

Lago was eager to aim the telescope at each and every star, but Crysta put a big cap on the front lens, a tiny cap on the eyepiece, then covered the brass tube with a white sheet. "That's good enough for tonight. You shouldn't stay up as late as I do, or you'll never make it to school in time. You'll be in class tomorrow," she stated, more than asked.

"I will. Oh, which reminds me"—he reached into his bag—"here's the book I borrowed."

Crysta took the book; it was *An Entomologist's Companion for the Isdinnklad Region*, by Hefra Boarmane. "What did you think of it?" she asked. "Aren't the illustrations exquisite?"

"They are! I didn't know there were so many types of bees, I thought there was just the one kind. Do you have one about birds? Alaia loves birds."

"I do have just the right one, also by Hefra, so I'm certain you'd both enjoy it. We studied together at the Zovarian Academic Institute, decades ago. Come with me."

They walked down to the library. Crysta pulled out the *Field Guide to Birds of the Loorian Continent* and handed it to Lago. "You'll find it a bit outdated. There has been a strange bird migration lately, they say of species entirely unknown. Hefra must be having the time of her life with her fieldwork."

"Weird," Lago said, then awkwardly mumbled, "Umm, also... do you happen to have any books about masks?"

"Masks? What sort?"

"Like, what people wear to hide their faces? Animal masks and such."

"I don't know, maybe? It's an odd request. Like they wear at the Feast of Plenitude, during Harvestlight?"

"Yeah, but not made out of plants, those look more like baskets. Doesn't matter, just curious."

"Maybe... All I can think of is a book of spritetales. It might be down here somewhere."

"Could we look for it?"

Crysta flipped through volumes on a shelf near the ground. The thin spines held no markings, forcing her to pull them all out.

"Here it is," she said. "*Acoapóshi Folktales*, collected by Lerr Holen Thar-Gerval. They are very old stories, very short too. I recall a tale that had a magical mask but—"

"Perfect!" Lago said and took the book. "It's small, I could read it in a day and bring it back."

"Take your time with it, no one will miss it."

Lago dusted the book's cover. It had a crude illustration of an animal face, but it was too indistinct to tell whether it was a lion, a deer, a wolf, or even a bird. The image could represent just about anything, yet it had a keen specificity in its vagueness.

"Speaking of spritetales," Lago said, then paused, seeming to regret saying anything. He went on, "Is it true that animals can speak to one another?"

"Have you not heard birds sing?" Crysta said, a bit confused.

"No, I mean, yes, I have. But I mean... Some people say they actually talk to each other, like we do with words, but instead it's all in their minds."

"If they did, how could we tell?" Crysta inquired. "Subjective perception is not something that can be dissected. Another being's qualia are, by definition, beyond our grasp. That is why scholars and artificers abstain from mingling with such follies—they fall beyond the scope of objective research, and therefore any supposition we can concoct about them is intrinsically moot."

"Yeah, that makes sense," Lago said, trying to count how many words he had failed to understand.

"But anyway," Crysta said, reaching into her handbag to pull out a perfectly formed Quggon block, "before you go, here's an advance for your troubles this week." She handed Lago his entire week's pay, figuring he could use it right away instead of having to wait.

Lago took the Quggon with trembling hands.

The main currency in Zovaria, the Tsing Empire, and several other realms was the Qupi. It consisted of chips of identical size made of metallic alloys infused with a tiny amount of magnium—the aetheric variant of iron—which made them magnetic. Each gnomon-shaped chip looked like three tiny cubes glued together, or like four cubes from which one corner cube had been removed.

There were six common denominations of chips. The smallest was the Lode, which wasn't really a full Qupi chip, but a single cube with a square hole running through the center. Made of a durable lead alloy, and almost imperceptibly magnetic, a Lode was worth a measly tenth of a Qupi. Then came the proper, whole Qupi, which was made of brushed steel. The chip after that one was the Hand, worth five Qupis, made of mirror-like chromium, bright and light. Then came the Cup, made of copper, which shone radiantly in warm tones, and was worth ten Qupi. Twice the value of a Cup was a Horn, which was cast from brass; the magnium infused in the Horns made them vibrant, closer to the look of gold. The highest-value chip in common circulation was the Hex, which was equal to sixty Qupi chips; due to being alloyed with cobalt, the compound metal took on a glossy, iridescent-blue sheen. Since the chips were magnetic, and each denomination had a particular angle of polarization, nine chips could be assembled into a larger cube, like a puzzle, adding up to exactly one hundred Qupi, or a Quggon. It took five single chips, alongside one Hand, Cup, Horn, and Hex, to make a Quggon block.

Lago stared at the perfectly formed block; it was heavy and cold, shining with cool and warm reflections. He had held Quggons before, when taking payments for his father, but he had never been given this much money for himself. From all the tips he had saved up, and which he had kept a secret, he had managed to accumulate merely twenty Qupi. The Quggon was a fair fare, nothing outlandish, but for a young boy of twelve, it felt like a fortune.

"Thank you so much!" he said, already breaking the Quggon puzzle into separate chips, so he could put it together again. "I'll buy only what I need, and save the rest."

"That's a good plan," Crysta said. "But now it's time for me to get to work. Go get some rest, and I better see you at school tomorrow."

"You will!"

Lago finished putting the puzzle back together, then ran back home.

Qupi

Quggon - 100

60 - Hex (Cobalt)
20 - Horn (Brass)
10 - Cup (Copper)
5 - Hand (Chromium)
1 - Qupi (Steel) x5
0.1 - Lode (Lead)

CHAPTER NINE

BROKEN PUZZLE

Something slid off Alaia's blanket as she sat up in bed. She reached down to find a leather-bound book embossed with a sparrow-shaped stamp. *Field Guide to Birds of the Loorian Continent*, by Hefra Boarmane.

"Where did you steal this from?" she asked, noticing Lago was already awake.

"Crysta let me borrow it," he said from his bed. "I thought you'd like it, it has really pretty drawings."

"That's so sweet of you. And what's that you're reading?"

"A book of spritetales. Crysta said it has stories about masks."

"You told her?!"

"I didn't tell her nothing, just borrowed a book. It's a hard one to understand though, old-fashioned language. But it mentions this king—his name is Ieron Mindrishim—who wears the mask of a black lion, and rides around on this big creature he calls a smilodon."

"Sounds wild. Fun story?"

"You'd think so, but then it gets weird. I really can't follow what happens. I think parts of it are in Miscamish, like they didn't translate all the words or something. And it doesn't have any characters turning into foxes, but it does describe the mask as being as dark and weightless as a crow's feather."

Alaia took the book and flipped through the pages, then eyed Lago as he leaned over to reach in his sock-covered crate. "Hey, put that cursed thing away!" she yelled as Lago removed the canine-shaped mask.

"I just want to see it," he complained. "Don't worry, I won't put it on, I'm only—hey!"

Alaia took the mask, shoved it in the crate, and stuffed the socks back on top. "Don't mess with it, not until we know more about it."

She handed the book back to Lago and picked hers up instead. "Your book is boring. *My* book is much more interesting, *and* it has pictures."

They ate crackers and purple Kirdu apples for breakfast, then heated water to steep star anise tea—a good choice before heading out on a cold day. As they waited for the water to boil, Alaia flipped through the bird guide. "Emerald starlings, iridescent green and purple feathers. Too bad there's no color to the illustrations, I bet these birds would look lovely if I—"

"Don't you dare deface Crysta's books."

"'Deface?' The nerve." She kept leafing through. "Look at this fat one! A voluptuous frigatebird. Cover those tits, Lurr!"

"Crysta said there are a lot of new species that won't be in the guide, something about a migration."

"That's what's going on? I've been hearing weird birdsongs lately, especially at night. Oh, oh, the other day, when I was swimming at the sinkholes, I saw a *massive* bird, straight above. Don't know what kind of bird it was, but I'd never seen one so big, much bigger than the glaive eagles we see in Spring. Feathers looked blue, but it was hard to tell with the bright clouds behind."

She flipped to the next page. "Here they are, mourning trogons, see? Just like the ones they use, I mean *kill*, at the mines." She showed him an illustration of a solemn bird: it had a majestic crest, a long tail, and wing feathers that when at rest pointed down like the teeth of an alligator. "I think ours have even longer tails, which makes me even sadder because they put them in these tiny cages, and their tail feathers bend and break. You can't see it here, but their colors are amazing, the deepest blues and reds you've ever seen."

"I don't understand why they have to kill them."

"Here's what's fucked about this," she said, closing the book as if ready to punch someone. "These birds sing when they are about to die, and all the birds who hear the call sing as well. It's the most dreadful song. They bring the birds in the mines so we are warned if there are deadly gases around. The assholes know that the bird who breathes the poison will sing until it dies, that's just what they do, and that makes the other birds nervous, and they all cry as one. You can hear the alarm all over the shafts, it's terrifying! And the bastards leave the poisoned bird inside, to make sure everyone hears it, and the bird just dies, screaming in the darkness. It's disgusting." Alaia was pissed off, breathing hard.

"Cool down, there's nothing you can do about it."

"Maybe," she said. "We just had a leak a week ago. Four birds died, but they keep shipping more from the south. The mine owners are evil, I tell you. They don't care about us, they don't care about the birds, we are all disposable to them."

"I wish you could find a better job."

"Not gonna happen for an Oldrin. These people tolerate us, but deep down, they hate us. Still, it's a better job than fighting the stupid Zovarian wars and dying for nothing. At least here we get paid a little bit."

"I hope one day we can get out of here. Maybe if we save up enough."

"Wouldn't that be something. To go out into the world and just watch all the birds there are."

While getting dressed for school, Lago told Alaia everything about seeing the moon through the telescope. Alaia listened intently, hoping someday she'd get to experience such wonders, but too embarrassed to ask if it would be possible. She decided it wasn't worth worrying about—the monks would never allow an Oldrin to desecrate the monastery grounds.

"I almost forgot, check this out," Lago said, pulling the Quggon out of his Qupi pouch.

"Now *that* you had to steal from somewhere. Do I see a Hex? Is that a whole block? What did you get yourself into?" She took the cube and began to pull the magnetic pieces apart.

"It's an advance for this week's work," Lago said.

"All of that for just one week? Boy, you Zovarians have it so easy."

She finished reassembling the puzzle in record time.

"How did you do that so quickly?" Lago asked.

"Bahimir let me play with his once. Wait, that sounded wrong. What I mean is, he found a golden bracelet in a Day of the Lost cache," she said, referring to the treasures hidden during the leap day celebration, which occurred every eight years. "When he sold it, he paraded his Quggon for everyone to see, and then let me play with it for a whole day."

She handed the completed puzzle back to Lago, then stopped him before he dropped it into his pouch. "Don't take that to school. Too much money gone to waste if you get mugged. Oh, and that silver coin you got from that blonde soldier? I asked around. It's worth a lot. A *lot*. Maybe three times more than your Quggon. I found someone who'll trade it for Qupi and—"

"No, I don't want to use it," Lago said. "It's... I don't know. It feels wrong. I'll keep it safe. I'll keep it all hidden." He removed a Hand and two Qupi chips from the Quggon, then hid the incomplete block inside a dirty sock, right next to the silver Krujel Fjorna had given to him, then shoved that in with the other socks that hid the dark mask.

Lago did not want to go to school that Moonday. Although his eye had had two days to heal, he still had quite a prominent bruise, and he was not looking forward to having to make up stories to explain himself. He climbed the switchbacks to the mesa, followed Feldspar Boulevard across Greisen Park, then hurried between the Twin Shrines of Takh, feeling a bit judged by the flanking statues of Takhísh and Takhamún. Once in the East Flank, he entered Birth-Light School from his secret passage through the arboretum and sat down for Lorr Felann's mathematics class. He didn't mind math too much; he didn't find it as hard as all the other kids claimed it was.

During recess, Lago avoided his classmates' questioning eyes by hiding in the arboretum. He sat on the bench by the turtle pond and unpacked his lunch: Kirdu apples and crackers again. Now that his father wasn't going to prepare meals for him any longer, he would have to buy groceries all on his own, and the thought scared him.

Alaia will help me figure it out, he thought, one hand holding an apple, the other fumbling inside his Qupi pouch, twirling the Hand and two Qupi chips he had dropped in there earlier. He had always preferred Qupis to the round Krujels of the Negian Empire, or the square Grunnels of the Horde, because those were not magnetic, always clinking too loudly over one another.

"Hey, stop!" he heard a voice exclaim nearby. Lago turned his head but saw nothing.

"I don't want to!" the same voice cried out. Lago stood. Beneath the fig tree, right next to the stone bridge, he saw Borris and Wailen terrorizing Penli, a Jabrak-Tsing kid from far south.

"Let me see it!" Borris said, pulling Penli's trousers down while Wailen blocked his escape. They were both bigger than Penli, particularly Borris, who was overweight on top of big-boned.

Penli tried to cover himself up, not to hide his genitals, but something he felt much more embarrassed about: his tail. The Jabrak-Tsing race had smooth tails that went down to their calves, where they ended in a furry tuft, similar to those of oxen. Most adults displayed their tails proudly, as they were not seen negatively by other races, unlike the spurs of the Oldrin. Children, however, tended to hide their tails to avoid showing their differences, further turning them into targets of the cruelty a lot of young people were so naturally predisposed to.

Borris's fat hands grabbed the base of the tufted tail and pulled it out. Penli began to cry.

"Hey, leave him be!" Lago called out, approaching with decisive steps.

"Fuck you, sissy," Wailen replied. "What do you care about the oxtail boy?"

Borris let go of the tail and faced Lago. "Coward, you hit us from behind last time. Can't do that now, can you?" He grabbed a solid stick from the ground and held it like a sword.

Penli moved back, stuffing his tail back in his trousers.

Lago suddenly remembered: when he'd picked up his belongings, he had dropped a knife in his bag. It was still there. He pulled it out, flashing it as he released it from its sheath.

"Leave him the fuck alone before I cut your balls off, you fat pig," he said to Borris.

Wailen took a few terrified steps back, but Borris did not want to back off; the chubby kid chewed on his lower lip and clenched a thick fist around the stick.

Lago picked up speed. "I said. Leave. Him. Alone!" He screamed in a rage and lunged with his knife.

Borris dropped his weapon and fled behind Wailen.

"Fucking better run, you fucking… fuckers!"

He tried to help Penli up, but the Jabrak child cowered on the ground. Lago realized how manic he must have seemed, bruised, panting, still holding the sharp weapon. He put the knife away.

"It's okay. They ran away, you are fine," he said.

Penli looked up and wiped his eyes.

They sat by the turtle pond, sharing their lunches. Lago gave Penli an apple and received a fried eel roll in return, which was breaded into a curling spiral. *Must be Jabrak-Tsing cooking*, Lago thought, and was not wrong. The spices were unknown to him, and he did not like the strong flavor at all, but he pretended he did.

"Were you really going to cut them up?" Penli asked, a bit of fear still tinting his voice.

"No, I was just bluffing. I mean, maybe. I guess it depends if they fought back. But I didn't intend to, I think."

"Carrying a knife to school could get you expelled. You could be sent to work at the rampart, or worse, sent to war like my uncle."

Lago considered. "Couldn't happen till I'm older," he said. "I've gone through this crap for years now, and I tell you, the only way to make them stop is to fight back. Maybe I overdid it a little, but it'll give them pause next time they try to mess with us."

"They won't mess with you, but they'll still come after me," Penli said.

He's probably right, Lago thought, measuring the smaller, shy youngster. "So… I've seen your parents before. They don't hide their tails, and they seem fine. Why do you?"

Penli shrugged. "Because if I keep it out, it'll be easier for them to pull on it, and they'll tease me more."

"Not necessarily. Here's something I learned from my best friend, Alaia. She's Oldrin, has this horn-like spur right here." He pointed to the right side of his forehead, right beneath his curls.

"Yeah, I've seen her with you."

"Well, she's much smarter than I am. Always has been. Instead of hiding her spur under a hat, she braids her hair around it, to show it off. She's proud of it, and she doesn't give a shit what others think. No one nags her about it. I think people are afraid of her confidence."

"I don't know, I'm not like that," Penli said, lifting his shoulders as if he could hide his head deep in his chest.

"Just give it some thought."

Penli nodded weakly. "So… You're quite bruised up, but you have no tail, no spurs. Why do they pick on you?"

Lago furtively looked at his nails, which were clear now, though there was still a hint of fingernail lacquer on the corner of his left thumb. He scraped it off. "It's… It's just… They don't like my curly hair," he said.

Lago was preparing tea, to warm up before heading to the observatory. Bear curled at his feet, tired from a day of exploring the Hollows on his own.

Alaia had just returned from the mines and was playing with the incomplete Quggon Lago had stowed inside a sock, trying to join the magnetic pieces in weird, new angles.

"Hey Alaia… Why do the Jabrak-Tsing grow tails?"

"I heard this one. It's not funny. Those kinds of jokes are never funny." She gave him a disappointed look.

"No, no joke. I'm asking for real. For that matter, why do you grow spurs? I just wanted to know where that comes from."

"Don't really know," she honestly answered. "The Tsing, like Lurr Hawal, the butcher, they don't grow tails. It's just the Jabrak farther south who have them, and their children, as far as I understand. And same with us, it's not all Dorhond or Bayani who get spurs, only the Oldrin."

She took out Lodes from her haversack and began to snap the tiny lead cubes into the Quggon puzzle.

"From what I heard other Oldrin say, we are all half-bloods. Bahimir says that way back we had many more spurs, all over our bodies. Glorious, like statues of flesh and bone, he said, but now our blood is all thin, and we got only a little left." She tapped her tiny nub and continued. "I wonder if the Jabrak-Tsing are like that too, and all they have left is their tails."

She finished assembling the puzzle, using nine Lodes in place of the three missing chips. She handed it back to Lago. "Done!"

"That's cheating," Lago said. "You can't make a Quggon with Lodes, it's supposed to add up to one hundred. And you swapped the positions of the Hex and the Horn, that's not how they fit!"

"Says who? They fit just as well. There are many ways of putting a puzzle together. This is *my* way."

Chapter Ten

Mourning Trogons

Nossday was particularly warm, with low clouds thinking about letting down some rain. But none of that was of concern to Alaia because the temperature in the mines was always constant. She found Dooncam and Ebaja on the trail to the mines, a brother and sister with very similar spurs cutting asymmetrical ridges on their scalps.

"Hurry up!" Dooncam yelled down a thirty-foot-deep sinkhole, where a friend of his was bathing. The vertical mine shafts had long been abandoned, now only used by miners for baths before or after work.

Alaia strode into the watermill, where spinning gears were making the giant bellows inhale and exhale tirelessly, circulating fresh air in the deeper shafts. Her lamp and shovel were already in her haversack, but she picked up a bucket and pickaxe from the rack. She checked in with her supervisor, Bahimir, who begrudgingly handed out the pay he owed her for last week's work.

Alaia counted her meager Qupi chips. *You cheap bastard,* she thought. *Lago gets more than this in a day, and it's only his first week at work.* She eyed Bahimir's necklace, made of a single Lode strung through a red thread. *Even your cheap-ass necklace is cheap.* She tossed her chips into her overalls pocket and headed down shaft fifteen.

She followed Ebaja, who carried round and split timbers to wedge into the seams as supports, to prevent them from collapsing; a cave-in was always a possibility in this dangerous job. Ahead of them were seven other miners who carried water, piping materials, and heavy tools. Dooncam was with them, holding a tiny cage in which their mourning trogon perched, looking hopeless and cramped. The bird was a female—Alaia could tell from the shorter tail feathers.

That poor bird deserves better, she thought. *Stop shaking the cage, you prick,* she voiced only to herself.

Alaia was intimately familiar with most of these shafts. She could navigate them in the dark by pure memory, feeling the change in the air circulation, temperature, and smells, assisted by the mental pictures the sounds of her footsteps drew.

She stood on her bucket, holding the split timbers to the ceiling while Ebaja wedged the round timbers below them as support columns by swinging her mallet to lock them in place. They could hear the chatter of the other miners just a little further down the mine, their picks ripping through the seam, bit by bit, hit by hit.

The Oldrin worked all day, with few breaks. Some of them came in and out to trade coal for more materials and tools; others kept picking at the seams. It was a grueling job, but strong camaraderie kept them civil and motivated.

"We are nearing the end of the seam," Dooncam said, some hours before their shift ended. He had already hit a wall of limestone and was now picking at what seemed like the last of the coal in that area.

"We should switch to the other shaft," Ebaja said.

"Let me finish here first. Once we are—" There was a loud crack, then a rumble. A cloud of dust filled the chamber, extinguishing the lamps.

A cough. "Is everyone alright?" a disembodied voice asked in the darkness.

"Dooncam?" Ebaja's voice called.

"I'm good," he answered. "Can someone light that thing again?"

One of the workers struck at the flint until his lamp came back to life, casting thick beams of light in the unsettled dust. A big chunk of black and tan rock stood mere feet away from Dooncam—he had nearly been crushed.

Alaia felt cold air brush her sweating forehead. "There's a breeze," she warned. "I think you hit a pocket."

That was when the trogon began her sorrowful wail, in a series of descending, guttural notes, like the raspy voice of an old woman crying for mercy. Dooncam rushed away from the cave-in. "Move, *move!*" he shouted, rushing to where Alaia and Ebaja were already picking up their belongings.

Alaia relit her lamp and looked down the shaft to where the deafening song was coming from—the bird had been abandoned in a corner, covered in dust. Other trogons echoed now, mimicking the cries of the first, alerting the nearby shafts of the noxious fumes.

"Let's go!" Dooncam screamed, pulling on Alaia's shoulder.

"Limestone again?" Ebaja asked, making conversation as they fled together.

"I think so. It just cracked right over my head," Dooncam replied. "Would've crushed me if—hey, Alaia!"

Alaia was rushing toward the wailing bird.

"Alaia!" he repeated.

"The bird! I'll go get her!" Alaia cried.

"It's dead. Let's go, don't be stupid!"

Alaia thought about Sontai, and how guilty Lago had felt about letting her die in the dark. *I can't let this bird go through that. Not alone. Not like this.*

"She is not dead yet, I can save her!" Alaia said, bolting down the shaft, holding the shivering flame of her lamp in front of her.

Dooncam looked at Ebaja and shook his head before she said or did anything. "Don't risk it. We'll wait for her up ahead."

The cries got louder, closer. Before stepping into the area they had been working in, Alaia inhaled deeply and held her breath. As she hurried to grab the cage, she tripped on the debris and dropped her oil lamp. The safety glass shattered, the light flickering once, twice, then bleeding away into blackness. *My flint,* she thought, feeling her pockets; but her flint was in her haversack, which Ebaja had carried for her. Either way, the fumes could be flammable. It would be reckless to strike a new flame with the safety glass broken.

With all the noise the bird was making, Alaia easily found the cage. She wanted to breathe again, but knew that if she gave in, and with how nervous she was, she would hyperventilate, and that'd be the surest, quickest way to die. It was the reason the miners used birds: they needed a lot more oxygen and inhaled the poisons more quickly, making them more susceptible to their effects. Instead of panicking, Alaia tucked the bird's cage under her arm, closed her eyes, and walked at a confident, moderate pace, listening for the shapes of the shaft ahead. *Just hold it, hold it,* she told herself as her lungs burned. *A little bit further. We are almost out of the dangerous area.*

The trogon began her descending dirge once more, a bit more defeated this time; it was echoed in a chorus that was both far away and all around. *Stay with me, little bird. I'll keep you safe.* She found it hard to focus with the tragic songs surrounding her, but at the same time, the sounds created the necessary echoes for her to visualize her way through the mine.

Her chest ached; her head pulsed. She pressed forward, then began to exhale, feeling little relief. A warm breeze hit her side, strong and steady.

The ventilation channel from shaft twelve, she figured. She let go of the last bubbles of stale air and breathed deeply from the fresh current of the intersecting shaft. It smelled like grass and sweat, and carried a reassuring certainty that she was close to the exit. *Almost there, don't need to cry now.* She picked up speed, no longer needing to hold her breath. Light from the exit hit her eyelids.

The trogon had stopped calling. She looked down at the cage. The bird wasn't moving. *There's still time. Just hold on, little bird,* she thought, as her eyes began to tear up.

When she reached the entrance, Dooncam was there to scorn her.

"You dumb bitch! What were you doing?"

Alaia didn't listen; instead, she kneeled by the entrance and opened the tiny cage. The blue and red bird was motionless, serene. She pushed at the bird's chest to make her react, but the trogon was dead.

"You should've known better, fool," Dooncam said. "Once they start singing, they be gone. Leave that stupid bird alone. I gotta go report the leak to Bahimir." He stomped away.

All the miners gathered around. Each of the groups had with them a caged bird, all alive. The birds had already cried their hearts out, as a response to the other trogon's call, but they had not been poisoned. They looked tired and confused.

Alaia hastened toward the nearest cage, and before the person holding it could react, she opened the door, letting the bird fly away. The trogon flopped weakly up and perched on a branch, catching her breath before taking off toward the mountains.

"What you doing? Get off!" yelled the youth who had been holding the cage. He violently shoved Alaia, who landed on the ground next to the dead bird. It was Carlo, a sixteen-year-old with scale-like spurs all across his forearms. Now that his bird was missing, he would have to make up some story to avoid getting in trouble with his supervisors.

Alaia grabbed the dead trogon from the dusty ground, then kicked Carlo in the shin. Twisting with pain, he lifted the empty cage, about to slam it down on Alaia, but Ebaja stepped between them. "Cool it, Carlo. She had a rough day."

"I don't give no shit, why'd she do that for?"

Ebaja walked Alaia back protectively, ignoring the teenage boy.

"She'll fucking pay for it!" Carlo yelled from behind. "Swear by the light of Pellámbri, she'll pay sixteenfold!"

Ebaja escorted Alaia toward the watermill. "Go home, girl," she said. "Don't let it get to ya. I'll deal with Bahimir. I'll tell him you got dizzy from the fumes, and I told you to take the rest of the day off." She kissed Alaia's nub and softly pushed her away.

Alaia held the dead bird tight to her chest and cried all the way home.

CHAPTER ELEVEN

SINKHOLES

Alaia plucked red and blue feathers from the dead trogon, not flinching at the sight of blood at the feathers' roots but cringing at how sad the bird's half-opened eyes looked. She used the feathers to adorn her hair, right around her nub, then placed the bird in the hollow of an oak, put an acorn in her beak, and after a solemn pause recited the same prayer she had chanted for Sontai. *Gotta stay strong in front of him,* she thought. She had lost her composure back at the mines, and she couldn't allow that to happen with Lago around. *That boy deserves better. He's been through too much.*

She expected to be scolded when she arrived at work the following morning, but that didn't happen. *I guess Carlo didn't tell on me after all,* she thought with relief. The cave-in had been checked, and although a bit of poisonous gas had leaked, the pocket had been small and was no longer a threat. Glad when her shift was over, Alaia dropped her tools by the watermill and hurried home.

"Moon lights," she greeted Lago, who was playing fetch with Bear at the rope bridges.

"Stars guide," he greeted back. "Hey, want to go for a swim?" he asked, sweat streaking his brow.

Alaia liked the idea. It was better to go before Sunnokh hid his face—the wind that snaked through the valley at eventide could get chilly.

They dropped their clothes at the edge of the largest of the sinkholes. Lago usually kept his underwear on, but seeing no miners around, he dared to go completely bare this time. A thick rope was tied to an old birch tree, with bulky knots along its length; they cast it down so they could use it to climb out later. The sinkhole had several boarded-up shafts that connected to it, leading to long-abandoned veins of the seam that had been exhausted, collapsed, or were not pure enough to bother with.

Lots of kids had gotten broken ribs from the high drop, but Lago knew how to dive feet-down to avoid getting injured. He took the plunge first, flattening his body into a piercing shape, tightening his butt as his toes cut into the water. Alaia jumped next, delighting in the freedom during the weightless moment before gravity reclaimed her. Bear barked at the edge; he loved water and would've been the first to jump into any creek, but he wasn't stupid enough— or brave enough—to jump from this height.

Alaia surfaced in a murky splash, coughing. "It got in my nose again! How do you shut yours without using your hands?"

"You just... tighten it? I don't know." Lago reached to pluck something from Alaia's head. "Hey, your pretty feathers are all coming loose."

"Oh shit oh shit." She swam in search of the trogon feathers. "Help me gather them, please?"

They collected as many feathers as they could and lined them to dry in front of one of the closed shafts. They climbed up and sat next to the feathers, dangling their feet in the water.

"Never seen you wear those colors before," Lago said, helping Alaia comb the feathers.

"I found them yesterday and thought they looked pretty," she lied, then began attaching the feathers back onto her tight braids.

Bear was barking again. Lago noticed a strange tone in his calls. "Bear, quiet!" he yelled. Then he heard Bear growl, and looking up saw a silhouette at the edge of the sinkhole, pulling the rope up. "We are down here. Can you leave the rope for us, please?" he asked. The rope kept moving up. "Hey, did you hear me?" Lago said, louder, to no response. He jumped into the water to grab the rope, but he was too late.

"Told ya you'd pay for it, bitch," came the voice of Carlo.

"You asshole!" Alaia screamed. "Leave Lago out of this. He has nothing to do with it."

"Not my fucking problem. They put me on shaft twenty-six because of your screw-up. You know that place stinks." He finished pulling up the rope, then tossed it away. "Don't stay out late, seems like it'll be a chilly night. Enjoy your swim," he said, then left.

"Come back! Hey! You can't leave us down here!" But no answer came.

"What in Khest was that about?" Lago asked. "How are we going to get out now?"

"I'll explain later. We need to go before it gets too cold."

"Go where?"

Alaia looked around. There was no way to climb up, and no one would hear them if they yelled. "We can take the mines," she suggested. "I think this shaft leads west, and we can—"

"That's east," he corrected her. Even though Alaia could find her way around in lightless tunnels, Lago had a much keener sense of direction outdoors.

"Shit. Okay. Then we can take that shaft over there. Follow me." Careful not to get her feathers wet, Alaia swam to the shaft on the opposite side. They climbed up and shook the water off, shivering as the chill air spiraled down them.

"We're gonna freeze," Lago said.

"The temperature is stable in the mines. We could wait till someone comes to swim in the morning, or we can try to find our way through."

Spending the night in the dark mines was frightening enough for Lago, but the thought of having to climb up naked in front of all the miners petrified him. "I need to get to the observatory," he said. "Crysta will be waiting for me."

"Then through the mines it is."

"But how are we going to see where we are going?"

"Don't need no light to find my way, Gwoli. If you make enough noise, you can hear your way around, kind of like seeing with sound."

"But what if we fall down a shaft or something?"

"There's nothing lower than this seam," she lied, confident in her abilities, but not wanting Lago too worried. "And maybe we'll get lucky and find an emergency cache. Help me pull this, will ya?" she said, tugging at one of the boards sealing the abandoned shaft. It came loose after a few hard tugs, making just enough room for the kids. Alaia squeezed her thin body through, scraping her torso on the remaining boards, then helped Lago. Once inside, she pulled two long, rusty nails from the loosened plank.

"Put a hand on my shoulder and follow right behind me," she said, venturing into the black void. As she rhythmically hit the nails, their muted echoes showed her wooden support beams and told her there were enough of them for the tunnel to have been properly stabilized. She figured the area had likely been closed due to exhausting its coal, rather than due to collapses. "This likely connects to shaft number seven," she said. "It opens near the sinkholes." She had worked that shaft before, years ago, and still remembered it well.

The darkness was complete, so dense that one could embrace it. Lago felt he could just lift both feet off the ground and float in it. It reminded him of playful times at their Diamond Cave, when they would close the round door and tell ghost stories in the dark, then sneak around and jump-scare each other.

Alaia began humming a lilting melody to keep them company, keeping the tempo by striking the nails.

"What is that you are humming?" Lago asked.

"An Oldrin lullaby I learned from Shao. Any sounds help me see."

"So, wanna tell me what happened out there?"

Alaia stopped walking, remaining quiet except for her faint breathing. "I'll tell you," she said, "but we have to keep moving." She resumed hitting the nails, but instead of humming, she told Lago everything that had happened the day before. Despite her impassive voice, she teared up recounting her story, but Lago could not see her eyes, and that comforted her.

Time was hard to measure in this underworld, where there was no reference other than the rhythms of one's breaths, heartbeats, and footsteps. They must've been walking for an hour when Alaia kicked something that made a hollow sound. "Yes!" she squealed.

"What is it?"

"An emergency cache. Hold on." She knew exactly how to open it.

Lago heard a creaking lid, then the sounds of rummaging. He tried to imagine what was in front of him, picturing a golden treasure chest filled with precious coins and clay vessels to match the sharp sounds, and a canvas map to correspond to the scraping rasp. He heard the crackling snap of flint being struck and was suddenly blinded by furious streaks of light. The silhouette of Alaia crouching down was temporarily burned into his retinas. A few more strikes and *fwhoomp!*, the oil-soaked wick was lit. Alaia studied the crate. It was ancient, the wood splintering apart—they were lucky that the oil had been properly preserved in a clay bottle.

Alaia stood straight and scanned her surroundings. "The seam is mostly bare, but still has some coal left to mine. I bet they closed this shaft due to outgassing, otherwise they wouldn't have abandoned a cache like this one."

"Great. So, we might die from gas poisoning."

"With this open flame lamp? Unlikely. We'd first die from an explosion. If that happened, we'd be roasted, then pulped by the collapsing roof." Alaia saw Lago's terrified expression and figured she was being a bit too insensitive with her not-really-joking jokes. "But don't worry, Gwoli, from the looks of it this was many years ago. There wouldn't be any gas left."

Lago took the metal box with the flint, canvas, and extra candles, just in case, while Alaia led the way with the lamp. It was a mystifying sight, manifesting something archaic and primal: a young woman perfectly silhouetted by a flame, walking naked in a tunnel with walls as dark as her own skin, guiding them out of the nethervoids.

Alaia took decisive turns around the passages. As she was turning right at one intersection, the lamp's flame flickered. Lago felt a chill coming from the left side.

"Did you feel that?" he whispered.

"Yeah... I thought the exit would be to the right, but there's a draft coming from the left. Might be a shortcut."

They followed the cold breeze to where the shaft widened and became shorter, forcing them to crawl on their knees.

"I don't get it, where did that wind come from?" Lago asked. "There's nothing here?"

Alaia noticed a pile of rubble and hurried toward it. "Check this out," she said, then stood. From Lago's perspective, it looked as if her upper body had disappeared into the ceiling, leaving only her legs behind.

He waddled his way to her and straightened up in a crack wide enough for both of them to stand side by side. The dim light of the lamp revealed a natural limestone cavern streaked with stalactites and stalagmites. Not only was there a cool wind blowing through the cavern, but there was also the sound of water inexhaustibly carving more passages. The cavern was spacious, branching into several paths, all equally unexplored.

The flame flickered in the breeze again.

"Do you think that wind is poisonous? Or... or flammable?" he asked.

"We'd be dead by now if it was. I smell something like clay and moss. It must be coming from the outside, which means it's fresh."

"So, we can exit through here?"

"Khest no, limestone caverns can exit just around the corner, or go for hundreds of miles, with not even a way out in the end. We could easily get lost, or step on a crack and fall hundreds of feet down."

"But you can feel the wind."

"But you can't always trust it. It could lead to a hole out of reach, or too small to fit through. It's damn pretty, though. Look at all these crystals! This one looks like it's growing hairs."

Lago squatted down to appreciate the forms. "And these colorful ones look like mushrooms. Like you could just pluck them out and eat them."

"And these stalactites are sharp!"

"Those are stalagmites, actually, because—"

"Shut it. Look, they almost look like teeth."

Lago touched their sharp points. "To me they look like the ridge of spurs on your spine."

"They do!" Alaia said, then counted the protrusions. "But there's only eleven of them, and I have thirteen sisters on my back. Mine are better."

Lago sat and leaned against a stalagmite; it was moist and felt slimy on his naked body, so he leaned forward again. "I miss our Diamond Cave," he said. "It'd be nice to have a new secret hideout, but this place doesn't feel the same."

"It does not. Too dangerous. Besides, it took us like an hour to get here, and we don't know how much longer it'll be before we make it out again." She looked at the lamp. "We probably have two more hours with this lamp. We should try to find the exit. Come on, Gwoli."

They left the limestone cavern and followed the path back to the intersection. Half an hour later, they reached a boarded-up shaft.

"Look, this was nailed from the other side," Alaia said. "This must be where they closed it off. Let's rip it apart."

Lago kicked through the boards, which were much easier to detach when pushed in that direction. The nails screeched, and the wood tumbled on the opposite side.

Alaia made her way through the opening and looked at a marking on the wall. "Yellow paint and a black line. Means outgassing *and* spent seam. That's why no one else bothered with it."

After a short walk, she recognized where they were. "It's shaft seven alright, the exit is this way."

They found their clothes by the sinkhole, and Bear, too, who was curled in a patient, whining ball. It was frigid outside, so they dressed quickly. It was late too, so Lago would have to skip going to the observatory. As they returned to the Hollows, they spotted a few lingering campfires from the communal kitchens. Dinner was over; the miners were packing up. Alaia's face turned furiously red when she saw one of the groups, then pale with shame. She kept her head down.

"Had a pleasant swim?" came a voice from the group, followed by a cackle from the other kids.

"Is that?... Is that the guy from earlier?" Lago asked. "What was it, Carlo?"

"That's him. Let's just go," Alaia muttered under her breath. "We had enough for one night."

Lago didn't listen. In a heartbeat, he was sprinting toward the teenager, who was four years older and much bigger, but was not expecting the attack. Lago jumped and punched Carlo in the ear, knocking him to the soil, making him cut his lip on the glass he was drinking from.

Lago didn't wait for a reaction. He had dealt with bullies before: if he gave Carlo one chance, the teenager would take him down. Lago was pure rage; he fought dirty. Before Carlo had a chance to regain his balance, Lago kicked him in the neck, then threw sand in his eyes and punched until his knuckles were bloody.

"Stop! Lago, stop!" Alaia uselessly yelled. The other kids were so surprised by the tiny flurry of violence that they had to laugh; they thought it hilarious to see Carlo struggle with a prepubescent little stick like Lago; some even cheered Lago on.

"That's enough!" Alaia said, pulling Lago back. Carlo was on the verge of unconsciousness, luckily for Lago; otherwise, he wouldn't have stood a chance fighting him.

"Keep your rabid puppy leashed, Alaia!" said one of the guys in the group, laughing all the while.

Alaia helped Lago up and looked around. "Let's get the fuck out of here."

CHAPTER TWELVE

ENCHANTRESS

"Was it Borris again?" Crysta asked, eyeing Lago's bandaged hands.

"Not him. It's nothing. Sorry I missed work last night."

"You can skip some days if you let me know beforehand, but your wages will be deducted accordingly. And I don't like you getting in trouble, you are too impulsive. I'm more worried about the other kid. What happened?"

"It was a guy at the mines. He was being an ass to Alaia and me."

"Did he hurt you?"

"Just my knuckles. His face deserved it."

Crysta gave him a stern look, blinked pointedly, then changed the subject.

"I talked to Chaplain Gwil," she said as she set up the telescope. "I won't be around tomorrow, but he will have some errands for you."

"What sort of errands?"

"Probably deliveries. Should be easy for you to handle."

The Sunnday errands were easy as could be for Lago, who was used to making deliveries around Withervale. Gwil sent him to deliver letters emblazoned with fancy wax seals, to drop off a box full of something that clinked like tiny glass bottles, and also to pick up leaves from an allgender botanist named Holfster, who lived in the East Flank, near the school. Lago knew Lerr Holfster from the deliveries he used to make for his father—they liked to buy fine silks and always tipped well.

Holfster was a portly trader from the Kingdom of Bauram: a distant, south-western island covered in blue, purple, and black sand dunes. They had told Lago stories of the ghostly desert where the blue sands shifted daily to reveal ruins from before the Downfall, only to cover them up again when no one was looking.

The walls of the shop were painted in a blue the same color as Holfster's eyes, and the same color as the sand they used to grow their imported plants. Most Baurami had those entrancing eye colors, ranging from the darkest blues that passed as black unless a bright light landed upon them, to bright turquoise like waters over a shallow reef.

Lago crossed through the plant nursery and entered the office. The incense and aromatic flowers turned the air in the shop exotic and remote. Perplexing plants were housed in transparent planters by the well-lit windows. *Succulents*, Holfster called them—Lago thought the name sounded icky.

"Lago? Your father was just here. Did he forget something?" Holfster said.

"No, I'm not here—" Lago began. "I didn't come because of him."

Lerr Holfster leaned on the counter and scrutinized Lago's evasive eyes. They were always well-dressed, attentive, soft-spoken, and particularly kind to Lago, who, unlike other boys, did not make fun of Holfster when passing in front of their shop's windows.

"I can nearly see a thundering cloud over your curly hairs," they said. "What's bothering you, lad?"

Lago was both saddened and embarrassed by the question. "Nothing. Dad and I had a big fight."

"I'm terribly sorry. If you want to talk about—"

"I don't. I'm not living with him anymore… He kicked me out."

The corpulent botanist leaned back and sighed. "If you need a place to stay, you know you can always—"

"I'm okay, thank you, Lerr Holfster. I'm staying with a friend now. I'm here to pick up some leaves or something."

"Still running deliveries?"

"For the Mesa Monastery now." He showed them the request Gwil had scribbled on a sheet of parchment.

"Chaplain Gwil is a fine man. You are in good hands." Holfster walked around the desk, out to the nursery, and plucked leaves from multiple plants. They wrapped them carefully and tucked them in Lago's bag. "Gwil will want them fresh, so don't delay too much. And be careful with those monks"—they leaned in conspiratorially—"I hear they get into some strange things."

"What sort of things?" Lago asked them, a bit spooked.

"Weird, spiritual things. Chanting, forbidden drugs, summoning spirits, talking to plants, that sort of thing. Well, I talk to my plants too, but I'm not *that* crazy, not yet. Just don't let them recruit you as one of their own, or they'll shave your head, and you'll look even worse than I." Holfster widened their bright-blue eyes and flashed their perfectly white teeth while running their fingers over their shiny, balding head.

Lago shivered theatrically at the idea. He liked his curly hair. "I'll be careful, don't worry."

They shared an awkward pause during which things were left unsaid.

Holfster walked behind the counter again. "Listen, Lago. I don't know if the friend you are staying with likes plants, but maybe this will make your new place more homey." They reached toward a window for a planter that seemed to hold only colorful, river-smoothed pebbles. "I know what you are thinking," they said. "These are indeed plants, not rocks. These babies are ruby-flecked stoneleaves. Like a lot of my succulents, they only grow in the blue sands of Bauram." The stoneleaves were a darker blue than the sands they inhabited, multiplying in clusters of strange symmetries. Their smooth tops were sprayed with crimson dots, like constellations of rubies.

"They look like gemstones," Lago observed.

"And they are just as precious to me."

Lerr Holfster used a pair of tweezers to pluck the smallest stoneleaf from the cluster; the plump offset detached with even tinier roots attached to it. They reached below the counter for a transparent planter not much bigger than a thimble, filled it with Baurami-blue sands, and planted the offset. They then dipped a pudgy index finger in a glass of water and tenderly tapped on the succulent, letting the stoneleaf absorb the moisture.

"Keep her in the sun. One drop of water a week will do for this size, but stop watering her at the end of Autumn and don't start again until late Thawing. She will take a long time to grow more offsets. Once she does, come and see me, and I'll give you a bigger planter as well as more sand."

"It's a beautiful, um, succulent. I'll take good care of her. I hope she grows as many babies as yours."

"Maybe more!" Holfster said, handing Lago the tiny planter. They smiled affectionately. "You've always been kind and well-mannered, Lago. I know you don't want to talk about what happened just now, but if you need anything, or just want someone who will listen, come and see me. You have friends in this city."

"Thank you, Lerr Holfster. I will," Lago said, then headed out.

When Lago returned to the Hollows, he placed his minuscule ruby-flecked stoneleaf on a window of the hole he had just begun to call home. He would give her a drop of water every week and make sure she was getting all the sunlight she could wish for.

The next day, during recess, Crysta approached Lago.

"How was working for Gwil?"

"Quite easy. He had me do deliveries in the East Flank, and a few more by Baurghost Street. Got 'em done super quick."

"He'll be sending you farther than that in the future, but nowhere farther than Withervale proper. Listen, if you have time to spare tonight, meet me at the observatory right at sunset. Two planets will be visible. We can look at them before we get too busy."

"Of course! I'll be there at sunset."

School went by too slowly; Lago could not wait to be done. He tapped his pencils rhythmically, as if that would somehow speed up time. *I'm going to see a planet! Through a telescope! Wait, two planets!* Magic hid in the brassy tube, urging Lago to want more, who knew he'd always see something unexpected. Those candles millions of starmiles away held his fascination, and the planets even more so. He arrived at the observatory a bit early and out of breath and waited in the library.

Crysta arrived soon after Lago. "Hey, so early? Let's get the telescope ready."

With Lago's help, Crysta moved the heavy telescope toward the west window of the octagonal room. The golden light of sunset became a streak sharper than a sword as it bounced off the polished brass tube.

"Can we look at the sun?" Lago asked.

"You'd burn your eyes out. So, no. We can try it some other day by using filters. Today we'll look at Ongumar and Iskimesh. They'll show up once Sunnokh's glow fades a bit. Give it a little while."

"How many more planets are there?"

"The days of the week should tell you. Moonday for Sceres, which isn't a planet but still counts, then Khuday for the Dawn Pilgrim, Khumen, Nossday for our own planet, Iskimday and Onguday for the two planets we are about to see, and Sunnday for the Sky Flame, Sunnokh. But that's not the whole story." She teased him with a smirk.

"There are more then?"

"Yes, there's also Senstrell, who is closer than Ongumar, but much harder to see because she is small and black. It means *obsidian* in Miscamish."

"Why is there no Senstrellday?"

"Because she was only discovered a decade ago. If we suddenly made our weeks have seven days, it'd be quite problematic for our calendars."

"I'd love to see a black planet... Can we look at her?"

"You wouldn't be able to see her with this toy. There's a telescope many times bigger than this one in the Yenwu Peninsula, the size of this whole room. That's how they discovered her."

"That's huge!"

"And we'd like to have even bigger ones! But they are not easy to construct. We don't even know how the ancients managed to craft the giant pieces of glass with such precision. But they survived the Downfall, and we can use the old glass today, just like we use their mathematical texts to make predictions of where the planets will be each night. They knew so much more than we do—we are barely beginning to understand all they left behind. Anyway, that's five planets we know of, including where we stand, but there might be others, either too small, too dark, or too far away for us to see."

Lago squinted at the horizon, as if trying to surpass the abilities of the telescope. "I see two stars there, are those it?"

"Not stars, but they are it. The left one is Ongumar, let's start with him. He's the one we call *Amberlight*, because of his orange color." She used a clean cloth to wipe the eyepiece.

"How do you know which ones are boy or girl planets?" Lago asked.

"Depends on each culture. Planets don't really have genders, but we like to make up stories about them, and once we associate characters that are male or female with them, they kind of stick. And since our own planet, Noss, is the source of all life, we see them as allgender."

"Like Lerr Holfster!"

"You know them too? Exactly like that." Crysta finished wiping the lenses, then fixed the focus. "Take a look."

Lago leaned his right eye over the eyepiece, covering the left with his hand; he was still having a hard time closing only one eye, and found it easier this way. "He looks like the sun at sunset!" he said.

"And he's not on his closest approach yet. In a few months, he will be even brighter. Pre-Downfall documents claim Ongumar is made of gas, like Sunnokh, but not as hot or bright. How the old scholars could know that, no one has yet figured out. But let's move on before the planets set." She took control of the telescope to make sure the next target was aligned. "Now take a look at the other one, the green planet."

"She has a trail of stars!" he said, then looked to the horizon without the aid of the glass, trying to spot the same dots with his naked eyes.

"They are not stars, but moons," Crysta said. "Right now, they are all aligned on the same side, so they look like a trail. We know of four moons, but there might be more we can't see. Ongumar has at least three moons, but only one was visible tonight, barely discernible against the backdrop of real stars."

"Do they have seasons, like Sceres?" Lago asked, eye still on the eyepiece. "Or a shard that glows like a beacon?"

"Maybe, who knows? They are too far for us to see them clearly. That planet is Iskimesh, the one we call the *Enchantress*. Tonight she looks green, tomorrow night she will look blue, some other nights a mix of both. Like in that Bayani lullaby, 'Oh, Iskimesh.'" She cleared her throat and chanted a tune that wove between mellifluous and wistful:

> Her coat was blue, bright green her dress,
>
> Of hues no poet could express.
>
> Her skin was pale, her eyes like pearls,
>
> And hair that twirled in teal-blue curls.

> Lurr Iskimesh by starlight shone
>
> Forsaken in her halls of stone.
>
> Lorr Ongumar left her in tears
>
> To journey forth to new frontiers.

> To not let sadness grief give way
>
> —To shun her loneliness away—
>
> She danced and spun and bared her chest
>
> Till milky pearls flowed out her breasts.

> Oh, Iskimesh your love has left!
>
> In jade azures your dress will spin.
>
> Enchantress who was left bereft,
>
> Keep dancing, twirling, till world's end!

Lago was staring at Crysta, entranced. "You sing it better than the music teacher," he said.

"Mennu is tone deaf. Don't tell her I said that. In that spritetale, Iskimesh and Ongumar were in love, but Ongumar had to leave her to go to war, so Iskimesh danced and danced every night, remembering his love, hoping that her dancing would bring him back to her."

"That's so sad. Why does she change colors?"

"We don't know, but we *think* that she's a planet like ours. Mostly green, with a big patch of blue, while ours is mostly blue with a patch of green. Her day cycle is different from ours, so each night we are seeing a slightly different angle, a different color."

"So, she's filled with fish and forests?"

"If there is life out there, maybe she has vast oceans, forests, or something analogous."

"Nalogoose. Never seen one of those."

"Analogous. It means *something similar*. But who knows? Life could be completely different out there. We have no idea."

Lago looked through the eyepiece again, "I can't find—"

"Use these two knobs, aim it down until she's visible again."

"She moves fast. She's almost at the horizon. Do you think you'll find a new planet someday?"

"It's not my field, really. It takes a vaster knowledge of mathematics. But your grades in math are good. If you keep that curiosity alive, maybe *you* will be the one to discover a new planet someday."

Without taking his eyes from the magical glass, Lago smiled, spellbound by the Enchantress.

CHAPTER THIRTEEN

DIRE WOLF

Lago spotted a frenetic gathering of gossiping kids when he arrived at school on Onguday.

"As big as a house!" said a mop-headed boy whom Lago didn't know.

"Can't be that big, Dad said as big as a Bergsulf bison," Phillin, one of Lago's classmates, corrected.

"While pulling a wagon," added Jasmeia, who was a year ahead of them.

The conversation devolved into a cacophony of hearsay and exaggerations.

"It took down fifty men!

"Teeth big as scimitars, and they said—"

"Took arrows to both of its heads."

"—the biggest dog you *ever* saw."

"A wolf, not a dog!"

"Same thing!"

Lago pulled on Phillin's shoulder, who seemed the most reasonable of the group, though that wasn't saying much. "What is everyone talking about?"

"Didn't you hear about the wolf?" he replied in a hush, but apparently not quietly enough.

"The three-headed wolf," Jasmeia corrected.

"Stop making shit up!" Phillin added with a glare. "Anyway, they killed this huge dog, wolf, this morning. A *one-headed* wolf. Dad told me it must weigh like sixteen tons, like some sort of monster from the nethervoids."

"It killed two guards by the wall," a fat, blond kid named Deon pointed out. Lago stared at the portly boy, listening intently. "Pat's mom said a whole pack of them came down from the mountains and—"

"A whole army of them!" interrupted Pat. "Got stuck at the river crossing, so they came straight for Withervale. This biggest one got separated and they shot him down. Went rabid and attacked the guards."

"Was it really an army of them?" shy Benneri asked.

"Yeah. Well, like five," Pat admitted.

The bell rang, sending the students scurrying to their classrooms.

"Hey Pat, what did they do with the wolf?" Lago asked, trying to keep up next to him.

"They dragged it to Fliskel Square, so everyone can see."

I need to go see this thing, Lago thought, trying to picture the mythical beast. *Maybe tomorrow, before it's gone.* He sat at his desk and paid no attention to class that day.

Lago rushed up the steps of the watchtower. Short of breath, he gasped, "Moon lights!"

"Takh smite me!" Crysta cried out, startled.

"H–hey, did you hear ab–about the wolf?"

"I heard about it indeed. No one has seen a creature of that size before, though they do have fossils of something like it at the museums in Zovaria." Crysta fumbled with the telescope and aimed it at a celestial object rising over the Anglass Dome.

"At school they are making up stories," Lago said, "it's hard to know what's true."

"I wouldn't trust anything the kids are saying."

"Does it really have three heads?"

Crysta rolled her eyes. "I won't even acknowledge that question. But I'm curious about it too. I heard rumors about giant wolves roaming around the Heartpine Dome, months ago. And lately we've had sightings of strange new birds, and insects too."

"You think they came from inside the dome?"

"We still don't know what's inside them, but I did get confirmation that part of the dome is collapsing. Maybe these creatures have something to do with it."

Crysta gestured for Lago to step toward the telescope. "But back to business. Before you look through the eyepiece, tell me what you see." She pointed east.

"You mean the bright star?"

"Yes, what is special about it?"

Lago narrowed his eyes toward the distant light. "It looks the same as the other ones," he said.

"Then why are you squinting like that?"

"I… I'm just having a hard time keeping it in focus."

"But you don't have the same problem with the other stars?"

Lago looked up. "No, the other ones look sharp. But this one looks stretched, like it's longer. Hey, is that one of the planets?"

"Exactly, now you can take a look."

Lago could smell the brass as he bent to the eyepiece. He saw a small circle of white, crossed by a luminous line. He described it to Crysta.

"What you are looking at is Khumen," the professor said, "the Dawn Pilgrim, after whom the second day of the week is named. The line you see is an enormous ring that wraps around the entire planet, like the brim of a hat. The ring is always flat to us, so we see it as a line."

"Then how do you know it's a ring, and not, like, a square?"

"We're quite confident it's a ring, not a square."

Lago seemed unconvinced. "Is there a song for Khumen, like the one you sang of Iskimesh?"

"There is! It's not Bayani, but a Zovarian tune. But I barely recall the words. My husband knows it, I'll ask him to teach it to me again, and then I can teach you. But enough of that, I have work to do on the new wisps." Crysta turned a knob to loosen the tripod head, letting the telescope drop a few degrees.

A bit shyly, Lago asked, "Do you think Gwil will have any errands for me tomorrow? Maybe down by the river?"

"I thought you didn't find his errands very interesting."

"Just wondering…"

"Probably. Come by in the early morning and see what he needs. The wolf will be at Fliskel Square."

Lago felt a bit embarrassed about how easy he was to read. "Yeah, I want to go see it."

"Be ready for big crowds," she warned.

On Sunnday morning, Lago darted under the arched gate of the monastery grounds and knocked on the observatory's door. No one answered. It was too early. He wasn't sure at what time the monks would leave their residence, so he decided to walk around the grounds while he waited.

The monastery was once a place of worship for a nameless religion from before the Downfall. The central nave of what used to be a cathedral stood as the observatory's library, a small annex of the Zovarian Academic Institute, with the watchtower jutting from its northern end. Bordering this structure were the garden and orchard, a few decrepit mausoleums, a cemetery, and a large building that Lago had never been in, but guessed was the dormitories, kitchens, and whatever else the monks needed for whatever it was that monks did.

Lago ran his fingertips over the ancient stones of the cemetery: most lay broken, coated in moss, and crossed by shimmering paths of slime that slugs had traced on them. He realized the bumps on the grass must have been tombstones, blanketed by soil, weeds, and forgetfulness.

He reached the sandstone balustrade at the north end of the cemetery and lost himself in the clear view of the fortified harbor city of Withervale. The city sprawled only half a mile north of the mesa, hugging the southern shores of the Stiss Malpa—the Great River—where it was crossed by the Old Pilgrim's Road. Lago's gaze drifted south from Withervale's eastern gate, down the Halfort Rampart, which ran all the way to the base of the Stelm Ca'éli, also known as the Pilgrim Sierras. The Union kept this choke point fortified, as it was of strategic importance, even if the rampart wasn't a particularly strong fortification. Pink banners flowed atop the turrets while tiny soldiers—clad in pink as well—dozed on the parapets.

Lago noticed a trail of leaf-cutter ants on the balusters he was leaning on. The soldier ants stood out with their huge, round heads, while the smaller workers carried polygonal cuts of translucent, green leaves. He picked one up by the leaf; the worker would not let go of it. He tossed the leaf and ant over the rail and watched them get picked up by the wind to be lost as a speck of green down the cliffside.

Using a tiny stick, he taunted one of the soldier ants. The ant chomped with its large mandibles, piercing the bark. Lago pulled the stick up, with the ant still holding on to it. He grabbed the ant's body and pulled; it would not let go of the stick. He pulled harder until the ant's head popped off, still biting hard on the indestructible enemy. Lago observed the wriggling, headless body and the thick mandibles pinching the stick like a nose piercing. He smelled his fingers and winced at the vinegary scent of formic acid.

"You know," Chaplain Gwil said, startling Lago, "they may look very different from us, but they do have feelings. Maybe not the same way you and I do, but all living creatures have a type of consciousness."

"Sorry," Lago said, casting away the evidence. "I was just playing around. I didn't mean to—"

"It's alright, son. It's not easy to put ourselves in that perspective, when we see creatures so small and different from us. It is like looking down at the soldiers entering the Loomdinn Gate, or leaving through the Shidendinn Gate"—

he gazed north toward the city—"they become tiny dots, abstract numbers. It's important to always put yourself at their level, to understand the world the way they see it, whether it be soldiers coming home from war, or ants carrying leaves to their nests."

Lago wasn't sure if Gwil meant he should lower himself to the ground, and how that would help, so he just stared uncomfortably.

"Don't look so mortified. But I will ask of you, when you are on the Havengall Congregation grounds, please treat each living creature with the same respect you would for, say, a friend of yours. And perhaps also when you are not at the monastery, but that is up to your conscience to decide."

"I will, Lorr Gwil."

"Just Gwil."

"Gwil... I was wondering, are there any deliveries you wanted me to help with today?"

"Quite an eager boy! Yes, I can think of some errands. Why don't you follow me?" Gwil wrapped a long-sleeved arm over Lago's shoulder and guided him away from the cemetery. "Professor Holt told me how helpful you've been to her. The tower is finally looking tidy once more—I no longer trip on her notebooks when I walk in."

He led Lago to the largest building in the monastery, which he called the Haven. Flying buttresses wrapped around the hexagonal structure, like ribs of a giant sea monster, crisscrossing the sandstone passages with confusing shadows.

The heavy oak door creaked in low, staccato reverberations when Gwil pushed it open. Past the entrance was a vaulted space connected to a cloister, at the center of which was a garden teeming with hundreds of carefully labeled herbs. Shaved-headed monks walked through the garden with their eyes closed, in some sort of ritual, somehow managing to avoid stepping on the plants.

The Haven was six-sided, with each side of the hexagon serving a different function. Gwil explained, "This vaulted space is the choir room. You should come hear our chants on Nossday. Our voices bounce from the curved ceilings to create a glorious harmony! If you follow the cloister clockwise, you have the kitchen and refectory, the chapel, the dormitories, the scriptorium—where we transcribe and translate books—and the laboratory. And of course, the cloister garth at the center, where we keep our sacred herbs."

They turned right, toward what Gwil had said was the laboratory. The chaplain pushed open a stained-glass door and led Lago into a clean room with bright, glass ceilings, nothing like what he had expected to find in a place like the monastery.

The shelves on the lab's walls were stacked with jars filled to the brim with colorful crystals, powders, and oils, as vibrant as the spines of the books they shared the space with. Eight worktables were laid out, covered with alchemical paraphernalia, where mountings held pipettes, burners, and coils. Microscopes, bellows, alembics, flasks, magnets, and magnifying glasses were spread all over the workspace. About a dozen monks handled the instruments to measure, cut, burn, mix, and bag strange substances.

"The Havengall Congregation guides our roots," Gwil lectured. "We strive to understand the metabolic processes, the essence of existence and awareness, and use our knowledge to preserve and improve life. Most of the medicines you've ever taken probably came from this monastery. We send our products south over the Ninn Tago, and ship from the ferries at Maulers Port, east through the Stiss Malpa, and west over the Isdinnklad. The garth you saw back there houses species found only in the most remote lands of Noss. The Havengall monks are trained in various scholarly and spiritual disciplines that teach them how to care for the herbs, and how the herbs can care for us."

"What were the monks doing out there, walking with their eyes closed?" Lago asked.

"It's an ancient form of divination. After decades of practice, some monks learn to see the threads that connect all life. The threads help us figure out which plant, fungus, or animal product could be used to cure a particular ailment. It's a monk's job to look into this complex tapestry and learn to identify the connections."

At a workbench, a monk was using a needle to separate spores of a moss growing on a piece of glass. Chaplain Gwil approached him. "Lago, I'd like you to meet Khopto."

The monk stood gracefully, letting his dark-gray robes drape. He extended his arms forward and clasped his wrists with the palm and fingers of the opposite hand, in a mirroring hold that bound his arms together, as if shaking hands with himself. The linked arms made a circular loop, over which he bowed his head. "Essence of one, soul of the many," he said with no inflection.

"Thank you, y…ou too…" Lago replied.

Khopto wiped his fingers on his peculiarly aquiline nose. The nostrils were black, as if he had smeared charcoal on them. He noticed the coloration on his fingers and pulled out a handkerchief to clean himself up, seeming embarrassed.

"Khopto is one of our most studious and well-learned monks," Gwil said before Lago could ask about Khopto's darkened nose. "He speaks twelve languages, including the humming songs of the far-gone Sheréli. He can write in

Tsing script, Miscamish runes, Khaar Du blocks, Wastyrian knots, and can illustrate quite fanciful letters when translating pre-Downfall texts into Common."

Lago stared in awe, still struck by the ludicrous idea of someone knowing twelve entire languages.

"Lago is Professor Holt's disciple," Gwil said to the monk. "The boy I told you about, who is helping us with errands on Sunndays. And how blessed our fortunes be that today is the day we venerate Sunnokh, for Lago has come to offer his services."

"Most blessed," Khopto said. "As it happens, there has been an incident by the Loomdinn Gate."

"The wolf…" Lago whispered.

"The dire wolf, yes," Khopto said. "Our fossil records of dire wolves date back to before the Downfall. We had thought them extinct. We must secure our chance to study it before too many parties get their hands on it. Would you be kind enough to bring us the dire wolf, Lago?"

Lago widened his eyes in a mixture of excitement and terror.

"I'm only joking," Khopto said, placing a hand on Lago's shoulder. "I need you to take some papers to Vicar Aurgushem. He's the Congregation's liaison down in Withervale, the perfect man to deal with the bureaucracy involved in these matters." He handed Lago an envelope closed by a blue wax seal. "These are the specimen requests from the Mesa Monastery. You will find the vicar at the Harrowdale Temple, which is just down the road from Fliskel Square, where I believe the dire wolf is being displayed to the public."

"They say it's bigger than a bison," Lago said. "Is it true?"

"Sixteenfold bigger than any dire wolf should be," Khopto said, "even for a male."

"How can they get so big?"

Khopto shook his bald head. "We don't know. Dire wolves were sizable creatures, but not much bigger than regular wolves, making this situation doubly unusual."

"Before I forget," Gwil added, "Lago, I'll need you to pick something up for me. The vicar has a box of insect larvae I requested last week."

"I haven't met the vicar," Lago shyly said. "How will he know to trust me with the box?"

Gwil considered for a moment, but Khopto was first to think of an idea.

"Wear this," Khopto said, "and he'll know you are one of us." He unclasped a bracelet from his wrist and handed it to Lago. The bracelet was woven out of a fine copper filigree, in a labyrinth of knots that ended in two hands.

Lago put it on, clasping the bracelet's two hands to form a loop.

Gwil nodded and said to Lago, "I have one last thing before you go, if you would follow me."

Khopto bowed to the boy and the chaplain, then sat back down to work. Gwil took Lago to the westernmost section of the cloister, through a long dining hall, and all the way to the end of a curved hallway. A balustrade protected a dark pit behind it.

"This here is our delivery lift," Gwil said. "If you see this flag up, rotate the crank to pull the correspondence up. Give it a try."

Lago leaned his head over the chute and saw it dropped through a natural cut from a dried-up waterfall, ending hundreds of feet down at the bottom of the mesa. He spun the crank on the pulley system and, after a brief moment, retrieved a wooden crate with a bundle of letters. He handed the letters to Gwil.

"Well done! Sometimes we'll also send packages down to our emissary. Her name is Svana. You should introduce yourself next time you are down that way. If it makes it easier, you can drop packages here and pick them up at the bottom, but nothing heavier than, say, a quarter barrel, just to be safe." Gwil flipped through the letters as he walked back toward the dining hall. "I'll deliver these now, but you may do so yourself next time, once I show you where to find each of the monks. Get going now, I can taste your eagerness. Come and see me once you are done."

Lago left in such a hurry that he simply rushed down Runestone Lane, passing close to his father's home. Right there on a corner was Theo Vaari, buying oranges and turnips from a street vendor. Theo straightened his back, lowered his brows. "Lago, get back here right now!" he called for his son, but Lago did not slow. "You wretched burglar!" he added hoarsely, with a weak voice that cracked at the edges.

Lago moved along briskly, not even giving him the satisfaction of a look back. He strode down the road with the longest steps he could muster—he was not going to let his father ruin this day.

"Ungrateful thiefling!" Theo barked, but neither Lago nor the loud marketplace could care less.

Lago hitched a ride with Lurr Gianna, a pottery artist who had just made her final Sunnday delivery. A fat caribou pulled her empty wagon quickly down the ramp to the East Flank. Lago sat at the back and stared at the gorgeous bracelet Khopto had given him, still feeling uncomfortable with how the monk had said Lago was 'one of them.' He didn't feel like one of them, didn't even know a thing about their strange religion and practices, but he thought it a kind gesture that they accepted him so openly.

"How far are ye going, sweetie?" Gianna asked.

"All the way to the gate, if you are," he said.

"Another delivery for your father? Or doing a bit of wildlife sightseeing?"

"I guess everyone is going to see the wolf today, huh?"

"Yeap, saw it myself when I left this morning. It was still dark, couldn't spot more than a dark silhouette. The thing is *ee*-normous. Must be a malign acolyte of Takhamún himself, for I see no other explanation. I'm just glad it's dead."

"Does it really have three heads?"

Lurr Gianna laughed. She chewed on a leathery strip of jerky and said, "I guess ye'll have to see for yourself."

They arrived at the southeast gate with no delay and continued to the Old Pilgrim's Road. "I'm turning right here, heading out through Loomdinn," Gianna warned him. "I ain't going to mess with them crowds. Ye're on your own from here on."

Lago thanked her and hopped off the wagon, watching her leave beneath the metal teeth of the Loomdinn Gate. Hundreds of people strolled in the opposite direction, under the same rusty jaws. Guards were patrolling the barbican in greater numbers than Lago had ever seen before, all as tense as the pink banners flying above them.

He followed the stream of crowds into the core of the city. It was unusually busy for a Sunnday morning, filled with excitement from curious adults and anticipatory terror from the youngest children. Lago passed the Riverbank Marketplace and pushed his way through the Great Shrine of Takh until he saw the tall sycamores that wrapped around Fliskel Square. Crowds were packing themselves like salmon at the Stiss Lalinuth in early Highsun. The closer Lago got, the tighter it became.

He wriggled his small body through the horde until he reached the gnarled trunk of a sycamore, then began his ascent. He wasn't an expert climber, but his curiosity gave him a little boost of carelessness. He managed to get high up the tree, but a curtain of yellow leaves blocked his view. He pulled himself onto a branch that extended toward the center of the square and wormed his way forward on his stomach until he settled on a spot with a clear view.

And there it was.

The dire wolf's dead eyes stared at Lago from below, timeless like drops of amber. He was a colossal creature, bigger than a Bergsulf bison. If he had been standing up, the wolf would have reached seven feet to the shoulders and over three strides from nose to tail. His body was a driftwood gray that whispered blue undertones, his head a black as ominous as the moon's shadow. An inky-black pattern of rosettes spread down his neck and back, shapes resembling those of a spotted cat; they helped transition the black of the head as it dissolved to cold and unassuming grays further down the spine. The dire wolf's fur was coarse and contorted from the struggle, yet remained silky and vibrant, except in places matted with dried blood.

The wolf was spread across two hay wagons, surrounded by dozens of Zovarian guards. The pink-clad soldiers made sure the public could see the creature, but their halberds came down as a warning whenever anyone breached their imposed safety perimeter. A gaggle of scholars worked closely with the dead beast, taking measurements, collecting samples, sketching. Two Takheist priests were also present, praying to the Twin Gods that the monster would not resurrect, that his wretched soul would go back to the netherflames of Khest whence he had come.

Lago noticed two well-dressed nobles making their way inside the perimeter of halberds; he recognized one as Seneschal Maree Oda, governor of Withervale, and the other as Consul Hanno Uzenzo, the trade representative for the Negian Empire. Big names. This was an important event.

A loud whistle pierced the air. The crowd parted as four bison were led toward the dead beast. The guards banged their halberds upon their kite shields, quieting the audience.

"As I said," Seneschal Oda voiced loudly, "please stand back, we'll be moving the wolf to a shipshed at the naval base. We will inform the public of our findings in the coming days. Make room for the wagons, and thank you for coming."

Consul Uzenzo seemed livid. He hissed something at the seneschal, who waved him off. The guards stepped forward, holding their halberds horizontally to force people back. Two tarpaulins were pulled over the wolf, and with nothing left to see, the crowds began to grumble and disperse. The bison pushed their hooves on the cobbles and dragged the wagons west.

Lago climbed down the tree and joined a pack of curious urchins, following behind the wagons for a few blocks, until the bison pulled into the naval base. The gates closed with a metallic clang of finality. The children dispersed, eager to tell aggrandized stories to their friends. Lago took one look back at the wagons, then sighed. He was just crossing the street to head to the Harrowdale Temple, when he saw a robe-clad monk turning the corner.

"Excuse me," Lago said, catching up to him. "Do you know where I can find Vicar Aurgushem?"

The monk stopped, eyeing Lago's bracelet. "You are a bit young to be a disciple of the Congregation," he said. "Where did you get that?"

"Khopto gave it to me. I'm running errands for the Mesa Monastery. My name is Lago, I have a letter for the vicar."

"Well, you have found him. I can take this now," Aurgushem said, taking the envelope and breaking the seal. "Move along now. Thank you for your help." The vicar continued his walk.

"Wait! Gwil said you had a box I'm supposed to deliver to him."

"I don't have it with me, boy, it's back at the temple. Why don't you come back later?"

"I can't, I live all the way up in the mesa."

The vicar's overwrinkled face fully displayed his annoyance, but he considered, rereading the letter Khopto had written. "Then come with me. It seems I have some business to discuss with the seneschal. After that, we shall head to the temple. Please stay quiet and mind your manners."

"Yes, Lorr," he said and followed silently.

Lago had been to the commercial shipyard before, and to the Oak Ridge Mill, where they also had a few shipsheds, but he had never been inside the naval base. The fortified harbor had multiple slipways that extended into the Stiss Malpa, as well as huge warehouses where the Zovarian Navy's powerful ramships and trimarans were built.

"Moon lights, Rodrik. The boy is with me," the vicar said to the gate guard.

"Stars guide, Pious Lorr," the guard replied and let them through the gates. They caught up to the wagons.

The thick-chested bison pulled the wolf not to one of the sheds, but to a slipway leading to a bulky collier ship. Crates overflowing with coal had been unloaded from the vessel to make room for huge blocks of ice, cut from icebergs shipped into town over the Isdinnklad Sea. Ice was an expensive commodity, harvested from the fjords and glaciers far west, where the wintry winds of the Quiescent Ocean froze the waters of Fjordsulf and Teslurkath even when Winter was still far from sight.

The bison hauled the dire wolf up a ramp and under the ship's blackened sails. Soldiers detached the yokes to let the beasts' burdens cease, while the seneschal and the consul argued next to the tarp-covered bundle. Vicar Aurgushem walked up to greet them, keeping condemnatory eyes on Lago to make sure the boy kept a polite distance but didn't venture too far.

"This is not what we agreed upon!" Consul Uzenzo exclaimed, raising his voice. "*We* chased the wolf all the way from Farjall. It was *our* arrows that wounded it first. We should be granted priority when it comes to studying it."

"It fell in east Withervale," retorted Seneschal Maree Oda. "And although you are a distinguished guest of our Union, this is not Negian territory." She straightened her dark-green and gold business suit, fully in control of the situation. "The Empire doesn't own whatever wildlife leaves their borders. I already promised we'd share all our findings with you. We have ice to keep the body cold, and artificers ready and waiting at the institute. We can move it swiftly by water, while you'd have to drag the carcass over the steppes to Hestfell."

"We have resources in Anglass for—"

"I have no time for debates, Hanno, if you'll excuse me—"

"Lurr Oda," interrupted the vicar, "if I may… Before the ship sails west, I have a series of requests from the Mesa Monastery." He handed the letter to the seneschal, who opened it with manicured hands and glanced over it.

"This seems reasonable, Lorr Aurgushem. Check with the boatswain, she can get you any tools you might need. And do hurry—as soon as the ice is tied down the sailors will cast off all lines."

The consul clenched his fists and face. "But my dear Maree—"

"Don't 'dear' me, Hanno, this matter is settled," the seneschal said, then hurried the consul down the ramp. "You can file your requests the same way our Pious Lorr did, and we'll provide you with all the information once the specimen has been studied."

The boatswain brought the vicar his requested tools: scissors, pliers, small glass jars, a ruler. She then loosened the tarpaulin and pulled it back, exposing the head of the dire wolf. He was lying on his right side, heavy tongue draping down like a wet carpet, daggerlike canines stabbing out from under purple-black lips. Lago stared at the tenebrous head, black as the space between the stars, lit by two amber eyes that stared achingly into the afterlife. *I'm sorry they've done this to you,* Lago thought, losing himself in those eyes. *You were so beautiful. I wish the world had been kinder to you.* The dark face reminded Lago of the mask—they were equally captivating and inscrutable.

"—help me with this. Hey. Boy, are you listening?"

Lago came back to his senses.

Vicar Aurgushem repeated, "If you are done staring, please come help me with this." He was pulling at the wolf's paw, trying to position it so that the claws were more accessible, but each leg was as heavy as his entire body. "Pull the fur back so that I can cut a sample from the claws," he said, readying the heavy-duty scissors.

Lago solemnly reached for the enormous paw. Each toe was larger than his own hands, with tufts of muddy, bloodied furs sticking out between each pad. He grabbed a paw pad and felt the hard skin, cracked like a dry lake. Touching the dire wolf made Lago feel as if he was stepping into a forbidden dream. *I hope you can forgive us for this,* he thought—but the wolf did not forgive, as he could not: he was dead, and forgiving was not within his power, and neither was holding a grudge.

"Not the pads, the fur! Pull it back!" insisted the vicar, snapping Lago out of his trance once more. Lago did as he was told, pulling the coarse fur back. Vicar Aurgushem snapped the claw samples and wrapped them in a kerchief. "Now for the teeth," he said, readying the pliers. "You hold the lips back, and I'll pull a tooth out."

They both hopped onto the hay wagon and walked to the voluminous head. Lago touched the wolf's lip right over the bulge created by a protruding fang but felt wrong forcing his hands upon the dead creature.

"Just push the lips out of the way, okay?" the vicar said.

Lago tried pushing the top lip, but it was heavy, like a blanket of meat. "I know, hold on," he said and walked behind the head, while the vicar stayed by the chin. Unlike the wiry mess at the paws, the fur on the wolf's skull was silky, smooth, well-groomed. Lago perceived a familiar musky scent, similar to Bear's breath, but mixed with the alkaline smell of rain splashing on dusty granite, and the sharpness of snow melting over pine needles. From the top side of the head, Lago grabbed two thick whiskers and pulled on them hard. The lips parted in front of the vicar.

"I'm only sampling the smallest teeth," the vicar said, "for these fangs are big as knives, and the roots go deep." He pulled with the pliers, but the tooth would not give. "Blasted thing is magsteel-strong!" he complained, pulling harder. He suddenly recoiled with his force, nearly falling off the wagon. "Heavenly roots, the bones of this creature are tough as diamonds!" He tried hammering at the tooth with the pliers, but it would not even chip. Soon he gave up, sweat streaking his scalp.

Lago let go of the whiskers. The lips smacked down, wet and loud.

"Please apologize to Khopto," the vicar instructed. "Perhaps we'll get him a tooth sample after the specimen has been processed in Zovaria."

Lago was distracted again, caressing the enormous whiskers.

"Hopeless…" Aurgushem grumbled. "Boy! Would you mind pushing the ear down for me?"

Lago did so, having to fold the ear down with both his arms, until the vicar could reach it to cut off a portion of skin and fur. It wasn't a thin cartilage, like a dog would have, but thick and meaty, yet the vicar managed to snap off a sample. "Give me a moment, I'll get a sample of blood," the vicar said, doing something gruesome by the wolf's chin that Lago thankfully could not see.

While Lago waited, he looked toward the wolf's shoulder blades and spotted something peculiar: some of the furs looked thick and wormy, almost like snakes. He stepped to the side to grab one of the unusual strands and saw it had been braided in a complex pattern, with silver beads distributed regularly along the braid.

He didn't know whether he should tell the vicar or not, but while he hesitated, the vicar noticed and walked curiously around the head. "Braids? How could this?—" He snipped one of the braids off with his scissors. "I wonder how this got here. Either way, this will do for a fur sample, if nothing else. We should let these good people work now."

Sailors had made a bed of ice blocks next to the hay wagons, spreading the tarps over it. As they readied a wall of ice around the cold bed, the vicar chipped off a few shards and placed them in his glass jars. "This will keep them from spoiling," he said. "Better if you return these samples with haste. Some cells might still be alive, and Khopto might be able to glimpse something in their threads." But Lago was not listening again—he was watching the wolf's body being pulled onto the ice.

Vicar Aurgushem wrapped the samples as best he could, keeping the ice separate so that it would keep them cold but not wet. He then led Lago out of the naval base and into the Harrowdale Temple, where he picked up Chaplain Gwil's box.

"You've been most helpful, boy, even if quite inattentive at times. Here you go, for your troubles." The vicar handed Lago a generous tip of one Horn.

Lago was surprised; it was an excessive tip for so little work. He stared at the brassy chip, then stuffed it into his Qupi pouch before the vicar had any second thoughts.

"Now hurry back," the vicar said. "These samples need to be delivered straight away. Essence of one, soul of the many."

"Yup!" Lago said distractedly, rushing to catch a wagon to carry him back to the monastery.

CHAPTER FOURTEEN

SUNNOGRAPH

During the entire ride up to the mesa, Lago exulted over the fantastic encounter with the dire wolf. He wished the event had been less gruesome, yet the discomfort had somehow made it all the more real. The mere thought of having the honor of being in his presence, and being able to touch him! He couldn't wait to tell Alaia about it.

A vivid vision of the wolf's face materialized as he reminisced. That obsidian head, with dead but vigilant amber eyes, suddenly transformed into the likeness of the mask. Eyeless, the mask stared at him just as intently as the dire wolf had. It called to an instinct Lago could not put to words, as if there was a connection, miles away, and a thread tugging him ever closer. Lago had thoughts about putting the mask back on; he knew not why, since the mask had brought him unmeasurable pain—yet something alluring tickled the back of his mind.

He snapped out of the daydream and looked around: the wagon had already passed Runestone Lane.

He clumsily jumped off the moving cart and tripped, dropping his bag on the ground. He cringed, hearing a banging and scraping from the items he had been entrusted with. *First important delivery and you fuck it up? Please, let it not be broken.* He got off the street and sat on a sandstone wall to check the contents of his bag. The dire wolf samples were fine. He took out the wooden box he was to deliver to Gwil and examined it. No scratches, but there was a dent in one corner and a clinking, glassy sound coming from the inside.

He undid the latch to inspect the damage. Inside were sixteen vials, all neatly tucked in slots on a wooden surface. The vials had weird, wingless insects and colorful things that reminded him of snail eggs, but they were all in their right places; no glass was broken. As he was about to close the box, he heard the glassy sound again. He poked at the wooden surface that held the vials, and it shifted slightly, then came loose. He lifted the board up, with all sixteen vials still comfortably attached to it. Underneath was a secret compartment, hiding four more vials of the same kind, held in special slots at the bottom of the box. One of them had come loose—the culprit of the rattling.

Lago picked up the loose vial and examined it; it was filled with a black powder, and so were the other three. He suddenly remembered Khopto wiping that dark substance off his nose. He reattached the vial to its slot, secured the wooden panel back in place, and closed the box. He peered around suspiciously, hoping no one had seen what he'd seen, then hastened up the road again.

He delivered the box to Gwil, too afraid of mentioning his dropping it or what his curiosity had led him to discover. He then hurried to the lab and handed the dire wolf samples to Khopto, who was utterly enthused.

"I thought I'd get the requested samples weeks later, shipped from Zovaria, all rotten and dried. What a wonderful surprise that you brought them straight away! It was providential that you found the vicar when you did. And what a great opportunity for yourself to see this inexplicable, fascinating species."

Lago could not agree more. "The vicar sends his apologies. He could not get a tooth removed; the bone was too hard to break."

"That will be alright—these samples will keep me busy for a while."

"I also heard…" Lago murmured, "well, *overheard* the consul saying that they chased the wolf from Farjall. He was angry because they wanted to take it east, but the seneschal wouldn't let them keep it."

"Farjall? By the Heartpine Dome? Fascinating. Perhaps Crysta's assumptions that these beasts have something to do with the dome's roof collapsing might have some validity after all. New species of that size are not something that just appear out of nowhere. I will have to reach out to scholars in the Negian Empire to see if they are willing to share any information."

"Oh, and here's your bracelet," Lago said, unclasping the copper ornament.

Khopto placed a hand around Lago's wrist before he could remove it. "You keep it."

"Are you sure?"

"As certain as the day has thirty-two hours, an hour sixty-four moments, and each moment sixty-four heartbeats. It is my wish. The bracelet will help our clients know you are with us."

After giving Lago a good tip and a pat on the back, Khopto mentioned that Crysta was at the watchtower and had asked about him. Lago hurried away but did not find the professor in the octagonal room. Hearing muted voices, he noticed that the trapdoor leading to the roof was ajar, so he climbed up. Crysta was there, using a strange instrument at the edge of the northern parapet, flanked by a monk in ashen robes. Lago rushed to Crysta, ignoring the monk.

"Crysta! I saw the wolf! I mean, more than that, I was right there, it was—"

"Lago! You should not be up here!" Crysta said, trying to cover up the instrument they were working with. But it was too late for that.

"But the wolf! The dire wolf, I even got to touch it and—"

"Calm down," she said, cracking a smile, but still seeming very uncomfortable. "Take a breath. I was just finishing here with Esum. You can tell me about the wolf once we are done."

"Greetings, Lago," the monk said, bowing with her arms in a loop. "I think I spotted you at the Haven earlier today. My name is Esum. You might see me working with Professor Holt sometimes, mostly on Sunndays."

Lago was taken aback by the monk's voice. He had assumed all the monks were men, since they all had shaved heads and wore the same kind of clothes.

Crysta once more tried to cover up the instrument she had been working with while Lago tried to peek around her. "Lago, could you go wait at the far end of the tower? We'll be just a moment."

Lago smiled awkwardly and went to sit between two merlons. From afar he watched them work on a device that looked a bit like a broken telescope made of suspended mirrors and lenses. Crysta held a piece of paper with something written on it while Esum flipped knobs on the peculiar instrument.

They were done quickly. Esum said her farewells, then disappeared through the trapdoor.

"Let's go down in the shade," Crysta said to Lago, who seemed about to burst. "Tell me all about your day."

Crysta enjoyed a fresh pomegranate drink while Lago caught her up on his adventure. She was particularly interested in the relationship between the seneschal and the consul.

"Look, I don't want you to overwork yourself on Sunndays," she said, once Lago finished his story. "Feel free to be on your way once you are done with Gwil's errands, no need to check in with me."

"Okay," Lago said with a slight tone of disappointment.

"What's the matter?"

"Nothing. I actually enjoy learning about what you do. I think it's fun."

Crysta's face lit up. "And we'll have plenty of time for that during week-days. But for a kid your age, it's important to also have time to play, as that is another way we learn. So, go home, and enjoy some time with your friends."

"Would you at least show me what that machine you were using is?"

Crysta hesitated, tightening her lips.

"Please?"

"You weren't supposed to see that, Lago."

"But I did. Is it like a telescope? Why is it all broken?"

Crysta finished her drink, then thought for a moment. "Look," she said, "I'll make you a deal. I'll show you, but you can't tell anyone about it. The institute has devices they don't want other realms to copy, and this is one of them. Do you understand what I'm saying?"

"Keep it secret. Got it."

"No, you have to promise. You already saw it, so I don't want you to go telling your friends about it. Not even Alaia. Can you promise me that?"

Lago pondered. "I guess."

Crysta's brows lifted.

"Yes, I promise," Lago said.

"Then follow me."

Up to the roof they went, toward the quaint contraption.

"This is a prismatic sunnograph," she explained, pacing around the arrangement of mirrors, levers, and tubes. "We use it to communicate with the Zovarian Academic Institute. It's faster than shipping letters, and much cheaper than flying magpies. It works with sunlight, that's why I'm here during the day on Sunndays, to send messages."

"How does it work?"

"See this mirror?" The main mirror was two feet in diameter, with a dark marking at the very center. "What I do is align the reflection of that dot to where I want to send the signal, which is toward the Wujann Observatory. You can't see it, but I know it's on a peak there to the northwest." She adjusted the mirror to show him. "And because we are in Autumn, I can't get Sunnokh to shine exactly on the mirror, so I use this other mirror to bounce his light." She positioned the larger, secondary mirror. "And by turning this knob, I can shift the angle of the main mirror, so my colleague at Wujann can see a series of blinking lights, like toggling it on or off."

"So, it's like a code?"

"Exactly. They have a special telescope-looking device there that is always aimed at us and reflects the signal down on a table. Makes it easier to transcribe the messages. There is a similar device downstairs too, although smaller than the one at Wujann. Esum usually takes care of receiving the messages."

"And why do you want to talk to the people in the mountains?"

"Oh, that's just one step. From Wujann they send the message west to the Nedross Observatory, close to the town of Chertwall, and from there south to Zovaria. As long as Sunnokh shines, we can instantly relay a message across hundreds of miles."

Lago inspected the instrument more closely. Unlike the telescope, the sunnograph was not assembled into a solid, cohesive shape. "What's this odd-looking tube for?"

"To focus the beam of light, so that other people can't intercept the message so easily."

"And what about this tiny knob here?"

"That's... Nothing. Just for calibrations," Crysta answered, a bit flustered.

What Crysta wasn't telling Lago was that the sunnograph was not made with an ordinary set of mirrors. The main mirror had two layers, acting as a prism when their angles changed, breaking the light into a spectrum. When she sent her signals, she used the light blinking on and off to encode her observations of wisps, stars, or planets: purely academic, scholarly data. But at the same time, she used the smaller knob to break the signal into separate colors, and it was in these rainbowy variations that an additional message was encoded, offering a second layer of protection in case someone intercepted the signal. The spectrum encoded figures on Negian troops by the Anglass Dome, as well as politically sensitive information that needed to reach Zovaria at once. The few scholars who knew about this messaging system were careful to keep it a secret, as it offered a unique military advantage to the Zovarian Union and was key in funding their academic research.

"So why is it so secret?" Lago asked. "If it's just like sending letters."

"Currently only Zovaria and Yenmai have these instruments," she said. "That's where we bought them from, at great expense. Quick transfer of information is very important, since it gives us an advantage over other realms. We wouldn't want the Negians to know about such a thing."

"Do you send messages every day?"

"No, usually just on Sunnday afternoons. They have to be timed properly so that someone can transcribe them at the other end. If there's an urgent message, we leave the beam on until someone notices, wait for them to signal that they are ready, and only then transmit our message. But that rarely happens."

"It reminds me a bit of the Ilaadrid Shard," Lago said, "how the moon's beacon lights up, and we can see it all the way from here."

"That's a very astute observation. Though Sceres's orbit makes her shard reflect light in a thirty-six-day cycle, every ninth and twenty-second day after a Hollow Moon. We send our messages every six days."

"Sure," Lago said, not really listening. He thought for a moment. "Do you think Sceres is trying to send *us* a message?"

Crysta gazed wistfully at the northern peaks. "Perhaps her message is that we are not alone in the universe. That even from far, far away, through the dark of night, a small speck of light can shine over the whole world."

CHAPTER FIFTEEN

LAGO'S DREAM

While Lago was away on his adventures with the dire wolf, Alaia spent the day helping a caravan of newly arrived Oldrin refugees. They were building a shack at Riftside, a shantytown just north of the Hollows, so that older miners could move into the new dwelling, leaving their old holes in the wall for the newcomers.

"Come on Bear," Alaia called once they were finished. Bear followed Alaia and her friends to the watermill, to return the tools they had borrowed. Muscles sore and streaked with sweat, they sat to chat and have a snack.

"I'm just saying, if Saled gets drunk one more time, I'm telling on him," Ebaja glowered. "He kept 'accidentally' turning off the lamp and getting all touchy again."

"Just slam your knee spurs into his groin," Maurin said.

"He probably has spurs in his cock," Ebaja said, "that's why he can't get laid."

The bickering continued, but Alaia had stopped paying attention. Her eyes were on a group of mourning trogons being carried by a courier, too tightly packed to possibly be comfortable. The courier hung the cage inside the chicken coop, alongside other equally small cages.

"Hey, told you to let it go, girl," Ebaja said, tracking Alaia's stare. "It's just dumb birds, not worth losing your job over them. Where else are you gonna find work in this Takh-forsaken place?"

"It's just so cruel."

"Didn't we all have chicken for lunch yesterday? Think about that for a moment."

Alaia didn't have a good response to that.

She headed back home once the shadows turned long, following Bear, who helped by spooking squirrels and doves off the path. The mesa looked beautiful this late in the day, when the setting sun scraped the valley floor and hit only the tip of the sandstone formation, making the observatory shine like a lighthouse of fire against a dark-blue sky. As the shadows crept up the sandstone walls, the Hollows began to light up with small fires in each eroded pocket. Alaia's own dwelling was dark, so she guessed Lago was still out doing errands— but it seemed to her, from far away, like her door panel was partially open.

Bear was way ahead of her, barking, agitated. He whined at the open door, but wouldn't go in.

Alaia trotted up, pushed the door panel out of the way, and saw Lago shaking upon the cold floor, as if he was having a seizure. The dark mask clutched his face like a leech. The boy gurgled a choked, guttural cry, drool darkening the sandstone floor. He weakly tried to claw the mask off his face, but his contorted limbs could not quite reach it.

Alaia vaulted in, ripped the cursed object from Lago's face, and hurled it at the wall.

Lago dreamed an endless dream.

He dreamed of a prairie that was wider than the sun. He dreamed of the smell of Summer, of the whispers of the canyons, of the six shades of the moon during a cloudless night.

The prairie was infinite, woven of looping threads that bound every particle together. Dewdrops decorated the very tips of every blade of grass, as if a forest sprite had carefully placed them there, one by one—they shimmered like a carpet of starlight.

All threads, all life was part of an immense tapestry. Every grassy hill was him, and he was a pack of timber wolves running over them faster than the mists of late Umbra. The soil at his paws was mud and blood and the memory of his father. The mist that evaporated from the dewdrops was his dead mother, whom he had never seen. The pollen in the air was his friends, Crysta, Alaia, Khopto, Holfster, Gwil—he had few friends, but here they were many;

in truth they were many. They were all connected to him, they were all the pack of wolves, and they were all the essence of nothingness, the empty space between spaces, the aether that better exists by unbeing.

Sunnokh was glowing white hot, yet the sky was black, and all the stars were out. Lago's countless legs danced through the prairie, the long grass tickling his dewclaws, the air becoming one with the undulating motion of his tails. His paws galloped weightlessly, as if barely touching the ground, making only a sound like that of a glacial creek rushing through pebbles. He/them was trying to reach a distant mountain with a snowy peak, but no matter the distance traveled, the mountain drew no closer.

His many legs soon tired and froze into trunks. He felt the sunlight feeding him, becoming tree rings, thickening the pillars that once had been his calves, his thighs. He was a forest now. He was the canopy, the roots, the bark. He was the soil, and the spores of a billion mushrooms and ferns. He was decay, he was the latent larvae in the sentient palpitations of a macroorganism beyond time. The forest burned, and he was charcoal and soot and prickly embers overflowing with energy. The blackened soil against the black sky was an obsidian mirror; it was the all-encompassing essence of below and above. The star-studded firmament became a verb of light; it became a tune of forgotten memories.

The charcoal sprouted, erupted, greenly and lustfully. He was a hummingbird, but also the flower, united in a sugary kiss of a sensual pleasure he did not yet understand. Mountains rose at his feet. The space between his toes became fjords, breathing chill air and biting sunlight. He became continents; he became all mountains, but not that one mountain, not the white mountain that was still out of reach. The continents gulped a breath of oxygen and sunk below the waters, and he was many more than before, for he was whales and unknown creatures from the deep; he was a colony of jellyfish, a cloud of krill, and each wandering, minuscule plankton. He settled onto the ocean floor as billions of diatoms of geometric bones smaller than grains of sand. He was the surface below the colossal pressure of the four oceans, and he rose, hardening as limestone, as a fertile field under the parting waters, still wet and salty and smelling of eternity.

The land was calm now. The only sound was the low rumble of the heartbeat of the planet. A flatness spread to every horizon, damp, filled with potential, reflecting the stars suspended in the tenebrous sky. He was himself, naked, walking on his bare feet, spawning ripples in the water, ripples that would extend beyond his understanding.

He looked to the stars. They began falling, like snowflakes drifting in an invisible breeze. As they landed on the water, the stars melted and faded, leaving only solitude in their wake. He extended a hand to catch a falling star; it sank into his palm and flickered through it, leaving a trail of phosphorescent air that shone through his bones. The star was extinguished in the eternity ahead but lived on in the eternity before.

The stars had all fallen, all withered out of being.

The world was dark. Not even the distant mountain remained.

There was no up nor down. The lightless sky was all, and he was but a transient shadow. In the distance, an orange light approached, like a candle, like a lamp in a dark tunnel, like a beacon. The light was warm and inviting; it was made of honey and embers and the ripples of light upon the smoothness of a pearl. The gleam ahead was pine sap, it was amber, it was a fluid that transcended the concept of time. The amber light split into two fiery gemstones, scrutinizing him without judgement.

The black void stared at him with melancholy eyes.

"To the stars, Lago. To the stars," it beckoned.

Chapter Sixteen

Masked in Darkness

Lago's head rumbled.

A distant sound edged him toward awareness, suspending him in a thin thread of consciousness.

He widened his jaws. His ears popped.

"—up!... Lago!... *Wake. Up!...*"

His eyelids parted. A blur of light smeared his turbulent perception.

"Please!"

Teeth, a wet tongue. *Bear.* A dog. He remembered that.

What was the other name?

He remembered a prairie, a mountain, two fiery eyes.

He remembered darkness.

He passed out again.

Shocking cold. Ice.

His body contorted, and through a gasp he sat up in a pool of freezing water. His sight was unfocused, but his mind had snapped back somewhere in his skull. Alaia was standing there, holding an empty bucket.

"What... happened?..." he asked.

Lago sat in front of the fire, wrapped in a towel, wriggling his toes by the flames, as if questioning them would unlock a secret.

"Drink this," Alaia said, handing him a hot cup of tea.

"Thank you. I... I don't know how to explain it."

The dark mask waited in a corner of the room, unblinking, unrepentant.

"That damn thing almost killed you," Alaia snapped. "You were trying to pull it off, and couldn't do it, but when I grabbed it, it came right off."

"I felt... so much pain, like the first time, but different. I was dreaming something. I was... I was... I can't remember it anymore. How long was I out for?"

"Don't know. I came back after sunset and found you that way."

"Must've been hours then."

"Do you mind telling me why? Just why? If it hurt so much the first time."

Lago felt around his temples, his shoulders—they were bruised, scraped. He was sure he'd find more injuries later on all the body parts he had slammed against the floor.

"I felt... an urge," he weakly explained. "A lot happened today."

He began the arduous process of recounting his entire day. Despite his clarity of mind returning, he couldn't explain the feeling, the *need* that struck him when he returned home.

"I just had to. I don't know how else to explain it," he bemoaned.

"I tried to break the fucker, you know," Alaia said, clenching her jaw. "Hit it with my shovel, it bounced right off. Didn't leave a scratch, but my shovel was—"

"Don't *ever* do that!" Lago shouted. "I made a promise, and I intend to keep it!"

"Suit yourself. I don't know how you'll find that lady's son—"

"*Grand*son. His name is Bonmei."

"Right, whatever. My point is, we can't keep this cursed thing here with us."

"I'm not getting rid of it."

"Didn't say you have to. I have an idea."

Long past midnight, when everyone at the Hollows was deep asleep, Lago wrapped the animal mask in an oilskin cloth, then placed it in his bag. He told Bear to be a good dog and wait inside, slid the door panel closed, and followed Alaia.

They took the back trail over the boulders, jumped the perimeter fence, and arrived at one of the mine shafts. It was shaft number seven.

As Alaia checked her surroundings, she spotted Lago's bracelet. "Wait, what is *that*?" she whispered. "Did you join their cult already?"

"Khopto gave it to me, so that the vicar would know I'm with the congregation."

"It's fancy! When are they shaving your head?"

"It's not like that."

"Just teasing. It looks pretty on you, but it'd be nicer if you painted your nails in copper, to match."

"Thanks, but I'm not taking fashion advice from Lurr Overalls."

They scurried into the shaft. Alaia was using her trustworthy lamp this time, one with a proper flame shield. She quickly found the boarded-up shaft they had kicked through recently. They scraped their way past the remaining boards and soon reached the dead end with the hole in the roof. Before climbing in, they dislodged old planks of wood from a wall and carried them to the hole.

"So, this is where we lay it to rest, unless we find Bonmei," Alaia said, climbing into the limestone cavern.

"*Until* we find Bonmei," Lago corrected. He took the oilskin cloth out of his bag—it was as light as if it had been empty. He searched for a cavity in which to tuck the mask away, but all the spots he found were too exposed.

"What about here?" Alaia said, pointing to a nook behind stalagmites that was well out of the way, hard to reach, and not very enticing. The row of stalagmites looked like a cage, and it would serve the same purpose.

"That could work." Lago scrambled up to the spot, slipping on the moist formations. Alaia gave him a hand, holding his feet up. Before placing the mask down, he unwrapped it and stared in its empty eyeholes. The flicker of the lamp and the droning of flowing water shifted Lago's memory to a place he had been before, or maybe hadn't. Wet feet. Black skies. A mountain. But like a word on the tip of his tongue, he was powerless to invoke it. The memory slipped away, and he was back staring at the mask.

"You can do it, Gwoli," she encouraged him.

"I'll find Bonmei, and I'll bring you to him, someday," he self-consciously mumbled to the inanimate object.

He wrapped the mask again and hid it behind the bars of stone.

Together, they lined wooden planks over the hole of the cavern, blocking the breeze that had once flowed through. On their way out of the shaft, they nailed back the boards they had kicked out before. The path was closed.

They walked home under the watchful eyes of a billion stars.

"It's done," Alaia said. "It'll be safe in there."

The new moon was rising to announce the approaching sunrise: a shy, amethyst sickle suspended in indigo.

Someday... Lago thought.

PART TWO
AGNARGSILV

CHAPTER SEVENTEEN

SIX YEARS LATER

Twenty-eighth day of Highsun, 1454 A.D.

The land developer was inspecting the progress on the newly dug trenches; they would make good foundations for new homes. They had to clear away debris from abandoned cabins, push small boulders out of the way, and split bigger rocks apart, but he was used to those hurdles—they were part of the job. He came from Hestfell, the capital of the Negian Empire, where rock was malleable as long as you had enough influence in the industry and Quggons in your pockets, and he had plenty of both. Consul Uzenzo had told him that this area used to be a logging town, abandoned hundreds of years ago, when resources ran low, and the population chose to move to the nearby mesa.

He walked by a creek that emptied northward, where he had assigned a lot for a mill, knowing that the glacial waters flowed constantly, even in Summer. It would make a very profitable lot. Across the creek, his workers were removing the stump of an oak and the remnants of a shack that leaned over a big boulder. One of his Oldrin workers waved at him.

"Lorr Kaspar, over here!"

"What is it?"

"Found something strange, you should take a look."

Kaspar crossed the bridge they had built over the creek and approached the Oldrin. The old shack his workers had been pulling apart was nothing but foundations and a tumbling wall. Broken bottles, colorful pebbles, and remnants of children's toys lay scattered in a corner, long abandoned. Behind the collapsing wall was a large boulder with a perfectly circular hole in its side, like a portal to an old cellar, filled with rocks.

"What in Takh's two names?"

Kaspar approached the hole and began pulling the rocks away.

CHAPTER EIGHTEEN

HARVESTLIGHT

"Hold up!" Lago gasped. "I can't breathe!"

"Beat you to it!" Alaia celebrated, also panting.

Their strenuous hike ended at the Ninn Tago Viewpoint, a saddle high on the Gray Pass offering outstanding views all around. For twenty miles they'd hiked to get here, having camped twice to break the long trek.

They sat on their usual 'lucky branch' of an old bristlecone pine, a tree so gnarled and twisted that it could not possibly grow any older. A few years ago, when they had hiked to this same spot and sat on this same branch, Alaia had spotted something hiding in a deep tree hollow of the pine, and out she'd pulled a woven, nearly spherical basket: a Day of the Lost cache; a treasure filled with memories of the deceased, left for others to find.

"Anything in the hole?" Lago asked.

"Empty again. Maybe we should leave something in there, during the next Day of the Lost."

"I wish it happened every year instead of every eight years."

"If it happened every year, it would not be a leap day, nubhead," she teased.

Lago opened his canteen and savored the chilled, glacial water. He poured a bit in his hands and let Bear lap at it. Thirst sated, Bear ran away to chase after pinecones. He had grown quite a bit, and his white-speckled brown coat had turned a bit darker, but he was otherwise the same careless mutt.

"I'm still a bit shaken from earlier," Lago said. "Had you ever seen a mountain lion before?"

"Not ever," Alaia said, grabbing the canteen and stealing a large gulp. "I swear I'm never hiking the Pilgrim Sierras alone. I'm so glad she was scared of us too."

"And glad Bear didn't think it smart to go play with her cubs."

Lago had turned eighteen only five days ago, while Alaia was very close to turning twenty. They had spent the last six years working, learning, getting in trouble, and living life to the fullest, or at least as full a life as the limited world of Withervale would allow. Lago was just about to start his last year at Birth-Light School and was considering studying cosmology at the Zovarian Academic Institute. He had become very adept at math, particularly calculus and algebra, and enjoyed studying the stars, but the thought of moving to the big city terrified him.

A year after Lago had the fight with his father, Theo Vaari had left Withervale, moving back to Old Karst. Thanks to the connections he had developed through his father's business, Lago now knew just about everyone in town. His work with Gwil and Crysta had become fruitful, both intellectually and economically.

Alaia, on the other hand, was still working at the mines. The prospects for an Oldrin didn't extend much beyond that. Although Oldrin miners were still grossly underpaid, she at least got Sunndays off, and a few holidays here and there when she could free herself from all responsibilities.

It was now Moonday, on the first of Harvestlight, the day the Feast of Plenitude was celebrated. Downtown Withervale would be filled with loud parties and drinking games, while the mesa would take the more traditional approach and celebrate with a boring sort of quiet penitence. The day after would also be a holiday, for the Vigil of the Famished: a day to pay respects and bring offerings in humility and solace, or to continue partying if you were down in the city.

For the past several years, Lago and Alaia had made it a sort of ritual to ignore the festivities and instead hike up the Ninn Tago, to enjoy the first sunset of Harvestlight from this most magical vantage point. The weather was always benevolent at this time of year, letting them see into the vast distance.

From this elevation, they could experience all the beauty around them at once: to the north was Withervale, the Isdinnklad, and the icy Wujann peaks; east and west were the sharp pinnacles of the Pilgrim Sierras; south was the Farsulf Forest of the Free Tribelands, wafting up a refreshing scent of pine needles. But also due south was the most intriguing sight of all: the Heartpine Dome.

Only fifty miles from the Ninn Tago Viewpoint, the viny wall of the Heartpine Dome rose interminably. Lago and Alaia were high in the mountain pass, and one would think that from such elevations the top of the dome would be below them, but the dome was higher, so much higher than any of the peaks, that no matter where one stood, the dome always broke through the line in the horizon. It was the same with the Anglass Dome, or any of the other fourteen domes Lago and Alaia had not yet seen. From this distance, one could truly appreciate the bulging roundness of the structure, but nowadays one could also glimpse into a small portion of its interior, thanks to the holes that had formed in the immense roof.

The Heartpine Dome was a light-green protrusion bulging out of an ocean of pines. Several great forests rose and fell around it, in hills that undulated like a deep-green sea. Waxy, always reflecting the sunlight in a peculiar soft glow, the dome looked so artificial and yet so in place in the natural world. The texture from the largest vines gave it a crackled look, which was appropriate, as it was cracking open.

Lago pointed to a peak that intersected the dome to create a sharp, triangular break at the base of it. "Look to the right side of Knife Point," he said, handing his binoculars to Alaia. It had taken him years to save up enough Qupi to afford the expensive device, and he never left on a hike without them.

"Another piece fell off," Alaia said. "That hole seems enormous. Did you see the supporting columns? Way in the back. Can barely see them through the haze."

"They remind me of funnel mushrooms, how they branch on top. And that new hole must be at least ten miles wide and half a mile thick. I can't even imagine the destruction it must've caused on the inside, something of that scale dropping down from the skies."

The roof of the Heartpine Dome had been collapsing for the past six years. Its vines had become more and more unruly, growing out of their once even margins, stretching sometimes hundreds of feet away from the main wall. Every time Lago and Alaia hiked to the viewpoint, the sight was slightly changed. Tendrils from where the roof pieces had fallen were now drying up, curling into gray, dead edges. Even the silhouette had changed: the dome no longer had a perfectly smooth curve but dipped in spots where chunks of roof had collapsed, while tentacle-like filaments stretched mindlessly to the sky everywhere else. A sizable portion of the domed ceiling had ripped apart, but the structure still held steady.

Professor Crysta Holt had entrusted Lago to make the hike to the Ninn Tago Viewpoint once or twice a year, to take note of the dome's changes over time. The massive holes were miles high, allowing for a distant view of the supporting vine columns connecting to the textured ceiling, but no one could see down into the land below. Not yet.

Lago distractedly rubbed his feet on the ground, staring at the distance with unfocused eyes. "I've been thinking, now that I'll be starting my last year in school... I'm still not sure if—"

"If you need to move to Zovaria, you move. It's your future, Gwoli. Treasure it, take advantage of it, live your life! You shouldn't waste the opportunity."

"You say that as if it's easy, but I'd need to find a sponsor at the institute. I couldn't afford tuition in a place like that, not even if I saved for decades. And I have so much in Withervale, all my friends are here. There's you, and Crysta, and Gwil, Penli, Kara, Lerr Holfster, Esum, Khopto, everyone at the monastery now. And Balek, and Pesh, and Deon, and—"

"Wait, wait, Deon? I thought you just broke up?"

"Well, sort of, until we didn't. Got back together last week."

"Is that why you've been lacquering your nails again? Trying to look pretty for your plump bear?"

"Oh, spare me, he doesn't like it. And he's not that fat."

"You wish he was, though," Alaia said with a smirky side glance.

"A bit more padding couldn't hurt. He can be witless at times, but he's got a nice cock."

"He's as thick-headed as an anvil! I'll find you a much better one, one who doesn't snore like a bison, one who can pronounce *ah-LAY-uh* instead of *ah-LIE-uh*. I'll find you the one with the roundest, hairiest belly in all of—"

Lago pinched the side of her torso, right over her hipbone.

"Hey stop!" she chortled. "Fucking s–stop, I can't breathe!"

"You don't deserve to breathe!"

Lago fell backward as he wrestled with her, dragging her with him by the straps of her overalls. Both landed on their backs upon a bed of pine needles, knees still wrapped over the branch, as if they were sitting again, only this time looking up at the sky.

Bear hurried to lick their faces.

"Get off, you are filthy!" Lago said, pushing Bear away.

He rested his head on the soil and stared at the transient clouds. "I just... I used to hate this place. Hated school, hated my home, hated my dad. All I wanted was to get out. But it's so different now. I have a good job, good friends, our new place—"

"Found *love*..."

"Hmph... I wish... And don't you start again. I haven't even *been* to Zovaria. It's so far, and they say it's so large that you can walk for hours and never even make it to the other side of the city. I wouldn't know how to live in a place like that."

"I wish I could go to a place like that... But there are no Oldrin scholars. No institute would take me. Not that I'd ever have the Quggons for something like that either way. But what's the harm in dreaming?"

Lago turned his head toward her. A cloud of jealousy passed through him, as if it was alright for him to have deep emotions about moving away, but not okay for Alaia to consider the same. It was an irrational sentiment that resounded dissonantly in his chest.

"What we need to do," she said, getting up and shaking the dirt off, "is to get Crysta to write a letter of recommendation, for your sponsorship. There must be a cosmologist that'll take you in, with your good grades and all. If you don't get the sponsorship, then we can debate what's next. But if you *do* get it, you move your ass to the capital, and you come visit me every Harvestlight, at least."

Lago was still resting on the ground. "I don't know. I hear you become indebted to your sponsor for years, and they make you work really hard. We can talk more about it, I'm still not sure. There's just a lot of—hey! Look up!"

"What is it?" Alaia looked above her and saw two enormous birds flying south. "Giant teratorns!" she screeched. The condor-like birds had a wingspan of fifteen feet. Their feathers were an iridescent indigo, their heads bright and yellow. "The binoculars, quick!"

"Around your neck, nubhead."

She fumbled with the binoculars and aimed them at the enigmatic birds. This species had been thought extinct after the Downfall, but they suddenly reappeared once the Heartpine Dome began its collapse. There had been a few dozen sightings and one dead specimen found at Lurr's Abyss in the Stelm Khull, but no one had been able to properly study them yet. They were extremely elusive birds, only spotted in the tallest mountains.

"They are just as blue as the one I saw by the sinkholes years ago!" Alaia said. "I see white legs, a bald, yellow head. The left one has a red ring around his neck, I'm guessing that's the male. Look at those wings, they are so wide! They don't even need to flap, they just glide."

"And they are going south."

"Toward the dome..."

"Keep your eyes on them for as long as they are visible," Lago said, standing up. "This would be good info to tell Crysta, and that naturalist friend of hers. I'll write it all down for reference."

"True. I first learned about them in Hefra Boarmane's books, saw her illustrations of their fossils. Maybe they are migrating south for Winter, back to their old home inside the dome. I wonder what it must've been like in there before it all fell apart."

A short while later, the birds became dots too small to discern, vanishing toward the dome like the floating specters of light one sees when looking at a clear, blue sky.

Sunnokh's daily journey had ended in the west. They were already in the shade, hiding between the craggy pinnacles of the Stelm Ca'éli, but the top of the Heartpine Dome reached much higher and would remain lit for much longer.

The snowcapped top glowed a fiery orange.

"Let's set up a camp before it gets windy," Lago said.

CHAPTER NINETEEN

THE DOCTRINE OF TAKH

Despite his grumbling protests, Lago had to return to class on Iskimday. The first day of his last year of school had begun.

"Don't fuck this up," Alaia said. "Just get going, or you'll be late."

"I know," Lago complained, slowly putting his clothes on. "But we are starting Codex Studies today… That class has nothing to do with cosmology!"

"But it's a requirement. And very important if you are going to move to Zovaria."

"We don't know if that's happening yet, so don't push it."

Alaia shrugged, as if more certain about Lago's future than he could ever be. "Don't matter," she added. "Go be a good Zovarian boy and worship your Twin Gods, alright?"

Lago flicked her an obscene gesture, then sat down to eat his breakfast: a bit of stale bread, huckleberry jam, and a glass of milk that was not yet spoiled enough to toss. They were doing better nowadays, but out of necessity they had learned to be resourceful, to the point of being a bit stingy.

They had both outgrown their little hole in the wall, and with their savings had managed to build a small shack at Riftside, just north of the Hollows. The neighborhood was littered with stacked buildings, narrow corridors, unsupervised pets, makeshift markets, and clotheslines territorially tangling over every street. They had erected their rickety place with wood, adobe, and sandstone blocks while conjoining it to similarly unsound dwellings. Although modest by all standards, their home gave them both some privacy, a place to cook, a table to work, and easier access in and out of town. They both missed their old home, just like they missed their Diamond Cave, but they were content with their new comforts.

Bear whined in feigned starvation, but Lago ignored him. Bear was mostly self-sufficient, even if unable—or perhaps too thickheaded—to hunt, but he was very much capable of begging his way around the marketplace or stealing when no one was watching. Lago guessed Bear ate better than he and Alaia combined, so he knew better than to sacrifice any more than the smallest of scraps to him.

Lago scratched behind the mutt's ears, picked up his well-worn messenger bag, and headed out. He strode distractedly down Feldspar Boulevard, reaching the school a bit later than intended.

"Do you know where Lorr Winnogard's class is?" he asked a schoolmate.

"Huh? Codex Studies? Down to the right, in the auditorium."

"Thanks!" Lago said and sprinted away.

By the time Lago entered the auditorium, the lecture had already started. The entire room froze, as if struck by Frostburn's chill.

Lorr Winnogard watched with impassive eyes as Lago took his seat. Once the young man was settled, he coldly asked, "Aren't you a bit old to be taking this class? What is your name, tardy youth?"

"Lago, Lorr. Lago Vaari."

"What year are you, Lorr Vaari?"

The undeserved honorific was wielded as an insult, and Lago knew it.

"Senior. Starting my last year, Lorr."

"I see. Checking off the bare minimum to graduate. The Doctrine of Takh needs to be studied for a minimum of six years to be properly digested."

Lago could see that all the students were much younger than he. "It's never too late to learn about the grace of our Twin Gods," he said. His efforts did not achieve the intended outcome—the professor was perspicacious enough to tell when someone was being disingenuous.

Professor Winnogard pushed his spectacles up and with a measured turn of his head continued his lecture. "As I was explaining before being interrupted, we Zovarians are not like the savages of the east, who pray to Pliwe, Wawumána, Raushamitt, and the profane gods of the sands. We are not like the inhabitants of old Nisos, who find solace in the incompleteness of the Lavra Scrolls and venerate animal spirits from spritetales. We do not follow the overly complicated creed of the Hi-Than-Mi Codices of the Tsing, nor sing the 'sacred' songs of the Horde, nor worship rocks like the primitive tribes in the northern wastes. We are children of the Twin Gods, Takhísh and Ta-khamún, because we understand the truth of the Takh Codex."

Winnogard leaned on the desk. "Would anyone care to tell us what the Doctrine of Takh professes?" he asked. "What is the core belief Prophet Gweshkamir wrote about, one century after the Downfall?"

A few hands went up.

"Yes, Lorr Vaari," he called out, even though Lago had not lifted an eye-lash. "You should be old enough to know this, I presume."

And Lago did know, a bit. He didn't *care* to know, but it was not as though anyone could live in the Zovarian Union without learning about the Codex.

"Um, it's like," Lago fumbled, "the doctrine talks about the Twin Gods, Takhísh and Takhamún, who act as the forces of creation and destruction."

Winnogard waved his hands, asking for more.

Lago continued, "Takhísh, the Demiurge, is our maker. He used the Shield of Creation to create all matter and imbued each particle with a spark of divinity."

"And what is the name of his shield?"

"Gaönir-Bijeor, Lorr," Lago said, certain he would hate every breath he took in this class. Getting no response other than a pair of raised brows, he went on, "And Takhísh's brother is Takhamún, the Unmaker. He used the Spear of Undoing—Tor-Reveo—to cut open the veil to the Six Gates of Felsvad."

"And just why would Takhamún do such a thing?" Winnogard asked, mercifully pointing to another student to answer. In a broken mumble, the singled-out girl managed to half-read from her copy of the Codex, "To bring f-forth death and decay, so that muh-more life could flourish."

Winnogard smiled, seeming to briefly forget about Lago. With pompous authority, he resumed his lecturing.

"In the times before the Downfall, all humans, plants, and animals were divine in nature," he said. "We were all made from the same matter that had spilled from Takhísh's fingers, and so we shared his divinity. Together, we chanted holy hymns in praise of our Demiurge's bountiful benevolence. And although Takhamún was equally important for maintaining a balance in the world of the living, for the Unmaker the plants and animals did not sing."

The professor's tone lowered dramatically. "Takhamún grew envious. Envious of his brother's creations, of the disquieting hymns, of the prayers never spoken in his name. Bitter and forlorn, one night Takhamún stole all divinity and ran away with it."

He slammed his hands on the desk. "Takhísh was furious! He took chase after his brother. In order to escape, Takhamún split himself into sixteen emanations and spread his forms across the continents. Why was Takhamún's theft of the divinity a problem, do you think?"

No one had been singled out, so no one answered.

"Because now that the creatures of land and sea had no divinity, they could be irreversibly destroyed!" the professor answered himself, with a bit too much glee. "Their slaughter could bring an ultimate end to those sickly, glorious songs Takhamún loved and hated. As a way to destroy all creation, Takhamún's emanations buried the Spear of Undoing deep into sixteen corners of Noss, summoning forth the netherflames from the Voids of Khest."

Professor Winnogard grabbed his leather-bound copy of the Takh Codex, opened the volume to a bookmarked page, and read aloud. "Sixteenfold did the conflagrations of death spill, in waves of green and black fire. Sixteenfold did they burn, scorching kingdoms of vanity, kingdoms of mercy, kingdoms of sorrow. But Takhísh was swift, for he was Divinity incarnate, and with Gaö-nir-Bijeor, rush he did to each spawning void. His Shield of Creation heavenward grew, splitting into two pairs twice doubled, trapping the erupting netherflames within the Voids of Khest whence they had come. But so did the domes ensnare all sixteen of Takhamún's emanations, and with them were caught the sparks of divinity he had stolen."

The professor paced around, no longer looking at his book. "Netherflames billowed within, expanding the domes like blood-sucking ticks. Takhísh witnessed their growth and knew it was a thing of evil. He sang for the vines to tighten, and by his mercy alone did their expansion cease. And so Noss was not fully consumed by the Voids of Khest. And so Takhísh cried. He cried, for he knew that his brother would be caged for eons. He cried, for he knew that the netherflames would scorch his brother's flesh sixteenfold."

The pacing stopped. "That was the Downfall," he said, closing the book. "But not all life was lost. Some of us endured, saved by Takhísh's song. But how did we rise from such tragic devastation to the glory of our Union of sixteen states? Lorr Vaari?"

Lago had been playing with Qupi chips, trying to force the magnets into a cube despite not having the proper denominations to form a Quggon.

"Lorr Vaari!"

Lago looked up. His unseemly assembly of magnetic chips snapped, realigning itself into a more cohesive combination, but one of the pieces shot away, clinking much too loudly down the marble steps.

Professor Winnogard walked up the rising rows of seats, pocketed the fugitive Qupi chip, and walked back down.

"What happened after the Downfall, Lorr Vaari?" he said, his back still facing the students.

"Uh, well. Um. The fires were put out, and then the cold came?"

"Are you asking me a question, or providing an answer?" The Professor did not wait for a reply. "What Lorr Vaari has so eloquently explained to us is that after the Downfall, Takhísh felt lonely without his twin brother, without his creations. He felt lonely with the emptiness of the ravaged lands, where the fires had run out of things to burn. And so, with the coldness of his heart, he brought forth the Enduring Winter. But the few brave humans who survived the Downfall felt the pain in the Demiurge's heart, and worked together to repopulate the lands, planting, sharing, spreading the surviving species to lands far away. For hundreds of years they worked, until Noss healed and thrived once more. And so did Takhísh's cold heart heal as well."

The professor stopped and took five measured breaths. "Takhísh was filled with gratitude toward humankind. He wanted to offer a reward for their help, but he could create nothing new, not with his shield still holding the nether-flames at bay. Let us see if he's been paying attention this time," he said, a bit disjointedly, but carefully not changing his tone. "What did Takhísh offer as a gift, Lorr Vaari?"

Lago *had* been paying attention, albeit briefly. He hated to play along, but he knew he'd have to deal with this class for the rest of the term, and so he answered.

"Depends on who you ask, Lorr."

"I'm asking you!"

"No, I mean, the Negians have their own version of the Codex, and Da-thereol yet another. Even the Bayani have a transl—"

"I didn't ask for the *opinions* of other realms, I asked for the truth. What was Takhísh's gift?" His dangerously arched brows pressured Lago to answer.

"Most Zovarians believe the Demiurge had sixteen sparks of divinity left, which he placed in the scepters of the sixteen Arch Sedecims of the Union. He told them to spread their will over other realms, to unite all lands into one."

The professor grunted, satisfied with the response, but not satisfied with being satisfied. "And so it was," he said, resuming his pontifical stride. "With their holy mandate, holding the sparks of divinity within their galvanum scep-ters, the Arch Sedecims have kept the Zovarian Union powerful and unified. Yet we still find ourselves in the Conquest Epoch. Like Prophet Gweshkamir did when he wrote and spread the Codex, we must work fervently for the same cause, for not until we teach the word of Takh to every living soul will the Ascension Epoch begin."

The professor then began a dull regurgitation of the aspects of all sixteen of Takhamún's emanations and their relationship with each of the domes. After an impromptu quiz, he went on to describe the Endfall Manuscript's contentious contents. The manuscript, written circa six hundred A.D. by Prophet Dargon, the last Oracle of Allathanathar, purported that Takhamún's emanations would one day use the Spear of Undoing to cut through the domes, at last freeing the Unmaker from his netherflame prison.

"The Endfall is forthcoming, and unavoidable," the professor professed, "for once the domes open, Takhamún will use Tor-Reveo to release the Voids of Khest, bringing forth the final epoch."

"It's total bullshit!" Lago complained to Crysta.

"What did I tell you about—"

"Sorry. It's bison dung. It's ox excrement. It's caribou fecal—"

"Stop it. Just because we aren't at school, it doesn't mean you get to use that language with me. I hope you didn't behave like this in front of Professor Winnogard. He deserves your respect, even if you don't agree with him."

Crysta kept one eye on the eyepiece while waving a hand behind her. Lago placed a slide rule in her hand and watched her use it to make calculations with only one eye.

Lago grumbled. "He gave the assignment just to me. He's trying to make me look bad in front of the entire class."

"Didn't you say you were late? I make an example of my students in a similar way."

"But the Endfall Manuscript is complete bull—It's a total fabrication, and now that the Heartpine Dome is opening, we know for sure it's all lies."

Crysta gave him a tired look out of the corner of one eye.

"You know it's not true," Lago continued. "If there were netherflames inside the domes, we would've seen them through the holes in Heartpine."

"Maybe the netherflames are black? It's one of the interpretations."

Lago gave an eye roll that Crysta could feel behind her back. "Now you are just defending him."

"Well, forget about Heartpine. Anglass still glows from the inside," she said, egging him on. At that very moment, she was observing a new wisp, a tenuous one. There *was* something aglow in the dome to the east.

"We don't know what the wisps are," he countered, "and Anglass changes nothing. If Takhamún was out there with his magical spear bringing forth the Endfall, I think someone would've noticed."

"Look," Crysta said, stretching her back. "The Endfall Manuscript is highly controversial outside of the Union. It is only here that it has been affixed to the Codex, while the Negian Empire and other realms reject it. They never recognized Dargon's divinity, because she was a woman."

She sat at the desk to jot down her observations. Lago opened his mouth, but she interrupted him, talking while writing. "But that doesn't make the manuscript any less important. You don't go to Codex Studies to learn about the nature of the cosmos, you go to learn about our history, our ways of thought—"

"He called the easterners *savages*, said they pray to the *profane gods of the sands*."

Crysta's brow tightened. Lago continued, "He insulted the Lerevi, the Tsing, the Dorhond, the Negians. I mean, the Negians deserve it, but he is so full of himself! He said the northern tribes worship rocks!"

"Well, they kind of do…"

"But it's the *way* he said it! He's not trying to teach what's in the Codex, he's trying to brainwash us into believing this nonsense."

"Hey now," Crysta said, feeling flustered, "I believed in this *nonsense* as well. It's still a part of who I am. It helped me overcome very tough times. It helped me find meaning when all seemed lost. My husband is a firm believer, as well as most of our family. And nearly all the scholars at the institute are as well. If you are going to be working with people who buy into this *nonsense*, you better make yourself familiar with what they profess."

CHAPTER TWENTY

FJORNA DARO

Chief Arbalister Fjorna Daro was oiling the sandalwood stock of her precious Whisper, a crossbow of legendary beauty that she had inherited after the Red Hand of Yaumenn took her father. Fjorna's silver-blonde hair fell over the crossbow's limbs, blending with the translucent yellows of the thick drawstring, which was spun from spine sinew harvested from the wild yak of the Falbagrish Range. She ran her short nails over the bone and copper inlays, then leaned back to sip at her wine.

She was at an alehouse, sitting across from two new, promising recruits who had come from the eastern edges of the Negian Empire, by the Lequa Sea. They were enjoying a well-deserved break after an exhausting training session.

The new members were Muriel and Waldomar Clawwick, sister and brother. They were properly skilled with the crossbow, but their mastery of the recurve bow was unparalleled: sharper eyes had never served Fjorna's squad, nor hands as steady as theirs, which could hold a pulled string as unflinchingly as a stone statue. They weren't twins, though they looked like they could be, sharing the same black, spiky hair and angular facial features of likely Khaar Du origins.

With the two newcomers, Chief Daro's squad had grown to a healthy fourteen. They were deadly, silent, self-sufficient, and shared a self-identity that tied them as a family. They were not mere soldiers, but specialists for covert missions.

Her squad was currently stationed southeast of the Anglass Dome, by the Great River. The fortified city of Anglass was a major training ground for the Negian army, making it a site of powerful influence for trade with the Zovarian Union, as well as not-so-subtle intimidation.

The Anglass Dome was an awe-inspiring sight, ever-present in those lands. In Summer it provided shade to the north end of the city, while in Winter it held a pocket of warm air that brought life into the deathly cold month of Frostburn, making it an ideal location for a permanent base.

The domes were incomprehensibly large, and the vines that weaved their impenetrable walls were mystifyingly thick. From many miles away, all domes looked like flattened cupolas, eternally bulging above the horizon. One expected to still see a curve when closer to them, but with eighty miles in diameter and seven miles in height, as one approached the domes, their vine walls went up so suddenly that they seemed perfectly vertical. Paradoxically, the curved sides receded into the distance in what looked like straight lines to left and right, as if slicing the entire world in half.

Six years ago, Fjorna became one of the first people to venture inside a dome—at least since the times of the Downfall—when the Negian Empire breached the Heartpine Dome. Six years, and so much had changed. Six years, and she still felt the sting of failure from that mission.

Fjorna rubbed wax on Whisper's drawstring as if playing a musical instrument. A waiter came to refill their glasses. "Leave it," Fjorna said, taking the bottle. She poured wine for the three of them, then leaned back on her chair, eyes following a passing line of slaves. Decrepit, tired, and muddy, the slaves were being whipped toward the east edge of the city, where new excavations were underway.

Muriel followed Fjorna's gaze and noticed two odd ones among the slaves, with red skin covered in tattoos. "Those inked ones aren't spurs, or mucks," she said.

"They aren't yennies either," Waldomar said. "What are they?"

"They are Wutash," Fjorna answered, furtively glancing around to make sure no one could hear their conversation. "The tribe that lived inside the Heartpine Dome. It's rare to see any bloodskins around anymore. Most died in the battle, the rest during the first collapse. My guess is that at most a dozen of them remain."

"And two fewer after they are done with these poor fucks," Waldomar added. "They are headed toward the Malhong trenches. That place gets flooded every time they dig. Steaming Wutash and Oldrin soup is all they are going to get."

A massive mining operation was being carried out at the Anglass Dome. Unlike the Heartpine Dome, which was resting on a range with veins rich in magnium, the ground beneath Anglass didn't provide the same natural resources. But the Negian Empire knew that the real treasure was not on the ground, but within the dome, and that the only way in was from below.

Nineteen years ago, the Farsulf Mining Company took over a mining claim at the south end of the Heartpine Dome. The enterprise soon became untenable, given that the vein of magnium wove through the roots of the dome itself, even more impregnable underground than it was over land. However, a small portion of the seam led straight down, so down they dug, parallel to the roots that sank deep into the rocky crust of Noss. It was a profitable enough venture, for magnium was the aetheric variant of iron, and hence possessed unique properties. As with all aetheric elements, magnium was hardly understood, but its rarity made it valuable for commerce and minting.

For years the miners dug deeper, discovering that a mile or so below ground the roots of the dome thinned out. It was then that the Negian army got involved. Taking over the operations, the Negians dug horizontally from the lowest shafts, through the gaps in the roots, then up into the dome itself, to uncover mysteries concealed for almost fifteen hundred years.

The breach into the Heartpine Dome was now in the past. The Empire guarded the secret of what they found there—and what they lost—with utmost care. Operations to enter the Anglass Dome began a few years after the Heartpine breach, but Anglass was significantly more problematic: the ground here was crisscrossed by underground hot springs, which unexpectedly burst and flooded the tunnels with boiling waters. It was a suicidal mission, but given that Anglass was the only dome in uncontested Negian territory, the costs were deemed worth it. Years of trials and failures were written in the flooded tunnels; years of investment, of promise, and of countless sacrificed slaves.

"This dome is sucking the blood out of our economy," Muriel said. "I always thought we should focus on the Lequa Dome. So glad we are finally being transferred there."

"It won't be long until we take Loompool and Mireinfield from the Bayani," Waldomar added. "Those animals don't belong on *our* continent. But even then, it could take years to dig under the Lequa Dome. Emperor Uvon hasn't provided us enough resources."

Fjorna's gray eyes stared east, to overcast skies of the same hues. "He will, once the area is secured. Tomorrow, we join the convoy toward Shaderift. Please be ready, and get some rest, it's a long road ahead. You did well today." They clinked glasses.

Fjorna noticed Muriel's eyes darting over her shoulder, so she turned and saw a member of her squad hastening toward them.

"Chief Daro, urgent news from the west," Osef Windscar said through shaky breaths. He wiped beads of sweat from his balding head, then added, "They've found her."

"Found whom?"

"Sontai, the Wutash leader. She is dead. An emissary of Consul Uzenzo delivered the message this afternoon. She was found by Eldius Kaspar, a land developer."

"Let's move to a safer location. Tell me everything." Fjorna stood, gulped the remaining wine from her glass, then hurried with her squadmates toward the barracks.

They entered a private hall. Osef produced a map of the Withervale area and spread it over the table. "They found an old cellar carved in rock, right here by the creek, where we lost her years ago."

Fjorna nodded. "I remember it clearly."

"The cellar's entrance had been blocked with stones," Osef said, "and inside was Sontai's dead body, well preserved from the cold. It seems an Oldrin funeral was performed on her. The tattoos match. It's her. You could swear by the Twin Faces of Takh."

"What about the—"

"The mask was not there. The consul secured the area for a thorough search, but it turned up nothing. But we might have a lead. The cellar had old toys and small footprints, and there was a name scribbled on one of the walls—"

"Lago…" Fjorna whispered.

"H-how did you know?"

"I never forget a name," Fjorna said, then sharpened her gaze toward Osef. "Who else knows about this?"

"Perhaps no one else, yet. The emissary reported directly to the consul and believes the information is secure, but we can't bet on it. At least three Oldrin workers were there when they found the cellar, so it's possible other parties will find out. He came as soon as possible, but it's been ten days since the incident."

Fjorna slung Whisper over her shoulder and commanded, "Muriel, Waldomar, gather the squad, make sure they are assembled before nightfall. We'll head to Withervale before morning. Osef, find Crescu, and meet me at the gates of the Fogdale Citadel. I have to report this to General Hallow immediately. Make haste."

Built within a thicket of vines that extended from the dome, the Fogdale Citadel was impenetrable. It rose in the western flanks of Anglass, fortified by the thorns and dense framework of the dome's natural, unchanging structure. Fjorna waited at the citadel's ample drawbridge, which curved over a pit of vines covered in thorns. Osef arrived, followed by Armsmaster Crescu Valaran, second-in-command of Fjorna's squad. Crescu was wearing a thin suit of fine leather and carried with him his crossbow and spear. Like all soldiers in the Empire, Crescu had his left temple shaved, revealing a ranking insignia that spoke of plentiful honors, but not nearly as numerous as Fjorna's.

They walked under the oppressive, rusting teeth of the citadel's gates.

A skeletal chandelier illuminated the war room, hanging over a long table of oiled hardwood carved with a map of Hestfell and the northern steppes. Sixteen twilight-blue banners circled the room, each adorned with blood-red laurels, the sigil of the long dynasty that had birthed Emperor Uvon dus Grei, the ruler of the Negian Empire for the past nine years. At the end of the table were two dignitaries from Hestfell, and the charismatic and intimidating presence of General Alvis Hallow.

"Chief Daro, Armsmaster Valaran, I was not expecting to see you until tomorrow's briefing," the general said with a courteous nod. Fjorna was used to seeing Alvis in the field, wearing plated armor and chainmail, but now he was wearing a red leather waistcoat with a black fur coat over it. Alvis was in his mid-fifties but did not quite look it. His complexion was stern, embellished by enough wrinkles that revealed unquestionable experience and ruthless ambition, but which also imbued him with an air of softness and grace. His sideburns were graying into the same sharp gray as his eyes, a common trait among the Iesmari race. He was a pragmatic man, amenable, constantly strategizing his next moves.

"We have urgent news, Lorr," Fjorna said. "For your ears only."

Alvis waved the dignitaries off, telling them he'd call for them when ready.

"General Hallow, we have reports from Consul Uzenzo in Withervale," Osef said.

"Please, sit down, Lorr Wildscar."

"It's Windscar, Osef Windscar, Lorr."

Alvis nodded.

Osef nervously dabbed his scalp with a kerchief, unfolded the map, and recounted the information he had just delivered to Fjorna.

"And there is no lead on the mask?" Alvis inquired.

"Nothing but that scribbled name, Lago Vaari, and an indication that an Oldrin was involved in the funerary ritual," Osef said.

"Oldrin have no family names," Alvis observed. "So at least two people were involved in this."

"Utmost speed is of importance now," Crescu Valaran said, leaning forward by balancing his weight on his spear. "Several days have passed. It is likely that the information will reach unfriendly ears. If the mask is in Withervale, the Zovarian Union already has the upper hand. Our squad is ready, Lorr, we can depart at your command."

"You mean the same squad who lost the Wutash leader six years ago?" Alvis inquired, walking toward a window that looked to the southwest. Even from over a hundred miles away, the Heartpine Dome could be seen through the haze, partially hiding behind the Pilgrim Sierras. "If you did not have the competence to secure this lone, old woman back then, why should you be leading this mission?"

"Lorr, you need a team that can infiltrate quietly," Crescu said. "We are the only specialist squad that is close enough and ready for the task. We are familiar with the mission, with the risks involved."

"If I may," Fjorna jumped in, "I'm also familiar with the lead, the boy named Lago. I would be able to recognize him. He should be around eighteen years old, brown skin, curly hair, from the looks of his clothing not a noble nor a miner. Probably lives in the mesa."

"And how do you know this boy?" Alvis asked, turning on his heel.

"I interrogated him after losing track of the Wutash witch. He was in the area."

"You are saying you were tricked by a boy, too? Splendid."

"We are unsure of the circumstances," she added. "Maybe they met after we departed. Lorr, our squad is the most prepared for this task, but we will do as you command. We failed you six years ago, but the turn of events was unpredictable. This time, we have a clear goal, a bigger squad, and greater knowledge of the situation. If you give us a chance, we won't let you down."

The general rubbed his freshly shaved chin as he sized Fjorna up. "Very well," he concluded, "but you will not be leaving alone. We have a merchant crayer that can be readied to sail by morning. I will go with you and take a small platoon of my finest."

"But Lorr, we could go much faster on our own."

"We will sail together. You will disembark at night, a few miles before arriving at the fortifications, to make your way into the mesa unseen. The Halfort Rampart is weak, especially to the south. Your small group can easily climb it unnoticed. I will fly a herald west to inform Consul Uzenzo of our plans, so he can grant passage to our crayer. My platoon and I will hide below deck, dock at Maulers Port, and wait on news from your squad before making our move. We will get into specifics once we are on board."

"If Seneschal Oda is alerted of this, she would send their entire army after us," Osef warned. "It would be a declaration of war."

"Then let's keep away from their eyes. If we make ourselves known, we hold our ground until their troops get too close, then escape east through the rampart, where I'll have horses waiting for us in the old forest. We go in, we go out. And if the mask is in their possession, we fight until we take it, for no one else merits its power. We are the ones who rescued it from the bloodskins, and by Takh's two names, we shall have it."

CHAPTER TWENTY-ONE

THE ASTROLABE

"I'll have it done by tomorrow, Professor Hayver," Lago said, stuffing a stack of papers into his bag. Biology class had let out early, so he headed to the courtyard to wait for the physics seminar.

"I'll save you a spot!" Penli said to Lago, holding hands with his girlfriend, Kara. Lago was happy for Penli, and proud, seeing him strutting around with his tail swishing in the open. Kara had braided red and yellow threads on his tail's furry tuft—it looked quite fancy.

Lago strolled over to the colonnade that overlooked the northern side of the East Flank and leaned on the balusters, facing away from the crowds. He dug in his bag, pulled out his wooden box of fingernail lacquers, and began to mix a bit of the paste with the solvent.

"You really want them to beat you up, don't you?" Deon's voice said from behind.

Lago turned around, startled, but not really afraid. "I don't give a shit what they think. If they want some, they can come get it."

Deon leaned next to Lago, but not too close. "I know you don't care, but it's awkward, you know?"

"What, you mean awkward for you?" He began to apply the lacquers, starting with his left pinky.

"Well, yeah, if they see us together, and you are doing this... lorrkin stuff... It's odd, they'll figure out what's going on."

"You are a big boy. If I can take them, you could pummel them to a pulp."

Deon was a junior from the Tharma Federation, just a year behind Lago. His rotund body supported a big belly and plenty of soft padding over his muscles. His pale skin and blond beard made a strong impression in these areas of the Zovarian Union, especially since most Zovarians didn't grow any facial hair.

I wish I could grow a beard, Lago thought, peeking sideways while he continued to paint his nails. He found Deon's beard irresistibly exotic and sensual.

Deon and Lago had never done more than nod at one another when passing by, not until one day a few years back, when Lago was out on one of his delivery runs. He had been carrying a crate filled with old trinkets that were no longer of use to the monastery, to drop it off at the Sharr Helm Antique Store, not too far from the school. The package was unwieldy, so the store owner—Deon's father, gifted with an equally alluring beard and plump body—asked his son to accompany Lago to the back warehouse to help him unload.

Lago followed Deon to the back and saw his belly poking from beneath his tight shirt. He'd found himself aroused. Even the sight of Deon's father had made his crotch tingle, and he'd felt guilty for having such thoughts. Deon noticed a furtive glance from Lago, and that was all it took; the portly boy was on him, kissing him and pushing him against a wall. Soon enough Deon dropped his trousers and pushed down on Lago's shoulders, shoving himself into his mouth a bit too eagerly. It was not Lago's first time, but it was the first time he'd felt truly physically attracted to one of his flings. Lago had returned to the antique store often after that, with or without deliveries to make.

Lago shook those memories off his mind and let his nails dry with the Autumn breeze that flowed from beyond the balustrade. He shivered, closed his little box of fingernail lacquers, and tucked it away.

A bell rang.

They walked together toward the courtyard.

"Physics?" Deon asked.

"Yup. You?"

"Alchemy."

"I didn't know you were taking alchemy," Lago said, truthfully surprised.

"There's lots you don't know about me," Deon said. He snuck in a half-lidded look. "Hey, it's Onguday. I'll be cleaning up at the store after Dad leaves."

"I won't finish till late at the observatory."

"I'll be working late too. I'll wait for you."

Although Deon could be obtuse, petulant, and a bit demanding, Lago couldn't help but go along with his requests. Deon was much more assertive in bed than any of the other boys he had been with, and that made Lago feel a thrill every time.

"So…"—Lago swallowed—"what do you want to do?" He slowed his pace down.

Deon's dimples punctuated his mischievous grin. He leaned slowly to Lago's ear and whispered something so salacious and daring, something so unimaginably raunchy to Lago's mind, that Lago could do nothing but freeze in place and slide his bag forward to cover his erection.

Deon glanced down. "I'll take that as a yes. See you tonight," he said, biting his lip as he walked away.

Alaia was cooking a stew when Lago arrived home. "Could you please lock Bear out? He keeps forcing the door open," she said.

"But it's chilly out," Lago said. He noticed broken glass on the floor. "What happened here?"

"Don't care if it's cold, he deserves it. That brainless mutt somehow climbed up the top cabinet and ate all the caribou jerky."

Lago walked Bear out and scratched his head while admonishing him. "Bad dog! Stay!" he said, then walked back into their rickety hut and propped a chair against the door to secure it.

He dropped off his bag, helped clean up the broken jar, and tossed away the bits of jerky he found, lest Bear chew on them later and find his gums bleeding from the glass. He then went to the window to water his ruby-flecked stoneleaf. The red dots adorning the pebble-like succulent glistened as brazenly as the blue sands that provided it with nourishment. The plant was precious to him; he felt proud of how the stoneleaf had grown a miniature grove of copies of itself. Lerr Holfster helped him with transplants once a year, giving him a larger glass planter and fresh Baurami sand each time.

Lago slumped on his flimsy chair to do his homework. Alaia placed a bowl in front of him.

After a moment, she asked, "Are you going to try it, or should I give it to Bear?"

"Sorry, thank you. I have a lot to go through. And I'll be home late."

"Mm-hmm. I see. Then you better wash before you go. I'll clean up the kitchen this time. I hope you two have fun," she said earnestly.

Bear always followed Lago to the observatory. He liked the walk up Runestone Lane, where he could boast about his independence to all the dogs locked in houses, feeling like the king of the street.

"You can't keep doing shit like that, Bear," Lago said, feeling the comfort of having someone to talk to. "If you keep breaking into our stash, we'll have to lock you out all night."

Bear mewed the saddest, most innocent of whines, but Lago did not buy it.

A few blocks before they reached the monastery grounds, Bear stopped and growled. The fur at his neck pricked up. Lago glanced to his side and spotted a dark figure darting behind a sandstone bridge. He pretended not to see anything and kept walking. He told Bear to go home, and the dog obeyed. After passing under the stone arches of the monastery and locking the metal gates behind him, he crouched in the shadows behind the short, stone walls and placed his right hand around a sturdy, fallen branch.

He held still for a moment. Then for a breath more, until he heard rustling, but the stones behind his head prevented him from pinpointing the direction of the sound. A shadow jumped the wall barely four strides to his left, landing with striking silence on the leaf-covered grass.

"What the fuck do you want?" Lago said, pulling the solid branch up and stepping menacingly toward the hooded figure. It was too dark to see anything more than a shimmering penannular brooch clasping the figure's cloak, shining leather boots, and the confusing silhouettes of sycamore branches over a darkening indigo sky.

The shadowy figure was startled and fled directly away from Lago, jumping the wall once more to escape down an alley.

Fucking creep, Lago thought. *You better fucking run.* He tossed the branch away and headed to the observatory.

Crysta was down in the library, standing on a ladder to reach books on the upper shelves. "Hold these for me, will you, dear?" she said.

Lago helped her bring down a handful of voluminous tomes. "Some person was following me. They jumped over the wall after I came in."

"Someone from school?"

"Don't know, I don't think so. Couldn't see their face, had a hood on. I made them shit their trousers though."

"Be careful out there. I know you can defend yourself, but you made quite a few enemies in the past." She stepped down the ladder and stacked the last few books on a work desk. She began flipping through them. "I don't want you getting in trouble. We'll walk out together after work, then we split off at Feldspar Boulevard."

"Well, actually, I'm going down the same way tonight. Spending time with a friend."

"Hmm. I did notice you dressed a bit too nicely for work, and your hair is all made up. And your nails, I love it when you color them blue—it's absolutely your color."

"Thank you," he shyly said.

"I hope he treats you kindly," she added.

Crysta had never directly asked him about his sexuality; the talk around it always sidestepped any concreteness. Lago blushed, thinking it was sweet of her to use that pronoun and acknowledge it so positively.

"Here, help me sort through these," she said, passing him a stack of books and a list of scholarly papers she was trying to locate.

"I was talking to Alaia the other day, about what happens after school and all. She thinks it would be nice if you could write a letter to the sponsorship committee. Maybe you know of any cosmologists wanting to take in new scholars?"

"She thinks? Or you think? Are you asking me, or are you again trying to dodge the responsibility?"

"*I* think, I think... I would. Yes. I would like to try out for cosmology. And I know it's gonna cost a lot and I don't really know anyone out there and—"

"Take it easy, I know it's hard. I had to move from Needlecove when I was your age. If you think Withervale is a small city, you have *no* idea. We had less than two hundred people in all of Needlecove. I practically knew everyone, and their pets, and their farm animals." She walked around to the side table to grab her cup of tea. "And yes, of course I'll do it. I've been waiting for you to ask of your own volition, and I'm glad you finally did. I know a handful of scholars who are looking for new talents to mentor, but it's not a Qupi giveaway, they'll make you work hard to earn their sponsorship."

"How did you know... I mean... How were you sure that you wanted to move out?"

"Oh, I never wanted to move out, but I wanted to learn. Let me show you something," she said, guiding him up the tower's steps.

The walls of the octagonal room had always been covered with odd instruments. Lago knew most of them, since they used them for work every day, but some were still obscure and seemed purely ornamental. As they reached the top step, Crysta turned around. "Right above you," she said, pointing to a plate-sized, metallic object that hung exactly centered on the keystone above the landing. The thing was ugly, rusted beyond recognition in teal, brown, and black growths.

"Do you know what that instrument is?" she asked.

"It looks like a wheel? A gear or something?"

"It's a mariner's astrolabe. It's my most treasured possession in the whole world. I put it up there decades ago, so that every night, as I take my leave, it reminds me to keep going in the right direction."

"Looks a bit crusty to be of help with any guidance."

"Show some respect now," she berated him. "It's metaphorical guidance."

"It doesn't look at all like the astrolabe we use."

"It works in a similar way. Well, this one doesn't work, it's rusted to the Voids of Khest and beyond. But it worked, once."

"Why is the hideous platter so special?"

"Be nice. When I was eight, living in my tiny world of Needlecove, I used to go play at the Ivory Cliffs. The sea stacks there are tall and steep, made of chalk, whiter than the snowy peaks we could see across the Isdinnklad. There is a path that goes down to the base of the cliffs, where waves carved enormous caves, needles, and arches out of the chalk. A very dangerous place. You could easily drown if you didn't know how to read the tides.

"My friends and I would venture down there during low tide, when the whole area turned into a white beach. In one of the caves was this old ship-wreck where we played pirate games, pretending the ship had just crashed on shore. We were castaways on a remote island, trying to survive without our parents, making up our own rules for everything. We had such a great time."

Crysta grabbed a step stool. "Would you mind bringing it down for me?"

Lago stepped up and removed the astrolabe from the keystone. It was as heavy as it looked, encrusted with ages of oxides and barnacles. Crysta took it to her work desk, where she rested it with a thump. They sat, and she continued her story.

"I was down by the shipwreck one morning, all by myself. I liked going on my own, before my friends showed up, because I could pretend I was the captain, otherwise only the boys would get that privilege. I was holding on to the mast—well, it was just a stick we planted within the ribs of the hull—when I saw a bright-red hermit crab dragging its shell under a rock. They were common in the area. We kept them as pets, called them *crab-berries*. I ran after it and stuck my hand under the rock, where I felt something odd. The white rocks there were rather smooth, but something underneath this one had an odd texture."

"It was the astrol—"

"Of course it was the astrolabe, don't get ahead of me, I'm trying to tell a story here." She cleared her throat and, a bit theatrically, continued, "*It was the astrolabe*. Of course, I didn't know *what* it was, but for a kid my age, who just found a chunk of metal next to a wrecked ship, it was treasure! I tugged it out, washed it as well as I could, and dragged it home. Oh, how hard it was to carry this burden up the steep path. I had to drag it on the loose chalk most of the way. It must've been heavy to begin with, but with the extra rust and barnacles, it felt weightier than a millstone.

"*I found the helm of a pirate ship!* I proudly told my father. *It's so heavy, it must be made of pure gold,* I said, and he played along, letting me have my little moment. He helped me clean it, but we couldn't get the bigger crusts off, so we weren't able to tell what it really was. He decided to call Sarina, who lived a few houses down—well, everyone lived a few houses down—since she used to cook for a trading ship that sailed the Isdinnklad. She immediately recognized it as an astrolabe, and with this enticing sparkle in her eyes she told me, *Little Crysta, with one of these you can read the stars like a book. You can uncover so many secrets, simply by looking up into the skies. I've seen them do it, it's like magic.*

"After that I asked my father where I could find a functioning astrolabe, told him I wanted to learn how to read the stars. He didn't know, but he guessed we might find answers in Zovaria. But the capital was so far, about three hundred miles from Needlecove! My father was such a sweetheart, Takhísh and Takhamún bless him. Without even questioning it, he planned a trip to Zovaria to search for answers. *A quest!* he called it, and the thought of it filled me with feverish joy. Mind you, my father wasn't wealthy. A trip like this would mean time off from his work at the hatchery. But he remained unfazed. He *would* have this adventure with his little girl.

"On an Iskimday morning, we hitched a ride south, and once on the Old Pilgrim's Road, we joined a caravan that took us west, straight to the capital. It took us weeks to get there, thanks to how muddy the road was, how frequent the stops. My father thought I would hate it, but I loved every heartbeat of it. It was wonderful seeing the landscape change, seeing the Moordusk Dome poking its snowy peak over the western horizon, and having my first glimpse of the pink capital. You can see Zovaria from many miles away, you know? The whole city rises as a shining, pink hill, due to the rose quartz they used to rebuild the walls after the Downfall. The Zovarian Academic Institute is unmissable, perched on the very top bulwark. My father had made arrangements to meet with a professor there, Artificer Grissem was his name."

"Wasn't he the one who sponsored you at the institute?"

"The same one, though that came nearly a decade later. Even after his death, I still feel indebted to him. My father and I took the Cliffside Lifts and met Grissem way up on the Sixteenth Bulwark, where he gave us a tour and everything. Can you imagine my excitement? Being led into those ancient halls full of history was an extravagance beyond anything I could've imagined. And the books... So many books... Their aroma is something I learned to treasure years later. Grissem took us to a museum collection of restored, pre-Downfall artifacts, one not meant for the public. They had old magnium gadgets for which we still don't know their functions, quaar relics from the Yenwu State, senstregalv arrowheads of Dorvauros origins, and all manner of mechanical and optical instruments.

"I proudly showed Griss my heavy, rusty astrolabe, which my father was more than a dear to carry all through the trip. He told me it looked like ones they used on trading crayer ships. They were still in use about fifty years ago, he said, but they had been forged three hundred years back. *Three hundred years!* And I had found it. He opened a glass cabinet and took out a brass astrolabe, much smaller and lighter than this clunky thing here."

Crysta ran her fingers over the encrusted wheel of metal and kept talking while her hand circled around it.

"He handed me white gloves and let me hold the astrolabe, telling me to be extremely careful. *This one is over seventeen hundred years old*, he said, and I gasped. He told me how we inherited all these fragments of technology from those who lived here before the Downfall. All those treasures from scorched civilizations, all that hidden wisdom had to be pieced together bit by bit, from epoch to epoch. There is still so much out there, temples buried under sands, libraries soaking below water, cities tangled beneath forests, with so much knowledge that may either be lost, or someday recovered by curious minds."

She paused for a bit. Lago waited, reluctant to interrupt her thoughts.

"My father, he did so much for me," she said. "After our trip to Zovaria, he saved enough Qupi to buy me alchemy and cosmology books, and had a sailor teach me how to read astrolabes. On my twelfth birthday, he surprised me with a pocket astrolabe, the same one I've been using this whole time." She took the instrument out of her coat's front pocket. "I never knew how much it cost him. I didn't dare ask. But for a poor family like ours, it must've been a fortune."

She slid the lightweight astrolabe back in her pocket.

"There's so much out there, Lago. I think about the wisdom we lost after the Downfall, and how, despite our primitive skills, we can still look back fifteen hundred years to the mysterious birth of the domes, ten thousand years to the Expansion Epoch, a hundred thousand years to the birth of our races. And we can go further, millions of years into the fossil record, to find beasts known to us merely from the lonesome traces they left in their wake. But nothing, and I mean *nothing* compares to the immeasurably deep time of the planets, of the stars.

"This universe is so expansive and abundant, and it needs inquisitive minds not to find answers, but to ask the right questions. That mentality should be treasured, more than any wheel of brass, gold coin, or precious stone. We are self-aware, able to contemplate ourselves contemplate the cosmos, and we are given this one chance to do something for life *now*, to serve those who will come after us. One chance.

"I am eternally grateful for the support my father gave me. I wish everyone could be given the same chances. I'm glad I followed my heart, and that I had someone there to hold my hand through it. Let the stars guide you, and never neglect your calling, for you will only face true regret by not following the path your heart knows is right for you.

"I think you have an exciting career ahead of you. Life has called you on an adventure, and you have to jump into it willingly, with passion. You have to let go of everything else and immerse yourself in your quest for understanding. And I'd be more than happy to be there to help you through it."

Lago was looking out the northern window, unable to face Crysta, as he did not want her to see him shedding tears.

CHAPTER TWENTY-TWO

THE DATE

Walking down Runestone Lane, Crysta and Lago saw no sign of the shady fig-
ure Lago had encountered earlier. They crossed the green bridges of Greisen
Park, passed between the Twin Shrines of Takh, and continued downhill on
Feldspar Boulevard.

"I almost forgot to ask..." Lago shyly said. "Alaia's twentieth birthday is
coming up. I wanted to do something special for her."

"And how am I involved in this?"

"You know what happens on Khuday. Well... I wanted to ask if I could
bring her up to the observatory for that."

"Merciful Takh! The monks would not take it kindly to have an Oldrin on
their sacred grounds. I don't know—"

"Chaplain Gwil has nothing against the Oldrin, I know that for a fact. Not
all the monks are as close-minded as the rest of the Havengall Congregation. I
just thought it would be nice for her. No one needs to find out about it."

"Well... If you promise to be quiet, and close up after yourself, and don't
tell anyone else. I'll be working through the afternoon, so I could leave a
bit early."

"It's settled then."

They reached the fork where they'd have to go their separate ways.

"Be careful the rest of the way," she said, eyeing the shadows.

"You too. See you tomorrow at school."

"Tomorrow is Sunnday. But have a good date!"

Lago smiled and hurried down the quiet streets.

"Hair looks good," Deon said, opening the door to his father's store. He peeked out to the streets to make sure no one saw Lago coming in, then closed the door behind them. He pulled Lago away from the windows and kissed him forcibly. Lago felt his back pressed against the wall, his front pressed against Deon's belly, and his cock pushing hard against his trousers.

Deon wriggled a hand under Lago's belt, held tight to his shaft, then said, "To the back. I got the old mattress back." He led the way.

In the warehouse at the back of the Sharr Helm Antique Store, Lago and Deon rolled over an old mattress, their bodies dripping sweat as they moaned with a shared lust. Deon's plump body, his cotton-soft beard, his pasty skin, they were all in direct contrast to his dominant assertiveness, his hard-pounding weight, his savage grunts. Their encounter didn't last long—they were both too excited and finished fast.

"Better get going, getting quite late," Deon said, unromantically wiping the cum off his pale cock and licking it off, before pulling his trousers up. "Maybe stop by tomorrow? We didn't get to try any of what we talked about."

"Of course. I, um, I'll have to get myself nice and ready for that," Lago replied, feeling a tingle running down his spine.

"See ya," Deon said.

Lago left, feeling full, and also empty.

"Where are you taking me?" Alaia asked.

"I told you, up the hill."

"Are we going to jump off the mesa?" she said, fixing the braids around her nub. She was dressed nicely as per Lago's request, but not too nicely. Clean trousers, no overalls this time, wearing a lace-back top which she somehow fastened by interweaving the laces with the spurs on her spine, enhancing the peculiarly grotesque beauty of the thirteen bony protrusions.

They were getting close to the observatory, which was calling for them like a lighthouse, lit by the very last rays of sunset.

"Is that where we are going?" she asked. "What is wrong with you? The monks would chop my head off and use it to fertilize their herbs!"

"They'll all be at the Haven by now, just trust me."

"Why are you taking me there? Do you need a servant girl to help you with your chores?"

"Shut it and go in," he said, unlocking the metal gate.

They walked under the stone arch, over the short path, then up the few steps to the library. "After you," Lago said, swinging open the heavy doors.

Alaia crept in under the light of dozens of warm lamps. "I've never seen a place like this," she whispered, admiring the columns of books rising up the intricate architecture. "When you told me there was a library, I thought it was like the one by the wharf. This is something else..."

"Feel free to browse through them," came the voice of Crysta. She walked down the tower steps, chomping down a muffin, satchel slung over her shoulder.

Alaia was woefully embarrassed. "Hey Lurr... Professor... Holt..."

"Nice to see you again, Alaia, your hair looks gorgeous. I'll take my leave now. Lago, please close after yourself. And again, no loud noises." She walked out the front door and closed it behind her. The door reopened just two heart-beats after. Crysta poked her head in and with a devilish smile added, "And have a nice date!" then closed the door again.

Alaia laughed out loud. "A date! Is that what this is?"

"Shhh, I promised her we'd be quiet!"

"Does she even know you are lorrkin?"

"Of course she knows, she's just being obnoxious."

"So, it *isn't* a date, then."

"It is whatever you want to call it. I thought you'd like to see where I work. You lived here your entire life and never once got to see the observatory. I figured it'd make a good birthday present, you know..."

"That's. Adorable. Really. And I'm *so thrilled!*" she said, raising her voice both in volume and in pitch. Then, quietly, "I mean, this place looks amazing! And I don't want to shatter your illusions, but my birthday isn't until the twelfth. Sunnday."

"I know, but this couldn't wait, you'll see why. Follow me, I'll show you around."

Lago gave Alaia a tour of the library, showing her his favorite book collections, letting her push the sliding ladder to browse around.

"Spit it out," she demanded. "You know what I'm after."

"Three shelves to your right. About half-way up."

Alaia followed his directions and found them, all the books about ornithology she could ever dream of. She flipped through their pages.

"Just make sure you put them back in—"

"I know, I know. Hey, this is the one you brought to me so many years ago, the one by Hefra, remember? I loved this book so much. I could read it over and over. Gorgeous illustrations, she's so good at capturing their emotions. Can you imagine what her life must be like? Getting paid to go out and stare at birds?"

"She probably doesn't get paid much for it."

"Still, living the dream."

"You done browsing? Ready to see the tower?"

"Fuck yes," she said, "race you up!"

Alaia found herself in a strange paradise, a forbidden place of artifacts and smells she could not identify. Lago gave her a moment, then showed her the telescope, and how it worked.

"Can we look at Sceres?"

"She won't rise till midnight. But Iskimesh is out. I had the telescope prepped for that already. Hold on." He aimed the telescope toward the south-western sky and adjusted the knobs until the Enchantress was in sight. "Take a look, quickly, before she sinks over the mountains."

"This... Whoa. She's so green!"

"The tiny dots to the sides are moons—Aelithem, Vallamowe, and Gormenn. So yes, you can look at moons tonight, just not our moon. Iskimesh has one more moon, Kelinei, but he's hiding behind her now."

Alaia started humming the Bayani lullaby, staring entranced.

"*Hmm, hmmm... danced and spun and bared her chest, till milky pearls flowed out her breasts.* Is that what those words mean? The pearls are her moons?"

"I think so. Whoever wrote the song must've seen her through a telescope."

"Glad we made it in time for that. But there's something more fun to see, follow me."

Up through the trapdoor they climbed, onto the roof of the tower. They rested their elbows on the northern parapet and stared out to the Stelm Wujann. The mountains were black, for no moon was shining, but the light of the stars was enough to draft a crisp silhouette, tinting the snowy tops ever-so-faintly with the greenish blue of a deep ocean trench.

"Lodestar guide me," Alaia said, staring at the Sword of Zeiheim, the constellation which dutifully marked the north.

"Pellámbri is glowing hot pink tonight," Lago said, referring to the Lodestar at the very center of the sword.

"She is." Alaia took in the rest of the panorama. "This view is much better than at the cliff's edge, you can see in all directions at once. You can even see tiny boats down in—wha?! Did you see that?"

"It's starting!"

"What is starting? Was that—"

"There's another one!"

"Where?"

"It was to your left, right over the Isdinnklad."

"Was that a falling star? What is happening?"

"You know it. Tonight is the peak of the Quindecims, the meteor shower from—there! Did you see that?" He pointed up.

"Again? I missed it."

"You can still see its trail, right there, crossing the constellation of Probo, the one with the two women chasing a javelina." He pointed at a cluster of stars that looked like anything but two women chasing a javelina.

Another shooting star blasted through, right above them, emerald-gold fading to lime-yellow.

"That was so bright!" Alaia yelled. "Sorry, keeping my voice down, sorry. I've seen shooting stars, but never this bright. Why haven't we seen this before?"

"This shower only lines up with our orbit every fifteen years. You might've seen it before, when you were five. If I saw it when I was three, I don't remember. And I must offer my apologies, for I couldn't reschedule it to Sunnday. I'll try harder for your thirty-fifth."

She punched him in the shoulder. "You are the best. This is absolutely fantastic."

"Hold on for a bit," Lago said and went down the trapdoor. He soon came back up, carrying a basket. In it were two cotton blankets, a bottle of red wine, and a few sugary snacks. Lago spread the blankets over the wooden roof and gestured for her to lie down.

"This is officially a date now," she said. "Wine, a romantic view, and are these fig pastries? I'm so gonna tell Deon. I'll tell him I'm going to have sixteen of your babies."

"I'm starting to regret this now."

"There! Two more! And over there! That one was even greener."

"Saw that, almost blinding."

They lay there for a long time, seeing nothing but the enveloping sky crossed by burning shards of an ancient comet.

"So, why all this?" she asked. "I mean, of course I love it, but it's a bit much, don't you think?"

"Maybe. I mean, several reasons. One is that it's something we couldn't miss. I'm not waiting fifteen years for the next one. Another reason is that we always do something fun for your birthday, and there's... There's a chance I might not be around for your twenty-first." He drew in a deep breath. "I talked to Crysta. I'm going to apply to the cosmology program. If I get a sponsor, I'll have to be moving west sometime after Pondsong, by Dustwind at the latest. That's less than a year away."

"I'm so proud of you, Gwoli! That's the best news I've heard all year. I always knew you'd go on to do great things. And by the netherflames, I'll miss you, but you have to take this chance."

A long pause, broken up by dozens of luminous streaks.

Lago took a sip of wine and rested his head down again. "If I get it, I mean, if I go… what are you going to do?"

"I wish I could go too, but they don't treat Oldrin as kindly in Zovaria as they do in Withervale. Honestly? I thought about this a lot. Once the Negian war with the Bayani is over, maybe I'll travel east, across the splitting divide of the Ophidian, all the way to Dorhond, to find my way to the White Desert. I always wanted to see my homeland. I don't know what life there is like, I just know I want to see those infinite white sand dunes, and live with people who won't call me a spur, or treat me like I'm some sort of animal."

She paused, stuck in a time far ahead. The stars continued falling over their heads—most were firefly-green colored; few took on warmer hues.

Alaia sighed. "But that's far in the future. And with how things are going, I'm happy where I'm at. I'm getting ahead at the mines. I might even become a technician if all goes like I'm planning. Take that position from Aiéma—that ass-kisser never deserved it."

More feeble nocturnal flames sliced gold-green veins across the infinite dome of the sky.

"For now, I'm just glad we have this," she said. "It might just be another moment in time, but to me, it is forever."

CHAPTER TWENTY-THREE

INFILTRATORS

Lago worked the monastery's lift crank. From hundreds of feet below, the crate dutifully rose to reveal two letters and an unbound book.

"Moon lights, Gwil," he said as he passed the monk on his way to deliver the correspondence.

"Stars guide," the chaplain replied. "The package for the Harrowdale Temple is waiting at my desk."

"I'll get it in a moment, I won't be long with Esum and Khopto."

Lago entered the scriptorium and handed the letters to Esum.

"Your line work is so elegant," Lago said, spying over the monk's shoulder, who was copying an illustration from a book titled *The Sacred Plants of Afhora*, carefully drafting it leaf by leaf, detail by detail. "You should try making a woodblock carving, it'll save you time."

"And use one of those fancy Tsing printing presses too while I'm at it?" she mocked. "You young ones have no appreciation for this fine art. It's not about speed, it's about understanding, and love."

Lago shrugged and went to find Khopto next, who was in the central garden performing his usual ritual. Lago stood under the arches to watch, always fascinated by Khopto's bizarre display of skills that mixed biology, spirituality, alchemy, and the study of consciousness itself.

Khopto walked around the cloister's garth with eyes shut tight, as if directed by an invisible breeze. His arms were looped in front of his chest, his feet sliding with the grace of a heron, always landing perfectly at the centers of the hexagonal tiles. Overcome by a sudden determination, he stopped, crouched, plucked two red leaves from a vine, and only then opened his eyes. Satisfied, he began to walk to the laboratory.

Lago caught up with him. "Crimson feverweed again, huh? Someone must be quite sick."

"It produces such magical oils, cures most ailments, I always say. But today, it is to add a little spice to my lunch."

"Did you need to do the whole ritual just for that?"

"How else would I know what flavors I will want to add?" Khopto asked.

Lago wasn't sure whether Khopto was joking or not, so he simply handed over the book addressed to him and followed him into the lab. While the monk ground powders and oils with a pestle, Lago helped by cleaning and calibrating the microscopes.

"You'll make a great disciple, the day you finally decide to join the Congregation," Khopto nonchalantly mentioned, not for the first time. He trimmed a sprout of needleclove and dropped it in the mortar. "I noticed you wear the bracelet even when you aren't out making deliveries."

"Yeah, I like the bracelet. I also like the curly hair atop my head. I think I'll keep both."

"We'll see about *that*," Khopto said, snipping the scissors toward him.

"I'm also smart enough to not get into drugs," Lago said, signaling to Khopto to wipe off the blotch of black dust smeared under his prominent nose.

"Spare me the judgment till you've tried it," Khopto said, wiping it off.

Six years ago, Lago had seen this strange substance by accident while delivering a package to Gwil. It wasn't until a year after that incident that he'd built up the courage to ask about it, but he'd asked Khopto instead of Gwil, as they had a more informal relationship.

Binding him under a promise of strict confidentiality, Khopto had told Lago about a substance called *soot*, the aetheric variant of carbon. The valuable powder was highly misunderstood, particularly because it was considered profane by the Takheists and a dangerous drug by most others, making it hard for scholars to secure grants to study it.

The coal mines of Withervale provided coal not just for burning, but also for an underground workshop in the Harrowdale Temple, where soot was processed and distilled. Those extractions were then sent to the Mesa Monastery, where monks purified them in the laboratory. Soot was, secretly, the primary source of income for all chapters of the Havengall Congregation, given that their medicinal ventures were merely philanthropical and not truly profitable.

Khopto had explained to Lago that soot was a psychedelic drug that made him 'feel the threads that connect all living beings,' in a similar way as it allowed the shamans of Wastyr to 'speak' to certain animals. It was while under the influence of this drug that the monks were able to walk around the garth with their eyes closed, although it took decades for them to learn the skill.

Tons of coal were necessary to process a single pinch of soot, but the deep pockets of rich realms were willing to afford it, for they needed a steady supply of it for their shamans. After inhaling the powder, shamans were able to communicate with their bird heralds and send them to deliver letters, track important targets, or keep guard as sentinels. Quick transfer of information was an invaluable resource in trade, politics, and warfare; other than Crysta's limited-range sunnograph, there was no faster tool than magpies to relay urgent messages to nearby cities, or cormorants to reach realms farther away.

This was the main reason Lago was so well paid for the simple jobs he carried out: he had been unknowingly involved in the trade of soot. Once he became aware of it, he didn't mind so much—as far as he understood, the substance was harmless. Besides, it financed the monastery's medicinal endeavors, supported Crysta's workplace, and covered his own living expenses.

Khopto took a gleeful sniff at his needleclove mix and put the pestle down. "I have something for you," he said, eyes glancing toward the lab's door. "And I know what you are going to say, you don't need to join our 'cult,' but here." He handed Lago the smallest of bottles. Inside was a pinch of the dark powder. "Consider it a late birthday present. It's from me personally, I'm not stealing from the monastery. Keep it, sell it, use it, do as you will, but if you are ever curious to truly learn about it, you know who to ask."

"I don't know about this," Lago said, trying to hand the bottle back.

Khopto raised his hands. "Again, sell it if you want to get rid of it. You know how valuable it is, and it's yours to do—"

The door opened. Lago hurriedly dropped the tiny bottle into his delivery bag. Gwil stepped in. "Lago, I nearly forgot. Could you also take these two letters to Aurgushem? And do hurry, it's getting late."

Lago delivered Gwil's correspondence to the Harrowdale Temple, ate a late lunch, then finished other errands in downtown Withervale. He sensed an odd tension in the streets, particularly by the gates of the naval base, as if the guards were on high alert. It was late afternoon by the time he made it back to the mesa, where he noticed something else that was strange: elusive shadows at the edge of his vision. Someone was following him again, but this time one pursuer was to his left, another to his right. He pretended not to notice and lost himself in the crowds of the Greisen Park Market.

"Lago, hey!" a voice called. Lago turned briskly. A bulky figure ran toward him: it was Deon.

"Hold on!" Deon said, catching up to Lago's brisk pace. "Seriously, wait up, gotta tell you something."

Lago slowed but didn't stop. "What is it? I'm running errands right now," he said, feeling on edge, having no time for distractions.

"Someone was asking about you this morning, at the store, I mean. This fierce-looking lady came in, said she was a collector. Asked my dad if he had any antique masks, like animal masks or something."

Lago stopped at once, feeling a chill crawl up his spine. "What does that have to do with me?"

"Not that specifically. Dad told her we have nothing like that, but she kept looking around anyway. But then… Then just out of nowhere, she asked Dad if he knew a young man named *Lago*. I mean, she was obviously not from around here, Iesmari I take it, from her gray eyes. Blonde hair just like mine."

Lago's heart thumped in his ears. "What did she want with me?"

"How would I know?"

"And what did your dad tell her?" he snapped.

"Told her you work at the monastery, that's all. What does—"

"I have to go," Lago said, hurrying uphill.

"Hey. Come on, what did I say? Hey!" Deon barked, as Lago left him behind.

Lago slammed the Haven's door behind him and locked all three latches.

"A woman was here looking for you," Gwil said. "Did you deliver the—"

"I did. What did she want?"

"I don't know, I explained you were out on delivery duty. Why did you lock—"

Bam! Bam! Bam! The metal knocker struck solidly behind Lago.

"What is going on?" Gwil asked, about to unlock the doors. Lago stopped him.

"I… I think I'm in trouble. Please tell them I'm not here."

Gwil flipped up the peephole guard and peeked out. "Yes? How may I serve you?"

"I am looking for Lago," a muted female voice said. "Could I please have a word with him, it's important."

"It's a woman, but not the same as before," Gwil whispered. "What should—"

"Tell her I'm not here, I will explain later."

Gwil spoke through the door, "He has not returned yet. Please come by later."

"Lorr, we saw him enter just now, we know he's in there. This matter is urgent, let us talk to him, it will only be a short conversation."

"One moment, please." Gwil turned to Lago and eyed him gravely. "What did you get yourself into?"

"I... I think they might want to kill me. I need to get out of here, I have to warn Alaia."

"Don't be foolish, no one is trying to—"

Crash! Glass shattered in the nearby laboratory. Someone screamed.

Lago ran through the cloister in the opposite direction. Behind him, a monk flew through the lab's stained-glass door, landing like a boneless puppet. A man wearing dark leather armor stepped out, wielding a bow. Gwil confronted him, but the man shoved him to the ground, eyes tracking Lago as he turned into the refectory.

Lago sprinted through the long dining hall, knocking chairs behind him. Three monks were setting up the tables, confounded by the chaos.

"Stop!" came a shout from behind. "I *will* take your legs if you keep running."

Lago turned at the end of the dining hall, sprinting toward the end of the building. A door. He closed it, locked it, and wedged a chair behind it.

"You know what we are after," the calm voice behind him said. "Stop running or I'll be forced to hurt you."

A scream. Another scream. Lago couldn't tell who; he simply ran and hoped the monks were alright.

"Khopto, help!" Lago implored, seeing his friend at the end of the curved hallway turning the crank of the delivery lift. Breathless, he stopped and said, "I need you to lower me, down the shaft, now."

"Have you lost your senses? What is the matter? What were those sounds I just heard?"

"Now!" Lago said, climbing over the handrail and holding on to the doubled rope: one side was static, locked onto the metal frame above; the other slid to lower the compound pulley.

Bang! Someone was trying to knock the door down. *Bang!*

"You'll snap the pulley, get down from there, right now!" Khopto said.

"You have to—"

The metal frame above buckled, dropping Lago several feet down. He loosened his grip too far, sliding ten feet more, but he clutched the ropes till his hands burned, stopping a deadly drop.

"Help me down or I fall!"

Khopto first tried to spin the crank up, but Lago was too heavy, so he eased it slowly in the opposite direction. "It's pushing back too hard, keep pressure on both ropes!"

The safety gear that allowed the crank to be turned in small steps snapped. The spinning handle delivered a hard blow to Khopto's stomach, but the monk held on to it and slowly lowered the young man.

Bang!

Lago's palms were raw and burning. His bag's strap tangled on the ropes as he tried to slide down farther.

Smash! A door was toppled up the hallway. Lago heard the whizzing of an arrow flying, then a muted impact, followed by Khopto's howls of pain. The moving rope slackened, then dropped freely with the pulley and crate, forcing Lago to hold his entire weight by the static rope alone.

"Khopto!" he screamed, tightening his grip.

"I can't... My leg!" Khopto wailed from above. "Hold on, I'll—"

The metal framing above Lago bent, creaked, and finally snapped.

Lago fell.

He crashed hard at the bottom of the shaft, breaking through a wooden platform, sinking into the sand beneath it. The metal structure came crashing after him, missing his face by a hair.

He couldn't breathe. He rolled in the sand, trying to restart his lungs. His diaphragm loosened in a sudden gasp, forcing him to inhale sand. He coughed it out and rolled onto his back.

"Bless the Twin Gods!" a woman's voice cried. It was Svana, the woman who helped send the correspondence up to the monastery. "Lago? Is that— you are injured, I should—"

"W-water."

She produced a canteen and let Lago flush the sand out of his mouth. Lago sat up, holding on to the remains of the platform. His clothes were torn, his shoulders and sides scratched. The back of his head was bleeding from a cut that still held a sizable splinter, which Svana helped remove.

"Lago?" she asked, pouring water over the wound. "You have to tell me—"

"Send... Send someone up to the Haven. Khopto is injured," Lago said, offering no more details.

"What happened? Are they in danger?"

Danger... Lago thought. *Danger... Alaia! I have to warn her, she could be in danger!* On a late Sunnday afternoon, Alaia could be anywhere, but he hoped he would find her at home. "Go!" he said to Svana. "Send help up, now!" He stood, stumbled, and ran toward Riftside.

Eyes were all over him when he entered the shantytown, making him feel paranoid. He then realized why: he was badly hurt, covered in sand and blood, and shambling breathlessly. He stopped at the well for a drink, shook the sand off, and washed his hair and face. Blood kept running down his scalp, but there was nothing to help that now, nor to help the monks he had to hurriedly leave behind.

He lumbered on, more careful now, checking around every corner for suspicious figures. Their little home was right ahead, tucked in a jumble of stacked shacks and torn awnings.

At least three people were after him, he surmised, and if they had found out about his work at the monastery, they probably also knew where he lived. *I don't care. I need to find Alaia.* He brushed the doubts from his mind and rushed across the narrow street.

Their home was completely trashed. Not that there had been much to trash, but they had done a good job of pulling apart everything they could. At least his precious ruby-flecked stoneleaf was still untouched, breathing sunlight at the kitchen's windowsill.

I need a weapon, he immediately thought, remembering the dagger he kept under his bed. He dropped his bag on the mattress, then froze. Right in front of him, through cracks in the flimsy boards, he saw a sneaking shadow. From the angle it fell in, it looked to be someone on the roof just across the street. Eyes locked onto the pacing shadow, Lago slowly reached under the bed for the dagger. But someone came from behind him, put a hand over his mouth, pushed him down onto the mattress, and twisted his arms till he dropped the weapon.

"Shhhh… Don't struggle…" a raspy voice pleaded right in his ear. "There are two of them patrolling the street. They didn't see you come in. Stay quiet and wait until they pass."

The stranger on top of Lago was strong and kept a solid hold. He whispered again, "I am not with them, I'm trying to protect you. I'm going to let you go now, but you will promise to keep quiet. Are we in agreement?"

Lago nodded.

The stranger slowly let go of his grip.

Lago turned around. The man looked to be in his forties, with strong lungs, probably from the mountains. Part Khaar Du, Lago suspected, due to the narrow, slit-like eyes and the hardened, freckle-sprayed skin. Under his broad nose dangled a thin mustache that was not exactly flattering but gave him a confident look. The man was wearing a green wool cloak matching a felted, short-brimmed hat with a tapered crown, and was carrying a scout's backpack.

The stranger hovered a calloused hand over a sheathed short sword, clasps unlatched and at the ready. "We need to get you out of here," he whispered, then looked around. "Where is the mask?" he suspiciously asked.

"Great. So that's what you are after. Why should I tell *you*?"

"Because we can't let the Negian army have it."

"I won't, but I'm not giving it to you. I made a promise to someone."

"To Sontai?"

Lago was stunned. "H-how did you know? I... I promised her I'd give the mask to one person only, and—"

"Bonmei..." the stranger whispered, his mustache stretching over a smile.

Lago raised his voice in surprise. "Wait! You are Bonme—"

The man put a hand over Lago's mouth. "Shhh... Behind you."

The shadow was back, not on the roof this time, but walking directly behind the wall.

The stranger flattened himself behind the door and gestured for Lago to hide under a blanket. Lago ducked under cover, feeling the brightness of the room through the thin cloth. It all darkened temporarily as a figure blocked the light at the entrance. Lago heard slashing, then a wet, gurgling sound, followed by a thud. He peeked from under the blanket and saw a soldier bleeding from her throat, and the stranger holding his sword through the soldier's lungs, preventing her from making any sounds.

It was gruesome. The soldier had been holding a dagger, and on her back was a crossbow. Her green eyes were still open, sharing a dying stare with Lago.

The stranger wiped his sword clean, then said, "Grab your bag, a weapon, and whatever else you need. I give you thirty heartbeats. Where is the mask?"

"It's... We have to go toward the mines, they are by—"

"I know where the mines are. Fifteen heartbeats, move it."

In his bag, Lago threw dried foods, a canteen, a few pieces of clothing, his Qupi pouch, and his binoculars. He clipped his dagger to his belt.

Arr rooff, rrowff! came the dangerously inconvenient barks of Bear, who had just poked his head through the front door. *Rrggrwouf!*

"Bear, no!" Lago quietly begged. But Bear kept barking. A dead body was splayed on the ground, a stranger stood in the room, and Lago was agitated, so Bear was reasonably alarmed. "Stay! Quiet!"

Bear turned around, growling, and backed into the room. Another soldier walked in, wearing the same type of leather armor as the woman bleeding on the ground. He wielded a switchblade in each hand.

Bear snapped at him, not enough for his teeth to make contact, but just enough to distract him. The stranger took the chance and jumped at the soldier, slamming him against the kitchen counter. Pots and pans flew everywhere. They tumbled by the window and knocked over Lago's stoneleaf; the glass planter shattered in an explosion of blue sands.

The stranger held on to the soldier's wrists to prevent the blades from slicing him, but elbows and knees beat him repeatedly. He smashed the soldier's hands on the windowsill, making him drop one of his switchblades. Their feet slipped on the blue sand, sending them crashing through the dining table. Now the soldier was on top, throwing his weight over his weapon. Bear bit his leg, received a kick in the face, and backed off, whining. The soldier pushed down again, switchblade slowly digging into the stranger's chest.

The stranger held on tightly with one hand, while with the other he unclasped the brooch holding his cloak and slammed it into the soldier's lower jaw. The soldier winced and growled, but the slender pin was not enough to stop him; he pushed harder, now scraping steel on the stranger's ribs.

The soldier's grip abruptly slackened. His wide-opened eyes rolled down, failing to see the sharp, red point sticking out of his jugular notch. Lago pulled his dagger out of the man's spine, feeling nauseated at the crunching of bones and snapping of sinew. The soldier dripped over the stranger, then collapsed on the carpet of blue sands.

"Lodestar guide me," Lago said. "I just... I just... Fuck..."

"No time to waste," the stranger said, pulling his brooch out of the soldier's face. "Let's go. And... thank you." He took the dagger from Lago's trembling hands, wiped it clean, and put it back on Lago's belt. "To the mines, now."

As Lago walked out the door, he took a quick look back and saw the succulent that Lerr Holfster had given him six years ago—the one he had taken such good care of—laying on the ground over a pool of red and sparkling blue. From all the sad things that had happened that day, seeing this somehow hurt him the most.

Lago led the way down the narrowest alleys and most obscure routes. Bear whined behind them.

"Ditch the dog," the stranger said, "he'll get us in trouble."

"I'm not leaving Bear behind. If I go, he goes."

They cleared Riftside and continued through the Hollows. Ebaja was sitting at a hanging bridge; she could tell something was wrong.

"Ebaja, have you seen Alaia?"

"She was just up by the watermill. Are you alright?"

"Thanks, we'll chat later."

"But you are bleeding. Lago!"

They hurried on.

"Is Alaia your Oldrin girlfriend?" the stranger asked.

"Yes," Lago replied, to make things easier. "She's in as much danger as I am. We need to get her too."

"This is getting too crowded. Let me lead. I know where we are headed."

They approached the mines from the back road, hiding behind the large boulders that marked the trail.

Shouting. A commotion by the watermill. Lago pulled his binoculars out.

He spotted a group of eight soldiers guarding the entrance to the watermill, dressed like the ones they just killed. *Murdered*, Lago thought, still feeling sick from what had happened. Five of the soldiers held crossbows; three more held recurve bows, also loaded and ready to shoot. They aimed their weapons directly at a circle of miners that had formed around them.

The soldiers suddenly parted, and then, to Lago's horror, out of the watermill came Alaia, with a white-hilted dagger held tight to her throat by Chief Arbalister Fjorna Daro. Alaia wasn't struggling, at least not anymore. Behind Fjorna exited a tall man wearing an imperious suit of red leather armor adorned with golden studs and silver pauldrons. The man unsheathed a daunting wave-bladed longsword and raised his voice for all the mine workers to hear.

"This Oldrin bitch refuses to talk," he snarled. "But maybe you will talk for her. We are looking for Lago Vaari, we need to have a little chat with him. We know you know who he is. If you decide to keep quiet, I'll start by cutting this ugly spur off this cunt's forehead." He pointed his longsword right at Alaia's forehead, to her nub. He kept the undulating blade steady, despite his arm being stretched all the way. "Then I'll cut whatever else I see fit, but not before my soldiers unload arrows on each of you. So, spit it out. Where is Lago?"

A dozen more soldiers came trotting up the hill. They were of a different sort, wearing plated armor, with red laurels emblazoned on their breastplates.

"That is General Alvis Hallow, and his private guard," the stranger said. "We are in deep shit."

"We have to help Alaia."

"There are dozens of them. Even if the miners help, we can't take that many. They are well trained, armored, and armed."

"I have an idea, but you have to trust me," Lago said. "Follow me."

They snuck behind boulders and sycamores while Lago explained his plan, until they arrived at the sinkhole where Carlo had pulled the rope away from Lago and Alaia six years earlier.

Bear whined excitedly, perhaps thinking they were about to go for a swim. Lago picked him up. "It's okay, boy. Calm down, relax." He handed Bear to the stranger and said, "Hold him just like this, don't let him slip."

"Hmph. Can we just let the dog go? Or toss him down?"

"It's thirty feet. He could break his ribs when hitting the water. He is my family as much as Alaia is. You either trust me, or we are all dead. Do you have tools to make a fire?"

"Of course I do."

"Then don't let them get wet. Clear up the boards by that lower ledge and wait for us."

The stranger went down the rope using his feet and right arm, awkwardly holding Bear with his left while the dog tried to wriggle himself free. Once the stranger was at the bottom, Lago tossed his own bag down to him, untied the rope, and dropped it into the water.

Lago stepped toward the watermill. He was fully in the open, but the soldiers hadn't yet noticed him.

"Hey!" he called out. "It's me that you want, let them go!"

The miners turned and moved to the side, leaving Lago in full view of the soldiers. Fjorna was in front of them all.

"How brave of you!" she exclaimed. "And just in time." She squinted, trying to get a better look at Lago's bruised, scraped body. "You look like shit. Were you hiding in a pigsty?"

She tightened the dagger under Alaia's chin and forced her to walk uphill, toward Lago. A drop of blood ran down Alaia's neck, disappearing between her breasts. The soldiers followed behind Fjorna, keeping their weapons aimed at the miners.

Lago swallowed, then slowly stepped back. "You... you let her go, and I'll give you what you want."

"You don't get to make the rules," Fjorna said. "First, I need to know if we are talking about the same thing. And be discreet about it, boy."

"I have your stupid fox mask," Lago belted out indiscreetly. "Let her go, and I'll take you to where I hid it. If you kill me, I promise you'll never find it." He had backed up as far as he could, standing at the edge of the sinkhole. Fjorna stopped too, many strides in front of him, but she was on lower ground, unable to see the hole behind Lago.

Alvis Hallow caught up behind Fjorna. He stood next to Alaia and grabbed her chin forcefully. So that only Fjorna and Alaia could hear, he whispered, "Let the uncooperative spur go. We'll take care of her after we are done with her boyfriend."

"We have the upper hand," Fjorna replied, without once looking away from Lago. "We could take them both now."

"They are unarmed, we'll run after her as soon as the boy is secured."

Fjorna nodded. Projecting her voice, she said, "Very well, but if you don't have what we need, we will come back for her, and next time you see her it will be just her head. And don't try to run, Muriel doesn't miss her shots." She signaled for Muriel to come forward, bow in hand. "Her arrow will not be aimed at you, but at the spur's back."

Lago stood defiantly. "I'm done with the small talk. Let her go, and the mask is yours."

Fjorna pushed Alaia. The young woman fell to the ground, picked herself up, and stumbled toward Lago. Once close enough to see each other's faces, they shared a conspiratorial look. Lago nodded, then jumped backward into the sinkhole and disappeared from Fjorna's view. Alaia took two big steps and jumped. While she was in midair, Muriel's arrow released and made impact, shoving Alaia forward and making her tumble through the fall. She hit the water head first.

Lago surfaced from the murky water. "Alaia!" he screamed. He dove and saw her twisting underwater, as if unsure of which direction was up or down. He helped her up to the surface and noticed the arrow—it was stuck through her haversack.

"Move, move!" he told her, as she regained a sense of space and balance. He pushed Alaia up on the ledge, then jumped up himself, just as a crossbow bolt struck near his heel.

The soldiers stopped at the sinkhole's edge. "Hold!" Fjorna yelled, preventing another one from shooting. She watched Lago and Alaia scurry into the shaft. "He might be the only one who knows where the mask is," she quietly said, "we can't risk killing him. Crescu, get the miners to talk. Osef, find me a map and place a sentry at each of the exits. Make sure every path is blocked. Elian, jump in after them. They can't escape now."

CHAPTER TWENTY-FOUR

LIMESTONE CAVERNS

"Into the shaft!" Lago hurried Alaia, who staggered in front of him.

They heard a splash behind them. Then a call. "Someone toss me a lamp!"

Alaia advanced into the darkness. "We'll need a light or they'll catch up to—"

A loud *rroowff* echoed through the abandoned shaft.

"Is that Bear?" she asked, now certain she hit her head too hard on the water.

"Don't stop, there should be a light up ahead."

And there was. Farther down the shaft, Alaia saw a bulky figure holding a makeshift torch, with a dog standing next to him.

"Take this," the man told Alaia, handing her a torn plank with a burning strip of cloth wrapped over one end.

"I have a lamp, it will work better," she said, reaching for her haversack. "Shit," she added, finding that Muriel's arrow had pierced her metal lamp, spilling the oil. "This thing saved me one last time. Never mind, let's go."

Once they were far enough into the shaft and they could slow to catch their breath, Alaia finally asked, "What in Noss is happening? And where in Khest are we going?"

"They came after the mask," Lago answered. "We are going to get it, and escape."

"Just give it to them, who cares?"

"They'll kill you if you do, or if you don't," the stranger said. "We have to get out of this city, take the mask someplace safe."

"Why is it so important? And who the fuck are *you*?" Alaia asked.

They heard hurrying steps behind them.

"Quickly," the stranger whispered, "you two go on ahead with the torch and wait around that corner." He hid in the shadows of a different tunnel, while Lago and Alaia went ahead of him. He took quiet breaths as he waited. The tunnel brightened near him. He could hear the careful footsteps of the enemy, the soft creak of leather armor. The light slowly faded again. The stranger stepped out and jumped the soldier from behind, stabbing him in the ribs. The soldier fell, trying to scream, but the blade only allowed him to hiss a gurgle.

The stranger peered behind himself, then pulled his blade out of the soldier's corpse. "It's clear! Come help me with this."

Alaia helped him turn the dead body over. The stranger looted the body for anything useful: a Qupi pouch with two Hexes and a handful of Lodes, a recurve bow, a quiver full of arrows, and a dagger.

"You should have something to defend yourself," he told Alaia, handing her the dagger.

"I don't know how to—"

"Poke the pointy end at the enemy. Let's hurry now."

Lago took the dead man's lamp and followed Alaia. It had been six years since they visited these tunnels, but Alaia remembered them like it was yesterday. They hastened through a series of shafts, turned left, and walked until the ceiling began to drop. Alaia squatted, then crawled on her knees. She pushed aside the boards that covered the hole in the ceiling, then tossed her torch through the gap. Lago lifted Bear up and climbed in, followed by the stranger.

They covered the hole in the ground with the boards, then sat down to catch their breath. "It's alright, no one else was following," the stranger said, "at least nowhere close. And once they see the dead body, they won't be moving in as fast. Take a break."

While the stranger more carefully covered the opening, making sure not a single streak of light could shine through, Lago climbed over to a row of cage-like stalagmites, reached behind them, and pulled out an oilskin cloth. "Here it is," he said, unwrapping the mask. It was dark as the depths of the cavern before their fire had interrupted its slumber, shimmering menacingly with reflected flames.

Lago drew in a broken breath.

"A long time ago, I made a promise to your grandmother," he said in a nearly rehearsed tone. "I promised her I would keep this mask safe and would only give it to her grandson. It tormented me for years because I did not know how to find you." He looked at Alaia. "Alaia, meet Bonmei. Bonmei, this is Alaia."

The stranger stepped closer, reverently gazing at the mask. "About that… There's been a misunderstanding. My name is not Bonmei."

Lago pulled back in a defensive stance but didn't know how to hold the mask with one hand, the lamp with the other, and at the same time reach for his dagger. "You damn liar, you told me—"

"Calm down," the stranger said. "Recall our conversation. You *assumed* I was Bonmei. I never said that was my name."

"But you didn't correct me either. What do you want with us? Alaia, get behind me."

The stranger backed off, hands in the air. "My name is Ockam. Ockam Radiartis. Bonmei is my adopted son. I've been on a quest to find his mask ever since it was lost."

"I don't trust this fucker," Alaia mumbled through her teeth. "Anyone could make that story up. Why should we believe you?"

"I could've easily pretended to be Bonmei to take the mask just now. But I didn't. I don't intend to deceive you. I'd prefer we work together."

"I'm not giving you the mask," Lago said. "Not you, not anyone else but Bonmei."

Ockam shrugged. "As you wish, you carry it. Lead the way, and we'll get out of here."

"Just how in Khest do you plan to do that?" Alaia asked. "They'll kill us if we go out the same way, and we don't know where these caverns go, or if they even have an exit."

Ockam shot a venomous look toward Lago. "I thought you knew this place."

"Well, how to enter it, yes, but I didn't plan ahead more than that."

Ockam exhaled at length, crossing his arms. "How far have you explored this area?"

Lago pointed fifteen feet away from him. "Till about that bend, I guess."

Ockam fumed silently, holding back his anger. "Alaia, what other ways out do we have?"

"The sinkhole connects to shaft number seven, which exits by the watermill, close to where the soldiers were. No other exit. But there is a breeze through these caverns."

Ockam took the lamp from Lago and lowered the flame to the bare minimum. "This is a serious situation. If we don't know how long our path is, we need to save our fuel." He looked down at the boards covering the entrance. "We need wood for torches." He handed the fickle flame back to Lago and removed the planks of wood from the ground. Then he looked around and began to snap the tall stalagmites off. "Use these to cover the hole instead."

They placed the stalagmites side by side, one facing left, the next right, like the closing maw of a wolf. With thick mud, they covered the gaps, until no light or wind could make it through.

Ockam ordered them around, "Alaia, help me snap the planks into thinner pieces. Lago, cut that oilskin into strips and tie them to the wood. I also have a log of heart pine in my fire kit. I gather I could cut it into ten strips or so, to use as candles. They don't last long, but it's something."

When they were done, they had eight torches in their bags.

"We better get moving," Ockam said. "We'll follow the wind and water, and pray to the Great Spider of Beyenaar that we don't run out of oil and wood before we find an exit."

"You have to tell us more about Bonmei, about the mask," Lago said.

"Long story. Let's save it for when we stop to rest. Now we need to move. These caverns look dangerous. I've never seen a place like it before."

"They can be tricky," Alaia agreed, "but I've explored limestone breaches from other shafts. I know what to look for, what not to step or lean on." She took the lamp from Lago's hand. "I'll go in front."

Alaia's keen sense of space made her an expert at navigating underground. She mostly followed the sound of water, as the wind was unpredictable, vanishing in some passages to later reappear farther down. The lamp's flame was nearly non-existent, letting only Alaia see ahead, while the others had to follow almost blindly.

About four hours into the strenuous walk, they reached a vast grotto with a stream of water snaking through its center.

"This would be a good spot to rest, and think," Ockam said. "Alaia, how much longer do we have on that lamp?"

Alaia checked the oil in the font. "With a small flame like this, two more hours. It was almost full when we started."

"Turn it off for now. We need to talk."

They sat in a pristine darkness.

Bear began to whimper, but Lago comforted him.

"We burned most of the oil already," Ockam said, "yet there's no sign of an end to this cavern. I gather we could light our way for about six more hours. Two with the lamp, two or three with the torches, and an hour or two more with the slivers of heart pine. After that, we'd be making it through with just embers." His voice turned raspier, pushed by stress and exhaustion. "We need to make a decision now. Either we continue together on this unknown path, risking being lost in the dark, or we turn around while we still can."

"Those bastards are murderers," Alaia said. "They killed Bahimir, right in front of me. If we go back, we're all dead."

"And we killed three of them, too," Lago recalled. "If we give them the mask, they'd have no more use for us. We've come this far already... I think we should keep moving, there has to be an end to this darkness."

"Light could be heartbeats or fortnights ahead, or there could be no exit," Ockam said. "If we go on, we need to be smart about it. We extinguish the flame when we rest, we ration our food, and we fill our canteens whenever possible."

They all agreed. After resting their legs, they drank from the stream, then adjusted their bags and belts. Alaia struck the flint to light the lamp and led them deeper into the belly of the Pilgrim Sierras.

Two hours later, the lamplight flickered once, twice, and was gone.

"That's it for the oil," Alaia said.

They switched to the first torch. The brighter flame was blinding, bouncing in wavering tendrils that made the colorful minerals on the walls sparkle. They could now see details with striking clarity: striations of oily colors, wet surfaces sprouting mushroom-like growths, bacterial mats blossoming like flattened flowers; there were even beetles crawling up the rocks.

"What's that there?" Alaia asked, pointing at the stream.

"A snake, be careful," Lago said.

"Bah, it's a harmless olm, a blind salamander," Ockam said, sticking his hand in the water. The pink amphibian swam away. "There is life down here, and that gives me some hope. Let's hope it can lead us somewhere."

Their last torch burned a slow, agonizing death, leaving only uncomforting embers behind. Alaia switched to a sliver of heart pine, attaching it to where the wick of the oil lamp used to be. It looked almost like a candle and burned just as brightly.

The passages continued with no end, sometimes uphill, sometimes down, but always merging back along the stream of water.

As their last stick of heart pine began to combust into charcoal and smoke, they entered a room with enormous selenite pillars, crossing diagonally like beams of sunlight through dark clouds. But the crystals were not sunlight; they offered no warmth nor hope, even in their unquestionable beauty. Alaia extinguished the flame before burning their last moments of light away. They sat on a horizontal crystal column, once more suffocated by the darkness.

Bear resumed his whimpering.

"So, what now?" Lago asked. "We burn our clothes? Our bags? Our hair?"

"I say we burn the dog," Ockam suggested. "Either that, or make him quiet down. I can't think like this."

Lago comforted Bear until his cries mellowed.

"I have an idea!" Alaia said. "I can walk ahead hitting the sparker, like this." She caused showers of sparks to light up the room. Every strike fleetingly described an unimaginable crystalline landscape, one that disappeared in less than an eye-blink. It was awe-inspiring, yet given the current circumstances, they could not appreciate its beauty.

"That'll make us move at a snail's pace," Lago said, "and it won't last long. We are stuck."

"Quiet down, let me think!" Ockam blurted. He was breathing deeply, as if meditating. Softly, to himself, he recited, "A young tree I am, the old forest I am not, yet forest and tree are of one soul. A small fish I am, the vast ocean I am not, yet ocean and fish are of one mind. A frail wolf I am, the strong pack I am not, yet pack and wolf are of one heart."

They waited for him to say something else, but Ockam remained silent.

"What were those words you just spoke?" Lago finally asked.

"An old litany from the Free Tribelands, to keep me focused. There might still be a way out for us, but I'm afraid to try it." Ockam sucked on his teeth, pondering. "We haven't had time to talk about Bonmei, and the mask, but now we have nothing but time, so we might as well talk. But first, let's get some food out of our bags. I'll need a bit of energy, and maybe stuffing something in Bear's mouth will make him shut his trap."

CHAPTER TWENTY-FIVE

OCKAM'S STORY

After a round of stale bread, peanuts, dried tomatoes, and salamander-infused water, Ockam began to tell his story.

"A few weeks back, a group of land developers found the cellar where you hid Sontai's body," he said, directing his voice toward Lago, "where you left your name conveniently written on the wall. That's how they came to trace you, how this whole mess began. I have my own contact in Withervale, who informed me promptly, likely before General Hallow found out. I have been following you for several days, trying to see if you would give away clues to the mask's location."

"Was that you at the monastery two nights ago?" Lago asked. "Behind the stone wall?"

"Yes, I apologize if I scared you. I thought I'd look through the windows to see what you were doing, and you surprised me, so I ran. I meant no harm to you."

Alaia was dubious, though no one could see her expression in the dark.

"I thought I recognized the brooch holding your cloak," Lago said. "Is it meant to be of Sceres?"

"And her shard," Ockam agreed. Although his penannular brooch was hiding in darkness now, Lago could picture its crescent shape, its sharp pin, and the sixteen-pointed burst meant to represent the Ilaadrid Shard.

Ockam continued, "I'm a sylvan scout from the Free Tribelands. We've always been at war with the Negians, trying to safeguard the forests around the

Heartpine Dome from their greedy generals, but they've been pushing us farther into the mountains every year. Decades ago, they took over our city of Farjall, and turned it into their military base. From there, somehow, they found their way into the dome. We suspect they dug a hole under the vines, but whatever it was, it was a massive enterprise, took them years."

"Was this when the dome began to collapse?" Alaia asked.

"Before the collapse. Something they did in there caused the dome to break down and grow out of bounds, like the Varanus Dome, though I have no idea of what."

"So, you've been inside it?" Lago asked.

"I haven't, but there is one person I know who has, and that person is Bonmei. He is one of the last of his race, the Wutash. They had been living inside the Heartpine Dome, taking care of it from the inside. Bonmei described it to me as a fertile paradise where giant beasts roamed, and where towers reached up to hold the sky."

"How does the mask play into all of this?" Lago inquired.

"I'm getting there," Ockam said. He cleared his throat and leaned back against a sharp selenite crystal. "Bonmei was a sort of prince, a *khuron*, in his tongue. He was to inherit Agnargsilv from his mother, Mawua, who inherited it from *her* mother, Sontai."

"Agnargsilv," Lago whispered, tasting the hard syllables. "That sounds familiar… it's something I heard Sontai say before she… before… What does it mean?"

"Agnargsilv is the name of the mask you carry. It's a compound Miscamish word, *agnarg* is their word for *canid*, and *silv* means *mask*. Sontai and Mawua were beginning to teach Bonmei about the mask, to prepare him for his future role as its keeper. This is where things get complicated… because Bonmei was not even five years old when the Negians breached the dome, and he only spoke Miscamish, so all he's told me has been only a vague translation. I can't tell how much of what he recalls is true, and how much came from his overactive imagination. His tales are often mixed up with pure fantasy, turning more confounded the more time passes. He said that when his mother put Agnargsilv on she would grow a long tail and snowy fur, becoming a white fox who walked on two legs."

Lago and Alaia gasped in unison, then let Ockam continue.

"He said the animals responded to his mother's voice and aided her and the tribe by helping them work the land. On giant wolves they would ride, all the way to the walls of the dome, which he said were sparkling like diamonds, as bright as the furs of the wolf spirit."

"Wolf spirit?" Alaia inquired, fully intrigued.

"He described her as a white wolf with silky furs that always blew in the wind, who sometimes took the shape of a jackal, a coyote, or a fox."

"I knew it!" Alaia said. "That's a Nu'irg, they do exist! They are living inside the domes!"

"Nu'irg is the Miscamish word he used for the spirit," Ockam said. "Like the creatures the Lerevi worship, from the old canticles in their Lavra Scrolls."

"They are mentioned in Dorhond legends too," Alaia noted, "and they say they went to sleep after the Downfall."

Ockam nodded in the dark. "Bonmei said the Nu'irg was elusive and would only ever approach Mawua. His mother seemed like a fine woman, Bonmei loved her so much. I wish I had gotten to meet her."

"What happened to her?" Alaia asked.

"It's a sad story, one that Bonmei still struggles to talk about. He said that one day, strange people wearing metal skins came into his lands. At first it was only a few, then dozens, then thousands. He was excited, having always thought the Wutash was the only tribe. They celebrated the arrival with a feast, and held great parties in honor of their guests, but then they all started to fight. He doesn't know why, but they tied his people with ropes and chains, and killed those who resisted. Wutash warriors rode their biggest wolves to protect what he calls 'the trunk,' an immense column of vines that grows at the center of the dome. Sontai, Mawua, and Bonmei were there, at the temple.

"He said armored soldiers forced their way in, killing the priests, burning their temple down. Bonmei's mother fought ferociously as the white fox, and then her fur was tainted red, and soon the fur was gone and only his dead mother remained, with the dark mask over her face. Sontai took Agnargsilv and carried Bonmei in her arms. They escaped by riding a giant wolf, holding on to his fur."

Ockam paused and recollected. "I've seen them, the dire wolves. A pack roams the volcano west of the Klad Senet, where no one can get to them. Dozens of them managed to escape, maybe more are still inside the dome. What is left in there we don't really know."

Lago sighed, remembering his encounter with the dire wolf. "I've seen one too. A dead one, the one they killed by Withervale. Why did Sontai and Bonmei separate?"

"As he recalls it, they rode on the back of the wolf through a dark tunnel, with screams all around them. Then he was outside, in a new world. He mentioned the first thing he looked at was the sky. He couldn't understand why it was blue! Soldiers chased after them, wounded the wolf with arrows, but the wolf kept running and running until he died. They hid in the forest for months, distrustful of everyone, foraging for food at the dome's perimeter. Unfortunately, it was only a matter of time—soldiers found the dead dire wolf, followed their tracks, and chased after them again, this time with hounds.

"Sontai tried to carry Bonmei, but she was old, and Bonmei was too heavy. She saw the soldiers following their tracks, getting closer, so she hid Bonmei in a fox's den. She told him to stay quiet, that she would come back for him. She waited until the soldiers could see her, to use herself as bait. Once they were close enough, she put Agnargsilv on, shapeshifted into a gray fox, and ran. The soldiers gave chase, unaware of Bonmei hiding in the den.

"That's where I found him. I was scouting the southwestern edge of the dome when I heard a child crying. I followed the sound and found my boy right there, still hiding in the fox's den. He called for his mother and for his grandmother, though I didn't know what the words meant yet. I pulled him out of the hole, and he ran away, but then stopped and fell to his knees. He cried over his grandmother's clothes, which sat empty at the spot where she had taken the shape of the fox. We still have her dress at our base in Thornridge. That's where Bonmei is now, and where I hope we can go, if we manage to get out of here."

"Actually, I... I haven't told you *my* full story yet," Lago said, "but the time I helped Sontai she was... Well, it wasn't Sontai exactly, it was a gray fox that came to me. She was tiny, and hurt, and seemed to be asking for my help. I felt like I understood what she wanted, so I let her crawl into the cellar to hide. When I went back in to check on the fox, Sontai was there instead, holding the mask."

"Well..." Ockam said, "I always doubted the shapeshifting part of Bonmei's story, but I've seen strange things in my years, and I can't say I'm entirely surprised to hear it's true. However, when Bonmei talks about his mother, he describes her as walking on two legs. *Part* fox, perhaps, not just a small creature. There is a lot regarding the mask we don't know about." He cleared his throat and continued, "But this leads to the reason I think Agnargsilv might help us. Lago, have you ever put the mask on?"

"Yes. Twice. They were two of the most horrible experiences of my life. It felt as if the mask was shooting pain into my spine, trying to make my head explode. I think I could've died from it this one time if Alaia hadn't found me. That's why we hid it."

"I see," Ockam said. "Agnargsilv, as I understand it, is a means of connecting to other living creatures, to feel them, maybe talk to them. Bonmei told me that on some cloudy nights his mother would place him over her shoulders and run in the perfect darkness, seeing everything around her, though for him it was completely black. With the mask she could *see the life in the looping threads,* he said."

"All I saw was pain..." Lago remembered.

"I think that's part of it. They had warned him sternly not to put the mask on, not yet. If he were to put it on, he would *feel the pain of every living creature around him.* It is something he remembers quite clearly, since they hammered it right into his mind, until they made him terrified of it. They said that once he came of age, he would be able to understand the pain, and be able to control it."

"I was twelve when I put it on," Lago said. "I really thought the thing was cursed, that only something evil could make me feel like that..."

"Yet you still tried it on a second time," Alaia reminded him.

"That was different. I can't explain that. It's like I was missing something, and the mask asked to fill that gap."

"I don't think Agnargsilv is evil," Ockam said, "but I think it could easily be used for evil purposes. The fact that General Hallow is after it is a clear indication—he's one of Emperor Uvon's most laureated war heroes. If after all this time they are still searching for it, and they risked going straight into enemy territory for it, it must be more powerful than we know."

"So, you think that if one of us wore the mask, they could see the way out of here?" Alaia asked.

"Or something like it, if my boy's story was more memory than confabulation."

"I'm not putting that cursed thing on," Alaia said. "I've guided you all quite expertly so far, thank you very much. That thing scares the spurs out of me."

Ockam made a sound of agreement. "That is fair. I will try it on and see if—"

"No. I will," Lago interrupted. "It's my responsibility. Sontai entrusted it to *me.*"

"Don't be a nubhead, Gwoli. Remember last time."

"That was six years ago. Maybe now I'm ready to face it. Even back then, abandoning Agnargsilv in the dark felt... wrong." Lago felt a tinge of awkwardness calling the mask by its true name, but he continued, "It was like Agnargsilv was calling me the whole time I walked out of the mines. I think I need to try it. I will have you by my side this time, Alaia, it'll be alright."

"I may know more about it, but you have more experience with it," Ockam said. "If that is what you've chosen, then I think it's time for you to put on the mask."

CHAPTER TWENTY-SIX

THE LABYRINTH

The remainder of their heart pine sliver was set alight as a final spark of hope. Under the candle-like flame, encircled by ancient pillars of selenite, Lago removed Agnargsilv from his bag.

Bear immediately began to whimper.

"Calm down, buddy, it's okay," Lago said, scratching the dog's chin, but he would not stop.

Alaia sat on Lago's right side, arm around his shoulders. Ockam sat across from them, palms clasped, eyes narrowed.

Lago stared at the unwelcoming concavity of the mask, feeling a sudden surge of anxiety and fear. He held the artifact but dared not place it on his face.

"I'm sorry," he said. "Can you give me a moment?"

"Take your time," Ockam said.

They watched Lago take exerted breaths.

"I can't focus," Lago said. His mind kept returning to the memory of the pain the mask had twice before given him.

"You need to keep your mind away from the fear," Ockam told him.

"I'm trying, but it's like I'm already feeling all that pain."

"Try this. Repeat after me, and only focus on the words, nothing else."

Ockam began to recite his litany, adding pauses at the end of each sentence so that Lago could repeat them right after. Together, one following the other, they chanted:

"A young tree I am, the old forest I am not, yet forest and tree are of one soul. A small fish I am, the vast ocean I am not, yet ocean and fish are of one mind. A frail wolf I am, the strong pack I am not, yet pack and wolf are of one heart."

Ockam began anew, letting Lago follow his lead more closely now that he knew the words better. By the third time, Lago's breathing was placid and controlled. He felt like closing his eyes was more strenuous, so he left them open and relaxed, as if staring at something distant. He cleared his mind, let his tense shoulders drop, and very slowly brought the mask to his face.

Agnargsilv attached immediately, as if fusing its shape onto Lago's skin, throwing his head back. Pain burst through, digging deep into his skull, through his spine, extending across every vein and cell. But he fought it, he fought it with everything he had.

The pain intensified, contorting his body. Lago struggled yet harder, grasping at a hidden courage that told him not to give up.

"Gwoli! Stay with me!"

He barely heard Alaia's call.

He pushed back against the anguish, but the pain doubled with his efforts.

"Stop fighting it!" Ockam called. "Let it run through you. Don't struggle!"

Lago tried, but how could he not fight against this? Why should he allow such agony into his body?

"It's not your pain," Ockam said, "it's everyone else's pain. Let it through you, acknowledge it, and let it pass."

Bear barked, terrified.

"Stay with us!" a voice called.

The last splinter of heart pine burned out, turning the darkness complete once more.

Lago loosened his muscles, toppling backward, but Alaia caught and held him. He tried to relax his back, his legs, his brain. Instead of pushing the pain away, he tried to face it, to see it. His eyes were closed, but he was staring, somehow, as if pain was an entity that surrounded him. He wasn't in the same room anymore, at least his consciousness wasn't. He felt as if he was standing on a black mirror that reflected only blackness. Sounds rang muffled.

He heard his name.

A distant bark.

Something in his mind snapped.

As if through a kaleidoscope, his awareness split into two pairs twice doubled, and sixteenfold his perception coalesced into something that was not seeing. No distinct shapes, forms, or colors became apparent, only presences.

One entity was in front of him and two others to either side of him, but there were also many, so many more. Each entity was made of threads, tied together in a tapestry of light without color or brightness.

He raised his hands in front of his face and stared at them with no eyes. His hands, too, were an intricate, interwoven network, with threads that looped in circular patterns, connecting to themselves and to everything around them.

He stood, gazing at nothing, seeing everything.

"Lago! Talk to me, please!"

Bear barked, whined, howled.

Lago turned his head. "Bear, it's okay," he said. And Bear was silenced at once.

A tense moment crept by like a cold breeze.

"I'm alright," Lago told them. "I'm here, it's passed."

Alaia hyperventilated next to him.

"Are you able to see anything?" Ockam asked.

"Maybe. It's… It's not like seeing, not with eyes at least. I feel it all, like there's a web around me, and everything connects to it. When I move, or when you move, the relationships change. It's very confusing, but clear at the same time."

Lago studied the essences filling the dark space.

"It's like I can see through things too, what's in front or behind makes no difference. But not everything is clear, some parts are 'darker,' some 'louder,' though it's nothing like light nor sound. You two and Bear are the brightest things around, until I focus my attention to myself, and then I see myself and the mask on me. Agnargsilv, it has this blue glow, like a blurry aura that follows it."

The aura Lago saw pulsated slightly, reacting to the movements of all life forms around him. Lago felt the aura as an intense indigo color, like a rich sapphire hiding in a cold ocean, despite being aware that the mask showed him no colors—yet the essence of indigo synesthetically remained.

"It's bizarre… If I stop focusing on something, it simply disappears," he said. "Right now, I'm focusing away from you, and you aren't visible to me. But without turning my head I can focus behind me and see you, or choose to focus all around me at once, though that becomes a bit more draining and confusing. Like when you suddenly decide to pay attention to sounds and only then hear all the crickets, or the wind, or a fire crackling, or your own breathing. Sounds that were always there, but you didn't notice until you consciously began to pay attention to them."

Lago paced around, admiring his surroundings. "Khest!" he cursed, bumping the mask's pointy ears on one of the crystals. "These crystals, I really can't see them."

"If I understand this correctly," Ockam said, "what you are 'seeing' are living creatures. There is nothing growing on these crystals, so there's nothing for you to see."

"Makes some sense," Lago said. "The water and wet walls are easy to see, where there must be millions of bacteria. But the tiny fish are brighter, like those eggs under that rock, and like these gnats that draw strange shapes in front of me. Over there!" he yelped, pointing as if his friends could see, "There are three salamanders in a room next to us, I didn't even know there was a room in that direction."

"Are you feeling any pain? Is that gone?" Alaia asked.

"It's not gone, but I can cope with it. I feel your pain right now, your fear. I feel Bear's anxiousness, and I feel the pain of everything in here that feels cold or hunger. But there are also feelings of joy, of comfort, although drowned beneath all the pain. But it goes further. I'm sensing down to the smallest creatures, to the even smaller cells that make them up, and it is as if their feelings of pain or joy or hunger connects them all. It's mostly very confusing, too much to process at once."

"Do you think you can find us a way out?" Ockam asked.

"I can try. You'll have to follow right behind me, and step carefully."

Lago guided them clumsily, too distracted by his new means of perception. He would stop often to stare at concealed invertebrates, finding delicate crayfish, weird-looking scorpions, spiders that scurried out of the way before they even entered the rooms, and snails holding to the undersides of every wet rock. He studied how his touch affected the threads and tried to describe what he was sensing, to give some imagined visuals to Ockam and Alaia in this space in which time seemed meaningless, and distractions were welcome.

"The water splits here," Alaia said, "I can hear it running in two different directions. Which side should we take?"

"Left. The smaller stream," Lago answered, showing no doubt. "There's more life on the left path, past the bend. The right one goes dark for me."

They reached a wide chamber with more sand than rocks at the bottom. "I think we should rest here," Ockam said. "Since our fires ran out, we walked for about five hours. That's my best guess. I've been counting my breaths. It gives me some sort of idea of how long it's been."

"My legs are sore," Alaia said.

"Mine too," Lago agreed. "And my head is pulsing. Wearing this is exhausting. It's giving me a headache, like it's been trying to cram something new inside my skull, making room for it."

Ockam dropped his backpack and sat leaning against it. "We went into the mines just before sunset. It should be around midmorning on the outside. We should sleep, regain some energy, and continue in the—well, not in the morning, but whenever we wake up."

Lago took the mask off. It was easy, as though it had never been attached to his face to begin with. He was dropped into sudden darkness, but with a lingering sense of the shape of the room. That feeling slowly faded, like an afterimage.

They lay down next to each other. They hadn't felt cold thus far, since their trek had been arduous and offered few breaks, but now that they were settling down, they could feel the chill crawling up their skins. They snuggled in a single pile and needlessly closed their eyes.

Lago dreamed. This was not like any dream he had before; it was not visual; it had no sounds. It was a dream of space and connections, a dream of interlacing meanings and feelings, tangling like a billion dendrites stretching from zealous neurons. Agnargsilv had summoned a new cognitive mode out of the depths of Lago's mind, and it kept developing, even as he slept.

When he woke up, he could not remember his abstract dream. Or maybe he did, but there was no way to put it into concise thoughts, as there was nothing concrete that could describe it.

He heard rustling nearby. "Ockam?" he called.

"I'm here. I'm preparing breakfast, crushing herbs and nuts together with water, to make a paste. Apologies in advance about the flavor, it's not an easy task to handle in the dark. I might've over-seasoned it."

Alaia yawned. "How long did we sleep for?"

"I have no idea whatsoever," Ockam answered. "But I feel well-rested, and this meal should give us plenty of energy to keep going."

"It's so confusing," Lago said. "I'm trying to recall what it's like to wear Agnargsilv, but I barely can. I remember the words I used to describe the threads, but I don't *remember* what it's like seeing them. Does that make any sense?"

"Nuh-uh," Alaia said.

"So... Imagine... It's like suddenly you couldn't picture what the color *blue* was. You remember blue things, and what blue stands for, and all your memories are intact, but the actual color itself is unreachable. That's kind of what it feels like."

Ockam handed Lago a sample of his paste and said, "What you are describing is something called *qualia*. It means our own conscious experience of things, what the qualities of our senses *feel* like to us. You've awakened a brand-new sense with the mask, and with that sense new qualia came to you. Subjective experiences are something ineffable to begin with, and since without the mask you can't experience those feelings, perhaps you also can't remember them."

"This thing better not fry your head," Alaia said. "You were weird enough already."

After breakfast, or lunch, or whatever it was, Lago readied himself to wear the mask once more. He had memorized Ockam's litany, but rather than reciting it out loud, he simply chanted it in his mind. Instead of snapping violently into place like the last time, the mask slowly fused with his skin through a subtle, nearly magnetic pull. It settled gently on his face, unhurriedly bringing his awareness back to that level that had just been unreachable.

"That... That was so much easier..." he said, surprised. "Yet the pain is there, available if I look for it, but not hurting me, if that makes any sense."

He scanned around him, willfully focusing to make all the threads that made up the chamber appear. To his side, he felt a strange motion and noticed some of Alaia's threads extending toward him, though she was not moving. Perhaps a heartbeat later, her hand reached forward and landed on his shoulder.

"That was peculiar," Lago said. "There's a new sort of sensation the mask is showing me today. I can understand the way the threads connect, or *will* connect, as if they are influencing this sensitive, invisible web. I can even see myself about to do something, but that becomes somewhat redundant."

"You lost me there, Gwoli," Alaia said.

"How do I explain it? When you moved your hand toward me, I could feel you were about to do that, I could 'see' it in the threads. Actually, it really *is* like a spiderweb, as if you touched a strand from the web and that warned me of what you were about to do."

Ockam stepped toward Lago.

"There!" Lago said. "The same thing! Ockam, before you stepped toward me, I felt you were about to do it, I knew the moment you made up your mind about it."

"Like you are seeing into the future?" Alaia asked.

"No, I don't think that's it. It's... it's like perceiving someone's intent? As if I'm understanding what you mean to do. In the same way I understand your pain, it's just there, clearly shown to me. But now I also see what you are thinking of doing, in a way."

"You better not spy inside my head," Alaia said, and to test things out she swung her arm to smack the back of Lago's head. Lago ducked right in time.

"Stop that," he said. "And it's not like I can read your thoughts. It's just... being more aware of everyone's feelings and intentions. But I feel it all through my body, not in my mind. What's that word? When you feel your own sense of space and balance and such."

"Proprioception?" Ockam offered.

"That's it! It's like I feel within myself what *your* intentions are. It's so confusing! I have to keep digesting this. I'll pay attention as we walk. Let's get going."

Lago concentrated on everyone's movements as they walked, trying to understand his developing sense.

"So, it's not just intent, it seems," Lago explained. "It's intent *toward* me. When you mean to come to me, to talk to me, to touch me, to avoid me, to hand me something, that is when I feel these vibrations in the threads. It doesn't happen when you do the same toward others, even though I still see your threads reacting. It is as if whenever we reach out toward each other, there's a new connection being made."

Long and tedious was the next part of their journey. Ockam stopped them for food and rest every four hours or so. By the end of their second break, Lago felt more at ease, enjoying the experience of wearing Agnargsilv to the point that he would sometimes run ahead of the others, forgetting they were unable to move without his guidance.

He approached a school of blind fish, to experiment. As his hand touched the water, and as the fish felt the slight change in pressure, he saw the escape path the fish thought about taking before they moved, and caught one easily, predicting the motion. He felt the fear the animal in his hand experienced, and it made him anxious. He let the fish go, satisfied with what he learned, yet disturbed by the thought that such a small creature could feel so much terror.

"The sound of water is growing louder," Ockam said, aiming to hurry Lago.

"Sorry," Lago said. "I hear that too. Several streams merge up ahead."

As they continued alongside the stream, Lago was so involved in his new way of seeing that he failed to notice the cavern brightening ahead.

"I see sunlight!" Alaia belted out. "Over here!"

Lago removed the mask, somehow seeing more clearly now that he could focus entirely on his normal vision. The light was painfully brilliant. He shielded his eyes and entered a room with a deep pond that seemed to be made of radiating light.

"The water is so bright!" Alaia said.

"There's a gap underwater that lets light in," Ockam said. "Right under that rock, there must be a large hole."

"We could swim under it," Lago said.

"It could be dangerous," Ockam warned, "the current looks strong and—"

"Bear, no!" Lago screamed.

Bear jumped right into the pool of brightness, as happy and careless as always. He tried to paddle against the current, but the current did not flow sideways, it went down, and pulled him under the bubbling pit of light.

Lago rushed to the edge and saw Bear dragged under the rocks and out of sight. "Bear!" he yelled and jumped after him.

Lago was sucked in, spun in circles, losing any sense of up or down. He felt weightless for a fraction of a heartbeat, then fell fast, slamming his back in a pool so bright he thought he must've landed on the surface of the sun.

He swam up and gulped a breath of fresh air. His eyes adjusted. He saw a forest, a creek that flowed north, a great waterfall, a pond of turquoise water, and Bear splashing happily in it.

"You stupid, silly, come here!" he said, trying to grab the mutt, who playfully swam away from him.

A high-pitched scream, followed by a lower-pitched one. Lago looked up and saw two shapes ejected out of the waterfall, framed over the sky, ending in twin splashes.

Alaia surfaced and swam to Lago. "Whoooaaah, that was wild! We are out, Gwoli!"

Ockam surfaced next, trying to hold his backpack over his head before everything in it got completely soaked.

"Well done, Bear," Ockam coughed, dropping to his knees right at the shore.

They spread their clothes and belongings to dry under the early morning sun.

Ockam stood naked by the edge of the creek, shaking the water off his boots. Lago stared at him, noticing his body was covered in way too many scars. Cuts crisscrossed his arms, his wide torso, his solid legs, his small belly. Lago didn't dare ask about them.

Alaia came around from the bushes, braiding her hair. "How far from Withervale do you think we are?" she asked no one in particular.

"Not too far," Ockam answered, "ten miles, give or take. We should climb over the falls to get a better look."

Ockam put on somewhat-dried clothes and led them up a steep outcrop to the side of the waterfall. Reaching the top, they gazed over an oak forest. Far northeast of them was the sandstone promontory of the Withervale Mesa, barely discernible from this distance.

"I know exactly where we are now," Lago said. He turned around. "The road to the Ninn Tago Viewpoint is somewhere right above us."

"Perfect," Ockam said. "The Gray Pass is the fastest way out of here."

Lago looked back toward Withervale. "So, we are leaving everything behind?"

Ockam pulled at his thin mockery of a mustache. "You won't be safe in Withervale, particularly now that they know your faces. They'll be looking for you, but they will probably spend a lot of time searching through the mines before giving up. Spies will be everywhere, ones who look like regular people, not like Negian soldiers."

"It's alright, Gwoli, it'll be an adventure," Alaia said, heading down to pack their belongings. "We always wanted to see what's beyond these mountains. Let's take that stupid mask back to that kid."

They ascended the winding Ninn Tago road until the oaks changed into pines and higher still until even the pines became scarce. They camped for the night, sheltering among rocks, and continued early the next morning, with little rest.

Ockam insisted they needed to move fast, hoping to make it to the top of the pass that evening. Lago and Alaia were exhausted by the elevation change, while Ockam's expansive mountain lungs were doing just fine.

The cold of high elevations hit them hard, compounded by the blasting winds and the sinking sun. Ockam shared whatever garments he could spare, hoping that at least no freezing rain would fall on them.

Through a narrow corridor between steep walls, they heard voices. Three strangers approached, carrying large bundles over their backs.

"Moon lights," Ockam greeted, tipping his hat as he moved past, trying to remain inconsequential.

"Stars guide," one of the strangers replied, stopping.

"If you are climbing to the pass, you are awfully unprepared," a woman added. "Sceres is in shadows, and the swallows have nested early. A cold night approaches."

"May we interest you in some wares?" the third one offered. "We are headed to the Alban Bazaar in Withervale. We have furs, as well as finished and unfinished garments of wool and cotton."

"Yes, please," Lago said, teeth chattering.

Alaia found a maroon cloak with a rabbit fur-lined hood. Lago found himself a blue tunic with leather elbow pads but could not find a cloak to his liking.

"Do you have any cloaks for men?" he inquired, as if fashion would be of any consequence when stopping the cold.

"Only for women," a merchant answered.

Lago resigned himself to buying a calf-length woman's cloak of dusky grays. It was beautifully embroidered with black leaf patterns at the edges, but Lago did not want to admit how much he liked it.

He pulled out his Qupi pouch, which he had tossed into his bag before leaving his home, but there were not many chips left in there; he had spent most of his savings on his expensive binoculars. As he counted his Cups, Hands, and few Horns, he found the silver coin that Fjorna Daro had given to him six years ago. After all that had just happened, he wanted to get rid of it, to expunge all memories of that vile woman. He offered it to the merchants.

One of them considered. "A silver Krujel? Odd coin for these lands. But I guess I'll take it, plus all of that," he said, pointing his chin at Lago's pouch. The single Negian coin was more than enough to pay for what he was buying, but Lago did not feel like bartering, so he handed all his savings away.

They said their farewells and kept climbing. Once the merchants were out of sight, Ockam said, "It was fortunate we found the merchants, though their prices were criminal. But this worries me. We don't look like we belong up a mountain during a cold evening. A Free Tribesman, a Zovarian, and an Oldrin walking up the Gray Pass. We are like a bad joke."

"And a dog," Lago reminded him.

"And a dog. Those merchants will have a story to tell once they reach town, our whereabouts could soon be known."

"Could we take any side roads to avoid other encounters?" Lago asked.

"Not until we reach Knife Point. The Ninn Tago is narrow, with few exceptions, so we'll have to stick to the path. Try to keep a low profile if you see anyone else. Quick greetings, don't call attention to yourselves. And Alaia, keep your hood over your... er..."

"My nub, is what I call it. And no thank you, I'm not covering myself up for anyone."

"He's right, though," Lago said. "Just to be safe."

"I'll only do it because it's cold," she grumbled.

CHAPTER TWENTY-SEVEN

UNRAVELING

Sunnokh had long since bled the last of his light. They set up camp close to the top of the pass, hiding from the cold between granitic spires.

"Tomorrow we'll need to hunt, if we want to keep eating," Ockam said, sharing the last scraps of food he had with him. "There's not much to forage among these rocks, not until we reach the forest."

Clouds rolled through, enveloping them in a dense fog. Bear curled up by the fire and slept. The others soon followed.

Ockam was up before dawn, gathering kindling for the road.

"The heart pine from these old trees is exceptional," he told Lago, making conversation as an excuse to get them up and running. "Though it makes me feel a bit guilty, knowing that these trees have been here for so long that they likely saw and survived the Downfall. I only take what I need for my fire kit, no more."

They had only hot tea for breakfast, as no food remained, except for a strip of jerky that Lago gave to Bear. They continued their climb and made it to the saddle of the pass before the sun fully rose.

Alaia rushed ahead, and from the fog she called, "Lago! Come sit with me on the lucky branch!"

Lago ran after her and found her sitting on the bristlecone pine they had sat on during the recent holiday of the Feast of Plenitude. Sunnokh was rising, slowly pushing the moisture away with his warm touch.

"You two! We barely started, it's no time for breaks," Ockam complained.

"Shush. This is *our* spot, you go sulk in a corner for a while," Alaia told him. "There it comes there it comes!"

The clouds parted under the pressure of the golden sunbeams, and the Heartpine Dome came into view. The sensuous curve lifted from a sea of clouds, like a nipple of Noss themself. There was nothing else: clouds below, sky above, and the distant dome floating in the middle. The unruly vines that had grown untamed in the past six years made the edges of the dome look fuzzy.

"There are clouds rolling into that hole on the right," Alaia pointed out, "like water spilling into the dome."

"Are you children done?" Ockam protested.

"Hey, I said shush. This is our moment."

"What do you think is left in there now, Ockam?" Lago asked.

"I don't know, but whatever was below those holes in the roof must've been crushed by miles of deadly, sharp thorns."

"Thanks," Alaia said. "Just what we wanted to hear."

Ockam started down the path. "Better keep your expectations low. The Negians likely pillaged and ruined all they could. My only hope is that those vines fell while enough of the bastards were still in there." He looked back and added, "If you want to hear more about it, let's talk while we walk, we should not waste time up here. It's a long way to the dome, but the road is flat and easy to travel. You have your predecessors from before the Downfall to thank for that—if it hadn't been for the old roads they built, traveling through this or any land would've taken much longer."

"What do you think happened to all the Wumash?" Lago asked Ockam, catching up with him further down the foggy trail.

"It's *Wutash*. Either they ended up as slaves or died fighting for their land. I heard rumors of red-skinned prisoners spotted on the road east of Farjall, probably sent to Hestfell. My boy had the luck of being protected by his grandmother, the dire wolves, and the mask—the rest weren't as fortunate."

"The mask is, um, intriguing," Lago said, "but I still don't see why it's so important to the Negian Empire."

"Maybe it's very valuable," Alaia said. "It looks like it's made out of quaar, since it's so light, dark, and durable."

"Quaar is rare and valuable indeed," Ockam said, "and if this mask is made of it, it'd be worth a fortune. But I don't think that's why the Negians want it. They have plenty of quaar artifacts in their museums, and they don't do anything special like this mask does."

"You told us that the mask has many powers," Lago said, "what else can it do?"

"Well"—he cleared his throat—"you've already discovered one aspect that Bonmei hadn't told me about, that strange perception of intent, of seeing what is coming to you. That, I believe, could be extremely advantageous in battle. But hey, look down there, the path is finally clear," Ockam said, changing the subject.

The fog was clearing at the bottom of the road, revealing the Farsulf Forest. The triangular peak of Knife Point rose from there, slicing right into the north side of the dome.

"She came all the way from there…" Lago whispered, considering how far the dome still was. "But why?"

"Why what?" Ockam said.

"Why would Sontai travel all this way? What was she after?"

"Minnelvad," Ockam cryptically replied.

"What is Minnelvad?"

"When they escaped, Bonmei said his grandmother was trying to take them to Minnelvad. He didn't know what that meant, or why they were going there, he just remembers the name. If I recall his exact words, Sontai told him, *We are going to Minnelvad, to ask our cousins for help.* I asked him to repeat those words many times, trying to figure it out myself.

"No matter how much I asked around, no one recognized the word. It was only recently, when I was in Dimbali, that I was talking to an old sailor at the Topaz Beck, and as was my custom by then with any new acquaintance, I asked if he had heard of Minnelvad. He told me that in ancient Miscamish, *minnéllo* means *waterfall*, and *ëovad* means *fire*, and that *Minnelvad* was the old name of a waterfall northwest of Brimstowne, before the sulphur miners came and changed its name to *Firefalls*. He said it's a steaming waterfall surrounded by hot springs, sunken deep in the Stelm Wujann."

"Sontai said she wanted to see her 'cousins.' Who are they?" Alaia asked.

"I don't know, but I aim to find out. The sailor said no one lives in that area, but he hadn't been up over the falls, he had only seen them from a distance."

They had descended enough to reach a semi-forested area where they could find better cover from the occasional traveling merchants and pilgrims. Their bellies grumbled as Sunnokh crested on his daily arc. Lago sat to rest beneath a grove of pines, while Alaia foraged for berries, and Ockam went hunting with the bow taken from the soldier he had killed at the mines.

Alaia found a few shriveled nuts, two mushrooms, and a handful of musk-berries, which Lago would forever refuse to eat, even if starved.

"Those are disgusting," he told her. "You are disgusting."

"But they leave such a sweet aftertaste! You just have to ignore the—"

"Rotten."

"—the rotten flavor at first. The rest is bliss."

Ockam soon returned, empty-handed. He dropped onto a fallen log. "We might have to hike lower to find anything substantial. The ground squirrels are more patient than I am, and the rabbits won't come out till it's darker."

"What if I use Agnargsilv to find them?" Lago asked.

"It causes you pain, boy, I don't want to put you through that."

"It does, in a way, but I've learned to control it. I've been wanting to put it on again and see if I can understand it better."

Ockam stood and approached the young man. "Lago," he said, squatting next to him. "I don't want you to take this the wrong way, but don't get too attached to the mask. It belongs to Bonmei."

"I *know* that. But in the *meantime*, if I can use it like I did in the caverns, I might as well."

Ockam eyed him carefully. "Only when necessary," he said and stood to scan their surroundings. "And we must stay far away from the road. We can't risk anyone seeing it."

"I want to see what happens when you put it on," Alaia said. "Mind if I peek around?"

"Sure," Lago said, "I wish I could see it myself."

While Alaia watched from a lower angle, Lago put Agnargsilv on. It settled effortlessly on his face this time, as if it had always belonged there.

"That's unreal," Alaia said. "It changed shape and conformed to your face."

The muzzle was still hollow, letting her see Lago's lips and nostrils from below, but the rest of the mask settled so perfectly onto Lago's nose, cheeks, and around his eyes, that it looked as if it had been masterfully cast from a mold of his own face.

Lago tucked his fingers under the mask, feeling how it contoured his anatomy. "It's not stuck to me though, it's just... shaped to me." He stood up and gazed upon the forest with Agnargsilv's sight. "But by the Steward of the Sixth Gate, in the light of day, this looks way different than in the caverns..."

Now that his eyes could see at the same time as the mask, the two layers synergized into a new level of comprehension, as if he had been looking at the world in shades of gray, and now all colors were revealed. What Lago perceived with the mask were not images, but they lived in the same conceptual space. It was not like a double image either, nor an interruption over a transparent field, but a separate layer of pure understanding, abstract in form but concrete in meaning.

Lago's compound sight found the trees were full of insects, the air saturated with invisible pollen, and the soil... The soil itself had layers upon layers of life: fungi, nematodes, latent larvae, and all manner of bacteria, hiding next to buried seeds eager to sprout. The cacophony of organisms piled on top of each other in a mantle of cells, of cycles of life and death.

He strode around, scrying for meaning from dirt, bark, and rock. He noticed a web under his feet, as if the tree roots extended far to touch one another, to speak with one another, but the mask told him the tendrils were some sort of fungus. He sensed five long-tailed voles in hiding under the expansive mycelial mesh, calmly waiting for the intruders to go away. Inside a tree he saw a mother red squirrel breastfeeding two furless, helpless babies. A bit higher, he spotted a blue nuthatch's nest cradling three eggs.

As before, more complex beings showed more clearly to Lago, but he was also learning to focus on their constituent parts, seeing not just the larger creatures, but the cells that made them up, even noticing things like networks of parasites and bacteria living within them. Each organism was a microcosmos of life woven into a cohesive whole, and the more Lago narrowed his focus, the deeper he could peer into their compound threads.

He thought of the word *unraveling* as a way to describe this new insight, but then reconsidered and figured it was entirely inappropriate. *It's not unraveling, it's the opposite. It's like weaving, putting the threads together. The meaning is not in the individual threads, but in seeing the whole.* He noticed nuance in the relationships between threads: The mother squirrel had a tighter link to the babies next to her. The nuthatch eggs grew a stronger thread as their mother crawled up the bark toward the nest. The threads of some pinecones were directly connected to the pines above them, while others seemed to be pulled toward trees farther uphill.

"Well?" Ockam asked, losing his patience.

"Give me a breath, I'm getting used to this."

He scanned for the brightest of threads. The mask showed him a plump rabbit, hiding in fear behind a rock, with nowhere to run to. "Over there," Lago said, "behind the boulder, there's a rabbit. If you approach from the right, there is no way for him to escape."

Ockam moved silently while Lago watched through the mask's eyes. Alaia held Bear's neck, so that he wouldn't run and scare the lagomorph.

Ockam spotted the target and stopped. He nocked his arrow and pulled on the bowstring. At that moment, the rabbit saw Ockam and became petrified with fear.

Lago had been paying attention to the threads of the rabbit, putting himself in the mindset of the animal. When the rabbit's fear increased, he felt the same sensation of terror.

"Stop!" he screamed and lunged toward Ockam, slamming into him. Ockam was knocked back, but the arrow flew and stabbed the rabbit in the chest. Lago fell to the ground, gasping, feeling the pain in his own heart.

"What happened?" Ockam asked.

"No... Please..." Lago cried on his knees while the rabbit flopped and bled on the rocks. "It hurts..."

"Gwoli, what is wrong?" Alaia asked, rushing to her friend.

Lago gasped for air, convulsing in tears.

As the rabbit died, Lago's pain eased, and he began to breathe again. He sat up, still gasping. He ignored Alaia and Ockam and stared at the dead animal. He couldn't see it in the same way anymore: the main threads were gone, but the countless individual cells from its body still made a tangle of threads that was somehow cohesive, with its order slowly breaking apart.

This is death, Lago thought. He experienced the complete shutdown of the links that bind one with the rest of the world, the essence of being, of awareness, evaporating, leaving nothing behind but a lump of incoherent cells. *This is death, and I felt it.*

He was clutching his chest, crying.

Lago couldn't eat the rabbit.

He sulked by the fire, chewing on nuts and grilled mushrooms.

"You could at least stop staring at me," he said.

"Not until you tell us what happened," Alaia said.

Lago was sitting next to Agnargsilv, which seemed to stare at him. He stirred embers with a stick.

"It's not something I—" he cut himself off and massaged his temples. "I don't know if I can properly explain it, you can't feel the way I feel. When the rabbit... when he saw Ockam, I *felt* it all. I was there, experiencing his fear like it was my own, and I reacted to it. And then the arrow—" he paused again, feeling a tightness in his chest. "The arrow, it hurt so much. It felt like it was me who was dying. The mask put me in the rabbit's mind, and I just... I wasn't ready for it."

"This sounds too dangerous," Ockam said. "Perhaps it would be best if—"

"I'm fine. It's fine. I'll learn how to control it."

Ockam chewed silently, eyes locked on Lago. "It is your choice, boy. But keep the mask hidden. We should only use it if strictly necessary."

Lago shoved Agnargsilv in his bag but felt its presence even after closing it.

CHAPTER TWENTY-EIGHT

THE GREEN HERALDS

"Yeap, all the way up the pass!" the merchant told his friend, then gulped half
of his ale in one go. "These city folk have no idea how to travel, wholly unprepared, they think it's just a happy strut up the mountain to see the sights.
We did them a good one, tripled the prices on all the wares, and they even
thanked us for it. Bunch of idiots. Odd thing, this boy paid with a silver Krujel."

Osef Windscar perked up, sitting alone at the bar. "One more, please," he
said to the barkeep.

"—and then he gave the cloak to his slave. What a waste, I tell you." The
merchant kept assailing his friend with complaints: about that pear-shaped girl
he was supposed to meet but who'd ditched him again, about how those scam-
ming hunters tried to sell him rex rabbit fur and make it pass for mink, about
how the silks from Wastyr were no longer what they used to be.

Osef waited, slowly sipping his wine, but no longer appreciating its complex flavor.

The merchant downed yet another pint, dislodged his body from the chair,
and stumbled to the privies. Osef followed.

A long trough lined the wall. The merchant leaned an arm on the discolored plaster, pulled his cock out, and pissed aimlessly.

Osef leaned next to him, trying to piss but failing to—the uric spectacle next
to him was much too distracting.

"I heard you saw my friends up the pass!" Osef said cheerfully. "I told those
ignoramuses they'd need warmer clothes."

"Oh, you know them?" the merchant said, turning around and spraying in Osef's direction. Osef took a step back.

"If it's the same people you mentioned, yes. Young boy, and an Oldrin girl with a little spur right here on her head, right?"

"That's them alright, funny-looking pair. And that Free Tribesman, what a weird sight."

"Free Tribesman?"

The merchant buttoned his trousers without shaking it off.

"'Twas three of 'em. Well, four, if you count the dog. Big Tribesman fellow was probably trying to swindle them by 'helping' them up the mountain or something. Can't trust anyone who walks that road."

The merchant pretended to wash his hands, as a show of courtesy. Before he exited the privies, Osef asked him one more question.

"How long ago did you see them?" He made it two questions. "Exactly where on the path were they?"

The merchant turned, coherently suspicious despite his inebriated state. "How much is it worth to ya?"

Osef placed a generous bribe on the merchant's moist hand.

A northern chill blew through Fjorna's camp. They were hiding west of the mines, in a concealed pocket of reeds where there was no chance the Zovarian soldiers could find them. They dared not make a fire, but they were used to living in the shadows, so they sat bundled in cold starlight.

Fjorna ruminated on her waning options. Two days they had spent combing the mines, two entire days bribing, coercing, and forcing mine workers to take them through every single shaft, yet they found nothing but Elian's dead body.

General Hallow had sent a striking force east of Withervale to buy Fjorna time to search the mines. Consul Uzenzo had arranged for an escape, but it wasn't a very discreet affair at that point; once the Zovarian reinforcements arrived, the consul was forced to flee east, following Hallow and his platoon.

Fjorna's squad was left behind, but for a good reason: to carry forth with the mission until every single lead was exhausted. She had lost two men and one woman, friends she had trained and fought with for decades. Only eleven remained in her squad. This was personal now, and she'd see it through.

There was a rustling in the reeds. Three of her arbalisters raised their crossbows, then lowered them once they saw Osef.

"Chief Daro, I found a lead," Osef said, clearing spiderwebs off his scalp. "Two nights ago, a merchant saw them near the top of the Ninn Tago. They must've escaped the mines somehow."

Before Fjorna even said a word, her squad began to pack up, silently and efficiently.

"The mask?" she asked.

"I don't know, it could've been in their bags, or it could still be hidden elsewhere."

"How far? Where are they headed?"

"Four miles before the saddle, traveling south. Once they reach Knife Point, my guess is they will head to the Thornridge Lookout."

"What makes you think that?"

"They weren't alone. A Free Tribesman was traveling with them. A sylvan scout, from the description I got."

"How did a bloody muck get involved in this? He must've been the one who got Jovan, Elian, and Salvina. Must've trained at Klemes."

"I thought so, too. I already left a note of our departure with the emissary. She'll inform General Hallow."

"Good. And good work, Osef. Now get your gear ready."

Fjorna addressed her entire squad. "You heard Osef. We leave in a quarter-hour. We travel light, we travel fast. We do not know if they are carrying the mask, so we need them alive once we catch up to them. If we can confirm the mask is in their possession, then they are as good as dead, do your worst."

Fjorna approached a Wastyrian shaman with short, red hair. Her face, her arms, and the parts of her body hiding beneath her leather armor were all covered in scarified bumps spiraling like galaxies. She had two green magpies perched on her right shoulder.

"Aurélien, I need you to send both of your heralds. Have Islav keep eyes on them while Aness shows us the path."

"As you wish," Aurélien said, petting her birds. "The boy and girl will be easy for them to spot."

Aurélien produced a small vial filled with a black powder. She sprinkled a delicate amount of it onto the back of her scarified hand, then inhaled it. Her eyes widened, her pupils became black holes, her breasts blushed with blood. Unblinking, Aurélien turned her head and whispered something unintelligible to Islav and Aness. She then looked up toward the stars and said, "*Va jambradikh frulv halvet alrull.*"

The green heralds flew at once, vanishing like dark meteors into the night sky.

CHAPTER TWENTY-NINE

THE PERIMETER

"We'll make it to the Farsulf Forest tomorrow," Ockam said, then spat out a sharp bone from the over-seasoned bluegill he'd just grilled. "It starts right around Knife Point, where the split of the Perimeter Road is. I'll show you a hidden path there. Almost no one but sylvan scouts from Thornridge move through it—it will be much safer than the main road."

By midafternoon the next day the road of the Ninn Tago began to cut between tall and monumental pines, where the dry ground was replaced by an undergrowth of mossy pine needles. They were entering the higher edges of the Farsulf Forest, a territory the Free Tribesfolk still held tightly under their control.

Lago and Alaia were much closer to a dome than they had ever been, feeling oppressed by its magnitude, by its everpresence. The wall of vines rose eternally across half of their field of view, sliced apart only by the sharp peak of Knife Point.

They arrived at a junction at the base of the mountain, where the Ninn Tago met the Perimeter Road that circled the dome. They followed an animal trail away from the main road and dropped their bags next to a clear pond. Only the Heartpine Dome and the tip of Knife Point remained lit by the dimming, orange sunlight.

"I'd love to climb up to Knife Point," Alaia said.

"Oh, no, not an easy task to undertake," Ockam said. "The dome makes it look smaller than it is, but it's a massive mountain."

Alaia paced around the pond, searching for a better view of the peak. "Let me see your binoculars," she said to Lago. "Are they still working alright?"

"I couldn't get all the water out. One side still fogs up."

Alaia stared through the clouded lenses. To the right side of Knife Point was the newest hole in the roof of the dome. Sunbeams were streaming horizontally through the gnarled, withered hole. She peered into it and saw how the massive vines had shriveled in the areas where the roof had ripped.

"It's like it dried up and fell apart," she said.

"There are five holes total right now," Ockam told them. "This one offers the clearest view inside, since we can see it from way up in Mount Zite and Mount Griss, but even those peaks are not tall enough to let us see what's on the ground."

Lago was distracted by a fluttering motion across the pond. "Alaia, there are a couple of birds for you, on top of the pine, right there."

"Where?" she asked, searching.

"Right over that dried up branch," he pointed. "Weird-looking magpies."

Alaia spotted the birds with the binoculars. "How beautiful! Those are jade stealers, you can tell by their green feathers and blue legs. Never seen them here before, they are from Wastyr. Maybe they are migrating?"

"Maybe they came out of the dome, like the teratorns," Lago said, as one of the magpies took off and flew back toward the north. The other perched still, watching without moving.

The bottom of the Farsulf Forest was much denser and overgrown. Ockam directed them to a hidden trail where the pines were colossal in height and the ground wasn't covered in just pine needles but in vines, bushes, ferns, and toppled trees that would've offered constant hurdles, except for a scout who knew exactly where to traverse.

They descended until they were enveloped by thick shadows of green and brown. Lago could no longer tell in which direction the dome lay, unable to see even a glimpse of the sky through the dense canopy.

At high noon, they saw the brightness of a clearing ahead of them and arrived at the first tendril of the Heartpine Dome. Lago didn't even notice. The wide glade rose into a leaf-covered hillock where no trees grew and the ground felt strange, slippery.

"Watch out for the thorns," Ockam said. "They are very big on the larger vines like this one. You can't miss them, but they are painful if you aren't paying attention."

Lago spotted dozens of sharp sticks poking out from the hillock, each between two and four feet tall. He had paid no mind to them at first, thinking they were dead sprouts of pine or some other plant.

They heard a *yip!* behind them. Bear came running and whining.

"My point exactly," Ockam said. "Don't worry, it's not poisonous, it just stings. You'll see how sharp the thorns truly get once we reach the wall. Careful now, the vine is slippery."

"This whole glade?" Alaia said. "We are standing on a vine?"

"We are," Ockam said. "The moss, dirt, and dead leaves disguise them well when they are half-buried, but it's only a few odd ones that crawl out of the way like this one. For the past six years, they've been growing out of their original bounds, even taking over entire settlements. Some of them have stretched out half a mile from the wall."

"Like the Varanus Dome," Lago said, "although its vines go out ten miles into the sea. I saw an illustration of it, and it barely looks like a dome, more like a thorny thicket. Do you think something similar happened here?"

Ockam shrugged. "If that's the case, it must've happened a long time ago."

They arrived at the wall moments later. Vines of all sizes tightened at its perimeter, from hundreds of feet wide, to tiny tendrils, all sharply toothed and rising so high that the scales became senseless. The first fifty feet or so of wall blended with the mosses, lichens, and crawling ivies of the forest, but after that narrow transition zone, the inexplicably numerous tendrils took on a waxy and pristine, yellow-green color.

Lago tried to bend one of the thorns; it was woody, not very flexible. He took out his dagger and cut it—a white milk came out, stickier than pine sap, yet not as thick.

"Don't touch it," Ockam warned, "it gives you the hives. Wipe your blade before it runs down it, or it'll rust to oblivion."

Lago did as directed, then asked, "How much farther till Thornridge?"

"About two days' march. We camp tonight, then tomorrow, and we'll probably arrive in the evening of the following day."

Ockam led them to a curled vine that worked perfectly as a circular shelter. They dropped their bags, rolled their sore shoulders, and lit a fire within the secluded nook.

All was quiet that evening. The air was as still as the sky was clear. The purple crescent moon was dropping in the west, breathing a dim amethyst glow at the edges of the conifer canopy.

A deep sleep took them.

Lago stirred, then suddenly got up. He wasn't sure why he awoke, or even if he was awake. He stood there in silence, staring at the dying embers. And then he heard them: wolves, howling far away on the mountain slopes, carrying echoes of moonlight down into the forest.

Without understanding why, he grabbed Agnargsilv and walked out into a clearing. He listened. When the howling resumed, he put the mask on and stood as unmoving as the trunks of the ancient pines.

Ockam found him, perhaps hours later. He put a hand on Lago's shoulder, breaking the spell. "Come on, boy. Let's get you to bed."

Lago followed in a daze, fell right asleep, and had no dreams he could recall.

After a snail porridge for breakfast—which Alaia did not want to admit she loved—they doused their fire and left their camp.

"Last night, were you afraid of them, or just curious?" Ockam asked, as they crossed a gurgling stream.

"Afraid of what?" Lago said.

"The timber wolves. There are many in the surrounding mountains. They sing to Sceres every night."

"I didn't hear any wolves."

"I thought that's what you were listening to when you got up."

Lago squinted, confused. "I got up because I smelled breakfast."

Ockam seemed equally befuddled. He stopped at the edge of the stream.

"Hmm… Late last night, I saw you get up and walk into a clearing. You were wearing the mask, listening to the howling of the wolves. You don't recall?"

"I… I don't… I didn't…" Lago mumbled.

Ockam thought deeply before speaking again.

"Agnargsilv is full of unknowns," he said. "I want you to be careful with it. It can do a lot of things you aren't aware of."

"Sounds like there's something you haven't told us about."

"There is one thing," Ockam admitted, "but that is not for me to divulge. I want to leave that up to Bonmei. It's his right to keep it a secret, if he wishes to."

"Then why tell me this now?"

"Because I want you to know that I'm not hiding anything because I distrust you, as I don't. But you'll meet my boy very soon, and I'm sure he'll be excited to tell you everything you want to know."

To Alaia, Ockam seemed almost giddy. He hummed in anticipation as he strolled carelessly ahead.

"What do you think that's all about?" she privately asked Lago.

"I think he's excited to see Bonmei."

"Hey Ockam," she called. "How long has it been since you've been home?"

"Oh, I'd say three months? Before this deal with you two, I was visiting a friend in Dimbali. She was on her last days, so I spent a few weeks making her feel at ease before the Red Hand of Yaumenn took her. I was on my way back when I got the news from Withervale, and headed straight there without stopping by Thornridge."

"What is Thornridge like?" she asked.

"It's nothing grand. Quaint town, friendly people, well defended by the Thornridge Lookout, which holds the gates some miles east of Thornridge proper. The lookout is surrounded by outgrown vines as a sort of natural fortress, kind of like our camp from last night, but way bigger. Very well protected, four watchtowers, strong gates. When I found Bonmei, he was on the Flasketh Mesa, about ten miles south of the lookout.

"Did I tell you I taught him to shoot the bow? He hit his first bullseye when he was eight. Eight! He was so happy, he couldn't believe it! For his birthday this year, I'm going to get him a blowgun. He saw my friend Jiara hunting squirrels with one and tried it out. His tiny little lungs couldn't handle it, but I think that now that he's older he—"

"Now he won't shut up about Bonmei," Alaia whispered to Lago.

"It's your fault, you brought it up."

"I asked him about Thornridge, not Bonmei!"

"—but then again, he's never liked the flavor of radishes," Ockam continued, unfazed.

That night they camped deep in an aspen grove. The warm air from their campfire rose, sporadically shaking the loose leaves off. Ockam plucked a dozen or so leaves from the ground and put them into a notebook, flat between the pages.

"They are his favorite trees," he said.

"Huh?" the other two replied.

"Aspen. They are very rare here, only grow in this patch of the forest. Bonmei told me that inside the dome they had huge groves of them. Running through the aspen forests while the leaves fell was one of his favorite things in the world. He likes how the leaves wave as you pass them by, as if greeting you. Like in the *Book of Marasal*, in the song Graumendel sings after he sails away across the Alommo Sea."

Ockam pulled a velvet pouch from his bag, from which he took out a small kalimba: an instrument made of metal prongs attached to a wooden board, about the size of his hand. He stroked his thumbs on the metallic fingers and played a haunting melody. The sounds were penetrating and warm, interweaving in an undulating dance—they sounded like distant bells through a fog.

Resonating over the melody of his calloused fingers, his raspy voice intoned:

> Wave your farewells till your leaves turn to gold,
>
> Fire to ochre then brown to transform.
>
> Skeletal branches like spiderwebs cold
>
> Hold them down tight from the wintery storm.
>
>
> Consort with poplar, with pine, and with oak,
>
> Sing vernal hymns to the blistering road.
>
> Tint gold your sorrows, dye yellow your cloak,
>
> Turn yourself back to a shimmering grove.
>
>
> Hands that held mine till I sailed to high seas,
>
> Hands that took care of our grove of old trees,
>
> Wave your farewells to me, shake in the breeze
>
>
> Like aspen leaves,
>
> Like aspen leaves.

Ockam finished the song with ascending, sparkling chords. The melody lingered in Lago and Alaia's minds, imprinted as a pattern they could not soon forget.

The last day of their journey to Thornridge began with a drizzle that soon turned into a downpour. Hoods up, they sloshed through the muddy undergrowth into an area where the vines curled on the ground in labyrinthine twists that allowed them to sometimes walk under them, although most times it was necessary to go above them. The Free Tribesfolk had made this area traversable by wooden bridges balanced on ropes, tied to thick pines, or stuck directly onto the thorns of the vines.

"The vines actually help us here," Ockam told them, crossing a shallow river via a hanging bridge. "It's less troublesome to build bridges over the overgrowth of vines. Makes the Stiss Lummukem easier to cross."

"Lummukem? Like the winged dragon constellation?" Lago asked.

"Same one. You know your stars well. There is a wider bridge on the main road just a bit west of us, but I prefer this hidden trail. Take a look to your left," he said, pointing to the dome's wall. The river was coming straight out of it, seeping through the holes between vines.

"So, this water is from a source inside the dome?" Lago asked.

"Either that, or it's a branch of the Topaz Beck, which enters the dome in the northeast. We don't know for sure. The vines get dense and tangled like chainmail inside the wall, but water seems to pass through them just fine."

The rain had finally stopped, but the clouds remained fat and obstinate, refusing to let sunlight through. Ockam slowed to take a breath.

"We are nearing the lookout," he said, "should arrive soon after nightfall." He paced around, chewing on his cheeks. "I know this situation is... complicated. Withervale will not be safe for either of you for a long while. You are welcome to stay in Thornridge in the meantime, it's a very open-minded community."

"What are *you* going to do? With Bonmei and the mask and all," Lago asked.

"I think Bonmei will want to go to Minnelvad. To the Firefalls, I mean, to see if we can find his 'cousins.' He needs to learn about Agnargsilv, and they might be the only ones left who know its secrets." He sighed deeply. "But that path goes right through Negian territory, and my boy looks as Wutash as they come. Maybe once he comes of age, I'll take him on that adventure. I'm also curious to see what is out there."

"It's so strange," Lago said, "I never thought I'd fulfill my promise, that I'd meet Bonmei and... And now we are almost there. It all happened so fast."

"And we still need to be careful," Ockam said. "We'll find the right moment for you to give the mask to him. Later this evening, after we finish dinner and most everyone has gone to their homes, we'll gather by a fire. Until then, keep the mask hidden. I trust our guards—they'll make sure to allow us some privacy."

"I'll wait until after dinner, then," Lago said, both excited and defeated.

Chapter Thirty

Thornridge Lookout

A dense night enveloped them as they neared the gates of the lookout. Ockam cut a small vine and let the white milk drip into a metal vessel he found hiding within a tree trunk.

"The sap burns slow and not too hot," he said as he set the white milk on fire. "And you can never run out of it, but it ruins most anything it touches."

The sticky sap burned green, with sudden yellow sparks, and not very brightly at all. It released a white smoke and shone an eerie, sickly gloom around them, barely enough to travel by.

Alaia spotted ribbons wrapped around nearby trees, sometimes braided, sometimes dangling loosely. Although their hues were hard to distinguish under the verdant light, Ockam told her they were blue, green, gray, ochre, and violet in color.

"What are they for?" she asked.

"The Free Tribelands fly no flags, wear no sigils," Ockam said. "We hang streamers of our five colors near our gates to indicate all cultures are equally welcome, as long as they are willing to abide by some rules."

A shrill whistle broke through the silence.

Ockam stopped. With fingers in his mouth, he whistled a response.

"Is that... Lorr Radiartis?" a voice inquired from up in the trees.

"Brahm?" Ockam answered.

"At your service! It's been so long, we thought you'd be back a month ago."

Lago heard a clang, a scrape, then something sliding down a tree, and soon saw a man running to them, who greeted Ockam in an embrace.

Brahm was a stocky but flexible sylvan guard. His gray-blue eyes looked green behind his round spectacles, which reflected the weak fire of the sap. He was dressed in all shades of gray, from leather armor to wool cloak.

"They have you on guard duty on a rainy night?" Ockam said to his friend. "You must've truly upset the marshal."

"Not the marshal, but Jiara. She is in charge until her sister returns. I got drunk, was late—she can be merciless." Brahm stared at Ockam's companions. "And what's this you brought from your travels?"

"These fine folk are Lago and Alaia, and they—"

"And Bear," Lago reminded him.

"And Bear. And they are to be treated as the most honored of guests. We bring stories, we bring news, but we did not bring any ale."

"We can take care of that! Shall I hurry ahead and inform Jiara? Make sure they prepare enough food?"

"We'd be most thankful if you did. We've traveled a long way and will not rush behind you. Is Bonmei at the lookout?"

"He should be, I'll make sure he knows you are coming. I'll see you soon at the gates," Brahm said, trotting ahead.

They entered a steep ravine. On their right, a canyon wall was growing taller, and on their left, the vines of the dome encroached ever closer, some of them curling above the group like bridges. The parallel walls converged into a natural chokepoint where two firepits burned greenly, framing a curved gate built beneath a snaking vine.

The Thornridge Lookout had three gates: the north gate, which they were about to enter, was the widest, set underneath the thickest vine; the south gate was small, opening to a trail to lookouts over the Flasketh Mesa; the west gate led to the town of Thornridge, four miles away, and to the forest road to Farsúksuwikh and the Klad Senet.

The Free Tribesfolk had created a fortified circle within the vines and the steep ravine, where half a dozen buildings stood. Four towers overlooked the perimeter, connected by battlements built atop the vines, following the natural shapes of the snaking tendrils. The organic nature of the fortress made it seem as if it had been designed by an architect who did not understand the concept of straight lines.

The gates opened wide to receive them. A young child came running toward them. Ockam rushed to meet him.

"My boy!" he cried with joy, picking Bonmei up in a big hug.

"Kaadi!" Bonmei said, giggling.

Bonmei was a sharp-eyed boy of elongated features, agile limbs, and soft, red skin. His hair was short and wavy, dark as the night that surrounded them. He had a few tattoos on his forehead and the backs of his hands but was not covered in them as Sontai had been—the Wutash tattoos told the stories of their lives, and Bonmei's short story so far only recounted eleven years.

Ockam placed Bonmei down and kissed the top of his head.

"Son, there is someone I'd like you to meet," he said.

Sylvan guards were in the process of locking the gates for the night, letting only the required sentinels remain inside the vine fortress. Brahm led Ockam and his guests to an outdoor table on which lay warm-enough food, although it had been sitting out a bit too long. Ockam sat next to Bonmei, Alaia and Lago across from them, while Brahm and a bunch of straggling guards helped themselves to seconds. Ockam seemed closely familiar with all of them.

"Tell me, Kaadi! Where have you been?" Bonmei demanded in his high-pitched voice.

"Like I said, after my friend's funeral, I had to spend time in Dimbali with her family. And then I ran late because my young friends here needed help."

"What did you need help with?" Bonmei asked directly to Lago.

"Well... We w-were..."

"Lago will tell you after dinner," Ockam said, pulling Bonmei into a side hug. "Don't get sleepy on me, because it's a story you'll be *very* excited to hear about."

The west gate was opened to let one person through and then quickly locked again. A muscular woman with a bossy demeanor pushed her way through. A thick, ash-blonde braid bounced over her generous cleavage, marking the rhythm of her heavy strut. She was wearing the gray leathers of the Free Tribelands, but the cloak belted over her armor was not gray like that of the sylvan guards, nor green like that of the sylvan scouts, but a dark walnut. From hood to cape, the edges of her cloak were trimmed with two strips of ochre, with a wider strip of teal between them, marking her higher rank. "You graceless stoolwaffle," she loudly voiced, stomping forward, "you were supposed to be back weeks ago! This demon kid of yours is a nightmare to take care of!"

Ockam stood to greet her with a powerful full-arm handshake.

"I'm sorry for the delay," Ockam said. "And watch your mouth, Jiara, we have guests."

Lurr Jiara Ascura vociferously introduced herself, straddled the bench next to Ockam, and downed a pint. She was a platoon commander of high renown and high warden of Thornridge, currently there only as an acting officer until her sister, Field Marshal Ascura, returned from Abafekh to retake her post.

"How is Biancall doing?" she asked.

Ockam forced a smile. "She didn't make it. Lasted only a day after I arrived."

"May Takh light that fucker's way to the Six Gates. I wish I had had a chance to grab one more drink with her." She lifted her next pint, took a large gulp in honor of the departed, then slammed the glass on the table and said, "Then what in the netherballs took you so long?"

"It's a long story. Could we have the hearth readied? I know it's late, but it's important we tell you everything after dinner."

"I'll see to it," Jiara said and left the table.

The hearth was a miniature amphitheater at the center of the lookout, a cozy circle for personal gatherings. Everyone who had joined them at dinner was there, except for two guards who'd had to return to the watchtowers.

Brahm fed two more logs into the bonfire, which burned fragrant and orange from the oily pinewood. The Free Tribesfolk had no problem burning vine sap out in the forests, but they considered it bad luck to burn it within their cities, or anywhere indoors. Alaia was glad for this, because she loved the woody aromas of a proper fire, while the burnt sap stank.

All the gates were locked. The only light that remained came from the single fire at the hearth. Heavy clouds lingered above, but no rain was forthcoming.

Ockam cleared his throat, then began, "First and foremost, I will ask all of you to keep this conversation private. I trust you, but what we are about to discuss is dangerous, and the fewer people who know about it, the safer we'll be."

Jiara, Brahm, and the eight other guards closed their fists and slammed their knuckles together twice.

Ockam continued, "After visiting Biancall, my trip took an unexpected turn. I received news that a body had been discovered near the Withervale Mesa, and I had to rush north to investigate."

He looked at Bonmei, who seemed to know where this was headed. "Yes, son, like we long suspected, your grandmother had long ago crossed into the Six Gates. But she was given a proper funeral by my friends. She rests with Noss."

Bonmei looked dejected. He uttered a quiet thanks to Lago and Alaia, then listened on. Ockam recounted the rest of the story, from the finding of Sontai's body by the land developer, to Fjorna's attack and their escape.

"And the reason they were after us, as at least Bonmei might have guessed... Lago, why don't you explain the rest?"

"I…" Lago drifted off, staring at the flames, then found the words. "When I met your grandmother, she entrusted me with something, and made me promise I would one day give it to you. I was just about your age when I made that promise. I'm here to fulfill it."

Lago opened his bag and took the mask out.

"Agnargsilv," Bonmei mouthed soundlessly, his breathing fully stopped.

Lago walked up to Bonmei, squatted in front of him, and handed him the mask.

The black, canine form stared at the boy who was meant to be its heir. Bonmei stared back, lost in the memory of his mother, of his grandmother, and all that they had lost inside the dome.

Lago sat next to him, unsure of what else to say. Ockam spoke in his stead, "Sontai and Mawua lost their lives to protect this treasure, and so did many other Wutash. The Negians are looking to harness its power, so it's imperat—"

"Northwest tower, trouble," Jiara warned, jumping to the side to grab her bow. "Take cover!" she commanded.

Ockam glanced up and saw a guard dangling lifeless at the northwest tower, then heard a muffled scream from the northeast tower. Before he could react, arrows and bolts flew at them. Two guards fell next to him, one screaming while holding her leg, the other toppling silently with an arrow in his forehead.

Bonmei clutched the mask to his chest, terrified, and tried to run. An arrow hit him in the back, making him tumble out of the stone circle. The mask flew from his hands.

Ockam rushed to Bonmei, picked him up, and ducked behind the stones for cover. "My boy! No, no, my son!" he wailed.

Lago and Alaia followed them, leaping over the edge of the stones, arrows sparking at their feet.

Two guards took cover under the long table where they had just had dinner. The remaining four guards instinctively rushed to the western wall to grab their weapons; three of them were shot down at once, while the survivor managed to grab a bow and quiver and hid underneath the arch of the gate.

"What the *fuck* is happening?" Alaia screamed, her back against the rocks.

"Bonmei! Stay with me!" Ockam cried inconsolably, trying to keep the boy from closing his eyes.

"They've taken the northern battlement!" Jiara called out. "Find cover!"

Brahm had run to a hut by the wall of the dome, where two round shields hung. He tossed one, making it roll toward the hearth. Jiara caught it. He tossed another, but the shield was struck by an arrow midway and tumbled onto the grass.

The guard at the southeast tower fell by a crossbow bolt, leaving only the guard at the southwest tower—she whistled loudly, hoping that anyone on the path to Thornridge was close enough to hear, but there was no reply. She released a well-aimed arrow, wounding one of the intruders on the north battlement.

"Now!" Jiara commanded, pulling on Ockam's arm. Ockam crouched next to her while cradling Bonmei.

Arrows flew by them, but Jiara held the shield steady and kept moving. Ockam picked up the other shield that had not reached them before, and together they hurried until they reached Brahm at the hut.

Alaia peeked over the stone circle. "Shit, shit, shit."

"Stay down," Lago whispered, pulling on her shoulder, "they can't shoot us if we stay behind cover."

"We can't stay here, they'll be coming around the side."

"Lago, catch!" Ockam called. He tossed a shield, but it was taken down at once, rolling too far to be used by either of them.

Jiara handed Ockam the other round shield. "Try again," she said, "but wait for my signal." She positioned herself in a dark corner where she could peek through a window. "There's a bit of movement on the north battlement, I just need a clear shot. Ockam, get ready."

Ockam readied the shield.

"Now," Jiara said.

Ockam tossed the shield toward Lago. A man stood at the battlements aiming his bow, giving Jiara's arrow a clear path. The man fell in a gurgling scream.

"You motherfuckers!" a shrill voice said near the fallen man. "You'll fucking pay for this, all of you!"

Alaia caught the rolling shield. "What do we do now?" she asked.

The closest cover was east, inside the hut with the others, but there didn't seem to be any way out of there. They could go west, to where the lone guard had taken refuge beneath the gate, but he, too, was pinned down. There were buildings by the north gate, but that was toward the enemy. To the south was a risky, open path, leading to the south towers, where one last tower guard remained. Bear was in that direction too, barking anxiously from the darkness.

"They are moving onto the western battlement!" the guard under the west gate cried out.

"We need to move away from them," Lago said. "Let's see if the tower guard can help us."

Lago waited for a flurry of arrows to be exchanged before making his move. He walked backward with the shield, leading Alaia toward the southern towers.

"Wait, wait, the mask!" Alaia said, rushing out of cover to grab Agnargsilv. An arrow struck her right forearm, making her drop the mask. *Fwip. Fwip.* The next two arrows barely missed her, but she managed to grab the mask again. *Thwump!* the next arrow hit, but on Lago's shield. Alaia was back behind cover.

"*Fffff... Aaaaaggghhnngg,*" she muffled a scream.

"Stay focused, just a bit farther," Lago encouraged. His shield stopped another arrow, followed by two heavy crossbow bolts that made him stumble. They took cover behind a corner where a ladder climbed up the wall. Lago checked Alaia's wound: the arrow was stuck between her forearm bones.

"Are you supposed to pull it out?" he asked.

"I don't... Just... fucking leave it. I can't," she gasped.

Bear barked next to them.

"Bear, quiet!" Lago said.

"*Psst,*" a voice called from above. The last tower guard had spotted them.

"How can we get out of here?" Lago asked her. "My friend needs help."

"I'm out of arrows," she said, "but I can find help in town."

"Then hurry before they take over the battlement."

"I'll make haste. May Takhísh's Shield protect you," the guard said, then slid down the tower's ladder. She hid behind a vine, then rushed over the battlement, directly toward the west gate.

Lago heard the woman scream. Then all went silent.

"That was your last sentinel," Fjorna's voice called from somewhere north. "You know what we came here for, Lago Vaari. But now we are after more than just the mask. You will pay for Jovan, for Elian, for Salvina. And now also for Waldomar, for Nikolina."

"Scorch your flesh sixteenfold, all of you!" warned the voice of Muriel, Waldomar's sister.

"And you led us right to that bloodskin flea," Fjorna continued, "who I saw spitting out his guts, as red as his cursed skin. It'll be the last thing he tastes, the last thing his blasphemous tribe tastes."

"Above you!" Jiara cried out.

Lago and Alaia cowered and looked up, but the warning wasn't for them, but for the guard beneath the west gate. Fjorna's armsmaster, Crescu Valaran, had crept onto a ledge overlooking the gate. He pulled the trigger on his crossbow. The heavy bolt pushed the sylvan guard violently back, impaling his body onto the vines.

"*Ffffhhnngg...* Themm... ask..." Alaia tried to voice. "Use th-themm... massssk," she whimpered, handing Agnargsilv to Lago.

"But what would—"

"You can—*hhnngg*—see them, it's dark up there, and they—"

"No more hiding," Fjorna called out. "Light them up!"

Lago stared as incendiary arrows cut brightly through the air, landing on the hut his friends were hiding in. The straw roof was wet with the recent rains, but that was not enough to stop the blaze—it would all burn, soon.

"Go, n-now!" Alaia implored.

Lago's heart pounded against his ribs.

Agnargsilv had a splatter of blood on the forehead, reminding Lago of the first time he had seen the mask clearly, with Sontai's blood drying on its brow. He felt angry, dismayed. With uncertainty and hopelessness, he put the mask on.

He made the mistake of focusing on the pain his friends were feeling, and once more felt a jolt of pure agony strike him. Bear barked. Lago stumbled backward, lungs pumping like strained bellows, then straightened himself and tried to clear his mind. *The strong pack I am not, yet pack and wolf are of one heart. Pack and wolf are of one heart. Pack and wolf are of one heart.* He tamed the pain, swallowed it, and let it run through his veins.

The pain settled into the back of his awareness.

"Bear, quiet," he ordered. Bear obeyed.

He focused Agnargsilv's sight and scanned the threads around him, searching for his enemies. A woman was sneaking across the platform above them. He hugged the wall, found the ladder, and climbed it, flattening his body against the steps. He sensed the woman leaning to look down. From the shadows, he reached up, pulling her hair straight down. The woman fell and smashed her face onto the ground.

Alaia ran and kicked her teeth in before she could call out, then went back to hiding behind the wall.

Lago climbed the rest of the way up, then snaked over the curving battlements. He spotted a man crouching by the ledge from where he had shot the guard. Unseen, Lago snuck closer and delivered a kick to his back before dropping down to hide again.

The man screamed as he fell from the ledge. His back smashed onto a vine, thorns piercing through his leather armor, leaving him stuck as he wailed.

"Who the fuck did that?" questioned a shrill voice nearby. "Someone pushed Crescu!"

Lago could sense the caller clearly through the parapet wall: she was slender and short-haired, and had two birds perched on her shoulders. The woman had just hung her bow away, trading it for a knife. Dead steel and wood did not shine with threads, except in small imperfections where bacteria grew, but Lago could clearly read the woman's posture and movements. He put himself in her mind to feel the pull of her threads, sensing what she was about to do. A man followed closely behind her, while others had mobilized toward the west gate, waiting in hiding.

It was dark as pitch up on the battlements. If he stayed low, hiding his silhouette, Lago could pass by completely unseen. He pulled his dagger out, holding it clumsily. He sensed his enemy making the decision to rush around the corner. He felt enraged as never before, more than when his father beat him, or the time bullies pissed on his face, or when Carlo abandoned them at the sinkhole. The rage exploded out of him as he charged before the woman could. He shoved her onto the man behind her, kicked her face as he passed over her, then stuck his blade into the man's torso, tumbling down with him.

The woman cried for help, her two birds flapping over her, but Lago rolled back to her and punched and kicked until she was unconscious or dead. The man pulled the dagger out of his chest and tried to stand. Lago took the fallen woman's knife and crawled away in the shadows.

"Aurélien?" Fjorna's voice called from far away. "What was that noise?"

"…*nnggd*fucker…" the man gasped, holding the bloodied dagger toward the darkness.

Lago snuck silently behind the man and stabbed him twice more, with a cunning precision that frightened him. He dropped down into hiding again, his rage easing slightly.

He forced himself to ignore the pain around him and gazed at the threads ahead, sensing farther with his narrowed focus. Two figures hid right past the parapet that arched over the west gate, in an area covered by a wide platform with circular holes through which thick-trunked pines grew. Two more enemies crouched at the edge of the battlement, arrows nocked as they peered below for survivors. The platform ended in a vertical rock wall permeated in gloom, with a ladder climbing to the northwest tower. At the bottom of the steps Fjorna hid, aiming her crossbow through a crevice between vines, waiting for Lago's friends to come out of the burning hut.

Lago knew the darkness would protect him, so he ran over the gate and jumped when he reached the far end. A sword and a dagger swung behind him, barely missing. He kept running toward one of the men at the edge of the battlement, who was turning his bow around. Lago jumped and slammed both feet into him, sending the man scraping over the thorny vines, then crashing on the grass below, where Jiara's well-aimed arrows finished him off.

Lago ran to the shadows and flattened himself against a pine's trunk. He sensed Fjorna and the three remaining soldiers sneaking toward him, their threads converging into his own, their intentions clear to Agnargsilv's sight.

With no enemies paying attention to the burning building, Lago screamed, "Ockam! Run to cover, it's clear!"

He could only hope they had heard him, but now he had given away his position. He sensed the four enemies moving with determination. No more bows or crossbows this time, all held daggers or swords.

"Stay back!" he yelped, making them briefly hesitate.

"Lago?" Fjorna said, sounding surprised. "How did you manage to—"

"Don't come any closer," he said, pressed flat against the wide trunk.

"You mucks killed my brother," Muriel spat.

"We'll make you pay, maggot, for those you took from us," Fjorna said. "I'll make you watch as I cut off your stupid dog's cock and shove it down that spur's throat."

Lago's rage boiled; he inhaled and exhaled so forcefully that his enemies knew exactly where to strike. All four of them jumped him at the same time, but Agnargsilv showed Lago their intended paths. He rolled away from the blades and slammed his heel on Muriel's knee, bending it at an odd angle. Hidden by the absence of light, he grabbed Muriel's bent leg and spun her small body like a mace, smashing another woman onto the tree. Lago felt stronger, though his muscles had not changed—it wasn't strength that he had gained, but a better understanding of where to apply his energy, and where not to.

A sword slashed by his face, sending sparks flying as it scraped the mask. Lago felt unhinged, rabid. He backhand-slapped the assailant, then grabbed a sword from the ground and drove its point up onto the man's chin, hearing the jawbone crack. The man toppled like timber. Muriel got up on her broken leg and swung at Lago, who parried the blow and punched her in the chest, then slapped her cheeks with the blunt crossguard of the sword.

Lago darted toward the stone wall and paused to breathe. Fjorna could barely spot him, but she could tell his back was to her. She bolted toward him. In the dark, all that was visible was the white hilt of Fjorna's dagger, but Lago didn't need to look back. He moved out of the way just in time, stepped behind Fjorna, and shoved her forward. She slammed against the rock wall, splitting her brow open. She turned, out of balance, slashing the air.

Lago felt his rage pulling him toward her. From behind the dark muzzle, he growled.

"What the *fuck* are you?" Fjorna cried. "I'll tear—"

Lago kicked her stomach, blowing the air and droplets of blood out of her lungs. Fjorna collapsed in a torn gasp.

Lago stomped on her hand, forcing her mangled fingers to release the dagger. He straddled her and began to punch. He pummeled, he hammered, he clawed. He saw his spit dripping down and felt like biting her fucking neck to shreds. He jabbed until Fjorna's face was unrecognizable, he smashed, and battered, and—

"Lago, stop!" a voice implored, seeming so distant. Lago's fists kept striking.

"Stop!" A hand on his shoulder.

He turned, ready to strike back, then stopped.

Alaia stood there, sobbing. Ockam was behind her, holding a torch. Jiara, Brahm, and the two guards who had taken cover under the table were farther down the platform, tying down the few soldiers who were merely unconscious instead of hopelessly dead.

"Stop…"

Lago pulled the mask off with his bleeding hands, then fell on his side.

The prisoners were chained by the north gate, faces to the wall, except for Fjorna, who was so heavily beaten that they let her sit on the mud, barely alive. Crescu had survived his fall onto the vines, but still had thorns stuck on his back, their white milk burning inside him. The other survivors were Muriel, Aurélien, Trevin, and Shea, all injured in different ways. Of the fourteen members of Fjorna's squad, six remained alive, while seven lay dead. But Osef… Osef was nowhere to be found.

Lago watched the Negian survivors from a distance, uncertain of how many from the squad he had killed, not really wanting to know. *They deserved it*, he thought, but he still felt like a monster. He focused on removing the loose skin from his knuckles, with Bear curled anxiously by his legs.

Jiara had pulled the arrow from Alaia's forearm and was washing the gash with cold water.

Ockam sat by them at the edge of a well, overflowing with sorrow. Bonmei was dead; the boy lay covered with a white blanket next to the fallen guards.

"I did this…" Ockam lamented. "I brought this death to our people, to my son. I didn't think there was a way for them to track us. And how could they break into our fortress?"

"It was a specialist squad," Jiara said. "They shot a rope from way up in the trees, slid over our walls in the dark. The ropes have been cut, but we'll have to cut down the old pines too. As beautiful as they are, they create a weak point in our defenses."

"There's a man missing," Ockam said. "I recall seeing a bald-headed man at the northern battlement, yet I saw no bald heads among the prisoners, or the dead."

"We've already sent scouts. If there's anyone else out there, we'll find them."

"I hope so. I don't want you to take any more risks. The Negians are after one thing only, the mask, and as long as it is here with us, they will come for it, and with reinforcements next time. They have too many spies. Now that we have alerted Thornridge of the attack, the chiefs will have questions, and word will spread."

"If that mask is responsible for the carnage we saw up there, I can understand why the Negians are after it," Jiara said. "It's too dangerous a weapon, could lure a war right onto our doorstep. I say we destroy it before—"

"No!" Ockam snapped. "It's a relic from the Wutash. From Bonmei. It's the only thing that… that… We have to find out more about it, but we cannot let it bring more death to our people."

"But how does it work? Why haven't we—"

A guard rushed in from the west gate. "Thirty more sylvan guards coming, Lurr Ascura, arriving within the hour. A hundred more will arrive with your sister by noon tomorrow."

Jiara stood, wiping her hands with a wet cloth. "Make sure there are sentinels in all the northern hideouts, and at least a dozen in the southern mesa. No fires, have them take their posts in the dark. We don't know if the enemy carried reinforcements at their heels. We seal the gates until our scouts are able to comb the forest."

The guard nodded and hurried away.

Jiara sat back down with an arm around Ockam's shoulders.

"I can't let this war fall upon my people," Ockam said, staring at the cloth covering Bonmei's body. "We are barely holding our ground against the Negians. If they were to send their legions, we'd have no way of fighting back."

"What do you propose?" Lago asked.

"We take the mask away from the Free Tribelands. I know where, but I'd rather not say until it's safe."

"I'll call for a ship to be readied," Jiara said, "to sail with haste over the Klad Senet."

"I don't mean to go west. The deeper the mask goes into our lands, the worse things will get."

"Too dangerous. If you go north, you risk finding other troops that might've followed. And the southern forests are constantly patrolled by troops from Farjall."

"But we can go east," Ockam said.

Jiara tilted her head, letting her big braid dangle next to her shoulder. "I don't understand. Unless you can climb over the dome, there's no way east from here."

"Maybe," Ockam said and leaned in. "Lago, come closer. I told you that Bonmei—" he stopped, wiped his reddened eyes, then quietly continued. "I told you my son knew of one other secret about Agnargsilv, one too important for me to reveal. He would've wanted to tell you himself, but now that he's gone, that burden falls upon me." He shot a look at Jiara, who without hesitation twice tapped her fists as a vow to secrecy.

"Agnargsilv has the power to control the vines," Ockam said. "The dome was meant to open at some point, with Agnargsilv being a part of that process. Bonmei told me that the mask could be used to walk through the vines, if you willed them to move."

"If that's possible, how come the Wutash never left Heartpine before?" Lago asked.

"They were not allowed to, not until the right time came. Bonmei didn't yet know when that would be, or how it would happen. But if the mask does control the vines, we could use it to enter the dome."

"You want to go in there to hide the mask?" Lago asked.

"Not to hide it, but to escape with it where Negians will not be able to follow. Lago, you are the only one with the experience of wielding it. I thought... perhaps you'd be able to figure how to open a path. We'd be safer in there anyhow, for now."

Ockam took a moment to gather his thoughts. "There's another reason," he said. "I had promised Bonmei that one day I'd take him back to his homeland. I'd like..."—he choked up—"... I would like to take him there for his funeral. It's the best I can do to keep that promise now."

Alaia leaned closer to Ockam. "I'm going with you all," she said.

Lago's eyes darted between them. "And after that, are we going to take the mask to—"

"Shhh," Ockam quieted him. "Yes, but we'll discuss that once we are inside."

"Then yes," Lago said. "I don't know how to do this, but it is as if the mask works on instinct. It teaches you what you need to know. I'll find a way, but I'm not leaving without—"

"Yes, Bear too," Ockam said.

Jiara huffed. "Whatever it is you are doing, you first need a good night's sleep, and then—"

"No," Ockam said. "You heard the guard. Thirty soldiers will be here in the next hour. A hundred more tomorrow. The sooner we can leave, the fewer people will find out, and the safer we'll all be."

Jiara shook her head. "But you are weak, and need supplies, and—"

"Then make haste and find us all you can. Food, gear, weapons, clothing. And talk to all the guards, make sure they say nothing to the others who will soon arrive."

"I'll see what I can do," Jiara said, leaving in a hurry.

Sylvan scouts traveled light, but with all the necessities: ropes, cooking supplies, extra provisions, warm clothing in layers, tools, medicine, weapons. Jiara and Brahm gathered all they could for their friends and helped them pack. The only thing they were unable to provide was a map of the uncharted land ahead.

"I'll be right back, I thought of a few more things," Jiara said and left again.

Ockam used his usual travel backpack, Lago his trusty and oversized delivery bag, while Alaia added a new backpack to go with her old haversack.

"Lorr Radiartis, I still don't understand why you need all these supplies," Brahm said to Ockam.

"Jiara will explain it to you. Thank you for all the help, truly."

Ockam carefully picked up Bonmei's wrapped body. Then the three friends plus Bear walked toward the dome's wall, next to where the hut had burned earlier that night. The vines in that area were singed, but unbothered.

Lago took Agnargsilv out. "I'll try it, just give me a moment," he said, then put the mask on.

He stared at the vines and focused to make the threads appear within his perception. Like every living organism, the wall was made of a network of threads expanding in every direction. The bigger vines had threads that felt more static, some of them looping back into themselves, while the smaller ones vibrated and shifted to link up with all the living mosses and insects that landed on them.

These threads had an odd shimmer to them, like a heat haze that made it slightly harder for Lago to see through them. He moved closer and placed a hand on a small vine, careful not to touch any thorns. With his mind he felt around and imagined the threads spreading, making room for him. He unconsciously imagined a flower un-blooming, a river carving a canyon, a calving glacier. The vines listened.

"I think it's working..." he mumbled.

Slowly, nearly imperceptibly, the vines began to contort and bend. The smaller vines moved out of the way first, wrapping themselves tight against the medium-sized ones, and those in turn began to wrap over the enormous, unmovable pillars of the larger vines. Some tendrils detached from the ground and shriveled upward, tightening into gnarled fingers, while others disappeared underground like shy earthworms. The larger vines didn't budge, but the space carved by the small ones was more than enough.

"What in the sixteen voids is happening?" Brahm asked. Ockam gestured for him to quiet.

The passage that was opening was about three strides wide. Lago took a step in, then turned to face his friends. "I can do this. It will be slow, but it's working."

Jiara came back, carrying another bag full of supplies.

"We have more than we can carry," Ockam said.

"That's fine," she said, "I don't mind carrying this one."

"Bah. You aren't—"

"Shut your cock trap, I'm going with you. You need help, and I'm not leaving you behind." She cocked a demanding eyebrow at Lago, then pointed at the vines. "Carry on, kid, stop wasting time."

Lago noticed that the vines had begun to close up while he had been distracted. He walked deeper into the hole and focused on the threads again, this time making the space deep enough for all of them to fit.

They stepped in.

Jiara turned to Brahm and slapped his hands. "Turn that lamp off! We can't let anyone else see this."

"You are really going?" Brahm said, extinguishing his fire. "But what do I tell them? They'll be looking for you!"

"Anything but the truth."

"And your sister? She'll be asking—"

"Make something up! You'll figure it out."

"I hate your stupid guts, you know?"

"I know. May Takhísh's Shield protect you!"

Brahm waited in the darkness. Once the tunnel fully closed, he left, mumbling to himself, trying to come up with some excuse he could spout when all the troops arrived.

At the north gate, ass in the mud, through blood-crusted eyes, and merely half-conscious, Fjorna had seen the group make their escape. She smiled through her shredded lips, her shattered jaw. She had now learned yet another secret about the mask, one that could prove even more valuable than any of the other powers she knew about.

CHAPTER THIRTY-ONE

LIKE ASPEN LEAVES

Behind Lago walked Alaia, holding a sap-filled vessel shining a green flame. She wrinkled her nose from the stench of the white smoke, holding the container away from her face. Lago didn't need the light to see by, but the others were glad for it, except for Jiara: the sickly green light made her uneasy.

"I can't believe we are walking into a dome," Lago said to no one in particular. "Just like Dravéll and Ishkembor in the *Barlum Saga*."

"Hey, I read those books in my youth," Jiara said. "Such amazing adventures the brothers had."

"Don't get him started," Alaia said, "or he won't stop yapping about them."

"You should read them sometime," he countered.

"Too unwieldy. And I prefer books about nature."

"My sister and I would act out the adventures," Jiara said. "But that oystertwat always got to play Dravéll, always had to be the one wielding the Sword of Zeiheim. By Khest, we dreamed about being the Wayfarers of the Sixteen Realms."

"Wayfarers…" Lago murmured. "I guess that's what we are now."

The wayfarers traveled in a slow procession. Not only was the passage opening at the pace of a glacier, but it was peppered with holes from where vines had retreated underground. The path was far from straight, forcing them to circle around for hundreds of strides when bumping onto the thickest, unmovable vines.

Alaia squatted to dangle her lamp inside one of the holes. She could see the vine retreating into the depths like a light-spooked snake.

Bear poked his head in and barked.

"How did they cut through rock?" Alaia asked the dog, but Bear didn't have an answer. "And where do they go to?"

"Alaia. Light," Ockam complained. Alaia lifted her lamp and ran to catch up.

"I'm totally lost," Lago said. "I can't tell where east is anymore."

"Still going the right way," Jiara said, checking her compass. "I can't believe you've been traveling this far without a compass."

"I use the sun, the moon, the stars to guide me," Lago said. "Never needed a compass before."

"It's not until the moment you need it that you regret not having it," Jiara said. "While we are trapped in this nethervoid, do you mind telling me more about this cursed mask?"

"Not now," Lago said. "I need to focus. We'll tell you about it once we make it through."

They continued in silence, except for the scraping susurrus of the shifting vines and the tumbling echoes when their movements dislodged ancient rocks. Every now and then, Ockam quietly sniffled, but he kept from weeping.

Two, maybe three, Lago thought. *No, if I count the man from Withervale, I've killed four people.* He was reliving the moments from the battle, seeing himself rabid and savage as he stabbed, clawed, and killed. *And I'm numbed to it, as if it had been someone else doing it, as if it doesn't matter. I don't want to be like this.*

"Kid, it'll be fine," Jiara said next to him. "I see it in your eyes. Find something else to think about. Focus on the vines, on what lies ahead."

"Yeah…" Lago said.

The constitution of the vines changed as they ventured deeper. Fewer holes littered the ground, and the thorns were soon replaced by fibers that tangled into a sponge-like netting, easy for Lago to push out of the way, as the hair-like filaments collapsed like a mesh onto the larger vines. The filtering fibers were soft to the touch, coated with tiny particles of dust.

The more Lago focused on his ability, the more he understood it. The vines were parting faster, letting them walk at an almost normal pace.

It took them nearly two hours to cross through the wall. Once the final vines moved obediently out of the way, they entered a perfect darkness. Their dim light showed nothing but grass at their feet, the vines closing behind them, and an enveloping void of fog everywhere else.

"We should rest now," Ockam said, carefully lowering Bonmei's wrapped body over the dew-speckled grass. "Our day was long, and yet longer our night. We'll be able to see what's around us when morning arrives."

"You go ahead," Jiara said, "I'll keep watch while you rest."

They spread their bedrolls over the soft grass and fell asleep, thoroughly exhausted.

Lago woke up next to Bear and Alaia. He glanced around but found no sign of Ockam or Jiara. It was bright out, but a clingy fog obscured anything beyond a few dozen feet.

He shook Alaia's shoulder. "Hey, where are the others?" he whispered.

She sat up and wiped her crusted eyes. "Don't know. Saw them get up a bit earlier," she said through a yawn. She stood in a stretch, then approached the wall of vines, examining it closely.

"Hey Gwoli," she called. "Did you notice the texture on these?"

Lago went to her and ran his hands over the vine. At first, he had thought the vines were covered in some sort of dry moss, but now he saw that they were different on the inside of the wall: instead of thorns, thin stems stuck out every handbreadth or so, with small capsules at the ends, like seedpods or minute flower buds. The pods were much more numerous higher up, entirely coating the vines, like a fuzzy blanket.

Lago plucked out a pod. It crumbled in his fingertips, dried out and dead.

"Do you smell that?" Alaia asked.

"Something's cooking," he murmured.

Through the fog, they followed the alluring smell of eggs, onions, and peppers. The mists didn't let them see much, other than short bushes with purple flowers and lichen-wrapped rocks that sprouted out of the dewy ground.

The transient mists parted slightly, revealing Jiara sitting by a cliffside, preparing a late breakfast. She gestured for them to join her.

"Where's Ockam?" Lago asked.

"He's praying over Bonmei's body," she answered. "Don't bother him. He needs a bit of time alone." She nodded toward the drop-off—there was nothing that way but whiteness. "It's quite humid in here, hard to see much. But just wait until those clouds part. They did so about half an hour ago, albeit briefly."

"What is it?" Alaia asked. "What's down there?"

"Patience!" Jiara barked. "Give it a moment. It'll be worth the wait."

Once the eggs were ready, Jiara passed the servings around. Before she took a bite, she helped Alaia change her bandages.

"It looks gruesome," Alaia said, staring at the open wound. She clenched her fist, and the hole seemed to blink at her.

"Don't force it," Jiara said. "You're lucky it pierced between the bones."

Alaia took a bite of her breakfast, watching Jiara rub a sticky ointment on both ends of the wound. "So, you are a chirurgeon as well as a commander?"

"We call them *physickers* in the Tribelands. But I'm no physicker, I just learned enough to be of use while at war." She wrapped the arm with a clean bandage. "Believe me, I'm better at causing wounds than tending to them." She tightened a knot, making Alaia flinch.

"She's a beast with the bow, as you've already witnessed," Ockam said, materializing from the mists. His eyes were red. He forced a smile and sat with his friends.

Jiara handed him a plate. Ockam refused with a shake of his head, then said, "This one time when we were kids, she hit a warbler from forty strides away!"

"That's awful!" Alaia cried.

"What's awful is that Ockam couldn't even pull on the bowstring with his weak arms," Jiara countered, then suspended Alaia's arm in a sling.

"Thank you," Alaia said. "But no shooting warblers, please."

"Don't plan to. Avoid rotating it. Keep it relaxed in this position. It'll take a few weeks to heal."

"I was catching Jiara up on our journey," Ockam said. "About all that happened in Withervale and the things we learned about the mask."

"Now I understand why the Negians are after it," Jiara said, glancing toward Lago. "The way you took down an entire squad, and you're only an untrained weakling."

"Hey now…" Lago said.

"Imagine what a true warrior could manage with such advantages. And that's before even considering all this shapeshifting business."

"That we still don't know much about," Ockam said. "But we were hoping to go find some answers."

"We are going to Minnelvad, aren't we?" Lago asked.

"Aye, if you'd be willing to come with. I wish I could take my son along for the journey. He always wanted to go, but we can let him rest here. This is his home, after all, and I'm sure he'd enjoy this magnificent view." As he spoke, the clouds in front of them parted.

A vast, decaying kingdom was revealed, with black rivers that fed into great lakes, and gray canyons that seemed lifeless yet sprouted sudden patches of lush forests. The landscape went on forever, interrupted only by enormous columns. Miles apart from each other the columns grew, spreading at their tops like the struts of a vaulted ceiling, where clouds were birthed from between their viny tangles. They counted thirteen columns, though they estimated there were more hidden in the distant haze. But one column stood out among the rest—almost straight east, growing from a peak at the center of the dome, stretched a column twice as wide as the others.

Slightly to their left lay an enormous segment of collapsed roof; a dozen miles in length, and nearly half a mile thick, it had left a raised outline of dirt, like a frozen wake, which oozed a dull, lifeless aura around it. Four other collapsed areas stretched far beyond sight, each underneath a corresponding hole in the dome's roof.

The light was strange, penetrating only through the giant holes above, revealing a realm awash in chiaroscuros, a solemnly shifting penumbra that crept in pillars of light and raked its warmth through the erratic expanse of the land.

Lago felt like he was inside an abandoned temple, one which held untouchable beauty despite the destruction the collapses had caused. *It's a whole universe,* he thought. *A world within a world, and we are but tiny ants within it. I wonder what it must've been like, before it fell apart.*

"I wish Crysta could see this," he said.

"Perhaps she will, here or elsewhere," Ockam said. "There are other domes than this, and who knows what might be found within them. What Bonmei described to me was much more colorful, pristine. Alive. This looks beautiful because of its scale, but most of it is dead, or dying."

"Do you think there are more Wutash in the other domes?" Lago asked him.

"All Bonmei knew about was Agnargdrolom, which is what he called this place. But I hope we'll find out more at Minnelvad—if we can locate the cousins Sontai spoke of. I'd like to know more about Bonmei's culture, the domes, and Agnargsilv itself."

Me too, Lago thought, losing himself in the vast view once more.

Ockam stood. "But if you are all done with breakfast, I could use your help now." He gestured for them to follow.

A grove of long-dead pines rotted down the hill. Together, they snapped off dry branches and carried them back up. Ockam built a bed for a pyre, short and small, by carefully interlocking the wood and filling the crevices with dry grass. He placed Bonmei's body on top of the bed, with the white sheet still covering him.

Jiara sprinkled oil over the sheet, creating a pattern of circles, like a fresh rain had just fallen on it.

Alaia gathered her courage, then timidly asked, "Is it alright if I say a prayer?"

"Why wouldn't it be?" Ockam asked.

"Because… it's an Oldrin prayer."

"We are not like most realms," Ockam said. "The Free Tribelands are free because we understand that life takes all shapes and forms, and these differences are what make us stronger. We have no race, no single culture that ties us down to one way of being. I won't deny there's still an unjust bias against your race, but Oldrin are welcome among our tribes. Any race is. Like when we took care of Bonmei, he needed not ask."

Alaia smiled. She reached into her haversack and took out the figurine of Pliwe that she had prayed to during Sontai's funeral many years ago. She placed the effigy of the contorted, tri-horned woman in front of the white sheet, kneeled, and said her prayer.

Once done, she returned to Lago's side.

Lago put an arm on her shoulder. "Did you ever find out?" he asked. "What that prayer means?"

"I did. I asked an elder who knew the old tongue. He told me the prayer said, *Let the sands of time carry your dust to the White Desert, where Sceres will shine her six colors onto you and be reflected in each grain of your soul.* It sounds prettier in Oldrin, though."

"It's very appropriate, thank you," Ockam said, nodding pensively. He walked toward his adopted son and placed his offerings underneath the wooden frame. For the forest sprites, he left a rhinoceros beetle horn. For the mountain sprites, a silver coin with one side scratched off. A fish tail bone for the water sprites. And for the sprites of snow and endless night skies, a wickless stub of a nearly exhausted candle. With his offerings in place, Ockam opened his notebook and from it took the leaves of aspen he had collected two days before. He placed them over the sheet, one at a time.

He lit the pyre.

As the flames rose, he took out his kalimba and played that haunting melody once more. The heat lifted the leaves, making them dance in a warm current, waving, shimmering gold and shimmering green as they flew away in the wind. Ockam was too choked up to sing, so he played and played, but both Lago and Alaia could not help but hear words repeated over and over in their minds:

Like aspen leaves, like aspen leaves.

CHAPTER THIRTY-TWO

RED LAURELS

General Alvis Hallow returned to the Negian capital, accompanied by Consul Hanno Uzenzo. Once at the fortress of Hestfell, they hastened toward the throne room, following the marble bridge that crossed above the luxuriant gardens of the Laurus Palace. Dark-blue banners waved before the palace's great doors, emblazoned with red laurels—the sigil of the Negian Empire.

A slender man waited midway across the bridge, casually leaning between two spiraling pillars. He turned, peeked over his thin spectacles, and hurried to shake the general's arm.

"Everything has been arranged," the man said, scratching his perfectly trimmed, dark beard. He eyed the consul. "And I don't believe we've met."

"You must be Artificer Urcai, a pleasure," Consul Uzenzo said, shaking arms. "General Hallow has spoken at length about you. I am Consul Uzenzo."

"From Withervale, yes," Urcai said. "I'm very grateful for your aid with the general's escape."

"Urcai, have any new heralds reached you?" Hallow asked.

"We received one last message from Chief Daro. They were at the Thornridge Lookout, readying to strike. The boy, the spur, and the Free Tribesman were still together."

"And?"

"And we know nothing else. It's been several days."

General Hallow leaned over the balustrade, tightening his grip on the hand-rail. "Was the mask with them?" he secretively asked, paying attention to the guards who patrolled the bridge.

"Fjorna did not know at the time their last magpie was sent," Urcai said, equally careful with how far he projected his shrill voice, "but she suspected the boy carried the mask. She mentioned the lookout was not properly se-cured—few sylvan guards, not enough to offer resistance to her squad."

"Then why have we not heard from her yet?"

"Unfortunately, we have to assume the worst. We might've lost it, again."

The general spat into the gardens below, where important dignitaries were prattling about trade and taxes and other nonsense he cared nothing about. His face reddened, but he took a deep breath and straightened up.

"Not a word of this to the emperor," he said to the artificer and the consul.

"But Lorr," Consul Uzenzo began, "if we are to ask for further—"

"Not a word," he repeated. "*I* will deal with this matter."

Each marble column at the long hall of the Laurus Palace was decorated with red wreaths. At the end of the hall stood two colossal statues of black stone. To the left was the Demiurge, Takhísh, holding the Shield of Creation; to the right was his twin brother, Takhamún, the Unmaker, holding the Spear of Undoing.

The Negian Empire, like the Zovarians, also subscribed to the Doctrine of Takh, although in their version of the Codex it was written that Takhísh had saved only one spark of divinity, not two pairs twice doubled, and instead of granting divinity to the sixteen Arch Sedecims of Zovaria, he had granted it to the first emperor of the Negian Empire. That made only the emperor and his successors divine in nature, and so the Empire justified their conquests and granted ultimate authority to the holy bloodline.

Takhísh and Takhamún looked impassive in their blackness. At their feet was a throne of white marble encrusted with veins of crimson rhodonite crys-tals. Slouching on the throne, Emperor Uvon dus Grei felt his precious heartbeats pass.

After his father had departed to the Six Gates of Felsvad, Uvon continued and concluded the work of breaching the Heartpine Dome. Beguiled by the advice of his inquisitor, he came to believe that one of the emanations of Ta-khamún had bred the corrupt tribe within. He was certain that the Wutash were of a lesser kind, one that only worshipped death and the flames of the nethervoids.

Uvon was young, in his mid-twenties. His light-brown hair was circled by red laurels, cut and embossed from a magnium and platinum alloy, with sharp sparkles of diminutive rubies. He was an arrogant youth, nothing like Emperor Grei dus Gauno, who had ruled mightily for fifty years and had brought the Negian Empire back from the ashes of the third Bayanhong War.

Before General Hallow reached the steps to the throne, the young emperor spoke. "I expect you have good news," he said, though he already knew the news was not good. His inquisitor and his political advisor, both standing to the sides of the throne, had already informed him of the failure at Withervale.

Hallow, Urcai, and Uzenzo kneeled down. As a sign of respect, General Hallow covered the ranking insignia tattooed over his left ear, then addressed the emperor. "Your Imperial Majesty, as you must surely have heard, the whereabouts of the Heartpine mask was discovered. Unfortunately—"

"Unfortunately, you brought back nothing," Uvon said, leaning heavily on a tired elbow.

"Correct, Your Majesty. But we have leads. A squad is following the subjects we suspect have the mask in their possession, while heralds are tracking them."

"And is there a reason why *you* aren't the one following this trail?" Uvon asked, fumbling with his red laurels, which kept sliding too far down on his small head.

"The mission required speed, and our specialist squad can move much faster than my heavy infantry. They are at the heels of the fugitives."

The emperor scraped his front teeth with his manicured nails, pushing an unpleasant underbite forward. "Is there another reason you came by today, General, other than to waste my time?"

"I have other news, from Anglass."

The emperor waved a dainty hand both dismissively and as a way to tell him to hurry.

"Artificer Urcai, would you mind covering the details?" Hallow asked.

Urcai stood, took a step forward, and kneeled back down.

"Your Imperial Majesty, we have found means of entry into the Anglass Dome, digging in a new sector. It is in a substrate that does not incur into flooding. Yet the hardness of the rock means we'll require additional slaves, as well as ingredients to mix sapfire."

"Sapfire? Why would you need sapfire?" the emperor snapped.

"I have found it weakens the rocks. In the long run, the sapfire will hasten our progress sixfold and reduce the total amount of slaves needed. I will provide the numbers to your artificers for confirmation, but the calculations are sound. We have plenty of sulphur from Brimstowne, but the other ingredients need to be purchased in quantities as great as the supply given to our Wyrmwash fleet."

"So, you've come to ask for slaves, and those… special ingredients."

"Yes, Your Majesty," General Hallow answered.

"What about your bloodskins? Your spurs?"

"The bloodskins are nearly all dead. And the supply of spurs is dwindling after all the floods."

The emperor whispered something to his political advisor, then sent him off.

"And how long will this new route take? Knowing that your previous errors have already stretched for years, with no success to show for them."

"Two to six months," Alvis answered. "Even in the direst conditions, we'll keep digging. The shaft already extends quite far beneath the roots. It's only a matter of time, but the more resources we get, the faster we'll breach the dome."

Uvon sneered. "I'll ask my advisors to confirm Artificer Urcai's numbers and determine how much of what you are requesting may be granted to you. This is your last chance, Alvis. You have six months, not a day more. I want those heathens, those hoarders, those worshippers of Takhamún's emanations to be taken out of their profane domes and killed. And I want their dark idols, those demonic countenances that mock my divinity, destroyed."

"So has the divine heir spoken," the inquisitor chanted.

"So he has," the general said. "May Takhísh's Shield guard you, Emperor Uvon, son of Grei, who was son of Gauno." He got up on his feet and walked away.

Alvis Hallow stormed out of the palace, eager to leave the presence of the spoiled monarch.

The consul hurried to match his pace, seeming pleased. "That was a most gracious offer, the emperor is kind and wise to—"

"He's a fucking tool," Alvis interrupted. "A puppet to his advisors, a believer of antiquated myths that only help that pandering inquisitor. He's a weak and useless infant who doesn't deserve his father's throne."

"But he's granting you the slaves you seek."

"Not as many as we asked for. And he wants to destroy the masks. He's so blinded by the doctrine that he doesn't see the power in the old relics."

"It'd be blasphemous to think that the—"

"It'd be wise of you to shut your damn mouth about this."

"I would take this as a win, General Hallow," Artificer Urcai said, making the general slow his pace.

"A win? We got shorthanded, how can—"

"The emperor's advisors know nothing of sapfire, of the strength of rocks, of how to administer slave forces. What they offered us in the end was exactly what we needed, no more, no less. I was hoping they'd give us this much. That is why I asked for so much more."

"I should've guessed as much, Urcai," the general replied. "I should've seen through your machinations."

Alvis Hallow let a furtive smile taint his face, but he quickly extinguished it and kept on walking.

CHAPTER THIRTY-THREE

INTO THE DOME

Bonmei's pyre lingered only as the scent of pine smoke in the air.

At the peak of noon, when the mists were abated by the pillars of sunlight streaking through the dome, they gathered at an escarpment with a clear view of the expansive lands. Ockam used a stick of charcoal to draw as big a circle on the ground as he could. He fidgeted with his thin mustache as he pondered over his drawing, smearing charcoal on his cheeks.

He sketched a small circle at the center of the larger one. "The thicker column that grows from that central mountain is the one Bonmei called the 'trunk,' and the mountain's name is Stelm Bir, which means *Home Mountain*. That's where the destroyed temple must be, where we might be able to find out more about the mask."

"With the dome's diameter being eighty miles," Jiara said, "that would be forty miles to the trunk on a raven's wing. Significantly more for us, having to make our path through collapsed vines, unknown landscapes, and changes in elevation."

Lago looked at the central trunk through his binoculars. "It's so big," he said, "it must be a mile wide."

"Nice toy, give me that," Jiara said, taking the binoculars from him. "I'm more worried about Negian troops. We have no clue whether there are any still inside."

"Aye, we must be on guard," Ockam said. He studied the angles at which the sunbeams fell, estimating the direction of each feature. He could read light and shadow as well as Lago could read the stars, or Alaia could read the sounds of a cavern, or Jiara could read her compass and maps.

Ockam placed his charcoal stick on the western edge of the circle. "We are here, by the lookout, at the edge of the Flasketh Mesa, which this escarpment seems to be a part of." He pointed north. "And there you can see Knife Point cutting into the dome. Farjall is southeast, just about here on the map." He made a mark, then he stood and pointed in the direction the Farjall fortress should be. "Past those columns, that's where the Negians would've come through."

Jiara spied through the glass. "That whole area is buried under a collapsed roof," she said. "I remember that earthquake. It was after that shake that the Free Tribesfolk noticed a segment of the dome missing."

"That must've crushed them to bits," Lago said. "Imagine the weight of that, like a mountain falling from the sky."

Ockam drew circles to represent all the visible vine columns, to act as the primary reference points. Then he added the two big lakes, the rivers, canyons, and mountains, and lastly the visible segments of collapsed roof, which took out a large swath of land. He was able to draw a relatively accurate map of the nearest half of the dome's enormous circle, while the farther side was left blank, as it was lost in the haze, or below the horizon. After he gathered his friends' additions and corrections, he traced a path that could lead them to the central mountain.

"From the top of Stelm Bir we should be able to see the rest," he said. "Ideally, we should exit the dome to the northeast, into the Kingroot Woods, and from there we can head north on Via Lamanni."

"How long will it take us to get across the dome?" Lago asked.

"I'd say three weeks," Jiara estimated, "if we don't encounter major difficulties. But with no one following us, we are in no hurry. As long as we can find food, we should be fine, and I can spot several patches of forest along our path."

Ockam diligently copied the map to his notebook, adding a few remarks for estimated miles and travel time. He closed the notebook and picked up his bag. "Let's go see what this forsaken realm is keeping from us," he said.

As they neared the bottom of the escarpment, the full strangeness of the dome became evident. They could only recognize about half of the living species they found, while everything else was new and exotic. An air of imbalance was manifest: ponds lay stagnant and lifeless near perfectly lively streams, and while most forests were dried up and dead, the surviving groves blossomed with whimsical flowers and swarms of bizarre insects. It was a sterile land punctuated by frequent, lavish oases.

Despite the decay, birds were doing just fine, presumably because they could easily fly from one green spot to the next. Alaia was ecstatic; she would not let Lago have his binoculars back. She spotted hornbills, warblers, slantwings, spritewrens, gushmaids, buntings, yifftails, cuckoos, rumpknives, and many more birds she could not name.

They stopped to fish at a creek, where they spotted strange shrews with thin snouts and beaver-like tails, who were quick to swim away when the wayfarers got too close. They chose to call them *ottermoles*. Jiara caught a few graylings and wipers—or at least something that reminded her of those types of fish—that provided scarce meat for the effort it took to catch, scale, and clean them.

"I'll do the seasoning," Jiara said, snatching a cleaned fish from Ockam's hands. "You set the fire."

"I've been wanting to ask something," Lago said, staring at Ockam, "but I don't know how..."

"Just belt it out, it's the best way, usually," Ockam said.

"Well... We used Agnargsilv to get in here, but I don't know if you'd feel comfortable with me wearing it again, after all that's happened."

Ockam blew on the kindling, then locked eyes with Lago. "Boy, as far as I'm concerned, there is no longer an heir to the mask. You fulfilled your promise, and by chance or fate the mask ended up back in your hands. As long as you are careful, it'll be your choice how or when to use it, not mine. And I'm sure Bonmei would agree, if his spirit could speak to us from beyond the Sixth Gate."

Lago's shoulders relaxed. He felt an alluring attachment to the mask, a pull asking him to wear it again, as if there were more secrets it wanted to share with him.

"I'd like to see how this place compares to the Farsulf Forest," Lago said. "Besides, there's not much to eat or hunt—the mask could help us again."

"See what you can find."

Jiara had not had a chance to properly admire the mask or see it function yet, so she tagged along. Lago put Agnargsilv on like it was the most natural thing in the world, feeling comforted by it. It wasn't only pain that the mask shared, but joy, fear, hunger, lust, disgust, love, and every other emotion the living beings around him felt; yet pain was somehow more essential and surfaced in a way that made itself more prominent. Lago's understanding of the mask was still thin, but his control over the pain now felt utterly natural, and the shared emotion no longer tormented him.

He explained to Jiara that the living creatures inside the dome all had a different 'flavor' than the ones outside, connecting to each other with stronger threads, while the tapestry overall felt thinner. He noticed Bear sniffing the ground, which led him to an ottermole's den. Their underground nests tunneled to air on one side and to the creek on the other. He could sense the fear of the little creatures. Underground he also spotted deer mice and gophers, and hiding behind a dry bush he saw a mangy raccoon dog scavenging on a lump of bones. He became aware that most larger mammals were entirely absent.

Jiara stared intently. Her eyes narrowed. "Are you wearing a woman's cloak?" she asked.

"It's all the merchants had available," Lago offered as an excuse.

"Not judging, kid, whatever suits your fancy."

"Hey, Lago," Alaia called. "I don't know this kind." She plucked a miniature grove of mushrooms from a rotten log. "Can you see if they are poisonous? Like the monks do?"

Lago approached. "I can't," he said. "I see the threads, and I can help you find more, but I can't interpret them like the monks can. Khopto said it took him decades to understand the meanings in the threads, and even then, it wasn't always accurate. I think what he saw is similar to what I can see."

"Safer to throw them mushrooms away," Jiara said, brows raised.

"But they look so delicious..." Alaia tossed the mushrooms behind the log. "The monks must've used quite a lot of soot over the years, to learn all that they learned."

Lago paused, suddenly remembering something. He walked back to get his bag and dug through it, tossing out his clothes, his equipment, his food, all of it.

"What's gotten into you now?" Alaia asked.

"The day we left Withervale... So much happened that day that I completely forgot."

"Forgot what?"

And then he found it, the tiny bottle of soot that Khopto had given him. He had tossed it into his bag when Gwil stepped into the room, and it was so small that it had stayed there unnoticed this whole time.

"Khopto gave me this," he said.

"Is that soot?" Alaia snapped. "You told me you weren't doing those drugs. I swear I'll beat your teeth off—"

"I'm not! He gave it to me as a present. I've never used it."

"Soot? That drug sells for a fortune!" Jiara said, taking the minuscule bottle from Lago's hands. "If this is aetheric carbon from Withervale, it carries a hefty price tag. Who is this Khopto?"

Although bound to secrecy in such matters, Lago explained how the Havengall monks secretly traded in soot and used the substance to study the same threads he was able to sense with Agnargsilv.

"I always thought those monks looked like devotees of more than just nature," Jiara said. "No offense, I see you still wear their bracelet."

"None taken," Lago said, making a conscious effort to not hide the bracelet. "I'm not one of them, but they are a sort of family to me. I wish I had known more about the mask while I was still in Withervale. There are so many things in common between what Agnargsilv shows me and what Khopto could see with soot."

He paused for a moment, seeming sadder and distant.

"I miss them," he continued. "I feel so guilty about what happened. I didn't even have time to explain, they must be angry and confused. And Crysta too, she must be so worried. I wish we could go see her."

"We will," Alaia said, "and we'll give her the greatest report on the Heartpine Dome she could ever have hoped for. No way she'll stay mad at you after that."

As Lago was about to stow the bottle of soot away, he looked closer. And even closer, bringing the bottle right over the black muzzle of the mask, having to cross his eyes to keep it in focus.

"Something seems strange," he said. He shook the bottle, spreading the particles a bit more. "It's by such a small amount, but the threads somehow bend toward the soot particles. It's like they are attracted to them, as if to a magnet." He moved his fingers around, directing invisible forces that only he could sense. "It looks… It looks like when I see myself wearing the mask, how all the strings bend back toward me. It's the same with these particles, but much more subtle and chaotic. I nearly didn't notice."

Lago stared at the particles for a while longer, trying to force his mind to make as many connections as the ones he could visualize in front of him.

"What do you plan to do with the bottle?" Jiara asked him.

"I don't know. I feel it'd be a waste to use it if it's so valuable."

Jiara smirked. "Kid, if you ever need a place to hide it, I have a nostril willing to help."

"By Teslur's sacred web, Jiara," Ockam said, "I thought those days were far behind you."

"Hey, just because you stopped going to those parties it doesn't mean I stopped too."

They traveled far that day, but not to the point of exhaustion, wanting to save energy for conversation and enjoyment once they found a comfortable place to rest. Due to the limited reach of Sunnokh's light, night in the Heartpine Dome fell sooner. Before it got too dark, they bathed in one of the healthy creeks, avoiding another one that had sickly, oily reflections on the surface.

Lago kept the mask on, as well as his underwear, not comfortable being naked in front of Ockam or Jiara, who were chattering on the opposite side of the creek.

"I guess she can't drown with those buoys," Alaia quietly joked.

Jiara was unmaking her braid, soaking the light hairs into the clean water while her ample breasts bobbed up and down. She was being playful with Ockam; chatting, flirting? Lago could not tell. Perhaps she was merely trying to pull Ockam away from his crestfallen mood, but the man was too deep in his own thoughts to notice; he swam to the shore and began to dry himself.

"Have you asked him about them?" Lago said to Alaia, looking at Ockam's scar-covered body.

"About Jiara's tits?"

"No, you nubhead, about his scars."

"Oh. I did a few nights back. He didn't say much. Apparently, he was tortured during the Barujan War, I guess before we were even born. That's way too many cuts for one body."

She reached back with both hands to wash her thirteen sisters, the ridge of bone spurs that protruded from her spine. Lago watched her, head half-submerged, as if it was only the dark mask floating in the water. He'd been told the spurs were not painful to the Oldrin, but they still looked painful to him, perhaps as painful as Ockam's scars seemed, but now that he saw them through the mask's sight, he knew for certain that they were not a discomfort at all.

They lit a bonfire and huddled close.

Lago stayed up to watch the fire after everyone else had gone to sleep. Sparks floated up in spirals of unintended beauty. With his eyes open, he found the fire blinding, pervasive, dimming everything else around him; but if he closed his eyes and looked only through Agnargsilv, the fire was the opposite, an absolute absence of threads and feelings, like dark netherflames, a perfect vacuum at the core of his perception.

Through the invisible void of flames, in the distance, Lago sensed something move. An animal. He stood and opened his eyes. Silhouetted against the blueish haze was a red fox. She was malnourished, skittish, and feeble looking, emanating an air of sadness. But Agnargsilv showed him something else: the red fox gave off a strange sort of glow, like the synesthetic indigo Lago saw when focusing his attention on the mask. The aura was nearly imperceptible, however, like the dark blues that are only glimpsed when one does not look directly at them.

Lago felt pity for her—she was a female fox, the mask told him—and tossed some scraps of grilled fish in her direction. The fox snuck forward distrustfully, grabbed the fish, then disappeared into the dry grass. Lago began to think that the blue aura had been but a trick of his imagination, of his tired senses.

For several more days they journeyed through the dying lands, hopping from one green oasis to the next. With no threats to worry about, Lago continued wearing Agnargsilv most of the time. His friends did not even seem to notice the difference between him wearing the mask or not, as if it had been a part of him all along, a part he did not have to hide any longer. Yet something still bothered him.

It's not my mask, he thought while caressing the muzzle in front of him—it was hard and foreign, despite it fitting so well on his face. *It was never my mask, it was Bonmei's. But he's gone now, and I chose to bear it. I promised Sontai I would keep it safe, but it still feels—*

"What's wrong, Gwoli?" Alaia asked.

Lago slowed his pace.

"You're doing that thing where you squint as if you're arguing with yourself," she added.

"It's nothing. Just... I'm a bit hungry."

Ockam marched beside them, eyeing Lago without saying a word.

They stopped for lunch in the middle of a forest of scarlet oaks. Half the trees were dead, eaten to shreds by some sort of burrowing beetle, but the other half stood green and lush. It was still only late Harvestlight, so the oaks were not yet a glorious scarlet, but green leaves were a refreshing break from all the gray dullness they had walked through that day.

Ockam closed his eyes and leaned on a tree, with his short-brimmed hat slid over his forehead. Jiara was telling Alaia about her training in the Tribelands, about mountains she had climbed far away. Bear was chasing ottermoles by the creek.

Lago felt relaxed, for a change. He placed the mask next to him, then pulled out a drawstring pouch of dark leather from which he took out his box of fingernail lacquers. He diluted a smidge of paste with the solvent, then painted his nails with methodical care, with not a worry clouding his mind. He chose green this time.

Ockam's nose twitched. He pinched the tapered crown of his hat, lifted it slightly, and opened one questioning eye.

"What is it you are doing?"

"Lacquering my nails," Lago replied. "Why, is it weird?"

"Aye. But no weirder than any of the things I've seen lately."

Lago half-shrugged.

"Never seen men do it though," Ockam added, "other than among the Khaar Du, who paint them black or red—only the lorrkin use women's colors. What's it for?"

"Nothing in particular, I just like doing it. It's something I've done since I was young, at least when no one was watching. Other kids didn't approve, of course."

"I can see what you mean. Bonmei went through something like it. Tattoos are for women, not men, and he had plenty of them! Imagine the faces of the other boys when they saw him."

"You should've seen Sontai's tattoos. When I met her, I thought she was wearing skin-tight lace."

Ockam chuckled. "Did you get those lacquers from Jiara?" he asked. "I haven't seen her paint her nails since we were teenagers."

"No, I brought them from Withervale. It was one of the few things that were in my bag when we escaped."

"What do you mean? Those solvents are flammable! We could've used them in the caverns!"

"Well… They wouldn't have helped in the end, would they?"

"But we didn't know that!" Ockam said, hurling a mossy rock at Lago and barely missing.

"We could've burned your kalimba, too. Good wood. And your notebook."

"Aye, good point, boy," he said, lowering his hat again. "Good point."

"These hills are as barren as the Charred Wastes of Fel Ukhagar," Jiara said with a scowl.

They were nearing one of the collapsed roofs. During the last few miles, they had been walking up and down smooth hills—the wakes that the crashing vines had left behind. The roof had plunged like a meteor, making the earth compress and ripple out as if it was a liquid, and then freeze, leaving a giant crater that wasn't round, but followed the irregularly shaped edges of the vines.

No life dared grow upon these hills. The soil was gray and rubbery, hardened with a crust that cracked like a sugary dessert.

"It must be the sap," Alaia said, leaving crackled footprints that disappeared as the stretchy film slowly fused back together. "Imagine how much sap must've dripped when the vines tore apart. It would've been like a white waterfall plunging from the sky."

"It does harden like rubber if you leave it inside lamps without burning," Jiara said, "and after a few years it turns into a yellowish crystal." She looked up. "Winds could've carried the sap for miles if it fell from that height. Could be what killed a lot of the forests."

"That and the limited sunlight," Ockam added.

"How did they get any sunlight before the roof collapsed?" Jiara asked him.

"Not sunlight, no, but something else. The dome was bright, somehow. Bonmei said the sky was a soft-colored white, like a pearl, but never blue."

"Like Sceres during her Pearl season," Lago observed.

"Perhaps, though they had no moon nor stars to compare to. It's those obvious things we take for granted that he was most stricken by once he saw the outside world. The moon, the stars, the sun, the sky—all pure magic to him."

"Crysta always thought that the insides of the domes were bright," Lago said, "and that wisps were a way to glance into them."

"I've seen one up close," Jiara said, "before this dome stopped having wisps and began its collapse. We used to camp atop Knife Point for weeks, training to handle ropes and ice. During a foggy night, this crack on the vines shot out a beam of light, as if opening a portal to Felsvad. I wanted to see what was inside, but only saw a diffused glow and tangled vines."

"Crysta would've killed to get a look at a wisp from that close," Lago said. "It's weird. After Heartpine began to crack open, she kept on with her studies, but it all seems rather pointless now."

They reached the bottom of the crater hill, where a mountain of dead vines lingered in decaying tendrils. The mass was enormous, forming a thicket of thorns and congealed sap that reached a thousand feet into the sky and perhaps a thousand more below ground. Like the unholy intestines of a fallen titan, the vines rotted slowly, solidifying in their own sap.

"They are all dead," Lago said, wiping a layer of white, mud-like crust from a vine. "I can't see their threads, yet they do shimmer in an odd way."

Ockam poked at a dead vine with his knife. A bit of sap bulged out without dripping, thickened and yellowed. The next vine he poked shattered like a crystal, entirely dried up.

"This collapse is already a year old," Jiara informed them. "The newest is the one by Knife Point, north of us."

"That one must still have a lake of liquid sap around it," Lago guessed.

"Let's not try to find out," Ockam said. "We keep heading east now. The edge of this crater should take us to the canyon we saw from up high."

They climbed back onto the rubbery hill and followed its sticky ridgeline toward the ever-present trunk that rose from Stelm Bir.

"The Great Spider bless us eightfold," Ockam said. "Are those bones?"

Ahead of them, the hips and ribcage of a gigantic creature stuck out from the lifeless ground. The bones were no longer white, but gray-streaked black, as if tar had covered them and the Void of Khest had sucked the light out of them.

"Poor thing," Alaia said, "probably died crawling away from the sap."

Lago crouched and walked between the cage of blackened ribs. "It's enormous," he said.

"Over there!" Alaia called out. "There's another one!"

The second skeleton had the skull partially exposed.

"Dire wolf," Jiara said, "look at those fangs."

The numerous teeth grinned at a macabre and eternal joke. The eye sockets—deep as caverns—retained only the memory of forgetfulness.

It must've been such a horrible death, Lago thought. He placed a hand over the brow of the beast. It was sticky, but he did not care.

The darkened skull reminded him of the mask he himself was wearing, making him suddenly aware of its presence. He thought he'd be able to visualize something through the mask, given he was in the presence of an ancient and noble creature of a countenance not unlike his own. He thought he would grasp a special connection, a bond that united the mask and the fallen canid. But there was nothing there—dead bones were dead, and the mask only saw that which was alive.

"Do you think…" Lago asked, a tad embarrassed. "Do you think you could help me pull one of its fangs out?"

"Whatever for?" Ockam questioned.

"I'd like to keep it. I don't know why, it's like finding an ancient fossil, a keepsake from this decaying land and all that was lost in here."

Ockam shrugged. "It'll be much bigger than it looks, the roots are longer than the exposed end."

"Even better. So, will you help me?"

Ockam swung his hatchet to carve a seam in the maxilla, but it simply bounced off. "This bone is hard as Graalman steel!" he observed.

"Same as the dire wolf in Withervale," Lago said. "Back then, I helped the Havengall vicar collect samples, but he couldn't pull a tooth out."

"Let me try," Jiara said, taking Ockam's hatchet. She swung it right into a natural bone suture, lodging the hatchet in. She used a giant metacarpal to slam the hatchet deeper, until the maxilla pried open, and the fang began to rattle.

"These beasts must've been tough," she said. "Ockam, give me a hand."

She wrapped the fang with a cloth, which clung easily to the sap and served to yank it out after a few heavy pulls. Roots and all, the canine tooth was about a foot long, half ivory-white, half blackened by sap. Lago wrapped it in the cloth and stowed it in his bag.

As they walked away from the skeleton, Lago felt a sudden tightness in his stomach. He turned around. Behind them was a wolf. Not a dire wolf, but a slinky maned wolf, scrawny and miserable-looking, like a skeleton on stilts, keeping her dark head down between her rust-colored shoulders.

Jiara reached for her bow, but Lago stopped her.

"Don't. I know her," he said. "I've seen her before, she's been following us. She was a fox, that was her."

The maned wolf felt too many eyes on her and scurried away behind the dire wolf's skull.

"I can see her aura," Lago said. "It's so pallid, yet blue…" He gestured for them to follow behind him. As they neared the skull, a tiny fennec fox jumped out and ran down the hill, dragging her massive ears behind her. There was no maned wolf.

Bear whined, looking bewildered.

"That was her," Alaia said with a too-wide grin. "That was the Nu'irg!"

"I'm so confused," Jiara said.

Ockam chewed on his cheeks. "If that's the Nu'irg, it's a bit of a disappointment," he said. "Each of the free tribes has legends about these spirits. It didn't look as magical as any of the stories I heard—it just looked hungry and sad."

"She," Lago corrected.

"Well, now this Nu'irg is following us," Jiara said. "Do you think she wants food?"

"She does look hungry," Lago said, "but I think it is the mask she's following, she must have some connection to it. I've only seen her in canine forms."

"Canid forms," Alaia corrected.

"That's what I said."

"No, you said canine. Foxes are vulpines, dogs and wolves are canines. Canids encompasses them all."

"You've been reading too many of Hefra's books," Lago complained.

Alaia shrugged.

CHAPTER THIRTY-FOUR

STELM BIR

The sap-covered ridgeline led to an eroded canyon of hard-packed sand, where the few traces of human influence had been mostly covered up by dust and vegetation.

Food was scarce, but with the help of the mask, their hunting was adequate enough. Lago still felt uncomfortable participating in the killings, but he learned to never again put his mind in direct connection with that of the animals being slaughtered.

The elusive shadow of the Nu'irg followed at the top rim of the canyon, always at the edge of their vision. She would take different forms each time, from a marbled wild dog to a sharp-jawed jackal, to a white greyhound, to a rusty dhole. Lago left scraps of food for her whenever possible, but the canid spirit kept her distance.

The long journey gave Lago ample time to reconcile his feelings; about Bonmei, about the responsibilities he'd inherited by choosing to wield the mask. *His* mask, for it felt now more like a part of himself, inseparable, essential. He kept thinking about Bonmei's stories, how the boy's mother and grandmother had used the mask to shapeshift into foxes. Without admitting it to his friends, he tried to find a way to shapeshift as well. He pictured himself as a creature with the shape of a man but with the head, tail, and sometimes paws of a fox. He imagined how it would feel to have fur all over his body, but despite his efforts, not a single additional hair grew on his skin. Sometimes he tried the same with the image of a wolf, a coyote, or even a dog much like

Bear. But that was not what Sontai and Mawua had done, so he always returned to the fox.

Their hike through the canyon ended at an expansive prairie which extended all the way to Stelm Bir, the central mountain under the dome's trunk. Scattered signs of habitation littered the grassy fields, including ancient rock walls, implements for farming and logging, and ramshackle remains of dwellings that collapsed or burned long ago.

"We should take a brief detour to explore that monster," Jiara said, referring to one of the gargantuan supporting columns. As they had suspected, the structure was formed out of the same vines as the rest of the dome, only sturdier. They estimated the column was about two thousand feet wide, massive enough to seem like a mountain when they stood close to it.

"It's enormous," Lago said. "And the one on top of the mountain is even larger. I can't imagine the scale of it now, standing next to this one. I can't picture anything bigger."

While circling the tangle of vertical vines, they encountered a warehouse-like building attached to the base of it. They followed its shallow curve, looking for an entrance, and found that the building stretched on for so long that it wrapped around an entire quarter of the column's circumference.

"What was this place?" Lago asked, pushing away toppled wooden supports. The ceiling had partially collapsed, and most of the walls had caved in, but they found a way into the ruins. The architecture was curvilinear and disjointed, unlike any construction they had yet seen.

"An earthquake must've torn this place apart," Jiara said, examining cracks in the walls.

"It reeks… like dried sap," Alaia said.

Enormous containers gaped open; one of them was broken from where a stone turret had collapsed upon it. From a wide crack, a cascade of white sap had long ago spilled, crystallizing into a sticky pool of dusty yellows.

"They must be silos," Jiara conjectured, crouching down to scratch at the dried sap, then smelling her nails. "They were collecting the sap. What for?"

The length of the building followed the same pattern, with silos upon broken silos, some spilled or empty, some still filled with drying sap. Finding more questions than answers, they journeyed on, leaving the silos behind.

After a few more days of walking, they reached the base of Stelm Bir. The grassland around the mountain was an old battlefield, where human skeletons hid repentantly among the tall grasses. They found abandoned kite shields emblazoned with red laurels, distinctively sharp Negian bracers, and rusty helms with dented crowns. From the Wutash army, all that remained were splintered spears with obsidian tips and tattered clothes. The dried carcasses of dire wolves rotted nearby, ribs opened to the sky like the hulls of ancient shipwrecks.

"This was a massacre," Jiara said. "A lot more Wutash skeletons. Very few are Negian here."

"Look, there are roads going up the mountain," Ockam pointed out.

The Wutash had cut wide, convenient roads to the top of the mountain, which were already overgrown with weeds. They chose the widest road and headed up to get a better view of the battlefield. The outcrops were littered with sacked Wutash buildings, stones only partially standing.

Ockam cleared his throat. "Everyone, very discreetly, follow me back here for a moment." He stepped behind a half-collapsed wall. "Lago, your binoculars, now. Stay hidden, stay quiet." He hurried him with a hand gesture.

Through a hole that might've once been a window, Ockam used the binoculars to peek down the path. "There!" he said. "We are being followed. Stay behind this wall. And Lago, put the mask away at once."

Lago obeyed without questioning.

"It's just one man, I can't spot any others," Ockam said. "Seems to be wearing rather standard clothes, what you'd see out by a settlement, no armor."

"Negian soldier?" Jiara asked.

"Soldier, servant, miner, could be anything. But definitely not Wutash."

"What should we do?" Alaia asked.

"If it's just him, I say we approach him. There should be nothing to fear if it's four—plus a dog—against one. He's probably a lot more scared of us than we are of him. Let's wait until he gets closer."

The man snuck up, hiding in tall grass, behind bushes, behind rocks, unaware that he was being watched.

"He's got a spear and a bow. Let's be careful," Ockam said. "He seems to be east Loorian, perhaps from Bergsulf, or from the Princedom, likely recruited in the Ash Sea. Light hair, tall, but I've never seen such a scrawny Bergsulfi before. Poor fucker, I bet he didn't expect this when he signed up. I'm going out to greet him. Don't mention the mask or how we got here."

Once the stranger was about a hundred feet away, Ockam stepped out right in the middle of the road. "Moon lights!" he barked.

The stranger jumped face-first into the grass. It was a terrible place to take cover, but the best he could do other than jumping straight off the cliff.

"It's okay," Ockam said in an effort to placate him, "we are not going to harm you. You've been following us, and we want to know why. Do you speak Common? Miscamish? Falbagrish perhaps?"

A timid head poked out the grass. "Y-yes, I speak Comm-mon. You aren't Negian or Wutash, where did you come from?"

"I'm a Free Tribesman, my name is Ockam." He signaled for the others to come out. "And these here are my friends, Jiara, Alaia, Lago, and Bear. Get up, we won't hurt you, we are as curious as you are. What's your name?"

"I'm... My name is Baldo," he said, clumsily leaving his hiding spot.

"For how long have you been following us, Baldo?"

"Just now, I saw you climbing up the road and thought you were antelope or elk, we don't see them in these areas no more. But then I got closer and saw you were something even rarer."

Ockam relaxed his shoulders, figuring that from a distance Baldo should not have been able to see Lago wearing the mask.

"If you promise not to hunt us, we promise to reciprocate," Ockam said. "Not that there would be much in it for us either way. Forgive my manners, but you seem more like dry jerky than meat."

"I'm starving, Lorr. Is there anything you could share?"

They shared some of their food. Baldo ate swiftly, as if the meats and nuts could suddenly run away to never return. Ockam offered him a sip of water from his canteen, then they continued their chat. "How many more of you are there?" Ockam asked. "How many Negian soldiers, or Wutash?"

"Haven't seen a bloodskin in a long time, they might all be dead as far as I know. There's a dozen or so Negians in my camp now, and there are always small groups spread around, but they don't last long alone. We've been lucky, so far." Baldo's eyes glazed over. Then, with sudden focus, he continued, "Other than that, there are two colonies. Fauborough in the far southwest, of maybe a few hundred, and one up north near Knife Point who call themselves the Watford Colony, of about eight hundred or so. Not good places to be, too many mouths to feed, too many people who are starving for food, and for power. How did you get here? We never saw Free Tribesfolk inside, and our Oldrin slaves have all died off."

Ockam stopped Alaia before she turned her glare into something more.

"I will have to keep that information private for now," Ockam said, "as I can't make any excuses that you will believe, and I'd prefer not to lie to you. But let's say we are new here, and—"

"So, you found a way in? A way out?"

"Maybe. But first and foremost, we are looking for answers."

"What sort of answers?"

"For starters, how long have you been here? Why haven't you gone back to Farjall?"

"Well, the latter should be obvious—the mines were crushed years ago," Baldo said, pointing toward the southeast. "And as to how long I've been here? Since the very beginning. I came in with the First Legion, under General Edmar Helm. I guess it's been six? Seven years?"

"What were the Negians doing inside this dome?" Jiara asked. "Why kill all the Wutash?"

"Excuse me, Lurr, you seem like fine folk, but I'm still sworn to secrecy regarding my orders with the army."

"Why would you give a shit?" she said. "They abandoned you, they aren't coming back for you."

"Maybe they are digging a new tunnel, you don't know."

Jiara chuckled a bit heartlessly. "They are not. They haven't moved new resources into Farjall since that portion of the roof fell. The Empire maintains the fortress so that they can keep pushing us back, but the slaves were transferred east years ago."

Baldo was crestfallen, even though he already knew this to be true.

"I will tell you whatever you want," he said, hiding a sniffle, "if you tell me how to get out of here. I suspect you found a tunnel, and I want to get out, that's all I want."

The wayfarers exchanged cautious looks.

"You'll need to excuse us for a moment, Baldo," Ockam said and took the others up the road for a private conversation. His eyes narrowed to razor-sharp slits. "We can't mention anything about the mask, but we could learn a lot from him if we give him just a bit of what he wants."

"And then what?" Jiara asked, gesticulating with her hands a bit more heavily than usual. "If that rawboned shit stain wants to get out, he'll have to follow us out, and that means he'll see Lago using the mask. And then we'll have a Negian soldier cavorting outside with all that information."

Lago nodded. "And there are a lot more of them at his camp," he said. "They'll all want to come with."

"It is way too risky," Jiara added, "but now we are stuck with him, and unless we kill him, we better keep him with us instead of risking him going back for reinforcements."

"And how do we do that? What do we tell him?" Alaia asked.

"Let me think…" Ockam said. He paced around, keeping an eye on Baldo, who was looking more and more like a beaten dog. Ockam bent the tips of his thin mustache into his mouth and nervously bit the tips off. Finally, he said, "Okay, we need to make sure he stays with us. No contacting his camp, just him. We could tell him that we know of a way out to the northeast, but that we'd only show it to him."

"He won't like that," Alaia said. "If they've been trapped here together for years, they are probably good friends by now. Family, even."

"Or maybe they despise each other," Jiara added.

"He's not Negian, he was just recruited by the army," Ockam said. "Maybe he's not as brainwashed as all the other soldiers. Maybe there's some hope left for him still, but we can't risk the others finding out about us."

"I saw him hatefully staring at my nub," Alaia huffed. "I think he's brainwashed enough. Oh, and didn't they murder thousands of innocent Wutash here?" She widened her eyes in mockery.

"That's true," Lago said, "but we can't just use him for information and then let him rot. What happens once we get to the wall, and he's still with us?"

"I... I don't know," Ockam replied. "I guess we can assess how much we trust him by that point. It will take weeks traveling through these harsh lands. We will have time to judge his character."

"We could blindfold him once we reach the wall," Lago said, "tell him it's part of the deal. And we'll also need the mask to keep hunting. We could blindfold him during those times too."

"It's worth a try, though he'll lose trust in us," Jiara pragmatically said. "It's unlikely we'll learn more without someone who can tell us what happened. And what we learn about the Negian army could be useful for the Tribelands."

"Very well," Ockam said. "Feel free to ask him questions, but let *me* do any answering."

They returned to Baldo, who flinched at any fast motions.

Ockam held a hand up to calm him and said, "Baldo, we are willing to show you a way out, and help you with food, in exchange for your story. We want to know what happened in this place."

"Yes! Yes, I will... I will tell—"

"But only if you stay with us and don't alert your camp."

Baldo froze, jaundiced eyes widening. "But... My clan, they have to get out too, I can't just abandon them."

"Maybe they'll find the way out on their own," Ockam lied. "But look at us, two Tribesfolk traveling with an Oldrin and a Zovarian... The last thing we'd wish to encounter is a Negian platoon. That wouldn't fare well for us."

"I can talk to my friends, tell them you are good people. You've been kind, and generous, and—"

"We are not up for negotiating, there's too much at risk for us. You either take our offer, or you don't," Ockam said, without specifying what the outcome of not taking the offer would mean. "Where is your camp at?"

Baldo stared at the ground.

"Your camp, Baldo, where did you come from?" Ockam insisted.

"To the south of the mountain, near where I saw you first," Baldo said.

"Then we won't have to cross paths with them. We first need to climb to the temple and from there make our way out across the other side. Will you join us?"

"The temple at the axis? Those are cursed grounds, Lorr, why don't we just head to the—"

"It's the path we are taking. Come with us, tell us your story, and we'll show you out of this place. Are we in agreement?"

"If you promise me a way out, yes, Lorr," Baldo said, distressed, but hopeful.

"And we have another request. It's an odd one, but I don't want you to feel like we are trying to trick you. When we walk out of the dome, we'll have to blindfold you. And we'll have to blindfold you whenever we go hunting, too."

"But w-why? That makes no sense."

"We won't tie your hands, it's nothing like that. We just have some things we want to keep private. It won't be long, it won't be often, it won't be tight, but we need to know you will not object to that."

"You'll abandon me!" he nearly sobbed. "You'll leave me there with the blindfold to die."

"What about... hmm..." Jiara thought out loud. "One of us can keep you company at those times, so you know we haven't abandoned you. If we wanted to get rid of you, we'd kill you, it'd be easier than snapping a twig. *But we won't*," she added, before Baldo turned even paler, "we don't intend to. We want your help as much as you want ours."

"Can't I just close my eyes?"

"Bah. Again, this is not a negotiation," Ockam said. "Either you take our offer, or we are done here."

"I... I guess?" Baldo said. "But I'm not letting you tie me up."

"We won't."

"Then, okay, I think. You are an odd bunch, but I need to get the Khest out of this nethervoid."

The malnourished soldier told them it would take a day and a half to reach the top of Stelm Bir. It would be a climb, for sure, but the Wutash road was mostly clear. Once night fell, they lit a fire atop the foundations of what had once been a dining hall. Now that they could use their lungs for things other than gasping for air, they took a bit of time to ask Baldo some questions.

"You came into this dome before most other troops. What were the Negians looking for?" Ockam asked, leaning his back on a burnt pillar.

"Before the collapse, this land was rich beyond compare, so full of resources. Obviously, we were here to take our fair share. The bloodskins were hoarding all of it, while our empire outside was in shambles. Mind you, I'm not into the politics of it all, I was just following orders."

"You can be at ease, we are here for information, not to judge you."

Baldo nodded. "Well… At first it was a friendly affair. The bloodskins welcomed us, we brought them gifts, they did the same for us. But when the emperor found that the bloodskins worshipped Takhamún's corrupt emanation, he called for them to be killed, or taken as slaves."

"Takhamún's what?"

"His emanation, took the form of a devil's face, of pure black. Turned the bloodskins into monsters is what they say, though I never saw it myself. Anyway, our orders were to secure the mountain." He half-shrugged. "That… didn't go so smoothly, they fought back like angered hornets. But we killed most of them, kept the rest as slaves to work in the Farjall mines. We needed bigger tunnels, you know, to extract resources more efficiently."

"Were the Wutash inside the mines when the roof collapsed?" Jiara asked.

"Aye, and so were thousands of soldiers from the second and third legions, the ones staying at the southern barracks. I was 'lucky,' I was up here working in the new armory, but most soldiers and nearly all the bloodskins were crushed."

"Stop. Calling them that," Ockam spat.

"Calling who what?"

"Bloodskins. They are Wutash."

"Whatever."

Ockam huffed, but let it go. "Do you know why the dome began to collapse?"

"I'm not certain, but I have a hunch. I can show you tomorrow if you want, when we arrive at the temple."

The remaining walk up the mountain was just as strenuous. They trudged by more signs of war, encountering rusted weapons, abandoned settlements, and dire wolf skeletons with hides dangling from them like unvictorious banners.

"Those dire wolves, Takh have mercy, they were terrifying," Baldo said. "Could easily take down dozens of our soldiers. They weren't the only giants either, there were overgrown foxes, and these coyotes or something? Nearly as big as horses, huge creatures. But them dire wolves were by far the biggest, and scariest."

"Are there any left alive?" Lago asked.

"Don't think so, no. We killed most of them, but I heard a bunch escaped through the mines at one point. The rest died after a while. They stopped fighting and fled north, where they starved. Most large animals died off after a few years, there's just not enough to eat for a big creature like that. I mean, it's hard even for us. And I should warn you, there's nothing to hunt at the top, unless you can hit bats midflight. Are you all carrying enough food?"

"Don't worry about that, we will take care of it," Ockam said.

At last, the road ended at a wide staircase that climbed up to the trunk. Woven out of thick vines of perhaps a thousand feet in diameter each, the scale of the trunk was incomprehensible. They estimated there were around twenty to thirty vines braiding themselves up to the sky, where they split into the umbrella that became the dome, similar to the struts inside a domed cathedral, or the fractal branches of dragonblood trees.

"Hey Alaia, look over there," Lago said. "Do you think those are—"

"Giant teratorns!" Alaia screeched. "Binoculars, now!" Lago dug around for them, and she snatched them at once. She looked up at the gyre of fifteen-foot-wingspan birds, who circled in a slow-motion tornado. "There must be thirty, maybe forty of them," she said. "Their feathers are so blue."

"You talking about those big birds?" Baldo asked. "We call them nether griffons. They are harmless, only eat dead stuff. They nest too high up on the vines, so we can never hunt them. Not worth it anyhow, pungent meat. Filling, but makes you sick. See those vines by the griffons that look darker and dried up? Try to follow them to the top, see where they lead you."

It was hard to follow the dry vines, as they wove between the others. Alaia was the first to make the connection. "The dry ones all go toward the fallen roof areas!" she said.

"Eeyup," Baldo confirmed. "All these thicker vines from the axis end up as one of the supporting columns. When you see one of them drying up, you can at least guess which part of the roof will fall next, though you can't predict when it'll happen."

"What made them dry up and fail?" Jiara asked.

"Follow me up and I'll show ya, we are nearly there."

At the top of the steps loomed a massive archway of stone and vines, narrowing into a tunnel of compound arches, in a splendorous display that mixed carved rocks and knotted vines. Animal motifs decorated the friezes, columns, and pedestals; all tapered in their muzzles, sharp in their ears. Triangular runes were chiseled onto the rocks, resembling serrated saw blades, or perhaps the pointed teeth of a predator.

"Miscamish runes," Jiara mumbled, running her fingers over the geometric forms trapped in the saw-toothed lines.

"You can read them?" Baldo asked, impressed.

"Nah. Not a clue."

The archway tapered at the top, with a keystone carved in the shape of the head of an ambiguous canid, much like Agnargsilv. On the canid's forehead was chiseled a triangular glyph, much more complex than the runes written on the other rocks. The glyph was partially shattered.

"The sigil on the devil's forehead used to be filled with enormous opals," Baldo explained. "The lucky soldier who hammered those out must now be as rich as the dukes of Bauram. If they got out alive, that is."

They walked northward under the heavy keystone, entering the barrel vault tunnel, heading directly into the core of the trunk. The ground tilted slightly uphill, at a shallow angle that was hard to perceive. By lamplight they saw the walls inside the tunnel were again a seamless blend of rocks and vines, though the vines had grown out of place, breaking through the rock.

"How deep does this go?" Lago asked Baldo, after one too many steps.

"Long ways," he said. "Half a mile to the altar."

Lago looked back. The entrance was a pointed arch of blinding light. The silhouette of a coyote trotted in front of it, stopped, and then hurried away.

As they neared the end of the hallway, the sulphurous air from an ancient fire wafted by, mixed with the tingly stench of burnt sap. Baldo said a quiet prayer to the Twin Gods, then led them into the temple. The room was so vast that their lamps only lit up a series of columns—all vines—rising into the empty void. The ground was littered with dried-up vines, weapons, skeletons, shattered masonry, and burnt wooden supports.

"Here," Baldo said, "set this on fire so you can see better."

They set a pile of wood and dried vines aflame. The fire went up in a green *fwoosh!* and slowly turned orange as it settled. The light described a circular chamber supported by columnar vines that acted as buttresses and struts for the arched ceiling. It looked like the inside of a titanic fungus, a desecrated basilica of forbidden geometries.

At the center of the room, six steps climbed to a raised platform, where a peculiar vine grew. It was a smaller vine, thornless, only two feet in diameter. It was dusty, dry, and dead, with a pool of yellowed-out sap crystallized around it. Heavy axes had cut a portion of the vine down, leaving the top segment dangling lifelessly from the vault above. Next to the core vine was a destroyed altar, broken into pieces too small to decipher. All around the broken altar and the core vine were pieces of a massive, chandelier-like structure that once had been suspended above the platform. The complex, geometric lattice had crashed and shattered, spreading hundreds of jet-black segments over the mosaic of cobbled rocks.

"What was this place?" Lago whispered.

"Don't know exactly," Baldo replied. "Some say it's where the bloodskins worshipped the corrupt emanation of Takhamún. Emperor Uvon is not fond of the unclean forms of the god, so he ordered the temple destroyed. They smashed the altar with hammers, chopped down the central vine, then spilled barrels of sapfire to burn the place until that dangling thing came down crashing."

Lago squatted to pick up one of the hundreds of sticks that had been part of the hanging structure; it came off the ground crackling out of a sticky, black crust. The object was a hexagonal tube that was light as a feather, about a handspan in length, almost two fingerbreadths in diameter. A subtle spiral twisted along its long axis, and strange notches marked its ends. The tube was hollow, with enough room to fit a small pinky finger, and was attached to a spherical form at one end.

The sphere connected to it was faceted in the manner of a geodesic polyhedron, with countless hexagonal faces evenly separated by twelve smaller, pentagonal faces. It was also hollow, with each facet digging a tunnel into a see-through center. Lago pulled at the sphere—it detached from the hexagonal tube, as if lightly magnetized.

"Alaia, look," Lago said. "They are covered in geometric patterns. They look like—"

"Don't touch those!" Baldo snapped. "They are cursed by Takhamún's magic. It's bad luck. Some soldiers snuck pieces out in their pockets, thinking they might be made of quaar. They say that's what caused the dome to begin its collapse."

Lago tossed the tube and sphere to the ground. He walked to a portion of the collapsed lattice that was still partially dangling from the ceiling, like a blackened spiderweb. He examined how the edge tubes and vertex spheres connected to one another; they were sliding joints of some sort.

"Don't get too close to it, Lorr," Baldo warned, "it can fall down at any moment. The sapfire weakened everything here. General Hallow didn't want the place burned, but Emperor Uvon insisted it be done."

"Alvis Hallow was here?" Ockam asked.

"Long ago. He commands the Second Legion, who joined in soon after us. He was in charge of most of what happened here. Until the first collapse, that is."

"Destroying this place is what caused it, isn't it?" Jiara asked.

"Some guess that, some others think it's the cursed artifacts, or the anger of Takhamún's emanation. It's why I wanted to show you this place. We should've seen it coming, there were enough warnings." He kicked at a bundle of dead vines. "A few weeks after the temple burned, some vines started losing color. And the dome, it began to flicker, like an oilless lamp burning its last filaments of wick. Segments of the ceiling suddenly went dark entirely, sinking us into a perpetual dusk."

"Is it true then?" Alaia asked. "That the entire sky was alight?"

Baldo was upset by the Oldrin addressing him without an honorific. He pretended not to hear her and continued with his story. "We all wanted to get out of this void, but we had our orders, and there were still so many resources to extract for the Empire, so they kept us working under the dim light. And then one day, it just went dark. I was having lunch with my shift mates at camp seventeen, when the whole dome blinked, flickered, and went darker than the deepest night. We all laughed at first, even howled and hollered, knowing that it'd light up again at any moment. But it never did.

"The next few months they had us working under those stinking green flames, since we didn't have enough oil to burn all day long, or night, whatever it was. Gather resources, haul them out to Farjall, repeat. Hunting was easy with the animals all confused, coming to our lights like moths. So many furs we got in such short a time."

A tattered smile forced itself upon Baldo's chapped lips.

"I loved going out on delivery, seeing the blue sky again, and the Farjall fortress. And to think I used to hate it there before. But then we had to light up our stinking lamps once more, and shuffle back in. I'm still bothered whenever I see green flames, we lived under them for months. Fire is supposed to be red and warm.

"After three months or so—it was hard to count the days in the dark—it happened. I was riding my wagon down this mountain, not too far from the axis, when my oxen stopped, feeling an odd tremor. Then I was blinded by a crack of light tearing the southern sky, where slowly, so slowly, this big piece of roof started to rip apart and come down. It looked like someone was lowering it carefully, making it take such a long time before it hit the ground. But if you think about it, that roof is maybe seven miles up—it must've come down with such speed...

"When it hit, this bubble grew from the spot, then vanished. Then a cloud of dust built up. It was so far though, like thirty miles away, there was no way it would reach us. But after a long moment, there was this *boom!* and the whole mountain shook. I thought the worst was over at that point, but Khest no, that cloud of dust was moving. It looked slow, but I knew by then that there was nothing slow about it. And then it hit us. By then I was already taking cover behind a rock. A blast of sand and wind sucked me forward and then back, but I held on tight, and only got cuts from flying debris. My oxen were hurled down the cliff, cart and all.

"And then it was done. The dust took hours to settle. It was all hazy, like a yellow mist around us, but at least there was sunlight again, Sunnokh's blessed light we so missed. The next day, my troop and I traveled south to see the mess up close, but a few miles before we got there, we got rained down on with sap and had to back off. The shit was spilling everywhere from the torn vines above, we all got the white hives from it. We returned a week later, once the sky stopped dripping, to find a whole lake of sap had formed. Thousands of bodies were floating on it. Bloated. Stinking."

Baldo stopped, digesting old memories.

"By Takh's two cocks…" Jiara blasphemously remarked. "That's a lot scarier than I imagined."

"You don't know the sixteenth of it," Baldo said. "And it's happened four times more since then. First it was south, by the Fauborough Colony, though it happened before the colony settled there. Then east near the Old Pine Forest, close to the first collapse… After that it was by the West Canyon, over the Klad Ommish. And the most recent one was by Knife Point. That last one was the scariest because it happened at night. Imagine sleeping soundly when your bed gets tossed to the side, and you think you've just been crushed to death. You stumble out and there's no light, and you can't breathe, choking on dust. Had to wait till morning to find out it had happened really far away, and we were safe.

"That's why I need you all to help me here, I don't wanna die crushed like those bloodskins at the mines. It's just a matter of time till all the other segments dry up and fall, though if Takh has mercy, I'll starve to death before then."

Baldo stared at the ground, crushing shards of dried sap under his toes.

"So, I hope that was enough to buy my passage out of here. I can tell you more, but there's not much more to the story, really. After that it's just been me and my friends trying to survive. It's been tough."

"Thank you, Baldo," Ockam said. "We'll keep our promise if you travel with us."

"Let's get out of here though," Baldo said, "this place is haunted, I don't want to be in here when night falls. You can't see the netherflames, but they can still burn you."

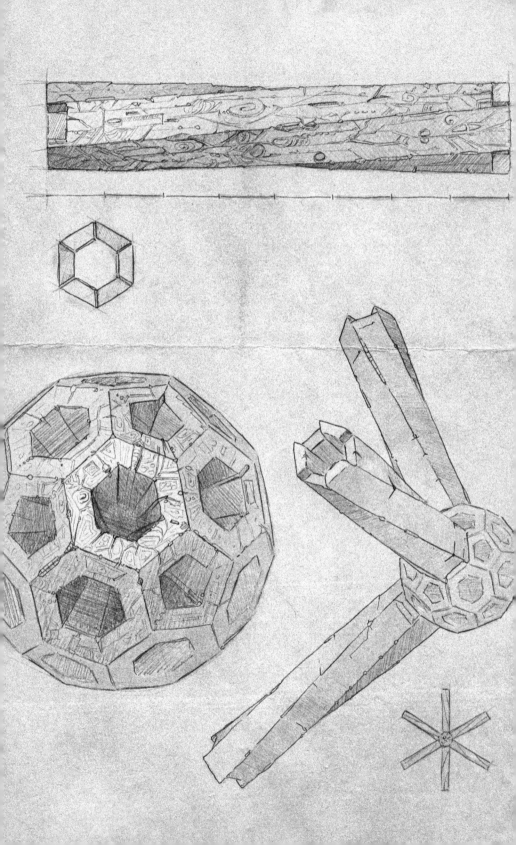

CHAPTER THIRTY-FIVE

CLIFF GALLOWS

Morning arrived in distant patches of sunlight. They were standing on a view-point at the northeast of the trunk, at the edge of a destroyed city. Ockam pulled out his notebook to sketch the missing parts of his map, careful not to let Baldo see it, for the map showed the path they had taken from Thornridge.

"We are going to follow the Topaz Beck northeast," Ockam mentioned, pointing at the river, "to where it flows through the wall and continues toward Dimbali."

"Bad idea," Baldo said. "Look above you, that vine that snakes northeast from the axis is weak. The roof could crash on top of the river at any moment. I know a better trail to the east that goes almost straight to the wall, it's one of the old bloodsk—Wutash roads, would be much easier than following the canyon's rim."

Baldo knew better, so they agreed to follow his recommendation. They traveled faster from there on, aided by Baldo's familiarity with the roads and forks on the mountain. When midafternoon arrived, they stopped to rest and to hunt.

"You won't find any game here," Baldo said. "We can eat tomorrow, there are mice at the base of the mountain, sometimes even rabbits."

"We are proficient hunters, don't worry about it," Ockam said. "But now, if you'll excuse us, we'll have to blindfold you as we hunt, as you promised you'd let us."

Baldo tensed up protectively. "Do we really need to do this, Lorr? You can see why it's… unnerving to me, can you not trust me?"

"I have an idea," Jiara said to Ockam. "Alaia and I will stay with Baldo inside those ruins, keeping an eye on him. He won't be able to see you or Lago. I need time to tend to Alaia's wound anyway. Does that sound better?"

"Yes," Ockam and Baldo replied in unison.

Lago, Ockam, and Bear headed out to hunt.

Baldo slouched uncomfortably on the rubble of a stone chimney, watching as Jiara took care of Alaia's injured arm.

"It's closed up quite well," Jiara said. "You won't need the bandages anymore, nor the sling. Just don't twist it too hard for another week or two."

Lago and Ockam returned in less than an hour, with five ground squirrels, two zebra doves, and a handful of truffles.

"How in Takh's two names did you manage that?" Baldo asked incredulously.

"Is that a canoe?" Jiara asked the following afternoon as they approached the sandy shores of the Topaz Beck, at the eastern base of the mountain.

"Eeyup," Baldo said, "just as I promised."

Bear hurried ahead and launched himself into the turquoise-tinted waters. The canoe bobbed up and down alongside the flimsy dock.

"Them waters are wide, but easy to row across," Baldo added. "We can camp on the east shore tonight, and I'll show you the road in the morrow."

It was a bit cramped in the canoe, and they almost tipped over once or twice. As they rowed across, Lago stared back toward Stelm Bir and saw the Nu'irg at the shore, in the shape of a tundra wolf, with furs that should've been white as snow, but were instead patchy and unhealthy. The white wolf paced back and forth, unsure of how to follow them. Lago hoped she would find a way.

The Topaz Beck was calmer at the opposite shore, ideal for wading and fishing. It was something relaxing they could do together to gather food without having to rely on the mask, and it put Baldo a bit more at ease, even if there were nearly no fish left to catch.

They camped by the turquoise river that night. It was the third day of Fireleaf, and Sceres was full and resplendent, proudly displaying her Amethyst season colors. Through the distant holes in the sky, beams of moonlight streaked into the dome, like purple crystals growing inside a monumental geode.

"It's so good to see the moon again," Lago said. "Even if it won't last."

They all watched Sceres as she glided past one of the holes in the roof. Soon enough she had disappeared behind the gnarly vines once more, but her purple pillars of moonlight still touched down elsewhere within the dome.

Baldo didn't close his eyes that night. After the campfire burned out entirely, after he felt certain not a soul was stirring, he quietly placed his bag and weapons under his blankets to create an inconspicuous mound, then crawled away, the sound of lapping waves concealing the noise of his footsteps. He snuck out of the camp, his tired eyes aided only by the purple moonlight.

His own camp—to where he had been leading them all along—was only two miles away, up on a cliff that overlooked the riparian lands. He hurried into the silent camp and pushed open the tarp door to an inky blue pavilion.

"Feilen, wake up!" he said, pulling on the shoulder of a sleeping man.

Baldo woke everyone up. His group amounted to twelve people total, including himself, most of them looking equally wretched and feeble. Once they were all gathered around their firepit—though Baldo insisted there be no fires—he told them everything that had happened since he met the outsiders.

"And I led them here, because I couldn't leave you all behind. They are afraid of Negians and did not want me to contact you."

"You are a fair and honest friend, Baldo," Feilen said, stroking his twice-braided beard. His hair was long and dark, shaved over his left ear, where his ranking insignia indicated he was—or had been—a renowned marshal, commander of an entire battalion. The two stumps where his legs should've been dangled out of his deerskin chair. Squalid and malnourished, Feilen retained his composure and pride.

"The Shade of Yza bless you sixteenfold for not abandoning us, Baldo of Barsubia," Feilen added, holding tightly to a pendant of a shield crossed by a spear. "All of us deserve to be let out of this Void of Khest. We'll be eternally grateful to you for not forsaking us. The motives of these strangers seem… strange. Are they spies? Why are they so secretive, even about hunting? It hardly makes sense to me, but they might offer us our only chance out."

"But how will we convince them to take us?" asked a woman named Noëliss, making her overlapping facial scars contort under the moonlight.

"You could follow us, track us from far away," Baldo suggested.

"We can't move at their pace, nor stay low, not while you have to carry me tied to this Takh-forsaken chair," Feilen said.

"They have a Tribeswoman officer and a sylvan scout, you said. They will undoubtedly spot us," a long-faced woman named Sharlett said while balancing a dagger on her fingers. She looked healthier than most, with some stringy muscles still holding on to her slender body. "I'm afraid they'll find our tracks as soon as morning comes, when they leave the shore. Those mucks are much more resourceful than you could imagine. You should've seen them at the battles in the Mugwort Forest, it was like fighting phantoms."

"You are right…" Baldo said. "And they hunt like… like gods, or like contraptions from a mad artificer."

"I say we go there now and take them as prisoners," Obris suggested with his cavern-deep voice. He was the largest member in their camp, an intimidating Baurami mercenary with deep-set, light-blue eyes who had kept his full size and strength despite their dire conditions.

"Aye—aye—I agree," said several voices at once.

"But they are friendly, they don't mean no harm!" Baldo pleaded.

"You told us one is a spur, another a Zovarian maggot, and the others mucks from the Klad Senet," Noëliss said, seething. "We swore an oath to fight against them. I don't give a griffon's turd how many rodents they fed you, I want to get out of this fucking nethervoid."

"Aye—scorch them—I'll strangle them myself—shhh, keep quiet," the voices said.

Baldo could not abandon his old friends to certain death, yet he began to regret his choice.

"Then it's decided," Feilen said, massaging his stumps. "We take them as prisoners and force them to show us where this exit is. We need to move immediately, before they realize Baldo is not at their camp. Bring them to me at once. We will interrogate them at the Cliff Gallows."

"Please," Baldo said, "just... treat them kindly, we'll have a better chance that way."

"All but that spur, perhaps," Obris said, clenching his purple-tinted, wide teeth.

Nine soldiers quietly got dressed, making sure to avoid metal armor. Baldo led them down toward the river. Feilen remained at the camp with Sharlett, who slowly carried him in his chair, up to the Cliff Gallows.

Jiara stirred in her bedroll, eyes half-open. She thought she had heard a whistle, or maybe it had been just a frog. She sat up with a big yawn. Obris's powerful arms reached out from behind her, covered her mouth, and slammed her to the ground. Bear barked, waking the others. Ockam spat curses as he was forced down by three soldiers, while Lago and Alaia were easily overpowered by the rest.

Baldo kept his distance while his friends secured the prisoners.

"You fucking traitor!" Alaia screamed.

"Shut your filthy spur mouth!" Noëliss said, then punched her in the face.

"Don't hurt them!" Baldo pleaded.

They were gagged, their hands tied behind their backs with ropes, inter-locked by a thicker rope that passed between all their arms, forcing them to move in a line. The knots were good—the Negians knew how to handle their slaves.

Jiara was made to walk in front, followed by Ockam, Alaia, and Lago at the back. Bear scampered helplessly next to them while the soldiers only half-joked about having mutt chops for breakfast.

Baldo and a few other soldiers carried the prisoners' bags. *At least they haven't opened them yet,* Lago thought, fearing for the mask, for *his* mask. He suddenly felt possessive and angry but could do nothing about it. Their captors were energetic, hopeful, chattering about all the things they would do once they finally left the cursed dome.

It was past morning twilight when they arrived at the gallows. The diffused light silhouetted a row of twenty-three splintering posts at the edge of a cliff-side, where skeletons dangled bleached and broken, contemplating the vista with hollow eyes. A handful of the corpses still clung to their red, tattooed skins.

Two forms waited near the edge of the cliff: Feilen, resting his stumped legs on his chair, and Sharlett, attentive by his side.

The soldiers pushed the prisoners in front of the old marshal and formed a circle around them.

No one but Feilen sat. The legless leader sucked on his concave cheeks, examining the peculiar group in front of him. "Baldo told us everything," he said. "I will make it easy on you, in the same way you made it clear to him that he could either abandon us to die here, or you'd dispose of him. You are going to tell us where the exit is. That, or you will hang with the bloodskins." He looked to his right, where six bodies hung from a thick post. "The gallows are crowded, but if you don't mind the company, they offer a delightful view." His ranking insignia burned darkly on his left temple.

"The nether griffons would be most pleased," Sharlett said. "They *love* fresh meat. But we'd prefer to get the Khest out of here instead."

A light breeze blew from the west, carrying the muddy scent of the river, mixed with a whiff of rot and decay.

"So. The tunnel. Where is it?" Feilen asked. "Did you dig through the Kingroot Woods? Or maybe you found an opening by the river? And don't lie, because you *will* be taking us there and showing us yourselves."

Obris and Noëliss removed the gags from all four prisoners, who promptly spat congealed blood and dirt.

Ockam exchanged a look with Jiara. "We can't tell you the exact location," Ockam coughed. "It's not a place we could describe to you."

"It's somewhere east, or northeast," Baldo shyly added. "That's where they were going to take me."

Feilen raised a hand to quiet Baldo. "Why can't you tell us where to find this place?"

Ockam grumbled. "We can find our way to the exit if we make it to the wall and show you then, but you'll have to take us there."

"Anywhere on the east wall?" Sharlett asked, doubting every word.

"In that general direction, yes, once we get there, we'll be able to follow the edge of the wall and show you the spot."

Feilen let out a mocking, resounding laugh. "Certainly, that sounds unquestionably plausible!" He kept his smile but glared at Ockam with eyes the color of aged driftwood. "Your short-brimmed hat, your calloused hands, your old but well-kept boots. You are a scout, probably from Farsúksuwikh. A well-trained scout who somehow does not recall the path he took in this land marked by giant columns. That terrible memory must be such an inconvenience to you. And you, big woman, you just happened to come across that walnut cloak? I see your teal and ochre trims, Lurr sylvan platoon commander." His fake smile vanished. "Do not take me for a fool."

Feilen gestured to Obris by tipping his chin, making his double-braided beard bounce.

With the help of a few soldiers, Obris made the prisoners stand right at the cliff's edge. At the bottom Lago saw dozens, if not hundreds, of skeletons.

"We can exit northeast, near the river!" Ockam pleaded.

"Truly?" Feilen asked. "Has your memory improved suddenly?"

"It has, we'll show you and walk out of here with you."

"How generous!" Feilen laughed. He hadn't yet decided what he'd do with his prisoners; there could be a handsome reward awaiting in Hestfell. "But first," he continued, "you will answer some questions. Why are the Free Tribelands in this cursed dome? Whose orders do you answer to? How many more of you await at that tunnel?"

"We are alone," Ockam cried out, "came out of our own free will. We are but a small party of adventurers."

Obris pushed Ockam, who teetered precariously at an impossible angle. He then shoved Alaia, who screamed as she fell, dragging Ockam down with her. Their arms snapped as the rope tensed, leaving them tethered to life only by the rope that bound them to Lago and Jiara, who were being held tightly by the soldiers. Obris pulled the two back up as if reeling in a pair of agonizing fish, then shoved the four prisoners back in front of Feilen.

"You lying mucks," Feilen said. "I will give you one more chance to tell me the truth, and if you do, we might even let you live after you show us the exit."

"Their bags, Lorr," Sharlett said. "They may have written orders from Klemes, or the Union."

Feilen nodded. "Obris, bring their bags to me."

Ockam exchanged a look with Lago that said *fuck*.

They opened Jiara's backpack first and found nothing of informational value, though they were already splitting up her gear. Alaia's bags had more of the same. Then they went through Ockam's, where they found his notebook. Obris handed it to Feilen, who didn't take long to find the sketched map.

"What have we here? Good draftsmanship." Feilen turned the notebook around to show the map to the prisoners. "According to this, you did not come from the northeast, but from the west. Right about where Thornridge is located. Are there multiple entrances, or were you planning to lead us into a trap?"

No one answered. Obris opened Lago's bag next.

"Wait, wait!" Lago yapped, seeing no other way to stop them from seeing his mask. "There is a way out northeast. Just take us to the wall."

Obris stared at him. "What you hiding here, maggot? Sounds like there's something you don't want us to find."

Obris opened the bag, rummaged through it, and pulled out the mask.

"What in the Last Oracle's name is this?" he asked, holding up the mask for everyone to see.

"That's Takhamún's head!—the face of the bloodskin witch!—curse of the void!" many voices called out.

Obris offered the mask to Feilen. "Take that profane effigy away from my face!" Feilen said, recoiling, not even daring to smack the mask away.

Obris looked to Lago. "Where did you get this?" he demanded, lifting Lago's chin with a heavy hand.

"At the temple. Found it at the temple," Lago whimpered.

"We've been there and found nothing of the sort," Obris said.

"That is an instrument of death, from the Void of Khest," Feilen said from his chair. "A blasphemous manifestation of the blight the bloodskins placed on Takhamún. You tried to put a curse on us. Obris, destroy it at once!"

Obris hesitated. "Lorr, it's nothing but—"

"Your commander has ordered you to destroy it!"

Obris threw the mask on the rocky ground. It bounced lightly, making no hard impact due to its feathery weight. He was angered at how weak his effort had looked. He unsheathed his broadsword and swung it down with the might of sixteen blacksmiths.

"No!" Lago cried.

The sword hit Agnargsilv right at the brow. Sparks flew, and a metallic *twang* resounded. Obris's arms bounced up in pain. He looked at his sword: it was lightly bent and had chipped at the point of contact. He picked up the mask—it had not a scratch.

The soldiers all laughed. "Their Oldrin slave could swing harder than that!" an anonymous voice said.

Obris was enraged and embarrassed by the eyes judging his weak display. He lifted his arm, ready to hurl the mask off the cliff.

"Wait!" Lago said. "Alvis Hallow will pay a fortune for that mask." That got Obris's attention, as well as Feilen's. "That's the thing he was after, when the Wutash leader escaped, riding the dire wolf."

"How do you know about that, boy?" Feilen asked. "You weren't here when that happened. Your balls probably hadn't dropped yet."

"I wasn't here, but I met the Wutash leader. I got the mask from her, not from the temple."

Feilen cocked his head. "Emperor Uvon ordered us to destroy the artifacts. Why would General Hallow be interested in this heretical instrument?"

Lago thought for a bit, then said, "Because it's an instrument of torture. He wants to use it on his enemies."

Obris chuckled, as he did not believe in the superstitions that tormented the Negians at night. "How so? What sort of torture?" his deep voice mocked.

"It will burn your head with the netherflames if you put it on," Lago dared him. "It will mangle your brain to a pulp and make you scream like a baby."

"Very funny, little boy, but your silly myths don't scare us," Obris said.

"Then try it out, big boy," Lago said.

Obris punched Lago in the gut. It was a hard blow, but Lago found the strength to swallow in a breath and said, "You p-punch like a toddler. P-put the mask on, fuh-fucking coward."

Obris punched again. "Your spritetales are even more ridiculous than your other lies," Obris said, lifting the mask toward his face.

"Obris, stop," Feilen ordered, somehow seeming more commanding when not raising his voice.

"Lorr, this lying maggot can't scare—*aaaaaaggggggghhhg!*" Obris wailed as the mask attached to his face. He fell, writhing onto the ground, feeling the immeasurable pain of everything around him piercing down his spine. He rolled toward the cliff's edge, madly trying to get away from the pain. Sharlett dragged him to safety and pulled the mask off his face, tossing it to the ground.

Obris kept on shrieking, scratching at his face.

Lago laughed. He laughed fully and fondly, from deep within his belly. He cackled, snickered, and chortled like a madman. "Told you, you idiot!" he said.

Obris contained his screams at last, got up, and jabbed Lago in the chin.

"You still punch like a butterfly," Lago laughed, lips split open. "You fell for my trap so easily!"

Obris snatched the mask from the ground. "Let's see how *you* like it, Zovarian maggot!"

He shoved Agnargsilv onto Lago's face.

A lot happened at once. While Lago was laughing and the soldiers watched Obris's spectacle, Jiara had furtively reached back to steal Noëliss's knife. She had quietly cut the ropes binding her wrists, then begun to slice at the thicker rope that held all of them together. Obris had then loudly rolled on the ground, making Ockam and Alaia exchange looks, not having a plan, but knowing something was about to happen.

Once the mask fully connected with Lago's face, he faked a scream while sensing with its sight. He saw Jiara had freed herself, so he tumbled backward, landing back-to-back against her. While Lago made a scene, Jiara cut through Lago's bindings. What happened next was very fast.

Lago stopped screaming, rushed forward, and slammed into Obris, shoving him off the cliff. Obris's shriek was sharp, quickly interrupted as he smashed into the rocks below. Jiara sunk the knife under Noëliss's chin. Ockam and Alaia together kicked at a group of soldiers, sending them tumbling.

No one was ready. No one had their weapons drawn or expected trouble.

Lago was savage. With the mask showing him how to use his limited strength wisely, he moved in a blur away from the attacks, hitting his enemies from behind, making them stumble off balance. Luckily, most of the Negians had been weakened by hunger, despair, and confusion, but there were three times as many of them, and Ockam and Alaia still had their wrists bound.

Lago dodged a mace and shoved the attacker's face into a splintered post, splintering it further. Jiara hurled Noëliss's body at two scrawny men, then finished the tumbling soldiers off with her knife. Lago was trying to protect Alaia but could do nothing when he saw Sharlett jump to Jiara, knocking her to the ground. Sharlett straddled her, but Ockam rushed to her aid and kicked Sharlett's ribs violently enough that she rolled to her shoulders to take the impact. Jiara seized the chance and jumped on top of Sharlett, trying to find a way to lodge the knife in her throat.

Ockam tried to stand, hands still tied, when a knife-wielding soldier came to stab him from behind. Bear lunged at the soldier, sinking his fangs into her leg. What could've been a deadly stab in Ockam's neck ended as a weak but still painful slash on his shoulder. Ockam stood fast when he felt the cut, accidentally hitting his head on his attacker's chin, toppling her over. While Bear still held the woman's leg, Ockam stomped down on her nose.

Baldo had stayed back this whole time, terrified. What curse had he brought upon his old friends? His only friends? He shakily took out his spear and ran toward Jiara to release his fury. Alaia jumped in front of Baldo, falling on her face and shoulders, but making him trip on her body and stumble out of control. Jiara lifted her knife and let Baldo fall right into it.

Sharlett took the chance to push Jiara off her and grab a sword from the ground. She stood and took a few measured steps backward, keeping her guard up. Lago was beating at the face of a soldier with a rock. Ockam made him stop, pointing out the fallen soldier's knife. Lago took it and began to cut Ockam's bindings when a gangly man tried to bury a hatchet in the demonic, black mask. Ockam was freed just in time; he punched the man in the kidney, allowing Lago to move out of the way. Lago sliced the knife against the man's thighs; he howled as he plummeted and bled.

Other than Feilen—who sat in utter terror upon his deerskin chair—Sharlett was the only one left standing from the miserable troop. She used a skeleton-draped post to take cover, but there was nowhere to go: the cliff was behind her, and the three warriors and the cursed emanation of Takhamún himself stood in front of her.

"Vanquish him! End him!" the cracked voice of Feilen commanded. "Cast him back into the void!"

Hiding behind the post, Sharlett switched her sword to her other hand, while with her dominant hand she pulled out a small dagger. She came out from hiding and flung the dagger directly at the masked demon. Agnargsilv could sense Sharlett's intentions clearly, announcing to Lago that something was being hurled at him, but Agnargsilv could not sense the intentions of the flying dagger itself, for it had none. The stabbing blade spun in a blur, directly toward his face. The young man had no time to react. It hit him right in the forehead. Agnargsilv took the hit, bouncing the dagger away with sharp sparks, but also detaching from Lago's face.

The canid mask fell to the ground. Lago scrambled to grab it, but Sharlett rushed him with a savage swing. Jiara slid in front of Lago, parrying the attack, pushing Sharlett back in a defensive stance. Ockam had found a spear and despite his wound took his position next to Jiara, brandishing the weapon.

"Burn them in netherflames sixteenfold!" Feilen cackled and wept.

Sharlett held her sword with both hands, measuring her opponents, sensing a weakness in Ockam's posture, in his bleeding shoulder. She sidestepped to place herself away from Jiara's reach, then headed toward Ockam, sword slashing. *Thud!* came the sound of a heavy rock slamming on the back of Sharlett's head. Alaia had cut herself free while the others fought and had hurled the rock just in time. Her injured arm burned with the effort.

Sharlett lost her footing and tripped toward Jiara, spinning her momentum into empty air. Jiara used the woman's own weight to push her further. Her gyrating charge yanked her to the edge of the cliff, where she keeled over and plummeted down the chasm dragging out a dreadful howl which ended in an unappetizing, wet crunch.

Lago drew in a shattered breath, surveying the battlefield. He was holding the mask tightly to his thumping chest. Alaia was rubbing her head: she had hit it hard on the ground, but the headache would eventually go away. Ockam dropped his spear to hold on to his bleeding shoulder, while Jiara carefully disarmed any lingering threats.

Not all the enemies were dead. Some were unconscious, some bleeding and trying to squirm away, some gurgling their last whimpers of blood.

Feilen sat crying, unarmed, knowing it'd be dishonorable to crawl away. He was too afraid to face the dark-masked demon directly, so he looked down at his stumps and held tightly to his pendant, asking the Twin Gods for mercy. Baldo was sprawled on the stony ground, with the knife still lodged in his chest, taking short, forceful breaths. Alaia walked next to him and looked down at his despairing face, feeling pity for the troubled man. She thought that maybe they could still do something to help him.

Baldo pulled the knife out of his ribs and tried to swipe it at Alaia's feet. "You disgusting... *cough*... spur cunt... I'll—"

She kicked his bloody mouth shut. The pitying stopped.

There were scrapes, plentiful bruises, a few minor cuts, and Ockam's deeply painful, bleeding shoulder.

"Your scapula took the hit," Jiara said to Ockam, holding a clean cloth to make the bleeding stop. "It would've gone through your ribs otherwise."

Five Negian soldiers remained alive, in terrible conditions, except for Feilen, who had suffered no flesh wounds. Jiara said they could not risk being followed and voted for the practical approach: killing them all. Ockam abstained from an opinion. Lago and Alaia both said they should just leave them be, and thus they won the vote. From the look of their wounds, the Negians would probably not have the strength—nor courage—to follow anyway.

As a precaution, they threw all the weapons they weren't carrying down the cliff.

The wayfarers repacked their bags and moved on, leaving the wounded souls to their own demise.

Feilen watched them leave, shaking in his chair.

"The Twin Gods smite you!" he cursed. "None of you shall meet the Steward! None! Long shall you be consumed by the netherflames, for sixteen eternities, you and all those whom you've ever loved!"

CHAPTER THIRTY-SIX

COLLAPSE

Baldo had lied about there being a wide road on the east side; he had said that only to lure them to his camp. Yet east they scrambled, making slow progress through blackened forests and acidic canyons.

Three more, Lago thought as they walked. *That makes seven I've killed. And I don't even remember their faces, just the sounds they made.*

"You're doing it again," Jiara said.

"Huh?"

"I've been there, kid. It's not easy to kill, but sometimes you do what needs done. It gets better with time though."

"I don't want it to get better," he said. "It's not who I want to be."

"No one wants war, death, pain, but it's part of life."

Lago grunted and kept scrambling up.

A long while later they reached level ground once more. Lago took a sip from his canteen, then as he put it away remembered something.

"Hey, Alaia, check this out," he said, pulling something out of his bag.

"Wait, you stole one?" she asked.

"Of course I did," he answered with a proud grin, "when leaving the temple, while Baldo wasn't looking."

It was one of the hexagonal tubes that had made up the chandelier-like, collapsed lattice. Lago took out his mask and held them side by side: they were indeed made of the same tough yet light material, with similar motifs in the intricate carvings.

I wish I had Khopto's microscope to better study all these details, he thought, running his fingers over the subtly twisting shape.

"Hey, thiefling," Jiara said, peeking from the side. She snatched the tube away. "What do you plan to do with this?"

"I don't know, what do you suggest?"

"It does look like it's made of quaar," she said. "You could sell it for quite a steep price. That shit won't break under a bison stampede. I wish I had taken a few myself. But who knows, maybe they *are* cursed, like that stoatfelcher kept warning."

"I do wonder…" Lago said, putting the mask on. He moved the tube closer to his dark visage, black on black. "It's… it's moving the threads…" he said, stopping his walk.

"Moving them? What do you mean?" Ockam asked.

Lago focused his second sight. "It's like the threads are sucked into one side of it and are pushed out the other end. They flow through the hole, like water through a pipe."

He rotated the dark tube in his fingertips. Some of the threads that got sucked into it were propelled outward into the distance, while others bent around it into a loop. Even Agnargsilv's indigo aura ended up trapped in the field, ejected far away as a dim, synesthetic glow.

"It may be some sort of pump," Jiara guessed. "Some mechanism that worked with these threads before that hanging thing collapsed."

Lago placed the object on his mask, right over his muzzle and spun it. At the moment the dark tube was aimed toward his face, he was struck by a most peculiar sensation.

"My sight, it's… farther," he ineloquently said.

"Huh?" Alaia asked.

"The threads, I can see them from farther away when I put this… thing in front of me. As if their essences are brought closer to me."

"Most strange," Jiara said. "I wish some of the Wutash were still around to explain all this. Keep that thing safe, kid."

Lago kept studying the way the tube affected the threads. He roughly estimated that his reach increased tenfold, though it depended on how much he focused his own mind, as that too further narrowed his sight in one direction.

"Just like a telescope…" he whispered.

Days passed. Miles flowed beneath their feet like a murky river, but at least they seemed to be in no danger.

No one followed. No one other than the Nu'irg, that is, who mostly took the shape of a shabby white wolf. The Nu'irg escorted them quietly, like a white glimmer, disappearing when too many eyes pointed in her direction. Lago was glad that she had made it across the river.

A narrow, overgrown path took them right next to one of the supporting columns, and next to its enormity they stopped to share a late afternoon break.

Little sunlight ever reached this area, so most of the large trees were dried up, or long-since-burned, but that allowed an unobstructed, distant view all around.

They leaned against a dry log to rest, staring toward the ever-present peak of Stelm Bir, trying to imagine what life must've once been like in here. Jumpy rodents and chirping birds skittered around them, hiding in nests tucked deep in the hollow trunks.

"It's those spritewrens again," Alaia said, eyeing a flock of bright-blue birds that landed near them. They were almost as small as hummingbirds, and equally energetic. She tossed crumbs toward the birds, who fought for them like ardent bolts of lightning.

"Keep quiet," she said. "Let me try something."

Alaia extended a hand, crumbs on her palm, and waited patiently. When one of the minute birds finally landed and pecked at the crumbs, her smile lit up as bright as the Ilaadrid Shard.

It's nice to see Alaia enjoying herself again, Lago thought, smiling with her.

Once the crumbs were gone, she leaned her head back on the log to look straight up at the column of vines. It went up in such an absurd perspective, converging into a distant point where it spread like a funnel mushroom.

"It's amazing to be so close to them," she said.

"Did you ever see the dragonblood tree at the arboretum?" Lago asked her, also gazing up.

"Only once. They don't like Oldrin around the school grounds. But I know what you mean. How this vine splits on top, it looks exactly like that old tree. One branch splitting into two, two into four, and so on. Detail upon detail until it's a jumble too small to see."

Sunken in utter peace and relaxation, they admired the sorrowful beauty of the mystifying land. The spritewrens rested on a gnarly branch, like somnolent sapphires. With no warning, they all took off at once, in an electric flutter of feathers.

Bear cocked his head and lightly growled.

"What is it, boy?" Lago asked, sitting up straight.

Bear looked into the distance, holding perfectly still.

Maybe he spotted an ottermole by the creek, Lago thought.

Rrroooff! Grrwwoouf! Bear warned, then stood, hackles raised.

"Shit," Alaia said. "The column!"

They watched in awe as a column miles to the northwest started to buckle. It was right over the Topaz Beck, on the road they would've taken if it hadn't been for Baldo's deceitful counsel.

The roof didn't collapse, but the splitting branches atop the column suddenly bent under the pressure. They saw a ripple beginning at the bent column, moving toward them across the ceiling. It took a long moment for the wave to reach right above them. They looked straight up. Miles above them they saw the enormous branches wriggling and twisting like snakes. The spiraling vibrations merged into the column they rested under and shot toward the ground.

"Move!" Jiara yelled.

They scrambled to their feet, but as they were about to run, the base of the column shook. The earth beneath them lifted, liquified from the vibrations, hurling them to the ground. The quake took a while to settle, leaving them covered in dirt, but otherwise unharmed.

"That was wild!" Alaia yelped, spitting out sand.

Bear shook the dirt off. *Rrrooowwwwll... Grrwooof!* he alerted, staring at the distance again.

At last, the roof gave in. Cracks of sunlight pierced through the shredded openings as the tangled vines tore like a rotten fabric. The column buckled, then snapped, spraying a white deluge from the heavens. Miles and miles of roof began to fall.

They watched the slow-motion spectacle as if in a trance. The collapse was so drawn-out that it didn't seem threatening at all. It reminded Ockam of seeing the calving faces of the glaciers of Fjordsulf in his youth, collapsing into the sea after being suspended in midair, weightless, for much too long. When the vines finally slammed to the ground, a shockwave bubbled around them, then dissipated harmlessly. Thirty heartbeats later, a piercing *crack!* knocked them all down. The land shook again, and then was still once more.

From the fallen roof, a cloud of dust was growing.

"Run," Ockam said. "Lodestar guide us, run, now!"

"Where?!" Jiara asked, unable to look away.

"Behind the column!" Ockam replied, bolting as fast as he could.

The column was so large that getting behind it was no easy task. They sprinted around the shallow curve, finding no particular end to this circle that felt like a straight line. As they ran, the column oscillated again, this time with the vibrations from the snapping of the faraway column. The earth shook more violently this time, tossing them into the air and practically burying them in dirt as they landed. Before they could dig themselves out, the cloud of dust reached them, flattening them against the softened ground. Rocks, branches, mud, and entire trees were flung above them in a hurricane of debris.

Once the rumbling subsided, they slowly unburied themselves. Their eyes were caked, their tongues thickened with mud. They saw nothing farther than a dozen feet away.

"Are you all okay?" Lago asked into the dust while he unburied his whimpering dog.

"I'll deal—yeah—let's get the fuck out of here!" came three replies.

They blindly plodded up the now softened trail. The dust cloud offered no sense of direction, so Jiara guided them with her compass. An hour later it began to snow, or so they thought at first. The flakes that fell were near weightless, light-brown colored, shaped like little cocoons.

"It's those pods I found at the wall, when we first came in," Alaia said.

"I guess there were a lot more attached to the ceiling," Lago said, catching one and crushing it in his fingers. The pod crackled to dust and blew away. Soon enough, so many of the dried husks had fallen that the entire ground was covered in them, making each step they took sound like they were stomping on layers of a flaky puff pastry. The warm winds began to spiral upward, creating sporadic currents at their feet, carrying the husks up in towering, crackling dust devils that rose like ghosts of the vine columns that had died.

The dust finally settled about an hour later, as the sun was setting. In utter disbelief, they stared at the spectacle created by the new hole in the roof. Thick, orange sunbeams burst into the dome from the holes on the far west side and continued horizontally in parallel tracks until they reached the brand-new fissure that had formed.

And the air itself glowed.

It glowed because of the torrents of white sap that were gushing from the ripped vines. As the long fingers of mighty Sunnokh caressed the sap, they formed a curtain of fire suspended miles in the air.

"Firefalls…" Lago whispered.

"Not the same kind, but close enough," Ockam said. "Let's go find the real Firefalls."

Benevolent winds pushed the rain of sap westward, while the wayfarers kept on journeying toward the east. Two days later, at the far end of a dead ironwood forest, they at last reached the Heartpine Dome's wall. Lago put

Agnargsilv on and stared at the vines; yet without turning around, he focused his mask's sight behind him—a dim, indigo aura followed them.

"We need to let her out," Lago said.

"Huh?" Jiara asked.

"The Nu'irg. She's been following us. Don't turn around, she's scared. I think she is trapped in here, like everyone else."

A shadow shivered, crouched behind a skeletal sagebrush.

"She won't come near us," Ockam said.

"She will," Lago said. "Once we enter the wall, don't look back, pretend she is not there. I will be able to see her without turning. I'll move as slowly as necessary to make her feel like she can trust us."

"You want us trapped in a dark tunnel with a hungry wolf? That's your plan?" Jiara mocked.

"Just trust me," he said.

Lago walked on, slowly opening a path through the vines, with Alaia bringing her warm light behind him. He felt more confident this time, able to make the passage wider, taller, as if they were walking into a large, circular home with ever-shifting walls. He could feel the Nu'irg—now shaped as a gray fox—hesitating, stopping at the entrance. He waited, they all did, never looking back.

Bear, however, did turn, and stared directly at the Nu'irg, as if having a conversation with her. Lago wanted to call him so that the dog would not scare the Nu'irg away, but he chose to remain silent.

The gray fox timidly placed her paws through the threshold and followed. Bear walked near her, but never too close, shyly darting his eyes to her from time to time, with his tail shaking between his legs.

Brilliant sunlight entered from a lush spruce forest once they reached the outer edge of the vines. The first of them to exit was the Nu'irg, who scurried beneath Lago and took a giant leap as a fox. She landed outside as a tundra wolf, letting her pristine white coat shimmer as she rushed away under the dappled light.

The squalid and mangy canid they had seen before was no more, and in her stead rose a regal creature from time immemorial. The Nu'irg leapt on the twisted log of an ancient spruce and stopped there, with her side to the travelers. Her head turned sharply, looking at Lago for a piercing moment, with bright-yellow eyes deeply lined with black. Her sapphire-tinted aura was no longer pallid, but resplendent, radiating from her white furs, which were set aglow in the sunlight and blew proudly in the Autumn breeze.

As if she had been nothing but a much-too-vivid dream, the white wolf jumped behind the log and vanished as an effulgent blur of light.

CHAPTER THIRTY-SEVEN

DISFIGURED

Forty miles south of Thornridge, in the fortress city of Maankel, Fjorna Daro sat chained up in a dark cell, hearing the faraway noises of the Autumn Equinox celebrations. Next to her, sharing her chains, were Crescu, her armsmaster; Shea, her sentryward; and three more of her arbalisters: Trevin, Muriel, and Aurélien.

It was past midnight, yet the celebrations were barely getting started. The night was thick and gloomy, only broken by the soft, lavender light from the waning crescent of Sceres, which washed in through the thick bars of the cell's only window.

Fjorna fumbled with her heavy chains. It had been a month since their failed attack at the Thornridge Lookout. The ranking insignia over her left ear was partly torn off, and the scabs that remained were being covered by her regrowing hair. The heavy beating she had received from Lago had left her disfigured; her bones were fusing at all the wrong angles, her scars mended in grotesque patterns, particularly on her left side, where her eyebrow drooped languidly over a bloodshot eye that was lower than it should've been. She was nearly unrecognizable.

Muriel Clawwick sulked, eyes sunken in shadows, still mourning the death of her brother, Waldomar. She felt incomplete without him. They had looked nearly like twins. They had felt nearly like twins. In her thoughts, she repeated the names of the seven murdered members of her squad: *Waldomar Clawwick,*

Jovan the Nimble, Emma Lightwood, Nikolina Marsh, Talled dus Muna, Elian Tiziano, Salvina Rhahe.

Crescu Valaran abstained from leaning against the wall, as his suppurating back was still suffering spasms from the thorns he had been impaled on. He still had nightmares about white sap burning deep in his wounds. His whole body was covered in the white hives.

Shea Lu chewed on her long, obsidian-dark hair, seething quietly, fantasizing of revenge.

Trevin Gobbar picked at the scabbing wounds on his broken leg, his mind a blank void.

Aurélien Knivlar meditated, hopeful and without concerns, and waited. Under the lavender moonlight, her short, red hair was the color of a violet twilight. The light falling on her was cut by the vertical shadows from the cell's thick bars, which drew elongated rectangles upon the rock wall and over the scarified, spiraling patterns on her face.

There was a flicker in that light, as a green magpie soundlessly landed between the bars. The jade stealer fluttered to Aurélien's shoulders. The Wastyrian shaman noticed a yellow thread tied to the magpie's left foot; she smiled. Tilting her head, she whispered something to the bird. The magpie flew off, as silent as the shadows it cast.

"He is on his way," Aurélien said.

An hour later, their cell's heavy door creaked open. Osef Windscar entered, his bald head covered by a sylvan guard's gray hood. He shuffled through a set of keys, unlocked the chains, and helped his friends up, handing each of them a hooded robe and their recovered weapons.

"Three horses," Osef said, "by the south gate, behind the stables. Watch your step."

They carefully stepped over the bleeding bodies of the guards and unlatched the prison's back gate. The sounds of celebration and merriment hit their deprived ears as they stepped out into the fresh air.

Chapter Thirty-Eight

THE CAULDRON

"Feels so good to be out of that death trap," Jiara said, hugging a spruce's trunk. "I really missed big trees. The live kind."

"Do you know where we are?" Alaia asked no one in particular.

"Not exactly," Ockam said, "other than somewhere in the Kingroot Woods. We should keep going east until we hit Via Lamanni. Lots of caravans pass through there, we can pay for a ride. I'm sick of walking."

They rested for the remainder of that day and the next morning began their journey away from the Heartpine Dome. The Kingroot Woods was a pocket of true wilderness, filled with fresh scents, lively fauna, and crystal-clear waters. Ockam gladly hunted without Lago's help—he had felt a bit inadequate every time Lago had intervened.

While Ockam stalked after deer, Lago helped Alaia gather berries.

"Not touching those," he said, watching her pick from a muskberry bush.

"Not sharing anyway," she said, popping a fetid muskberry into her mouth.

Lago was feeling cheerful again. His mask's sight blossomed in the fruitful diversity of the forest, so he kept experimenting, learning to see the connections between different species, studying their relationships. He noticed that earthworms had a stronger bond to certain bird species, that blackberries had points of tightened loops in them where their seeds waited, that certain butterflies had a deeper bond with specific flowers.

He squatted next to a cerulean lupin and inspected the elongated flowers from as close as his dark muzzle would let him. Bees of different species were buzzing drunkenly over the softly ciliated petals, searching for a nectar reward.

"Alaia, see these bees here, the fuzzy ones?" Lago said. "It's strange, but I know these two are from the same hive, while these other ones that look exactly the same are from a different one."

"You know what that means, right?"

"Um... no?"

"That there's honey nearby! I've been craving something sweet for weeks. Hey, Jiara!" she hollered. "Want to help us gather honey?"

"On my way!" Jiara replied.

Lago concentrated on the two bees, trying to sense a pattern. As with most small creatures, their threads weren't as easy to spot, so he narrowed his focus as they buzzed away. With their pollen baskets nearly full, the bees trailed a flickering tangle of threads back to all the lupins they had visited recently. Alaia and Jiara followed closely behind while Lago squinted at the two fuzzy insects like a masked madman, running while half-crouching. What he saw next made him stop with his mouth agape.

Stuck between an outcrop of basalt and a weathered juniper was the hive. Though the bees each had their own threads, which all partially bent toward the hive, there was also a colorless aura around the hive not restricted to the area of the hive itself, not even to the area where most bees flew, but reaching further, in a diffused, pulsating shape.

"Hey, what happened?" Alaia asked.

"It's the hive. The whole hive. It's alive."

"Of course it is, it's full of bees, and delicious honey."

"No, no... It's the pattern. I can't describe it. It's brighter than the whole, more than the sum of all the bees that make it up."

Lago kept staring. They let him have his moment.

"Are you still okay if we get the honey?" Jiara asked after a while.

"Huh? Y-yes. Yes, you can get it, sorry."

He watched as Jiara masterfully removed the honey without getting stung—or not caring about the stings—and filled a glass jar with slabs of gold-dripping honeycomb.

The glowing volume that made up the hive's aura shrunk, then turned to chaotic lines. In a silent snap, the glow vanished from Lago's sight, though all the bees—each with their unique threads—were still there. Lago stared at the space where the complex pattern used to throb, getting so close to understanding it, but falling short.

The far-reaching trade route known as Via Lamanni wrapped around the great mesas of the Negian Empire, covering over six hundred miles: from Nool, south to Leedock, and then far to the northeast, into Wyrmwash. Plentiful wagons rolled over the smooth road, eager to pick up hitchhikers for a fee, or sometimes purely in exchange for good conversation. Yet for the foreigners, finding a ride was not an easy task, not with their conspicuous looks.

Before all the light faded, they hid in the forest and checked the approaching wagons with Lago's binoculars, guessing at the best candidates before casually stepping out onto the road. On their first try they hailed a muskoxen-pulled cart, which would've been just big enough for all of them. The driver had a Yenwu complexion, and the empty cart indicated he was on his way back from a delivery. The driver whipped the oxen and sped up, spitting on the ground right by Alaia, barking a Yenwu obscenity at her.

"You should cover your head spur," Jiara told her, pulling at her furred hood. "And you'll hate me for this, but you should pretend to be our slave while we are in these territories, at least until we get to Nool. Keep your eyes on the ground."

"You are pushing it," Alaia grumbled, lifting her hood up.

Fourteen more carts hurried by, not interested in whatever foreign ideas the travelers might have been selling. Next came a freight wagon, pulled by eight Bergsulf bison. Slow-moving, but still better than walking. The wagon's tall sidewalls were tarped to protect the merchandise from the rain, which could offer a private way to travel.

The wagon stopped. A pot-bellied man with a haystack mustache secured the reins, hopped off, and hurried to the side of the wagon.

"Just in time!" he said, unloading a torrent of piss behind a wheel, like a dam had just broken. "I've been holding that since Haedshire." He buttoned his fly up and fixed his straw hat, then regarded the group. "Traveling north?"

"As far north as old Lamanni can take us," Ockam said. "To Nool, if you happen. Do you have room for all of us?"

"For a price, there's always room. I'm trading cargo in Nool, then taking the Steppes east. Got a few more stops along the way, should be 'bout a week of travel. Name's Davy," the man said, shaking Ockam's arm. "If what you are looking for is privacy and discretion, it'll be a bit extra," Davy added, eyeing their faces, their gear, and paying special attention to the trims on Jiara's dark-walnut cloak.

They agreed on a price and set off north. Although not comfortable, the private space was cozy and a great relief for their worn-out legs.

The week passed uneventfully. Through slits in the wagon's walls, they saw the Heartpine Dome shrinking, then hiding behind the Pilgrim Sierras, all while they moved closer to the Anglass Dome. On Khuday they arrived at Nool, thanked Davy for the safe passage, and handed him a handsome tip so he would forget ever having seen them.

That night they stayed at the Five-Legged Elk, one of the smaller inns at the north end of town, aiming to keep away from the crowds. They shared a wobbly table at the inn's humble restaurant, tasting the bitter local brew.

"Withervale is so close now," Lago said, wiping foam off his top lip. "Do you think we could stop by? I have to tell Crysta and Gwil what happened. They must be so worried."

"That's exactly what I'd expect you to do, if I was General Hallow," Ockam said. "It's been but a month and some. They will have spies looking for us, and they will definitely be keeping an eye on the monastery. Even here in Nool I don't feel comfortable, too many soldiers stomping through this city."

They discreetly left the inn early in the morning and caught a ferry loaded with squealing hogs. Once they disembarked on the northern shore of the Stiss Malpa, they spotted a man hefting yellow boulders from his cart into a freight boat, carrying them on his bare shoulders. Once done transferring the minerals, the man sat down, streaked with sweat, his stringy body and graying hair covered in yellow dust.

"Are these blocks from the Sulphur Pit mines up north?" Ockam asked.

"Aye Lorr, pure as the Steward of the Sixth Gate. I'd offer you a good price, but 'tis all I brought today." He gestured toward his now empty cart.

"Not looking to buy, but we are headed to Brimstowne, and we could use a ride. Seems your caribou could use more weight to haul, and we have some Qupi to spare."

"You've found the right man for the job. Mallaren, ready and willing," he said, offering a yellowed hand.

This lighter cart was fast. Though the road was mostly smooth, there was no spring under the wheels, making for an uncomfortably bumpy ride, even more so for those sitting at the back.

"Should arrive by tomorrow evening," Mallaren said, looking at his shaken passengers. "Rest easy and enjoy the smooth ride."

Lago watched the Anglass Dome to their right side. Though they were traveling at good speed, the dome remained static as a mountain range. He noticed smoke darkening the western base of it and pointed it out to Jiara.

"Say, Mallaren," Jiara asked. "What is that burning there by the dome?"

"Negian troops, Lurr. They've been clearing the slopebrush to build more barracks. Lots more battalions moving in lately."

"Anything to worry about?"

"Nay, same old, burn and build. They always use as much land as they can, but they respect the borders with our colony. They don't venture into Brimstowne, if that's what yer askin'."

"Good to know, thank you!"

"Don't mention it," Mallaren said. "But now that you *do* mention it, may I ask what your business in Brimstowne is? You don't look like mine workers, except for the Oldrin gal—I'm closely familiar with those calluses. You don't look like investors either, or land prospectors. Honestly, I don't have a clue *what* you look like, Takh forgive my impertinence."

"It's alright, we do look like a queer bunch," Ockam responded. "We heard there are famous hot springs in the area. Do you know what I'm talking about?"

Mallaren turned his head like an owl, staring at the two men and two women in the back. He raised a bushy eyebrow and said, "I do think I know, Lorr. I'll drop you off exactly where you need to go, no need to say another word."

As sunset encroached on them the next day, an overly flashy sign arching ostentatiously over Silverkeep Road made sure they were aware of the fact that they were undoubtedly entering Brimstowne. The frontier town was an independent Bergsulfi colony in the washed-out borders between the Unclaimed Territories and the Negian Empire, belonging to none. It climbed the lower slopes of the Stelm Wujann, following the edge of the tawny-colored Stiss Minn. Of black clay were all the brick houses, and yellow all their roofs, yellow like the sulphur mined at the nearby pits. The contrast on the hillsides was striking.

Mallaren broke off from Silverkeep Road and drove the shaky cart to a livelier area of town, one teeming with small shops, taverns, and street artisans. He stopped abruptly, right in front of a large building that seemed like a sort of inn, with a round sign hanging over the front doors that read *The Yeast Cauldron*.

"There it be, glad to be of service," Mallaren said. "Not the cleanest place, but the hot springs you seek through those doors you shall find." He winked.

The passengers hopped down. Ockam handed Mallaren two Horns and one Cup for his troubles, then waved him goodbye.

The four of them plus Bear stood there looking at the building.

"I'm confused," Alaia said.

"We all are," Jiara concurred. "But let's see what this place is."

They shyly pushed open the double doors and walked into a reception lobby. Behind the counter was an angular-faced, thin-lipped allgender. They had androgynous features, a shaved, glossy head, and were twirling a pen in their long fingers.

"Moon lights, gentlefolk, welcome to the Cauldron," they greeted with a hand flourish. "Just the tubs, or looking for rooms?"

"Er, we are new in town," Ockam said uncomfortably. "We were told something about hot springs?"

"Certainly. Since it's your first time, you get a six Qupi discount per person," they said, pointing at a list of room prices on a board. Seeing no response, the receptionist leaned over the counter to point down a hallway. "The hot spring tubs are in the back, just around the corner. There is more fun down the stairs in the back, but do be careful, it gets slippery, and it's very dark. If you want to stay away from the steam, head to the grill through the glass doors. The rooms are right above, if you take these spiral stairs. How many rooms?"

"Just... one?" Ockam said, looking at the others, who shrugged, equally befuddled.

The allgender eyed them curiously, then turned and checked a panel with keys behind them, flicking through them.

"I'm sorry, Lerrs," they said, turning back, "our large room is taken, but I can give you two regular rooms for the same price. And please, no dogs in the tubs. Do you mind leaving him in one of the rooms first? I won't charge a pet fee, as long as he behaves."

They paid, got their keys, and walked up to the rooms.

"I guess we ended up in some sort of spa," Jiara said.

"After that bumpy ride, my back is in pure agony," Ockam said. "I would *love* to lounge in a hot tub. We were lucky to land here. Shall we go soak?"

They left Bear in Lago and Alaia's room, then walked downstairs.

In the hallway they passed by a tanned woman handing out towels. When Alaia reached for one, she pulled the towel back and said, "Sorry gal, no Oldrin in the tubs, but you are welcome to order at the bar."

Alaia half-expected this, but it still upset her.

"Don't worry," Jiara said, "I'll keep you company. Let's grab a drink."

The four entered the steamy room with the tubs and bar. About twenty pools hollowed the ground, like massive potholes, with bamboo armatures that piped hot water into them, creating a permeating, splashing sound. The far ends of the chamber were entirely lost in the heavy steam. Jiara and Alaia pulled up stools and sat at the bar.

Lago shrunk between his shoulders, unsure of what to do.

Ockam took his tunic off, pulled his trousers down, and tossed them over the back of a chair. "Come on boy, don't be shy!" he said.

Lago scanned around nervously. He hid behind a planter to take his clothes off, then swiftly covered himself with his towel. He tiptoed behind Ockam. Most of the tubs were overflowing with rowdy clients, all drinking and guffawing, pints toppling and spilling right in their tubs. Ockam chose a quieter tub, where only one man was soaking. The dark-skinned man half-opened his slanted eyes and smiled at Ockam's approach, keeping his arms stretched around the rim of the tub. He was slender and muscular, and though his body was mostly hidden under the foamy water, they could tell he was very tall. His deeply black skin glistened like velvet covered in dew.

"Moon lights. May we join you?" Ockam said.

"Please, stars guide, be my guests." The dark man waved a welcoming arm over his kingdom of foam.

Ockam walked right in, sighing in boisterous delight as the hot water immediately relaxed his aching muscles. It had been three weeks since he got stabbed in the shoulder, and he was no longer wearing bandages. His wound began to hurt in an oddly pleasurable way.

Lago checked his surroundings, hung his towel on a wooden pillar, covered his crotch, and snuck into the tub, glad for the presence of the shrouding steam. He sat on the same side as Ockam.

An attendant crouched behind Lago, startling him. "Something to drink?"

"Large mead for myself," Ockam said, then looked to Lago, who was utterly lost. "And a cider for the boy," he added, with a wink to Lago. "Let's spoil ourselves a bit, it's been a long trip."

The attendant nodded, then left.

"I don't think I've seen you around before. Are you two together?" the dark man asked.

"We are," Ockam said. "First time here, though I have been to Brimstowne on my own, long ago. This is quite the nice establishment, friendly people." Ockam stretched backward, with his small belly briefly poking out from the water. His back popped, and he let out a satisfied moan.

The dark man smiled.

Just a handful of strides from the tub, Jiara and Alaia sat at a steamy bar.

Jiara slurped the foam at the bottom of her pint, then quickly ordered another one. "You've barely touched your drink," she said to Alaia.

"I'm just… I was looking around. I think I just realized what this place is."

"Took you a bit," Jiara said, half-lidded. "It's a nice spa, but not to my taste—all they serve is hard-boiled eggs and sausages."

"Are. You. Serious?" Alaia said.

"I'm as lurrkin as they come. Don't worry gal, you are too young for me. And I like a bit more meat on them hips. Juicy, like the sweet pears of Cairngorm," she said as a stocky barkeep passed by them.

Alaia laughed. "I'm such a nubhead. I was so clueless!"

"Not as clueless as poor Ockam over there, I'm afraid."

Ockam thanked the attendant and took a large gulp of his mead. Lago held his cider with both hands, taking small sips, as a way to avoid conversation. He felt the dark man's toes caressing his leg and flinched, almost spilling his drink. But he didn't pull his legs back. The dark man then tried the same with Ockam, who jolted straight up, shrinking his feet and body back. Eyes wide, he stared uncomfortably at the stranger.

The dark man sensed the tension. He finished his own drink and stood to leave. As he walked out by Lago's side, his long cock—covered in foam—dangled just two feet from Lago's face. But more dangled behind: a tufted tail, dripping with warm water. The man was a Jabrak-Tsing, like Penli, Lago's old classmate.

The man leaned down and whispered in Lago's ear, "Room thirty-seven, after dinner. I don't think your lover is into me, but he's welcome to join us."

He let his tail subtly caress Lago's neck as he left the pool. Lago was very glad that the water was foamy enough to hide his excitement.

"What did that man say?" Ockam questioned nervously.

"That... um... To order the chicken pie. Best in town, he said."

"I... I think he was... not just a Jabrak, but... a lorrkin," Ockam whispered.

Lago raised his brows in feigned surprise and did his best to contain his laughter. He would tell Ockam later.

They sat for dinner at the grill, which was in a separate area where the steam wasn't as oppressive. Lago and Alaia chose to share a sampler of skewers, while Jiara asked to try the tiger trout. Ockam ordered the chicken pie.

"...and out the back, I swear, I saw this man walking around with his... with um... with an erection!" Ockam complained. "He didn't even bother to cover himself up!"

"Ockam, dear, I think it's time you realized something," Jiara said, then fully explained the situation.

Ockam blushed like a beet and filled himself with more ale once he finally understood. He had known Jiara preferred women; he had flirted with her *and* her sister many years ago, quite unsuccessfully, but he had never figured Lago out. He felt utterly embarrassed now. And to top it all, the chicken pie wasn't very good at all.

They paid, dropped a handful of Qupis and Lodes as a tip, then took the spiral steps back up.

"See you both at the grill for breakfast," Jiara said, following Ockam.

Bear was ecstatic when Alaia and Lago walked into their room, and hungry. They gave him a snack, walked him out to do his business, then returned to drop flat on their beds, happy to finally lie on springy mattresses. Though Alaia passed out quickly, Lago did not. Once Alaia was snoring, he silently sat on the edge of his bed. Aided only by the dim light that fell through the window, he lacquered his nails. *Purple will look best tonight*, he thought.

He stowed away the box of fingernail lacquers and opened the door as quietly as possible. The hinges creaked. Bear raised his head, cocked it, and whimpered. Alaia turned to face him, opening her eyes.

"You dog!" she said, smiling at Lago.

"It's been months. And he seems nice."

She yawned and turned back around. "Don't stay up too late."

Lago closed the door behind him and searched for room thirty-seven.

The dark man opened the door, already naked, cock and tail dangling between his muscular legs. He ushered Lago in by pulling him by the nape of his neck and watched silently as Lago took his clothes off. The man pointed his chin to the bed, watching all the while as Lago positioned himself on his back. He then approached, crawling like a shadow over Lago, and after an unspoken moment of exploration with his tongue, he slowly pushed himself in.

Lago relaxed, somehow. He felt the man was eager, but at the same time patient enough to allow Lago to enjoy himself. He flinched, feeling something tickling his belly, then noticed the dark man had bent his tufted tail forward, to brush it on Lago as he slid in and out, sweeping in the same soft and even rhythm. Lago closed his eyes. *I wonder what this would feel like if I was wearing my mask*, he thought. *What one person inside another would look like. All these connections, the weaving in and out of two bodies, the sharing of each other.* The idea aroused him and made him moan and sweat. He pushed their lips together, grabbed onto the tuft on the dark man's tail, and pulled on it to force him deeper.

They were laying on their sides when the man came. He embraced Lago from behind and stayed inside him as they quietly chatted.

"The two of you make an adorable couple," the dark man said. "Too bad he couldn't join us, but I'm happy you did."

"Me too," Lago said, ignoring the *couple* comment. He didn't want to have to lie or make this nice moment awkward with the truth.

"Many people travel to this town to enjoy the pleasures of this locale," the man said, caressing Lago's curls. "This Bergsulfi colony doesn't share the prejudices of most of the Empire, or the Union. Is that why you came?"

"Sort of. We actually heard about other hot springs. Do you know about the Firefalls?"

"I do. There are hot springs on the trail at the bottom, but quite far from the falls themselves. No one goes there other than a few old miners. You won't get much action at those pools."

"That's fine. We enjoy seeing places on our own."

"How romantic. I love it."

"Can you tell me how to get there?"

"The first part is easy. Head west to the Sulphur Pit, until the road turns into a trail." He traced a finger on Lago's belly, as if drawing a map. "It's hard to spot, the trail hides among rocks, and it looks like it ends abruptly, but try to keep near the Stiss Minn and follow it northwest. The steaming river will be yellow and brown close to the mines, but once you see it turn clear, look for the trail again, and follow it. It's quite a long hike, but you'll find the pools right as you crest a ridge. And you can see the steam of the Firefalls from there too, although way in the distance. It's a very private spot."

The tufted tail wrapped around their hips, flicking up and down unconsciously. Lago caressed it and asked, "Do all Jabrak-Tsing have tails like yours?"

"It's not the Jabrak-Tsing who have tails," the dark man mumbled, half-asleep by now. "It's the tail that makes us Jabrak-Tsing."

"That… makes no sense."

The man softly chuckled over Lago's neck. "I'm sure you've seen some of us before. We come in all different colors and shapes. We are a mix of races, like most of the Tsing Empire. There's only one thing that ties the Jabrak together." He flicked his tail over Lago's balls, making him quiver with goosebumps. "It's… complicated. Two Jabrak together will always have a tailed child, but when we are mixed, tails only rarely sprout. No one has figured out exactly how to predict the outcome. Only my mother was Jabrak, my father was plain-old Tsing."

"How does it feel?" Lago asked.

"To have a tail? Well. I don't know. How does it feel to have a leg? An arm? It is the way it is—I don't know any other way of feeling or being. Though now that I think of it, the only thing strange about it is that it sometimes moves of its own accord, giving away my thoughts."

The dark man's tail caressed Lago's cock, making him hard once more. Lago had not yet finished, but now that the tail rubbed on his cock in just the right rhythm, he simply let himself go.

They dozed off for a bit, tired but still glowing. After a while Lago shifted up slowly, then got dressed. As he was pulling his trousers up, he realized they didn't know each other's names, and felt strangely comfortable with that. The dark man gave him a soft kiss, then a tender slap on the butt cheek. Lago left the room.

CHAPTER THIRTY-NINE

THE FIREFALLS

"Well, that was unexpectedly refreshing," Ockam said, walking out the double doors of The Yeast Cauldron. "Now, how about we head to the Crooked Teeth and ask the locals where we can find Minnelvad?"

"No need, I know how to get to the Firefalls," Lago said. "Let's head west and I'll show you."

"How do you know? When did you—"

"Don't be so nosy," Alaia said.

They followed the dark man's instructions, climbing up a trail with a view of the Sulphur Pit mines. From above, the pit looked like an enormous, yellow-ridged tub. It had a spiraling road with hundreds of miners carrying sulphur blocks up and down. The bottom of the pit was steaming in an eerie blue cloud that turned greenish as it blended with the sulphurous dust.

The trail was tricky to follow. The rocks didn't show enough wear to indicate a path, but Lago assured them that if they followed the steam, they'd get there eventually. The yellow waters turned emerald green, then bright cyan, then ghostly clear. It took them many hours to arrive at the ridge, and from the crest they saw a cluster of blue pools below, partly shaded by a circle of tenacious poplars. Far to the northwest, two sharp peaks cut through the clouds, and from between them spouted a misty waterfall that poured down as much as it steamed up.

"It looks more like a cloud than a waterfall," Alaia said. "But it's so far away."

"It's likely the main tributary feeding the Stiss Minn," Jiara said. "At least the portion of it that hits the ground, instead of billowing up into steam."

As they scrambled down the trail, they suddenly stopped upon encountering what seemed to be a dead body sprawled next to the pools. The skeletal figure was wrapped in dry skin, naked, face up, with a feathered hat covering his face. As if summoned by a necromantic force, the desiccated figure pulled its hat back and arose.

"Welcome to Geo Springs!" the man said through friendly, scant teeth. It looked like vultures could rain down upon him at any moment, not that they'd manage to scavenge much.

"Make yourselves at home, *all* of you are welcome," he said, making sure Alaia heard him. He lowered his leathery feet into the blue pool. Bear ran, eager to jump in, but the old man reacted quickly, blocking his path and holding him down. "Eaaasy boy. I don't recommend you try this one, it's near boiling hot." He looked at Lago. "Keep an eye on your dog, unless you want him for stew. You'd all be happier in the cooler, lower terraces. Might suit you amateurs better."

Ockam tipped his hat and said, "Thank you, but we aren't—"

"Like Khest we aren't," Alaia barged in. "I didn't get a chance to enjoy this yesterday. Now I'm definitely jumping in."

All of them, including Bear, went to soak in the lower terraces. The pools at Geo Springs were certainly cleaner than the ones at The Yeast Cauldron, although the sulphur still gave them a bit of a rotten egg scent. The old man joined them, happy for the company, striking up a friendly conversation. His name was Jilpi; he'd been a miner for sixty-some years. "From way back before the Snoring Mountain began snoring," he said. He came to the pools to relax his bones and to try to 'moisten his shriveled noodle,' as he put it. It didn't happen often, but sometimes he got lucky.

"Heavy bags you carry, not for a day trip," Jilpi said. "Best spot to camp is yonder past the grove, plenty of room."

"We were actually looking to go to the Firefalls," Lago said. "Do you know if there's a way up there?"

"Aye, but it's not an easy trail. Few people ever go that far into the Unclaimed Territories. There used to be an old mine somewhere up there, got flooded with boiling water, which wasn't so healthy for the miners. You won't find any settlements left."

"So, no one lives up there?" Ockam asked, a bit disheartened.

"Not at the falls. But beyond? Who knows, the land past the twin peaks is unexplored. Would take you several days to get up, I wouldn't recommend it."

"We are well equipped, and know a thing or two about mountaineering," Jiara said.

"This is not like any place you likely encountered before. The weather changes at the whims of the Twin Gods, mistdrafts come and go unannounced. And lots of bears in these areas, too."

"Never seen bears before," Jiara said.

"They only live in the northern mountains. Ancient creatures, long-furred, clawed, and fanged. The black ones are harmless and come down to Brimstowne at times, to dig through the scraps the miners leave behind. The brown ones you need to be careful with, especially if they have cubs with them." He looked to Ockam. "You seem like a scout, you'll be able to spot their tracks. Look for claw marks on tree trunks. There's also the long-tongued ones we call honey bears, or sun bears if you are from the eastern steppes. And a bit more rare in these areas are the kiuons. Smaller bears, look closer to wolverines. Mighty smart fellas who hunt in packs, but they wouldn't attack a group your size, as long as you don't wander around alone. Farther north I hear there are white ones that sail atop icebergs, but that's hundreds of miles away."

"You make it sound quite treacherous," Ockam said. "We'll be careful."

"Don't say Jilpi didn't warn you. At least do me one favor and walk around singing, or banging sticks on rocks, or dragging your feet. The bears are numerous higher up, but they will make room if they hear someone's a-coming. And don't leave food near your camp when you sleep. They don't look for trouble, and neither should you. And if after hearing all that you are still set on going, I can at least point out the safest way up."

They nodded and listened.

"See the pile of rocks over that hill? That's the first cairn of the 'trail.' Once you get to it, look for the next cairn, which will be visible from that spot. Then do whatever you must to get to *that* cairn and look for the next. They are far apart, and don't expect a trail between them, but at least the cairns are always there, unless it mists or snows. It's only Autumn, but you can feel the first winds of Umbra creeping in."

They dried their warmed bodies, thanked Jilpi for his help, and resumed their trek, crossing the hot river by jumping on strategically placed boulders. Once on the other side, they made their way to the first cairn in just half an hour. From there they tried to find the second cairn, but that proved to be no easy task: the landscape was rugged, vast, hard to read.

"Got it!" Alaia said, pointing at a distant bump.

"That can't be it," Lago said, "it's too far, you can barely see it." Yet he checked with his binoculars. Alaia was right—that *was* the cairn, unexpectedly distant. Finding a path between the two points seemed unlikely, but Jiara showed them how to do it, leading them from cairn to cairn.

"You think it's safe again?" Lago asked, pulling Agnargsilv out of his bag.

"I think so," Ockam said. "I've only spotted old tracks. I don't think we'll find anyone else on this... road, if you can call it that."

They were walking alongside rainbow-hued pools. With his mask on, Lago noticed the unique 'flavors' of the bacterial mats in the differently colored rings. Toward the inside, where the yellow mats turned lime-green due to the blue waters, Agnargsilv showed a tightly cohesive system of just one particular species. In the outermost bands of rusty oranges, the sensation was chaotic, as if thousands of different kinds of bacteria shared the same space. Although his human eyes perceived the color transition as an even gradient, through Agnargsilv he could see the separation, the specialization, the uniqueness of each ring.

For three more days they traveled, higher each time, along a path closely following the river that the distant falls birthed. They left behind the tremulous poplars, the gnarly birches, and the stalwart maples; trading them for furrowed firs, fragrant hemlocks, and whiskery larches. Near the hot river, no plants grew; that was the realm of hissing fumaroles, bone-like terraces, calcified trees, and bubbling mudpots. Every once in a while, a geyser would erupt next to them, lifting a transient curtain that separated them from the opposite cliffside.

They saw their first bear, too, on the other side of the river. She was a cinnamon-colored black bear with lush and glossy furs, who stood on two legs to pluck berries off a thorny bush.

"Look, she's climbing up the tree," Alaia said, spying with the binoculars.

"Let me see," Jiara said, taking them. "There's a beehive up there. I think she's going for the honey." And the bear did. She expertly harvested the honey, slathering her claws and muzzle with it.

The bears grew more numerous at higher elevations, so they followed Jilpi's advice and banged sticks, noisily dragged their feet, and sang. Ockam taught them his favorite war songs from the Free Tribelands and the lullabies from the Khaar Du fjords, where he had lived until he was eight years of age. No bears bothered them.

On their fourth night, they camped within a grove of dead cedars. The earth had boiled their roots years ago, leaving only their crystal-covered skeletons, with spiraling minerals rising around their roots and trunks.

The Firefalls were clearly visible from their camp. After night fell, as they sat to enjoy dinner and a quiet conversation, Lago stood up abruptly and looked toward the falls.

"What is that?" he asked.

They all moved away from their campfire to get a better look.

The falls were alight, glowing red like fire, but deeper. They had only seen the falls during the day so far, not yet in the dark of night. The brightest things around were the stars, the violet moonlight on the mountaintops, and the glowing waterfall. The twin snowy peaks on either side of the falls looked like fangs with a trail of blood dripping between them.

"Minnelvad," Ockam said, almost to himself.

"Is it a volcano? I'm not sure what we are seeing," Lago said.

"I think there's either flowing lava or very hot rocks behind the falls," Jiara conjectured.

The red light vanished as the steam thickened with a change of the wind. Then it lit up once more, brighter than before, like a furnace being given new breath by powerful bellows.

When they woke up the next morning, the red glow—if it was there—was too dim to see. A fresh coat of snow blanketed the landscape, brittle and shimmering in the sunlight.

"I'm a bit worried now," Lago said as they broke camp. "This path seems to be taking us to the bottom of the falls. If our goal happens to be at the top, we still have quite a hike to struggle through. That is, if the cairns even lead that far up."

"And the snowfall will make things harder," Jiara said. "It's not enough to hide the path, but it can make it slippery."

"Bah," Ockam dismissed her, "with your ropes and expertise, it should be no problem. I've never met a better climber. Not counting your sister, that is."

Jiara wrinkled her nose, as if smelling something bitter.

Lago began to walk, carving a path in the pristine snow. "We have to give it a try," he said. "Let's first get to the bottom of the falls and see if we find any sign of those 'cousins' of the Wutash."

The base of Minnelvad was roaring, deafening. The falls emptied into a basin large as a city block and mottled with hundreds of rainbow pools, all separated by crunchy walls of mineral buildups. Surrounding this depression were steep cliffs, making the steaming basin seem like a large frying pan with the fire burning below.

They kept their distance from the falls, as the hissing steam seemed as if it could singe their eyebrows off. Lago had to put a collar and leash on Bear, something he rarely did, too afraid of the dog accidentally falling—or purposely jumping—into one of the pools. They balanced over the brittle minerals, making their way to the center of the basin, and from there to one of the walls.

Despite the steaming waters, there were icicles—and much more bizarre ice formations—covering nearly every surface. The temperatures were below freezing when away from the pools, helping the steam crystallize in wing-like shards, compound blades, or fragile dandelions; like a hoarfrost that traced the emotions of the wind, listening to the whims of a sculptor of impermanence.

They searched for clues, for anything that would tell them why they came this far, or who they were looking for. Alaia walked while sliding her hands over the brittle ice, leaving a trail of sprite dust behind her. She stopped, noticing something on the wall she had just exposed.

"Here!" she said, "There are writings!"

Her friends rushed to her. Hiding behind the tremulous crystals were petroglyphs, carved directly onto the rock face. They were triangular in nature, flowing up and down in a sharp zigzag.

"Same kind of runes as we saw on Stelm Bir," Lago said.

They used their cloaks to more quickly clear off the crystals and uncovered more runes and indecipherable drawings. The etchings merged toward travertine terraces not too far from the steaming Firefalls; there, the limestone had built up over the centuries, covering the remaining petroglyphs under carbonate deposits. Lago climbed on the terraces easily, as if they were a staircase, searching for more clues.

"They continue above, over there," he said, pointing up and to his right.

"I see another cairn up there too," Ockam said. "This path does go up the falls after all."

"Let's make sure we aren't missing anything down here," Jiara said, "and if there's nothing else to find, we can make our way up tomorrow."

They found petroglyphs all around the basin, even entire walls carved into niches and altars, but no signs of recent habitation. Once the shadows of the evening crept in, they made their camp inside a crack on the wall that protected them from the crystallizing steam and from the overbearing rumble of the falls.

They stood at the mouth of the crack to look at the falls one more time. Minnelvad looked like a constantly shifting tower of lava, tinting red the entire bowl they were inhabiting. A bit of moonlight still shone from the west, turning the vapors into lavender specters far above, where the redness reached not; and into a magenta veil below, where it merged with the warmth of the heart of the mountain. They watched in awe, listening to the mountain's roar.

A few more fingerbreadths of snow had fallen overnight, but the next cairn up the pathless path was still clearly visible, at least for those who knew where to look.

"It could take us all day to climb to the top," Ockam said. "Jiara, what do you think?"

"This steam worries me. It moves with the shifting winds, and aside from blocking the view, it can grow ice in unexpected places. We don't have crampons, nor ice axes. I wasn't expecting an ice climb when I packed our equipment. I think we should go back to Brimstowne and pick up better gear."

"That would set us back more than a week," Ockam said.

"It'll get colder the longer we wait," Lago said, not looking forward to having to walk all the way back.

"True," Ockam agreed. "Dewrest will be here in only four more days, yet the sky is clear as crystal today. I can't imagine we'll find better weather later in the season."

They debated, then decided that they had better get started right away, aiming to get to the top before nightfall, since there might not be any safe place to camp on the hillside, and climbing in the dark was ill-advised.

They set off on their journey up the travertine steps, with the great falls looming to their left. All the runes they found seemed to follow a clear direction toward the cairns. By the time they reached the fourth cairn, about two-thirds of the way up, the crystal-clear skies were no more.

"Winds are picking up," Jiara said. "Keep your center of balance close to the walls and at least three contact points at all times, you hear me?"

The temperature abruptly dropped. The rocks up here had cracks through which steam congealed in pockets of hoarfrost, which melted again to form icy puddles. Bear was getting anxious, and he kept sliding, or breaking through the thin ice and getting his paws wet and even colder. Lago was wearing Agnarg-silv, which somehow helped calm Bear down, but wasn't much help at all when traversing the treacherous path.

Geysers hissed near them. In slow and methodical fashion they progressed, constantly reminding themselves not to step too close to a hole that might suddenly erupt in boiling steam.

"I think that's the last cairn before the top," Ockam said, looking up with hope in his eyes.

"Shit," Jiara said. "Here it comes."

A soft-moving avalanche of clouds rolled down from the twin peaks, sinking them in a thick fog.

"Stay together!" Ockam ordered.

Jiara pulled out her rope and made sure they were all holding on to it, so that no one could be left behind. The fog was biting cold, hastily freezing all the puddles. After a sluggish, near-blind climb, they found the final cairn, where they stopped to pile on more layers of clothing.

"We are nearly there," Jiara said, shivering as she tightened her hood. "I think I might be able to figure out the rest of the way, if we keep on moving."

They had stopped close to a perfectly still, blue pool. It steamed soothingly.

Bear whined, feeling the cold dig into his paws. He stared at the pool.

"Bear, stay," Lago said.

Bear looked at the pool, then at Lago, then at the pool again, and ran for it.

"Stop!" Lago said, bolting behind him. If it hadn't been for Bear's clumsy paws, Lago would not have reached him in time. He tackled the slipping dog, and with their momentum they slid toward the scalding—yet never bubbling—blue pool. In a moment of panic, Lago took Agnargsilv off and slammed it into the ice, pointy ears down. The scraping ears created barely enough friction to make them slow, then stop, mere fingerbreadths from being boiled alive.

"You stupid, stupid dog," he said, kicking away from the blue water. "You almost cooked yourself to death." He put Bear over his shoulders and hurried back to the others.

Crack! the ice below them went, weakened by the cuts Lago had scored in it. The ice began to split in a frigid spiderweb. *Crrr-rrack!* it went again, then shattered. Lago's left leg dropped through and splashed into boiling, acidic water. He hurled Bear toward the others, barely able to see them through the fog, then was struck by a searing pain. He lifted himself up and rolled on the ice, as if trying to quench a fire.

Lago screamed in agony and crawled away from the weak ice. Ockam grabbed his shoulders and pulled him over the snow-covered rocks.

"It burns!" Lago shrieked as he tried to pull his trousers off.

"You have to help him!" Alaia begged.

"Be calm!" Jiara said. "Don't do anything rash."

"But he's in pain!" Alaia said.

"Just get it off!" Lago howled.

"Stop thrashing!" Jiara ordered. "Roll your leg on the snow, let it melt on you." She helped Lago pack more snow over his leg, which melted quickly and diluted the blistering waters of the hot spring.

"Easy, easy, it's cooling off," Jiara said. "If you were to pull your trousers off, you could rip away all your skin with them. Let's be patient."

Once the heat subsided, Jiara cut the trousers from ankle to waist and helped Lago take them off, careful not to pull too hard on the blistered skin.

It was horrendous. Up to his knee, Lago had burnt off most of his skin. His feet had been saved due to his tight boots, but the rest was peeling off in agonizing pain.

"I'm going to wash it off with fresh snow," Jiara said, packing more snow around it. "The water is highly acidic, we need to get it all out of your leg before bandaging it."

Once the leg was clean, Jiara took out the jar of honey she had collected at the Kingroot Woods and spread the sticky nectar over the leg. "This will help the inflammation go down." She then tore a shirt and wrapped the shreds around the pink, throbbing limb.

"Chew on these, for the pain," Ockam said, placing lazuline claw leaves on Lago's tongue, making sure he swallowed the bitter herb.

It was still daytime, but it felt like night in the opaque fog.

"Can you walk?" Ockam asked, after giving Lago barely enough time to compose himself.

"I think so. It hurts like the netherflames, but my feet are fine," Lago said, glancing at his legs. Alaia had sewn the trousers back together after washing them. They were wet and cold, but not too bad when worn over his other pair of trousers, which alone were too thin for the current weather.

Ockam helped Lago up and said, "We should go back to town and find better care for you—"

"No," Lago snapped. "We are almost at the top, let's get there and find a safe place to rest."

"The kid's right," Jiara said. "With all this ice, it's harder to go downhill. Let's hurry before it gets too dark."

Lago picked up his bag and held on to the safety rope. The climb resumed.

The fog quickly turned into a blizzard with no sense of direction. The snow blew down, it blew sideways, it blew up. The winds hammered in a mix of extreme cold followed by short respites of warmth from the waterfall's fiery breath. Their clothing was blanketed by crystal needles that would break off in the slapping winds, only to be replaced by twice the number.

Lago was once again wearing Agnargsilv, which was now white and spiky and had icicles elongating where its fangs would be. His head was throbbing from the cold, and he could not pull his hood over his mask's tall ears, so he took it off, removed all the frost from it, and stowed it in his bag. Lago's reddened, brittle ears thanked him greatly once his hood went up.

"We are almost at the top!" Ockam screamed over the blizzard.

Bear was whining, paws cold once more. They had wrapped a jacket around him, which was not fit for a dog, but helped a little.

"We'll be there soon," Lago said, but Bear found no comfort in his words.

The winds changed again, and the steam from the waterfall hit them hard. The mineral-infused fumes smelled different up here: sharp, pungent, malign. They soon felt dizzy from the smell, but there was no escaping it.

"Keep moving, over that rock!" Jiara encouraged them once the cliff became less steep. She jumped on top of a flat and steady rock, making sure it had no ice built up over it. She tied the rope around a rotting tree trunk and reached her hands down to help Alaia up.

"Hand me your gear," Alaia said to Lago.

Lago slung his bag up to her. He then picked up Bear and was lifting him up, arms outstretched, when his weak leg slipped on the ice. With both arms holding Bear up, Lago was no longer grabbing on to the safety rope.

"Hold!" Ockam cried, reaching over to support Lago, but his hands grabbed onto nothing but cold air. Lago tumbled down, with Bear right above him, landing on a soft pile of snow. He tried to crawl out of the pocket he had carved, but the snow broke apart in small cracks, then in large chunks began to slide down the hill.

They tumbled and rolled in a white avalanche. Lago held Bear tightly to his chest, protecting him. He felt his legs scrape, his shoulder impact, and then came a sense of weightlessness. In that brief moment, he recalled the time not too long ago when they had escaped the limestone caverns, and he had tumbled out of the waterfall into the bright light. He had landed on water back then, but this time he landed on harder snow, on his back, knocking the air out of him while more snow fell and buried him.

He was pinned down in the white darkness.

He tried to move but didn't know in which direction to go. He tried to breathe, but his lungs did not answer, and there was no air around him either way.

He felt a scraping above him.

Rrrwwoof! Rooouff!

A shard of gray light, followed by Bear's tongue licking his face.

Lago's arms reached through the hole and pushed snow out of the way, until he managed to sit up, bottom half still buried. He hugged Bear and turned him this way and that, making sure he wasn't injured. The dog seemed fine, although terribly scared.

Lago crawled out into thick mist. He noticed a cold draft blowing on his shoulder, where his clothes had ripped and his skin had cut. For a moment he forgot about the pain of his burned leg, until it returned throbbing back to him.

The Firefalls steamed right next to him, too close for comfort. Travertine terraces capped by oily films rose in complex structures all around him. He did not recognize this place, nor could he see the path they had been following. He tried to estimate how far he had fallen, but he could find no reference points. He walked on, sidestepping stinking pots of bubbling mud, which made him feel nauseated. The steam was thick. His mind was reeling.

"Bear, stay with me," he said, raising his voice to overcome the roars and hisses near him. Bear followed with his tail between his legs, terrified of the alien environment.

Lago staggered forward, coughing, wheezing. The fumes were not just water vapors, but were mixed with something metallic and rich, like a greasy smoke. He felt dizzy, losing his balance, his sense of space. He nearly prayed for the Lodestar to guide him, but no starlight could pierce the grayness.

He stumbled onto cleaner snow once more, and although he had moved away from the falls, the fetid steam was yet thicker here. He shambled uphill, dragging his feet as the snow packed deeper, reaching to his hips.

Colors changed in his eyes, his vision blurred, and he began to suffer hallucinations. The snow looked purple, then green, then fuzzy and bubbly and somehow remorseful. His fingers looked way too long, like rubbery icicles, and they felt like they did not belong to him. The dead trees up ahead twisted and grinned their galls at him. He couldn't tell in which direction he had been heading. He turned around, searching for a sign.

The rumbling of the waterfall was all around him, dissonant, percussive. No, that was the sound of his heart. He heard Bear barking next to him, looked down, and could barely keep his eyes on him, as if every reaction from his muscles landed two heartbeats too late.

Bear yipped and ran in circles, trying to get his attention, but confusing him even more. Lago felt cold. So cold.

He lumbered farther uphill, or down, he could not tell. The mask felt cold on his face, so he reached forward to take it off, but he had no mask; it was way up in his bag somewhere.

Everything was gray and white. Waterfall. Bark. Snow. Fire.

He collapsed onto the snow. He felt Bear licking his face and could smell his breath, and thought he heard him bark again, but the bark sounded distant. Bear ran into the snow, losing himself in the mist.

"Bear!" Lago cried. "Bear! Come back!"

The softened silhouette of Bear stood still in the distance, peering back at him through the haze.

"Bear!"

The shape came in and out of view through curtains of mist.

A distant bark.

"B... Bear..."

Bear's figure vanished like a breath.

Lago waited.

Bear did not return.

A long moment passed, perhaps an hour. He felt stunned, delirious, curling tight into a ball. Shapes in his vision merged into senseless abstractions.

"B-bear..."

A faraway bark.

He saw Bear approach, but the dog seemed larger. Too large. His form was enormous.

The shadow loomed closer.

It wasn't Bear, but *a bear*, mountainous, formidable, and with a creamy, sparkling-yellow fur.

The golden bear stomped forward, pink nose snuffling.

Lago gazed upon a huge, moist muzzle. It contacted his face, smelling, snorting, tasting, grunting.

It... It smells like lemongrass.

Lago passed out.

PART THREE
BANOOK

CHAPTER FORTY

URGSILV

General Alvis Hallow paced around the war room of the Fogdale Citadel. He had sent for the prisoners nearly an hour ago. *What is taking so long?* he wondered. He sat again, clenched his hands upon a wooden desk, then forcefully let his fingers relax. *They better bring them back to me alive.*

After years of failures and countless wasted slaves, they had finally managed to breach into the Anglass Dome through a route that did not suffer any flooding. Artificer Urcai had found that by slathering the shafts with sapfire and letting them burn, it weakened the rocks, letting the slaves cut through an otherwise impassable, hard substrate. Their tunnel was not yet wide enough to let the battalions march in safely, so they had sent persuasive emissaries in their stead.

Alvis ran his fingers through his graying temples, over the complex tattoo of his ranking insignia. Those old markings were no longer important to him—his face, his name, that was all the proof of rank he needed.

"They are here, Lorr," said a servant at the door.

Alvis stood. "Send them in."

Guards pushed in two chain-bound prisoners. They were the chief of Urgdrolom—the Anglass Dome—and his daughter. Both had long and lustrous black hair and faces seeping despair. Their fine silk robes were white, splattered with red.

"It wasn't that hard to get you, after all," Alvis said, pacing before them.

"Should I translate that, Lorr?" asked the interpreter as he hurried in behind the guards. He spread open a voluminous Miscamish dictionary.

"No need. And the blood? I said not to hurt them."

A guard took a step forward and answered, "They killed two of our finest when they realized they'd been deceived. The blood is not theirs, General Hallow."

"Feisty. Is the entrance tunnel secured?"

"Yes, Lorr."

"Good," Alvis said. "Tell me their names."

"Antástis is the chief," the interpreter said, to which the man in chains reacted by raising his head. "His daughter is Dena." The teenage girl kept her head down. "As you can see by their hair and skin, they are not Wutash. The race that lives in this dome call themselves the Teldebran, or Teldebran Miscam."

"And where is the artifact?" Alvis asked, already looking past the prisoners.

A guard pushed past the others, carrying an object covered in a vermillion cloth. He placed it on the desk.

The general reached forth a calloused hand and pulled the veil away. There lay Urgsilv, the mask of cervids, fifteenth of the Silvesh. It was shaped like the head of a deer, or elk, or some kind of antelope perhaps, with a small crown of antlers that was imposingly regal, yet not cumbersome. Hallow took the mask to closely observe it. Too beautifully stylized Urgsilv was, swimming in details too fine for human eyes to see.

Chief Antástis looked up in fear and said, "*Esathuk khe Silv wäeth henet nu'irg ilm däenn enn khuársaash trafólv!*"

Alvis arched an eyebrow at the interpreter.

"I couldn't pick up all of it," the interpreter said, "but he spouted something about Urgsilv—the cervid mask—filling your soul with pain."

"I know about the pain," Alvis said. "It doesn't scare me, and neither do his words."

Alvis stepped right in front of the Teldebran Miscam chief and to his face said, "Your kind amassed fortunes and riches for generations, concealing them from every realm in Noss. You are nothing but selfish hoarders, self-centered heretics. You have been sucking at the marrow of our lands with your damnable domes. It's time we took it all back."

The interpreter strained to keep up. Alvis continued, speaking over him.

"All your profane, Miscam kingdoms shall fall. Your uncivilized tribes will perish, while I—I will lay claim to the power of this relic, freeing Takhamún's emanation from the curse you cast upon it." Alvis lifted the mask to his face. He was making a show of it, not as much for the Teldebran chief and his daughter, but for the soldiers who stood guard behind them. He knew the soldiers would talk; he expected them to.

As the mask connected with his face, Alvis felt a surge of uncontainable pain. He staggered backward, falling to his knees, but he did not utter a moan. A guard rushed to help, but Alvis waved him off. Straining his breath, he reached up as if to pull off the mask, but soon stopped himself and focused instead.

The pain he felt, it wasn't his own, he now realized; it belonged to others. This soothed him. This felt invigorating to him. He let the pain run through him as a grotesque smile creeped up his contorting face. Alvis stood, seeing twofold, revitalized by the agony fed into his spine.

The power of Urgsilv was self-evident, but Alvis knew it had secrets to be uncovered. He approached Dena—the chief's daughter—pushing his cervid countenance uncomfortably close; a light-sucking shape of dread. *She is terrified, and she should be*, he thought.

Alvis caressed Dena's long, black hair and said to her father, "Now you will teach me how to take the shape of the beasts, and how to control them, or I will have you watch as my guards make good use of your daughter's body."

The interpreter had to look up a few words in his Miscamish dictionary, but he knew the rest. He spoke the words, uncomfortable with what he was saying, but conveying the meaning quite clearly.

◑

For weeks, Fjorna Daro rode alongside the surviving members of her arbalister squad. After escaping the Maankel prison of the Free Tribelands, they reported to the fortress of Farjall, where they were informed that General Hallow was close to breaching into the Anglass Dome. Aurélien Knivlar sent Islav—one of her trusty magpies—to notify the general that they'd be heading his way immediately, to deliver information of utmost importance about the masks.

When Fjorna and her squad arrived in Anglass, they were directed to the holding cells of the southern keep. They hurried down into the dungeon, walking past mostly empty cells. At the end of the hallway was a metal door. A guard unlatched the heavy bolts.

Stone steps descended into a torture chamber, windowless and cold. The dreadful space had thick walls, to prevent screams or even prayers from escaping. Fjorna forced herself not to cover her nose at the reek of decay. *Dying bodies stink just the same here, in Hestfell, or in Fjarmallen*, she thought.

The seven arbalisters passed by rusty artifacts crafted solely for the infliction of pain. A servant mopped something sticky off the floor, nodding a weak salute at the group. At the back of the chamber, lit by the only two torches in the room, they saw two naked prisoners hanging from opposing walls. Their limbs were spread open, their long hair spilling like curtains of tar. One was a pale man, his yellowish skin streaked with sweat, but clean. Facing him was a young woman covered in bruises, with trails of blood oozing from her lips, from her nipples, from between her legs.

Standing between the prisoners were three men. One was a thin man with even thinner spectacles, of slicked-back black hair that matched his sharply cut, short beard; he had the habit of constantly peering over his spectacles, as if he might as well dispose of them entirely. The next was a bulky man holding a substantial book, who was trying to avert his eyes. The third man was the oddest—he wore a suit of red leather armor decorated in gold and a disconcerting mask that resembled something like an elk.

The third man strutted to the arbalisters with confidence. He removed his mask and said, "Crescu, Shea! Welcome back! I thought I'd never see you again. Will Chief Daro be joining us, too?"

"I'm here, General Hallow," Fjorna said through her disfigured visage.

"Fjorna? By the Twin Faces of Takh, what happened to you?"

"It has to do with the masks, we came here to… Is that?—"

"It is," Alvis answered, proudly showcasing his trophy. "Its name is Urgsilv. I've had it in my possession for three days now. Our dangling guests are the chief of Urgdrolom—as they call it—and his daughter. We took a subtler approach this time, more persuasive than what we tried with the bloodskins. We tricked them into joining us outside of the dome, locking the shaft behind them."

"And the general has already managed an astounding level of control over the mask," the thin man behind Alvis said, stepping forward as he adjusted his splattered, orange doublet. "General, if I may—"

"Certainly. This is Urcai, one of our keenest artificers. Trained in Afhora, of course. He has not only devised the majority of the toys in this chamber, but also our most ingenious weapons of war, such as the sapfire cannons."

Artificers were multidisciplinary academicians who mixed engineering with fields like alchemy, cosmology, theology, and physics. They were crafters and scholars, highly versatile and well-learned. Urcai happened to be one of the best, not only for his contributions to warfare, but for his vast knowledge in politics and commerce.

Artificer Urcai bowed with hands to his chest, following Afhoran customs. He further lowered his spectacles and said, "I've been studying Urgsilv and the effects it has on the general. It's fascinatingly powerful, but there's a lot more that the Teldebran Miscam are keeping hidden from us."

"It's just as the bloodskin prisoners once described to us," Alvis said. "The masks grant an ability to perceive well beyond what mere eyes can see. I have learned quite a lot, but the chief has not yet revealed the method for changing forms, nor explained how he controls the herds."

"We know the Teldebran chief was able to shapeshift at will, just like the Wutash witches," Urcai said. "Before we tricked him into taking off the mask, he had been in his half-form of a marsh deer."

Alvis addressed Fjorna directly, "The letter said you carried important knowledge about the mask. I was hoping it was referring to the secret to take these forms. Is that the information you came to deliver?"

"Not exactly," Fjorna said, "but I feel that what we discovered could prove even more valuable than that."

Alvis's ash-colored eyes glinted with curiosity. "Tell me everything," he said.

Fjorna recounted in detail all that had happened since they had followed Lago's trail across the Pilgrim Sierras. She described Lago's increased sense of awareness, his ability to see them in the dark, and how Agnargsilv had helped him fight so many of the arbalisters at once. She then recounted how Lago had made his escape, straight through the vines.

"A key to enter the domes?" Alvis murmured. "And we spent all these years digging through miles of rocks. We could easily breach the Lequa Dome and get *their* mask, use their resources to take over the Bighorn Dome, and the Moonrise Dome after that. We could take over the entire Jerjan Continent, one dome at a time, with no time wasted in digging."

"Have you taken precautions to prevent Anglass from suffering the same fate as Heartpine?" Osef asked uneasily.

"Lorr Wild… Windscar, I remember. Emperor Uvon ordered us to destroy the temple at once, but I told my troops to hold back. Not only that, but once we secure the dome, I will send a platoon to protect the axis, to make sure no one steps near the lattice." Alvis sniggered, "Uvon… that gullible child still believes in those ridiculous myths of the Takhamún emanations. No offense, if any of you are believers."

"None taken," Osef said, taking offense.

"Do not underestimate the power of those stories, Lorr," Urcai said.

Alvis nodded. "I know, Urcai. I do not doubt your knowledge of the Takh Codex, which has been exceptionally useful. I will follow through with our strategy."

"And the animals, Lorr, how will you deal with the dire wolves?" Aurélien asked from the shadows while caressing her two magpies.

Urcai took the question. "There are no dire wolves in this dome. However, there are other colossal creatures, of a similar sort. Stronger beasts, antlered, not fanged, who respond to the whims of the one who controls Urgsilv. We are trying to find out how to harness that power, but Antástis—the chief here—has not been cooperative, despite all the persuasive methods we've tried on his daughter."

"If I may…" Fjorna said, inspecting the prisoners with her misshapen face. "No offense, Artificer Urcai, but I think you have it backward. Don't waste your time hurting her, make *him* suffer instead. I know her kind. She will break if you flip the roles. And she's old enough, she must've been training to become the mask's heir. She will know all that you want to know."

"It's worth a try," Alvis said, "as long as we don't kill him yet."

Throughout that night, Urcai worked his most callous tools and harrowing skills onto the body of Antástis. Hour after hour, trapped between echoing wails, he pierced, and snapped, and tore, and crushed. He cut, and burned, and scraped, and ripped, until Antástis could no longer beg Dena to remain quiet, his energy drained, his soul crushed, his tongue shredded. But the burning and breaking continued until Dena shouted it all out; she shouted everything they asked to know: the secret to Urgsilv, the secret to all the other masks that waited in the sealed domes.

With Urgsilv on his face, General Hallow could tell Dena was not lying, so he listened intently. In utmost secret, day and night he prepared, following her advice. For three suns and three moons he strained in the depths of the dungeon, until at last his mind snapped in the right configuration; at last, he understood.

That night, from the depths of the dungeon came out not General Alvis Hallow, but a formidable creature, noble and chilling. Walking on heavy hooves, thickly matted in brown furs, wearing a mighty crown of antlers that sprouted sixteen sharp points, Alvis Hallow had been transformed into a being with the rough proportions of a man, but the anatomical features and power of an elk stag. His dark eyes scanned with Urgsilv's two-fold sight; his dewlap waved pendulously beneath his long muzzle. His red leather armor snapped seams as his muscles bent and tightened with each step.

He was followed into the courtyard by the seven arbalisters and his chief artificer. As the crowd around him swelled, he rose onto a platform and belted out a high-pitched bugle, a screech like that of an unholy banshee, of a ruthless wraith, which commanded reverence and devotion from all who heard it.

His thunderous call proclaimed a new dawn for the Negian Empire.

CHAPTER FORTY-ONE

BANOOK'S CABIN

Lago dreamed.

He dreamed of white and gray, of a cold so deep that it turned his bones to crystal shards. His skull was covered in triangular runes, glowing blue, green, and gold. Like steaming geysers, his breath shot out his nose and ears. His mouth was a pool of rainbow acid both boiling and frigid; around it, his mineral lips crackled like breaking glaciers. His pores grew hair-like icicles, his tongue tasted metallic and glowed red like the falls at night. His injured leg pulsated, bubbled, and hissed like enraged mudpots.

He dreamed of Bear, as a distant silhouette that kept running closer but never reached him. Bear's face was black, like the dead dire wolf's; his bark sounded like the roar of a waterfall. Bear kept running, no longer a dog, but a golden-furred bear, as big as a mountain. His muzzle dripped hot lava and honey, his eyes bespoke fire and comfort.

He dreamed of being lifted and carried by the mist. He floated in a pool of forgetfulness, in a viscous vapor of sulphur and solitude and fear.

He dreamed of the warmth of hibernation, of the giant bear holding him tight against his belly, his enormous arms wrapping around him, paws dangling long knives in front of his face. The golden bear's muzzle steamed a white aurora.

He dreamed of a deep darkness where he had lost his friends, where he could not wake up. In the darkness all that remained was the memory of a distant mountain and the pulsating ache of his burning leg.

Lago slept.

Lago awoke.

His crusted eyes cracked open. He was disoriented, not sure whether he was still asleep; the only thing he was certain of was that he was warm, and that the cold was nothing but a faraway memory. He wiped the gunk off his eyes and found that his cheeks were resting on soft, brown fur. He looked toward his belly and saw a massive bear paw, with claws longer than his fingers, wrapped around his waist.

He jolted up, shoving the paw away from him. It was a bearskin, paws and all, wrapped around him like a blanket. The fast movement made his injured leg itch and throb; he saw it was expertly bandaged with clean cloth.

Lago was wearing his underwear, as well as a long-sleeved shirt with a button-up neck, a few sizes too large. *Ockam's?* he wondered. He looked around the space. He was in a cozy log cabin crafted of walnut and oak beams, expertly fitted together. His bed was a cushiony couch, comfortably tucked in a corner across from a stone fireplace, where fragrant pine wood released furtive sparks up the chimney. Stairs led to an interior balcony that hung above his head, all made of wood. Shelves covered the walls, overflowing with books and wood carvings. He saw snowflakes—barely perceptible out the tall windows—weaving like moths in the dark night.

Among the aromas of hardwoods, leather, and smoke, Lago smelled something that made his dry mouth water. *Is that chocolate?* he wondered. He heard a spoon stirring in a metal cup, the pitch of the clinking sound lowering as something dense and sugary dissolved in the liquid.

He leaned forward in his bed to spy further down the length of the cabin and in an open kitchen saw the back of an enormous man. Nearly nine feet tall, the man was fat and bulky, but smoothly carried his weight. His loose belt wrapped around a simple tunic, revealing the curve of a plump belly. The short sleeves displayed his heavy forearms, which were covered in wispy, strawberry-blond hairs. The mountain of a man reached up toward a cabinet, allowing Lago to see the side of his face and the short ponytail his hair was tied into. His strong neck supported a bushy beard that shimmered in light, reddish colors like a waxy cedarwood, and sparkled in gold like fresh pine sap in Summer. The man had thick eyebrows, a pudgy nose, and wide lips that widely smiled.

Should I say something? Where am I? Lago noticed that the cabin was built with strange proportions. Some chairs were extremely large, others normal-sized. The front door was unseemly wide, yet short enough that the man in the kitchen would need to duck to walk under it. Lago heard a scrambling noise on the interior balcony, and down came Bear, clicking his claws on the extra-wide steps. The dog immediately jumped onto Lago, dropping him back against the bed in a torrent of licks, releasing quiet yips of unconfined joy.

"He's finally awoken!" the giant quietly said, tiptoeing toward Lago while holding a mug that looked ridiculous in his colossal fingers. "Cocoa, honey, and a touch of cardamom. It's very hot," he said, squatting down and handing Lago an enamel mug. The man had honey-colored eyes and was smiling the warmest smile Lago had ever seen—the fireplace and the sweetened chocolate felt entirely redundant.

"My name is Banook, and I presume you must be Lago," he said, holding his hand out.

Lago put a timid hand forward. Banook enveloped it with his fist and shook it.

"I... I am..." Lago said. "Thank you, Banook, for th-the chocolate... How did you know my name?"

"Bear here told me, of course!"

Bear jumped onto Banook's belly and licked his face, making him lose his balance. The giant tipped backward and fell on his ass, unleashing a small earthquake. The rustic decor took a short while to settle back into place.

Banook laughed, then put a finger to his own lips and made a *shhh* to quiet his own laughter. "We must be quiet as a moonbeam in the Spring. Let's not wake up your friends quite yet, they are fast asleep."

"They are here!?" Lago said, raising his voice. Banook placed a massive finger to Lago's lips and *shh'd* again. The finger smelled of lemongrass, leather, silt, and pine.

"They are indeed," he replied, with cheeks lifted in a perpetual smile. "Hopefully still sleeping, if my little fall did not shake them as much as it shook the belly of the caldera below us. Your friends are eager to see you rise, but they also need rest. They have cared for you with open hearts, for six moons and six suns. You must count yourself lucky to travel with such committed companions."

"I am. I... I was so scared I'd lose them, are they—"

"They are as healthy as the Summer days are long. Come with me, and I will tell you all that has happened."

Banook walked surprisingly quietly, leading Lago to a dining table in the kitchen. Something was cooking on the iron stove.

"I heard you mutter as you came back to consciousness and thought you might be hungry," the big man said with his low, meadow-smooth voice. "It's almost ready."

"I'm starving, actually," Lago said as his host pulled up a normal-sized chair for him.

Banook stirred something thick that had a meaty fragrance, with hints of thyme. "It's caribou stew," he pointed out, then served a hearty portion in a bowl and placed it in front of Lago, before sprinkling it with crushed juniper berries and pepper.

"Fill your modest belly while Banook tells you the story," he said, then sat on a larger chair.

The stew was dense and filling. Lago wolfed it down, hardly chewing, feeling a bit embarrassed by how quickly he was ingesting the meal.

"Six nights ago," Banook began, "I was sauntering back home when I was engulfed by the mistdraft. It's common among these piercing peaks and ample mountains, particularly in early Umbra. It crawls over granite like a ghostly blanket, pulling its cold tendrils in every which direction. Mist or not, I know my path, but I heard troubled calls nearby—three voices hollering your name. I cut my way through the fog and asked your friends what had happened, then jumped down into the white to search for your tenuous tracks."

He poured mint-infused spring waters into a blue glass goblet, then pushed it toward Lago.

"Mind you," he continued, "I know these mountains well, but you fell near the pernicious vents, where I dare not venture, as their fumes can be as lethal as the Frostburn gales. But a call for aid I heard, and heeded it. It was this brave hero here"—he stroked Bear's back—"who loudly ran to search for help, and he found me, as I found him. My breath I held and followed Bear's lead, until I found your beaten body and carried you away from the noxious vapors.

"You were frigid, your lips and eyes sealed like icy catacombs. I held you to my chest until you warmed up enough to take full breaths again, then carried you back to your friends. Night had settled upon the mountains by then. My cabin is not too close to Minnelvad, but your tired friends followed me tirelessly. For eleven hours we walked in the gloom, pushed fore and aft by the unrelenting mistdraft.

"We arrived here in the morning, but your friends did not rest even then. Jiara tended to your wounds with expert hands, Alaia fed you and kept you clean, and Ockam helped me find medicine and hunt for food. And Bear, he kept you company and kept you warm, sleeping by your side."

Bear panted happily.

Lago finished his bowl of stew. Banook offered more, but he refused, fully satiated. The big man shrugged, picked up the whole pot, and with the ladle as a spoon gulped the remaining stew down in an instant. He scraped the inside of the bowl with one bulky finger and sucked on it.

"Where are we, exactly?" Lago asked.

"In the mountains, which I call home. Northeast of Minnelvad, tucked between the Snoring Mountain and the five peaks of Drann Trodesh. It's a land that offers repose like no other, a borderless country for wanderings and freedom, where the only roof is the starry firmament, where the fragrant woods are filled with song of bird and wind and flower. I can't wait for dawn, for I am eager to show you my home. I hope you will rejoice in the beauty of this land as much as your friends and I have."

"I can't wait to see it either," Lago said. "Thank you, Banook, for... for saving me, and taking care of me, and my friends."

Banook placed a tenderly heavy hand on Lago's shoulder. "I am equally thankful to all of you for coming here and allowing me to be your humble host. But let us both rest now, and once Sunnokh rises, we can all saunter in his sunbeams."

He stood, towering over the table.

"I am taking the guest room just down this hall, while your friends sleep in my bed upstairs, as it is warmer up there. My door will remain open. Do come and see me if you need anything. Moon lights, little cub."

Lago felt bashful and warmed by the affectionate pet name. "Stars guide," he replied and went back to rest under the bearskin.

The alpenglow bounced pink radiance across the fresh coating of snow, seeping in through the tall windows. The mountains blushed. The flames at the fireplace had died down to purring embers that shyly lingered between blackened logs. Bear snored by Lago's feet, his paws shaking, perhaps chasing an ottermole in his dreams.

Lago heard people talking. He smelled fresh-ground coffee and eggs. He sat up and through the windows saw Banook and Ockam sitting side by side on a bench upon an ample wooden terrace overlooking a vast pine forest that was turning from pink to orange. He was ambling toward the kitchen when he heard Alaia's voice.

"Gwoli! You are up!" she said, hurrying down the steps to deliver an improperly rough hug. "I'm so happy to see you awake. How are you feeling?"

"My back hurts, and my leg itches, but I'm fine. I woke up last night and—"

"And you didn't tell me?!" she yapped while smacking his shoulder. "Why didn't you—"

"You were all sleeping, and Banook said to let you rest. He told me everything that's happened."

"So, you met him already. He's such a love, I could not imagine a kinder person. He saved all of us, really, not just you. That storm turned so cold, it nearly froze my nub off. We would've been lost without him. Come sit," she said, pulling up a chair, "breakfast is still warm."

"I'd like to say hi to the others first, and take a look at that view."

"Oh you have no idea. Bring your mug, let's go."

The wooden terrace was covered in a finger of fresh snow, with indentations delineating the spaces between each of the boards. Alaia led Lago around a sugar pine that pierced right through the center of the wide platform, stairs spiraling around its trunk. Farther toward the edge of the terrace was a firepit—the coals dormant and chilled—and farther by the handrail were chairs, and benches carved out of solid logs, where Banook and Ockam were sitting.

Ockam heard the crunching snow and turned around. "The boy is up!" he said and rushed to welcome Lago. His embrace was less rough than Alaia's, but equally warm.

"Banook told me you ate plenty last night. Come, come, you have to see this." Ockam walked Lago toward the edge of the terrace and had him take his seat on the wide bench, next to Banook, who smiled kindly at him.

The cabin was built as a sort of treehouse, partly suspended on several large pines, with the back of the structure balanced at the edge of a prominent rock. The spacious terrace hung above a white-tipped pine forest that snaked into a deep valley, circling ridges of cracked granite and ancient volcanic flows. Creeks streaked the valley, some hot and steaming, some frigid or already frozen. Far toward the southeastern horizon was the Anglass Dome, velvety yellow green under the morning light. Brimstowne could also barely be seen due south, right by the Stiss Minn—the dark buildings with yellow roofs looked like a patch of infinitesimally small flowers.

Lago took in the grandeur, together with a sip of coffee, enjoying the steam that warmed his nose.

"I'm glad you rose early," Banook said, right by Lago's side. "The light of morning softens this jagged landscape with a picturesque palette of harmonizing hues. Your friends and I have been enjoying this view each morning, waiting for the alpenglow to set the peaks alight while we hold warm drinks between our tittering fingers. Well, Alaia has been sleeping in a bit more, but who can blame her? The blankets are much too inviting."

Banook was dressed quite differently this chilly morning, wearing heavy leather boots, green trousers of a thick and durable weave, a long-sleeved shirt with the cuffs rolled up, and a bearskin that acted as a cape, with one arm wrapping around his neck and the paw clasped as a brooch over his left shoulder.

Jiara arrived moments later, carrying two mountain hares and a handful of aromatic herbs.

"You live!" she said, coming behind Lago for an embrace, her bulky braid dangling over Lago's chest. "Feeling better?"

Lago nodded. "Can't get much better than this view."

Banook glanced toward Jiara. "Great catch," he said, then stood up. "I will dress them and get them ready for a slow-cooked lunch."

"Found these too," Jiara said, handing Banook a bundle of trident-shaped, red leaves.

"Crimson feverweed!" Lago said, remembering the plant from his time at the Mesa Monastery. "Khopto always said it's great to treat pain. Thank you, Jiara."

"It's not for you," Banook said, "it's to spice up the meat. To add a bit of pain, if you will, not to take it away. But I may save some for you, too." He winked and left to dress the hares.

"We should show you the rest of this place, it's an architectural marvel," Ockam told Lago. "And we need to talk, just amongst ourselves. Are you well enough to take a walk?"

Lago followed his friends through a path that circled the cabin, up a stone-carved staircase to the east wing, onto a rocky overhang from where the entire structure could be appreciated from above. The cabin was connected by wood and rope bridges to other smaller structures, all hiding at different heights among the tall trees. There were warehouses, guest rooms, workshops, pantries, places for leisure, for reading, or for cooking special meals. Like a spiderweb on treetops, the paths sometimes ushered them nowhere, or led to a tree that happened to have a special quality Banook appreciated, or to a rock that seemed like a comfortable place to sit on to ponder and wonder.

"This must've taken ages to construct," Lago said. "How many people are living up here?"

"Just Banook," Ockam said. "It's quite a secluded nook. We never would've found the secret path without his guidance. He mentioned he hadn't seen anyone in these mountains for many years, not past the falls."

"So… no Wutash…"

Ockam sighed. "It doesn't seem like it, but we haven't directly asked. We didn't want to reveal our intentions just yet, not without consulting you first. Besides, Banook seems quite eager to please us—we've been having a wonderful time."

"You should see the view from the north side of the mountain," Alaia said, "so much vaster than the one at the Ninn Tago. Herds of caribou in the hundreds of thousands roam down the valley, they look like ants. And flocks of birds just as large, covering entire lakes. And lots of bears too, of different sorts. They usually forage up there by that butte."

"It's a very fertile land," Jiara added. "It's cold now, but Banook says it gets all six seasons. It must be thriving and lively in Spring."

On the north side of the rocky promontory, steps led them yet higher.

"I have a good feeling about Banook," Lago said, "even having just met him."

"We do too," Ockam said, arriving at the top of the rock. "Watch your step here." Below them, to the north, was a vast meadow steaming moist fragrances into the morning light. Fresh snow melted at the tips of golden grasses while a forest of hemlocks dozed off in the periphery. The meadows were part of an elevated basin, which farther ahead ascended to immense peaks that revealed the true scale of the Stelm Wujann.

"Is this the view you mentioned?" Lago asked Alaia.

"Oh no, past the meadow, over that distant hill, from there you can see for miles and miles. I'll take you there once your leg is better, it's a bit of a walk."

"I think…" Ockam said, then paused. "I think we should ask Banook about the Wutash, but without revealing our purpose, or the mask. We could ask him about the runes we found by Minnelvad, and that will open up the conversation more naturally."

"Last night he told me we are northeast of Minnelvad," Lago said.

"We are," Ockam said.

"No, no. What I mean is, he used the word *Minnelvad*. He didn't call it the Firefalls."

Ockam scratched his thin mustache. "That's a good sign. He might at least know where to point us to next. Do we agree this is what we should do?"

They all nodded, then strolled together through the meadow. Bear joined them, chasing hares, quails, and a small herd of deer.

"We should ask him today," Ockam said, "once we gather for lunch. I'm very curious."

"What makes *me* curious," Jiara said, "is why *he* hasn't asked *us* why we are here. Even though he has an inquisitive nature. It's been days, and he's been most welcoming, but he hasn't questioned us being here at all."

They ambled leisurely, letting Lago get used to the feeling of his leg again. They came back down through a different route on the west side, following a creek that softly cascaded down to the west wing of the cabin.

Banook was back at the terrace, slow-roasting the hares on the firepit.

"It smells delicious," Lago said. The smell carried a tinge of homeness, but also a nostalgia that he could not yet comprehend. He felt at peace. He felt guilty for feeling at peace.

Chapter Forty-Two

Jugged Hare

Banook tossed red coals around the clay pot, even over the lid, to let it heat evenly. Once the jugged hares finished cooking, he brought out fresh-baked bread and served the food at the terrace.

"Banook," Jiara said, leaning an elbow on the long table, "you've been so kind to us this whole time. Yet you never asked us why we are here."

"I have not," he said, slurping a hind leg and spitting out a bone like it was a seed from a grape. "I didn't think it necessary, as there's only one reason I could imagine."

"What reason do you suppose?" she asked.

"To bask in the glory of the mountain range, tasting the moonlit radiance of glaciers yet untamed. To feel creeks cascade through your veins as they tickle your minds and replenish your souls. To watch the tiniest of flowers bloom like crystals of salt, and bathe in the warmth of a campfire during the coldest of nights. To sway like grasses on sweeping meadows, to leap through icy falls, to feel squirrels crawl on your bellies as you dry them in the sun. To lay witness to the immortality of starlight on a clear night, and heed the call of the mountain, who thumps to the heartbeat of life."

"I…" Jiara said, "well, mostly yes."

"But there's another reason," Ockam said. "Banook, are you familiar with the Wutash?"

Banook straightened his ample back, looking taller than was necessary for a man sitting down. "There are no Wutash here. What reason do you have to ask?"

Ockam's brow puckered tightly. "So, you do know of them?"

"As I said, you won't find any Wutash here, nowhere in these mountains."

"Bonmei, my son…" Ockam continued, "my adopted son was Wutash. His grandmother wanted to bring him to Minnelvad, to see his cousins. But they were both murdered, so we took the pilgrimage in their stead."

"A Wutash son? Unlikely, unless he came from Agnargdrolom."

"How do you know that word?" Ockam asked.

"It's only a Miscamish name, which is a tongue I speak. The Heartpine Dome is what you'd call it."

"That is where Bonmei was from," Ockam said. "The dome was breached years ago by the Negian Empire. They dug a tunnel under the vines and sent in their armies. Most if not all the Wutash there were killed."

Banook's perpetual smile suddenly faltered. "This brings me great sadness. Even more so, given that I cannot lead you to where you wish to go."

"Why not?" Lago asked. "If the Wutash are no longer here, can you tell us where they went?"

"I would rather show you," Banook said. He shook crumbs off his beard and gulped a jar of water down. "You will understand once you see for yourselves. Will you follow me?"

They all got up, taking a last bite of hare; it was too delicious to leave behind without one more taste. They followed Banook up the steps that led to the backyard meadow.

Banook cut northwest through a cottonwood forest, into a canyon of black rock zig-zagged with white veins of quartz. After about half an hour, Alaia asked, "How long is this hike? How far are we going?"

"Hike?" Banook said incredulously. "This is no hike. You can't call it a hike unless it takes you at least a week out into the wilderness. We are going just around the corner, follow closely."

He peered back and noticed Lago's discomfort, only then realizing how tactless he'd been. "How careless of me!" he said to Lago. "I had not considered the situation in full. I oftentimes overlook what is obvious to most. Allow me." Mindful of the injured leg, he picked Lago up in his arms and softly carried him.

He can be tender as a cloud when he means to, Lago thought. He felt Banook's beard tickle his ears and sunk in deeper. Through the gold-and-copper curtain he watched the landscape roll by, letting his small body rumble with each breath of mountain air the big man inhaled and exhaled.

Hours passed.

Drenched with exhaustion, they at last arrived at a cliff's edge with an open westward viewpoint.

"Like I said, just around the corner," Banook claimed, unfazed, with not a drop of sweat upon his brow. "We haven't even left my back yard yet." He carefully lowered Lago, then straightened up to look west into the mountains.

In the haze behind the sierras was the circular depression of an enormous caldera covered in ice, fifty miles across. Year after year, the accumulation of snowfall had solidified into an extensive, unmoving glacier. It looked smooth, a soft line of blue-tinted white flattening the mountainous horizon.

"If you are looking for the Wutash," Banook said, "that is where they lie, in the city of Da'áju, deep beneath the ice. There have been no Northern Wutash for a thousand and a half years, since the times of the Downfall."

Ockam leaned his weight on a rock wall and slid down to the ground. "All I wanted was to find some answers for him, some way of telling him, *Your kaadi did it, he followed through with his promise.* But this crushes my already shattered heart."

"How do you know about all this?" Jiara asked Banook, being unapologetically skeptical.

"I know Miscamish, and can read their runes, which I'm sure you saw on your way up the falls. There is some history written there, though not much. The Wutash are gone. They have been gone for epochs."

"Is there a path to that city?" Lago asked. "Some way to reach it, to find out more about what happened there?"

"The ice is cracked by the steaming caldera it sits on," Banook said. "The city lies somewhere in that labyrinth of ice and steam, on top of a hill where the springs used to run hot, a hill that is also buried beneath the ice. If by chance or foolishness you risk venturing into those bottomless crevasses, you will be rewarded with nothing but forsaken ruins."

"But how do you kno—" Jiara began to say, but Banook cut her off.

"It saddens me as well," he said. He picked Lago up once more, then began his walk back. "But there's much more magic to rejoice about in these mountains, your journey has not been for naught. I hope that despite this dire news, you will still join me as my guests, until you grow tired of my presence and decide to wander through the mountains in solitude, as we all must someday."

Ockam willed his defeated body to stand. They all followed Banook, not saying a word more, having a hard time appreciating the beauty Banook was so eager to share with them.

They returned to Banook's home when the western peaks were casting long, jagged shadows upon their eastern sisters. Banook went inside to load fresh dough in the oven while the others sat around the outdoor table where earlier they had abandoned their last bites of roasted hare.

"There's something unsavory with this whole ordeal," Jiara said, eyes on Banook, who she could see busily preparing dinner. "I'm beginning to lose trust in that lovely man. He's not telling us the entire truth. How does he know what he knows?"

"He read it in the runes," Alaia said.

"It doesn't quite fit. He was bothered as soon as we mentioned the Wutash. And he didn't ask a thing about the Heartpine Dome when Ockam mentioned Bonmei. Why wouldn't he be curious?"

"He's a hermit," Alaia replied.

"No, there's more to this," Jiara said, scrunching her lips.

"I would still like to try to find answers about the mask," Ockam said. "I feel it's important, to me personally, but also in the larger scheme of things. There may be no Wutash here, but there are many other domes."

"The Anglass Dome is the nearest one, but it's surrounded by Negian forces," Jiara said. "The closest one we could safely travel to would be the Moordusk Dome, by the bogs west of Zovaria. But what are we doing here? How far are we willing to travel for this?"

"If Agnargsilv is the key to enter the domes, it's too powerful," Lago said. "We should keep it away from the Negians and learn more about it, whatever the cost."

Alaia nodded. "There's also the possibility of—"

Scrreeech, crack!

"What was that?" she asked.

Behind them, up on the sugar pine that pierced through the terrace, they saw a tiny brown bear clumsily sliding down the bark of the thick tree.

"He's adorable!" Alaia said. "He's got hare ribs right in his cute muzzle, the fluffy little thief!"

"Alaia, no!" Ockam said, as Alaia approached the cub.

The terrace jerked as a massive grizzly bear stomped toward them, growling to protect her cub. They tried to get up and flee, but there was nowhere to go to but over the rail and down to their deaths.

The bear swiped her claws at Ockam and shoved him onto the ground, then advanced toward the crawling man. They had taken no weapons on their impromptu hike, so Jiara hurled the lid of the clay pot at the bear. It bounced off the thick fur and distracted her for only an instant. The bear huffed, turned back toward Ockam, and lunged, shredding his cloak with her curved claws. Ockam tried to kick at the bear's face, but his leg was met by a powerful bite.

In mere heartbeats it happened: As Ockam's leg was pierced by the bear's fangs, another bear roared his way onto the terrace. This male bear was yet larger, covered in yellow-gold fur. He charged toward the female bear, who cowered and scampered away. She and her cub found the stairs around the tree and fled in shame.

The enormous bear growled in tones so low that the terrace trembled. Everyone froze, unsure whether it would be safer to run away or jump into the abyss.

The bear rose on his hind paws, golden fur seeming patchy from the strange shreds of fabric dangling from it. In a trick of light and shadow, his fur turned ethereal and refracting, as if it was part liquid, part smoke. Swimming within this enveloping, refracting substance appeared the bulky shape of Banook, as a silhouette floating within the larger silhouette. The shimmering substance shrunk and congealed until only Banook remained. Only Banook and the shredded clothes draped around him.

Banook hastened toward Ockam, who was bleeding on the ground.

"I apologize if I scared you," he said. "I will explain, but let's get your wounds cleaned up right away." He picked Ockam up in his log-sized arms as if he were a child, then carried him into the cabin.

Chapter Forty-Three

KERJAASTÓRGNEM

"Thankfully, your bones did not break," Banook said, keeping pressure on Ockam's leg while Jiara packed the puncture wounds. "Drink some of this." He handed Ockam a bottle of plum liqueur.

Ockam didn't complain, didn't moan, he hadn't even screamed when the bear bit him.

Bandages secured, they turned Ockam around to deal with the scratches on his back. The new slashes crisscrossed his many old scars and would probably not be noticeable among them once they healed up.

"These will be fine with stitches," Jiara said, getting the needle ready. Ockam gulped down more of the strong spirits.

With the wounds taken care of, they sat Ockam on the softest couch. Banook went to his room to change into a loose-fitting tunic that wasn't shredded to bits.

"She is usually a very tender momma bear," Banook apologized as he returned, buttoning his cuffs. "Please forgive her, she was afraid for her cub. I should've known better than to leave bones out when company is present. I forget to consider these things, since I have nothing to fear from my bears." He seemed genuinely embarrassed.

"What happened out there?" Lago asked. "You were... Are you..."

"I am many things, and now those things I can no longer hide from you. I am Banook the man, but I am also Kerjaastórgnem the bear, known by the Miscam tribes as Nu'irg ust Urnaadi, the spirit of ursids, and known to beark-ind as *Barrghnukhurrrgk*." The grumbling roar had no recognizable vowels.

"A Nu'irg!" Alaia exclaimed. "You are the bear spirit? But… you can take the shape of a man?"

"As I said, I am many things. I am also known as Golden Claw by the Steppe Nomads, as Tomut-Kich gur Hathar—the Light-Furred Serac—by the Eastern Khaar Du, and as Quoonbe the Terrible by the precursors of the Horde, though I do not know what I did to deserve the latter epithet."

"We met another Nu'irg, one who could turn into wolves, foxes, and coyotes," Lago said.

"Nu'irg ust Agnarg, known as Safis among the ancient Miscam. Isn't she a beauty and a mystery? I do miss her songs to Sceres, her hushed paws, her tender whiskers. But how did you come upon her? How is she faring? I have politely recused myself from prying into your private matters, but matters of the Nu'irgesh I do feel entitled to inquire about."

"There's been trouble at Heartpine," Lago said. "We've actually… traveled through it. The dome, it's collapsing. Most of the creatures inside have died."

"I heard about Heartpine's collapse, from travelers in Brimstowne, but I did not know people were venturing inside of it."

"That's… complicated," Lago said, still not sure how much to reveal. "The Nu'irg, she seemed malnourished, hopeless. She followed us as we traveled through the dome, and we showed her a way out. She seemed better once she exited, healthier somehow. We don't know where she went to after that."

"A good deed, you did. As long as Safis is near her canids, she will return to full health. Why was she following you? I cannot believe she would approach any but her own kind."

Hesitant looks were exchanged. All eyes suddenly landed on Ockam, asking for guidance.

"Fine, if you can't make decisions on your own, then I'll speak," Ockam said. "As far as I'm concerned, this precious man has saved us enough times, and has now told us his truth, so we owe him *our* truth. Lago, your bag is upstairs, by the bed. Bring it down if you are comfortable doing this."

Lago nodded and went upstairs. Banook's bedroom was a wide, open loft with angled ceilings and snow-covered skylights. There was an ample writing desk and a door exiting to a balcony that wrapped around the exterior of the cabin. An enormous bed sprawled at the center of the room, where Lago's friends had been sleeping. Next to a stained walnut nightstand was Lago's trusty messenger bag. He quickly returned downstairs, already untying the bag's flap. As he sat down, he pulled his mask out.

"Agnargsilv!" Banook yelped, his pitch higher than Lago expected given his size. "You carry the fifth face of the Miscam! How did it come to pass that you were entrusted with such an honor? Tell me your tale, and I will tell you mine."

With his friends' help, Lago told Banook their story in full detail, aware that this man—or bear—would become an integral part in helping them unravel the mysteries of the masks, the riddles of the domes. They continued while Banook prepared dinner and only finished the story once they were done eating.

"Luck follows you, as much as tragedy does," Banook said, drying the dishes. "I've been secluded in these mountains for so long that I lost touch with most humans and had not taken heed of the recent conflicts among the current emperors, sedecims, and kings. It's been over fifteen hundred years since I settled into the northern mountains, because where the bears go, I have to go, and the only bears that survived the Downfall were here in the Stelm Wujann, the Stelm Nedross, and farther still into the Khaar Du Wastes of the icy north."

"Are you trapped, then, unable to leave?" Lago asked.

Banook went to sit by the fireplace, asking the others to follow.

"I cannot leave unless my bears also leave, and they have chosen to make these mountains their home, comfortably away from the dangers of humankind. But I am as free as the wind that caresses the meadow reeds, in this land that is as vast as it is beautiful. The evergreen gardens and crackled glaciers are but a few of the imponderable, sacred chambers in the uncountable mountains of the north. And I have ventured too, beyond the mountains, albeit briefly. Black bears are becoming accustomed to humans once more, prowling the berry-filled forests around Brimstowne. I travel there once or twice a year, for supplies, tools, books, and all the things I cannot find up here, by myself in my back yard."

"I'm curious," Ockam said, "wouldn't the Brimstowne folk recognize you and think, *by Noss, that man hasn't aged a day in centuries?*"

"My ample body is hard to miss!" Banook laughed. "I am well known amongst the townsfolk. Every so often I stop visiting, for a decade or two, so they forget me. I take trips to the northern wastes to trade with the Khaar Du instead, while I visit my polar bears. Or I venture far west to lounge with the giant pandas by the Fjordlands Dome. Then I show up once more, albeit with a shaved face, and the Brimstowners think me the son of myself. It's not too hard a ruse to play, except for the shaving part—I am not fond of that aspect."

Lago tried to imagine Banook's face with no beard. His features had a warm, baby-like tenderness to them. *He is so handsome. Charming, in a scruffy way*, Lago thought. *His round body is captivating, his plump lips so tempting.* He found himself staring and felt self-conscious. He changed the subject. "Are other Nu'irgs able to change into humans too?"

"*Nu'irgesh* is the plural form in Miscamish. I've known only three others who can. The first one can do so because the human form comes naturally to her, since she is the Nu'irg of all primates, including all of you. Her name is Buujik. She is a colorful monkey when in her primal form, a red-shanked douc, to be precise."

"Humans have a Nu'irg as well?" Alaia asked.

"Indeed," Banook said, "although humans have distanced themselves from others of their kind, for reasons I do not understand. Buujik always found it harder to relate to her human side, struggling to understand the clumsy human languages, and much prefers her other forms. The second Nu'irg who can take a human form is... was... I would... rather not sour this evening with sad stories, so let me speak of the third instead. The third is my friend Mamóru, who before the Downfall lived far away in southwestern lands I rarely visited. A most well-traveled, sophisticated individual."

Lago was intrigued. "What type of Nu'irg is Mamóru? Of which kinds of animals?"

"He is a steppe mammoth himself, when not in human form. His kind are other mammoths, mastodons, and elephants."

"Elfents?" Lago said. "Never heard of those before, or any of the others."

"I'd describe them to you, but you would not believe me," Banook said.

"I'd still like to know," Lago said.

"Well... Depends on the species. But elephants are as big as a house, with skin like cracked mud, legs like earth-shaking granite columns, a nose so long that it drags on the ground, tusks so large that they twist in strange curves in front of their faces, and ears like wings. Oh, and tiny tails."

They did not believe him, but they let it slide.

"You said you knew Mamóru from before the Downfall. You've been alive that long?" Jiara asked.

"I have, and for much longer before that epoch."

"How old are you?"

"That I do not know. My memory is diluted in youth like a snowflake fallen upon a roaring creek that washes into the ocean. It would be like asking for your memories of the day you were conceived. At one point in the past, and for the eternity before that moment, I was not. But here I am now, and in those thousands of years between not being and being here, I was becoming who I am today. There is no moment of birth for my kind. Perhaps there is none for yours, either."

"Most cultures have lost their memories," Lago said. "It's like we are scavenging from the scraps the previous civilizations left behind. There is so much confusion. Would you tell us what happened during the Downfall? We don't even know that. People tell so many different stories that not even scholars seem to agree."

"I carry more memories than any human life could wish for, or withstand, yet my ability to recall is still limited. But I will try my best to remember what happened in that faraway time. The story of the Downfall is tightly woven with the story of the *drolomesh*, the domes." Banook took off his right slipper and put a massive foot over his knee.

"About five hundred years before the Downfall, the Miscam tribes were summoned to a great council, where all Nu'irgesh were also to attend. At that council, it was decided that the construction of the domes would begin, aided by the power of the eighteen Silvesh, including Agnargsilv. One Silv for each of the domes."

Lago's eyes lit up. "There are more masks like this one?"

"There are more masks, but none like Agnargsilv. They each are bound to different clades of animals, the same way we Nu'irgesh are the embodiments of those clades."

"Hold a moment," Ockam said, "you said eighteen masks, one for each dome. But the domes are impossible to miss, and there are only sixteen of them."

"The plan was to grow eighteen of them, but one was never to be. I will get to the reasons for that in a moment. Why another of the domes seems missing is something that has tickled my curiosity for a long time, but I have not been able to dig out answers."

"Prophet Gweshkamir would be angry indeed to find he got the wrong number of emanations of Takhamún in the Takh Codex," Ockam said.

"And the Arch Sedecims got the wrong number of sacred states for the Zovarian Union," Lago added. "What happened to that dome that was never grown?"

"This is where the story of the Wutash comes in," the bearish man said, playing with his hairy toes. "The Wutash were not one, but two of the eighteen Miscam tribes. The Northern Wutash lived between the Stelm Wujann and Stelm Ca'éli, close to where Withervale is today. The Southern Wutash lived in what you now know as the Free Tribelands, just east of the Klad Senet.

"With Agnargsilv's help, the Southern Wutash grew Agnargdrolom in the now called Farsulf Forest. The Northern Wutash were supposed to use Urnaadisilv—the mask of ursids—to grow their dome among these glorious mountains, but stubborn they were. They treasured freedom, refusing to be sequestered under a false firmament. No dome would be needed for them, they claimed, for Noss had built mountains around the Da'áju Caldera that were thicker and stronger than any wall of vines. That caldera is the round glacier you saw earlier today, where the Northern Wutash city is buried."

"But why did they need to build the domes?" Lago asked.

"To survive the Downfall," Banook answered. "The ancients prophesied a cataclysm was nearing, one that would wipe out most life on Noss. They foresaw that growing the domes would be the only way to assure the survival of key species. I believe they were right, but not everything went according to their plan. The domes were meant to open up once the threat was over, and the land habitable. I do not know why the domes are still sealed, why the old species have not returned to repopulate Noss. All the wondrous life you see in these forests, in the deserts, in the oceans—all of it is but a fraction of the glory that we shared in the lost epochs."

"And the Northern Wutash, what happened to them?" Ockam asked.

"Wielding Urnaadisilv they called forth bearkind, urging us to move into the mountains. From your story, Lago, I got the impression that you do not yet understand the full power of the Silvesh. They are conduits through which humankind can communicate and work together with other species. Bears followed Urnaadisilv because it spoke to us. In a way, it also controlled us."

Banook's eyes looked distant. He ran thick fingers through his reddish-gold beard, then continued.

"The Da'áju Caldera was one of the most fertile oases in Noss, one entirely protected by the ring of mountains. The Northern Wutash, alongside bearkind, labored to construct a new natural balance, working their claws on the land, bringing in animals and plants that were needed to sustain the biomes, to maintain order among species. In this same way, wolves, foxes, and other canids helped at Agnargdrolom, and other kinds helped in their respective domes.

"For five hundred years we cultivated the caldera, making sure the mountains were safe, storing food for the longest of Winters, preparing, learning, all while living as free as only the Northern Wutash knew how to live. When the domes at last began to close, the Northern Wutash laughed, for they had the sky, the stars, and would never trade them for anything."

Banook put his feet down and interlaced his fingers between his knees.

"Then the Downfall came. I was up in the Snoring Mountain, who had not yet begun snoring. From there I could see Urgdrolom, entirely sealed up, as it had been for the past year. It was Winter, so the sky was cloudy, but even through the clouds I could see something strange was coming. It was in the middle of the night when the clouds turned green and gold, flashing as if the entire dome of the sky was an enraged firefly. The clouds lit up in the distance, as if struck by green lightning, although none as bright as a light that came from the southwest. Blinding it was, even from far beyond the horizon, briefly turning the clouds to white, fading to orange, and then green once more. It was so distant a flash that it wasn't until an hour later that I finally heard the rumble, and many hours after that until the fires became visible, and the embers fell to litter the landscape."

"Was it a comet?" Lago asked. "Or a meteor, like some artificers claim?"

"I do not know what specific kind of celestial body. I had only heard that a great fire would come from the skies. The Miscam tribes were purposely secretive about it, knowing that not everyone could be saved, and that revealing too much to the non-Miscam would put their plans in peril."

"I bet it was a comet. Crysta always said—"

"Let the man tell his story, Lago," Ockam said.

Banook carried on. "Before the fires reached us, I climbed down into the safety of the caldera. From there we all looked up as the sky turned red, and later gray, when the ashes fell in remorseless clumps. All the forests outside of the caldera burned, but the mountaintops had only granite, and granite would not burn like the hearts of pine and hemlock, so the great fire did not venture into our domain.

"Months later we dared climb up again and attested to the absolute devastation. The Northern Wutash were right, in a way—their paradise did not burn in the conflagration. But what they did not expect was the cold that came after, as chilling as the icebergs of Teslurkath are blue. No resources were left to gather from the charred outside, and our crops soon failed under the sickly gray snow. The humans had plenty of stored foods, years' worth, but years don't compare to decades. Soon they starved, and we did too, but us bears could hibernate, use less energy, and gather near hot springs where we could sometimes find food when we temporarily reawakened. In that way, we barely managed to survive, half-starved, half-frozen. We lost many species of bears during those cold years. I miss them dearly. I know I will never see their kind again, nor take their forms as I once could."

Banook briefly closed his eyes, then went on with his story. "When we awoke from our long hibernation, the entire caldera had been covered in snow. Layer upon layer, the snow solidified under its own pressure, trapping the city of Da'áju in ice. There was a temple there, named Ommo ust Urnaadi, where Urnaadisilv was kept. It had a map carved in rock, pointing to the locations of all the domes. Perhaps the missing dome could be found by studying this map."

"It's something we should strive to find out," Ockam said. "Is Urnaadisilv still resting at this temple?"

"That is likely, yet uncertain. The mask was in Da'áju at the time the Wutash perished, but most of us bears were not. We were in caves, hiding close to the warm arteries of the mountains."

"If Urnaadisilv is as important as Agnargsilv, we should try to find it," Alaia said. "We can't let people like Fjorna or General Hallow get their hands on the masks. It would be the end of the domes and of everyone living inside them."

"If that mask is under the ice," Jiara said, "and that cocksucker finds out about it, he'll go after it. We should find our way to it first."

"Banook, do you think you could take us to Da'áju?" Lago asked.

Banook contemplated, thick eyebrows merging into one. "Like you saw with your own eyes," he said, "Da'áju is covered in ice. But there are paths under it, unsafe, unexplored. I myself tried venturing through once in the past and found myself utterly lost. The ice is so vast that there's no telling where the city lies below it, where to enter the deep cracks. The crevasses are deeper than the box canyons of the Fractured Range."

"Maybe I could use Agnargsilv," Lago said. "When I look at Agnargsilv through its own eyes—I know, it's hard to explain—it has a glowing, indigo-colored aura. Urnaadisilv must have one too. Its aura should be visible more than anything or anyone else around, through ice, mist, or snow. We could find exactly where the temple is, assuming Urnaadisilv is still there."

"The crisp snows of Dewrest are already here, as you have clearly witnessed," Banook said, glancing at the falling flurries behind the tall windows. "The paths of the caldera are sealed. The ice is not just ice, but countless feet of snow upon solidified snow, hiding deep cracks that are invisible when fresh snow is obscuring them. By the month of Fogdawn, the mistdrafts will be as opaque as the obsidian trapped in the Laaja Khem mines. By Hoartide, the snowpack itself will turn to ice and crack under your feet, cutting through your shins like Dorvauros blades. By Frostburn, it will be so cold that not even a hibernating bear could survive without shelter. I could take you there, but no sooner than Mudfront, or Cloudpour, depending on how warm the Thawing season begins."

"Bear mask or no," Ockam said, "I'd be happy to go there to learn more about the Wutash. I'm afraid the Heartpine Dome will not last long, and once it collapses, all their history will be lost under miles of sap and vines. But here, in the ice, perhaps more has been preserved. If anything, the day I cross through the Six Gates of Felsvad, I will be able to tell Bonmei that I learned more about his people, that I helped carry their memory."

"I will be glad to tell you more about the Wutash, Ockam," Banook said, "although my knowledge is more rounded on the Northern Wutash, and not as much on their southern cousins."

"You've talked a lot about the Miscam," Alaia said, "like from the old Miscamish language. Are they the same as the Wutash?"

"The Miscam are not one tribe, but many, who were spread across all corners of Noss. The original tribe who made the Silvesh was the Acapóshi. They gifted the Silvesh to those tribes they deemed worthy, as a sign of respect and union, and those tribes joined under the collective name of Miscam. Together they birthed the Miscamish language, which became their main tongue, while most realms spoke Common, or Yenwu."

"The Acapóshi created the masks so that they could grow the domes?" Lago asked.

"Not so, although that was a good guess. The Silvesh were made thousands of years before then, I don't know for what original purpose. With the Silvesh the Miscam tribes were able to assist in the growing of the domes, but that was incidental and not the reason for their creation."

Banook yawned, then caressed Bear's neck. The mutt was snoring on top of a deerskin pillow, which had quickly become his favorite, as it always rested near the fireplace.

"What about the other powers the Silvesh have?" Lago asked. "It's mostly by chance that we've discovered some of what Agnargsilv can do, but I still don't really understand it."

"I do not know *how* they work, but I know of some of the things they can do. That is, perhaps, a longer story, and it is well past our bedtimes. Why don't we discuss that when the morning light adorns the proudest peaks? We need rest, and Ockam needs healing."

They thanked Banook for his story, then got ready for bed. Lago offered Ockam his spot on the living room couch, but the scout refused—he liked the oversized bed upstairs.

Lago dropped on the couch, then crawled under the bearskin. It took him a long time to fall asleep. His mind was fitting too many puzzle pieces together. Some fit just right, some he had to force into place to be able to begin comprehending them, but there were so many more pieces still missing.

CHAPTER FORTY-FOUR

ACOAPÓSHI FOLKTALES

Crysta stepped around the piles of notebooks, then sat heavily at her desk. Books from the downstairs library now built precarious towers on the floor, hoping to someday be placed back in their proper shelves.

It had been two weeks since she hired Kedra, a trustworthy scout who knew her way through the mountains. Crysta had sent her to gather news and observations of the Heartpine Dome's most recent collapse. But of course, Kedra gathered not only information about the dome, but also about the movements of Negian troops; she had been recommended to Crysta by the Zovarian army, after all, for she was good at keeping secrets that needed to be kept.

Any day now, Crysta thought. Not having all the data was holding her back, serving as an excuse to avoid working on anything else. She hoped the new hole in the dome was low enough to get a glimpse at its insides. She'd give anything to be able to know what was down there.

She absently flipped through a stack of homework she needed to grade. Her mindless rifling stopped when she found a half-filled page—the incomplete letter of recommendation for Lago's sponsorship at the Zovarian Academic Institute. She drew in a disconsolate breath and let it seep out.

It had been two months since Lago had mysteriously vanished from Withervale. She missed him. She missed his enthusiasm and passion, his jokes and dedication. They hadn't been able to find any clues as to his whereabouts, or that of his best friend, Alaia. She was worried to the nethervoids, unsure of what might have happened to him.

Crysta stepped to the tower's east window and stared at the clouds of dust being raised by the construction of the taller, thicker walls of the Halfort Rampart. After the strange attack at the monastery and the infiltration of Negian troops at the mines, the Zovarian Union had decided to reinforce the fortifications, to better protect Withervale's border.

Chaplain Gwil came up the stone steps, carrying a freshly brewed pot of tea. "Emberwood?" he offered.

"Thank you, Gwil, you didn't have to."

"It's no problem at all. You could use some help up here," he said, carefully stepping around the piles of books. "Maybe hire another one of your students?"

Crysta smiled dismissively.

Gwil left the pot on the desk and leaned against the wall next to Crysta. The delicately embroidered sleeves of his blue robes draped over the windowsill like heraldic standards. "I miss him too," he said, "but all we can do is hope he is alright and move on with our lives." He chewed on his cheeks and looked out toward the distant Anglass Dome. "Did Lago ever tell you something about a mask?" he asked.

"The ones you weave for the Feast of Plenitude?"

"No, no. I'm not sure if this has anything to do with anything else, but the strangeness of what happened here seems to connect a lot of disparate situations. I've been talking to a lot of people in town. There's this kid, Deon, who told me an interesting story related to Lago."

"From the Tharma Federation? Fat and blond? He's in one of my classes."

"That's the one. I was delivering some items to be sold at his father's antique store, when I heard Deon mention the name *Lago* to a friend of his. While I waited for his father, I struck up a conversation with the boy. He told me that the day Lago went missing, this lady had come by the store. Tall and blonde, light-gray eyes, he said. Sounded Iesmari to me. And she wore a garment on her head covering just the portion where the Negians tattoo their ranking insignias. He said the lady came asking about an animal mask of some sort, and when Deon's father said they had nothing like it there, she asked if they knew where she could find a boy named Lago."

Crysta straightened her back and gave Gwil a look that told him to go on.

"So, I went around and asked, and found some others who were questioned about a mask. And Lago's name came up again, several times. I think it's related to that dead body they found, up where they are building the new mill. Lago had something to do with that, I don't know how."

"Something to do with a murder?"

"That's not what I meant. It's just another of the oddly shaped puzzle pieces that I can't seem to fit."

They sat at the desk. Gwil poured the now lukewarm tea for both of them, pretending to enjoy the smoky flavor. "Anyway, I don't mean to disturb you, I just thought that—"

"He did mention something once," Crysta said, eyes suddenly darting while she tried to recall a hazy memory. "It was the oddest thing. Out of nowhere he asked me whether I had any books about masks. But that was years ago... Hold on," she said and walked down the tower steps.

Gwil waited, looking over the desk while pointedly avoiding the strong tea. He saw the partially written letter for Lago's sponsorship, pulled it closer, and began to read it. He heard Crysta stomping back up and put the letter back in place, pretending he hadn't seen it.

"Here," Crysta said. "*Acoapóshi Folktales*, this is what he borrowed. One day he was extremely excited about masks, and the next day he'd forgotten all about it. I don't know what Acoapóshi means."

"It's the name of the first Miscam tribe, from before the Downfall. Very few of their tales made it through time. Oral traditions, later transcribed in little volumes like this." Gwil flipped through the book. "This one was copied at our very own scriptorium, hundreds of years ago. My mother used to read me some of these stories. I remember this one here, with the dark lion mask, but there were many more. *Silvesh* they were called... They were not just any old masks, but magical artifacts that communicated with Noss themself. If the stories are to be believed, the Silvesh were made out of quaar, or something quite similar to it."

"If they are to be believed? So now you believe in spritetales?"

"They may be based on some truths. We've been studying quaar artifacts, on loan from the Zovarian Museum. There's something about them we can't quite figure out. They affect our monks' abilities to perceive the threads, how the effect of soot works in their bodies."

Crysta shook her head. "Or is it the soot you inhale that affects your rational minds? You know I don't approve of those drugs." She covered her mouth. "I'm sorry, I should be more respectful. I am your guest here, after all."

"Relax, I'm not here to change your views on that matter. What *does* matter is that quaar seems to sometimes make these threads act in odd ways, depending on its crystalline structure. There is a force at play we don't yet understand."

"I fail to see how this connects to Lago."

"I don't know exactly, Crysta. But if that mask, that Silv, is real, it would be invaluable. Other than the uncountable Qupi it could be sold for to a Tsing collection, if whatever it does is even remotely similar to what those old stories describe, then it makes sense why the Negian Empire was willing to risk so much to get it. And if Lago had anything to do with it, it would've put him in great danger."

"This is just becoming more confusing," Crysta said, standing up and leaning her arms on the backrest of her chair. "You are talking about magic, monsters, legends. All I care about is finding that innocent child."

"Not so innocent, and not a child anymore." Gwil sipped his tea, his salivary glands tightening. "So, you were getting ready to send him to the institute?" he asked, nodding toward the letter.

"I wasn't sending him anywhere, it's what he wanted to do," she said, covering up the letter with a stack of papers.

"Didn't mean to pry. Anyway, I thought you would want to know about this." Gwil stood and pushed the chair back under the desk. "I will leave you to your work. If you think of anything else related to what we talked about, do let me know."

"Thank you, Gwil. Sorry, my mind is scattered today. I'll ruminate on it."

As soon as Gwil left, Crysta sat to read the folktales from the book. They made no sense to her, despite her reasonable understanding of old Miscamish. Too much magic, too much allegory, too many unknowable names. She closed the book, closed her eyes, and thought for a moment.

It was Sunnday afternoon. In only half an hour more she would have to ready the prismatic sunnograph and send her report to Zovaria. She didn't have much to report to the institute, but she did have a lot of information about the movement of Negian troops by the dome, data that had been pre-written, containing numbers, movements, statistics. To properly encode that data in her report, she needed a slightly longer non-secret message to hide it under. She thought about what to write down, then picked up a quill.

30-Fireleaf-1454. Light fluctuations nominal for past week, wisp E2SW172 vanished on 28-9. Linear decay rate starting on 26-9. Nothing else to report.

Odd request for Artificer Balstei Woodslav: Before you depart, find any books related to old Silv myths, Miscam artifacts, and the Acoapóshi tribe. Anything related to their masks, or mentions of quaar (your papers, too). If you could bring them along with the other reports and items, I have a student who needs them for a thesis. Sorry for the late request. I will cover the costs for the extra weight. See you in a few weeks. -C

CHAPTER FORTY-FIVE

THE RED STAG

General Hallow needed to reach the capital before news of his achievements at Anglass made its way to the emperor. Word would spread fast, so faster still he rode, followed by Artificer Urcai and his seven arbalisters.

The steeds galloped up the vast mesas of Hestfell and across the miles of ramps connecting the three great gates before reaching the city at the top. Hallow hurried to the Laurus Palace, strode over the bridge, and continued down the lengthy marble hallway toward the rhodonite throne, keeping the cervid mask concealed in a bag. The enormous statues of Takhísh and Takhamún stared down at him and his followers, silently judging.

Emperor Uvon dus Grei was standing near the throne, next to his political advisor, while his inquisitor whispered something venomous in his ear. All three turned as the general reached the bottom of the steps.

Uvon adjusted his slipping, red laurels, wincing at the sight of the general. "General Hallow, I received no warning of your arrival until only moments ago. I expect your unannounced visit isn't to ask for more troops nor sapfire, for I have provided more than was deserved, and am currently in the process of reassigning three of your borrowed battalions to the Sixth Legion." The political advisor leaned in to mumble something. "The Seventh Legion," the emperor corrected himself, displeased with his advisor.

Alvis Hallow kneeled and covered his ranking insignia. "Your Imperial Majesty, I had promised you success within two to six months. The two-month mark is soon approaching, yet I've come to tell you that we've already achieved what we were after, thanks to the resources you provided."

"The Anglass Dome has been breached?" the emperor said incredulously.

"It has, with nearly no losses on our part, and—"

"Why has no one notified me of this?" Uvon turned a blaming gaze toward his advisor.

Alvis interjected, "It was I who wanted the privilege of delivering the report directly, Your Majesty. We have captured—"

"I want their temple burned! Those blasphemous savages will finally witness the wrath of the Twin Gods." The emperor paced, smiling fiercely. "I'm pleased with your expedience, General Hallow. This is an unexpected surprise from you. Your next goal should be clear—you must find that profane countenance of Takhamún's emanation and destroy it and any of its wielders."

"Your Majesty, there will be no need to hunt for the mask. We have secured it. I bring to you a token, proof of our success, of the strength of my Second Legion. I present to you, Urgsilv." Alvis removed the mask from his bag and held it up toward the emperor.

Uvon cautiously stepped down, sneering with disgust. With a handkerchief he examined the mask at arm's length, then quickly tossed it to the ground. It landed soundlessly.

"How dare you desecrate my throne room with such a sacrilegious effigy!" Uvon said through his teeth. "I want this abomination destroyed at once!"

Keeping his knee on the floor, Alvis picked up the mask. "Its power is greater than you suppose, Your Majesty. It is more valuable than any general, than any legion. Than any emperor."

The emperor took two vigilant steps back. He raised his arm to command his guards, but before anyone could react, Alvis put the mask on.

The arbalisters surrounded Alvis, aiming their bows and crossbows all around. While on his knees, Alvis changed into the powerful half-elk, his armor splitting seams, his antlers stretching like sharp-clawed hands. The emperor gaped in horror, trying to exhale a signal to his guards, but all he could do was stumble backward up the steps, while his inquisitor and advisor cowered behind the legs of the Twin Gods. Alvis looked up at the emperor, then lowered his head once more and charged, stabbing Uvon with the sixteen points of his branching crown.

The few guards who managed to react were shot down at once. The elk rose next to the throne, with the young emperor impaled above him like an offering. Uvon's laurels fell to the ground, clinking weakly; his blood dribbled on the elk's brow and down to his muzzle, tinting red his entire face.

"Witness forth!" Artificer Urcai called out, pretending to cower near the befuddled guards. He fell to his knees in exaggerated praise. "Witness the return of Takhísh's twin brother. The first of Takhamún's emanations has been freed!"

The powerful elk raised his arms toward the meek body skewered above him and proclaimed, "There is no holiness in this wretched, heirless child. The true grace of the Twin Brothers has returned. I am the embodiment, proof that the divinity that was once lost to us can be ours again. Ours, for the entirety of the Negian Empire, not just for one immature ruler whose head could not fit in his father's laurels."

With a mighty twist, the elk swung the emperor free from his antlers, hurling him down the long hallway, smearing a red trail on the white marble. The elk raised his bloodied head and bugled for every guard to hear—and they all heard, they all listened, and they all knew who to follow.

"Each of Takhamún's emanations carried a spark of divinity with them," the elk said. "This mask of power holds merely one such spark, but I intend to bring them all under our rule, so that Takhamún can be whole once more." The elk gestured toward the statues behind him. "The Twin Gods share no enmity toward one another. In order for life to thrive, both of their blessings are needed. Let us be the ones to reunite them, as we unify our empire and bring divinity back to humankind. This is how we conquer the lands of the savages, how we vanquish those whose faith is broken or untrue. Follow me into power, into conquest, into glory and divinity!"

The elk stomped his cloven hooves down the steps, following the emperor's trail of blood as if parading over a wet, red carpet. His arbalisters followed, but needed not defend him, as no guards dared object to his rule.

The elk walked across the bridge, headed to a balcony that overlooked the great Zaugfell Plaza, where his citizens had been called forth in advance.

Rumors flooded through the stronghold. Crowds gathered tightly, eager to see their new ruler. As the bloodied countenance of the elk appeared over the balusters, a man shouted loudly from among the crowds, "The Red Stag has come! The Red Stag has come to save the Empire!" A thundering chant for the Red Stag broke out, one that would not cease, as more people gathered under the supremacy of the god-like figure.

Blue banners were taken down, and with wide brushes the citizens began to paint a red triangle, point down, right at the base of the red laurels that used to be the sigil of the Negian Empire. The laurels now looked like a crown of antlers over an elongated, skull-like form.

The paint dripped like red sand down an hourglass.

CHAPTER FORTY-SIX

THE THREE STAGES

Warm winds had melted most of the snow overnight. The morning was clear, the sunlight sharp and penetrating. Ockam sat to enjoy the views with a warm cup of chocolate while the others went out for a walk, following Banook.

With no big secrets left to hide, Banook spoke openly about his wonderful home. He had built the cabin by himself over hundreds of years. He'd even carved the stone steps, which were now worn where his heavy feet had trodden countless times. The cabin was a project that was constantly evolving, as Banook gathered inspiration and new tools every time he visited Brimstowne or the cities of the Khaar Du, and used what he learned in his renovations.

He showed them tunnels under rocks that he used as cellars, which reminded Lago and Alaia of their old Diamond Cave. Banook said he would sleep there at night as a bear, too, but they weren't sure whether he was joking or not. Around the cabin a handful of creeks flowed, some frigid, some hot, from which Banook piped waters into his home, allowing the guests to take hot showers for as long as they wished.

"There are wondrous hot springs farther north," he said, leading them along a mossy trail underneath his cabin, "with pools big enough to hold my substantial frame. I will show you, when the time is right. My garden extends for hundreds of miles. You must saunter through every crevice, keenly observe every stone, talk to every drop of dew upon each and every wildflower. The other bears will not bother you. I will have a talk with them, so you have nothing to fear even in the dying of the light. Feel free to take walks at night, knowing the stars will always be there to guide you back."

"Like the response to the greeting, *May the stars guide your heart*," Lago said. "As a kid, I guess I took it too literally. I learned about the stars and how to read them, and how I could use them to find my path."

"It's a beautiful greeting," Banook said. "The stars guide us not just back to one place, but to wherever fate takes us. They inspire us to explore paths we do not know about, encourage us to rejoice in being lost, as that is one way to find ourselves. You'll be even more inspired by the stars here in the mountains. The last few nights have been a bit cloudy, and Sceres is almost full, but if you could see a clear, dry, moonless night from these piercing summits, the stars would turn you into a devout worshipper of their beauty."

They spiraled their way up the sugar pine and arrived back at the terrace, where they joined Ockam, sitting in a circle under the dappled light.

"This morning has been a pleasant respite from your worries," Banook said, "but I know your minds are still filled with curiosity. The day is young and as glorious as can be, so if you want to talk more about Agnargsilv, bring it out, and I'll explain what I can."

Lago hastily brought Agnargsilv out and took a seat next to Banook.

"May I?" Banook said, then took the mask from Lago. It looked like a toy in his hands. "I never had the honor of holding one myself. Thank you for indulging me. It looks as pristine and beautiful as it did during the Equilibrium Epoch, so many millennia ago. Much lighter than I expected, too." He twirled the miniaturized canid form in his fingers.

"As I was telling you last night," Banook continued, "the masks' true purpose eludes me, but I've seen them work. The Northern and Southern Wutash kept their Silvesh as family inheritances. Other tribes conducted trials to see who would be most deserving of the honor, consulted oracles and visions, or let it be decided by votes from all tribe members. I was always close to Urnaadisilv, and I met each one of the wielders from the generations of chiefs who inherited it."

He handed the mask back to Lago. "You've learned a lot on your own. Given that there are no Wutash left to train you, I would be honored to at least help with what I can. If you'd like me to."

Lago's wide-open smile was enough of an answer.

"There are several stages I saw the heirs go through," Banook said. "The first seemed like the hardest, but it's actually the easiest. That is learning to deal with the pain that the mask brings, to understand it, to find the right frame of mind to let the pain pass through you. With their coming of age, most heirs find a way through that phase. I've seen only a few who failed at this stage, who gave up after countless tries, having to pass the mask on to a sibling, in shame. The abilities the mask grants in this stage are the ones you are familiar with, such as that special kind of seeing without seeing, the understanding of the threads around you, the perception of intentions, and, of course, the gifted curse of pain. It may also seem to grant you strength and dexterity, but that's a mere side effect from the increased understanding of your surroundings. Reaction is dependent on perception.

"The next stage is one I'm familiar with in an intimate way, and it is that of shapeshifting. All Nu'irgesh are able to shapeshift, though we are limited to those forms of our very nature. Just as you saw Safis move through canid forms, I can only shapeshift into bear forms. Black bears, polar bears, any bears. We all have one species that feels more personal to us, our primal form, and that's the one you saw me take last evening."

"But you are also able to take the shape of a human," Jiara said.

"And quite a shape it is!" Banook said with a laugh, slapping his belly with both hands. "That, I'm afraid, is a long story for another time. The shapeshifting of a Nu'irg like myself is very similar to that of a Silvfröa—"

"A Silvfröa?" Lago asked.

"It means *voice of the mask*, the title of all those who have wielded the Silvesh and with their aid taken their half-forms. Bonmei's mother and his grandmother—given their particularly canid case—were known as the *Agnargfröash*, and once you learn to shapeshift, you too will be an *Agnargfröa*, or the *voice of the canids*. Shapeshifting is an experience that requires the wielders to know themselves very deeply, to have little doubt about who they are. And, perhaps just as importantly, shapeshifting requires the person to discern what species they feel most connected with."

Lago nodded attentively. "During our journey, at times I would be walking with the mask on and trying to force my body to change, to see if I could work it out somehow. I would picture myself as a fox, trying to feel my skin as fur, looking at the dark muzzle in front of me and imagining it had whiskers. I tried many times, but it never worked."

"You, little cub, do not strike me as a fox," Banook said. "You have not found the right essence to focus on. It will come to you, in time. There's also a particular frame of mind needed to shapeshift, and it's one that might take you time to learn, though I've seen some who have mastered it in merely a day or two."

"It's been a while since I've worn Agnargsilv," Lago said, eyes down. "Sorry, we were cautious, and trying to keep it a secret from you—"

"I take no offense. That was smart and prudent of you."

"—but I've missed it. It has become an extension of me, somehow. Hiding it was like leaving half of me behind, like having to forget those things ever happened. Even just holding the mask makes me feel at ease."

"I have seen plenty of *Urnaadifröash*—wielders of the mask of ursids—struggling through the same conundrum. The mask changes something deep within your mind, particularly during the first week of wearing it. It becomes an extension of yourself. It is one of the reasons many tribes never shared the masks with anyone but their direct heirs, as it was too painful to part with a portion of their own souls."

Banook looked into Lago's eyes, a beaming smile lifting his flushed cheeks. "You should wear it proudly, cub, there is nothing to fear here. My cabin is well hidden, no lost hiker nor wandering pilgrim will find this secluded pocket. I'd love to see you wearing it and being your full self."

Lago felt goosebumps from the encouragement of that smile. He put the mask on with an ease he'd never felt before. He once again sensed the energy of the threads around him, of all the connections of this exotic yet familiar forest, but his eyes—and the mask's eyes—were on Banook. The Nu'irg's aura was intense, vibrant, alluring. The synesthetic color Lago perceived from Banook was not indigo—like the auras of Agnargsilv and Safis—but an iridescent gold swaying in copper undertones, like a dewy field of barley scraped by a Highsun dawn. The mask expressed Banook's intentions and said they were not just benevolent, but selfless and loving.

"There you are," Banook said, as if he too could glimpse beyond what his eyes showed him. "It suits you well, and you look very comfortable wearing it. I think you could learn the next steps with just a little nudge from this old bear. Your first lesson will begin in the morrow, we still have much more to discuss."

Banook got comfortable, took a drink of chilled water, then continued, "The Silvfröash were entrusted to guide the animals of their clades, as once they shapeshifted into their half-forms, they were able to communicate with one another. I vividly recall the time I met the first Urnaadifröa, about eight thousand years before the Downfall. Her name was Gwarnamíshkhul, she was in her half-form of an ursavus, or a dawn bear, the oldest species of our kind. She was swimming in the glacial creeks that feed the Stiss Khull, chasing after the elusive pearlescent trout. She mindspoke to me, but somehow more clearly and pointedly than my bears could."

"Mindspoke?" Alaia asked.

"Mindspeech is how all members of a clade communicate with one another, in the way Bear likely talks to other dogs, or foxes, although what he says I could not tell you, for I am no canid. It is not the same as the language you are familiar with, for it uses no syntax, grammar, or sounds. We communicate in feelings, emotions, sensory images. We can convey the idea of words too, which is useful when it comes to names, but their true essence is much more... essential.

"But back to where I was. During the second stage, the Silvesh grant the ability of mindspeech, at least with those of the mask's own clade. That second stage is the one your son"—he looked at Ockam—"described about Mawua. The one we call the *half-form*, both animal and human. It is a sort of bridge that only the Silvesh can provide, so I cannot take it. It is unnatural to my kind. There is a third stage, as you must've guessed, which is what you saw"—he looked at Lago—"when Sontai approached you in the form of a fox. That is the feral form."

"Like you, as the golden bear," Lago said.

"Exactly, cub. It comes effortlessly to me, as feral is my very nature, but it's not something easy nor safe for the Silvfröash to undertake. Other Nu'irgesh have told me tales of Silvfröash achieving this feat and returning to their human forms, after much struggle, but those are the exceptions. The one case I personally witnessed did not end so well."

Banook pursed his lips, making his beard tighten while he recalled long-gone epochs. "It was in the time the Northern Wutash were migrating to Da'áju," he said. "A Wutash caravan was moving supplies when they were attacked by marauders. Chief Cturk, protecting his wife and daughter, shapeshifted into a feral polar bear. He fought ferociously, and saved them, but at a high cost. His mind was lost in that state, as if he had not enough human cognition to return to. Unable to understand human language, he ignored the pleas from his wife and daughter. Instead, day in and day out he plodded north toward the ice fields of the land you now know as the Khaar Du Wastes. Wutash warriors followed him, and I did too, and though I was able to speak to him in our bear tongue, I was unable to help. Cturk did not recall much of the Wutash, of being a chief, or even what being chief meant, for polar bears do not have the same social hierarchies the human tribes do. His human mind was quickly vanishing. For months he hunted seals atop the icebergs of the Ash Sea, then deeper in the Unthawing Ocean, until eventually his own warriors grew tired and hunted him down. As he died, he turned back into his human form. The Wutash warriors took the Silv that still dangled from his face and brought it home to his wife and daughter. The warriors told them that their father, their husband, had been slain by fur hunters, and never confessed the truth."

"When Sontai turned into the gray fox," Ockam said, "maybe she did so knowing it was her last recourse to carry the danger away from Bonmei."

"It is not something I've seen the chiefs teach their heirs," Banook said. "It happens instinctively, perhaps only in the direst of circumstances. It's just one of the mysteries of the Silvesh, as I'm sure there are more. I myself did not know of the power the Silvesh have to control the vines. The makers of the masks—the Acoapóshi—were a secretive kind. But there you have it. Those are the main stages I wanted to tell you about, the rest is legends and spritetales, filled with exaggerations and hearsay. Stories about the Silvesh controlling the weather, birthing animals from the ground, shutting off the stars, talking to the moon, bringing back the dead, or turning the wearers into animals the size of mountains. I don't believe the other legends to be true, but most spritetales tend to grow around a nugget of truth."

Lago took the mask off and looked at it, at the other part of himself. "I don't understand how something so small can hold so many secrets. It's like when you try to peer into the tiny ridges carved over the mask." He put his eyes very close to the muzzle, running a fingernail through the darkly filigreed lines. "There is so much detail, so much complexity that the eyes can't resolve. We just aren't capable of understanding it."

"But it doesn't mean you never will," Banook said. "The Acoapóshi understood them, they *made* them. Whatever knowledge they had may still be out there, or it might be long lost, but it is not beyond reach. Think about your body, and how complex you are, made out of billions of tiny cells which somehow function as a whole. The mask might be just the same. You are seeing one complex thing, but it could be broken down into less complex parts, or it could be part of something even more complex that you are yet unable to perceive."

"I'd love to have Crysta examine it," Lago said, caressing the angular ears. "Or Khopto… He's one of the monks there, who I… I… I hope he's still alive… They have microscopes at the monastery and many books, and decades' worth of knowledge I could never hope to master. And they know a lot about soot. There seems to be some connection between that and the Silvesh. I have a little bottle of it that Khopto gave to me."

"Ah, yes, soot," Banook said. "The aetheric carbon contains myriad mysteries. It would not surprise me if soot or any of the other aetheric elements were involved in the making of these relics. The Miscam tribes—who called it *ustlas*, not *soot*—used the powder so that their shamans could better communicate with the animals, in a similar way the Silvesh do, but not remotely equal to it."

"Shamans from the Wastyr Triumvirate do the same with their heralds," Jiara added. "They are costly mercenaries, but their birds are well trained, and fast communication is critical in warfare."

"An unfortunate consequence, but yes," Banook agreed. "The substance also helps in learning. Those under its influence more easily find the meaning and emotions behind words, learning much quicker, particularly when it comes to languages. It is an expensive way to learn, however, with how pricy the powder is."

"Khopto knows like twelve languages," Lago said. "I wonder if that's why he's so smart. Do you know any more about these aetheric elements? They don't teach us much about them at school, since they are so rare and hard to study."

"I am no scholar," Banook answered, "all I know is that certain elements have a kindred counterpart that acts similarly yet possesses unique properties. Like soot acts in the manner of carbon, but also somehow is linked to these mysterious threads you perceive. Magnium, which you use for minting—a most belittling use if you ask me—behaves just like iron, but it imbues its magnetic properties to elements it alloys with."

"That's why they can mint Qupi with just an infinitesimal fraction of magnium," Jiara added.

"Exactly," Banook replied. "There are others. I know of pharos, an element that glows bright like the kenzir stones of yore. I also heard of brime, a special kind of sulphur that retains heat, as if you are holding a perpetually hot stone. Very useful to start fires. And I know of aether itself, but only from hearsay. They claim it's an invisible gas indistinguishable from common hydrogen, but I know not what magical properties aether possesses.

"More was known about the aetheric elements in times before the Downfall, but that knowledge was lost. The Takheists consider them profane substances, particularly soot, so research has been limited, just as my knowledge of them is limited. As I said, I am no scholar."

"I bet the monks will find answers way before the artificers do," Lago said, then furrowed his brow. "I wish we could ask Khopto more. When do you think it will be safe to return to Withervale?"

"Give it time," Ockam said, "it's not been long, they'll still be looking for us. And when we do return, we will still need to be very careful. Which reminds me, Banook, we do not mean to impose on your hospitality, but—"

"As long as you'd like!" Banook replied. "You are my guests, and my home is yours. You are welcome to stay here through Umbra and Winter if that will suit you. The cold is invigorating, and so are the hot springs, much more so once they are covered in snow. I've had no guests for decades. There's so much room to entertain that it'd be unfair not to share it with kindred spirits such as yourselves."

"I would love to take a break here," Jiara said, "and see what other surprises this bear has for us." She leaned on Banook's wide shoulder.

"I agree," Alaia said. "But are we going to go to Da'áju?"

"After the snows begin to melt, I can take you there," Banook said. "But I'm afraid it's not easy to crawl in those crevasses, they are deep and steep. A bear like myself can cling with claws, but on the fickle ice your flimsy nails will not suffice."

"We've got months before the Thawing season," Jiara said. "I could teach you how to climb on ice, how to rappel down safely, so you can build the muscles you'll need for that adventure. It's not something you can learn in a day. Banook, do you have ropes you can spare?"

"That I do, and the best kind, just wait and see."

"But we'll also need climbing equipment," Jiara said. "Ice axes, crampons, anchors, pitons, ice screws, better boots perhaps."

"Although a stroll to town might be too risky for you to bear, for this bear it is not. I can take a quick trip to Brimstowne for supplies, while you stay here and keep your hinds away from those enemies chasing after you."

"Then we'll start the training as soon as we get the gear ready," Jiara said.

Banook nodded. "I'd be happy to be your host as you pull the ropes and learn the knots, as you craft and climb and admire the allure of this land from up high." He looked to Ockam and Lago. "Though before that, we also need time to heal and snore, as you two should be doing for several weeks more."

CHAPTER FORTY-SEVEN

NAKED

After breaking fast the following day, Lago went for a walk by himself. His leg was raw and itchy under the bandages, but as long as he took his time, he barely even noticed it. He felt at ease in this landscape and could only imagine what it would look like during the other five seasons. He sauntered—as Banook said they should—all the while wearing Agnargsilv, to let the beauty the mask revealed envelop him.

When he returned from his walk, Lago went into the cabin and opened his bag. The massive dire wolf fang waited inside of it; he still wasn't sure why he had decided to carry it. He placed the cloth-wrapped fang on a side table and kept digging, finding the hexagonal tube from the temple at Stelm Bir: another odd memento that felt somehow important and useless at the same time. He dug around some more and found what he was looking for.

He went to sit at the terrace, leaned back on a log chair, stretched his legs, and rested his feet on the base rail. He placed Agnargsilv on a seat next to him, weighing it down with a rock so that it would not blow away in the breeze. He then pulled out a small pouch and began preparing the lacquer to paint his nails.

Banook's wide shadow came up behind him. Lago knew he was coming before seeing the shadow, feeling the terrace's boards bend with each step.

Banook leaned on the handrail and looked out toward the Anglass Dome. He didn't seem disquieted in the least by Lago painting his nails, to the point that Lago felt as if he was ignoring it on purpose.

"I don't lacquer them often," Lago said. "I always liked to, but it's hard to find a place where I feel comfortable enough to do so."

"Blue suits you splendidly, it's a beautiful color," Banook said. Lago wasn't entirely sure whether Banook understood the cultural biases he was alluding to. Maybe they meant nothing to him—he was a bear, after all—or maybe he understood way too well but was completely immune to the puerile irrationality of humans.

"I also like your bracelet," Banook said, "yet you don't strike me as a disciple of the Congregation."

"You know about them?" Lago said, pulling his sleeve back to fully reveal the copper bracelet. The hands that formed the clasp held each other securely by their wrists, creating a loop that was at once two and one.

"I've met a few monks in the past, they have a temple in Brimstowne. They share a misguided yet intriguingly benevolent philosophy. Their teachings have evolved a lot over time, branching off from Miscam ideologies from before the Downfall. What you mentioned about their relationship with soot is something I didn't know, however, but now it all makes sense."

"I used to make deliveries for them in Withervale. Actually, I guess I was more like a drug dealer. They didn't only *use* soot, but secretly traded in it, purifying it right there at the monastery. I moved packages back and forth for them. Khopto always wanted to turn me into a monk. I think offering me the drug was a push to lure me in."

"I'm glad you did not join, as your dark curls suit you well," Banook said.

"That's exactly what I told him!"

"And I do not believe you have a need for that drug, for there are other ways to witness the same truths. And I don't mean Agnargsilv. I mean all it takes is a bit of empathy to see how, from the biggest bear to the smallest flea, we all share a special connection with each other, and we need to care for one another."

"Gwil used to say that even ants have a consciousness. I don't know if I truly believe that. I don't think of an ant as being the same as I am."

"Ants are as beautiful and complex as any of us, but in their own way. I think the problem lies in trying to box things into too-tight categories, assuming something either belongs, or doesn't. The fact that we share connections doesn't mean we are the same."

Banook placed a finger on the handrail and let a tiny ant crawl on his thick fingernail. He observed the insect closely with his honey-colored eyes.

"We are not the same," he said, "we are *different*, and that makes us all even more special. The similarities tie us together, while the differences make us stronger. An ant might not be conscious in the same way you and I are. Perhaps it's a matter of degree, perhaps a matter of kind, most likely a mixture of both."

Banook carefully placed the ant back onto the handrail, then gazed at the vista once more. "It's a fine day," he said, "the wind weaves glad tidings through the waving trees. No better time for a first lesson. Would you like to get started after lunch? Jiara is preparing a savory mushroom pie. I could serve berries for dessert, so your belly will be full and ready to get started. The process can be a bit draining."

"I would love to," Lago said, stowing away his lacquers. "I've been eager to begin, but didn't want to be pushy."

Banook's smile widened.

After lunch, Jiara, Ockam, and Alaia sat beneath the shade of the terrace's sugar pine to witness Lago's first day of training.

Banook stood by the edge of the terrace, with the distant dome barely visible in the glowing haze. "This might come to you easily," he said, "or it might take until the last sycamore leaf of the year has fallen, so do not lose hope if it takes you long to figure it out. You are a few years older than the age at which the Wutash heirs inherited their masks, a prime and proud age of discovery and development."

He took a step forward. "Shapeshifting is achieved through a particular state of mind. It is about intention, but it's also about detachment and about awareness. Self-understanding and self-acceptance are most important. It is about knowing not just who you are, but who you are trying to become, and understanding that that form is and always has been a part of you, even if you hadn't realized it before.

"Equally important is recognizing what species you feel the strongest connection toward. For each Silv there is one and only one way you could answer that question. At times, I've seen Silvfröash take on the shapes of hybrid species of the same clades, though that is not as common."

"You mentioned the clades before, what do you mean by that?" Lago asked.

"They are higher orders of animals, bound by a common ancestor. Such as a tiger, a house cat, and a mountain lion all descend from the same lineage."

"What is a tiger?" Lago asked, having heard the word only in reference to tiger trout before.

"They were ancient, striped cats from before the Downfall, bright orange with black stripes. Like most big cats, they too seem to have gone extinct. But back to the clades. All canines and vulpines would encompass Agnargsilv's clade. You must by now have an idea of the species you feel connected to, but

I do not expect you to be certain. It is not as simple as recognizing the species, however, but you must picture the very essence of the animal who is the other part of your soul, to the smallest detail.

"The physical process of change comes next. It's one I can't very well explain, but I'll try. As you shapeshift, you consciously guide the threads—the same ones you see with the mask—to aid you and pull from the nature around you. There is a moment of weightlessness as you are suspended by these threads when you must carefully guide each connection and weave them together into your new form. This comes naturally to me, it always has. For you, Agnargsilv will be the conduit. You must trust it, listen to it, as much as you need to trust and listen to yourself."

Lago swallowed. He found the words inspiring, but at the same time utterly confusing. He could only think of one inconsequential thing to ask.

"Does it hurt?"

Banook chuckled. "No, little cub, it does not. You should not fear it. If you are ready, I can first demonstrate, and then see how well you fare."

"Yes, I think I'm ready," Lago said, not believing his words.

Banook unclasped his bearskin cape and let it drop to the ground, then pulled his tunic off, revealing his hairy chest and round belly.

"Another important thing," Banook said, stepping out of his boots, "is to be careful with your clothing, as you don't want to"—he unbuckled his belt—"ruin them the way I did the other night." He dropped his heavy trousers and loose briefs and stood there in front of Lago, completely naked.

Lago stared at Banook's belly, then at the wide cock dangling in the shadow beneath it.

He is beautiful, he thought, utterly frozen. Why was it that larger men attracted him so? Something irresistibly sensual was embodied in Banook's curves, in the shapes and folds beneath his arms, in the plump pad around his cock. Something primal and assertive concealed in the fullness of his beard, in his imposing height, in his enormous hands. Something innocent and youthful softened his features, his playful demeanor, his flushed skin. Lago understood he could be crushed by the bearish man yet felt reassured by his very presence. Dominant and acquiescent, tender and rough, Banook was the epitome of all that he had desired, and he was standing there, naked, exposing himself with no hint of self-consciousness. *His body is perfect. I wish I could hold him, I wish I could bury myself in his hairy chest, I wish—*

"Come on, cub, take them off," Banook said. "When I said there is no pain in shapeshifting, I hadn't considered clothing—it can be quite painful, particularly if you are ripping through leather."

Lago's heart began to thump, anxiety boiling through him.

The three spectators tried to read the scene, unsure of what to do.

"Could I... just watch you do it first?" Lago asked, hot embarrassment reddening his face.

Alaia walked up to rescue him. "It is a bit cold out for skinny people like ourselves, let him warm up to it first." She placed her cloak over Lago's shoulders, knowing full well that Lago would have a tough time removing his clothes in front of a crowd.

"Very well," Banook said. "Pay attention, and study how my body conforms into the next shape. You won't need Agnargsilv yet—I prefer you watch with your own eyes this time." He stepped uncomfortably close to Lago and Alaia, perhaps unaware of the taboos against nakedness.

Lago's face barely reached a handspan over Banook's deep belly button. He looked up.

Banook stood towering in front of him. Tendrils of gold and gray smoke rose from his reddish hairs, from his supple skin. The smoke did not blow away in the breeze but grew into the larger shape of a translucent bear, forcing Lago and Alaia to step back. Banook's toes lifted, floating within the smoky frame. The figure inside became soft-edged, the smoke refracting almost like water, yet with a peculiar directionality, as if translucent shards were swimming in the transmuting volume. Threads stretched within the smoke, connecting Banook's anatomy to the corresponding points of the forming bear's body. Nose, nipples, eyes, toes, ears—threads flowed from every portion of his body, from every cell, in a burst of dark radiance that soon became opaque.

The refractions subsided as the smoke congealed the twin silhouettes. There stood a bear on his hind legs, a dozen feet in stature, covered in fur more golden than a ripe wheat field.

The bear dropped onto four paws that wielded twenty knife-like claws. He was so large that he was eye to eye with Lago after dropping down. His nose was pink and moist, and flexed over his muzzle as he sniffed around. He grunted bear noises that made no sense to the humans. Lago looked shaken, while Alaia beamed as if she was staring at the most adorable puppy.

"Can I... touch?" she said excitedly.

Banook nodded and took a step toward her.

Alaia caressed the silky fur. It went deep, separating into soft clumps.

Banook turned so that his side would brush Lago's arm. Lago's shyness partially subsided; he dared to rub his fingers in and then his whole hand, exploring the velvety-warm coat. From within the fur, he could smell something like damp leaves and wildflowers, but he was not brave enough to bring his nose any closer.

Alaia could contain herself no longer; she lunged to Banook's thick neck, shaking it like she did with her unusually tight hugs. Banook laughed in grunts and soft roars.

The golden bear then took a few steps back, stood again on two legs, and the inverse transformation process began.

This time Lago felt a bit more at ease and walked around the shapeshifting bear, hoping that in the details he would see something to help him understand the process.

The refracting smoke vanished, and there stood the naked mountain of a man.

"It's that easy!" Banook said, putting a friendly arm on Lago's back.

Alaia was too curious now. "Were you not able to talk as a bear?"

"Not as a bear, but I could understand you, though your words sounded muddled and detached. Were you able to observe all the details?" Banook asked Lago, squatting down to be eye to eye with him again.

"Yes, those lines in the smoke… they look just like the threads that I see with the mask, but somehow made solid, or liquid, or whatever they are."

"A keen observation. What they are, who knows? Maybe the Miscam know, or my old friend Mamóru might know, as he always was the smartest of us all. When shapeshifting, you must visualize them moving and connecting to the corresponding points. And I should mention, the process can be much swifter once you properly learn it. It can be performed in the blink of an eye. I only did it slowly so you could appreciate the nuances. Now your turn has come. Did you warm up enough beneath Alaia's cloak?"

Lago nodded uncomfortably. He gave the cloak back to Alaia, who traded it for a reassuring smile that did not reassure him in the least. Alaia wanted to save Lago from the awkwardness again, but knowing she could not protect him forever, she chose to sit back down with Jiara and Ockam.

Lago removed his tunic, then his boots, then pulled his trousers down while covering himself with the mask. He dared not remove his underwear.

Banook nodded, encouraging him. "You must be wearing your mask for this to work, I believe," he pointed out.

Lago kept one hand lowered to cover his crotch, shoulders tensed up. He timidly arched his back as he raised the mask.

"What is wrong, cub?" Banook asked, a hint of concern clouding his face.

"I'm okay. I'm trying to focus and um, remember what y-you said."

"You seem very uncomfortable. Is it because you are naked?"

Lago looked away. "Y-yes," he said, almost whispering. "I'm not... I'm ashamed of... I'm not comfortable when others look at my body." His eyes darted over the floor.

Banook reached down and pulled Lago's trousers up, then quietly said, "It *is* a bit chilly out today. Why don't we go inside and warm up? We can always continue this another time."

They got dressed. Lago followed Banook into the cabin.

"What was that about?" Ockam asked once the cabin's door closed.

Alaia explained and suggested they stay outside for a bit. It wasn't cold really, and she thought it better to let the two have a moment alone.

Banook boiled water for tea while Lago brooded at the kitchen table.

"I'm sorry," Lago said. "I'm not good at this... It's something that's bothered me for a long time."

"The only one to apologize should be me. I forget sometimes about certain aspects of human temperament that are learned through culture, which are hard for me to even conceive of. It's not in my nature to be modest. I walked these lands naked for thousands of years as a bear, unaware of my own nakedness."

"Alaia and I used to have this cave. It was the size of your cheese cellar. We used to play naked in there, just me and her. We were simply kids being kids, exploring, and I had no problem with it. But I never felt that way with strangers, or in public. When my friends went out swimming, I would always make up an excuse not to go."

"What do you think it is that makes you feel this way?"

Lago sat remembering, without answering.

"I do not mean to put pressure on you," Banook said, "but in order to take your half-form, this is something you'll need to overcome. How could you be comfortable finding your true forms, if you aren't comfortable in your own brown skin? It's a fear that you have to face, but it was wrong of me to force you, no matter how foolishly unaware of the situation I was."

"Don't apologize, it wasn't your fault. There are things I haven't told many people, only Alaia." Lago looked out the window and saw his friends having a lively conversation—it didn't seem likely that they'd come in to bother them.

Banook placed a cup of sweetened black tea in front of Lago, then served himself the rest of the pot. He sat in front of Lago and looked at him with sympathetic eyes, quietly sipping his tea.

"When I was a kid," Lago said unprompted, "like five, or I think six... My dad, he worked selling textiles, importing them, cutting them, sometimes making his own garments. It was my mom's business from before she died, and I knew my dad hated having inherited it. But he wasn't smart enough to get any other jobs."

Lago looked outside again, fingers trembling around his warm cup. "Two Tsing tradesmen had come in. They were in the living room, negotiating with my dad over silks, the expensive kind. Dad had this shipment of mulberry silks in his bedroom, and I saw them and touched them and they were wonderful, I had never felt something so soft in my life. I was only wearing a tunic, so I took it off and wrapped myself in a cut of the silk. It must've been a shawl, or something not too large, but it covered my body. I thought, *If those men want to buy silks, and they see me wearing something this pretty, they will surely pay a fortune for it!*"

Lago cringed as he pathetically laughed. "Just the kind of thing a foolish kid would think… I was such an idiot. I walked into the living room, wearing this dress and doing a stupid walk, trying to look graceful. I was excited, thinking I was being clever and that my dad would later thank me for it. I just wanted him to be proud of me.

"It was… that look he gave me, that's what I keep seeing when I am naked. It was those hateful eyes, so disappointed and angry at me. He slammed his fists on the couch and through his teeth told me to *take that off*. I stood there in the middle of the living room, all three men staring at me, and he yelled, *Take that off now, you sissy lorrkin!* And I cried. He yelled at me more until I slowly had to undress myself and stand naked in front of them."

Lago was tearing up, stuck in the memory.

"I just… I hated him so much after that. He never loved me, always wanted to get rid of me, and from that point on he had an excuse to treat me like shit."

Banook reached out with giant, tender fingers and wiped the tears from Lago's cheeks. "The insecurities of your father should hold no purchase over your own heart," he said. "He cast his own fears onto you, and you may—when you feel ready—let those fears go, as they are not and have never been yours to bear."

He let Lago have a moment, then promptly returned to his joyous self. "I know just what to do," he said with a smile, then trotted away down the hallway, leaving Lago alone and confused. When Banook returned, he dropped an exceedingly oversized shirt on the table. "You can wear one of my shirts! Even if you shapeshift into the direst of netherbeasts, there is no way you'll grow bigger than this belly."

Lago laughed, lifting the blanket-sized shirt. He caught a whiff of lemongrass from it; musky, but fresh.

"But we need not do it today," Banook said. "We'll take our time and work through it. I am sorry I am not better at dealing with these matters, but I want you to know that despite them being foreign to me, I do understand them. Life can be cruel enough to all of us. The joy of a Spring breeze, the warmth of a fire, the spawning of salmon, and Sunnokh caressing a flowerbed of lilies… all these wonderful things that I treasure and devote myself to, they all sometimes pale in comparison to the amount of suffering, wickedness, and cruelty that inhabits the shadows in our hearts. But that has never put my hopes down, because I know that all it takes is one kindred soul, one act of compassion, one moment of empathy, and all shadows vanish back into the void."

"You've been able to lift my spirit like no one else," Lago said through a sniffle. "Thank you, Banook. I don't know what I did to deserve you."

Banook reached out from behind Lago to hug both him and his chair. He ruffled Lago's hair, which was a thing Lago usually hated but somehow didn't mind when Banook did it.

"Would you help me prepare dinner?" Banook asked. "I've never seen you cook. We have plenty of time, and I can teach you a thing or two."

Chapter Forty-Eight

Endless Forms

Over the next few days, Banook took Lago on walks to share his knowledge of shapeshifting and conjecture about the workings of the threads. No matter the topic, however, all his ruminations ended up, sooner or later, on a tangent about the beauty of the mountains.

Despite looking awfully silly, Lago did wear Banook's oversized shirt. It helped him feel at ease, but more than anything it was a happy memento for him, a symbol of a moment when a dear friend had cared for him.

"How do you do that with such large fingers?" Lago asked.

They were inside Banook's woodcarving workshop; not the one he used for cutting logs for his cabin—that was at the mill, by the creek—but one for delicate carvings. His creations decorated the shelves, crossbeams, knobs, coat hangers, windowsills, and even the handles of the tools themselves. Lago had seen these carvings inside the cabin, but he hadn't till now realized it was Banook himself who had brought them to life.

"Tender fingers are tender no matter the size," Banook said, using a bent chisel to delicately carve the eyes of a bear figurine.

Lago tossed the sleeve of the huge shirt over his shoulders, like a scarf, and leaned in to watch. He did feel naked when wearing nothing else underneath Banook's shirt, but at the same time he felt comforted.

"Did you also carve the bear on the walking stick you let Ockam borrow?" Lago asked.

"That I did! From a branch of a mighty ironwood tree who died half-sunken in the ice of the Klad Mahujann. Best of woods are found in those areas, if you are not afraid of digging in the ice and know how to treat the wood after carving it."

Banook finished a clump of fur detail with a veiner, then let the tiny bear rest on the worktable. "I will stain it later," he said, admiring his creation. "I think of wood carving as similar to shapeshifting. It's not about making something new, but about finding something that was already within, then uncovering it, bit by bit, until it's clear to your heart." He considered his words for a moment, then frowned. "But I'm afraid my simile shatters when I consider all the wood shavings I removed to make this little bear. You mustn't remove Lago from the equation. Once you find your half-form, you will still be Lago, yet be more. And once the mask comes off and you return to your human self, you'll still be your canid self. We are many in one, yet only few of us ever realize it."

Later that day, they strolled across a meadow, watching warblers and shrikes flutter by.

"That morning of my first lesson," Lago said, after walking in silence for a while, "you said you could take the forms of other kinds of bears. What kinds? I've only seen the black and brown ones around here, and you as a golden bear, of course."

"There are a few others. Polar bears, who lurk under the icy-blue waters of the north. Sun bears, with tongues as long as snakes. Spectacled bears, with their fanciful markings and humble demeanors. Giant pandas, with their plump and curious faces. Kiuons, as small as they are smart. And others that are unfortunately extinct, as they did not survive the fire and ice of the Downfall."

"Can you tell me about those?"

"Precious and unique they were, each and every one. Moon bears, with their crescent hearts of Sceres imprinted on their welcoming chests. Sloth bears, long-maned and tender-hearted, with claws like sickles. Short-faced bears, with jaws that could put a dire wolf to shame. Cave bears, as hard-headed as their skulls were dense. Agriotheriums, long-legged and nearly as large as yours truly. Dawn bears, the oldest kind, who could be as small as cats, and just as agile. And arctotheriums, the largest of all, of which I am the very last."

"You as the golden bear, you are the last arcto... um—"

"Arctotherium. My primal form is the last remaining manifestation of arctotheriums. We were a prodigious and proud kind, but like many of the others, did not manage to survive. Except for one."

"I assumed you were a brown bear. You look just like them, except for the golden color."

"Our anatomies are slightly different, but we do look like the browns. Except you will not find a brown of such size, not even among the grizzlies at the shores of the Unthawing Ocean. Gold is my color, but other arctotheriums ranged from copper, to steel, to dusty brass. I have one and one form only for each species, as one is my true nature for each. It is the same in my human form, which is this one and this one alone."

"Could you show me the species I haven't seen before?" Lago asked, embarrassed by his own directness. Banook seemed delighted to hear the request.

"The non-extinct species I surely can, and it would be my pleasure! But I will not yet show you the kiuons, for you have to see them marauding as a pack to truly appreciate them. I'm planning on having you meet them in the near future, I know just where to find them."

Banook undressed for the demonstration. It still made Lago a bit uncomfortable; it was part embarrassment, part excitement about seeing a naked man who was exactly the type he desired. He hoped he was properly managing to conceal his arousal.

"I won't be able to talk to you while in those forms, but I hope you'll recognize each species in turn. Do step closer to feel the differences—the furs are highly specialized and need to be appreciated by sensitive hands."

Banook's body began to turn smokey. He shapeshifted more quickly this time, and in an instant, there stood a sun bear, balancing on his hind legs. Lago was surprised at how much smaller Banook was now: as a sun bear, he was only the size of a large dog. His furs were dark with a stunningly symmetrical, cream-colored marking crossing his chest, and skin that drooped loose as a velvety fabric. Lago caressed the furs; they were downy and warm. Banook's jaw then dropped open and out came a lengthy tongue, wrapping around Lago's arm; he squirmed and quickly pulled his wet limb away.

"Gross! How is it so long?"

Banook's tongue draped down all the way to his belly button. He grunt-laughed while he rolled it back into his mouth.

While still on his hind legs, Banook grew taller, surpassing Lago's height once more, until his form congealed as a spectacled bear with gorgeous, marble-like patterns of white and gold over a sparkling, black coat. The fur felt coarser to Lago, as if it would be impossible to get it wet.

"I love these patterns," Lago said. "They remind me of the quartz-veined canyons we walked through the other day. And your nose, does it remain pink in all your forms?"

Banook nodded, then closed his eyes. The cloud reformed around him and turned colorless. He shrunk in height but made up for it in girth, dropping down to his butt in a black-and-white pile of softness, as a giant panda. Lago had never seen anything like this animal before, not even in books. Banook was so bewitchingly cuddly that Lago came in for a hug. The panda embraced him back, then showed him his dexterous paws, which had an additional pad that could grab on to Lago's fingers as if it was a thumb.

"This is… too cute," Lago said. "You have to show this form to Alaia, she will squeal."

The panda smiled with surprisingly sharp teeth. He dropped onto all fours and closed his eyes again. This next transformation seemed more strenuous. Lago took a step back. The refractive cloud grew, lifting the plump panda within it. It kept growing, bigger than Lago expected. The threads stretched until the shape coalesced into a massive polar bear, almost as large as the golden bear had been, but slenderer, longer necked, and furred in pristine whites with cream undertones.

Lago felt the dense and deeply insulating fur, thinking that each hair looked like an elastic crystal shard. The massive jaws were rimmed by black, glossy lips with purple highlights. It was a terrifying figure, but Lago feared not.

"How beautiful," he whispered, losing himself in the whiteness. "Do you think that—"

The white bear took a sudden step sideways, losing his balance. He dropped on his haunches and slowly shifted back into human form. "Sorry," the naked man said, eyes closed. "It takes effort to go through so many species in so short a time. And the polar form makes me weary—they live too far from here, making it harder to tap into their essence." He slowly opened his eyes.

"I'm sorry," Lago said, "I shouldn't have asked."

"It's alright, cub, I had a good time showing you. But I think it's time we return home. This old bear needs to take a long nap."

CHAPTER FORTY-NINE

STAR-HEART

"I just don't get it!" Lago snapped. "I tried to do it exactly as you've been telling me, but I can't seem to—"

"Relax, cub," Banook said. "It's only been a week since you started."

"Maybe it only works with the Miscam people. Maybe I'm not cut out for this."

"You should try to enter a calmer frame of mind, and then—"

"I *am* calm!" Lago said, a bit too loudly. He stopped his pacing. "I'm... sorry. I just don't know what I'm doing wrong."

It was the twelfth day of Dewrest, the sixth day of Lago's training in shapeshifting. He had been learning from Banook non-stop, yet still not a whisker had he been able to grow.

"Come with me, cub," Banook said. "There is a place I enjoy sometimes, when my mind becomes cloudy. It might help."

Banook led him to a blue-green creek with shimmering white sands. It was no grand landscape, nothing extraordinary, but the simplicity and familiarity of the place felt reassuring. They sat next to each other, listening to the running water. Banook did not try to impart any further wisdom—he simply let Lago enjoy the calm.

The gurgling stream gradually eased Lago's anxiety, reminding him of the creek near their old Diamond Cave, where he would sunbathe naked on the rocks with no one else in sight and no worries on his mind. Even the smell was the same.

Cascades softly splashed into a pool that was sprinkled with fallen leaves, tracing spirals in fiery colors. The two of them quietly gazed into the vortex for what must have been hours. It felt oddly comforting to be so at ease while saying nothing at all, in those times when words were not necessary.

Lago focused on the movement of the leaves.

"Thank you," he said, after a long silence. "I think I needed a moment to just... to just not think so hard."

"It is good to step back sometimes."

"I've just... I've been trying to figure out what species to picture. At first, I only thought about foxes, since both Mawua and Sontai were foxes."

"And I still don't see you as a fox."

"I don't, either. But lately I've been focusing on this new image... It's the dire wolf that I saw in Withervale. I don't like picturing it, because I see his dead face, his dangling tongue, his fiery eyes always staring at me. That seems the obvious choice, it's what most deeply ties me to the mask."

"Perhaps it is, or perhaps it's much too obvious. It's not just a species that you must seek. It's finding the precise personification that calls you, the one voice you hear even when you are asleep."

Lago suddenly recalled a moment in the Farsulf Forest, something that had intrigued him at the time, but which he hadn't given more thought to afterward. Ockam had said that Lago had sleepwalked away from their camp to listen to the sound of wolves howling. Not dire wolves, but timber wolves. And as if spellbound in a dream, Lago couldn't remember the incident the next morning.

But I've tried focusing on a timber wolf, a tundra wolf, even a steppe wolf, and those didn't work either, he thought. *But there is something about that night that feels important.* He felt on the verge of a realization, more of a gut feeling.

"I think... I think I want to try this again," he said, standing up.

Banook pulled his feet out of the cold water, turned around, and leaned against a boulder.

Lago paced around the edge of the creek, deep in thought. Something brewed in his mind, an image, an idea that had always been inside of him yet was entirely new to him. He stopped pacing. Instead of trying to wear Banook's enormous shirt, he let it drop to the ground and put Agnargsilv on.

He faced the pond of spiraling leaves and let his mind be carried by their hypnotic motion. He forgot for a moment about this place, about his shame, about his scarred leg, and even about Banook, who sat staring at him. He didn't close his eyes but let them take in the circular motion of the leaves while through Agnargsilv's eyes he connected to the myriad of organisms that danced in the same spiral. They all blended as one.

His mind echoed a distant memory. He was a mountain, no, he was searching for a mountain. He was a meadow, a valley, a wolf. No, not a wolf, an entire pack, dozens of legs trotting in unison. He was a hummingbird, a flower, and the depths of the ocean. *Have I dreamt this before?* He was microorganisms and consciousnesses all bound into one. He was the stars, and the aether between them. *Where is this memory coming from?*

He stood alone, in a pure darkness deep within his own mind, and looked down, unable to see his own body. He stopped trying to see himself as a half-man, half-canid, and instead pictured a presence in front of him, of a creature separate from himself, but who was still himself. A timber wolf manifested, fur weaving with the breeze. The timber wolf's coat colors were the same as the dead dire wolf's had been: subtle grays that dreamed of blue; tail, paws, and head as dark as coal; and dusky rosettes that transitioned the two colors smoothly across his back. The wolf's eyes were drops of luminous amber. The dusk-coated canid was standing in mist, beneath softly falling snow. His left side faced Lago, his head turned in the same pose Safis had briefly held after they had rescued her from the dome, before she'd vanished to freedom. The snowflakes froze in midair and burned brightly, turning into a field of stars speckling a clear night. The wolf's blue-gray coat blended with the delicate hues of the Galactic Belt, the black face turned one with the dark beyond, and the eyes—like fiery beacons—held their warranted place among the stars.

To the stars, Lago. To the stars, a memory reverberated.

When Lago came out of his hypnotic trance, he was in a new form. His muzzle was no longer of hard quaar, but of bone and flesh covered by soft furs. His whiskers pulled upward in a smile as he looked at himself in wonder. He felt a few fingerbreadths taller; with his leg anatomy changed, he now stood on his toes, over leathery pads. The scars on his burnt leg made his fur patchy there, but everywhere else his fur shone lustrous and dusky. His coat was a crepuscular gray with inky blue reflections, lighter at the belly and down to his sheath, and transitioning with black rosettes across his back. He saw the blackness of his muzzle and was certain that the rest of his head, up to the tips of his pointed ears, would also be tinted in night. And he knew without a doubt the color of his eyes.

He examined his hands, or paws, as they were a blend of both: shaped mostly like human hands, they had soft pads on them that were pink in color. Each of his wrists held a calloused, highly sensitive carpal pad. He was very glad that instead of tiny dewclaws, he still retained useful thumbs, even if they looked quite different now.

He suddenly noticed he was wagging his tail, which he had not even realized had been behind him all along. He pulled his tail around his hips and caressed it: the fur was much longer there and pitch black, like his head, his footpaws, and his handpaws.

He looked at Banook—still sitting against the boulder—and shared with him a smile. Lago leapt on Banook's belly and hugged his chest. The Nu'irg held him fondly and stroked the silky fur, giggling with excitement. "You did it, cub! Quite a stunning wolf you are!"

Lago stepped off Banook and said, "*Thaarrkk grrwouww,*" and his brow whiskers dropped. He cocked his head like Bear sometimes did.

Banook laughed from the depths of his belly. "It's okay, cub. Your tongue, your throat, they are not as they were. You will have to learn how to use them again. Speech will come to you in time." He kept laughing.

Lago gave him a half-lidded stare and growled, which he could easily do.

"Easy, boy," Banook said, still chuckling. He pushed himself away from the rock and squatted in front of the wolf.

"I'm very proud of you, cub," he said. "There is a tradition among all Miscam tribes, Wutash or otherwise, for the day a Silvfröa finds their new self. And what better temple to grant these honors than this most magnificent manifestation of nature? The mountain range itself, serenaded by cascading streams, enveloped by the incense fragrances of pine needles and moist soil."

Banook took Lago's handpaws in his hands, looked straight into his amber eyes and said, "The Miscam had the honor of choosing a name for the Silvfröa's new half-form. You are still Lago Vaari of Withervale, but I also name you Sterjall, which means *star-heart*, as your eyes tell me that that is your true calling."

"*Grstrellsharrll,*" he uttered clumsily.

Sterjall turned to observe the threads of life around him. It was similar to seeing with his mask and eyes at the same time, but not exactly the same. The two views were truly mixed now, conjoined into a single level of understanding that was no longer two separate layers. Everything carried with it a new sensation: from how his fur felt when he stroked it, to how his pads were rough yet tender, to how it felt to swallow, or to bend a leg up, or to flare his nostrils. Through his wet black nose, he drew in a filling breath, fascinated by how refined the aromas of the forest were. He found himself mesmerized by how well his ears worked, how directional and clear sounds were. He instinctively learned to turn his ears, to flatten them, to focus them far, near, or behind.

As he contemplated his surroundings, his keen ears picked up a throbbing sound; he turned and realized it was Banook's heartbeat, echoed by a beating coming from his own chest. Sterjall suddenly saw the man, the bear, with brand-new understanding. He now knew what it was like to be two and be one, what it meant to fall in love with the mountains, to revel in the details of the tiniest of creatures. He saw the bonds, the threads that made up Banook's large body, and how they inextricably looped back into themselves, but also connected to Sterjall's own canid form. And he also saw that strange aura that emanated only from the Nu'irgesh and the masks, which was sparkling gold and welcoming. Sterjall knew him then, and he knew Banook was looking back into his own soul and knew him back.

Banook turned away in shame, as if he had pried too deeply into something he shouldn't have. The moment was gone.

"We should share this great news with our friends!" Banook said, jovial once more. "But first, let us see if you are able to shapeshift back to your human self. It should be much easier."

Sterjall simply had to focus on the young man he already knew himself to be. With a clear goal in mind, he felt himself turning to that smoky substance, yet this time being fully aware of the transition. He caressed the translucent fur on his arms and was surprised to find that the smoke was solid, even though it swam like a cloud while the transformation occurred. He saw his whiskers vanish in ethereal vapors and his muzzle flux from refracting smoke back to the nightly charcoal of the mask. He pulled Agnargsilv off and looked down at his naked body, feeling no hint of self-consciousness.

The first to greet them upon their return was Bear, who jumped into Sterjall's arms and fiercely licked his muzzle. Alaia came right after, mouth agape and shaking her hands as if they were on fire. Jiara and Ockam followed behind her, while Banook introduced Sterjall by his new name and explained all that had happened.

Sterjall tried on his blue tunic over his fur, which fit fine as long as he kept the drawstring at the neck loosened. His trousers and boots, however, would not fit: though his waist was the same size, his tail was now in the way, and his legs and footpaws did not have the same proportions. Jiara brought out a sewing kit and sat with Sterjall to see about remedying that.

"Weeneedgth too cutha hol fwor my thail," Sterjall mumbled incoherently. "Dooyou haff eny eckkstra battons?"

"I know, sit still," Jiara said, taking measurements of Sterjall's legs. "I think the boots… if you shapeshift, you'll have to ditch them, or tie their laces to your belt. At least your wolf paws are narrower than your human feet, meaning you won't break through your boots as you shapeshift, like our friend here." She glared amiably at Banook.

"Ifft like I dound neeff them eeanygways," Sterjall said, barely noticing he was barefoot.

"This is so weird, but I love it," Alaia said, playing with Sterjall's neck fluff. Ockam stood to the side, not sure what to do, but unable to look away.

Sterjall tried to convey the experience, forcing his tongue to fold in the proper shapes. It didn't take long until he was able to speak almost normally again. He told them about the vision he had, how he found his focus, and how that triggered the transformation.

"By now I can doeet at will, it omly takes sha heartbeat," he said, shapeshifting as he sat on the chair. Sterjall's fur turned translucent, revealing Lago's smaller body inside the refracting smoke. Agnargsilv was not yet visible, but as the smoke shrunk and coalesced, a dark silhouette appeared within it, solidifying into the black mask. Sterjall was gone and there sat Lago, wearing just the tunic and the canid mask.

"Alright wolf kid, try these on," Jiara said, after spending some time sewing. She handed Lago the modified trousers.

Lago stood up, surprised by how comfortable he was with being half-naked in front of Jiara and Ockam. He would still feel that insidious shame around others in the future, but he had at least found a way to be at ease among his close friends.

"I put magnetic buttons on the back," Jiara said, easily pulling the back fly open and letting it snap close again. "I sewed a row of Qupis within the seams. Clever, huh? And I widened this part of the legs just a bit. The waist didn't need any adjustments."

Lago put the trousers on, then slowly shifted into Sterjall. The Qupis on the back fly popped open with the pressure as the tail sprouted out.

Sterjall grimaced. "Shtill a bit tight on the thail, but it vill gwork," he said.

Caribou ribs were served for dinner, out on the terrace, to take advantage of the benevolent weather before the Umbra season turned truly cold. Sterjall tried out his acute fangs on the ribs, cleanly cutting through the tender meat. He guessed he could chew through the bones, too, if he wished to. Even eating was a new experience to him, not only the physical process of chewing the food, but also the tasting. His nose was more sensitive, yet also more forgiving to strong smells, and his wolf tongue perceived flavors in a different way than his human tongue. A single meal could be two entirely different experiences if he shifted forms while chewing.

As he cleaned his handpaws with his long tongue, he got a lot of his own hairs in his mouth. "It's weird," he said, licking his chops, "the hairs in my mouth don't bother me, they are barely noticeable. They would've irritated me to no end in my human form." He had wondered before why Bear didn't mind grooming himself and now understood that it was all in the manner in which their minds perceived different stimuli.

"There is something else that looks strange in this form," Sterjall said. "Agnargsilv's indigo aura—now that I'm in my half-form—is no longer focused only on my head. It extends down through my body in glowing tendrils. It's as if I am seeing my own, I don't know, maybe my spine and veins or something, but as a dim blue glow."

"Like it's truly a part of you," Alaia said. "So... can you talk to Bear now?"

"I already tried," Sterjall admitted, "but nothing's happening."

"It could take a while," Banook warned, finishing a whole stack of ribs. "The next lesson is one I cannot directly teach you, as I am unable to mindspeak with canids. There are different qualia and ways of perception for each group of animals, inaccessible to the other clades. If you were a bear cub, not a wolf pup, we could be mindspeaking right now."

"I feel as if my brain had to make room for all these new ways of sensing," Sterjall said. "When the mask is off, it's hard to remember what it felt like to see the threads, as if that part is shut off from me. And even now, as a wolf, I find it hard to recall what it felt like to have smooth skin."

"I get something like that during Winter," Alaia said. "Those nights when it's been cold for so long that you try to think of what a warm Summer day is like, and you can't, as if there's no memory of it. But it's there, once you experience it again—it had always been there, you just have to rekindle the feeling."

"I think language must be similar," Banook said, standing up to clean off the table. "Other animals don't use words the way humans do. When I was just a bear, I could understand only a dozen or so words, which had to sound very different from each other. It wasn't until I became a human that I was able to comprehend how the spoken words are put together. And now, even after taking my bear form, those meanings remain with me, albeit a bit less concretely. Learning about spoken language was fascinating. I marveled at how such tiny things like syllables could be combined into such wide a range of meanings."

"And so you became a poet!" Sterjall said.

"Far from it, cub. It is nature who is a poet, silently caressing the underside of a bird's wing, lifting—"

"There he goes," Alaia said, "you started this one, Lago. I mean, Sterjall."

"—joyful praise, and exulting devotion, in all their forms."

Sterjall yawned. "It's still so early, but I feel exhausted."

"You've changed far too many times in one day, Lago-Sterjall," Banook said. "Fret not, shapeshifting is not a danger to you, but it will wear you out."

"Well, I'm not tired," Alaia said. "Banook, can you finally tell us about how you became a human?"

"There's a time for food, a time for tales, and a time for sleep," Banook said, walking away with the dishes. "The former two we've covered. The latter we must focus on next."

Lago was getting ready for bed. The fireplace cradled a reticent fire, warming up his couch and bearskin blanket. Banook had gone to bed long ago, and the others were settling upstairs, lamps already extinguished. Yet there was a brightness all around, not from the dim fire, but from the Ilaadrid Shard. Sceres was in the late stages of her Amethyst season and would soon be sprouting her first tendrils of Jade. Lago could see her, violet and white, with her bright shard enticing his tired eyes.

A beam of vibrant moonlight framed Bear, who dozed atop his favorite deerskin pillow, right in front of the yawning fire.

The stillness was palpable.

It was Lago's first moment alone since his transformation. He began a slow, careful ritual he had performed countless times before, starting by loosening the drawstrings of a small pouch and removing a tiny wooden box. He unlatched the box and from within its colorful compartments scraped off a bit of lacquer paste. He mixed the paste with a few drops of solvent and stirred it with his delicate brush. He quietly painted his nails by the moonlight, not caring that he was about to go to sleep. It was a way for him to relax and introspect. He thought about all that had happened that day, and all he was yet to experience, and decided he wanted to go to bed as Sterjall, to see what that felt like. Too many times he had shapeshifted through the day, to the point even his whiskers were tired. Yet he put the mask on to do it one more time.

He stared at the spindly flames, letting himself drift into the mental state that allowed him to shapeshift. He slowly changed into his wolf half-form.

When he looked down at his handpaws, he noticed the fingernail lacquer had broken off and fallen like glitter to the ground. *I should've expected that*, he thought. He didn't mind; it was all an experiment. He peacefully mixed a new batch and repainted his claws, enjoying the extra effort it took to pull the fur back so that it wouldn't glue itself to the drying paints. His muzzle covered the view when he held his hands in front of his chest, so he had to tilt his head as he worked. The blue lacquer reflected the sparkling firelight as it dried. *I wonder if the tips of my claws will be trimmed after I cut off my human nails,* he thought. An experiment for another time.

Content with his new look, Sterjall stripped off his clothes and crawled under the bearskin. He had time now to fully explore his new body. He felt underneath his black lips, pulled at his long tongue, fondled his sharp teeth and his even sharper fangs. His nose was always moist, something he found disconcerting; he wiggled it, then forced it up in a snarl, noticing it was oddly detached from his bones. His ears were deep, and pushing a claw in made him ticklish, forcing him to reflexively shake them. He noticed other whiskers he had not paid attention to yet, not just on the side of his muzzle, but on his chin, his eyebrows, and near his wrists. The eyebrow whiskers made him blink involuntarily at the slightest touch, while the chin whiskers gave him an additional perception of space in that area below his muzzle where his eyes didn't reach. Together with his fur, the whiskers created a mental construct of anything that touched them, similar to how the mask gave him a sense of space that wasn't visual.

He squeezed his arm muscles; they felt about the same, except for the volume the fur added. He dragged his claws on his thickened neck, down to his sternum, which felt narrower, more pointed forward. He kneaded his long chest and belly fur, and to his surprise found extra nipples. He had three pairs now, the new ones down by his belly—he hadn't even noticed them underneath so much fur.

I wonder what's down there, he thought, then explored the mystery of his new sheath and what hid within it. He noticed he was hard without being erect, marveling at the presence of his penis bone. His handpaws traveled all the way down to his balls—they were one of the few furless spots on his body, and extremely sensitive.

It was all too intriguing, making him feel too excited, too exhausted.

Sterjall fell asleep with his handpaws between his legs.

CHAPTER FIFTY

BALSTEI AND KEDRA

"Here is fine, right on the table," Crysta said, showing Artificer Balstei Woodslav where to place the first of several crates of books and artifacts she had asked him to bring from the Zovarian Academic Institute.

Balstei dropped the crate inside the library. He was an older but very much in-shape scholar. The light gray of his well-trimmed beard and the darker gray of his mustache matched the colors of the striped doublet he wore. He had detached his doublet's sleeves, showcasing his thick arm muscles. Crysta thought it looked quite out of place for an academician, or a man his age, but she was not about to complain.

"What's with the Union guards?" Balstei asked, eyeing the two pink-clad soldiers stationed by the gate to the monastery grounds.

"Just safety measures," Crysta explained. "Haven't seen anything suspicious since the attack, but you can never be too careful."

"They let Scholar Fulmen go, did you hear?" he said. He had the disconcerting habit of biting his lower lip while waiting for a reply.

"Fulmen? When?"

"Just a couple weeks ago." He picked up another crate; his biceps bulged under the striped shoulder wings. "No benefits, no honors. He had been impregnating his younger students. *Again.* Who knows where he'll end up. Maybe Umarion will take him, they don't mind a scandal or two."

"That's a bit of a relief, actually," Crysta said, "but I'll miss his lectures."

"This crate is for the monastery, where should I—"

"Down by the door is fine," Gwil said, strolling down the path. "I'll carry it to the Haven. Thank you, Balstei."

"Hey Gwil. Sorry I couldn't get all the samples, Lurr Crestreaver is too protective of her herbs. Where's Khopto? I want to see what he's been working on."

"Join us for dinner. Khopto will be happy to tell you more. Your usual room is ready. This time we made sure to clear most mice droppings from your pillow."

"Kind of you. It'll only be a few weeks. I'll be out of your way soon."

Balstei picked up the last crate, which he lifted much more easily than the others. "This one has the books about Miscam myths," he said to Crysta. "Simza helped me dig through the archives, and still we couldn't come up with more than this. Lots of stories about the Silvesh. Not much is published about quaar, but I included my two papers in there. I'd love to talk to your student, what is their focus? Maybe I can help."

He handed the crate to Crysta. It was mostly empty, but still contained enough books to keep her busy.

"Miscam myths, huh?" Gwil mocked, peeking inside the crate.

"Don't read too much into it," Crysta said. "I'm just curious, nothing more."

"I thought it was for someone's thesis?" Balstei half-asked.

"I lied. I'll tell you about it once we are done sorting everything."

Balstei helped Crysta unload the books into their respective shelves, then they carried the rest upstairs. "You really need an assistant up here," he said, looking at the mess that had accumulated in the tower. "What happened to that kid who used to work here, Lango?"

"Lago. He's gone. It's a long story, oddly related to this whole mess I asked you to help with." She nodded to the crate of Miscam literature. "I'll explain, but it's complicated, alright?"

"You are a snappy one today," Balstei said. "And sorry for asking, but where will I fit in? There's no room on this desk. I need a clean worktable to take the telescope apart and change the lenses, and I need to write my reports, too."

"I'll clean some of this up tonight, I promise," Crysta said, squaring the edges of some papers as if that was any help at all.

"So, what is it with you and Miscam mythology?" Balstei asked, leaning too casually on the desk, in a clear gesture of, 'I won't let you dodge this any longer.'

Crysta dropped into her chair, a bit flustered. She poured some lukewarm tea for them both, then told Balstei all she could about Lago's mysterious disappearance and the potential connection with the masks, and with quaar. Once done, she waited, unsure whether Balstei would say something supportive, or make fun of her.

"I would've said you'd gone mad as the Arch Sedecim of Holv-Yanan, Crysta," the artificer said. "I would've said that a few years back, that is, before I got serious about studying the aetheric elements. The Havengall monks have had the right idea about soot all along, Takh bless them." He grasped the magnium-infused pendant resting over his ashen chest hairs—it was shaped like a kite shield, with a spear crossing it.

"Oh, Bal, don't tell me you are getting into those same drugs."

"No, of course not. I mean, it's only for research. Soot is damn expensive, I was only able to afford a few doses through grants, though of course I wasn't entirely honest about where the Quggons went to. The monks here have it easy, the stuff that comes out of these coal mines is quite pure, and relatively inexpensive."

"Is that why you want to see Khopto?"

"He gets me a decent price, but that's not it. You know me, I'm no addict, I couldn't afford to be one. We are in academia, for Takh's sake! I'm interested in Khopto's studies. The best stuff we've been discovering, the most intriguing data, all of that we can't publish because, well, we'd get busted, lose our funding, get thrown out of the institute like lecherous Fulmen and his cohorts." He combed his mustache down, then continued, "There's this cosmologist at the Yenmai Institute, Professor Lai-Nu, who—"

"I know about her. It's from her that the institute bought the glass for this telescope."

"I figured. Anyway, she's been doing research on soot and quaar. They say she's developed a theory on how it originated, which could be groundbreaking. If you knew how soot was created, you would know where to better find it. But the bitch won't reveal anything, she hasn't published a single paper."

Crysta shot him a chastising look, but Balstei went on.

"I won't apologize, I didn't use the term lightly. She's an irascible, maddening piece of work. I'm afraid Empress Pian-Thi is forcing Lai-Nu's hot-tempered mouth shut, as keeping her findings confidential could mean a huge boom for the Tsing economy. I want to break into her lab just to steal her notes. Perhaps also to punch her conceited nose."

"So, what is it about soot, quaar, and these Silvesh? How are they related?"

"You should read the stuff I brought ya, you'll immediately see the connections. But mainly, the way the masks are described, from the blue dunes of Bauram to the white towers of my old Elmaren home, it matches all we know about quaar. Color, texture, weight. That's a given. And their powers... I think most of it is pure legend and exaggeration. Most, but not all." He leaned back and bit his lower lip.

Crysta rolled her eyes. "Go on, you don't need to savor the moment so much."

"When using soot, someone with *experience*, like Khopto, can 'see' these interwoven threads, like the stuff they describe in the myths. I've had a glimpse myself when using, albeit briefly. And the connection—hear me out here—I think quaar and soot are exactly the same material."

"You mean carbon?"

"*Aetheric* carbon. You know how hard it is to distill that stuff, for every ton of coal they get but a speck of it, if they are lucky. And I've analyzed quaar artifacts. You won't believe how hard it is to scrape a sample from them, they are tougher than bloody diamonds! When analyzing those samples, quaar seems to be made mostly, if not entirely, out of soot. With sensitive-enough equipment we can measure the oscillating mass, it's a telltale sign. But imagine if one was able to pulverize those old artifacts, they could sell that dust for a fortune. That's a big *if*, no way any machine we know of can do that."

"What are you actually saying? This doesn't fit with the myths of the Silvesh."

"But I think it does, Crysta, can't you see? Hmm... Put it this way, what if the masks from the legends were made of quaar? Imagine you were wearing a mask that was able to channel these immeasurable forces the way soot does, but without having to burn your nose and make you look like a spur digging at a coal mine."

This time, Crysta's piercing look made Balstei raise his hands in surrender.

"Just an expression, just an expression. Anyway, if that was the case, you'd see all sorts of miraculous things, maybe that's what inspired the myths to begin with. Hey, who knows, maybe those masks were nothing special, but they filled their muzzles with a spoonful of soot and their shamans got high as drunken whores from all of it, writing those perplexing spritetales while rolling around in some deranged orgy."

Crysta waved him off, shaking her head in disgust.

"You know I ain't just saying stuff, Crysta, it could be! Either way, we found some quaar artifacts that channel better, distributing the threads in perfect, geometric patterns. And we don't even know what in Takh's two names that force is, as you can only see it while under the influence, and there's no way to measure it outside of one's subjective perception. You know that doesn't bode well when you are begging for Quggons from the foundation."

"Exactly. It's not scientific," Crysta said. "It could be all in your head."

"It's the same with all aetheric elements, they make no sense either way!"

"But you can measure the magnetic pull of magnium. You can light a room with particles of pharos. You can quantify the energy of burning ignium."

"Yet we know nearly nothing about them. The little we know is from texts written before the Downfall, and even those advanced scholars could not figure the elements out. Other than magnium, there's not enough of them to go around to study properly. Each of the aetheric elements holds secrets, soot perhaps more than any of the others."

Balstei reached inside the crate and handed Crysta a leather-bound folder. "Start with this one. Unpublished, and likely never to be published, if I want to keep my job. If there's any connection between those masks, soot, and quaar, this is it. And if Lago was involved in this shit, this would easily explain how he got so deep into those Negian asses. Wasn't he doing deliveries for the monastery?"

"Yes, but that's only errands, nothing to do with—"

"You are too naive, Crysta. Where do you think they get their supply? Do you think all they make in that laboratory is cough drops?"

"Now you are spouting conspiracies. Sorry, Bal, but I won't entertain the idea that the monks—"

"I don't need to speculate, I *know*, I'm one of their clients! They are good people, they do it to fund the monastery, and with that they are able to provide cures for people in need. It's not some conspiracy, it's just economics. You have the mines, a good supply chain, talented scribes, and a high demand from the west, be it from rich fucks who don't know where else to stick their Qupi in, or from poor academics like yours truly who just want a fair chance at running their research."

"Okay, okay, I get it," she said, dropping the folder back in the crate. "I'll go through all of these, I promise. Give me a couple of days. And I'll help you clean this mess up."

"You mean I'll help *you* clean this mess up."

"Same thing, but let's get started before it's too late. You have to make it to dinner with your dealer."

For the next few days, Crysta submerged herself into all the documents Balstei had brought. She was glad Balstei was there to answer questions; the technical papers were as far from her field as they could be. Balstei also helped install new lenses in the telescope, a much-needed upgrade Crysta had been waiting on for years.

On a Nossday evening, Balstei was walking down the tower steps, ready to head to his dormitory, when he heard a knock at the front door.

"Don't tell me Gwil forgot his keys again," he grumbled and unlocked the doors. Beneath the threshold stood a young woman with short, dark hair, carrying a backpack much too large for her petite body, but which didn't seem to inconvenience her. She was wearing muddied leather trousers and a long-sleeved linen jacket with the neck popped up.

"Is Crysta at work tonight?" she asked.

"Who's asking?"

"My name is Kedra, she'll—"

"Kedra!" Crysta's voice said from behind Balstei. "It's so late, you could've found me tomorrow. Did you just arrive?"

Kedra pushed her way in and looked around, lowering her backpack, quiver, and bow. "Just walked in from the east. They are almost done reinforcing the rampart, had to sneak around the southern edge to get here faster. Sorry it took me so long. There's a lot to discuss, some you might want to know about right away." She peered to her side. "Excuse me, you are?"

"Balstei Woodslav, I'm an artificer with the institute. I don't mean to intrude, I was just headed to my dormitory."

"I'll catch you up tomorrow," Crysta said as Balstei walked out the door. She locked it behind him, then turned to Kedra. "Come sit upstairs, I have a fire going. What is so urgent?"

She pulled two chairs in front of the fireplace and served Kedra a goblet of chilled water.

"I have all the information about the Heartpine Dome's northeastern collapse. It's all here," Kedra said, handing Crysta a wobbly edged notebook. "Fascinating stuff, but that's mostly inconsequential right now. I scoured around the perimeter road, trying to gather more information about the collapse. A sylvan scout told me about an attack that happened in Thornridge. Apparently, a Negian squad snuck there from the north, right after the infiltration here in the mesa."

Crysta perked up.

Kedra crossed her thin legs, then continued, "I went to Thornridge to find out more. Only a few guards had been there when the fight happened, and I overheard the name *Lago*. Wasn't that the name of your student?"

"Lago! Yes, he is in Thornridge?"

"He was, but they wouldn't tell me anything else. Only one guard seemed to know more. He was terrible at hiding it, but he wouldn't talk. The others just knew the name they heard and the rumors that Lago had disappeared after the battle. A scout and a high-ranking officer went missing too."

"Any idea why they were looking for Lago? Did they mention anything about a mask?"

Kedra's shoulders tensed. "How did you know about that? I was going to mention it. The prisoners they took, apparently they were after some sort of mask. Is this related to what is happening in Anglass?"

"I'm not sure I know what you mean," Crysta said, now more deeply confused than before.

"That was the other thing I wanted to tell you about. I came back through Nool to look closer at the movements in the east. You heard anything about the Red Stag?"

"The red what?"

"About three weeks ago, something happened in Anglass. Merchants in Nool talk about a creature that came from the nethervoids to take control of their army. Some say it's an elk taking the shape of a man, others say it's just a man wearing a dead elk's head. This coppersmith was saying it's one of the Negian generals wearing a mask from the old legends. Whatever it is, they say he went to Hestfell to take Emperor Uvon's throne. They call him the Red Stag."

Crysta recalled one of the folktales she had just read about; it mentioned a mask called Urgsilv, *urg* being the Miscamish word for *cervid*.

"Does that mean that…" Crysta thought out loud, "if Lago had that mask, if that's what they were after, that means he was captured by them?"

"I can't think of how. The Free Tribesfolk defeated the squad that attacked Thornridge. None of this makes sense. They are preparing for something big. Several battalions are advancing from the south, marching behind the sierras. And the merchant ships at Nool are scarce for this time of year, they are likely supplying the forces in Anglass instead, or perhaps they are stationed at Dormendal, being refitted for war. I'm afraid there's only one place they could be looking to attack."

"We have to tell Gwil and Balstei about this. And I need to send a message to the capital as soon as dawn arrives. Zovaria needs to mobilize their fleet, posthaste."

CHAPTER FIFTY-ONE

ANGLASS SIEGE

Alvis Hallow was very pleased with how well the speech Urcai had written for him had been received by the crowds at Hestfell: the artificer's words had convinced everyone that the emanations of Takhamún were alive and needed to be freed from the domes that held them prisoner.

Urcai had guided Alvis with utmost care, telling him exactly how to rile up the citizenry. It was he who planted a man in the crowds to yell the name of the *Red Stag*—a name he had come up with himself and which had picked up like a wildfire. Alvis was so pleased that he'd named Urcai his viceroy, to help him rule the empire while he was busy conquering. An entirely new hierarchy of governance was being constructed from the ground up, but Alvis had no time to spare for the politics involved.

"The empire's sole goal is finally clear," Urcai said to the new chancellors, ministers, and other bureaucrats of Hestfell. "When Prophet Gweshkamir wrote, *From sixteen to one I shall return. From dark my light shall emerge, to shine upon the chosen Shten-Havúr*, he was not telling us that Takhamún would emerge from the domes to bring forth the Endfall—as the blasphemous manuscript of the Zovarians proclaims—but to return divinity to us, his chosen people. Freeing his emanations, rescuing the sparks of divinity from the heathen tribes, that is the goal that unites us today."

Urcai peered over his spectacles around the long table, then looked to Alvis, who held the dark mask to his chest. "The divine nature of the masks cannot be denied," Urcai said. "Takhamún's emanations are not trapped in the Silvesh, they *are* the Silvesh. The Unmaker has chosen Urgsilv as his voice."

Alvis lifted the mask to his face, then stood while he took the form of the Red Stag. Even those at the table who had previously seen his elk half-form gasped in awe.

"I have heard Takhamún's voice," the Red Stag solemnly intoned. "It is a voice of pain and desolation. I have felt his anger, but also his hope. Takhísh has wept enough for the loss of his brother. Takhamún has wept enough for the errors of his past. They are brothers of love, of forgiveness, who wish to be reunited. Let us bring them back together. With their unity, ours will follow."

"We must release Takhamún from his sixteen prisons," Urcai said, "and help him reunite with his twin brother. Once all the Silvesh are in our control, the Twin Gods will help us rule under their holy mandate."

Everyone listened to the new viceroy. Whether they believed him or not was inconsequential, given that their vested interests compelled them to support him. After all, those who had defied the new order had been swiftly replaced.

Of course, Alvis himself did not believe a word of the Takh Codex. To him, religion was nothing but a tool, a convenient way to gain support from the masses, to grant himself permission to do whatever needed to be done.

"There is more than the sparks of divinity within the domes," Urcai continued. "There are resources beyond imagining, greater riches than what was found within Heartpine. With the wealth of the Anglass and Lequa domes alone, we could feed our nine impoverished states. Our legions could at last sail over the Ophidian and begin their march into the Jerjan Continent."

When the new emperor rode back into the fortress of Anglass, he did so as the Red Stag, with his muzzle and antlers painted in bright, dripping reds. Dried elk skulls had been dipped in red dyes and hung on the fortified battlements to announce the new emperor's arrival. The banners around the fortress had all been painted with the down-pointed, crimson triangle, making the laurels of the old sigil look like antlers over a cervid skull; in the same manner were shields emblazoned, capes embroidered, and cuirasses etched.

Crowds cheered their new leader as he galloped into the fortress, chanting that the Red Stag had come to conquer the dome for them, to bring back the golden centuries of the Reconstitution Epoch. The Red Stag exuded a terrifying charisma, inspiring a desire for devotion, not just from the cervids the mask was naturally inclined to connect with, but from allgenders, women, and men alike. Perhaps it was an effect of the mask, or simply the very nature of the weak minds of his subjects, who were carried away by their own desire to worship a powerful leader.

The Red Stag dismounted his steed at the Fogdale Citadel, followed by Viceroy Urcai and his personal guard of arbalisters, with Fjorna and Crescu at the lead.

A soldier approached and said, "General Jaxon Remon is waiting for you in front of the barracks, Your Imperial Majesty."

The Red Stag visibly recoiled. He disliked the pompous honorific; it sounded so archaic. He composed himself and replied, "Jaxon is here already? I was not expecting him so early. Urcai, would you mind setting up the pavilion for us?"

"At once, Your Imperial Majesty," the thin man said.

"And Urcai, I was thinking, could we drop the *Majesty*? I think referring to me as *Monarch Hallow* would fit best. Something new, to wash away the old customs. I do not want to be linked to Uvon's wretched dynasty."

"Of course, Your... Imperial Monarchy?"

"Just *Monarch Hallow*. *Excuse me, Monarch Hallow. As you wish, Monarch Hallow. Monarch Hallow has requested your pitiful presence.* Or even *the monarch has ordered his head served on a platter.* It has a better ring to it. And of course, among the crowds, referring to me as the Red Stag is preferred, when I'm in that form."

"Certainly, Monarch Hallow. It will take some time for everyone to get used to it, but I will communicate the request. The name sounds auspicious, for a stag with a sixteen-pointer of a rack is indeed called a *monarch*. This has a good ring to it, that I can incorporate into the lore I'm crafting for your mythological persona."

"Good. Now ready the pavilion if you please."

General Jaxon Remon—who commanded the Third Legion—waited for Monarch Hallow in front of the barracks, leaning his weight over his heavy mace. He was a robust and tall man, with short, dense hair the color of a rusted scythe, and a jawline like a miscut brick. He was missing his entire left arm, where he kept a single brass pauldron over the empty shoulder. The general covered the tattoos of his ranking insignia and sank to one knee as the Red Stag approached.

"Jaxon, there's no need for those formalities with men of your honor and rank, spare me."

"Yes, Your... Majesty?... Your Red Eminence?" Jaxon said and stood. "Honestly, Lorr, since you are asking me to be at ease, I'd like to ask what the proper honorific is?"

"This again?" the Red Stag sighed. "Jaxon, for you, as we did on the battlefield, our first names will be fine."

"Glad to know it's the same old you inside that filthy sack of fur, Alvis," Jaxon said, offering a strong armshake.

The Red Stag smiled; it was an uncanny expression, with that long face and wide, wet nose—it had an appeal that felt ghastly.

"You know why we are here, Jaxon. Tell me what you've learned."

"Come with me, I'll show you."

They walked inside the dark-blue pavilion while Fjorna, Crescu, and the other arbalisters stood guard at the entrance.

Jaxon unrolled a round-cut map of the Anglass Dome over a table.

"Our second tunnel breached in through this sector a week ago," he said, pointing at a series of lines on the map. "We sent three vanguard scouts. Only one returned, but she's brought us a lot of useful information. The Teldebran Miscam are still unaware of our second breach. It's well hidden."

"Are their warriors as useless as those from Heartpine?"

"Unfortunately, they are much better trained. They are not bloodskins, as you saw from their chief and his daughter. They are better armed and armored. Nothing we can't overcome, but a bottleneck like these narrow tunnels will make it hard for us, we'd lose a lot of soldiers going in. They have archers behind good cover, and enormous beasts patrolling the entrance."

"Their beasts, Urcai, are these the 'companion species' the chief's daughter mentioned to us?"

"Yes, Your Imperial Ma—Monarch Hallow," Urcai said. "They are big, and smart enough that they need little to no direction from their shamans. They have been bred to help their race, like the dire wolves and other giants at Heartpine."

"I never saw the dire wolves, but I heard the stories," Jaxon said. "But just wait until you see these fuckers. Urcai, what are their names again?"

"There are three," Urcai answered. "The first are tufted deer, like the ones that breed in the Everbloom Forest."

"The tiny, fanged ones? I used to hunt them when I was but a toddler," the Red Stag mocked.

"Yes, but this species was bred bigger, the size of war caribou. They seem to travel in small packs, or squads, assisting the human soldiers. Their second species is a stag-moose that our scholars had thought extinct, the *cervalces,* which has also grown taller than any fossils we ever encountered. But the biggest colossi they have are the ones we call *megaloceroses*, also a species we had thought extinct. They are giant elk, twice the height of the biggest moose from the Fjarmallen marshes. Their antlers are sharp and wide and can scoop up a whole squad in one swipe. All three species are well trained and follow the Teldebran army closely."

"But Urgsilv is no longer under their command," the Red Stag needlessly pointed out. "Why do the beasts still answer to them?"

"Out of their own free will, Monarch Hallow. Their companion species are sapient. They understand many Miscamish words, although they cannot speak themselves. It makes those creatures sixteenfold more dangerous."

Jaxon nodded. "Like the viceroy says, these beasts have tremendous power. They patrol our exit tunnels, and one of them is enough to trample hundreds of our soldiers."

"This is great news, Jaxon!" the Red Stag said, smacking a hand down on Jaxon's armless shoulder.

"Excuse me?"

"I've learned a few tricks since my trip to Hestfell," the Red Stag said. "I was aiming to show you later. Come with me."

They exited the pavilion. Crescu opened the gate to the nearby stables and ushered them in, leading them to a corral. The Red Stag looked to the back of the corral, where a troop of war caribou was circling.

The caribou all froze in place, in utter terror, staring at the Red Stag with their heads lowered. The Red Stag made a gesture toward them, waving fingers that ended in calcareous tips, like small hooves. A single caribou approached, pathetically, stopping in front of him. The Red Stag touched the cervid's chin, lifting his head almost tenderly. The caribou's muscles spasmed, as if receiving mixed signals, one telling him to run, a more powerful one ordering him not to move. Carefully, methodically, the Red Stag reached out with his right hand. He grabbed the caribou's left antler and with a swift move snapped it off.

The caribou flinched but held still. The stump where his antler had been flowed with fresh blood, squirting rhythmically in the hurried pattern of his heartbeat. The animal's dark eyes stared and tried to not see at the same time. The Red Stag snapped off the remaining antler. The caribou remained subdued, barely daring to breathe.

"Completely under my control," he said to General Jaxon Remon. He turned back to the miserable creature, and with no more than a thought, commanded him to go bleed somewhere else. The caribou hastened to the farthest end of the corral to suffer, alone.

"You... You can control them?" Jaxon asked. "Like the bloodskin witch controlled the dire wolves?"

"Any and all cervids who come within my reach, Jaxon. They are mine to subdue, they will obey my every command, even if it leads to their deaths."

"We must continue to evaluate the limits of your abilities," Viceroy Urcai said, wiping a droplet of blood off his spectacles. "There are tests I wish to perform before you risk venturing into the dome."

The Red Stag nodded. "We can work on those tests as we wait for our soldiers to arrive. Jaxon, how far away are the legions?"

"The Third is at the eastern barracks, and patrolling the northeast quadrant, but they could be readied at your command. The Fourth will be arriving tomorrow. The Sixth will take a few weeks more. And the First was stationed in Dormendal a month ago, to help with the shipyard, but could be recalled if necessary. I don't foresee us needing that many soldiers."

"I agree, there is no need to wait for all the others. In three days, we strike. In the meantime, Urcai, let us run those tests of yours."

Right outside the thick walls of the fortress of Anglass, the Red Stag was demonstrating his abilities to Jaxon. With Urcai's aid, he had learned that not only could he command cervids of all species, but he could keep them under his control indefinitely, or at least for as long as he retained his elk half-form. A herd of caribou, elk, deer, and even a handful of moose were following him now, unwillingly waiting for his orders.

"They don't look so well," Jaxon said, noticing the wobbling gait with which the cervids followed. Their eyes looked empty and unfocused; their bodies shuddered with uncertainty.

"They are mindlocked, as the Miscam would call it," Viceroy Urcai explained. "Their minds are conflicted, struggling to break free, but Urgsilv's voice is more powerful. They are healthy, obedient, and deadly. Even the small ones."

With a nod of his sixteen-pointed rack, the Red Stag directed a spotted fawn to charge toward a wall of rocks. The terrified fawn obeyed without hesitation, galloping at full speed to smash her head in. She collapsed with a shattered spine.

"Even the harmless-looking ones could help break through a line of infantry," the Red Stag said. "It's like hurling boulders with a trebuchet."

"But what if you removed your mask, Alvis?" Jaxon asked. "You'd lose your entire force."

"This is why we are performing these tests now," he replied. "And I am glad we are, for once I capture those giant cervids, I do not wish to lose them." He glanced to Urcai, prompting him to elaborate.

"We performed some tests," the viceroy explained. "The mindlock is indeed broken when Urgsilv is removed, even when Monarch Hallow shapeshifts to his human form while still wearing the mask. It's a regrettable outcome, but not unexpected. This seems to be related to the threads the monarch sees when wearing the mask. All links are severed when the half-form is lost."

"There are other inconveniences too, however," the Red Stag mumbled, with more than a hint of disappointment in his tone. "My new soldiers follow only simple orders. They do not change strategies when the situations in the battlefield require it. If I tell them to trample, they will simply keep on trampling. They do nothing but feed and shit without my guidance."

"That will do to command the giant ones," Jaxon said. "But with an army of thousands of creatures, you can't possibly be issuing them orders individually."

"I can focus on more than one at a time," the Red Stag said, "but it takes effort to isolate the orders, instead of sending them all at once. And it also requires *their* attention. Urcai, how would you explain it?"

"You see," the viceroy said, "these links established by the mask are two-fold. When two creatures sense each other, when they are aware of each other's presence by any means within their perceptive capabilities, an empathic channel is opened. That is the channel the mask can exploit. It's not exactly dependent on distance, it seems, but has more to do with the reach of each creature's perception and subsequent awareness."

"If they see me or hear me, they'll obey me," the Red Stag said, oversimplifying matters. "But only me, and no one else. I can't delegate to my generals, marshals, captains, or chiefs, for they cannot mindspeak to the creatures the way I can."

"I think you underestimate your powers, Alvis," Jaxon said with a smirk. "They won't listen to any of your current officers, but that does not mean they will not obey a simple chain of command."

The Red Stag simply stared and tried to guess at what his old friend was implying.

"Say, for example," the one-armed general said, "that you bestow upon one of your creatures, a moose, an officer rank. Commander Moose, you can call him."

The Red Stag smiled, unsure of where this was headed.

"You only need to command Commander Moose," Jaxon said, now feeling a bit uncomfortable about the foolish nature of his example, "and tell him to trample the nearest muck village, or to disembowel any spurs in his way. But before the battle, you tell a squad, or perhaps a platoon of deer, elk, or any mix of animals, to keep an eye on Commander Moose and trample anything he tramples, to do as he does. Send the moose into battle, and all others will follow."

"That might just work, Jaxon," the Red Stag said. "Urcai, what are your thoughts on this?"

The viceroy seemed partially convinced. He was already envisioning countering mechanisms, calculating viability, and scheming failsafes to the strategy, but overall, he seemed to agree. "We should run tests," he said. "But this could offer a way to command a larger army. We can't have thousands of these creatures following the monarch so closely—they will overwhelm him, if only with their smells."

"I do feel that they will simply rush forth and die, however," the Red Stag said. "They have no concept of what is happening, only that they should follow a simple set of rules. If our own soldiers are in the midst, they will get equally trampled."

"Let the animals go first, then," Jaxon said. "Let them open a path for our legions. They are nothing but meat covered in sharp antlers—no offense to you, of course. Send them to kill, to die, and when the battle is won, we'll have enough venison for the most opulent of feasts."

The Red Stag stretched his lips in a macabre grin.

Soldiers had taken their positions inside the long mine shafts, ready to rush through once they heard the signal, which would come at the break of dawn.

The Red Stag and the arbalisters gathered by the edge of the dome, many hours before sunrise. When the Red Stag stepped forward, the vines in front of him opened, as Fjorna had taught him they would. They ventured in.

There was beauty beyond comprehension within the Anglass Dome, a beauty the Red Stag was entirely blind to. He ignored the hot spring-steamed vistas, the peculiar source of the light emanating from the branching tops of the dome, and the complexities of the biomes, focusing solely on his goal. He had designated Fjorna's squad of arbalisters as his own private guard, and they followed him closely, retaining a circular formation around him, shields like a dome to protect the Red Stag from any arrows—but the precautions proved unnecessary, as not a single arrow was to reach them.

The Red Stag spotted a herd of elk nearby. As soon as he got their attention, the elk stopped with blank stares. He mindspoke to them from a safe distance, seeded himself into their brains, and ordered them to trample the Teldebran Miscam warriors stationed near the still-locked tunnel his forces waited in. His instructions were simple: kill any human they found along their path. The elk rushed manically, stomped, stabbed, and died for their master.

The Red Stag heard a tremor behind him and turned to see two colossi galloping down a wide road—megaloceroses had come forth to help contain the chaos he had unleashed. When they passed close enough to see the Red Stag, he mindlocked them and ordered them to demolish the enemy's trenches. The beasts could not help but obey his insidious command. Terrified warriors quickly assembled their shields into carapace-like walls, but the megaloceroses easily scooped them and their fortifications up in their giant antlers, tossing them dozens of feet into the air, then stomping down the survivors.

Archers high on a cliff were trying to shoot down the colossi. The Red Stag found their actions displeasing. He spotted another of the so-called *companion species*, a pack of five tufted deer who had been sent on patrol. They were of much greater stature than the small deer he used to hunt as a child. The Red Stag's mind captured the five as a group, then sent the peculiarly fanged creatures to beat their sharp hooves and fangs onto the unsuspecting archers.

As the massacre raged on, a blaring signal resounded. Then the mine shaft doors opened, flooding the battlefield with Negian soldiers. It wouldn't take them long to wipe out the Teldebran survivors.

"Apologies for the delay," the Red Stag said to Jaxon, entering the war room of the Fogdale Citadel. "How many have entered so far?" he asked.

"We have two battalions inside. The tunnels are narrow, but we'll get the rest through."

"Capture as many slaves as possible. I instructed the cervids to continue their attacks farther inland, but hopefully they won't kill too many. Don't get your soldiers too close to my creatures—they will attack anyone they find."

"Already warned my troops," Jaxon said.

Fjorna jumped in. "We have sent seven squads to infiltrate the axis and trace a safe passage for the main infantry. They will be deployed at the temple's entrance, to make sure no one is allowed in."

Viceroy Urcai shot a sharp look at Fjorna. "Good. We must take no chances. The core vine needs to remain intact, or the dome will suffer the same fate as Heartpine. Our riches, our legions, are at risk."

"We will see it through," Fjorna said, then looked to the Red Stag. "Monarch Hallow, Anglass will soon be secured. We should shift our focus back to Withervale."

"Your spies have found nothing there," he said, "the tracks are cold."

Fjorna's misaligned face spasmed. "But Lago could've made his way—"

"I don't care about the maggot!" the Red Stag snapped. "The mask is all that matters, and we have no lead pointing to Withervale at this moment."

Fjorna scowled, but no one could tell the difference.

"Mask or not," Crescu interjected, "if we could take Withervale's port, we'd have control of the mouth of the Isdinnklad and the mountain pass."

"It's too risky a move," the Red Stag said, "we do not have enough ships on the Great River. But maybe… Let me speak to General Helm, once he returns from Dormendal. I may persuade him to take on an assignment." He looked derisively at Fjorna and added, "There are other masks for which we know their locations, starting with the one inside the Lequa Dome. So, east is where we will head next. General Broadleaf waits for us there with the Fifth Legion."

"They've only just started excavating there," Jaxon complained. "You could walk right in, but your troops would have to wait for months until the tunnels are ready."

"Fret not, for Urcai has devised a plan to lead us in much more expediently."

"What sort of plan?" Jaxon asked.

"It has to do with the Shaderift aqueduct," Urcai answered. "I will show you all the strategy during tomorrow's briefing."

Jaxon cocked his head toward the monarch and said, "Alvis, if you don't mind me asking, what is your goal once you gather more of these masks?"

"Perhaps the first will be a reward to my right-hand man!" he said, slapping Jaxon's only arm. "I'm only half-kidding. There is no fixed goal yet, there is only a vision. A vision to unite our lands under the same banner, to rescue our citizens from poverty by taking back the riches the Miscam stole from us. To make them pay for the cancer they grew on our lands."

"But the domes contaminate realms thousands of miles away, protected by armies much greater than ours," Jaxon said. "Half of them are not even in this continent."

"One step at a time, Jaxon. We take one step at a time."

CHAPTER FIFTY-TWO

QUAAR RELICS

Sterjall was returning to Banook's cabin after a stroll when he heard a metallic chime coming from the building. Ockam was at the kitchen table, carefully tuning his kalimba by tapping the handle of a knife onto the metal tines. He had been teaching Banook how the instrument worked, but Banook's large fingers kept strumming nearly all notes at the same time.

Ockam handed the retuned kalimba to Banook, who, despite his delicate touch, could not figure it out.

"Playing this thing is infuriating," Banook complained. He gave up, placing the instrument on a side table, next to Sterjall's dire wolf fang. "Cub, you collect strange keepsakes in your travels," he said, glancing at the fang—only the roots were exposed, the rest still wrapped in sticky cloth. "What kind of animal did this strange bone come from?"

"I've been meaning to show you that," Sterjall said. "It's from a dire wolf we found at Agnargdrolom. It's a fang."

"A fang? Of this size? Impossible."

"I think the roots make it seem bigger than it is," Ockam suggested.

"That is not what I mean," Banook said. "I thought this wrapped bundle was some sort of leg bone. When you told me the story about the dire wolf at Withervale, I thought you were exaggerating for effect."

"I was not, that dead wolf was so big they had to use two wagons to pull it," Sterjall said.

"Uncanny. I've seen dire wolves, many a time, who would fight for the prey my bears hunted down. Well, perhaps it was my bears trying to steal the game the wolves caught, but my point is, this tooth is much too large. Dire wolves were the biggest species of canids, but not by much. Perhaps twice the body weight of timber wolves, or three times as heavy for the larger males. This could not possibly be a canid fang, it's unwieldy."

"I haven't yet seen one alive," Jiara said as she walked over to prepare herself a drink, "but I've seen their prints and a few skeletons in Heartpine. Definitely wolves."

"Odd indeed are these times," Banook said. "I wonder how those beasts reached such majestic sizes. Something must've happened inside the dome."

The talk about the fang made Sterjall remember something else he wanted to ask Banook about. He placed his bag on a chair and removed the hexagonal tube he had picked up at the Stelm Bir temple.

As his handpaws handled it, the threads Agnargsilv showed him bent and shot out through the tube's hole, exiting on the opposite side in a more organized, linear path.

"Banook, what do you make of this?" he asked, tossing him the tube. As Banook reached for it, his golden aura too pierced through the hole.

"A Miscam artifact?" Banook said, examining it.

"It is. Found it at the temple in Heartp—in Agnargdrolom. There were hundreds of them, part of the big lattice that was above the altar."

Banook scraped his nails on the subtly spiraling tube, smelled it, then licked it. "It's made of quaar, the same material as your mask, or at least something very similar. The Miscam used it for their sacred artifacts, weapons, and tools."

"When I look through it with Agnargsilv, if I place it at the right angle, it lets me see the threads much farther away than usual," Sterjall explained. "It's like it extends my reach in one direction."

Banook peered through the tube as if using a microscopic telescope. The hole was perfectly circular and smooth, but he could not see farther into the distance like Sterjall described; to him it just looked like a dark pipe.

"Quaar reminds me of graphite, or charcoal," Banook said, "but light as a hummingbird's daydream, and hard as the Corundum Monolith of Khaark-adesh. Quaar relics are less rare in the Jerjan Continent, where most Acoapóshi Miscam ruins wait in abandonment. The few recovered artifacts are used in machinery for mining, for smelting and smithing, for weapons of war, or for proclamations of power and wealth. Legends tell of a mystical quaar bow with a quaar string that would never break nor slacken, and of entire suits of armor forged for invulnerable knights. I have a few quaar items I collected over the years, but other than the Silvesh, I'd never seen one carved as intricately as this."

"What sort of items do you have?" Sterjall asked.

"I shall bring them. I was going to show them to you all soon, for a different reason."

Banook ducked under the cabin's door and took a rope bridge toward one of his workshops, then another bridge to a warehouse filled with cobweb-collecting items. When he returned, he placed his quaar artifacts on the kitchen table, one at a time.

"This quaar helm I recovered from the Aedellok Battlefield, now known as the Artad Slopes, where no more signs of the ancient battle remain." The helm had a cross-shaped slit for the eyes and nose and a slightly beveled crest at the top. It was perfectly smooth to the touch, yet exquisitely adorned with geometric patterns, as if the sheen itself was textured, reflecting the light differently depending on the angle one looked at it from. The inside was padded with a durable, springy material. Sterjall spun it in his handpaws; something like moist soil fell from it.

"My large brain won't fit in it, unfortunately," Banook said, "but it made for a good planter for snowbells and alpenroses. Don't let your whiskers worry, I transplanted them to another pot, but their seeds might want the helm back at some future date."

Banook placed a few pieces of armor down, from an incomplete set. "This shoulder guard and shin guard came from the same battlefield. A gruesome war that was." He placed a much smaller piece down. "And I believe this was a pendant, or earring. I use them to shape curved metals and woods when I work in my foundry and mill. And this"—he dropped a kite shield on the table—"is a shield I found in ruins deep in the Stelm Nedross. I use it as an anvil, pounding metals over it. It has never scratched, despite my incessant pummeling."

Like the helm, the shield was smooth and covered in reflective patterns, but of a more organic nature, like a ripple of water transforming into knotted roots at the edges. It had two enarmes on the back—for a non-Banook-sized arm to grip—and a strap to let it hang over one's back.

Banook next placed two ropes upon the table: thin yet sturdy, glossy in their darkness, subtly textured. Jiara abandoned her drink on the kitchen counter and stepped closer.

Banook untied one of the ropes and let it droop over the edge of the table. "These here are some of my most prized possessions. The Miscam also crafted quaar cords, then wove them together. These ropes can hold as many Banooks as you care to dangle from them."

Jiara picked up one of the nearly weightless ropes and felt the perfect friction of their weave. She noticed the ropes ended in heavy, sliding magnium tips, so that there was some weight that could be shifted around in case one needed to toss them. The opposing magnium tips attracted each other to tie the ropes as loops in a quick snap.

"This is incredible," Jiara said. "How can they be so light? So solid? There is nothing like this that we know of, not even in the Tsing Empire. I can't wait to get started with the training, these will make it all a breeze." She caressed the rope like it was a kitten. "How did the Miscam craft these artifacts?"

Banook shrugged, an expression that felt heavily overdone for his size. "It was only the original Miscam tribe, the Acoapóshi, who crafted quaar. Their knowledge of quaar was perhaps the most well-guarded secret they kept. I haven't seen anyone craft artifacts of such wondrous durability since the indomitable domes were closed."

Sterjall inspected the artifacts. Like his six-sided tube, they had a strange effect on the threads, but rather than propelling them through, they simply made them bounce at odd angles, as if the threads aligned themselves to the internal structure of the crystals of the nightly material. When he spun the quaar items around, the threads shimmered, as if snapping into new alignments.

Sterjall explained what he was seeing.

"What the Acoapóshi did was all purposeful," Banook said. "I do not understand their magic, and I don't think any other realms at the time did either. They knew how to control this force you are perceiving, how to bend it to their will, but also knew how to respect it."

"All your relics are beautiful," Sterjall said, "but they react in a completely different manner than this one." He put a dark claw inside each of the tube's ends, watching his own threads and aura flow through it. "What do you think this was for?"

"From what you've described," Banook said, "it seems to be a sort of focusing instrument, or part of a much larger focusing device. Whatever its original purpose in that lattice was, it is no more, but it could be repurposed for anything that does not require cutting it or bending it, as there are no tools I know of that can manage that. What do you plan to do with it?"

"I don't know. It reminded me of Agnargsilv, and I thought it would be good to examine it more closely. Maybe I'll take it to Crysta someday."

Banook was mulling over something, eyes thin as slits. He tapped a finger to his plump lips and nodded.

"I do have an idea. Would you let me have both this wondrous… umm… tube, and that sap-stained, oversized fang of yours?"

"Why? What will you do with them?"

"It will be a surprise," the Nu'irg said. "But be warned, it will take me some time."

Sterjall felt Banook's giddiness, which he could tell the Nu'irg was trying to hide. He found it endearing how Banook sometimes failed at containing his emotions. He handed the long fang to Banook and said, "I think the cloth is stuck to it now."

"It will do just fine."

CHAPTER FIFTY-THREE

INFORMANTS

Sterjall leaned against the edge of the terrace. The cloud-dappled, midafternoon light made for quite a view of the faraway Brimstowne and of the ever-present Anglass Dome. He placed his binoculars over his muzzle and scanned the waxy green textures of the dome.

"May I see that?" Banook asked, taking the binoculars. "Fascinating instrument. At the old Yenwu Theocracy, before the Downfall, they had highly advanced glasses, like the one you described from Withervale, but much larger. Incredible machines. Entire buildings were designed to house them."

"Crysta told me about that," Sterjall said. "Most old observatories burned, but the Tsing artificers found a way to rescue the Yenwu technology. It's the same with most knowledge that we have today... About mathematics, alchemy, just about anything. It was all discovered epochs ago. We sometimes use the old formulas without even knowing why they work, they simply do."

"The Miscam tribes did not use advanced gadgets like this one here. If there was something that united them all, it was their distrust of technology. Sometimes that played in their favor, sometimes not."

Banook used the binoculars to peer at the distant dome, forced to look through only one eye, since the device wouldn't spread wide enough for his huge face. He lowered his arms, looking troubled. "There is something unsavory stirring by the dome," he said. "A cloud of smoke rises from its base, near Dormendal."

"We saw movement in that area when we rode up to Brimstowne," Ockam said, stepping in behind them. "A man told us they were burning slopebrush to make room for new barracks. But why build at Dormendal? Their fortress is in Anglass."

"They have a port there," Banook said, "and a shipyard, and access to sulphur, as well as a solid supply line. But the Negians have never pushed their military camps that way before."

"Maybe they found a way into the dome from there," Sterjall conjectured.

"Maybe," Ockam said, chewing on his thin mustache. "But it's also uncomfortably close to Withervale."

Banook returned the binoculars. "I think it's time for me to take a brief trip to Brimstowne," he said. "I'll find out more about what is happening in our neighborhood. And I could pick up the climbing gear Jiara wishes to hamper our bodies with."

Banook packed an oversized satchel with snacks, two Qupi pouches, and a book he intended to use for trading—those were all the items he'd need for what he thought of as a quick stroll down the hill.

The Nu'irg knew these mountains like he knew the scents of all wildflowers. He could traverse them at great speeds when not held back by slower companions, or by the usual distractions caused by a colorful feather, a seedpod with an uncanny symmetry, or a pebble that sparkled too fiercely under the sunlight. He ignored the distractions along his path this time around and strode down the cairn trail, only stopping briefly for a nap or two.

"Oy, Jilpi!" he called after passing the last of the cairns. Next to a nearly boiling pool of blue was the old man the travelers had encountered a month earlier, still working on melting off the crackled skin his bones greedily clung to.

"Lorr Banook!" the old man called back through gaps in his teeth. "Doing a run for Winter supplies?"

"You know me well, old friend," Banook said, already stepping out of his boots. "I won't be long. I need to be home before the snows block my path. How are the waters treating you?" He sunk his feet into the pool, then sat at the edge.

"The Geo Springs are as fine as a Dathereol wine," Jilpi said. He sat up on his razor-sharp hipbones and massaged the pruning calluses on his feet. "Say, big man, you carry something else with you this fine day. What might it be?"

Banook looked at his nearly empty satchel, which held only the bare necessities.

"No, not in your bag, in your eyes," Jilpi said. "There's a sparkle to them, a fire, even. Whatever it is, it must be quite special."

"Perhaps it is my yearning for the incoming Winter. It is the best of the worst seasons, and sets my soul alight."

"Well, that must be it, then."

"Say, Jilpi, any news on what is happening by the dome? From my cabin I can see clouds of black and clouds of gray."

"Portents of bad times to come, I'm afraid. The Negians are readying for war. The new emperor is bringing his army."

"New emperor?"

"Of course you haven't heard, you are lost in the mountains! Only you, Sunnokh, Sceres, and the eternal granite. You must not yet know about the Red Stag."

"I am afraid not, old Jilpi. Is it a new tavern in the sleazy side of town?"

"Oh no, something fouler than that. Some say he is a demon come from the voids. Some say he's a god, Takhamún reincarnate. I think he's just a fool wearing a dead elk's head."

"An elk's head? Now I'm more confused than ever."

"He is the new emperor, who killed Uvon dus Grei and took over the rhodonite throne. They say he looks like an elk who walks on two feet, that's what they say. Face streaked red with blood. Two pairs twice doubled is the number of points of his antlers, stretching like spears defying the very heavens."

"This is dire news, Jilpi," Banook said, pulling his feet out of the hot waters. "How long has it been since this occurred?"

"About three weeks since Uvon was killed, is what I heard, but I don't know too much either. Like yourself, I prefer to stay away from the troubles of empires and despots. That is why I like this colony, where we aren't so bothered by them. As long as the Negians don't come bother me or my hot springs, this frail body will not wage war upon their empire. You'll find out more in town, whether you ask or not. Gossip abounds."

"I shall do just that, old friend," Banook said, stepping into his boots. "Thank you for the information. It concerns me, for reasons I cannot say."

"Keep your secrets, you secretive man, I will not pry. I see you are in a hurry, but do stop by for a proper soak on your way back up. You know these waters are cleaner than the ones in town."

"That I shall do. May the moon light your path, Jilpi."

"May the stars guide your heart."

The Alpine Hut, the only place Banook could think of where he'd find climbing supplies, was already closed by the time he strode into town. He walked down the streets of Brimstowne, sensing unease in the faces of the locals. At the doors of the Crooked Teeth, a rowdy tavern in the east side of town, he spotted a scuffle.

"Take that shit down!" a barkeep screamed at a man. She was the tavern's owner, who Banook had spoken with many times before. The man she screamed at had just climbed onto a wooden beam to hang a banner from the balcony above it.

"This is a private business, not your piss-stinking barracks!" the barkeep spat.

As the man was sliding back down, he was aided by a solid kick from the barkeep. He fell shoulders first onto the cobblestone path, scraping his face and arm.

"Fucking wench, I'll tell the general that—"

"Shove a rusted spear up your general's ass. This is an independent colony, not your playground. Fuck off now, we don't want your business here."

The man staggered up. He was wearing partial Negian leathers, probably a low-level infantry recruit. A strange, red mark was painted on his cuirass. He aggressively stomped toward the barkeep.

Banook walked between them, placed an enormous hand on the soldier's chest and said, "The kind woman asked you to kindly fuck off. Will you do so kindly? Or will you be needing my assistance?"

"Y... yes, I was just—" the soldier said, stumbling backward. He ran around the corner and disappeared down an alley.

"Thanks, Banook, nice to see you in town again," the barkeep said. "But I could've enjoyed smashing that vermin's face a bit more."

Banook looked up at the banner the soldier had hung. He plucked it as easily as a leaf loosened by the Autumn chill.

"Lurr Oxana, what is this?" he asked the barkeep, showing her the banner.

"The Red Stag's sigil, of course. Those taint sniffers stationed nearby come here to drink at night and act as if this is Negian territory. Well, someone has to show them who's the boss."

The banner in Banook's hands was of a midnight blue, with the red laurels of the Negian Empire emblazoned at the center, and a red triangle with the tip down underneath it, hastily stroked in red. It did resemble the face, or skull, of an elk.

"Well," Banook said, "if I see any more of these macabre decorations, I'll be sure to take them down."

"Thanks, big man. You coming in for a drink?"

"As is tradition. Have you seen Ardof, by the by?"

"The ranger? He's in town. He'll likely stop by at some point tonight, to harass my customers. If he wasn't such a good tipper, I'd kick him out just like I kick all these Negian scumbladders. Are you here to break the ranger's bones?"

"Nothing so ungracious, just wanted to ask him a thing or two."

Banook was searching for more than the usual gossip that travels from loose tongues; he needed trustworthy, insider information, and the right man to provide it seemed to be in town. He sat in the back corner of the Crooked Teeth, from where he could keep an eye on all the patrons and the front doors. The crowd was boisterous that evening, but no more fights broke out. Banook was not too fond of the Crooked Teeth, but it was the only place where he could get a decent meadowsweet mead.

"One tankard of the finest metheglin, for the man of the mountains," Oxana said, bringing the drink before Banook had a chance to order it.

"Thank you, Lurr Oxana," Banook said and struck up a conversation with the barkeep to learn more about this Red Stag. Customers came and went. Couples fondled each other in the dark corners of the tavern. Men, women, and allgenders alike approached Banook, curious about the exotic giant, but Banook kindly turned down their offers and focused on the front door.

A few hours later, when the more interesting crowds began to filter in, Banook spotted a ranger with a light-brown beard pushing open the front doors, scanning the tavern like an owl.

"Oy, Ardof, I saved you a seat!" Banook said, patting a chair next to the two he was using. Ardof approached, face shaded by his wide-brimmed hat.

"Banook? What brings you to town, eh?" Ardof asked, taking the seat and leaning his elbows on the table. The peculiar white wraps around his forearms contrasted heavily with his coppery skin and the dark wood.

"Picking up Winter supplies, trading goods, the usual."

"I'd ask you to trade some books, but I didn't bring any with me this time."

"You did not, but I did," Banook said. He reached into his satchel and pulled out a gray book with embossed letters that read: *The Last Voyage of the Gauffor*, by Captain Erimus Tier-Erimus. He slid it across the table.

Ardof picked the book up and quickly flipped through it. "Haven't read this one. Is it as bland as his journeys in the Charred Wastes?"

"Nothing like that dreadful account. It's more poetic, deals with his adventures in Fel Varanus and his escape to Allathanathar. A bit more adventurous, you'll enjoy it."

Ardof placed the book on the table and slid it back across. "Thank you, pal, but like I said, I didn't bring any to trade with."

"That's alright. Perhaps I can trade it to you for information instead."

Ardof pushed off his hat to let it dangle on his back by a strap, revealing his thinning hairline. His grass-green eyes studied Banook with skepticism. "Huh. I'm usually the one doing this sort of inquiry. What is this about?"

"Mere curiosity," Banook said, producing the banner with the Red Stag's sigil he had torn down earlier. "Saw a scoundrel hanging this outside, and it upset Oxana, so it upset me as well. She told me a few things about this Red Stag fellow, but I thought I'd ask the person who'd know most." Banook pushed the book back. "Here, it's yours. I'd rather you have it, anyway."

"Well, if you insist," Ardof said, taking the book. "But you probably know the gist of things by now. Way too many myths surround the Red Stag, but you have to look past all that. This whole deal—and you won't believe this, pal—it has to do... Well... You know those Silvesh mentioned in the spritetale books you borrowed?"

"The animal masks of old?" Banook asked, pretending to vaguely remember.

"Same ones. Well, it seems—no, we now *know*—that they are real. Somehow, they let the wearers transform into half-beasts, that is why there's so much talk about this elk taking over the throne. It's General Alvis Hallow. You know the one?"

Banook shook his head, although he had heard about the general through his friends.

"Ruthless scoundrel, that man. He found one of these masks inside the Anglass Dome, used it to kill Uvon dus Grei, and now he's bringing entire legions to take over whatever else he can find inside the dome."

"Inside the dome? How did he manage that?"

"Mines," Ardof answered, then ordered a strong firewater. "There are mighty riches to be found in the domes, or so the rumors say. I was in Anglass a week ago when they were bringing in all the battalions. I saw too many marching toward the shafts, not nearly enough coming out. Something big is going on."

"I could see smoke near the dome, all the way from my cabin."

"That's for the Dormendal barracks, shipyard, and the sapfire refinery. It's something else entirely. They have no mining equipment there, and that worries me most."

Banook leaned in. "How so?"

"I think the dome is just the first of their plans. If they are manufacturing sapfire and readying ships, they might be going after Withervale next."

Banook sighed with trepidation. He could not divulge his connection to Lago, to Withervale, so he sidestepped the issue. "You said *masks*, plural, so this Red Stag has more than one?"

"No, but he's after another one, one they lost in Withervale, of all places. That's why I think they might be planning on taking over the city. It's a strategic choke point either way, and the relic is as good an excuse to attack as they'll ever get. They have spies everywhere, who've been making my job... complicated. It's not been easy lately."

Banook leaned in. "What are these spies expecting to find?"

Ardof took a sip of firewater and winced. He tried to measure Banook, but there was too much to measure, and he seemed confused by the questioning. He answered, nonetheless.

"They are looking for some kid, an Oldrin gal, and apparently some Free Tribesfolk who got involved in this. Plenty of spies asking about them here in the colony."

"But why here?"

"Who knows?" Ardof replied, finishing his drink in one big, courageous draft. "But there was word about a month ago of a spurred gal visiting the Yeast Cauldron. An Oldrin should know better than to go to a place like that, they have their own filthy springs by the pits. She was noticed by a few customers, who saw her with others that fit the description. Either way, no one knows where they went to."

Ardof stood, slapped a few Qupi chips on the table, and patted Banook's shoulder. "Anyway, I better hurry, I see a friend over there I need to get to. He's in that perfect spot where he's too drunk to later remember what he told me, but not drunk enough that he'll pass out while telling me everything."

"Go do your thing. And thank you for the information."

Ardof's keen eyes scanned Banook's expression one last time. "I'll make sure to bring a book with me next time," he said. "Be careful out there. Moon lights, pal."

"Stars guide."

Banook headed to the Alpine Hut early the next morning, where he bought pitons, ice axes, and all the climbing equipment Jiara had requested. He could not find crampons or a harness for his size, but he was confident he could use his workshop to modify what he'd bought.

He spent the day in Brimstowne discreetly gathering information, then began his trek toward the Firefalls. He once more stopped by Geo Springs—as he had promised Jilpi—to take in a soak before heading up the mountain.

"Spies all over Brimstowne?" Jilpi asked, his body submerged up to his handle-like clavicles.

"That's what I heard. Looking for some Withervale fugitives, it seems. They think they might've come through town." Banook waited for a reaction, trying to hide his nervousness. He leaned his back against the edge of the pool, displacing yet more water—the rocky ground outside the pools was utterly soaked.

"A lot of people pass through Brimstowne," Jilpi said, "it's hard to keep track of who goes in, who goes out. You know I hate those Negian invaders as much as the next person, so if there is a side to be taken, I'm with the fugitives on this one, no questions asked. Whoever they are, I hope they are not found."

"I believe we are in agreement, old friend."

Jilpi understood more than he let it show. He sucked on his few teeth and said, "And if those runaways happened to pass this way, I would've turned a blind eye to them. My eyes are not as good as they used to be, either way, so they should not worry. This old man has seen nothing. I may even forget I've talked to you—my memory hasn't been so sharp either."

"Understood. I'm sorry about your eyes, about your memory," Banook said as he stood.

The blue pool suddenly vacuumed itself in due to the loss of Banook's volume, leaving the old man sitting in water just up to his waist.

"Sorry, I always do this to your beautiful pools," Banook said, naked body steaming as he shook the water off.

"It'll fill back up. You should head back up before night falls. Go warm up your home, for Winter is arriving early this year. And rest safe, for there is no safer place than the mountains."

"Shit," Jiara said. "I can't believe they tracked us all the way to Brimstowne."

"They found out *after* you were in town," Banook corrected, "no one tracked you directly." He spread the Red Stag's banner over the coffee table. "This is his wretched sigil. I am afraid that if this Red Stag has managed to obtain the cervid mask in this manner, he will soon be visiting the other domes."

"If there are Miscam tribes living in those domes, we need to warn them," Ockam said. "We can't risk General Hallow doing there what he did at Heartpine."

"It's too late for Anglass," Jiara said, squeezing hard on her thick braid as if trying to strangle someone in her mind. "We can't fight an entire army, but perhaps we could go to the Moordusk Dome, the one just west of Zovaria."

"That's quite a journey to undertake," Ockam said. "But at least it's through lands that are safe for us to cross."

"We can go there after Da'áju," Lago said, his mask resting over his knee. "If a Silv is to be found in the Da'áju Caldera, we better be the ones to get it."

"I agree," Banook said. "I would hate to see the Red Stag finding out about the Northern Wutash and deciding to send a legion into my own back yard. We must secure Urnaadisilv before it's too late."

"There's only one other dome in the Negian Empire," Ockam said, "the Lequa Dome, east of the Fractured Range. We can bet that's where he'll be headed next. But after that, who knows? It's all too unpredictable."

"There's no use worrying about places beyond our reach," Banook said. "For now, you are safe in these mountains. Stay in my humble cabin and keep me good company. I will lead you to Da'áju to find Urnaadisilv, and then your journey might take you to domes beyond many horizons. The time for struggles will be ahead of you, but do not let fear cloud your thoughts."

Zovarian Union

Negian Empire

Free Tribelands

Tsing Empire

Yenwu State

Kingdom of Bauram

Republic of Lerev

Dorhond Tribes

Bayanhong Tribes

Graalman Horde

Elmaren Queendom

Tharma Federation

Kingdom of Ashora

Wastyr Triumvirate

Khaar Du Tribes

Vathereol Princedom

CHAPTER FIFTY-FOUR

UNEMAR LAKE

The day after Banook returned from Brimstowne, he wanted to wash away some of the stress caused by the unsettling news he brought. He decided to take his guests on a fishing trip to Unemar Lake, at the base of Drann Trodesh, commonly known as the Five Peaks.

Short trips with Banook were never short, so they carried enough comforts to spend several nights away. It made no difference to Banook whether he made it home one night or not, for he could fall asleep on the grass, on a rock, even on the snow while watching flurries get stuck to his eyebrows. The old bear was trying his best to be conscious of his choices when the weather was unkind, but sometimes he still forgot. Fortunately, they were met with good weather; although snow still cradled the crevices between rocks, there was warmth in the clear, crisp air.

They were nearing the wide lake as the twilight-blue sky began to puncture itself in starlight. From an elevated trail they approached, watching the five fang-sharp peaks turn into ten in an awe-inspiring reflection, while the constellations also inverted themselves in the glass-smooth waters.

They were sliding down the loose shards of slate that marked the trail when Sterjall stopped suddenly and turned around. Banook was still up on the ridge they had crested, a faraway look in his eyes. From Banook's point of view, his four friends were silhouetted against the reflections, as if standing among the stars with mountains floating over their heads.

Sterjall could sense Banook's unease. He trotted back up.

"What's on your mind?" he asked.

"Nothing but a mirage, a glimpse into long-lost moments. Do not let your whiskers worry."

Sterjall waited next to him, gazing at the reflected mountains. "It must be a beautiful memory," he said, but Agnargsilv told him that there was more that Banook wasn't saying. He felt guilty then, feeling he was invading Banook's private emotions.

Banook looked at Sterjall and smiled. "Let's go down with the others and catch some trout. The biggest ones always come out after dark."

They woke to the sound of squawking jays, who swarmed the shore's junipers in sudden bursts that made the trees lean and shiver. Flycatchers hovered over the lake, wings brightly backlit as they intercepted dragonflies and damselflies.

Jiara had gone fishing, while Alaia had ventured away to spot more birds.

Sterjall was watching the glints of sunlight on the water when he noticed two red foxes prowling on an isthmus, their movements reflected upon the lake in a warm smear. Bear also noticed them, perking up his ears.

"There are not many canids near the cabin, other than yourself," Banook said, approaching Sterjall from behind and handing him a steaming mug of juniper berry tea. He sat next to the wolf, sipping from his own mug. "You should practice your mindspeech while you can. Your attempts with Bear are always useful, but you two seem to have your own way of communicating already. Perhaps that has been misleading you."

"I've tried so many times, and I just don't get it," Sterjall complained. With Bear, it was as if they were always reading each other's minds, understanding one another through microexpressions, posture, context, or experience. "I still can't understand how you can hear each other's thoughts, while the thoughts aren't supposed to have words," he said.

"It's not hearing nor seeing. It is also not talking. You must put those preconceptions away. You will directly communicate—and understand—ideas, emotions, feelings, and sensory perceptions. The meanings will be clear, that is all that matters."

"But whenever I—"

"Quiet now. The foxes are getting closer. Try and see if you can mindspeak to them."

The foxes had reached the mainland and were sniffing the shore, having picked up the scent of the bones left over from dinner. They scurried with their heads down, only perturbing a few phalaropes who were resting in the sand. Bear stood up.

"Bear, stay," Sterjall whispered, and Bear obeyed, but his eyes and ears remained locked.

The foxes fought over a few scraps, then kept searching.

Sterjall put his mug down, then focused, trying to conjure what a thought in a fox's mind would feel like. Come on, foxes, tell me how you do this, he thought. What does it feel like to talk like a fox? Is talk even the right term? That word Ockam used, qualia, I need to find it within myself, understand what it's like to feel as foxes feel. Sterjall envisioned abstract concepts that a fox might grasp and tried to project them mentally. Was it about smells, or the feeling of the breeze on one's whiskers? Were there vocalizations involved? Did it deal with fears of hunger, the joy of the hunt, the rhythm of paws during a trot, the feeling of the passing of the seasons?

"They just don't seem to hear me," Sterjall said.

"You forgot an important aspect, cub. In order to mindspeak, you both need to be aware of each other's presence. They haven't seen you, their noses are too distracted with the scraps to smell you, and they have not heard our whispers."

"Okay, I'll try to get their attention without—"

The foxes tensed up, noticing they were being watched. They both made eye contact with Sterjall.

Banook subtly nodded.

One of the foxes took a tentative step forward. Sterjall felt a tingling in the depths of his awareness, like a synesthetic jumble of the concepts of redness, affection, strife, fullness, wet soil, the rustling sound mice make underground, the scent of a hollow log, the satisfying crunch of a tick between sharp fangs. The disjointed meanings were close to solidifying into a semblance of a thought, but they were getting tangled in an incoherent soup of senses.

"Caught a huge gar!" Jiara yelled nearby, jogging back to the camp. The foxes were spooked, vanishing in twin blurs.

"There will be more opportunities," Banook said, then stood to help Jiara with the fish.

The next two months were dedicated to training for their icy hike to Da'áju. Jiara was eager to teach them everything she knew about ice climbing. Luckily, the quaar ropes would hold even Banook's weight, though he stubbornly insisted he'd prefer to climb using nothing but his bear claws.

Ockam's leg was healing well. He knew how to use ropes to clamber up rocks but had nearly no experience with ice. He had trained in Klemes, not in the Stelm Ankrov, but he was confident he could catch up quickly once he had properly healed. He made himself useful by adapting two harnesses into one to fit Banook, by sharpening and balancing the ice axes, and by making sure their crampons fit perfectly around their boots. Ockam also stayed up late to help with the secret gift Banook was making for Lago-Sterjall, but did so discreetly.

Banook took them on hikes (true hikes) up treacherous peaks, where they could test their skills on rock before training over ice. The quaar helm became indispensable: whoever was being belayed at the time had to wear it, except Banook, who instead wrapped a bedsheet like a turban around his head. Many a skull was slammed, but none cracked.

They tried to find a way for Sterjall to climb, but human boots and helms did not fit him, and his muzzle got in the way when he needed to rotate his head while keeping his center of gravity tight against a wall. His footpaws were convenient only because he barely felt the cold when barefoot, but they had fewer corners to tighten footwear to and a lot less surface area to support crampons. This forced Jiara to make a decision: Sterjall would have to keep the mask off and learn to climb as Lago.

Their true training over ice and snow began once the cold mists of Umbra thickened. Jiara first took them to shallower ice slopes, where she taught them how to walk flat-footed, how friction and surface area were critical. They progressed to steeper slopes, where she showed them how to dig the crampons in and how to sidestep without snagging them on their own legs. She demonstrated the proper methods to squat and stand, how to set screws and pitons, how to find anchors, how to create ice bollards to hold their ropes. It was a tiring affair, but they always allowed themselves a perfectly relaxed rest at day's end.

Banook surprised them all with his flexibility and agility. He was able to jump over wide gaps with the nimbleness of a squirrel and could run fast—like most bears could—unhindered by his size. Banook's grip on the quaar ropes was tremendous; the only problem for him was finding strong-enough attachment points, forcing him to use a generous number of pitons and anchors to hold himself up.

"How did you learn to do so much, anyway?" Alaia asked Jiara while being belayed down into a crevasse. "I mean the climbing, the skills with medicine, and hunting, and—"

Bonk!

"Watch your head, girl," Jiara said, cringing as Alaia slammed her quaar helm onto the ice.

Alaia quickly recovered her balance, unharmed. "I'm still curious," she said.

"Jiara had the best teacher, that's all," Ockam said from above, waiting for his turn to be belayed.

"What, you taught her?" Alaia asked, finally touching her feet to the ground.

"Of course not," he said, "though we did train together, at times. I meant her big sister. She's a power to contend with, taught Jiara all she knows."

Jiara huffed. "Shut your filth hole, I learned most tricks on my own. And I'm younger, and can hold my drink much better—"

"Sorry to strike that sore nerve!" Ockam mocked.

"Yeah, you better shut it. She's a bossy and rude pain in the ass. Now get *your* ass in the harness, old man, you aren't using that mauled leg as an excuse today."

Chapter Fifty-Five

Banook's Story

The month of Hoartide arrived to open wide the gates of Winter.

Banook had taken his friends atop the middle of the five peaks of Drann Trodesh, where they were resting after a long day of training on the slopes. The night was as cold and serene as the lake below.

"Why do they call it Unemar Lake and not Klad Unemar?" Alaia asked as they warmed up by a crackling fire.

"Unemar is not a Miscamish word, but Khaar Du," Ockam explained. "It simply means *mirror*. Most landmarks are named with Miscamish words, but not all."

"Our friend of Khaar Du blood is correct," Banook said. "This lake was once called Klad Wuári, meaning *toothed lake*, for the peaks that look like teeth when reflected upon it. But the lake had not been on any maps, at least not in any that survived the fires of the Downfall, so its name was lost. When the northern tribes rediscovered it, they gave it a new name, but a few of us still recall its original one."

"That's why mountains tend to have Miscamish names," Jiara said. "Those were clearly marked in most maps, so their names persisted through the epochs. Same reason why most forests *aren't* named in Miscamish, since they all burned, and new forests grew in their stead."

"Precisely," Banook said, "although it's not always consistent, giving us some variety." He placed a few more logs into the fire. "Miscamish is a peculiar tongue. The Miscam tribes needed it to endure the sands of time so that once the domes reopened, all the tribes could once again speak to one another. Before the domes closed, they crafted strict phonetic rules, extensive dictionaries, and laws on how to address the advent of new words, and compiled them into a tome called the *Miscamish Grimoire*. They did the same for Common, knowing it was much too common a tongue to ignore. That is why Common and Miscamish remained nearly unaltered through the ages, while other languages have drastically changed."

Sceres was in her Jade season, beginning her transition to Tourmaline, while Umbra was making room for Winter in Noss. Bright-pink fringes spiderwebbed the moon's green face, noticeable even on her unlit half. She was in her first quarter phase that night, her Ilaadrid Shard shining sharply and beacon bright. Lago said he wanted to move away from the firelight to see her better and to look at the stars.

"Wanna come with me?" he asked Banook, as he began to walk away.

Banook nodded. "Aren't you taking Agnargsilv?" he said.

"I don't need to wear it all the time. I like being Lago as much as I like being Sterjall."

Lago and Banook found a comfortable nook with an overlook of Unemar Lake. The luminous beam of the Ilaadrid Shard was birthing a streak like an icy sword on the freezing waters. The surrounding mountains looked sharp and cast even sharper shadows.

Banook spotted elongated shadows far below, by the lake's shore—two bulky, brown bears, searching for food.

"There go the brothers," he said.

"You recognize them from this far away?" Lago asked.

"Yes, by the manner of their walk. Quite the pair they are."

"Do you ever give them names?"

"I have names for all my kindred in my head, though sounds or words they are not, but rather the impressions they conjure for me while I'm in my bear forms. A mixture of smells, mental images, abstract emotions that create this… I can't truly explain it. You'll understand it one day. It comes naturally to me since spoken language is something I learned much later."

"I think you should name them something you can pronounce, so you can talk to us about them."

"I wouldn't know what to name them."

"How about… Hmm… Wadrook and Cashe?"

"That sounds familiar somehow."

"They're the lost brothers from the *Barlum Saga*. Have you read it?"

"Oh, yes! A long time ago. I have it in my library alongside the *Chronicles of Aubellekh*."

"I felt like I was one of the Wayfarers of the Sixteen Realms when entering the Heartpine Dome. Like I was living a chapter from the books."

"Wayfarers you are, although of only one realm thus far, not yet sixteen. It surprises me that you've read the Saga—the volumes are quite unwieldy."

"It's one of the things that got me interested in the domes," Lago said, smiling fondly. "The adventures of Dravéll and Ishkembor through the sixteen domes fascinated me. Though now that I've been to one, I can see Loregem's speculations were massively wrong. Still, he was very imaginative."

"You'll have to show me your favorite chapters when we get back, I want to see which ones make your mind and eyes sparkle. Maybe we can read it together. It's been a while since I flipped through those dusty pages. What should we call the momma bear who lives by the cabin? The one Ockam's leg is intimately familiar with."

They thought for a short moment, then at the same time both yelled, "Sabikh!" and laughed.

"We read each other's minds," Banook said. "And Frud for her cub, like the despot queen and the bastard prince, wonderful idea! I could find names from the Saga for all my bear friends."

"You could also find good names among the stars," Lago said, "the constellations are filled with mythical creatures, you'll never run out of them. Crysta has been teaching me, but there are far too many to memorize."

"Not all are myths, some are based on true stories. I know a few of the old names myself. Do you know this one?" Banook pointed at a cluster of stars.

Lago leaned on Banook's arm to properly estimate the direction he pointed to. The night was a bit hazy, with a thin veil of high-elevation clouds, but he could pick up the most vibrant constellations. "The one with the two bright, yellow stars?"

Banook nodded.

"Of course I do," Lago said, feeling cocky. "The stars are Metheglin and Meodu. The constellation is Kerja, the yellow-eyed ogre."

"Ogre!? Is that what they teach you nowadays? How rude. Its complete, original name is Kerjaastórgnem."

"Like the name the Miscam used to call you?"

Banook blinked his honey-hued eyes and smiled.

"Wait. It's you!? You have your own constellation?"

Banook's smile widened. "All eighteen of the Nu'irgesh do, or did. As you've just proven, some might've changed over time."

"This is thrilling! I'm in the presence of a mythical beast!"

Banook laughed. "I am no ogre, but beastly I can be, when necessary."

"Which other Nu'irgesh can you spot?"

Banook craned his neck around. "Let's see... There are not too many visible tonight, but I can tell you more about those who are." Banook began to point at one constellation at a time. "I can see Muri, the honey badger, over there. Quite a temperamental fellow he is, but tender-souled once you get to know him. He was worshipped by the Dorvauros tribe, but it was the Jojek Miscam who held the mask of musteloids, and so with them he went to live. The Jojek are a fierce race who wear leaves on their bodies, making them nearly invisible in dense foliage. Muri and I don't agree on much, but our love of honey keeps our hearts entwined."

Banook tilted his finger a bit to the side. "There I see Ishke'ísuk, the basilisk, displaying his double crest upon a starry branch."

"The one with the greenish star?"

"The very one. His non-primal forms are some of the scariest you could ever encounter, not even the giant megalenhydris otters dared venture in waters with such creatures. The Mo'óto Miscam worshipped my reptilian friend Ishke, though I never got to meet them, as they lived on distant islands where bears roamed not."

He went on to the next constellation.

"There is Sovath, the chital, a spotted deer whose furs look like the very stars in the sky. She lives in the dome closest to us, alongside the Teldebran Miscam, a kind tribe with lustrous hairs that drape darkly to their ankles, like waterfalls of night."

"Do you think Sovath is faring well? With the Red Stag and all..."

"I hope so, cub. Perhaps she found her way out of the dome, somehow. If not, I fear Urgsilv might be used to... But no, this is not the time to talk about such things. Let us have a moment of joy with the stars and not dwell upon such thoughts. Take a look this way, just a bit to the right of Sovath is Däo-Varjak, the ribbon seal of the Alommo Sea. The constellation is in the shape of her tail flippers, quite symmetrical."

"We call that one the *Sphinx*. Looks like a sphinx moth, too."

"Fits it just as well, but don't go telling Däo-Varjak that she was replaced by an insect, no matter how beautiful those moths are. My dear Däo-Varjak had too many unfortunate tragedies in her past, tales that are not proper for such a glorious night." Banook scanned the skies. "I think those are all the Nu'irgesh constellations I can see at this time. Wait, there is one more, but you won't be able to see it, as it's dimmed by the bright light of the moon. The one hiding behind Sceres's glow is Probo."

"The javelina being chased by two women! I know this one."

"I don't know where you see two women in such a simple cluster of stars, but yes, the Nu'irg ust Nagra's primal form is a javelina. Probo used to live in these very mountains with the Puqua tribe, before they moved west to grow the Fjordlands Dome. How the Puqua could tolerate Probo is something I'll never understand. He can be quite a pest."

Lago could not keep himself from smiling. Banook was not just a man, not just a bear: he was a myth, a legend that transcended the epochs. Lago was in the presence of someone too renowned and at the same time too warmhearted and approachable.

"Once the skies of Winter clear, I will show you more constellations," Banook said, "and teach you about the other Nu'irgesh. I hope you get to meet them all someday. They are each unique and magnificent in their own ways."

"I would love that," Lago said, then drew in a long, cold breath. He was shivering a bit, palpably nervous, as he had not yet revealed the real reason why he had dragged Banook away from the others. "Last time we were here, at Unemar Lake, I mean," he said, holding on to a thread of courage, "we were just cresting the last ridge before the shore, when you stopped. I knew something was wrong, but I felt like I was prying into something personal. I get that feeling sometimes with Agnargsilv, guilty that I shouldn't be allowed to read into people's emotions unless they choose to open up on their own. That's why I asked you to come with me tonight, why I didn't bring the mask. I wanted to ask you about it."

Banook looked at the shard of moonlight reflected on the icy lake. "There was a moment that evening that reminded me of something that happened here long ago. It's a memory that brings me joy, and brings me sadness."

"I'm sorry," Lago said, tucking his hands between his knees so that his fingers would stop shaking. "I'm being too nosy, I was feeling curious and—"

"It's alright, cub, I will tell you. And canidkind is nosy no matter what." He tapped a finger on Lago's nose. "It has to do with the time when I first took my human form." Banook looked up at the stars and considered where to begin with his story. "Beyond six lands, beneath six seas, centuries before the Downfall, the Northern Wutash were on the move through these mountains, searching for the best place to grow their dome. This was before they decided *not* to grow it, of course. During those times, I was still only a bear, a foolish bear who helplessly fell in love with a human.

"It happened not too far east from here, by a shallow creek that seeps from the Stelm Khull's hidden core and overflows with salmon in late Autumn. The tribe was moving west, and all bears were migrating with them, to help with their cause. I had met the Urnaadifröa of that time, who was named Jento-Arlu, but he had gone south for decades. His caravan had returned with news of his death, but they also brought with them Urnaadisilv's new heir, his daughter, Nifréne."

Banook's eyes lit up suddenly, as if consuming the light of the Ilaadrid Shard. "I first set my eyes upon her from the shores of that shallow creek. She was in her half-form of a spectacled bear, of dark fur with golden patches that drew forms so mysterious that no oracle could decipher. I saw her fishing with her spear with the grace and speed of an egret."

"Sounds like she was truly beautiful," Lago said.

"She was. Her fur shimmered brighter than the scales of the zircon salmon she caught. But behind her, concealed beneath the shade of an old willow, was Khaambe, her brother, though his name I did not yet know. And my eyes... my eyes could not stop gazing at him. He sat in silence, alone, with sadness held tightly in his heart. His nightly hair and charcoal eyes joined together with the patterns inked on his body, dark against dark twice shrouded in shade.

"Nifréne saw me then. She had never seen the Nu'irg ust Urnaadi before, so she mindspoke a greeting to me. She told me they were traveling west, that she was happy bearkind would be joining them in the Da'áju basin, and that my presence was an honor. I told her the honor was mine. Nifréne smiled, said her farewells, and left with her catch. I looked back under the willow, but Khaambe was there no longer—his somber sadness had vanished before I could catch another glimpse.

"I walked alongside their caravan as they plodded west, trying to get another look at Khaambe and his melancholy. After a fortnight of travel, the tribe camped just west of here, over that hill behind the lake. I watched them from the slopes as they fished and cooked and laughed. Khaambe was a good fisherman, he could dive in and toss trout straight out of the water without the aid of any tool. When wet, his black hair turned glossy and penumbral, like polished onyx.

"When the tribe returned to their camp to sleep, Khaambe lingered behind with the company of the stars. He sat there, on that distant promontory. He sat there and waited until the night was as dark as obsidian and the stars dragged the Galactic Belt out with them.

"I crested right on a path behind him, and saw him silhouetted against the lake, with the lake in turn reflecting the heavenly lanterns. Khaambe sat wrapped in starlight, and in the quiet of the night, with no more than a chorus of katydids and loons to accompany him, he sang a most haunting song. I knew he was singing words, but I did not understand words, yet I understood the feeling that bled from that doleful tune. I needed to know what he was singing about, where his sadness came from.

"Khaambe came back the following night to sing once again. As I sat behind him and listened, a few pebbles must have slid from under my claws, and Khaambe heard me. He turned and saw me looming behind him. I tried to say something, but only managed to growl and roar. He got scared and ran away, and I felt as if I had broken something special.

"I came back the night after that, but Khaambe was there no more. I stood on that same rock and recalled the melody he had sung. I imagined him, his beauty, his sorrow, and wanted to be with him. I wanted to know him, and I wanted him to know me as well.

"That was the night I became a man," Banook said, tapping a fist to his chest. "I was lonesome. I was yearning for Khaambe, and I needed to fill a void within myself. I stood on two paws and pictured myself as a human. I was familiar with some human customs, with their ideas, even if their language and motivations escaped me. My eyes swam on the reflections of the saw-toothed mountains, focusing on their mirror image until I found my form, and I became like them, though nothing like them still. My body was the size of ten of theirs, my beard imposing, my eyes too bright, my skin not red. I was still a foreigner, a strange man who did not yet speak their tongue. I dared not come near them.

"The caravan continued west into the Da'áju basin. I followed from far behind, sometimes as a human, sometimes as a bear, listening to their speech, learning their words. Once they settled into their newly built city, I approached and introduced myself. I chose not my Miscamish name, but a Common one, so that they would not recognize me as Kerjaastórgnem, but know me as Banook. By then I had learned enough words to say I did not speak Miscamish, but also to tell them I could learn fast, and that I had strong hands, and could do good work.

"I helped them plow their fields, raise buildings, shape wood and rock. I learned how to work metals and leather, and how to cook. It took time, but I eventually learned their language. Yet I still did not dare approach Khaambe, not until I had learned enough, so that he would not see me as a stranger and fear me as he had feared me that one night."

Banook swallowed, then continued after a short pause. "Nifréne had been away for a long time, on diplomatic errands with the Puqua tribes. The day she returned, she approached me and mindspoke to me. *Nu'irg*, said she, *I can see your honey-colored aura. I know you, I've known you before. Why have you taken a human form? Why is it you hide from your kind among ours?* I replied to her in their own tongue, and told her I had heard Khaambe's lament and wanted to understand his song.

"Nifréne shapeshifted into her human form, for which her name was Ofréia, and with cherry-red lips told me that Khaambe sang for a love he had lost. His lover had drowned, and ever since that day Khaambe had been overtaken with sorrow and could love no more. She said I should meet her brother, but that I should not tell him or the tribe that I was the Nu'irg, as they would not see kindly for our different kinds to be together in such a manner. I was afraid, but I accepted.

"Ofréia introduced us that very day. When Khaambe shook my hand, he saw my cheeks blush and my eyes sparkle. We worked together, hunted together, slept together, and in time we fell in love with each other... But that part of the story would take many nights to properly tell. What matters is that I loved him, more than anything, yet I was not sure whether he loved me back the same. He seemed happier with me, but always a touch distant.

"One night I heard him humming that sorrowful song, and I asked him what it was. He sang it for me." Banook started humming a melody that soon wove into Miscamish lyrics. His voice was cavernous, yet silky, oscillating in rumbling notes, some of which were so low that Lago felt them in his chest. The melody vanished like ripples upon a placid lake.

"That was achingly beautiful. What do the words mean?" Lago asked.

"It would take a true poet to translate the rhymes, meter, and hidden meanings behind the words. It's an old Miscam song of a sailor who fell in love with the sea, who seduces him and asks him to join her in her entrancing waves. The sailor gives her his food, his water, his clothes, his sails... but that is not enough to appease her. He chops off the mast and casts it into her depths. He then gives her his entire vessel, and with nothing else left, he gives himself to her and drowns. The night Khaambe sang it to me was the first time I truly heard the words, the first time I understood them."

"Did he know you'd heard him sing it before?"

"I confessed it to him, after he finished singing. It's something that greatly pains me to this day. I told him the truth about who I was, and he felt betrayed."

Banook's eyes welled with tears. Lago wanted to comfort him but did not know how.

"Khaambe thought it was wrong for a man to lie with a Nu'irg," Banook continued. "He said we were of different kinds, that I could never fully understand him, and he'd never truly understand me. He said I could never mean to him what his long-lost love had meant.

"I lost him then. He went back to the shadows and became the sorrowful man I'd first seen that bright Autumn day. Nifréne tried to speak sense to him, but she confessed to me that this had happened before—her brother had been briefly infatuated by others but could not love them the same way they loved him. Nifréne apologized for bringing me so much pain. She had known deep inside that Khaambe was lost and would live the rest of his life in a distant memory.

"For a long time, I went back to being a bear, utterly disheartened. I thought that humans would never accept me in the way bearkind could or understand me like Nifréne and other Silvfröash did. Long after the Downfall, during the Reconstitution Epoch, when capitals were being rebuilt and kingdoms were birthed from ashes, I dared to change back into Banook and venture into the new world the humans were building. That is when I started to build my cabin and realized that both the human and bear forms were fit for me. It took me long to understand that, to accept both sides of myself and stop living in a distant memory. Thread unravels, cut, and sewn, and so the story goes."

"I'm sorry that happened, Banook," Lago said. "I don't understand why someone would find it wrong to love someone else only because they are different."

"Thank you, cub. I think Khaambe was a lost cause, but it was my fault too, for falling for his mystery and sorrow. He merely used our differences as a way out. He was in love with tragedy, and there was no way for him to change. Nifréne knew that, and Khaambe knew that."

"And while you were together, the tribe accepted you?"

"They did, for none other than Nifréne knew I was the Nu'irg."

"But I meant… Because of you two… being men."

"The Wutash made no such distinctions, and neither do bears, for that matter. That is just the Wutash, mind you, as the Miscam are a union of disparate tribes with entirely different cultures, and not all of them would have taken too kindly to see two men love one another. I always found that odd, for lerrkins among all species are as natural as dewdrops in Umbra. I could love any gender, sex, or kind—those categories are meaningless to me."

"It's been hard… for me. Because I'm also—I… I'm lorrkin. I've always liked men, not women. And Zovarians are not as accepting as the Wutash about that. The Doctrine of Takh doesn't allow it, and most follow their rules blindly, even the ones who don't believe in the Codex. I feel like I don't have anyone to talk to about it. The three of them know"—Lago nodded toward the remote campfire—"but it's not something comfortable to bring up. It's like they accept me, but don't necessarily understand me."

"That's been my entire life, cub."

The night was green, the shadows purple.

Lago watched as the mountains traced their sharp contours onto the icy lake, struggling to find more courage within himself. He felt his heart drumming. "M-my first time as Sterjall..." he stuttered. "There was a moment... a moment when I truly saw you for the first time, and I understood what it was like—at least in some way—to be two and be one. And I saw those bonds, those threads connecting the two of us, and they weren't the same as I had seen them before. You were looking back at me, but suddenly turned your eyes away."

"I did. And I felt those same bonds too, in my own way."

"But... then why did you—"

"I will tell you a short story, which might help you understand. Back when the council of all Miscam tribes was summoned to discuss the threat that could soon destroy our planet, the attendance of all eighteen Nu'irgesh was requested. The Northern Wutash chief who wore Urnaadisilv back then—her name was Tajo-Sol—asked me to follow her to the homeland of the Acoapóshi Miscam, on the southern slopes of the Stelm Tai-Du. Our ship was met by storms at the Ophidian Sea, leaving us stranded for much too long. To make up for the lost time, Tajo-Sol decided to take a shortcut across the sierras, through lands once inhabited by the Dorvauros tribe. But despite the splendor of those mountains, no bears lived around the elevated pass.

"As we traveled, I could feel the distance from my kindred draining me. My golden fur began to turn gray and sparse. I lost weight, turning into a skeletal shadow of my former self. I was forced to take the form of a squalid kiuon, so that Tajo-Sol could carry me in her arms. I agonized, feeling the finality of death settling into me.

"I believe the only source of energy sustaining me was Urnaadisilv itself. If it had not been for the mask being so close, I would've perished. Urnaadisilv is part of bearkind, in its own way. It feeds me, as I feed it. But alas, Tajo-Sol carried me across the sierras, back to bear-filled lands that were no longer forbidden to me. I regained my shape, my color, my youth as soon as I felt the presence of bearkind. That time I was away from my bears was one of few in my life in which I felt true fear, utter despair."

Banook massaged the bridge of his nose, then blinked heavily. "I turned away from you that night... because I see something special in you, Lago-Sterjall. But I know you have untrodden roads ahead of you, in places remote where I cannot follow. My paws go where the bears go, and the bears have settled in this land, and so I am a man of the mountains. This is my home. I am as much a part of these mountains as the valleys that delineate the spaces between them—you can't have one without the other."

Banook drifted forlornly in thought, with eyes reaching beyond the sawtoothed horizon.

"I understand," Lago said, drooping his head. "But I still feel a connection. Even now. Even without the mask."

Banook turned his head and looked at Lago. His honey-colored eyes were overflowing with yearning, fear, and compassion. He took Lago's small hand in his, then looked back to the horizon. Lago tilted his head up and fixed his eyes on the unreachable constellation of the golden bear. They sat side by side, holding hands, without saying one more word.

CHAPTER FIFTY-SIX

EMEN RUINS

It was the Winter Solstice, and Winter had indeed arrived in the mountains, though not yet in full force.

Sterjall was taking Alaia to a dead-end canyon just west of the cabin, where a grove of snow-covered sugar pines grew.

"What is it? Where are you dragging me to?" Alaia asked.

"Up this tree," Sterjall said, stopping by the tallest of the pines, "there's an amazing view. Banook just set these steps up yesterday." He offered Alaia a handpaw, then spiraled his way up behind her.

Above the canopy was a platform big enough for one large bear, or for Sterjall and Alaia to lie down comfortably. They wiped off the snow and sat down.

"You were right, this is quite the view," Alaia said. "Is that creek over there the Stiss Minn?"

"Yep, the Firefalls would be just behind that peak." He pointed to a towering cliff of granite.

The Anglass Dome was visible from up there too, though its left side was partially blocked by a ridgeline. At wintertime, the snow piled thicker on the dome's cap, making its entire top half take on a textured white look, while the sharp-sloped bottom retained its waxy greenness.

Alaia dug in her haversack for a handful of fruits and nuts and shared them with Sterjall. She snickered as she watched him try to chew on the nuts with his sharp teeth, which didn't work quite as well as human molars.

"Stop that," he said, glancing sideways.

"You look like Bear when he has something stuck in his gums."

"You brought almonds on purpose."

"Maybe... So, what was it you wanted to talk about?"

"Well," Sterjall said, tonguing the last shards of almond from between his cheeks, "the other night, when we were camping by Unemar Lake, I... I'm not sure if I'm supposed to tell you this. Banook finally told me about when he first became a human."

"I've asked him so many times, and he just went on about mountains and sunsets and ignored me."

"It's not exactly a happy story. I can see why he didn't want to talk about it."

"But you're gonna tell me anyway."

Sterjall swallowed his guilt, then nodded. He told Alaia Banook's story, as well as he could recall it. He didn't yet mention what had happened *after* Banook finished his story, when Lago had confessed his confused feelings, and they'd held hands.

"Poor guy, that's so sad, and so unfair," she said, then she eyed Sterjall carefully. "But there's something else, isn't there."

"Well... Yes. And then... I told him that *I* could understand him, in some ways, because I know what it feels like to be two things at once." He gestured vaguely at his furry body. "The day I first turned to Sterjall, I saw him clearly for the first time. There was something special there, some strange connection the mask showed me that I haven't felt with anyone else. And I knew he could see it too. He's not like any of the men I've been with before, he really understands me."

"Wait wait wait, you mean you *like him* like him?"

Sterjall shrugged and cringed, offering both a confirmation and embarrassed dismissal.

Alaia chuckled. "Gwoli, I knew you liked them big, but I had no idea you—"

"See, this is what I mean—even you, you know me so well and still make fun of me. You accept me, but don't really understand me."

Alaia's smile faded. That had hurt a bit.

"That's not fair. I wasn't trying to—" she began, then got stuck on her words. "It's not like I don't—" she stopped again, catching a glimpse of Sterjall's evasive eyes. As much as the words had pained her, she could deal with that, but she could not deal with seeing the anguish in her best friend's face. "I'm sorry," she said. "That was uncalled for. I was just trying to lighten things up. I mean, yes, I see why you like him, he's amazing! But what did you expect? He's a Nu'irg! He's like the demigod of the mountains. And excuse me but I *have* to mention this—he's maybe ten thousand years older than you?"

"He's ten thousand years older than anyone alive!"

"That's… a good point. I—"

"And I think he feels the same way about me."

Alaia turned to watch Sterjall's expression; it was bittersweet, wistful with a touch of hope.

Sterjall huffed weakly. "And with how stupid I am, I couldn't help myself and told him what I felt. Well, vaguely. I mostly just hinted at things. He took my hand in his, and I just didn't want to let go. Then we walked back to the camp without saying a word. What am I supposed to make of that?"

"Maybe he's trying to protect you. We are not going to be staying here long. Once Winter is over, we'll head to Da'áju, and then who knows where?" She put a hand on Sterjall's knee. "Remember that time with what's his name, the big-bellied guy with the silly haircut—"

"Conny."

"Yeah, Conny. You hit it off and then, when he had to move back to Old Karst, you were devastated."

"But that's different, I hated his hair to begin with. And he was selfish, and always tried to—"

"You are making my point. You'd miss Banook even more, it would be sixteenfold harder."

"I'll miss him either way," Sterjall said. He stood up and leaned against the trunk of the tree.

"Look, I don't know what is right or not," Alaia said, standing up as well. "But one thing I know for certain is that you don't know how to be clear with people. If you are going to tell him something, be direct, do it right. Might be a terrible idea, but I know otherwise you'll go about second-guessing yourself and feeling depressed. He's as much of an adult as you're going to find. Hit him with the truth and see how he reacts."

"I'm scared of pushing him away."

"He's the most welcoming, caring, squishy bundle of joy in all of Noss. I don't think that'd be possible."

"That he is. Thank you. Maybe I will, one of these days. If I find the courage to. I'm already trembling just thinking about it."

Alaia embraced him and rubbed his arms back and forth. "It's just the cold making you shiver."

Sterjall let a tiny smile escape.

"Be brave, and be you," she said, letting go of him. She sniffed the air. "I think he's cooking caribou again. Let's get back there and help him set the table. But as much as I've encouraged you to be yourself, don't ruin lunch for us. Take some time to think, then speak to him when you are ready."

Now that the snow was piling thick on tree and creek and rock, their ice training took place much closer to the cabin, allowing them to return to the comfort of the fireplace every evening. Ockam's leg had fully healed, and he was not just catching up fast, but becoming a great mentor to Banook, who was still hesitant about dangling from ropes. Lago's leg had healed too, though he would wear the burn scars for the rest of his life, in whichever form he took.

On a cold morning, when the snow had piled up so high that it blocked the cabin's front door, Banook seemed particularly jubilant. "Now that the real cold is here, I must show you a place of incomparable beauty," he said. "It's four days' walk away, so pack what you must."

"Four days?" Alaia yowled. "But we were just getting used to this. It's so cold out. Can't we keep training here?"

"It's not for training that we go, but to raise our spirits while we rejoice at my favorite spot in these mountains. I will show you a wonder beyond anything you could imagine. The Day of Renewal is less than a week away, and what better than a special place, during a special time, with special friends, to welcome the new year?"

They packed all they thought they'd need, then ventured out. Banook plowed the way with his wide legs, prancing and whistling with anticipation.

For days they battled through the cold: crossing frozen lakes, crawling under dormant forests, clambering over icy crags, and struggling against frigid winds. At one point, they entered a wide meadow where only a foot of snow covered the ground, revealing a landscape of dry reeds and muddy pockets where warm springs thinned the snow. Banook spotted paw prints streaked across the path and stopped. He searched the distance, then smiled.

"I thought I'd find them here!" he said. "Here they come, my beauties!"

From up the meadow, a pack of a dozen or so creatures was running to them, fluffs of fur poking in and out of the snow as they hopped along. They seemed like dogs at first and moved just as fast, but once they broke through the last patch of snow, they revealed themselves to be small but fierce-looking bears.

Around Banook they galloped, making a sound somewhere between a bleating and a low hum. They had slightly longer snouts than other bears, and medium-length tails that snapped up and down instead of wagging from side to side. Their fur was a rich yellow marbled in brown patterns, with burnt umber at the heads and paws.

"Hey, hey! Watch those claws!" Banook said, pushing a few of the viciously friendly creatures away. "These are my kiuons, the most ancient species of bearkind who still roam Noss."

The kiuons bleated and hummed. Bear tried to join them, barking. The kiuons all turned to face Bear and slowly backed away, growling and slapping their tails down in defiance.

"Easy, boys, Bear is our friend. All of us are friends here," Banook said.

The kiuons resumed wagging their tails up and down, then inched closer to sniff at Bear.

"There's something strange about them," Sterjall said.

"Strange indeed are these fellas!" Banook bellowed.

"No, I mean, Agnargsilv shows me they have an aura of their own. Though it has no color, and it's not always there. It reminds me of this beehive I saw once."

"They look nothing like bees to me, cub, although their humming can sometimes sound like a buzz."

Sterjall kept watching. While the kiuons moved about, the tenuous aura flickered in and out of his perception. Like a shy specter, the aura seemed to vanish the more he tried to understand it, and he began to question whether he had been seeing anything at all.

"What do you think the auras are?" Sterjall asked, squatting down to pet the small bears. "Yours, and the kiuons, and even the one from my mask?"

"I cannot see them myself," Banook said, "and although I fancy myself as smart, I'm not as smart as these kiuons here, so I'm afraid I do not know the answer."

For the rest of the day, the kiuons joined them on their trek, randomly running circles around Banook. When the snow was higher than a few feet, it looked like Banook was surrounded by a wake of humming, rippling snow. Every now and then a kiuon would stand up on their hind paws, head poking out like that of a gopher, before sinking again with a sharp bleat.

When night came, one of the kiuons brought a rabbit to the camp and dropped it at Banook's feet. The other kiuons stood attentive, waiting as one.

"Thank you kindly!" Banook said to them, taking the rabbit. "You are most gracious, and most hospitable. May your lands remain as fertile as your seed and your wombs."

Content, all the kiuons ran away at once, heading back to the meadow that was their home.

Banook waved goodbye. "Smartest creatures they are," he said. "Smartest of all bearkind."

On the fourth day of their journey, they woke up in the deepest cold. Banook's increasing enthusiasm was contagious, but the cold was draining, and the rest of them were too tired to feel joyful. At least they were getting close, or so Banook claimed, if one could trust him with distances.

Sterjall was exhausted. Tiny icicles grew beneath his moist nose, which he had to lick off, making the edges feel raw and chapped. His ears kept trapping snowflakes when he forgot to fold them down, which sometimes melted and dripped inside, forcing him to shake his head the same way Bear did when drying off after jumping in a pond. His lower legs piled up snow that froze clumps into his fur and settled in the spaces between his toes, as bothersome as pebbles inside a shoe.

They surmounted a snowy ridge from where they had a good view of the Telm Klannath, a glacier-fed valley in the lands of Khaarkadesh. Herds of caribou roamed the creek-streaked landscape, scoring miles of muddy tracks.

"We are finally here," Banook said, admiring the view. "Most of the caribou have migrated south by now, but this lazy herd prefers to stick around in the hot tributaries of the Stiss Khull, where Winter never fully settles."

"It's a nice view," Jiara said, meaning it, yet plainly unconvinced that it had been worth so much trouble.

"And you should see it in Spring! But in Winter we come here for another reason. Follow me."

Banook took them just a bit farther over the same ridgeline, to an unimpressive set of ruins. Half-buried in the snow rested three broken columns, an angled wall with a circular opening, and hints of tile work that might have once been colorful. The opening yawned descending steps, leading into the unknown. An ice dam had built up above the entrance, draping curved icicles like a giant, frozen eyelid.

"This place is the Emen Ruins," Banook said. "Or rather, that is what I decided to call it, for I don't know its true name." He pointed at the snow around the opening: wolf prints, fresh ones. "Your kin seem to have found my secret spot," he said to Sterjall. "Why don't you go strike up a conversation with the pack? Ask them if we are welcome to join them."

"You mean go in there knowing there are wolves inside?" Sterjall asked.

"With Agnargsilv, you have nothing to fear," Banook said.

"It still hasn't worked that way for me. I tried mindspeaking with wolves at least five times, many more with foxes. They all just get confused and bolt away."

"They aren't confused, it's you who have been confused. They will listen to you. Go on. We will wait here."

Sterjall swallowed. "What will I find down there?"

"You'll see very soon."

Sterjall handed his bag to Banook, then balanced on his way down the slanted opening, spreading his arms against both curved walls to keep from slipping on the icy steps. He smelled the silty aroma of wolf fur, similar to his own, and a sort of electric tingling that permeated the air. After dozens of steps, he reached a wide room with no distinct features. Through Agnargsilv's eyes he could feel the shape of the walls as well as a round tunnel that led deeper. Five wolves huddled in a corner. Two of them, the largest, were standing alert.

His eyes slowly adjusted to the dimness, catching flickers of the wolves' reflective retinas glowing in the gloom like shimmering coins. He shook the ice from his frozen paws, then squatted against the wall by the steps.

Hi, wolves, he thought, feeling like an idiot. *Don't mind us, we're just visiting. Please don't eat us.* The wolves did not growl, but they also did not seem pleased by the intrusion. Sterjall noticed he was shivering, partly from the cold, but mostly from his nerves. He tried to calm himself down. *A frail wolf I am, the strong pack I am not, yet pack and wolf are of one heart.*

Instead of trying to talk, or think with words, Sterjall let his mind drift into more visceral emotions: he tried to project his cold, the idea of shelter, the need for warmth, the feeling of wiping icicles off his whiskers. He conveyed the love for his friends—his pack—and his urge to lead them to safety.

The wolves stared, perhaps listening to the wordless thoughts. The ones standing were the parents; their pups—fully grown, being over a year old— kept still on the ground. The wolf mother huffed, turned to look at the pack, then stepped around nervously. *It's alright*, Sterjall attempted to mindspeak, *I just need you to—*

The wolf parents both approached, eyes aglow, clicking their claws on the icy floors. Sterjall froze in place. The pair moved yet closer, right up to Sterjall's face, and began to lick his muzzle, lifting Sterjall's lips to lap at his teeth. They then playfully chewed on his face, wrapping their maws around his muzzle and biting tenderly, in their own way of greeting each other. Sterjall returned the gesture; it felt oddly natural, though he had never done that before, as if Agnargsilv had shared that instinct with him. He kept himself from using his handpaws and instead mimicked the wolves' body language and gestures, even vocalizing small grunts of gratitude. His tail wagged unconsciously.

Sterjall understood the wolves' signs and in his mind sensed the warmth of hospitality and of kinship. It was not quite the mindspeech Banook was trying to teach him, but for the first time, he felt a reciprocating signal, even if it was a dim one. The wolf parents then went back to lie down with their pups, closing their eyes in complete trust of their new guest.

Sterjall stood and walked back up the steps.

"I think I understand it better now," he said, wiping the slobber off his face. "It's like feeling the meanings without the words, but I have to put myself in their own minds instead of being a stranger. I still can't hear them, but at least I'm getting somewhere."

"Wonderful news, cub," Banook said. "It will become second nature to you soon enough."

"There are five of them. They welcomed me and tried to make me feel at ease. They don't mind us sharing their den, but it's cold down there, and there's not much room."

"I'm surprised," Banook said, "the chamber should not be cold, but warm like the breezes of late Thawing. Let's go down and see what the matter is."

They went down, aided by Alaia's lamplight. The wolves dozed in the corner, paying no attention to them other than a quick raise of an eyelid whenever their guests were being too noisy. The chamber was indeed frigid, but it at least provided shelter from the wind. Banook pointed to the only tunnel that sprouted from that chamber and led them down. A few hundred feet deeper into the rock, they reached a wall of ice.

"Water must've seeped through that crack," Banook said, pointing above them. He asked Alaia for her lamp and waved it around the icy wall, trying to look through it. He handed the lamp back and reached into his bag for a blanket.

"Stand back, if you please," he said, wrapping the cloth around his knuckles.

He leaned back, then swung his heavy arm at the ice, once, twice, and on the third punch the ice cracked and collapsed into the tunnel. A warm air current rushed past them, traveling up the tunnel. It was invigorating and reassuring, carrying a fresh aroma with a mint-like tinge—they could almost taste it.

"Help me clear the rest of the ice off," Banook said, "so that our wolf friends can easily travel down the passage if they so desire."

With the ice sheet completely removed, they continued deeper inward. The circular tunnel here seemed naturally formed, although it had been polished in parts and carved with columns, niches, benches, and other ornamental forms. Despite the warm air, icicles grew in the deeper cracks and nooks.

Ockam noticed runes carved on the stone trims that followed the ceiling and floors; the shapes resembled spirals, crescents, and circles. "These runes aren't triangular like the ones at Minnelvad. They aren't Miscam writings, are they?"

"Not Miscam, no," Banook answered. "This place is much older than them. The Dorvauros tribe etched these runes, many thousands of years before the Miscam migrated north. The Dorvauros dug numerous caves and mines, and then mysteriously vanished, leaving behind treasure-filled ruins, most of which are still to be discovered. They worshipped Sceres, and who could blame them? Don't we all worship her as well? Beautiful and kind folk they were, of long hairs the color of a gilded sunrise, like Jiara's."

Jiara caressed the thick braid over her shoulder, nearly blushing. "These Dorvauros folk knew how to work stone," she said. "These rocks are similar to the ones in the Stelm Sajal, and just as black. It seems to be a lava tube, one carved quite masterfully."

"What's a lava tube?" Sterjall asked her.

"It's when molten rock flows like a river, and the outside gets cold first and solidifies, like a crust. The liquid insides continue to flow like water out a hose, and leave a solid, natural tunnel like this one. They are common near volcanoes."

"There is indeed an old volcano dozing beneath these mountains," Banook said. "But I fear no anger from it, it's been tame since the Dorvauros built this place, though its mountain blood still runs warm."

Numerous smaller tunnels branched off, some to larger halls with stone tables, some to altars with broken-down statues of badger-like animal figures, or abstracted human forms. They stepped into a room much warmer than the rest, where a subtle gurgling sound permeated all the walls. Soothing, yet disconcerting.

"It's warm!" Jiara said after sitting down. "The stone bench is warm as a courtesan's cooch!"

Alaia felt it, then dropped to her knees and felt the stone-tiled ground: it was warm too.

"This chamber has hot waters running under the floors," Banook said. "The hot springs feed into the Stiss Khull, which snakes its course north of here. But don't let your behinds get too comfortable yet. Follow me deeper, for there is more you must see."

Just past a bend, sunlight shone into a low, rippling mist, making it flow against the walls like lapping water. A curtain of icicles decorated an ample archway, sparkling with the streaking light behind them. Banook stood to the side and let them go through first, careful not to block their first glimpse of the magic beyond.

As they crouched under the icicles, the flowing steam parted to reveal an enormous chamber with five round openings in the tall ceiling. Half a dozen columns had been carved to keep the natural roof from breaking down further.

Light poured through the holes in the roof in shining pillars that diffused in the steam, illuminating a dozen pools of hot water scattered in stepped levels.

"By the eyes of the Great Spider, this chamber is glorious," Ockam mumbled, inhaling the inviting vapors.

"It looks like the Heartpine Dome," Sterjall said. "With columns and holes in the roof and all." He instinctively held on to Bear's neck, just in case the dog decided to go for a swim.

"The pools are hot," Banook said, stepping in behind them, "but not enough to burn. You can let Bear wander. Follow me down to the lower tubs."

They meandered in awe between the hot pools—each of different colors—until at the far end they reached a bright opening much larger than the holes above, also delicately curtained by sharp icicles. The lava tunnel opened on the side of a mountain, where the streams from the pools merged their colors and plummeted off the sharp edge. As they leaned forward carefully, they saw a perfectly vertical drop birthing a waterfall so tall that the waters never reached the bottom as a stream and instead floated as a diffused, rainbowy cloud. The view opened into the valleys of Khaarkadesh, with the hundreds of thousands of cervids moving like ants among the hot creeks.

"This place is truly magical," Sterjall said, looking back inside. The light kept shifting and reforming. The steam sometimes flowed up the ceiling holes in ephemeral tornadoes, while at other times it draped itself over the edge of the cliff and flew away like a ghostly blanket.

Banook had stayed further back in the chamber, rejoicing in his friends' fascination. "The views are wonderful in all six seasons, but the rejuvenating warmth of the springs is best appreciated after a long, tiresome walk in the cold. The icy, northwestern winds are a blessing in these chambers. Let us drop our bags in the hall we just passed, where I recommend we set our camp."

They dropped their equipment, but rather than setting up their beds or anything else, they took care of a much more urgent matter: they all removed their clothes and rushed their shivering bodies into the colorful pools.

Their cold toes throbbed with delightful agony inside the hot, mineral-rich waters. They explored each pool in turn, realizing the hottest ones were on the highest steps, turning colder as they flowed into the lower platforms. The one by the far opening had the best views, but also had a thick sheet of ice over it. Banook happily broke through the ice to soak into the frigid water; the others weren't as brave.

"Follow me into the cloudy rift," Banook said, once they had a chance to properly explore all the pools. He showed them to a crack in the wall through which he could barely scrape through sideways, which widened to a natural steam room filled with hissing vents. The fissure rose high, revealing a rift of bright sky. At one end of the narrow chamber, melted snow showered down on them, freezing their shoulders and making them flinch.

It was the last day of Hoartide, and Frostburn would welcome the new year in the morrow. The arduous trip had indeed been worth the struggle. Sterjall was beginning to understand Banook's philosophy of finding the best angles on beauty by sheer contrast. This place would always be beautiful, but its most glorious beauty only manifested itself against the freezing cold of Winter, the same way the simplest of foods tasted most sumptuous when one returned home hungry after a long walk, or how a single wildflower could shine more glorious alone in a desert than a million could together in a flowery meadow.

The long soak had left them starved. Across the hallway from where they set up their beds was a room with a smoke vent and rectangular stones that served as benches and a table. They had brought firewood, as well as frozen trout and tubers, so they set out to cook what to them then felt like the kingliest of feasts.

Once night fell, they snuck under their blankets. The room's cozy warmth and sound of running water had made them all the more sleepy. Souls sated, they gave in to the exhaustion, to the comfort.

CHAPTER FIFTY-SEVEN

TOURMALINE MOON

Sterjall woke to the sound of hushed rustling. He saw Banook get up and walk out of the room, becoming only a silhouette against the moonlit steam that filtered through the round doorway. *Where is he going so late at night?* Sterjall wondered. He got up as quietly as he could and followed the Nu'irg.

As he rounded the bend, he saw Banook beneath the icicle-rimmed arch, naked, shapeshifting into the golden bear as he dropped onto his four paws. The bear vanished into the pink-tinted steam. After a short while, Sterjall heard a splash of water.

He removed his clothes by the archway and tiptoed into the steam, searching for Banook. Five pink pillars shone down from the holes in the roof like angled, luminous twins to the stone columns that supported the ceiling. A gust of cold air pushed the steam for a moment, letting Sterjall spot golden ears poking out from the mists. Banook was sitting in a pool with his eyes closed, leaning forward, his massive nose almost touching the bubbling water.

Sterjall hesitated at the edge of the pool, shivering, though not from the cold. In a surge of sudden commitment, he dipped his footpaws into the water and slowly sank to the right side of the bear. Banook jolted his head up as he heard Sterjall's tail splash, snorting—he had been dozing off.

"Sorry," Sterjall said, sinking deeper. "I heard you getting up and came to see where you were going."

Banook smiled and grunted. His bear eyes were so small in that giant face; they glinted like citrine crystals.

"I almost never get to see you as an arctotherium," Sterjall said, with the water now warming up his shoulders. "I only saw you like this the very scary first time, the first day you taught me about shapeshifting, and then only a few times out in the mountains. That day of the first lesson, I was... well, a bit stunned. I wanted to know what your fur felt like, but I was so nervous, too shy to reach forward and touch you. I was happy you leaned on me like you did."

Banook voiced something like a chuckle, exhaling in such a way that the water under his thick, pink nose splashed a bit. He reached a furry arm over Sterjall, pulling the wolf up against his plump body. It was a little nook of warmth and comfort in an already balmy and cozy place.

Sterjall was tense, but he let himself relax and sink into the fur under Banook's arm. He leaned back, looking at the holes in the roof: the dark rock was starkly contrasted by the snow capping its edges, which shone in pink crescents so vibrant they seemed magenta.

He focused on the feeling of the moisture drenching his muzzle, dripping down his whiskers. He felt the tips of his ears freeze when the breeze flowed from the north, and heard the symphony of the syncopated bubbles, the staccato of the leaking ceilings, the drumming of Banook's pulse. Banook's heartbeat was diligently slow, his arm tightening around the wolf ever so slightly with each thump. It felt good to be this close to him. He didn't want the moment to end.

He began to play with Banook's fur, digging into it with his claws, spreading the clumps open. "It's such a lovely color," he said. "Though it feels very different now that it's wet. You'll have to show me again when you are dry."

Banook nodded.

"Sceres is so flushed tonight," he continued. "Her Tourmaline light warms this place up even more than should be possible. I always loved her most in Spring though, you know? When she's dressed in Obsidian. I've been trying to figure out why. She's dull and dark then, but I feel like she calls to me even more."

It felt oddly liberating to chat with Banook in this way, with him as a bear only listening, at most grunting a reply or flashing an understanding smile. It felt like a confession, but without the negative connotations; a moment of sharing with a friend who listened and cared.

"You have ice growing on your ears," Sterjall said. He reached up and scraped the crystals off the right ear; it was so soft and bent down easily under his handpaw. Banook tilted his head to offer the other side, and Sterjall wiped it clean as well. He patted Banook's muzzle when he was done. They both smiled.

Sterjall leaned back again and closed his eyes, sensing the threads of the room he was in, feeling his body next to the golden bear. The warmth-gilded aura of the Nu'irg and the oceanic coldness that came from Agnargsilv both were merged into one, becoming nearly indistinguishable.

Sterjall found Banook's heavy paw under the water and lifted it up. The paw emerged, with the arm still wrapped around Sterjall's shoulders. He inspected the long claws, the leathery pads. "These are even bigger than your human hands. And these look deadlier than knives."

The bear lifted an eyebrow and smirked as if saying, *You don't know the sixteenth of it.*

Sterjall let the paw drop back under the water but dared himself to keep holding it. "I've been wanting to talk to you," he said, "since that time up in Drann Trodesh, when you held my hand. But I just didn't have the courage to say anything more."

Banook sighed. Sterjall couldn't tell whether it was a sad, pensive, relieved, or upset sigh.

"I still feel—well, that's not true… I feel more certain now than I did back then about this strange connection. I know you do too. We aren't the same, we'll never be the same, and that's one of the things that draws me nearer to you. And I'm learning so much from you, and with Agnargsilv I'm learning about myself, and I feel like maybe I'm still a teenaged, inexperienced kid, but that doesn't mean I'm not able to understand my feelings, and I haven't—"

Sterjall felt an odd tingle around his shoulders and saw Banook slowly shifting back to human form.

When Banook was done, he stared up into the rose-colored shafts of moonlight and said, "I do feel it, cub. And perhaps I speak from experience, perhaps from fear. But the reality is that these have been some of the most enjoyable days of my long life, having you all here with me, discovering, teaching, learning, sharing. But Winter will soon crawl back north, and like waking up from a long hibernation dream, these last months will be but one wondrous memory, and I will once again be by myself in the mountains. You know I cannot follow where you are going, Lago-Sterjall. I am bound to this life, and you have much greater things to do with yours."

Sterjall felt a knot in his throat. He let tears cloud his eyes but wasn't even sure whether that was possible in his wolf form; he had never cried as Sterjall. He remembered words Crysta had spoken, which at the time had meant something entirely different to him. "Back when I was in Withervale," he said, "I was terrified of change, of moving to Zovaria to study. It was Alaia who convinced me to ask Crysta for her support." He swallowed. "Crysta told me her own story one night, of how she took chances in life and never regretted her choices. She said that you can only face true regret by not following the path your heart says is right for you." Sterjall drew in a pink breath, then said, "You are right, our journey will take us on separate paths after this, but while we are here, while *I* am here, I don't want to regret not following my own heart."

Sterjall stood, put his handpaws on Banook's soft cheeks, and brought his lips closer, until there was nothing left between them but their shared breaths.

It was strange. It was awkward. It was arousing. He didn't even know how a kiss with his muzzle would work; he didn't care; it was an instinct deeper than anything rational. He smelled the scent of lemongrass once again, but it was deeper and more complex. It was flavorful, intoxicating. Banook tasted like meadows, like granite, like pine, like smoke. Like mountains. Sterjall could hear Banook's heart pumping, and he felt his own chest pounding with the same ferocity. Banook let himself be taken by the moment and closed his eyes.

After an eternity in that brief moment, Sterjall pulled his lips away and leaned back, afraid and uncertain. Banook slowly opened his eyes and smiled, just like that first time he had smiled at him, the night Lago had woken up in his cabin and Banook had brought him a warm mug of cocoa with honey and cardamom.

Banook reached a tender hand behind Sterjall, caressed his neck and back, then pulled him into a much deeper kiss. Sterjall lost himself in the weaving of their tongues, in the fiery warmth that flushed his groin, his heart, his senses.

With a sudden movement, Banook pulled the wolf all the way up and dropped him on top of his belly, laughing, then noticed his loudness and covered his mouth to stay quiet. Sterjall hugged Banook's chest, sinking into his beard while the giant's arms wrapped around him.

"There are wonders to discover beyond the mountains," Banook whispered, "and I'm glad one does not need to travel to encounter some of them, as they come to you. You are a gift to me, cub. You rekindle the fire in my heart with youth. I am glad that you are more courageous than this cowardly old bear." He kissed Sterjall between his pointed ears.

Sterjall suddenly became aware of his nakedness, of his erection where his bare legs wrapped around Banook's belly. Though he felt a bit shy about it, still uncertain of how far his courage would take him in just one night, his tail began to wag with eagerness. He pushed himself up with his arms to see Banook's face once more.

"If a few months is all we have, let's make the best of them," Sterjall said, then leaned his black nose against Banook's.

"And there are things we'll need to discuss. But I'm happy you care for me so, as I do care for you too. I was not holding out hope of finding this kind of shared joy any longer, it had been much too long."

As their mouths met again, Sterjall slowly rediscovered what a kiss was. He'd had many lovers before, but they'd been variations of the same essential experience; this was something undeniably new.

Banook slowly got up, with Sterjall still on his belly, and carried him through the fog toward a pool closer to the north opening. Their warm bodies breathed out tendrils of pink steam that followed them until they sank back down into the warmth.

The view was breathtaking. The Tourmaline light of Sceres set all the shadows dimly aglow. The stars reflected on the distant rivers, and so did both Iskimesh and Ongumar, glowing blue-green and amber, orbiting so far apart, yet seemingly so close to each other.

A chill wind made Sterjall shiver. Banook lowered himself further into the pool and placed Sterjall over his knee, letting them both face the pink-bathed vista. Sterjall leaned back against Banook's belly, letting his arms dangle in the water, when his handpaw bumped against Banook's own growing arousal. He would've flushed if he hadn't been covered in black fur. He pulled his arm away, ashamed, feeling his cock grow out of its sheath.

"There is nothing to fear, cub," Banook urged him.

Sterjall swallowed. He felt his jaw and fingers tremble, and in one last bout of courage reached down and grabbed hold of what he lusted for, but quickly grew frightened again, feeling that Banook's cock was proportional in size to the giant's body. He fumbled to pull the foreskin back, but once he managed it, he knew not what to do next. To remedy the uncertainty of the situation, Banook planted a kiss between Sterjall's ears, then rose to sit at the edge of the pool, balls dipping into the water, fully displaying his erection to the wolf. Sterjall stared, then shyly looked away.

"Close your eyes, cub," Banook calmly said.

"Wuh-why?"

"Close them, and see me truly."

Sterjall did. Eyes closed, he visualized the threads and the enticing aura of the Nu'irg. In that perceptive state, he was well aware of Banook's body, yet sensed no particular shape, volume, or silhouette to things, but only the synesthetic essence of their being. Banook seemed less threatening then, even delicate and ethereal. Sterjall waded closer, eyes still closed. He felt Banook's enormous hand at the back of his neck, opened his muzzle, and slowly let himself be pulled forward.

Banook was a tender, considerate lover. After letting the wolf explore his body, he placed him on the edge of the pool and wrapped him in his warmth, softness, and eagerness. His size was both intimidating and reassuring, and though anatomically it seemed unlikely for their body parts to find ways to match, they were both willing to get creative and explore the possibilities.

They quietly made love under the moonlight, with their bodies wrapped in rosy mists while caressed by the chilled breeze. The constellations glimmered enviously.

Warm, satisfied, and glowing, they snuck quietly back into the hall, careful not to wake the others. As they lay down together, Lago removed his mask and wrapped himself in Banook's arm, then the big man spread a blanket on top of them both. It felt so different, the feeling of Banook against his smooth body—an experience they'd have to explore at another time.

The big man's breathing was steady and quiet, his heartbeat as meticulous and slow as the passing of the seasons. His beard—a soft pillow—invited Lago into its golden-red depths.

Lago sunk into a blissful, dreamless sleep.

CHAPTER FIFTY-EIGHT

BRAND-NEW YEAR

Banook had rolled onto his back overnight, leaving Lago cradled between his side and arm. The wind direction had shifted, now wafting in from the south, replacing the warm steam with a wintry breeze. Lago woke up in the chill and pulled the blanket back up to his neck. He opened his eyes.

Alaia was sitting up in her bedroll, staring straight at him with her eyebrows up to the ceiling. Lago forced a smile and a shrug; she retorted with an overdone sigh and a shaking of her head, then mouthed, "I'm going to make breakfast," before quietly standing up and tiptoeing to the room across the hallway.

Lago got dressed, then kissed Banook softly on the forehead. Banook smiled but kept joyfully snoozing. Lago stepped around Jiara and Ockam—still asleep—and went to help Alaia.

"You're gonna tell me everything," she said.

As they boiled water and cooked eggs, Lago told her what had happened during the night, leaving out the most salacious details. They discussed what this could mean for them.

"I guess we'll see what happens when it happens," Lago said, "but for now, I'm very happy with what I have. And I don't just mean Banook, I mean all of this." He gestured widely. "You and Jiara and Ockam and Bear, all of us, and all that we are going through together. I used to be terrified of leaving Withervale, and now I see this as the best thing that could've happened to me."

"You have no idea, Gwoli. I thought I'd settle for working the mines till I grew ancient and decrepit. Though it also feels a bit like we are escaping from responsibilities, but we can't be running away for much longer. Are you going to tell Ockam and Jiara about—"

As if summoned by the words, Ockam and Jiara stepped into the room, lured like hounds to the scent of breakfast.

"Tell us what?" Jiara asked, reaching for a mug.

"Why is it so cold here this morning?" Lago dodged.

"There's a breeze coming from the wolves' den," Ockam answered. "It's blowing the opposite way today."

They sat on the rock benches and split the food into small plates, lowering a portion for Bear and saving a sizable chunk for Banook right on the pan.

The light dimmed as Banook ducked under the doorway and entered the room. He sat on Lago's right side, pulled Lago's chin up with one finger, and gave him a soft kiss on the lips. Then he grabbed the pan and spatula and began eating.

Jiara and Ockam were stupefied, looking around for answers. Alaia mouthed, "Later," as she refilled their mugs.

Lago leaned on Banook's arm, which hugged him instinctively, while the other arm continued working on the food.

"Okay, no 'later,'" Jiara barked. "What is going on here?"

Banook pulled Lago tighter and said, still chewing, "Nothing but two men who love each other."

Lago felt a rush of excitement at hearing Banook use that word. He wasn't sure if it was appropriate yet, but what was there to lose by saying it?

Banook continued, "After you went to bed last night, my dear Lago and I had a chat and decided we'd be happier if we could be with each other during this short time we have together."

Ockam and Jiara were speechless.

"We didn't think we needed to ask for your permission, exactly," Lago said.

"I wasn't saying anything," Jiara said, half-laughing. "Whatever brings you joy." She lifted her coffee mug at them and tilted her head down.

"B-but..." Ockam stuttered.

"But what, exactly?" Jiara asked him.

"I... It's just..." Ockam lifted his hands up in surrender.

"What Ockam is trying to say," Jiara said, "is that you make the oddest couple we've ever seen. And this is while seeing *you*, Lago, not even Sterjall. But your smile tells us you are very happy, so we share the happiness with you."

"Brand-new smiles for a brand-new year!" Banook said. "And that calls for a brand-new soak, and then another, so that we welcome this Day of Renewal with replenished souls and rekindled hearts. The morning's chill and the mineral waters beckon our shivering bodies."

They cleaned up the table, dropped their clothes, and hurried to the hot springs. Alaia was the first under the icy archway. She stopped suddenly and cried out, "Shit!"

Lago held still behind her and saw the five wolves exploring around the pools. They all stood alert, their ears piercing out of the vapors.

"I left the mask in the other room," Lago mumbled, breathing harshly.

"Lago, they already know you," Banook said. "They weren't under a spell. You greeted them, they know who you are. You shouldn't fear them."

"That was Sterjall. I can't—I'm not able to... It's not the same, I can't feel them, can't communicate the same way."

"You do exactly what you did yesterday, and they'll understand. If you show fear, they will see fear. They are your friends, and right now we are guests at their home. Be brave and greet them kindly."

Banook nudged Lago with a subtle push.

Lago trembled and tried to turn back, but Banook shook his head.

The wolves stared from within their misty shrouds.

Lago took a tentative step into the steam, then tried to remember exactly how he had felt and what he had done the day before. But now he was just a naked boy surrounded by five large animals. He couldn't help but feel fear.

He thought about how he had once let pain control him, and how he'd learned to internalize that pain, to let it become a part of him without pushing it away. He did the same with his fear now; he swallowed it, accepted it into his body, and walked forward without hiding it, but without letting it control him either.

He reached the center of the room and squatted, balancing himself with his fingertips. The two wolf parents approached him, a bit more hesitantly than the day before, as if they recognized Lago but couldn't remember where from. Once they were close enough to smell him, they relaxed and saluted him by licking his teeth and chewing on his face again. It made Lago chuckle, and the tension was released.

The three younger wolves approached next and curiously greeted Lago, sniffing every part of his body with their cold noses, making him twitch. Bear playfully ran toward them, making the wolves raise their hackles. They slowly relaxed when they saw the dog meant no harm and just wanted to be a part of the fun.

The young man stood up, dressed only in steam, surrounded by the five wolves and Bear.

"It's okay, you can all come in," he said to his friends.

The remainder of the day they spent soaking, relaxing, exploring the multiple tunnels and chambers, then going out to the snow to find overlooks of the western and eastern slopes. They returned to the Emen Ruins a bit before twilight, joyfully cold once more, knowing it wouldn't be long until another replenishing soak.

"How is this place so well maintained, if no one's lived here for thousands of years?" Alaia asked, walking down the icy steps.

"All it takes is one laborious person to keep the majesty of a place like this," Banook said. "I come up a few times a year, scrub away any mineral buildups, remove the dried bones from the wolves' hunt, or the bones of their dead friends, and only sometimes do I have to redirect streams to the right pools, or close off springs that sprout in the wrong rooms."

They shared a quick snack and then rushed back into the pools.

Jiara and Ockam were sharing one of the higher pools, discreetly watching a lower pool where the new lovers were hugging and kissing, being themselves without any fear of what their friends might think.

"But he's so... big!" Ockam whispered to her.

"Big he is," Jiara said. "But why should that matter? It's not so odd. I like some bigger women."

"You like them pear shaped, not bear shaped. And not bear *sized*, as far as you've told me."

"Hey, I wouldn't rule it out," she said. "Either way, what bloody difference does it make to you? You are not the one fucking him."

"Don't even mention that. I mean, you've seen his... My brain is having a hard-enough time picturing how it even works between the two of them."

"Seems you've been giving it quite a lot of thought," Jiara said, then cackled while making an obscene gesture with her hands and tongue. Ockam elbowed her ribs, making her stop. "Just let them be, for Takh's sake," she added. "They look so happy together. Can you imagine anyone better for Sterjall? Anyone better for Banook?"

"Well... It's not... But he's a bear! It's just so wro—"

"There's nothing wrong. Look at them! Seriously, point your stupid eyes at them and tell me they aren't beautiful in the oddest sort of way."

Ockam slowly shook his head. "But he's so big..." he grumbled.

After dinner, during their sixth soak that day, Sterjall was sitting at the edge of the pool where he'd first kissed Banook, playing with the Nu'irg's wavy wet hair, legs dangling over one of his hairy shoulders. They watched as the others dared each other to jump in the pool of frigid water, dipping their toes in and wailing. Alaia was the first to dip her entire foot in, balancing at the edge of the pool on her other foot and one outstretched arm. Bear suddenly came up behind her and put his cold nose right on the dimples of her lower back, making her twitch and slip into the cold water.

They all laughed, except for Alaia, even though she had won the dare.

"Remember that night I first woke up in your cabin?" Sterjall asked, resting his muzzle on top of Banook's head. "You called me *Lago* when you saw me wake up, and I asked how you knew my name. You said Bear had told you. Was... was that true?"

Banook started laughing, making his weight shift, submerging his head. He came back out, still laughing, and turned to face Sterjall.

"Of course not, cub. Your other friends told me your name. I was just being silly."

"I... I actually believed you, and then I was just confused and too embarrassed to ask."

"Sorry. The only canid whose mind I can somewhat read is you. Bear escapes me. He's a weird fellow."

They switched positions, Banook sitting at the edge with Sterjall soaking in front of him. Banook slowly massaged Sterjall's neck. *His hands could crush me at any moment,* Sterjall thought, *but he is always so gentle.*

"That reminds me," Sterjall said, "another thing I've been meaning to ask about. The day you rescued me, I was having strange hallucinations when I was down in the vents. The memories are all jumbled together, but one thing I clearly remember is calling for Bear. I called his name, and instead of Bear I saw you, but you as the golden bear, coming to rescue me. Did that really happen?"

"That, hmm. Not quite. I came down as I am now, although more clothed, and picked you up in my human arms, not as an arctotherium. I found shelter behind a rock, shielded from the fumes, where I sat and held you to my chest, rubbing on your body to make the blood flow. Bear was there too, curled next to me. Once your body was warm enough, I wrapped you in my bearskin cape and went to search for our friends."

"I clearly remember you as the golden bear, coming straight to me as I passed out. I even recall your muzzle tasting my face, the scent of your breath. Maybe my memory is mixed up from all that happened, but that's one of the clearest things I recalled as soon as I was conscious again."

"Maybe even then, before you even knew me, you already somehow saw me. I don't know, cub, but it makes me wonder."

They sat there thinking while Banook kept massaging Sterjall's shoulders. By now all three of the others had managed—coerced or pushed or 'slipped'—

to find their way into the frigid pool and had decided to retreat to the hottest pool to cleanse all memory of that trauma.

Sterjall and Banook were getting too warm, so they decided to move to one of the cooler pools. Banook leaned back and let Sterjall sprawl face down on his belly.

"It's amazing how pure and pristine these hot springs are," Sterjall said, paws dangling into the water. "Even the smell, it's so different."

"Very different than the hot springs south of Minnelvad, which smell more like rotten eggs," Banook said. "And they are even filthier down in Brimstowne, where the rowdy patrons let their pints tumble right into the water, no respect at all."

"In Brimstowne? Do you mean at the Yeast Cauldron?"

"How do you know about the Yeast Cauldron?" Banook asked, belly suddenly tensing as he bent forward a bit.

"How do *you* know about the Yeast Cauldron?" Sterjall retorted, lifting and cocking his head.

Banook laughed from the depths of his belly, sinking Sterjall into the pool. He rescued the wolf, containing his laughter, and said, "My dear cub, as a bear I have all I need up here, but as a man I still have my needs."

"So, is *that* why you go to Brimstowne, then?"

"I'm popular among a certain clientele, you can't blame me. And it's not the only reason. I hope that doesn't make you feel jealous."

"No, I think it's funny to picture you there. You'd overflow any of those pools in one dip."

"It's not unheard of. But I much prefer these pools here and your sweet company," he said, offering a tender kiss.

"Wait… This makes me wonder," Sterjall said, after giving it some thought. "Does this mean you have children? Or rather, *can* you have children?"

"I can. I have not had human children, as far as I am aware, as I have taken precautions with women. Ursid children, however, I perhaps have hundreds alive today, of all living species. My grandchildren, grand-grandchildren, and further on, well, they'd be too numerous to count after thousands of years. Perhaps all living bears today are related to me in that way, whether closely or from ancient blood."

Over the next three days, Lago-Sterjall and Banook would sneak out at night to explore all aspects and combinations of each other's bodies. Then they would talk for hours about their favorite books, about Banook's long history—

and Lago's shorter one—and about the wonders still undiscovered in the vast lands of Noss.

The wolves were always present and followed Lago whether he was wearing Agnargsilv or not, and even shared some of their hunt with him. They didn't see him as their leader, not remotely; the wiser wolf parents saw Lago as perhaps a lost pup who needed a sense of direction, who could use better training on how to use his fangs and claws.

On the morning of the third day, their last day at the Emen Ruins, Banook made sure to leave everything tidy. They picked up their bags and ventured into the snow once more. The wolves followed for a bit, to make sure Lago was safe. After a while, they tired and let the cub go his own way—he would learn the rest without their help.

Chapter Fifty-Nine

SOVATH

"It reeks of sapfire in here," the Red Stag muttered.

"Apologies, Monarch Hallow," Viceroy Urcai said, "this was the last of the tunnels we made, so the smoke is still clinging to the stone. We are almost there. She's just a bit deeper down this shaft."

The tunnel was wide and tall, made to fit more than simple mining equipment or human troops.

"Is everything well?" Urcai asked, noticing the exhaustion in his monarch's long-muzzled face.

The Red Stag glared at his viceroy and answered, "It's... something a bit embarrassing, I'm afraid. It bothers me that I can no longer take my human form, lest I lose the mindlock on the cervids I already captured. I have not slept well due to this. Do you have any idea how hard it is to rest with a rack of antlers preventing you from turning on your pillow?"

"I... had not considered that, Monarch Hallow. Perhaps I could engineer a new kind of resting device, one that your army could carry for you during the upcoming campaign."

The Red Stag huffed, interested in the proposal but too proud to acknowledge it. He decided to shift the conversation to more pressing matters. "Did she cause as much trouble as last time?"

"More, I'm afraid. Took down two hundred of our soldiers before she fell into our trap."

"Takh have mercy. I hope she's properly secured."

"That she is," Urcai said, just as they arrived.

In front of them was a mesh barrier of metal bars interwoven in a dense pattern, overlapping two more meshes of the same kind. Behind the diamond-shaped holes was darkness, but in the darkness something sparkled, like a field of stars, with two of the stars shining brighter than the others. The two bright stars blinked.

"Her Miscamish name is Sovath," Urcai said.

"Sovath." The Red Stag tasted the word. As his eyes adjusted, he began to more clearly see the creature behind the protective meshes. Standing on four spindly legs was a chital doe, slender, small, with orange furs spotted in a constellation of white dots. Her eyes reflected the flame of Urcai's lamp in a dangerous green.

"She's so tiny, so innocent-looking," the Red Stag said. "She's afraid. I don't need the mask to feel that."

"Be careful, Monarch Hallow, she is much more—"

SLAM!

An enormous megaloceros hit the triple mesh, then backed off from it with her forehead bleeding. Sovath had moved so fast that the Red Stag had not even seen her shapeshift.

Dust and rocks fell from the ceiling. Sovath shook her heavy shoulders and stared with anger-filled eyes.

"I was earnestly scared, for a moment," the Red Stag said with a small chuckle to defuse his tension. "Are you certain the mesh will hold?"

"Yes, it's a magnium alloy stronger than magsteel, highly resilient. We could not use simple bars, for her smallest form, that of a pudu, could've snuck through them. This mesh won't hold her forever, but—"

SLAM!

More rocks tumbled; cracks appeared on the wall.

Sovath's forehead bled openly.

"She's injured," the Red Stag observed.

"Do not concern yourself—she heals surprisingly fast."

"But no antlers? What a shame."

"She may look less threatening than the antlered males, but she's sixteen-fold deadlier."

Sovath huffed, blood steaming off her forehead. Her back scraped on the ceiling, barely fitting in the tunnel.

The Red Stag stood firm, then took a few decisive steps toward the mesh. As he moved closer, Sovath reduced herself back to her primal form and backed off to the farthest reaches of the dark tunnel. The spotted deer reached another triple mesh on that end, and there she stopped, thin legs quivering.

Come to me, Sovath, the Red Stag mindspoke, and the Nu'irg ust Urg obeyed.

"Be careful," Urcai warned, "she might be faking it."

"No," the Red Stag said. "I can feel her, I can read her. She is so much smarter than the others." He pushed his hoofed fingertips through the mesh and caressed Sovath's bloodied head. The chital's tense muscles spasmed sporadically, struggling with her awareness of her impotence.

The Red Stag tightened his grip within Sovath's mind, mindlocking her to his will. "She is mine now," he said. He turned to Urcai. "Release her."

"But what if—"

"She is fully under my control. Release her. Now!"

A dozen Teldebran Miscam slaves pulled the heavy mechanisms that had sealed the meshes shut. With the barrier removed, Sovath simply stood there, eyes empty as a dry well, staring at the open tunnel that could lead her to freedom if only she was able to run away.

Chapter Sixty

FANG

"Warm... bed... at last!" Alaia cried, dropping her bag at the cabin's terrace and hurrying inside.

Jiara picked the bag up and to Banook and Sterjall said, "I'll let her nap, but we'll move out of the upstairs room after that."

"No need," Banook said. "I'm quite fond of the guest room, and I'm sure my cub will be as well. You three can keep the big bed."

"Bear, help me hunt some logs for the fireplace," Ockam said, heading in as well. Bear followed.

Sterjall was struck by a wave of nostalgia as he entered the cabin, as if the Emen Ruins were but a distant, vivid memory he could not return to. Despite the wistfulness, he was happy to be back, eager to share a comfortable bed with Banook.

After a few days of much-needed rest, they returned to their arduous ice training, and the more they trained, the more they understood the necessity of it. Their biggest problem now was Bear. They tried to get him used to being carried in a sling, but the mutt would always try to wriggle out, preferring to drop to his death rather than being suspended from ropes. He was also inept with ice, not knowing how to stop. Lago-Sterjall began to have recurring nightmares in which Bear ran on an ice sheet with a dark-blue crack at the far end, slowly sliding to his death.

Bear's recalcitrance soon turned dangerous, forcing them to reconsider their options.

"We can't take him," Jiara said as they trudged back to the cabin. "This whole time we've been training so that we could avoid unnecessary risks. Taking Bear is taking a tremendous risk, and a highly unnecessary one at that."

"He's not *unnecessary*," Sterjall snapped.

"Yet he is," she retorted, "at least for this trip. He was a street dog before, who found his own food around the slums. Once Thawing arrives, there'll be plenty for him to hunt."

"He's never hunted, he just chases things. He wouldn't know what to do with a rabbit if he caught one. The food he got at Withervale was scraps from people who would feed him, or that he'd steal from the kitchens."

"I know what we can do," Banook said. "I can ask Sabikh to bring him food while we are away."

"Who in the voids is Sabikh?" Ockam asked.

"She is the lovely bear who had a good taste of your leg," Banook answered.

"Bah. And you named her after that evil queen from the, what's it called, that saga? Very fitting. I don't like her."

"She seemed to like *you*," Alaia replied.

"And we could ask if Frud would be willing to keep Bear company," Banook said.

"Let me guess, the cub," Ockam said.

"The very one. He's still playful and not much bigger than Bear. They would get along. I will have a chat with them and see if they would be willing."

Every morning after breakfast, Banook—and sometimes Ockam—would spend time working with Sterjall's dire wolf fang and quaar tube. Sterjall could hear the banging and scraping and sawing, but could not guess at what they were doing, and Banook inflexibly refused to let him peek into his workshop.

After the coldest part of Winter had passed, on the very last day of Frostburn, Banook was preparing a particularly extravagant banquet. Pies were ready to bake, and fresh dough was rising. Rabbits and pheasants were dressed and stuffed, sauces and beans were simmering, and spices and fruits were infusing into the wine.

"How are we going to eat all of this?" Sterjall asked.

"Never mind your own tiny belly," Banook said, "there will be plenty of room in mine for whatever you leave behind."

"But what's the occasion? You've never cooked anything like this before."

"You will see tonight, be patient." He gave Sterjall a kiss and returned to his busywork in the kitchen.

They cleared the snow off the terrace and readied the outdoor dining table. The firepit was roaring by the time the feast was served.

Sceres was still in her Tourmaline season; during this waxing gibbous phase, her Ilaadrid Shard was shining fervently, illuminating the terrace in pink-tinged white, with the fire contributing a still warmer glow.

They feasted, they drank, they sang. They reminisced of all their adventures and awkward moments. They speculated about the future and avoided talking about certain futures they did not want to consider yet. Bellies and hearts full, they sat around the firepit to contemplate the rising sparks and crackling embers. Banook and Sterjall held each other.

Banook suddenly nodded to Ockam, who got up and went into the cabin. He returned promptly with an item wrapped in blue silks, which he handed to the Nu'irg.

Banook's big hands were trembling with nervousness. He turned to Sterjall and said, "Cub, you've been a precious gift to me, and I want to offer something precious to you in return. This is yours." He handed the silk-wrapped object to him.

Sterjall took it and slowly unwrapped the cloth. Inside was a dagger, sheathed in an intricate scabbard of brass and cedarwood. The grip was made of the spiraling quaar tube, attached to a crossguard of dark steel and copper inlays, and a white pommel enveloped by a steel band. One side of the pommel had a delicate carving of a wolf's head, the other that of a bear's head. Sterjall unclipped the scabbard and slid the blade out.

The dagger was slender and delicate but felt solid and strong at the same time. The core of the blade—like the pommel—was also white, bending in a pleasing curve. The edges of the blade were sparkling black.

"Th-thank you…" Sterjall mumbled, spellbound by the outstanding craftsmanship and exotic forms. "It's so… so beautiful." He was about to use his pads to test the sharpness of the dark blade when Banook stopped him.

"As you must have guessed, the white parts are carved out of the dire wolf fang. It was far stronger than I expected, not like bone nor walrus tusks, but denser, as uncannily resilient as Bra'uur steel. The blade you must be careful with." Banook took the dagger to show him the details. "It's made of a series of obsidian bladelets, six on each side, embedded into the bone around the whole edge. Ockam showed me how to work the dark glass with precision, something my indelicate hands were not so good at." The obsidian shards were masterfully cut and inserted so as to flow as one, leaving no gaps. They converged into the sharpest of tips.

Banook ran his fingers close to—but never touching—the edges of the dagger. The blackness glinted, reflecting the fire at one moment and the beacon-like light of the Ilaadrid Shard at another. "This is no ordinary obsidian," he said, "but a rarest kind called *senstregalv*, birthed in the volcanic belly of Laaja Khem, northwest of the Da'áju Caldera. There are ancient black glass mines there that tunnel deep within the heart of the mountain, dug by the Dorvauros tribe in times before the Wutash settled these lands. It's the strongest obsidian known. It will not shatter, it will not lose its sharpness."

Sterjall peered at the dagger with Agnargsilv's sight and noticed something peculiar happening at the edges of the black glass, separate from the effect the quaar tube had on propelling the threads. "The threads that pass through it, they bend upon it," he said. "I think there are small filaments of quaar embedded in the obsidian. It acts as quaar would."

Banook nodded. "You are quite perspicacious. Although perhaps it's not exactly quaar, but some crystalline form of aetheric carbon, one birthed naturally, under great pressures. Very few seams of senstregalv have been found, where the marrow of mountains crystallized in this most perfect infusion of materials." Banook handed the dagger back to Sterjall. "Its name is *Leif*. It means *fang* in Miscamish. A bit on the nose, but appropriate, I believe."

"Leif..." Sterjall whispered, caressing the curves of the weapon. He inspected the bear and wolf carvings on the pommel: they were marvelously rendered and stained to give them further depth.

He playfully swung the blade, then straightened his arm and held Leif in front of him, staring down the length of the blade. As before, the quaar tube pulled the threads in its unusual manner, expanding Sterjall's second sight in the direction the senstregalv tip pointed to.

Banook put a hand on Sterjall's shoulder and said, "May it keep you safe and hold me in your memory until your return."

Sterjall deflated, dropping his arm. His eyes darted up to Banook. "You say that as if you are saying goodbye."

"Not yet, cub, but the day will soon come, and we must both be ready for it."

Banook kissed Sterjall's forehead and wrapped his arm around him again.

Sterjall held Leif over his lap, rotating it in his handpaws, but his eyes were looking past it, through it, to nowhere.

"Sorry I got quiet after dinner," Lago said, lying in bed next to Banook. "I didn't even properly thank you. Leif is truly beautiful. You have no idea how much it means to me. It's just that it now dawned on me how little time we have left. And it made me think, do we really need to hurry? I mean, we could try and—"

"As much as it hurts me to say so, yes, you must hurry. After Da'áju—whether we find the city or not—your goal should be to journey west, or south, and seek the Miscam tribes in other domes, and perhaps recruit their aid. The Negian Empire has not been at rest during Winter, they know not how to hibernate. Instead, they have been scheming, readying their troops around the Anglass Dome. It worries me that war may be coming to your lands."

"What am I supposed to do if the Negians attack? I don't even know how to use a dagger."

"You must learn. Wars are ugly things, they make us do things counter to our natures, but sometimes fight we must. Plenty a war have I fought in, and many a soldier have I slain to protect the innocent. When war comes to you, you must put aside some parts of yourself you hold dear and fight for what you know is right."

"I didn't know you fought in wars before."

"I have, and so have most of my Nu'irgesh friends. I battled wielding my claws as an arctotherium, in times long before the Downfall, but twice also as a man, wielding long glaives and pikes, though I've also been known to hurl boulders when needed."

"I can't imagine you killing people. You are too kind, care too much for others."

"You know some sides of me, cub, but not all. Some hidden aspects present themselves when needed and are there out of necessity, not out of the callings from my heart. Believe me, I much prefer to love than to hate. I value hope over despair. I will honor kindness and reject her ugly, sinister opposite. You must strive to do the same."

"I will try..." Lago softly spoke, then turned his head and saw Leif sitting on the nightstand, its cedarwood sheath sparkling under the lamplight. "I wanted to think of Leif as just a gift, a practical tool, but now I realize it's more than that. It's a weapon, and it scares me to think of it as that."

"The light shines darkest in the sharpest end of the glass," Banook said.

"What does that mean?" Lago asked.

"It's an old Dorvauros aphorism. It means what it means to mean. But do not worry about Leif's nature, for it will be what it must be. You will learn to wield it, in time, and it will help you when violence becomes not a choice, but a necessity for survival, for the protection of those you love."

"I don't think I'd be fit for that. Ockam and Jiara know about warfare, strategy, politics, while all I know about is the stars. I've been thinking, maybe they could be the ones to go, while I could stay here with you."

Banook turned on his side to face him. "Lago-Sterjall, I do not believe in fate nor providence. I don't believe you are destined for greatness nor misfortune. Life cares not for hopes, injustices, or wishes. No matter what oracles tell us, or what visions we dream of, what we are left with is nothing but our own choices and the paths we ourselves decide to tread. The stars do guide you, in a way, but they don't dictate a particular path for you to take. They have no influence other than the way they brighten your heart and inspire you with wonder and hope. I know the curiosity that feeds your soul, and I know you would regret neglecting its calling."

Banook wrapped a hand around Lago's head and quietly said, "The mountains will still be here when you return, and so will I, waiting for you."

Lago sunk himself deep into Banook's chest. He closed his eyes tightly and said nothing more, surrendering to the pressure of joy, and sorrow, and a longing for something he had not yet lost.

CHAPTER SIXTY-ONE

I HEAR THE MOUNTAIN SONG

One eventide, as Sunnokh's descent painted the entire snowy wilderness with his palette of warm colors, Lago and Banook were warming up in front of the fireplace, sitting on the couch on which Lago used to sleep.

Snow had piled up at the bases of the tall windows, melting into icy crystals in the corners near the stone chimney. Through the glass they watched Jiara, Ockam, and Alaia, who were laughing as Bear tried to catch snowflakes, which fell like golden fireflies under the scraping sunlight.

Banook sat with his arm around Lago, who had book two of the *Barlum Saga* on his lap. It had been four years since Lago read the saga, and about forty since Banook had. Now that they were reading it together, they felt like they were experiencing it all anew, able to discuss the intricate story as they went along, to take note of the pacing of the words, to introspect about the hidden meanings, and await eagerly for their favorite moments.

They took turns reading aloud, one chapter each, though oftentimes Banook would jump in during Lago's chapters when his deep voice was needed to bring life to the netherbeasts of Hasuth and the nethervoid dragons.

Written by Ansko Loregem, the *Barlum Saga* told the story of Dravéll and Ishkembor, and their journey through the sixteen domes. The sixteen gemstones that held the universe in balance had been stolen from the staff of Shaman Umbaarlis, and the heroes had been sent on a quest to recover them from the Khest monsters who hoarded them. From dome to dome they traveled, defeating the netherbeasts before they used the gems to grow their domes yet larger, and no land was left to save. The books had been banned by the Takheists, as they presented a blasphemous interpretation of ideas taken directly from their sacred codex, full of too much whimsy and imagination.

In this part of book two, Dravéll had journeyed across the Cobalt Desert of the Kingdom of Bauram and entered the Azurean Dome by cutting the vines with the magical Sword of Zeiheim, a legendary blade forged not in steel, but in lightning. Dravéll journeyed into the dome to rescue Ishkembor from the two-headed nethervoid dragon Talaemánwe, who knew that by kidnapping Ishkembor, his friend would come to his rescue, bringing with him the three gems they had already recovered.

"Armies hundredfold more vast than any from the Mistdraft Nations have met their doom beneath my netherflame breath, between my fangs of steel," Banook's voice resonated. As the two-headed dragon, his throaty, rumbling vocalizations were terrifying. "Say now, prince of Lumerenith, say why I should not crush your skull like a grape instead of listening to your poisoned words?"

Lago flipped the page; here Dravéll tricked the dragon by pretending to trip, tossing one of the gems down into the Void of Khest. Talaemánwe flew below the aurora bridge to catch the sparkling object—but it wasn't the gem; it was one of the crystal cherries from the underwater orchards of Strethema, which Dravéll discovered during his adventure through the Moordusk Dome. Dravéll took the chance to swipe the Sword of Zeiheim through the magsteel cage that held his friend, unsure of how they would escape once the nethervoid dragon returned.

"I've wondered lately," Lago said, pausing in his reading, "now that the story is coming back to me, if later in the books, when they decide to destroy all the gemstones instead of taking them back to Umbaarlis... Was it a metaphor about taking power away from the Zovarian states? Are the gemstones supposed to represent the galvanum scepters of the Arch Sedecims who rule the Union?"

"I honestly believe you are reading too much into it," Banook replied. "Loregem clearly stated that he did not care to make a political statement with the Saga, he only meant to tell a captivating story."

"Maybe he said that to cover his ass. I also wonder, if he were alive today, and we could tell him that there were supposed to be eighteen domes—if you count Da'áju and the missing dome—if he'd write a new book that dealt with those two. I'm curious what weird new worlds he'd make up for each. I really love the imagery in the Azurean Dome, it's one of my favorites, how the whole dome is made of stardust, and they walk in light bridges made from the aurora."

"I loved those descriptions, too. They really capture the essence of the northern lights."

"Have you seen them before? Well, what a question, of course you must've."

"I have, many times, and each time is more magical than the time before. I was hoping we could enjoy them together when we were at the Emen Ruins, seeing them tint the pools magenta and green. Alas, they are unpredictable, and rarely are they seen so far south."

"At least I have Loregem's descriptions to go by. They sound magnificent."

Banook leaned back more comfortably. "Loregem's wondrous prose can be magical, making us see the lights in our minds. Books have been a blessing to me. Sometimes I spend much too long by myself and forget certain aspects of the human side of my nature. But books are always there to help me remember. They can also be filled with songs, like my favorite chapter in the Saga, that of the Bighorn Dome."

"I can't wait to get to that chapter, then you can sing the songs for me! It's so hearty and carefree how the characters just break into song as they travel."

"I may or may not have made up my own melodies for most of them. I'd be happy to sing them for you, except for that dreadful tavern song. Any buffoon could write a song better than that."

"Your words would translate well to verse, you have a natural cadence for it. I think you should write."

Banook ruffled Lago's curls. "You are too kind, cub. Do you really think so? I don't believe my writings are really that good."

"So you *have* written before?"

"Well, maaaybe," Banook teased.

"Now you have to show me!" Lago said, placing the ribbon bookmark before closing the book.

"Well, perhaps one song. Allow me a moment." Banook got up to search through the bookshelves and pulled out a leather-bound notebook from between a row of similar volumes. Lago had never browsed through them, as they were high up and looked bland, with no titles on the spines. Banook sat back down next to Lago and flipped through the pages.

"What are all these writings?"

"They are observations of the natural world, of beautiful insects, pebbles, clouds, sunbeams, anything I may find here in my back yard. Sometimes, when I feel alone, I write, and it is as if a friend sits with me, and we converse in prose and verse."

"There is so much in here. Are all those other books—"

"Yes, all those notebooks are my own. There are very few poems, however, I'm searching for one I know you will like." Banook flipped through half-scribbled and crossed-out writings in Miscamish runes, and some in Common letters. Finally, he found what he was looking for.

"This one here is called *I Hear the Mountain Song*. I wrote it hundreds of years ago, with a few recent additions. It deals with my journey with bearkind as we migrated north and settled into our new home."

"Is it a poem? Or a song?"

"Both. I will sing it for you." Banook picked Lago up and sat him on his left knee. He kept the notebook open over his right knee, so they could both see the handwritten words. He cleared his throat and began to sing in a low bass that interwove with baritone highlights. His voice was sweet, tender, and wistful; and intoned:

> The alpenglow on snowy peaks calls forth where I belong,
>
> I lend an ear, the granite speaks! I hear the mountain song.
>
> The Silv has summoned all bearkind to follow it along;
>
> An offer that can't be declined, Urnaadi's voice is strong.
>
> In caverns deep I'll build my keep, in meadows I shall sprawl,
>
> For fish I'll leap and full I'll sleep behind clear waterfalls.
>
> In mounts so high I'll claw the sky and touch our turquoise dome,
>
> Yet bluer still the fjordic ice entices me to roam.
>
> The day soon comes to travel north through landscapes yet unknown,
>
> My brother bears and I set forth to find our sacred throne.
>
> I hear the wind caress my fur, sharp claws resound along,
>
> The spruce and pine, and cones of fir all join the mountain song.

Lagoons we cross, upriver swim, beyond the shining dunes,
But not all brothers heard the hymn, some settled for their doom.
Moon bears not heeding her request neglected Sceres' call,
The crescent marks upon their chests will Sunnokh kiss no more.

Nor shall their lush, black manes e'er comb our brethren named as sloths,
Where once grew forests they called home lay buried sickle claws.
Old bears of yore are laid to rest, more species lay entombed,
Their bodies trapped beneath, at best in song shall be exhumed.

Yet we all march to brand-new homes through snow and wind and rain,
For mountains call for us to roam and make them our domain.
The Pilgrim Sierras far behind now seem so frail and small,
We'll soon be home to rest, unwind, and hear the valley's call.

At last we reach the Wujann peaks and climb their steep gray walls,
Fresh trout and berries we shall seek amongst these hallowed halls.
But doomsday rears its evil head and sets the skies ablaze,
Hot ash and fire blast and spread, suppressing Sunnokh's rays.

Unending Winter snows are blown once burns at last abate,
The cold sinks deep into our bones as bears all hibernate.
When morning breaks, the tribe is slain, ill luck the Wutash fared,
But bears and cubs will thrive again, for some our lives were spared.

I build a cabin with my hands and contemplate my past:

Where paws were then now two feet stand and home I am at last.

I saunter lonely in my back yard and listen for birdsongs,

My heart feels full, and like a lark, I sing the mountain song.

At this point, Banook turned the page. The next stanzas were written on a newer, whiter piece of paper, as if it had been added recently. He continued singing:

But something's missing from my soul, a yearning I can't bear,

With clouded thoughts I take a stroll to breathe fresh mountain air.

In Minnelvad through ice and steam I rescue a frozen boy,

The wolf cub thaws through fevered dreams and lifts my heart with joy.

At Emen Ruins we drop our clothes and bathe in lustful bliss,

By moonlight pink he reaches close and plants a furtive kiss.

This kindred spirit steals my heart and teaches me to love,

I hope we'll never be apart, I pray to stars above.

And now he sits upon my lap—my love I ought proclaim.

I place my lips upon his cap and sing one last refrain:

Banook leaned down and kissed the top of Lago's head, then sang the last few lines:

I hope he knows that we can be together all along

When far apart he thinks of me and hears the mountain song.

Lago hugged Banook so tightly that he lost himself in his beard.

"I hope you approve of the latest additions," Banook said. "The night I gifted you Leif, I felt I left you uneasy, and my words were not as comforting as they could've been. But a song… A song lives in your heart, like you live in mine. Here"—he handed the notebook—"so you can remember the words and read through some of my other writings, if you'd like."

"Thank you, Banook," Lago said, teary-eyed, falling tenderly into his arms. "I will treasure this song, it's the greatest gift of all." He wiped his eyes and stared curiously at Banook. "So, you planned this, all along? Even me sitting on your lap, and the kiss?"

"For the past week or so, as I wrote the new stanzas. But I wasn't sure when the right time would come—it just presented itself."

"I love you," Lago said. "I will read through these verses and memorize every word."

"Don't be surprised if I still make a few changes. Songs are stories, after all, and stories are alive and as ever-changing as rivers and canyons."

CHAPTER SIXTY-TWO

THE EIGHTEEN NU'IRGESH

"Come on, cub!" Banook said, trying to shake the wolf awake.

"It's so late," Sterjall moaned. "Can't you show me in the morning?"

"Now is the perfect time. There is no other, and so your padded paws must follow."

Sterjall clumsily and much too slowly got dressed.

Banook tossed his bearskin cape over Sterjall. "This should do. We are not going far, I promise."

"I don't know if I should believe you…"

"I blame you not, but follow me still, little cub." Banook hurriedly walked out of the room.

There was no point in arguing with Banook when he got in these strange moods, so Sterjall humored him, despite his heavy-lidded eyes. As he was about to leave the room, he turned back around, grabbed Leif from the nightstand, and clipped the scabbard to his belt.

The fire in the living room had died out long ago, leaving only ghostly embers. It was a moonless night, in the darkest hours before twilight.

Banook swung the door open, letting in a chill breeze and the smell of wet pine needles.

It was the last week of Winter, and with Thawing peeking over the horizon, some of the snow was already melting. Sterjall folded Banook's cape in half so that it wouldn't drag on the ground, pulled it tightly around his neck, and followed him outside. Banook was wearing only his loose-fitting under-wear, seemingly unaware of the cold.

"You did not need to bring your dagger with you, cub," Banook said, bare feet crunching on the new ice crystals that had formed on the terrace. "I prom-ise I will not get us in trouble."

"I just like carrying it with me. It makes me feel better just to have it. I've been meaning to ask… If senstregalv is unbreakable, how did you cut it?"

"You can't cut senstregalv, nor mold it as you would with steel, as far as I know," Banook answered. "But you can shatter it if you first heat the glass to a certain temperature and strike it at the right angles. Ockam and I spent long nights in my humble forge until we knapped the bladelets into their proper shapes."

"You did a marvelous job of it," Sterjall said. He unsheathed his dagger, to admire it under the starlight. The bone-white core mirrored the snow at his footpaws, but the sharp edges of obsidian shone the darkest, like a starry night trapped in dusky amber.

They strolled west of the cabin, over a hill and into a rocky canyon.

"Can you not see it yet?" Banook cryptically asked.

Sterjall had been distractedly staring at his blade. He put it away and looked around. "See what? It's very dark out."

"Exactly!" Banook said, walking into a grove of sugar pines, toward one that had spiraling steps around it. It was a tree Sterjall had climbed before, the time he brought Alaia to show her the view and to confess his feelings toward Banook.

Banook climbed first, making the wooden boards creak in discomfort. Ster-jall followed a safe distance behind. The big man cleared off the snow from the top platform, then sat his nearly bare ass down, leaning his back against the trunk. "Come on cub, sit right here."

Sterjall sat on Banook's lap, straddling one voluminous thigh. He looked up and at last understood, eyes fixed on the Galactic Belt. The core of the galaxy was exposed, glowing in faint oranges, elusive magentas, and tremulous ocean blues. He had seen this view countless times, always in awe at the im-mensity of the greatest of all domes, but he had never seen it with such clarity, such vibrancy.

"It is two hours before twilight," Banook said, "on the night of a Hollow Moon, when Sceres shies away with no dress to cover her body. The clouds of Winter have at last fled, the air is dry as the Fractured Range in Summer, and we are as high as the sugar pines dare hold us. This, my dear cub, this is the true magnitude of the Stelm Wujann's stars."

Sterjall's eyes twinkled. "It's so crisp, so colorful. It's... confusing. I can't even see most constellations, there are so many more stars visible that I can't pick any patterns out."

"They are all there, hiding among friends." He caressed Sterjall's whiskers, then added, "I had promised you once that I would teach you about all the Nu'irgesh, some of whom I've spoken about in the past. Not all their constellations are visible in this intangible moment before twilight, but there are stars to spare in their absence. I can tell you about them, with or without their starry eyes watching us from above."

"Finally. I'd love to hear about them," Sterjall said, fully awake now. "Every time I've asked you about them, you've been evasive."

"Only because I was waiting for the right moment, for the right conditions, which presented themselves this blessed night. Now, do not feel guilty if you do not remember all these names. There are many, and I've had some millennia to get to know them. I just want you to get a sense of who my friends are."

"I'm sure I'll forget most of them, and I'll ask you about them later." He pulled the cape tighter over his arms and tucked his back further into the nook between Banook's arm and chest.

Banook cleared his throat. "You well know of Safis, the proud queen of white, praised by the Southern Wutash for her dignified nobility. We have briefly spoken of Probo, the javelina, and the Puqua tribe who tolerated his pestering and followed him west toward the Stelm Nedross. I have also told you of Sovath, the chital, and of Ishke'ísuk, the double-crested basilisk, and of the sorrowful ribbon seal named Däo-Varjak."

Banook pondered for a moment, trying to recall which other Nu'irgesh they had discussed in the past. "Oh, and I told you of Muri, my temperamental honey badger friend. And of course, I spoke of Mamóru, the steppe mammoth who could take the form of a man, but I had not yet pointed to his constellation, for it was hidden last time. Tonight, you may gaze upon him, if you look over those peaks and search for an odd symmetry between the stars."

"You mean the stars that line up in two curves?"

"The same ones! Those are his tusks, extended like sinuous scimitars. Though I knew Mamóru well, I did not know the Toldask Miscam in the same fashion, as I always saw him while he traveled through my lands and not as much around his own. I think those are all the Nu'irgesh I've already spoken of."

"There's one more," Sterjall said. "Some kind of ogre, if I recall?"

"Perhaps you are referring to the handsomest of Nu'irgesh? One with twenty long knives for claws, and furs so silky that they'd put a golden orb spider's gossamer to shame. They say he could take the form of a man, one with a slightly plump body, and a lush beard as flushed and sparkling as the cherries of Strethema sprinkled with flakes of mica from the Falbagrish Range."

Sterjall caressed Banook's belly. "You are a bit more than slightly plump. And your beard is sparkly, but I think you might be exaggerating a bit."

"I would dare not speak anything but the truth. You can't appreciate all the tones of my beard, nor the shapeliness of my figure, under this dim starlight."

Banook wrapped his arm a bit tighter around Sterjall and with his other arm pointed to the stars. "Now pay attention. Up there near the core of the Galactic Belt is Skugge, the Nu'irg ust Kroowin, from the clade of avians. They are the only allgender Nu'irg. In each of the thousands of species whose form they can take, they do so under a different sex. Skugge used to spread their wings over the steep, bladed mountains of the Yenwu Peninsula. Some sort of owl is their primal form, though the species name I'm not familiar with, as there are far too many avians to remember."

"An owl? Alaia will pop her nub off when she finds out! You gotta tell her about Skugge in the morning."

"I shall do just that, cub. Now focus those amber eyes of yours toward the horizon. Right there is Fuuriseth, the leaf-nosed bat. She is fresh white as sugar-coated snow, with bright-yellow ears and nose. To be honest, she looks a bit like a fried egg. Last time I saw her, she was sharing her caves with the Bikhéne Miscam, a tribe who learned to see in the dark by clicking their tongues."

"Like Alaia does at the mines! Well, she sings, or taps onto metal objects, but sometimes she clicks her tongue."

"Quite a skillful gal she is. I'd say she'd enjoy visiting the caves of the Bikhéne, but to be quite frank, it gets too loud there with all the clicking, and the guano gets everywhere. Let's see, who is next? Hmm… Oh, yes, I can see Beiféren the bootherium, right over the snowy cap of the Anglass Dome."

"Bootherium?"

"Some called them the *helmeted muskoxen*. Big fellow, dangerous horns. He's a solitary kind who likes the mountains as much as I do. He mostly spent his time near Mount Rashúr, the mightiest peak you may ever lay your eyes upon."

Banook squinted toward a dark area of the sky, away from the core of the galaxy. "Do your wolf eyes spot that small blur over yonder?"

"You mean the Glires Nebula?"

"If you wish to call it that. It does look a bit nebulous. But it also has those four stars extending from it, the ones that sort of look like a tail."

"I've seen them with Crysta's telescope before. The nebula next to them is a gas cloud, like the one from Pellámbri, but instead of pink, it's sort of greenish in color. In pre-Downfall texts they claimed it to be the ghost of a long-dead star, though we don't know how they figured that out."

"You seem to know more about this one than old Banook! But perhaps you do not know that the tiny 'nebula' and the short tail make up a constellation of their own. It is that of the Nu'irg ust Okri, a hazel dormouse by the name of Gwit. He's a strange rodent, who likes to travel with people on their boats, live in their homes, but cares not too much for their presence. If ever there was anyone who could beat me at hibernation, that fuzzy dormouse is the one."

Banook scanned the skies. "Who are we missing? Oh, speaking of rodents—well, some of their kind look like rodents, though they aren't really—I just recalled the Nu'irg ust Quaju. He is of the clade of marsupials. Ëalcor is his name, a beautiful thylacine he is."

Sterjall did not know what a marsupial nor a thylacine were, so he expressed his confusion with a tilt of his head.

"Marsupials are like rats," Banook explained, "and like foxes, and a bit like raccoons, but also some are a tad like bears—the tree-climbing kind—and shrews, since some also live below ground. And a thylacine is exactly like that, but also like a tiger, but only in their hindquarters. They have cuts in their skins where they can hide their babies. And their testicles are upside down."

"I... Okay, sure. You lost me there."

"Ëalcor once told me his homeland is one of blue, purple, and black sands. One we read about recently, in the Barlum Saga."

"The Kingdom of Bauram? I have a friend from there, who lives in Withervale. Lerr Holfster is their name, the kindest person I've ever met."

"Other than yours truly, I presume."

"Most certainly. Wait, you said this Nu'irg told you about his lands? You can speak to marsupials?"

"No, cub, their clade is distant to mine. But all Nu'irgesh can mindspeak with one another, for we are similar in the ways that matter most."

"Is there a constellation for, what's his name, Ëalcor?"

"There is, of course, but it is below the horizon at this time. Actually, right next to him should be Estriéggo, Nu'irg ust Almel. He is a woolly rhinoceros, and though his wool-like fur can at times be soft, it is usually a matted clump more like armor than a blanket. He has told me countless times that I need to visit the stone arches of his lands, but I have not had the time to go visit."

"No time? Haven't you been alive for thousands of years?"

"Well, perhaps it's just that he's a bit grumpy, and I have made up excuses so I don't have to be near his curmudgeonly presence so often."

"So Almelsilv is the mask of rhinos?"

"And other kinds, too. Paraceratheriums, horses, tapirs. Those are some of the forms I've seen Estriéggo take in the past, all belonging to the odd-toed kind."

"What's so odd about them?"

"Odd as in *not even,* cub. One or three or five-toed."

"I have five toes too. Well, not now, but when I'm Lago, I have five. When I'm Sterjall, one of them goes away."

"A fine set of toes those are, but you are not an ungulate," Banook said, playfully tickling Sterjall's footpaws. "They have hard hooves, unlike yours, which are soft and pink like my nose when I'm a bear."

Banook looked up again and turned his head far to the right. He adjusted his posture so Sterjall could see as well.

"I spot a friend we have not spoken of, farther down the Galactic Belt. That bright cluster belongs to Pamúnn, of the bovid clade. I'm still confused as to why Beiféren is not one of them, as their horned kinds look much alike, but I will leave that discussion to proper taxonomists. Pamúnn is a beautiful nyala. A very discreet and evasive one, who can disappear in an eye blink."

"What is a nyala?"

"They are like a striped antelope, with bright-orange socks and fashionable, white dots adorning their fur. Beautiful horns Pamúnn has, spiraling softly like calcified tornadoes. He always enjoyed grazing and browsing in the thickets of Kilkarag, where the Tjardur Miscam built enormous walls to protect themselves from the endless wars of the now called Jerjan Continent. Great with forging steel the Tjardur are, masters of all kinds of alloys I could never concoct in my lowly furnace."

"You did an outstanding job with Leif's crossguard and pommel."

"It's just plain steel, cub, anyone could do that. Nothing like the Bra'uur steel of the Tjardur—their skills do not compare to my amateurish attempts at metallurgy."

Banook lifted Sterjall up with one arm and went to sit on the opposite side of the tree trunk, placing him between his legs.

"I nearly missed the ones behind us," Banook said. "The next one is the largest of all constellations. She is hard to see, as she takes up such a vast space in the sky that it is hard to describe." He gestured vaguely toward an ample portion of the heavens. "I'm a bit uncomfortable with this one, as it brings painful memories. It is the constellation of Allamónea, the great sperm whale. Thousands of years ago, I saw her die."

"Die? What happened?"

"The Nu'irg ust Amá'a was killed by whaling ships. She took down a dozen vessels while defending herself, but they got her in the end. She was dragged ashore, still alive. I saw her essence vanish in front of my very eyes." Banook sighed deeply, obviously distraught. "The cetaceans have always had it hard among our kind. They are deeply misunderstood."

"What... what happens when a Nu'irg dies?" Sterjall dared to ask.

"Eventually a new Nu'irg for that clade is born, or *appears*. None of us know how it happens, or when, for we cannot remember the beginning of our own existence. But I know there were other Nu'irgesh ust Urnaadi before me, but those tales are for another time. There is a new Nu'irg ust Amá'a now, who was born from the essence of all living cetaceans, but who is not Allamónea. I have not met them, nor do I know their primal form, but I can feel their presence as surely as they can feel mine. The new Nu'irg likely lives with the Isdinnuk Miscam in the Capricious Ocean."

"You mean in the Seafaring Dome?"

"Yes, Amá'adrolom, the very distant one."

"How does a tribe end up growing a dome in the middle of the ocean?"

"That I do not know. No bears dare swim so far south. But let us move on. Who are we missing?"

"I think... I've been keeping count. With yourself included, you've spoken of sixteen so far. There should be two more. Isn't there a Nu'irg for felines?"

"Oh! Of course! Felids, not felines, if you please. They prefer the former. And that would be Nelv, Nu'irg ust Mindrel, whose constellation is unfortunately contained inside Allamónea's, right over there. Nelv may look like a lovely spotted kitty, but take my word—do not *ever* try to pet her. You will lose more than your fingers. She is the most ferocious Nu'irg of all. Nelv has lived all over Noss, from jungles to deserts to mountains and islands. I would not wager she is happy with her sequestration, enclosed in a dome only eighty miles across."

"Which dome does she live in?"

"I'm not certain. I did not see most domes being grown, since I was focused on helping the Northern Wutash alone. I only learned of the final location of the sixteen much later, after the Downfall. Perhaps she is in the Moordusk Dome, or maybe in the Old Kingdom one you call the Nisos Dome. She could be in the Moonrise Dome for all I know."

"One more to go, then. Who's the last one?"

Banook explored the sky but could not find the last constellation. Then he looked nearly straight down, where the roots of the sugar pine would be.

"Aha! Buujik has been hiding right below us. I will show you her constellation when she pokes her colorful face out once more. Buujik, Nu'irg ust Hoombu, the painted monkey of the Sai-Salóm Forest, a forest which likely exists no more."

"You mentioned her before, the Nu'irg of primates, right? The one who could shapeshift into a woman?"

"That is her indeed. Even though her primal form is referred to as a *red-shanked douc*, her shanks are more terracotta in color. Silkier, more velvety-smooth furs and hues you will never see. She is majestic, smart, and can hop the treetops as swiftly as Skugge and Fuuriseth can cruise the air. The ones who hold Hoombusilv are the Acoapóshi, the original tribe who made the Silvesh and gifted them to the other seventeen tribes. Buujik was never very fond of them, but she still helped the tribe, in order to help Noss. Legends say that Hoombusilv was the first mask to be created, and thus it was weaker than all the others, but still held its own secrets."

"What secrets?"

"If I knew them, they would not be secrets, would they? But there you have it, cub, my sixteen friends who are, and one who is no more. Safis, Skugge, Pamúnn, Beiféren, Sovath, Allamónea, Fuuriseth, Nelv, Ëalcor, Muri, Buujik, Mamóru, Estriéggo, Ishke'ísuk, Gwit, Probo, and Däo-Varjak."

Sterjall had kept count while Banook recited. "You remembered them all!"

"Your sweet presence mended my mangled memory."

"Can you really feel all of them? Right now?"

"In a way. It's more of a gut feeling, which luckily I carry plenty of with me!" Banook laughed, smacking his bare belly. "Yet I don't feel them all equally. It is as if some of them are always more distant. Skugge, Ishke'ísuk, even Ëalcor always felt elusive to me, but they are there, somewhere in the back of my awareness. I feel a tighter connection with Muri, Safis, Nelv, and Däo-Varjak. But just because I don't feel them all as closely, it does not mean I don't love them all the same."

"They all sound lovely. I hope I get to meet each and every one of them. But I'll always have my favorite." Sterjall snuggled closer against Banook's chest. Banook unfolded the bearskin cape so that it would cover not just Sterjall, but also his own legs and parts of his bare chest. He was getting a bit cold and didn't want to admit it, preferring not to ruin the moment.

Sterjall closed his eyes, safely sheltered in Banook's cradling body, with the red-and-gold beard tickling his pointed ears. He fell asleep, thinking of the domes far away, of the mythical Nu'irgesh he could not wait to meet. His dreams sparkled of starlight.

CHAPTER SIXTY-THREE

TO THE CALDERA

Sceres had changed to Pearl, beaming white with gold and peach reflections. The last days of Mudfront were at hand—the Thawing season had begun.

The final weeks of Winter had not been particularly cold. Banook's cabin was soon clear of ice, and the white creeks around it roared with replenished vigor. The wayfarers had decided to leave for Da'áju before the month of Mudfront came to an end, and one day was all that remained.

Sabikh had come by for the past few weeks with her cub, Frud. Today she had brought a portion of a deer's ribcage for Bear, dropping it at the terrace. Sterjall had shown Bear how to open a small door they made for him, so he could take shelter inside the cabin while they were gone, while Frud had tried to show him how to climb trees, without much success. Bear was a bit confused by the whole affair, but he was at least enjoying the presence of the friendly bears. Ockam, however, had a hard time remaining at ease, despite Banook's assurances.

"Let me see those binoculars," Ockam said to Sterjall, before he packed them in his bag. He took them to the edge of the terrace to spy at the base of the Anglass Dome, hoping he'd see something that would hint at the Red Stag's next move.

"You won't be able to see them from so far away, my dear Ockam," Banook said, "but the soldiers are there, preparing for something."

Banook had taken another trip to Brimstowne the previous week, to stock up on last-moment supplies and gather as much information about the Red Stag as possible. Unfortunately, he could not find Ardof, his ranger informant, but from the locals he heard that the Red Stag had moved an entire legion to

Dormendal, the port city west of the dome, while he himself had traveled far east, leaving Anglass behind.

"It worries me," Jiara said. "If he already stole that cervid mask, why bring more people here?"

"Do you think they might be going to Da'áju as well?" Sterjall asked.

"Doubtful," Banook said. "More soldiers would be a detriment, not an advantage. If they were somehow suspicious of the ursid mask's location, they would've sent scouts, seen that the caldera is impassable, and turned back. They would not be as foolish as we are to venture in there."

"It all points to Withervale," Ockam said. "It's a strategic position that's been denied to them for centuries. But Zovaria would put up all their strength, and they have a huge advantage in the water. It doesn't entirely make sense."

"What are we going to do if they attack?" Alaia asked. "We have friends there. It's still our home."

"Events like these are too large for any one person to influence," Ockam said. "We can be certain that the Union is tracking this menace and is ready to defend the mouth to the Isdinnklad."

"I wish there was a way to know how Withervale is faring," Sterjall said. "I already abandoned Crysta and Gwil once, after I put them in danger. And Khopto, I don't even know if he survived the arrow wound. If the Empire attacks, it will be because of the mask. I can't help but feel it's my fault."

"There is a pass that looks south over the Stelm Wujann," Banook said, "with a distant view of Withervale. We'll cross it before we climb down into the glacier. With the aid of your binoculars, if the day is clear, we might be able to see the port, maybe even the mesa. They will be but mere specks on the horizon, but it might ease your worries to at least see your home from afar."

They finished packing their bags that afternoon, making sure to take the quaar ropes, shield, and helm. They had nothing else to do now, and it felt strange, as if they couldn't use the remaining hours to rejoice in the beauty around them. The air was tense, almost electric with anticipation.

Their sleep was unrestful that night. A growing preoccupation clouded their thoughts.

"It's okay, Bear, we'll be back in a few weeks," Sterjall said, letting Bear hop on his lap and lick his muzzle, the mutt whimpering all the while. "Sabikh will bring you plenty of food. And who knows, maybe you'll actually learn to hunt while we are away, and on the day we come back, you'll surprise us with the biggest elk we've ever seen!"

Bear agreed with a lick.

"All is set!" Banook said, ducking under the front doors and closing them behind him. "This will be a proper hike. Whether or not we find a path through the icy caldera, the views will be magnificent."

The day was warm. The snow had all gone by now, leaving the soil moist and filled with energy, but no new green had yet begun to sprout. Banook tied two heavy ladders to his large backpack, swung it over his shoulders, and led the way southwest.

Sterjall was keenly aware that these could be his final weeks with Banook. He walked beside him, trying to hold hands, which was difficult as their strides were of much different length, and there was no way to keep their arm swings synchronized.

They traversed the secret mountain paths that kept Banook's cabin private, weaving through a labyrinth of canyons and passages, crossing streams that seemed to lead nowhere. The following day they reached the top of Minnelvad and went a little off their trail looking for the rock Lago had been trying to climb on that mistdraft-sunken evening when he had lost his footing. They all stood on the rock together and looked down—now that the snow was gone, a fall would mean certain death.

"I'd recommend you keep your mask hidden while we are near the falls," Banook said to Sterjall.

"How come?"

"Sometimes hikers from Brimstowne come up to the top. It's not often, but now that the snow has cleared, they'll be more likely to come. You can wear your whiskers and tail again once we move out of this area."

Lago put his mask away, scanning around for signs of human tracks but finding none.

Banook pointed at a distant spot. "Over yonder, where that geyser gushed up. That's where the noxious vents are, where I found you and Bear."

"That is much farther than I imagined," Lago said. "I must've bounced and slid down that hill. I can't believe you were able to find me that far away, and in the mistdraft."

"I have good ears and an even better nose. Bear was barking loudly, and you, my sweet love, smelled like honey," Banook said with a wink.

"You two are bloody disgusting," Jiara said. "But I'm taking credit for that honey. I got stung plenty to get it."

They had never gotten a chance to appreciate the beauty of Minnelvad from above before, so they climbed to an overlook between the two fang-like peaks that framed the falls. They soaked in hot pools with outstanding vistas, and from there they could spot some of the cairns they'd once followed and the cauldron at the bottom of the falls, but not the creek itself that turned into the falls, for that stream grew within the mountain, ejecting sideways from the vertical cliff.

For nearly a fortnight they traversed a glacial valley where giant boulders had been left abandoned by long-gone ice. During their times of rest, with Jiara's help, Sterjall learned to measure the reach Leif granted him to see the threads of life, hoping his extended sight would help him more clearly find a path into the icy caldera. After many a test involving a compass and long ropes to measure distance, Jiara estimated that Sterjall could see the threads up to half a mile away when assisted by the blade. Without Leif, the wolf could see at most three hundred feet in front of him if focusing his sight as a narrow cone, or forty feet when focusing it around him like a sphere.

A dense growth of conifers and deciduous trees embellished their trail. Pinecones littered their pathway, and many streams cascaded down to further erode hillsides and feed a lush river that ran loudly through the valley's core. Countless lakes formed in these hallowed mountain halls, offering great fishing and attracting plentiful bears.

"Bear species used to spread widely over most of Noss," Banook said as he scratched the ears of a sun bear who had briefly joined them. "To survive the Downfall, they had to adapt to a new diet, learn to live together, and find ways to share. Some species, like the cave bears of old, were too proud to follow, to change, thinking they'd be safe in their caves. They died by fire or starvation. Others were unable to handle the diet of these mountains or the cold decades that followed the fires."

The days turned slowly, until one late afternoon they arrived at a cross-roads. One path led north, toward the caldera, and another went south. The view of the caldera from here was spectacular, describing a massive bowl of white spiderwebbed by bright-blue crevasses. Near the center of the caldera, a cloud of steam billowed, occluding the far reaches of the glacial horizon.

It was a warm day, so they were surprised when they got hit by a sudden gust of icy wind.

"The caldera is always cold," Banook explained, "even in Summer. The northwestern winds always blow coldest, passing through the Klad Mahujann to then settle their frigid fingers in these mountains. That frozen lake is quite a mystery."

"What's so mysterious about it?" Alaia asked.

"Lakes that far south should thaw in Summer, yet the Downfall seems to have stirred something in Mahujann's belly, for it's been crystallized ever since.

When snow blows from it, it blows colder than it should, then piles up at the Da'áju Caldera, hence why the caldera too remains unnaturally cold."

"The Khaar Du believe it's something to do with impish snow sprites who live in the nearby craters," Ockam said. "Although I once heard an artificer say that perhaps the lake has a high content of an unknown aetheric element, one yet to be studied or understood."

"Sprites, aetheric elements, or not," Banook said, "your Winter clothes will be very needed."

Ockam studied the view of the caldera, then said, "We should make use of this elevated viewpoint to plan our path."

"And there's more we need to do," Banook added. "There won't be any food once we enter the ice, so we need to stock up all we can and drop off anything unnecessary. We'll hunt tomorrow."

"Is this southern trail the one that leads to Withervale?" Sterjall asked.

"Yes, although it is not much of a trail. There's a good view of the Isdinn-klad over that crest and a nook among rocks right at the saddle. It will make for good shelter for tonight."

They followed the last rays of sunlight up the southern pass until they reached the rocky saddle. From up so high, they could clearly see the valley of the Isdinnklad. Withervale was nearly straight south, but far too distant to be spotted by unaided eyes.

Sterjall took out his binoculars. "It's so far away," he said, aiming the glass at the base of the gray-streaked Stelm Ca'éli. "I can't make out anything." He sharpened his focus toward the river. "But I do see something in the water. I think those are ships, pink sails. They are too small to see any detail, but I'm guessing that's about where the naval base would be."

Jiara took the binoculars from him. "That must be a very large fleet to be visible from this far away. Pink sails are Zovarian Navy, a good sign at least. It makes me both nervous and relieved—it means they are aware of a threat, but also confirms that there's danger ahead."

They gazed into the distance until Sunnokh dipped behind the mountains.

"Let's rest," Jiara said, dropping her backpack, "and tomorrow we prepare for the ice."

They hunted and foraged, gathering as much food as possible. The center of the caldera wasn't exceedingly far away, but there was no straight route to their destination, or even a clear way in. Banook estimated it could take about a week to journey in and another week out.

From a high vantage point, Ockam stood on a large flat rock and drew a map with a stick of charcoal, noting the obvious cracks on the shattered glacier. Banook did his best to pinpoint where Da'áju was located: somewhere near the center of the caldera, but a bit closer to the south end.

"Banook, do you know how deep the ice is?" Jiara asked.

"That would depend on the terrain below it. The temple was located on a hill, perhaps a thousand feet higher than the city that surrounded it. With that in mind, knowing there's no hill poking out from the caldera, the ice would be at least a thousand feet thick in some areas. Ommo ust Urnaadi could rest a fingerbreadth below the surface, or much, much deeper. There is no telling."

Banook scribbled a few guesses on the map. "The temple was built around a hot creek named Fressálv," he said, "which was fed by several small streams, all sprouting from the top of the hill. The creek ran northeast from there, to become one of the main tributaries of the Stiss Khull. That barrier of steam you see here"—he drew a line on the map—"might be the creek cutting its way through the ice, by means of vents and boiling waters." He pointed to the corresponding spot in the landscape, where a wall of steam rose as white upon white.

Once the map was finished and a tentative road planned, Ockam copied the drawing into his notebook, adding notes on distances as well as estimated days of travel.

They were ready. In the morning, they would venture into the Da'áju Caldera.

"I'd never seen a cuter thing in my life!" Lago said to Banook, as he unrolled their shared bedroll. The others had already laid down, dozing off around the dying campfire.

A bit earlier that day, Banook had pointed out a black bear mother and her cubs. The cubs were just weeks old and made of pure, adorable fluff. The mother bear had let them pet her cubs, but then grown tired of their curiosity, their oddly high-pitched voices, and of Alaia's overpowering motherly instincts, so she had decided it was best to take her offspring back to the safety of her den.

"When we come back from Da'áju, I'm grabbing a dozen of them and taking them home," Alaia said, tucking herself under her blanket.

"It is rare to see them this far south," Banook observed. "Bears don't tend to venture on the southernmost mountains." He threw the last logs into the fire and sat down. Lago nestled between Banook's legs and leaned back onto his belly, looking up at the stars.

"Seeing those cubs made me curious," Lago whispered, not wanting to bother his sleepy friends. "What would happen if someone got pregnant while in a half-form? Or got someone else pregnant? Not that you and I need to worry about that, but, you know."

"It is a great taboo among the Miscam," Banook said in a serious, hushed tone. "They consider it a terrible disrespect to make love while in their half-forms. What we've been doing is perhaps a mixture of nearly every taboo you could concoct, except perhaps—as you observantly pointed out—that I do not think we'll bear any children, try as we might. But do not fret, I believe those rules might've been there for a reason, but it doesn't mean they are entirely rational and apply equally to all situations. The Wutash are gone, and you and I are not Wutash nor Miscam—we must use our minds to figure out what is right or wrong instead of holding on to antiquated rules."

Banook played with Lago's curly hair as he continued talking. "What you described, conceiving a child while in a half-form, is something I have heard about once before, but I'm sure it must've happened more times than one. The case I'm familiar with is that of one of the wielders of Trommosilv, named Bum-Vaor, who would take the half-form of an aurochs, a primordial kind of bull. I never met Bum-Vaor, but his story was told to me by the Nu'irg ust Trommo. Do you remember his name?"

"Pamúnn is the Nu'irg of bovids, his primal form is a nyala," Lago recited.

"That is correct," Banook said. "Pamúnn said that Bum-Vaor's wife, Walu, got pregnant while Bum-Vaor was in his half-form, and they had a baby who was born with a tufted tail. I never learned their son's name, Pamúnn didn't even know if they ever named him.

"To avoid being executed by their own tribe, or by the Acoapóshi if they ever found out, Walu decided to keep their newborn a secret. She pretended the baby had died at birth, then ran away with him to never return. Bum-Vaor remarried and had another child, fully human, but I do not know what happened to the aurochs child and his mother—they were lost in myth and time."

"That's very unfair, especially for the kid. It wasn't his fault."

"Yet it was a merciful outcome compared to what could've been. Deep-rooted beliefs will make people act in ways counter to their own hearts. Not everyone is that way, but most humans quickly become afraid of that which they do not understand. They find it simpler to categorize things as right or wrong, black or white, and will clutch onto their narrow preconceptions to their graves. I believe that is why most Silvfröash seem to be open-minded, because the Silvesh are bridges into understanding other points of view, and that helps them find common ground and understand others, even when faced with great differences."

"I see what you mean. I don't only feel like I understand other people better, but also understand how other species feel. Particularly canids, of course, but other clades to a lesser degree. With Bear I always had that connection, because we grew up together, but when it comes to other animals, I really had a lot to learn. I think that without the mask, I would never have become the person I am today."

Lago pondered for a moment, making his head comfortable on Banook's belly. "Do you think the Jabrak-Tsing have anything to do with Trommosilv?" he asked.

"You mean the tailed race from down south?"

"Yeah... I wonder... Maybe Bum-Vaor's half-aurochs child made it, then had kids of his own, and all the Jabrak are his descendants."

"I would call him quarter-aurochs, not half, as he was a mixture of a half-form and a human form. But perhaps the Jabrak are a product of Trommosilv, or maybe Rilgsilv, or Almelsilv, or Nagrasilv, as their clades too have species with tufted tails."

"Maybe," Lago said, suddenly remembering how the tail of the dark man at the Yeast Cauldron had felt in his hands. He was getting sleepy, and his thoughts began to drift into increasingly unrelated tangents. "I wonder how Bear is doing," he said. "I miss him already."

"He's likely prancing in meadows with the company of his new friends. Worry not for him, you will see him again soon."

"How long do you think it'll be?" Lago said, quietly. "Before you and I see each other again?"

"I do not wish you to dwell on those thoughts. It is not something we can foresee. But whether you return in a few months, a few years, or a few decades, it will make no difference in how much love I hold for you, nor how much I will rejoice when I see you."

"It hurts me to know you'll be left alone."

"I am never alone in the mountains, my cub, I am by myself. There is a difference."

"But still... It's something we haven't discussed... But like you said before, you have your needs, and—" Lago felt uncomfortable saying it, but he had to get it out. "I want you to know I'll be okay if you go to Brimstowne and find other people when I'm not around. Or bears, as weird as that sounds. I'm not the jealous type. What we have is something else entirely, sex is just one part of it. I don't see why a pleasure like that should be kept locked up and forbidden, just as I would not forbid you to read books while I'm gone, or to watch the stars at night."

"I will be in no hurry, but I appreciate your thoughtfulness," Banook said. "And I would offer the same to you, as you are young and have a lot to discover about yourself. Be free, lust, and crave. Find whatever kindles your desire, but you must do so under one non-negotiable condition."

"Um, sure... What condition?"

"That when you come back, you must tell me about your experiences, of all I have been missing, and teach me all that you've learned." Banook leaned in and with a warm breath whispered very close to Lago's ear, "All aspects of pleasure are there to be explored, and shared."

"There's a lot I haven't tried," Lago nervously said.

"There's a lot *we* haven't tried," Banook added, pulling him closer.

Lago felt the pulse between the big man's legs, then felt his own crotch warming up. "I thought we were going to sleep."

"The night is young and so are we," he replied, with his hand caressing the young man's crotch. Lago shivered with pleasurable goosebumps. Banook picked him up in his thick arms and walked away with him, in search of a private nook beneath the stars.

CHAPTER SIXTY-FOUR

KROSTSILV

A megaloceros finished pushing a heavy wagon down a long pipe through which his wide antlers could barely fit. Once the wagon reached the end of the tunnel, with nothing more than a stare, the Red Stag commanded the colossus to bring forth yet another piece of cargo. The giant elk obeyed, having to walk backward the entire way, unable to turn around in the tight space.

"Move, move!" Fjorna Daro commanded a group of thick-backed workers, who hurried to the wagon to pick up three hefty pipe segments, then struggled to align them at the end of the partially built tunnel. "Faster!" she said. "The second pipe needs to be finished before sunset, or I'll scorch you all myself at the pyre tonight."

"Cut them some slack, Chief Daro," said General Behler Broadleaf, commander of the Fifth Legion. "My troops won't be ready to move in for a day or two." With the lamp he held up by his face, the rawness of his snub nose looked gruesome. Behler stepped away from Fjorna and the workers, approaching the Red Stag. "You look tired," he said to his monarch.

"And you look like a fucking rat just chewed your nose off," the Red Stag replied, waving away the bright light the general carried. "Let me focus, Behler, I wish to finish this today. Go bother someone else." He held his position impatiently, standing at the center of what seemed like a cathedral of vines.

They were deep within the Lequa Dome's walls. Not long ago, the Red Stag had arrived at this eastern frontier of his empire to pursue a strategy devised by Viceroy Urcai. Given that Urgsilv only opened the vines wide enough to allow at most a hundred soldiers to march in at a time, Urcai had recommended they build a more permanent tunnel, so that Monarch Hallow would not need to be present every time his troops marched in or out. Urcai requested that pipe segments from the Shaderift aqueduct be brought to the Lequa Dome's perimeter, where the Red Stag would set the vines to part a bit at a time, watch as the triple-split pipe segments were assembled in the newly opened space, and then let the vines collapse over them, tightening the segments into place without even the need of cementing them together. He would then move in a bit deeper to wait for the next segments of pipe to be brought in and assembled, then continue until the dome was breached.

It had been an arduous process, but over the course of merely a few days, the Red Stag had been able to lay down tunnels for traffic in or out of the dome, both large enough that even his megaloceroses could fit, as long as the colossi lowered their heads and turned their massive antlers sideways while they marched. Two days, instead of the years it had taken to dig the tunnels at Anglass and Heartpine.

"Thank Yza's Shade, that is the last of them," the Red Stag said, once the final pipe segments were secured. Inside the Lequa Dome waited not a Negian battalion, but only Fjorna Daro's small arbalister squad, who were there to make sure none of the locals became aware of their operation. "Any sign of them yet?" the Red Stag asked Crescu Valaran, second-in-command of Chief Daro's squad.

"As with the other tribes, all their cities are located away from the walls, Lorr," Crescu replied. "None have noticed us yet."

"Good. What of their creatures?"

"We spotted only one kind of giant so far, a big badger of some sort."

"Jarv wolverines," Aurélien Knivlar offered. She was the squad's shaman, knowledgeable about not only the different species of Noss but also about the beliefs and history of the ancient Miscam tribes. "An extinct musteloid species. Or thought to be extinct. The Miscam bred them big as grizzly bears, and though they seem tame, I doubt they will remain that way for long."

"Very well," the Red Stag said. "As long as we can secure the mask before those creatures attack, we should have no problem whatsoever."

But the Red Stag's plans were foiled, for the Jojek Miscam tribe had been spying on the army assembling by their walls. To remain undetected, their shamans had sent forth myna birds to perch near the pipes, to overhear and memorize the sounds their mouths spouted and later report back to the tribe. The shamans had listened to the strange words the mynas carried back, translated them to Miscamish, and at once understood the danger their dome was in. They were forced to plan an ambush of their own.

The warriors of the intrepid tribe wore no armor, but instead were dressed in leaves that rendered them invisible in the lush vegetation. They waited in hiding behind the swaying grasses of meadows, over the wide fronds of the jungle, and among the stiff reeds of marshes, then attacked once night fell.

"Form a perimeter around the pipes!" General Behler Broadleaf commanded. The Negians knew there would no longer be a way to lure the Jojek chief out to steal her mask, not as they had done with the chief at Anglass. Now their priority was to protect the pipes while the entirety of Behler's Fifth Legion stormed in.

Behler's soldiers advanced to make room for more battalions, but the frontlines were quickly taken down by the vicious jarv wolverines, who stalked throughout the forests and pounced with open maws at the invaders. The wolverines were frightening foes yet did not compare to the threat lurking near the rivers: megalenhydris otters prowled the shores, nearly twice the size of the wolverines, and with fangs like daggers. With a swipe of their tails alone they could take down a dozen soldiers before disappearing back into the waters.

To help clear the way for Behler's forces, the Red Stag sent forth his cervids, asking them to trample anything they found in the tall grasses.

The battle raged for nearly two weeks.

The Negians had moved in closer to the mountain at the center of the dome, from where the mile-wide trunk grew, and where the Jojek capital of Dïer was located.

"We believe their leader is close," Fjorna Daro said to the Red Stag, from within the safe perimeter of their new garrison. "The large animals seem to be acting of their own volition, but those small ones who attacked today are most certainly mindlocked. We could use them to track the heathen who holds the mask."

In an act of desperation, the Jojek Miscam had resorted to mindlocking their smaller species. Weasels, skunks, raccoons, and all kinds of musteloids were sent to distract the Negian soldiers while the hidden Jojek warriors pounced on them. The strategy was working, but it also highlighted the waning power of the defending army. The Jojek had even sent the very Nu'irg ust Krost into battle, although he had gone willingly.

"He escaped," Fjorna reported to her monarch. "The Nu'irg could not be held by our nets. He took a small weasel form and wriggled out the holes. But we wounded him severely. He must be fleeing back to their leader."

"Good," the Red Stag said. "Can you track him down?"

"Aurélien is on it. I'm waiting for her heralds to report back. The leader doesn't seem to be at the capital but hiding in the mountains beyond it. If you gift us with a distraction large enough, we could sneak deeper in."

The Red Stag nodded his sixteen-pointed rack.

Under the cover of night, the Red Stag sent out Sovath, Nu'irg ust Urg, to demolish a nearby village, with Behler's troops rushing behind her. At the same time, Fjorna and her arbalisters dressed themselves as the Jojek, and while clad in nothing but leaves, tracked the direction from where the mindlocked critters were being sent.

"There is the witch," Aurélien whispered while crouching behind a jagged rock. She handed the spyglass to Fjorna. "Up on those trees."

After several days of tracking, Fjorna, Crescu, and Aurélien alone had infiltrated the forests near the Jojek capital and spotted the silhouette of the Jojek chief hiding in a tall tree. Her name was Krobbar when in her ferret half-form, or Faóla when not, but none of the arbalisters had cared to learn the name of the woman—they simply wanted her dead.

Krobbar was far beyond the reach of their bows and crossbows. She was calling up a long line of critters, then sending them into battle. Among those animals was Muri, the musteloid Nu'irg.

"There's that fucker again," Aurélien said, watching the Nu'irg limp his way to the Jojek chief as a jarv wolverine, then stop in front of the tree. A group of Jojek shamans approached him, removed the arrows from his body, then chanted prayers as they circled him, with all the other animals circling about as well. Muri took deep breaths, then shapeshifted into his primal form of a honey badger and rushed away again. Aurélien watched him go and said, "Should we try to—"

"No," Fjorna said. "Let him go. We cannot hope to defeat him, but we could capture him later, once the mask is under our control. Crescu, cover my back. Aurélien, find your way to those rocks and take down the two sentinels. I'll push closer."

Fjorna ventured into the forest, moving as invisibly as a breeze. She got within range and loaded a bolt into Whisper, her precious crossbow. She heard a bird-like whistle—Aurélien's signal that the threats had been dispatched—and aimed up toward Krobbar. She immediately felt the eyes of the ferret on her, knowing she'd been spotted. Fjorna released the bolt in a metallic *clang!* and watched it fly toward the Jojek chief. The bolt cut through the air, then slashed through the ferret's throat, slamming hard into her spine. The ferret did not even have a chance to scream.

Fjorna hurried toward the falling body, stabbing three of the nearby, stupefied shamans as she ran. By the time the body reached the ground, it was no longer Krobbar, but Faóla who lay there dead-eyed, with a dark, almost canidlike mask resting near her face.

Chief Arbalister Fjorna Daro knelt as she presented Krostsilv, the mask of musteloids, to her monarch.

The Red Stag took it and inspected it carefully, scratching off a streak of dried blood from the sharp muzzle. "It seems you have won us more than a mask," he said. "You won us the entire battle."

"How so, Monarch Hallow?" Chief Daro asked, standing at attention. "We've been too busy keeping undercover, and just arrived without knowledge of how the battle is faring."

"We all felt the very moment the leaf-crotched chief died to your bolt. All her mindlocked critters simply scattered away, and the heathens hiding in the grasses became frightened and fled. They all seem to know what happened. They are leaderless now, hopeless. We've been capturing hundreds of them, and few are fighting back."

That evening, the Red Stag ordered General Behler Broadleaf to march with the full force of the Fifth Legion to clear the dome of all the Jojek Miscam warriors who had not given up their weapons. He also asked Behler to capture the musteloid Nu'irg, but Muri had vanished without a trace.

The Red Stag would not stay to see the end of the battle, for he was to take Krostsilv west. Once he returned to the fortress of Anglass, he asked General Jaxon Remon—his right-hand man, as he liked to call him—to meet him at the Fogdale Citadel.

"Learn to wield it, and quickly," he said to General Remon, handing him the mask. "You must learn to command your own kind as soon as you find your form, Jaxon."

"I'm not complaining," the general said, admiring the black complexity of Krostsilv, "but what will I do with a bunch of weasels?"

"There's more than just weasels," the Red Stag said, putting a hand on Jaxon's pauldron. "Come with me and you'll see." He led Jaxon to a balcony, then pointed down to a row of enormous cages by the stables. "Although we could not find that Nu'irg, Behler captured a few presents for you."

CHAPTER SIXTY-FIVE

THE ENDLESS GLACIER

"Alaia, help me set up the ropes," Jiara said, examining an overhang of rock that extended over the ice. It had proven difficult to find a suitable place to cross into the glacier, given that its periphery had melted from contacting the warmer rocks, carving out drops wider than their two ladders tied together.

Ockam went down first. The ice below him looked pitted and rusty, covered with holes from dark rocks that had fallen from above, captured more sunlight, and melted their way through. He could look straight down a crack from there, which started in muddy grays, then changed into deep blues, and sunk in a pitch black.

It was their first test, and it went mostly well. Their harnesses held, as they knew they would after months of putting them to the test. Alaia banged her head on the overhang once, but the quaar helm protected her and her nub. Banook went last. He slid down a bit too fast, falling hard on the ice and making them fearful of causing a new crack, but the ice took the hit without too much complaint.

Once they all made it down, Jiara pulled on the retrieval rope, which was set up to untie and drop all the ropes at once. Lago kept his mask stowed away, needing his human feet so he could use his boots and crampons. They began their walk over the sheet of ice, leaving the comfort of the rocks behind.

They followed Ockam's directions northward for a handful of miles. This was a flat and easy area to traverse, yet there were still dangers, particularly the abundant meltvoids—circular shafts where melting ice had carved deep, vertical holes. Just a month ago, many of these pits would have been hidden by the snowpack, becoming invisible traps for anyone unknowingly walking over them.

"What are you doing?" Alaia asked Ockam, seeing him stop and lower his backpack.

"This thing is getting heavy on my shoulders," he said. He placed the quaar shield on the ground, detached one end of the strap from it, lowered his backpack onto the shield, then attached the strap to his belt. He continued on, pulling his load like a sled.

"Someone's getting lazy," Lago said.

"I didn't bring my whip, or I'd make you pull it for me, wolf boy."

After many hours trudging over flat ground, they reached their first real crack. It was a larger gap than they had expected, cutting a chasm fifty feet wide. Its depth they could only guess at, as it was nearing sunset; without Sunnokh shining straight down, they were unable to see too far in. They walked around the impediment, following the crevasse for a few miles to where the two blocks of ice wedged themselves into one, their pressure lifting towers of serrated ice.

Jiara looked up at the icy pinnacles. "Those seracs could come down at any moment. It's better to cross here, over the crevasse, than to try to climb even a few feet on those unsteady death traps."

They tied up the ladders with a quaar rope; their combined length was just enough to bridge the gap. They used the other rope as a lifeline, making Banook keep a hold of one end, as there was no way for any of the others to drag him down with their puny bodies if they fell.

Banook was the last to cross. Lago was terrified and could barely watch, but Banook had constructed the ladders with the finest woods, and crossed the gap with no hint of hesitation, balancing with the grace of a cat.

As the caldera fell under the shadows of the western Stelm Wujann, a frigid air began to blow from the northwest. They camped by the seracs that Jiara deemed the most structurally sound, taking shelter from the menacing winds.

It was a painfully cold night. They could not carry weighty bundles of firewood for this part of the trip. All they had was enough kindling to boil water for hot drinks and small meals. They used the quaar shield as a firepit so that their fire would not melt the ice and cooked a meager dinner. For warmth, they bundled up in layers and snuggled close to one another. Banook became their main source of heat: he slept on his side, with Lago cuddled at his chest and the others leaning on his back and legs.

By the time they woke up, they were covered in a layer of crunchy, grayish snow. Ockam got up first, lifting the solidified wool blanket they had been using and shaking off the shards of ice that had formed over it.

"Snowing? Isn't it Cloudpour already?" Alaia asked, shaking the snow off her cloak.

"Just a ground blizzard," Ockam answered, "carried from the mountains by the high winds, not snow fallen from clouds."

"It looks filthy," Alaia said.

"Must be mixed with ashes from Laaja Khem," Jiara said. "It's a volcano past the far northwest of the caldera, where we saw that dark cloud on the horizon yesterday."

Lago crawled out of the cave Banook had made for him between his beard, chest, and arms. His neck ached, and his back felt like his vertebrae had fused together. A draft of cold air had bothered him all night, no matter how he contorted his body. He stared at Banook, who was still sleeping while wearing a satisfied smile.

"It's like he's hibernating," Lago said. "I wish I could sleep that soundly. I should've gone to bed as Sterjall, but I didn't expect it to get so damn cold. I just passed out."

Banook perked up once he smelled the coffee they were brewing. His beard and hair sparkled like a chandelier. He shook the crystals off, releasing a flurry of snowflakes into the crisp morning sunlight. They had a light breakfast, saving as much of their scarce provisions as possible, then carried on traversing the endless white.

"Have you given thought as to what to do with Urnaadisilv, if it is to be found at Da'áju?" Banook asked as they walked.

Lago looked at Alaia and said, "I've been telling Alaia that she should try it on."

"Khest no," she snapped. "I've been terrified of them since I had to rip Agnargsilv off your face that time in Withervale. Besides, I'm happy with who I am."

"A great responsibility being a Silvfröa is, and one that must not be taken lightly," Banook said. "If we do find Urnaadisilv, to whoever wields it, I want you to carefully consider the power it can hold. There is one aspect of the Silvesh I have not yet told you about, perhaps because I was being too wary, perhaps scared." He slowed his pace down.

Lago slowed next to him. "What is it?" he asked, feeling unsettled by Banook having kept things from them.

"When I helped the Wutash, I did so willingly, and so did my bears. But the masks, in the wrong hands, can be used for coercion, even a form of enslavement. They have the power to mindlock those creatures of their own clades in a most devious, heart-wrenching way."

"Mindlock? What do you mean?" Lago asked.

"A mindlocked animal is trapped within their own mind, unable to do anything but obey the commands of the Silvfröa controlling them, all while still being conscious of their atrocious actions. It is what happened to my friend Däo-Varjak, when long ago a mad prince took Gwonlesilv—the mask of pinnipeds—under his command. He sent Däo-Varjak with her seals, sea lions, and walruses to tear apart his enemy's fleet, then to murder all within their island cities. In the wrong hands, any of the Silvesh can be as dangerous as an entire army."

"Let's hope the Red Stench never learns about such powers," Jiara said. "Imagine what an army of cervids could do."

"I'd rather not imagine such things," Banook said.

"Wait..." Ockam said. "If one of those masks is the mask of primates, wouldn't that mean it could control any allgenders, men, and women it crossed paths with?"

"Luckily, not so, my dear Ockam," Banook said. "That would be the mask held by the Acoapóshi, the original Miscam tribe. Hoombusilv was the first mask to be created and was known to not be able to mindlock at all. The weakest of all masks, all legends claimed. But the others... the others could be far more frightening, including Agnargsilv and Urnaadisilv."

"I want that thing even less now," Alaia said. "You can all take turns with it, as far as I care."

"I would like to learn to wield it," Jiara said, "then show my sister something she can't do, for once." She sighed. "But I feel it should be Ockam who does. He's a Wutash at heart. And Bonmei would've been proud to see his kaadi hold the honor."

Ockam contemplated the white passing beneath his heavy boots. "I am as terrified of it as Alaia is," he admitted, "but it's pointless to debate it. I don't want to live under false pretenses again, I've been disillusioned too many a time. We'll figure it out *if* we find it."

Every day their legs grew more tired, until the wayfarers began to stagger. By the fourth day of their walk, the vents were near enough to spot through the binoculars, but the cracks they hissed through ran for many miles. Figuring out which steaming crevasse was the right one to venture into first seemed impossible. They decided to approach the closest one.

"Be careful," Jiara said, "the steam will be freezing at the edges, making it extremely slippery."

Lago approached the edge, and after stomping around a few times, said, "It's okay, the crampons are digging in." Once the wind shifted and shoved the steam away from him, Lago leaned his head over the edge of the crevasse, holding on to a safety rope. "I can only see twenty feet down, then it's a river of steam."

Jiara stepped next to him. "This would be like climbing down blind. And we don't even know where it leads, if anywhere."

"Hold on," Lago said, pulling the mask out from his bag. With Agnargsilv on his face, he peered down.

"Anything?" Jiara asked.

"Nothing alive, at least not close enough for it to matter."

They moved away from the crevasse and sat on the ice. It crackled lightly beneath them, like a coat of solidified grains of sugar. Ockam pulled out his map and jotted down a few notes.

"I think we are about here," he said, pointing with his pencil, "and Da'áju could be anywhere within this—"

A loud *crack!* snapped near them, followed by a metallic *twang* and an eerily high-pitched, bouncing echo. The sound took a long while to dissipate.

"It's just ice cracking," Jiara said. "It wasn't where we are standing, we would've felt it."

"Anyway," Ockam continued, "we need to find the hill the temple is on, otherwise the climb down will be too deep for us. We should move on that way"—he pointed northwest—"and see if there's any hint of ground at the bottom of those crevasses."

They kept track of the locations they visited on a new map Ockam was drafting. Most of the cracks seemed to drop into a bottomless black. Other cracks ended in a light-gray curtain of steam that swayed like water at the bottom, and yet others were steaming so hard that there was no way to even get close to the fog-drenched edges.

Lago had been trying to find life with his mask, but his perception of the threads was not as sharp when in his human form. He tried with Leif's extended sight, and could detect something vague at long distances, perhaps bacterial mats, but there was no way for him to measure his findings, given that his second vision followed no rules of perspective, parallax, or anything to provide him enough clues.

"I think the hill must be somewhere around here," Ockam said, pointing at his updated map and then gesturing toward the landscape in front of them. "It's the only place where Lago has been able to see any threads, but it's still an area several miles wide."

"I can search one block of ice at a time, until we cover the area on your map," Lago said. He put the mask on again, then untied his boots and loosened the drawstrings around his collar.

"What do you think you are doing?" Jiara asked.

"I can't see well enough as a human. As Sterjall, I'll be able to pick up the threads better."

"You can't go around without your crampons, it's too slippery around the edges."

"Don't worry," he said, shifting into Sterjall. "I don't need to go near the cracks, I'll do it from the middle of the ice fields. Urnaadisilv could be anywhere, and Leif can see very far. Just follow me."

"Just don't do anything stupid," Alaia said, picking up Sterjall's boots.

They followed behind the wolf while he did his best to comb the vast area. He walked slowly, aiming his dagger at odd angles, dowsing for tenuous tendrils of life.

"I can feel the hill, somewhat," he said, miming a round shape with his left handpaw while his right one held Leif at a downward angle. "It's a dim image, right below us. It started about fifty feet back, and now it seems to be getting closer, higher. It's hard to comprehend. With Leif it is like looking through a straw. I'm focusing on only a tiny piece at a time, and I have to assemble the puzzle in my mind, recalling all the previous pieces."

The ground was slippery, but Sterjall was able to dig his claws down for traction. When it came time to cross crevasses to explore other ice sheets, he would take the mask off, put his boots back on, and cross safely before returning to his wolf half-form.

They tried tossing chunks of ice down the crevasses to listen to their impacts, as a way to guess the height of the drops. In some spots they never heard a sound, while in others they heard a splashing at the bottom. Ockam took notes.

"Hey, are you alright?" Alaia asked Banook.

He had a strange look on his face. His usual wide smile had drooped, and his skin looked discolored.

Sterjall turned around and walked back to his lover. "What is it?" He noticed Banook's worn appearance and felt guilty for not having spotted it earlier, having been too focused on reading the threads.

"I'll be alright, cub. I've simply strayed a bit too far from my bears, that's all. They are all around us in the mountains, but none for dozens of miles within this icy caldera."

"Can you go farther?" Jiara asked him. "We still have more ground to cover."

"I can. It's not a pleasant feeling, but I can handle this and some more. I will let you know if it becomes too much to bear for this old bear."

Sterjall held Banook's hand.

Banook's smile returned, lighting up his face for a brief moment. "Now hurry," he said, "find us that temple, cub, worry not about me."

It was getting windy, a portent of the approaching dusk. Sterjall continued steadily with his search, right arm extended, senstregalv and bone blade aimed slightly down. He halted, then turned around, eyes closed and brow whiskers down.

"Have you been walking around with your eyes closed?" Jiara admonished him.

"Shhh. It's okay, I can focus better this way. I felt something, but only for a moment. Hold on." He scanned around, tracing a path left and right, shifting the dagger's height ever-so-slightly each time, aiming to comb the entirety of his field of view.

"There! I see it! A golden glow!" he exulted, pointing his dagger toward one of the steaming cracks. He then seemed to doubt himself. "Shit. I lost it." He began his careful scan once more. He focused and seemed to be almost listening to the threads in one direction, subtly cocking his head. "There it is again, that's it! It must be really far, at the edge of Leif's reach."

He sheathed his blade and hurried toward the vents. "This way! Follow me!"

"Don't go so fast!" Jiara warned him. "Hold up!"

But it was too late. Sterjall was still hundreds of feet from the nearest crevasse, but the steam had melted and refrozen that entire surface, making it frictionless and giving it a slight downhill slope. He began to drift toward the crack. He dropped to his knees and used all his claws to try to hold himself in place, but he kept sliding, pulled faster by the weight of his bag.

Banook dropped his gear, grabbed one of the ropes, and ran toward Sterjall, his crampons digging hard into the ice, causing tremors with every stomping step.

Crack! The entire sheet of ice vibrated, then seemed to tilt slightly, throwing Banook off balance. He pulled himself up and rushed forward once more, while Sterjall slid closer and closer to the edge.

"Banook! I can't stop!" Sterjall cried, digging his claws so hard into the ice that they left a trail of blood on the perfectly smooth surface.

Banook hastened, then fell to his knees and began to slide as well.

The slope became steeper, making Sterjall gain speed. He could feel the heat from the steam behind him. He tried to pull one of his ice axes from his bag, but as he fumbled with the straps, he reached the edge of the chasm.

"Hold on, cub!" Banook yelled. He found a strong footing to dig his heels into and tossed an end of the rope blindly into the mist.

Sterjall saw the rope through the vapors: a twirling spiral of gray and black in a perfectly white universe. The rope uncurled itself like a snake, reaching toward him as he reached back. He clutched with his handpaws tightly but held only mist. He fell into the palpable whiteness, seeing hundreds of years of time compressed into glacial ice flash by his sides, until the white turned blue, then gray, and he was swallowed into a black void.

"Lago!" Alaia cried. She and Ockam rushed toward the crevasse and also felt their feet slide. Jiara pulled them to the ground and slammed her ice axe down before they suffered the same fate as Sterjall. Alaia stared and saw only steam billowing out from a crack and a giant silhouette standing near the edge.

Banook pulled the weightless rope back, tears welling in his eyes. "I won't let you down, cub. I won't let you go like this."

He hurled the rope toward the others, removed his boots, and said, "Find another way in. I will go after him."

Quietly weeping, Banook took off his clothes.

"Wait, Banook, let's find a way down together," Ockam screamed.

"I will meet you at the bottom," Banook said, then dropped onto his hands and knees, already shapeshifting into the golden bear.

With a despondent grunt, Banook entered the steam by sliding backward toward the chasm, digging his claws into the ice. As his body dropped past the edge, he reached over to the opposite side, spreading his limbs across both walls to slide down with his knife-like claws digging between the compressing walls. He scratched his way down, carving twenty white trails, sinking into the steam until the darkness took him. The crack widened at the bottom, to the point where Banook could no longer spread his limbs far enough to reach both sides. His claws broke through the last bit of ice. He fell in a tumble.

Splash!

The golden bear gasped, pushing his head out of the icy water. He tried to swim and found footing when he stood on two paws.

Grrrwooarrw! Rroarrggg! he howled into the void. All he could see was the dim blur of the crack above him, like a dark-gray lightning bolt stuck in the sky. He shifted back to his human form, but he was naked, and the icy water quickly vacuumed away his body heat.

"Lago! Cub! Where are you?!" he screamed while wading, searching with his arms. "Sterjall!" The only response was a hollow echo.

His arms touched something: Sterjall's bag. He wrapped the strap around his shoulder and searched on. His fingers found wet fur, a muzzle, a floating body. "I'm here, cub, I'm here. Stay with me."

He grabbed the limp body and slogged through the cold water until he found solid ground. It was muddy, and he could feel sharp pebbles digging into his skin as he kneeled.

Sterjall wasn't breathing.

Banook placed the wolf over his left arm, face down, and smacked his back with his right hand. He could hear water spilling out of Sterjall's lungs, but no breath. He placed him on the freezing ground and compressed his chest, then wrapped his mouth around Sterjall's muzzle and shared his own breath.

Sterjall coughed and wheezed, spitting out freezing water as he turned to his side.

"My cub, my love," Banook said, holding him close. "I need to get you warm." He carried Sterjall against his chest and walked blindly through the crevasse, stomping through puddles and over sharp rocks.

"I'm so... cold..." Sterjall said. "It's so dark..."

"You'll be fine, cub. Your big bear is here to keep you warm. Stay with me, cub, stay with me."

Banook reached a chamber that opened wider. He heard hissing to his left and followed the sound until he felt steam blowing on him. But it wasn't hot; it was only slightly warmer than the frigid walls, and he could not get away from the moisture and constant dripping. Still, it was better than nothing. He placed Sterjall down on the mud and removed his wet clothes. He shapeshifted back into the golden bear, then wrapped himself around his cub, keeping him as dry as possible within his chest furs.

Sterjall's head pounded. He felt dizzy and sore all over. He could not feel his own handpaws, yet he held tightly onto Banook's fur, feeling as if he had lived this moment once before. He was confused, so tired, and so cold.

He inhaled deeply, filling his lungs with the scent of lemongrass.

He passed out.

CHAPTER SIXTY-SIX

DA'ÁJU

"Keep away from the sloping ice and dig your crampons down," Jiara told Ockam, tying one side of her rope to his belt. "And Alaia, hold him down too, just in case."

Jiara let herself slide toward the edge of the crevasse while the other two anchored her rope. The steam enveloped her, letting her see nothing but the rope and her hands holding it. Her feet found the sharp drop, where she lodged her axes and prayed for the wind to blow the steam away.

"Banook! Sterjall!" she screamed into the pit. The steam changed direction, but even then, she only managed to see a few feet down.

"Banook!"

She kicked off a row of icicles and listened. It took too long for them to splash at the bottom.

Shit, that's too deep, she thought.

Something resounded over the howling winds.

"Banook! Is that you?!"

Now she heard it, a distant roar, from much farther down the crevasse. The bear was alive.

"Banook, we'll find another way down! Every once in a while, roar like you just did, and we'll follow the sound!"

Another roar came in reply.

Jiara pulled herself back up, picking up Banook's clothes along the way. She moved away from the dangerous slope and grabbed her backpack. "He's down there somewhere," she said, a bit out of breath. "It's too deep, wet, and dark. Let's find a safe place to climb down. Sunnokh will set soon, let's hurry."

"You carry my bag," Ockam told Jiara. "And you both carry the ladders. I'll handle Banook's backpack."

Ockam could barely lift the backpack, but he forced his muscles to deal with the weight. Jiara took the front end of the ladders while Alaia took the back. They walked as near to the cracks as was safe, searching for spots where the steam wasn't blowing so densely, but they soon found themselves too far from where their friends had fallen, with no luck.

"What about the other holes?" Alaia asked, "What did you call them, deathvoids?"

"Meltvoids," Jiara said. "Maybe. They tend to drip down to the very bottom. One could connect to these cracks."

They backtracked and inspected the meltvoids they had passed by before. The first was too small. The second didn't seem to go all the way down, ending in blue ice. The third was a possibility, being close to one of the crevasses that connected to the one Sterjall had fallen into. They tossed a chunk of ice down the meltvoid and heard it smack onto something moist and hard.

"Ockam, hold me up," Jiara said, dropping the ladders at her feet. "I'll go first to check. If it looks like it will connect, we'll set up the ropes properly so we can all go down." She looked at Alaia. "Get your ice axes out, start carving an ice bollard for the ropes to save time while I go down. Make it deep and sturdy, but don't crack the ice."

Alaia obeyed without complaints.

Jiara tied a lamp to her belt and descended into the blue pipe. It was about eight feet in diameter, mirror-smooth on the sides. As she neared the widening floor of the pipe, she saw frozen mud and stones, and an opening on the side where the water had run off, leading directly toward the nearest crevasse.

She asked Ockam to pull her back up. "There's a path," she said, once she reached the top. She quickly attached her rope to the ice bollard. Harnesses on, they went down one at a time, then lowered their ladders and bags.

"Leave it attached," Jiara said, regarding the quaar rope. "I'll carry the other one." She hurried into the tunnel, which did indeed cross the area they meant to enter, but it did so from too far below. They could see the light of the cracked ice above them, but no way through. They continued down the narrowing path and hit a wall. A tendril of steam seeped out from beneath it.

Alaia ducked and peered into the steam. "We can crawl under here," she said. She pushed through, frozen mud cracking under her weight, ice shards breaking across her back. She pulled her backpack in behind her.

"This looks good!" she said. "Follow me!"

"I can't fit through there," Ockam complained.

"Move out of the way, Alaia," Jiara said. She swung the tied ladders like a battering ram, and with a few crunching hits broke an Ockam-sized hole through the thin wall of ice. Alaia was waiting on the other side with her lamp.

They entered a wide, dark-blue cavern, with a ceiling curved like a barrel vault tunnel. Farther ahead, the tunnel sunk into a waving wall of steam.

"Hold on," Jiara said, pulling the compass out of her pocket. "Good, this path leads mostly north. The crack they fell into was slightly northeast of the meltvoid. Let's keep this way. Ockam, keep an even stride, count your steps to measure the distance."

"Already have been," he replied.

They ventured into the tunnel, with Alaia's lamp reflecting into thousands of icy copies of itself in the myriad concave pockets on the ceiling.

"Where are we?" Sterjall asked, stirring in the bear's embrace.

Banook grunted and tenderly rubbed his muzzle against Sterjall's ears.

The wolf poked his head out of the furred shelter. He stopped trying to see with his eyes, using Agnargsilv's vision instead. He could feel Banook's intense aura next to him and see the bacterial threads on the muddy ground. He realized he was naked.

Banook suddenly roared.

"What is it? What is wrong?"

Banook's frozen fur crunched as he sat on his haunches. Without letting go of Sterjall, he slowly took his human form, letting the ice slide off him. He was shivering. "I've been r-roaring so that our f-friends could hear us, and co-come help us," he stuttered. "I'm happy to s-see you awake. I felt around and could not tell if you are woun-w-wounded. Are you in p-pain?"

"Everything hurts, but I don't know, I'm too numbed by the cold. Did you fall too? Where are the others?"

"I came down t-to help you," he said through chattering teeth. "The oth-thers are trying to find a safe way in."

"Thank you for coming down for me," Sterjall said in his arms. "I'd be so lost—I'd be dead without you."

"I love you, c-cub, I'd n-never leave you b-behind."

"I love you too."

"I am f-freezing in this th-thin skin. Maybe we can find a w-warmer spot, if you can see with Agnar-rg-gsilv."

"I'm getting cold too, now that your fur is gone. There's barely anything alive here to see my way, but I can manage. Follow me."

"We should not m-move too far, or it will be hard-der for them to find us."

"But let's at least find a hot vent. We won't stray too far."

"Alright, c-cub," Banook said, and gave him a little kiss in the dark. "But now, I n-need to go back to being a b-bear, or I will freeze to death. Do not be af-fraid of my roars, I'm only calling for them. Keep close to me, we'll be warm-m-mer together."

Banook unwrapped his arms from Sterjall. He shapeshifted into the arctotherium once more, feeling immediate relief under his thick furs.

Sterjall looked around, feeling much colder now. "This way, I think," he said, keeping a handpaw on the bear's fur as they walked.

Alaia's orange flame pulsed in the steam. The ground was wet and slightly warm, carving a path through the crevasse for them, but also cutting dangerous drops.

They dropped their ladders horizontally to cross a narrow chasm; Alaia squatted at the edge, studying a rock half-buried in ice and mud. "Look. It's square, like a brick." She shined her light around and realized the icy wall was hiding an old stone building.

"Da'áju..." Ockam whispered. "We made it after all."

"I just hope we can make it out as well," Jiara said, leaning close to see through the sheet of ice.

Farther down, the building intersected the icy tunnel. They walked into one of the rooms until their path was partially blocked by a collapsed wall overflowing with ice. They climbed over the obstacle and continued through the tunnel, hoping they were still going in the right direction.

The path split into three. Jiara consulted her compass and picked the rightmost path. In there they found more rocks—some carved with Miscamish runes—and crossed through more frozen dwellings. Northern Wutash bones sat on icy chairs or lay on cold floors. They hurried past a crystallized bed where two skeletons held each other, grinning humorlessly with sparkling crystal teeth. Some bodies were entirely contained within the ice, not even touching the ground, as if floating in cold amber; those were remarkably well preserved—not just bones, but tattooed skins of rusty reds, wrapped in clothes that still showed their original colors.

"How did they even get there?" Alaia asked.

"Maybe they died trying to crawl out of the piling snow," Jiara guessed, "and then it froze on top of them. I don't know, but it's terrifying."

They found the source of the steam: it was a wide channel carved in rock, splitting into smaller channels in hexagonal patterns. It was untouched by the ice, as it had always flowed with hot water, but the lower splits had built up a thick crust of minerals around them, making the water spill out to form the long tunnels of mist.

"These might be part of the hot springs near the temple," Ockam said. "They had similar motifs at Stelm Bir."

Gggrroooooaaarrr came a distant rumble.

"It's Banook!" Alaia exclaimed, lamp held high. "He can't be that far away." But they couldn't tell where the sound had come from—it echoed all around them.

They turned a corner and saw an odd glow. Alaia blocked the lamplight with her cloak and saw that right above them, blurred out by the mist, was the undeniable shape of a long crack. The rift was glowing pink, tinted by vibrant cirrocumulus clouds.

"This is it," Ockam said, checking his map. "If we turn right at this crevasse, it should connect to the one they fell into."

"And that pink tells me we'll spend the night down here," Jiara said. "Let's find them fast, and look for a place to rest and warm up."

Another roar, closer by, and they could pinpoint its direction this time.

"We are getting closer," Alaia said.

The crevasse ended at an intersection where it connected with a perpendicular crack. Jiara consulted her compass, just in case. They turned right at the split.

A roar thundered even closer. "Can you hear me?" Jiara called out.

"...can... ear you..." said a muffled voice. Sterjall.

The vents of hot air that hissed by them offered a slight respite from the cold, though they made it much harder to see by. They marched on, with the steam so dense that they could barely see their own feet.

"Over here! We can see the light!" Sterjall's voice said.

"There's room for all of you!" Banook's voice added.

As they finally got close enough, they found Sterjall and Banook shielding their eyes from the bright light, sitting naked in a pool of hot water.

Jiara stepped forward. "We risk our lives to save you and find you lounging in hot springs?!"

"We were freezing!" Sterjall replied. "Even Banook was about to pass out from the cold."

Alaia came up behind Sterjall and leaned down to give him a hug. His fur was soaking wet, but she didn't mind. "Are you hurt? Let me see your head."

Now that there was light, they saw that Sterjall had suffered several cuts during his fall. He had been bleeding from his arm and the side of his head. The blood was flowing freely into the hot pool.

"Get your tail out of there," Jiara said. "I'll take care of those wounds."

They debated making a fire. They didn't need it if they stayed close to the warm vents, but Sterjall's drenched clothes would not dry in the humid cavern. He had taken his human form to dry his body more easily; after Jiara was done bandaging him, he turned back into Sterjall to keep warm. He tried on Ockam's extra set of clothes and found that by wearing the trousers backward, he could stick his tail out through the fly. The clothes were baggy, but they would do.

"We found Da'áju," Alaia said. "You might not notice, but we're right in it. Old stone buildings, water channels, lots of frozen people—it's quite unsettling."

"I could see Urnaadisilv's aura from just a bit farther up that way," Sterjall said. "The temple has to be nearby. Should we go find a path?"

"We are not going anywhere until the sun rises," Jiara said. "You need to rest, you need to heal, and though you two have already had your fun, we still haven't had our warm soak."

Banook and Sterjall found a comfortable spot where a warm air current blew. There they cuddled themselves to sleep while the others bathed in complete darkness.

They woke up to the sound of cracking ice while shrouded in a dim, enveloping grayness. They were all startled, even more so when they realized they couldn't move—their clothes and blankets had been absorbing moisture overnight, freezing them onto the floor and wall and even onto Banook himself.

"Sorry," Banook said. "I was trying to get up quietly, but the ice cracked. I really have to pee."

He forced himself to his feet in resounding cracks, removing the parasitic warmth stealers from his body. He relieved himself in a nearby corner, further steaming the chamber.

"How did it get so cold and so warm at the same time?" Alaia asked over the sound of Banook's interminable stream.

After a small breakfast, and after spending some time by the vents to unfreeze their clothes, Sterjall led the way by following the lure of Urnaadisilv's dim glow.

They reached the intersection.

"We turned right here last night, when we heard you," Jiara said. Then she pointed to the path leading left. "That way is where we came in, where we found the buildings in the ice. It's not a crevasse, but a tunnel carved by the steaming water."

Sterjall looked at the possible paths. "There's only one other direction to try, but Urnaadisilv seems to be to our right, straight through the ice." He extended his arm, pointing Leif in the direction he spoke of. With the focusing power of the quaar grip, he managed to just barely feel the aura of the distant mask. He lowered his arm and said, "Banook and I took another crevasse last night, before we found the hot pools. From there the mask seemed closer, but it led to a dead end."

"Then we should take this last path, see what our curious feet can find," Banook suggested.

The mist cleared as they walked, letting them see farther ahead. The ice began to glow blue as the sunlight hit directly above. They suddenly realized they were in the middle of a building. It had been frozen in its entirety, and the ice had later cracked and split the building in half. It was as if they were looking at a mirror image, nearly identical on both sides, with protruding bricks and planks of wood that revealed the internal structure of an ancient dining hall. They could make out tables, chairs, and even a crystal chandelier that looked ghostly, with the crystal almost entirely disappearing in the equally refracting ice. Alaia found half of a dead body sticking out from one wall, then turned to find the other half on the opposite side.

"I know this place," Banook said. "Gwenolm Hall was its name. It is located near the temple. It brings back memories of great banquets, of roaring fires, and even louder roaring laughter. It also brings great sadness, seeing it this way."

The crack led in only one direction, so they followed it.

"We've been going the wrong way," Jiara warned, checking her compass. "We need to turn right, and then right again, until we are heading north."

An ice tunnel intersected the crevasse. The water running at its bottom was not hot, so there was little steam blocking the view.

Jiara shrugged and went in, following the path to the right, which climbed into a vaulted cavern of sparkling, dripping blue. The muddy path got darker the deeper they went, to the point that no more sunlight penetrated through the ice. Alaia lit her lamp once more.

"Over here," she said. "More portions of walls sticking out. They are totally frozen, though."

They followed the debris and found the entire tunnel blocked by a stone brick wall.

"This might be good," Jiara said. "If the wall hasn't collapsed, there could be air instead of ice behind it. A hand, Banook?"

Banook nodded. He put an ear against the stone wall and listened, then tapped with his knuckles. "Move back, please," he said, and the others did. He landed a heavy kick on the side of the wall. One of the bricks shifted slightly. He kicked again, the stone pushed through, and a section of the wall collapsed.

"Sorry for the mess," he said. "Let me remove the ones still stuck above. I don't want them falling on you."

Banook cleared the way and walked in. The vaulted hallway he had uncovered was wide and tall, with stone columns spread evenly across the entire length. He was glad he still had his crampons on, as the floor was sloped and covered in an even sheet of ice. It went uphill to the right and downhill to the left, both ways toward total darkness.

Clang! Thock. A distant sound echoed. A few heartbeats later, a distant *splash.*

"What was that?" Ockam asked.

"The rocks I dislodged," Banook replied. "They slid down and just reached the distant bottom. Let us not go that way, it sounded like a long way down to certain death. Cub, it's time to bring Lago back. Put your boots on."

Sterjall nodded as he changed forms.

"This icy tunnel bears forth glad tidings," Banook said, peering into the darkness. "Ommo ust Urnaadi was reached by walking up a long, gentle ramp."

"Like the Stelm Bir temple," Lago said, putting his boots on. "There was a ramp that led up to the central room at Agnargdrolom. This tunnel looks similar to it, minus the vines, that is." Lago kept the mask on as he tried to see farther up the tunnel.

"Let me go in front," Jiara bossed around, making her way past them. "Keep your ice axes in your hands, but try to stick to using just your feet, leaning slightly in. Banook, you go last. If you were to fall in front of us, you'd take us all down."

"And if you fall ahead of me, I'll catch you," Banook said, patting his belly. "It'll be a soft landing."

They slowly made their way up the sloping tunnel, making sure to keep their crampons firmly lodged before taking each step. Farther up the icy ramp, the tunnel narrowed abruptly. Once they arrived at the tight spot, they realized it had been offset due to the shifting ice sheets, which had displaced a portion of the hallway with them.

"This must be where the water seeped through," Jiara said, "to freeze the ramp beneath our feet." She used her axe on the icicles blocking the fragmented tunnel. The spears of ice screeched as they slid down the ramp. A long while later, they slammed, cracked, and splashed.

They stepped over a small crevice and onto the other side of the tunnel. But Banook could not fit: the way the shifted halves overlapped left only a narrow gap to walk through, and even sideways he was having a hard time pushing his belly through. Banook handed his gear to his friends, then tried to force his way in. They all helped by pulling on his arm—glad that their side of the tunnel had no more ice to slip on—until Banook's belly popped through. He landed on his knees, nearly crushing Alaia.

"Just a bit tight," he said, shaking it off.

They strolled easily now, without any worry of slipping. Lago had shifted back to Sterjall and could sense Urnaadisilv's golden aura clearly in front of him, waiting in the icy gloom. It was not long until they reached the end of the hallway.

"Enter now the hallowed halls of Ommo ust Urnaadi," Banook announced. "The temple of ursids beckons you."

They could tell right away that the temple was similar to the one they had visited at Stelm Bir: an enormous, round chamber with columns that weaved upward into complex struts and knots, holding vaulted ceilings where the lamplight could barely reach. This time, however, the columns were all beautifully carved from hard woods, not grown from vines. Banook turned pensive, recognizing that each of the columns was carved to honor a different species of bear, many of which had been extinct for fifteen centuries.

All surfaces, even the ground itself, were coated with glittering ice crystals that had remained undisturbed for epochs. Their feet crunched on the minuscule shards as they walked up the steps of an elevated platform at the center of the room, where a curved, table-like structure sat, convex on top, like a giant lens carved out of stone.

Right behind the curved table was a central column that sprouted toward the dark ceiling. The column was six-sided, carved with triangular runes interwoven with animal patterns. A few feet from the ground it split into six segments that spiraled around one another, like a rope that was becoming unwound and rejoined back above, hollowing a space between the divisions. Inside this space, resting upon an ivory pedestal, Urnaadisilv awaited.

Sterjall looked back at Banook, almost as if asking for permission. The old

Nu'irg still looked pallid and weakened, but he forced himself to smile. He seemed to be doing a bit better down here, as if being near the ursid mask gave him a spark of energy.

Banook nodded.

Sterjall reached between the spiraling columns and picked up the bear mask. It was as light, as beautiful, and as dark as Agnargsilv, though it looked almost white from all the crystals that had grown over it. The muzzle was shorter, the nose larger, the eyes and ears smaller. It had a blockier sort of stylization, in a design that spoke of each and every bear. It conjured strength and respect, and almost felt heavy despite weighing nearly nothing.

Sterjall turned to Ockam and said, "You made it." He handed him the mask. "I'm sure Bonmei would be proud."

Ockam hesitated. He looked into Sterjall's eyes, then solemnly took the mask. He ran calloused fingers over it, dislodging a sparkling cloud of glitter.

"I bet he is," Ockam said, seeming equally happy and sad. "I don't know what this mask will mean for us, but being able to visit Da'áju makes me feel as if I fulfilled my promise to Bonmei. It's not the same without him here, but it gives me some closure. Thank you. To all of you."

Banook placed a hand on Ockam's shoulder. "Ockam Radiartis of the Free Tribelands," he said, "son of Bero and Ur-Viv of Baysea Beyenaar, do you accept the role of steward of Urnaadisilv, and swear to bring honor and pride to bearkind, as the previous Urnaadifröash before you have?"

"I gave it some thought," Ockam replied, "and I will try. But I don't know if I'm capable of what Sterjall has accomplished. Give me time to think, to rest. I'm not ready yet."

Banook nodded. "There is a lot you must learn. As the Nu'irg ust Urnaadi, I feel power in Urnaadisilv's presence. It nurtures me and feeds me as if I was drinking honey and tasting salmon, but it can also be dangerous to me. Once the mask settles upon your face, I ask that you remain aware of its influence on me. I will follow you no matter what, as a friend, but I want to do so out of my own volition."

"You are my friend too, Banook. I'd never ask you to do anything that you did not want to do. I will be careful, and treat you and Urnaadisilv with the respect you deserve." He tried to shake Banook's hand, but Banook pulled him in for a hug.

"Is this what I think it is?" Jiara asked, exploring the curved table at the center of the room.

"This is the map of Noss I once mentioned to you," Banook said. "It shows the location of all seventeen domes. I'm not good with these kinds of abstractions—I read the mountains by exploring their saw-toothed silhouettes from within, not their view as a raven would from without, but I can at least tell that this"—he placed a finger on an indentation over the curved surface— "is the Da'áju Caldera, where the eighteenth dome never was."

All the features of the map were carved in a striking relief, from domes to seas to mountains, with the mountain ranges lifting the surface like the spines of buried snakes.

"Here's Heartpine, and Anglass," Ockam said, pointing at two circular bulges protruding from the map. On top of each of the bulges—and in the indentation of the caldera—was a unique glyph, like the one they had seen above the archway to the Stelm Bir temple.

"Banook, what do these runes say?" Sterjall asked.

"I cannot read these. They are not Miscamish runes, but glyphs, much more complex in their meaning than the phonetic runes I studied. I had never seen this map myself, but only heard about it. Only the Urnaadifröash and their high priests were allowed in these hallowed halls."

"You can see the Isdinnklad here," Ockam said, walking around the table, "and Zovaria would be in this area, though I guess it didn't exist when they carved this map. Why is it curved like this?"

"It's the curvature of the planet," Sterjall rightfully guessed. "Imagine the rest of Noss below it, like a sphere of water."

"That would be an awful lot of just water," Alaia said. "I hope there's more out there."

"What is this dome here?" Jiara asked. "Look at these peaks, these would be the Stelm Sajal, with Mount Loor and the great Laaja Khenukh, but there's a dome here in the west that I'm not familiar with."

"Isn't that the Moordusk Dome?" Alaia asked.

"No, that's this one, near Zovaria," she answered. "This odd one would be right at the volcanic fields, over the Brasha'in Scablands. Is this the missing dome?"

"That whole area is nothing but a dry lava field," Ockam said. "Hundreds of miles of black rock, nothing else."

"Does that mean the dome was swallowed by lava?" Alaia asked.

"Seems like it," Jiara said. "There's nothing else there, and although Khenukh still fumes it has not erupted since the early Reconstitution Epoch." She cocked her head, trying to pinpoint something else that felt off.

Sterjall looked at Banook, who seemed mournful. "I'm sorry," he said, hugging his arm.

"It's a great loss," Banook said. "All those species, all the knowledge from that dome, forever lost. They were a part of Noss, a part of all of us."

"And the Nu'irg too," Alaia said. "That makes me so sad…"

After an uncomfortable pause, Banook continued, "But this is quite peculiar, for we feel each other's presences—all the Nu'irgesh do. I've felt five Nu'irgesh die in the past, in ages untold, including Allamónea, who I saw perish with my own eyes. This is strange, because I do not feel any of my friends missing, I have felt none of them die. I wonder what that could mean."

"Is there a way the Nu'irg could've survived?" Sterjall asked. "Do you know which one it was?"

"I do not know who made their home in that dome," Banook said. "But as hard as we are to kill, I could not have survived molten rock over me. None of us could've. And Safis, I don't know how she survived the loneliness, the tragedy of seeing her dome collapse, but she would've certainly died if those vines had crushed her body."

"So, what do you think happened?" Sterjall asked.

"I don't know," Banook said. "I only know that I have not felt any of my friends cease being, and that is a comfort I dearly welcome."

"Has anyone explored those volcanic fields?" Alaia asked. "What about the mask that was inside that dome? Could it still be there?"

Jiara shook her head. "The Scablands are impassable. It's not flat rock, but shards as sharp as knives, black and scorching hot. There are three hundred miles of deadly rocks where no life grows. The Union and the Tribelands loosely mapped it from the tops of the Stelm Sajal and the Steps of Odrásmunn, but never ventured in. If the mask is there, it's buried under rock. We got lucky here—the ice didn't breach into this chamber, but a sea of lava would've washed this temple away like a sandcastle."

Jiara carefully studied the map again. "Ockam, the time you traveled from Zovaria to the Yenwu Peninsula, did you take the pass between the two sierras?"

"Of course, it's the shortest path to the port of Cairngorm, by the rim of the Sajal Crater. But that is not by the Brasha'in Scablands."

"I know, but look at the map. The Stelm Sajal continues in a straight line to meet the Stelm Ankrov. There's no crater dividing the two ranges."

Ockam looked closely. There was indeed an unperturbed line of mountains, but he knew for certain that a massive crater lake should have flattened that area—it was a well-known route, and the crater an unmissable landmark.

"I think the Sajal Crater must've been an enormous volcano," Jiara said. "Could be what caused so much to burn during the Downfall, and why it is not on this map."

"Maybe the comet crashed on that spot," Sterjall postulated. "What about the Varanus Dome? On this map it looks perfectly round, but I've seen illustrations of it, and that dome looks more like a spiderweb, spreading all over."

"I've never been there," Jiara said, "but I've heard tales of it. It's like what's been happening at Heartpine since those bumsquirts destroyed the temple. Maybe Varanus is collapsing like the Heartpine Dome?"

"No, it's definitely not collapsing, nor drying up," Sterjall said. "If anything, it's more alive than the others, spreading farther. It's what inspired Loregem to write the *Barlum Saga*, fearing all domes might someday grow out of bounds and take over all of Noss."

Jiara pointed at a dome on the far southwestern corner of the map. "The Nisos Dome," she punctuated. "I heard from a Lerevi friend that it too used to look gnarly like Varanus, but then shrunk back to normal, leaving holes in the mountains all around it. But that was hundreds of years ago. If Nisos went back to normal, maybe there is a way to fix things. Hey, Ockam, could you copy this map?"

"I was just about to get started on that," he said. "Would you be so kind, Alaia, and hold your lamp near me as I do this?"

Over a two-page spread, Ockam sketched the outlines of the map using blue ink, then in reds he copied the delicate glyphs in their corresponding locations. While Ockam worked, the others collected wood for a bonfire. They felt a bit guilty about burning old relics, but it didn't seem as if any of the skeletons would miss the many chairs piled up at the back of the chamber. There was no wind blowing inside the temple, but it was gelid; once the fire burst into being, they felt extremely grateful for its presence.

They did not know what time it was, but Jiara guessed it must be about sunset and recommended they set up their beds by the fire, dry their belongings overnight, and trace their way back whenever they woke up.

Sterjall emptied the wet contents of his bag near the flames. The smoke billowed up and settled on top of the tall chamber, with nowhere to escape to. They sat on their bedrolls and looked up into the complex patterns of the ceiling, now swimming in an upside-down, gray-orange sea of smoke.

Ockam left without saying a word, trudging down the dark tunnel, accompanied only by Urnaadisilv. It made Sterjall anxious. He stood up.

"Let him be," Jiara said, grabbing his arm and forcing him to sit back down.

A little while later, they heard an echo from the depths of the tunnel as Ockam played that haunting melody on his kalimba once more and sung a raspy, choked tune. A song for Bonmei. Ockam's deed was done. Sterjall could almost feel the breeze of Autumn around him. He looked at the sparks lifting from the bonfire and imagined aspen leaves flying into the sky.

17 Cloudpour
1455 A.D.

CHAPTER SIXTY-SEVEN

A Young Tree

Sterjall was sitting on his bedroll, examining Urnaadisilv under the firelight. He handed it back to Ockam and said, "I don't mean to rush you, but I think it's better if you try on Urnaadisilv while we are down here. Remember in the limestone caverns, how I was able to control Agnargsilv for the first time? There weren't many living creatures around for me to feel their pain. The feeling once you are in a forest is overwhelming, much harder to deal with."

Ockam nodded without looking at him, and instead focused on the mask's small eyeholes. The fire flickered behind them.

"I will give it a try," he said. "I've learned a lot from watching you, and from hearing Banook's stories. I don't know if I'm cut out for this, but I will try. Jiara, could I have you close to me, in case I need help pulling the mask off?"

"Of course," she said and came to sit next to him.

Sterjall turned his attention fully in Ockam's direction. "Don't try to fight it, you have to let the pain—"

"I know, I know, I've heard it all a million times before. Thank you, Sterjall, but what I need now is peace and quiet."

Ockam crossed his legs and closed his eyes, focusing entirely on the crackling sound of the fire, the heat licking his face, and the scent of smoke and damp rocks. He sat there for so long that Sterjall thought he had fallen asleep. He then recited his litany:

"A young tree I am, the old forest I am not, yet forest and tree are of one soul. A small fish I am, the vast ocean I am not, yet ocean and fish are of one mind. A frail wolf I am, the strong pack I am not, yet pack and wolf are of one heart."

With methodical precision, he raised Urnaadisilv, feeling it snap on and accommodate to the shape of his face.

Ockam didn't scream; he didn't fall down in tears like Lago had his first few times. He tensed up with eyes closed, the veins on his neck and forehead engorging, his face red, his knuckles white. For a long while he held statue-still while Jiara held her arm around his back. He inhaled rhythmically, in small amounts, faster and faster, and suddenly exhaled all at once, looking as if he had just lost control of his muscles, but soon tensed up again and straightened his spine.

He let out a miserable moan. Tears and sweat streaked his face under the mask, but he kept still. His body began to shiver and tense further, then suddenly the tension released.

Ockam began to breathe normally. He sighed deeply and opened his eyes. He turned to Sterjall and said, "Sterjall, my friend, I don't know how you managed this at your age. I've been through some horrible pains in my life, ones that my many scars can attest to. This was much harsher, for it was not my own pain, but all of yours."

"Are you still hurting?" Jiara asked, not letting go of him.

"I am. But it's inside me now. I don't know how long you've been here with me, but to me, it felt like hours."

Ockam focused his new sight around the room without having to turn his head to do so. He saw the threads at last, like filaments of a complex tapestry weaving all around them. He saw as well the golden auras of his mask and Banook, and the indigo fullness of Agnargsilv.

"I see now, Sterjall. I finally understand. I can see."

Ockam dreamed of endless whiteness. There was no land, no horizon; only white, only cold. The air was made of bright aetheric particles, like infinitesimally small snowflakes, like minuscule suns in a galaxy with no bounds. He tried to make sense of what was in front of him, but it was all too bright, and he could think of no words to describe it—words were not even a concept, they did not exist in his mental state; all he knew were feelings, emotions, and the endless bright.

Each particle he observed was a small cry for help. He looked at himself and saw he was nothing more than one of the many points of light; a small one, an inconsequential sparkle in an infinity of pain. The particles all suddenly gleamed and elongated, extending toward him as if merging into a loom. Each luminous thread sunk a small stab into his heart and dug its tendrils deeply, clutching at his soul. He wanted to cry out, but fought against it. He wanted to let go, but did not know how.

Ockam woke up sobbing, with the bear mask watching him from the shadows.

CHAPTER SIXTY-EIGHT

RETURNING HOME

Lago put on his dried clothes when he finally rose, then returned the ones he'd borrowed to Ockam. They packed up, put the fire out, and walked toward the exit. Lago was wearing Agnargsilv while in his human form, and Ockam was wearing Urnaadisilv next to him, still not fully comfortable with it. They looked at each other, observing how the masks twisted and bent all the threads around them, glowing all the while.

After a short walk down the gently sloping ramp, they arrived at the shifted segment of the tunnel.

Jiara handed the quaar rope to Banook and said, "You barely fit last time, and fell after squeezing through. If you fall down on the icy side, you could be sliding down all the way. Tie yourself to this column, just in case."

"Good idea," Banook said, "you can't trust me to be as graceful every time." He dropped his gear in the corner, then tied one end of the rope to his belt and the other end around a stone column at the edge of the split corridor. "I'll go first. You might have to give me a push," he said, walking sideways, sucking his gut in and trying to compress his frame into the tight gap.

He got stuck, his belly pushing hard against the column. The others helped with a push, then with a mighty shove managed to squeeze Banook through. He landed on his knees and began to slide down.

"It's okay," he said, trying to stand while he slid, but he fell again, now sliding faster. He reached the limit of his rope and sighed with relief as he stopped. *Cr-rrak!* the column reverberated as it shattered off the wall.

The large cylinder of rock slid toward Banook, but he dodged it and sunk his crampons into the ice. He then looked down the ramp and saw the column fragment rolling toward the dark tunnel, with the rope still tied to it, still attached to his belt. The rope tensed up and pulled Banook down.

Sliding on his back, Banook swung his two oversized ice axes down, but the pull was hard, and he was moving too fast. He lost his grip on the axes, safety cords snapping under the tension. They flung off, lighting sparks on the side walls. Banook screamed, unable to slow down.

"Banook!" Lago shrieked, running toward him. Jiara stopped him before he hit the ice, holding him down. "Banook!" he screamed again.

At that same time, Ockam fell twitching onto the ground, feeling Lago's pain of losing Banook fed to him through the mask. It was unbearable, devastating, and Ockam found no way to control it.

"Banook!" Lago screamed once more, and from the depths of the dark tunnel a tremendous roar made the rocks and ice tremble. Another followed.

"We have to help him, now!" Lago said. He dropped his bag and walked onto the icy ramp.

"Slow down!" Jiara said. "We'll go together. Ockam, are you able to stand?"

"Yes," Ockam croaked, having removed Urnaadisilv with Alaia's help. "I'll manage."

"Lago, wait!" Jiara yelled.

They followed Lago down the tunnel, but he was going carelessly fast, slipping and catching himself as he went. He couldn't wait for them, and he could see without Alaia's light, either way.

"Slow the fuck down!" Jiara called from behind him.

Another roar, closer this time.

Hold tight, be brave, don't be afraid, Lago prayed to himself, or to Banook. *I'm right behind you. I won't let you go like this.*

Through his mask, Lago saw the golden bear sprawled on the ramp, all twenty claws digging through the ice and into the rock underneath. Banook's back claws had pierced through his boots; his shirt, trousers, and jacket were shredded to pieces. His thick belt was still attached, with the rope tied to it, with the heavy column relentlessly trying to drag him into the void.

"I'm here," Lago said, putting his hands on the bear's muzzle. "I'm here, I'll get you out of this, hold tight."

He walked to Banook's side and tried to untie the rope, but it was pulling too hard, and he could not undo the knots. Banook lost his grip and slid down once more, pulling Lago with him. They were both picking up speed, until Lago remembered Leif. He unsheathed it and tried to cut the rope, but the quaar was much too strong; it would not succumb to any blade, no matter how sharp. They rushed past the opening Banook had kicked into the wall and kept on speeding down. Lago then realized how stupid he had been, and with one clean swipe of the senstregalv dagger cut through Banook's belt instead. It sprung up like a beheaded serpent, whipping around as the rope pulled through it. Banook clawed at the ice and slid to a halt, with Lago holding tightly onto his fur. The stone column took the rope down, dragging showers of sparks down the length of the hall. Shortly after, they heard a boom and a distant splash.

Banook grunted, breathing hard. Lago cautiously moved to hug his neck.

"I thought I'd lost you," Lago cried. Banook turned his head and held Lago between his cheek and shoulder. "I can't lose you. I don't want—I thought you..."

The others arrived, finding Lago and Banook holding each other. They joined in the embrace.

"Everyone fine?" Jiara asked, checking for wounds.

Banook growled softly.

"Your boots are shredded," she said. "I wouldn't trust them. Can you claw your way back up as a bear?"

Banook nodded.

Jiara lowered her backpack to the ice. "Ockam, take my bag. Carry it low, don't get too top-heavy. I'll go back up and get Lago's and Banook's gear."

Banook took a step forward and huffed, shaking his head *no*.

"Quiet, big bear," she said. "It's fine, I'll lower it all in front of me with a spare rope. It's easy to do downhill. I can take care of this. You climb to the exit, get yourself to safety."

Jiara lit an extra lamp and headed uphill on her own.

Ockam patted Banook's forehead and said, "When she gets bossy like this, you better do as she says. Let's head out of here, carefully this time."

They walked slowly up the ramp, with Banook overeagerly gripping the sheet of ice with his claws. They exited the hallway into the ice tunnel; a dim blue light shone at the far end of it.

Banook leaned against the rock wall and shapeshifted back into his human form with a painful sigh. Lago held him tight.

"Thank you, cub. I would've been lost without you."

"You're bleeding," Lago said, looking at Banook's torn nails, scraped knees, and raw elbows.

"I will heal. My boots, however, are past the Six Gates by now," he said, lifting a leg up and inspecting the shredded toecaps. "My poor clothes too, but I have a few spares to wear."

Jiara whistled to let them know she was arriving, lowering the bags with the two ladders beneath them as a makeshift sled. They helped her get the gear through the hole, then sat down to rest.

Jiara took care of Banook's wounds while they planned what to do next. "We lost a precious quaar rope," she said, "but we have one more tied at the meltvoid and yarn backups for good reason. I'm more worried about your boots. We can try to fix them, but they won't seal. Your mangled toes will get cold."

"I can deal with cold toes," Banook said, letting Jiara clean the loose skin from his elbows. "It's not too many days of travel until we are out of the ice."

They did their best to fix Banook's boots but could do nothing about his clothes. His bearskin cape was still intact, at least, and would keep him warm enough. He put on his few spare clothes using a segment of yarn rope as a belt, and out they went, following the tunnel's blue light.

"One more soak as we take a lunch break?" Lago suggested when they reached the next fork. They all were too cold to argue, so they took the brief detour to the hot pools they had visited earlier.

After their soak, Alaia, Jiara, and Lago prepared lunch in a dry corner, while Ockam and Banook stayed in the pool for a bit longer.

The ursid mask floated lightly, bobbing up and down as if suspended by steam. Banook took it in his massive hands and examined it. "I've always been a bit afraid of it," he confessed. "Afraid of what it can do. Back in the Unification Epoch, before all eighteen tribes joined under the banner of the Miscam, some masks fell into the wrong hands. They were used for warfare, with their Nu'irgesh trapped under their spell, forced to fight wars they did not believe in, to commit atrocities they would never forget. Not all suffered that fate, luckily, only a handful. And though I was not one of them, their stories scarred me, nonetheless. I wonder why the Acoapóshi did not consider this danger when creating the Silvesh. It is as if they had full confidence that the other tribes would follow their rules and vision."

"That's a lot of trust to give," Ockam said. "I don't understand it either. I'm curious, what would happen if a Nu'irg like yourself were to wear their own Silv?"

"You mean like this?" Banook said, lifting the mask.

"No! Wait!"

Banook laughed. He stopped without letting the mask touch his face; it looked more like a small muzzle in front of his wide nose. "Sorry if I scared you, dear friend," he said. "I doubt it would fit this unwieldy skull of mine. But I am glad Urnaadisilv is not my burden to carry. You and Lago are much better fit for the Silvesh."

Ockam took the mask from Banook's hands, just in case. He slid closer and quietly said, "He really loves you, you know. When you fell... I felt his pain. It was unbearable, felt the same as when I lost my son." Ockam leaned forward and inhaled the steam. "You've been so good to him, to all of us. It will hurt him greatly when we have to depart."

"I know. I feel it already," Banook said, his voice soft in the mist.

"Lago has... He has become a bit like a son to me, you know? I want you to know that I'll take care of him. I'll protect him no matter the cost. I promise you that much."

"Thank you, Ockam. You ease my worries. I know he's in good, loving hands. He couldn't have asked for better friends." Banook wrapped an arm around Ockam and pulled him in, squishing him tenderly.

Alaia materialized through the fog. "Don't you make my gwoli jealous now, Ockam. You two need to get out and get dry. Food is ready."

The light dimmed above them as they continued down the crevasse. It was the eighteenth day of Cloudpour, and the clouds were fattening. Thunder rumbled above.

"We need to get out of here before the rain arrives," Jiara said. "This place could flood at any moment."

They hastened across the long tunnel, then into the round chamber they had climbed into two days ago.

"This is the meltvoid we came down through," Jiara said, looking at the circular hole above them. The quaar rope was still there, but she worried that the ice bollard Alaia had wrapped it around might not be strong enough to hold Banook. She scurried quickly up the rope, expertly climbing with her ice axes, setting up screws and pitons while Banook belayed her with a yarn rope in case she lost her footing.

The meltvoid widened at the bottom, making for a complicated upside-down climb before hitting the vertical segment. It started raining as Jiara reached the top. She secured the quaar rope to a series of strong holds—as many as she could spare—to support Banook's full weight.

Banook wrapped a blanket around his head for protection and climbed up next, using borrowed ice axes that were too tiny for his hands. His boots were weak, especially the crampons at the front caps, which did nothing but further injure his toes. The two ladders helped during the inverted part of the climb, with the others balancing them below Banook, hoping he wouldn't come down crashing on them. The rain was now flowing freely down the walls of the meltvoid. They kept their hoods over their heads and tried not to look up.

Banook fought through the stream, digging his axes and feet in, as the water poured over his arms and flowed onto his face. After popping at least two pitons out while ascending, Banook finally swung the ice axes over the edge of the meltvoid, which was beginning to look more like the edge of a whirlpool. He crawled out of the hole.

His boots were twisted oddly, the crampons bent between his wet, bleeding toes. His feet were so cold that he hadn't felt the injuries. Jiara helped him up and away from the slippery hole.

"I'll help you with your wounds as soon as the others are out," she said.

More thunder roared over them, and the rain fell harder, sometimes compact like sleet, sometimes as enormous drops that felt like hurled pebbles.

Rather than climbing up, the others let Banook pull them up one at a time while they used their axes to keep some distance from the wall. Alaia went first and was pulled up and out before the water flowed too strongly. She tossed down the quaar helm to Lago, who hurried up next, bracing against a torrent of water.

Ockam went last. Before attaching the rope to his harness, he tied the gear to the rope and let Banook pull it all up, including the ladders. Ockam's boots were now sunken into cold, running water. He wanted to retrieve the anchors and pitons on his way up, but the cylindrical waterfall was thickening, so he watched them pass by as Banook pulled him up. Once he reached the top he dug deeply into the ice for traction and crawled out, utterly drenched.

They were all soaked with water and cold. Banook's feet were freezing and bleeding, but they had to keep moving. They found a serac to take shelter behind, and there they waited for the rainclouds to pass overhead. They wrung out their clothes and made a small fire with a bit of wood they had carried from the temple.

"Keep them by the fire," Jiara said, after once again taking care of Banook's bleeding toes. "You don't want frostbite to take them."

"Let's pray to the water sprites we don't get any more rain in the next few days," Ockam said as he helped fix up Banook's shredded boots. "We have a long way to go, and we won't be able to dry off easily, not with so little wood left."

Once the sun was back out, the winds picked up again. The loose snow from the north blew over the rim of the serac and turned to yellow ribbons above them, twirling in floral curves as it howled through cracks. Afraid the serac might topple, they walked away from it, into the lacerating winds.

They followed their tracks back as closely as they could, aided by Ockam's careful notes as well as by various landmarks they could spot from a distance.

For five days they journeyed through the ice, climbing, sliding, crossing chasms, and battling the strong winds. Rain hit them twice more, more forcefully, as if trying to test their determination and endurance.

"Your boots are coming apart again," Sterjall told Banook as they rested for the night.

"I'll be alright, cub. I have more at the cabin, and most of the time I go barefoot anyways." He pulled his boots off, then unwrapped his bandages and massaged his toes by the dying fire.

"You are all healed already?" Jiara asked, inching closer to examine the bulbous toes. "A wound like yours should've taken weeks to heal and should've left nasty scars and twisted toes behind."

"As I said, my dear Jiara, I heal fast. All the Nu'irgesh do. Though we still suffer, and from greater wounds we may fall. And you should all be glad we heal fully. If I had scars for every wound I collected over thousands of years, I'd be but a shapeless, furless mound of scabs by now."

"You are looking better, too," Ockam said. "Overall, I mean. Warmer, even younger somehow."

"And like a newborn cub I shall soon feel. We are closer to my bears now that we are nearing the end of this caldera, and they fill my soul with energy, helping me recover faster. "

Once they finally reached the rocky cliffsides, they had to find a new way up, as the overhang they had climbed down from was too high up. It took a detour of several miles before they found a ledge of ice they could climb down, to then trudge up the eroded rocks, legs throbbing and worn out.

This edge of the caldera was a talus slope, made of very loose rocks that piled on the cliffside. The rocks tumbled down easily, impacting and eroding the ice below, turning the pitted surface a muddy, rusty color. They moved carefully up the slope, making sure they were not in direct line with one another, as the loose rocks slid beneath each and every footstep, releasing torrents of deadly, tumbling shards. Banook went last, as his heavy feet dislodged boulders large enough to besiege a castle.

It was close to sunset by the time they found their way off the talus slope and back onto the trail.

"We should take cover from the whirling winds," Banook said, walking ahead of the group as if not tired at all. "Up, over the edge of the pass. We could use the same campground from last time. Let's go, before night swallows day, and let's pick up wood while on our way."

They arrived at the fork in the road and continued south a bit longer, toward the pass. It was already quite dark when they reached the saddle. The clouds to the south had an eerie orange glow to them, though Sunnokh had set long ago. Something seemed awry.

Lago scrambled ahead of the others. He stopped abruptly, staring southward in terror.

"Withervale is burning," he said, peering through his binoculars. "The city is on fire!"

From their high vantage point, they saw dozens of fires lighting the undersides of the billowing smoke. Bursts of sickly yellow light flashed from time to time.

Ockam took the binoculars. "Those yellow flames, the white smoke... That looks like sapfire cannons. Only Negian vessels use those cursed weapons."

"What do we do?" Alaia asked.

"Crysta, Gwil, Khopto. I can't abandon them again," Lago said. "What if the Red Stag reaches the mesa? We have to help them! This is all my fault, I led him to Withervale."

"It's not your fault, cub," Banook said behind him, trying to hold his voice and expression steady. "It would take two weeks to get to Withervale if we went back to the cabin first, and then the road south of Minnelvad would be much longer and swarmed with spies and Negian troops." He swallowed, then considered his next words. "If you must go, you must do so now, before your city burns. Through this southern pass it will still take you about four days to reach the river, but only if you hurry. Hopefully the Zovarians can hold the enemy off till then."

"But what about Bear? And you? We still had weeks to be together," Lago whimpered.

Banook lowered himself to his knees and stared straight into Lago's teary eyes. "I will take good care of Bear, don't worry about him. And I will go with you down this path, but not for much farther. The bears don't venture south of the mountains, and I already feel their pull behind us. You must continue on your own after this."

"We should hurry," Jiara said. "We can hike down for several more hours, then get a bit of rest before morning. We'll need sleep if the road will take several days, but we can do with only a few hours each night."

The thin crescent of Sceres was in Pearl, shining like a sliver of sunlit nacre near the horizon, sharing but a thin light to walk by. She had tear-like streaks on her unlit face—wispy clouds rarely visible when not in her Obsidian season.

Lago held Banook's hand as they descended the long switchback road, watching the distant fires that lit up the southern horizon. They said not a word.

For two days and most of the nights they walked down the mountain road, getting very little sleep. Lago was wistful, but he spent as much time close to Banook as he could. There were no bears on this side of the mountains; they hadn't seen any since the edge of the caldera, and Banook was looking more worn down with every step. Lago tried to ignore Banook's lack of energy, believing perhaps that he would be able to continue as long as he pushed himself.

Dusk settled upon them as they reached the bottom of the mountain path. After crossing a white creek in the middle of a sugar pine forest, Banook stopped and fell to his knees.

"I'm sorry, cub, I cannot go any farther," he said.

The aroma of pine needles and moist soil permeated everything around them. The creek roared.

"Please, I need you, could you come with us just—"

"I wish I could," Banook said, short of breath and feeble-eyed. He looked ancient and seemed to have lost a lot of weight. The wrinkles around his eyes did not look like those he got from so much smiling, and the eyebags below them drooped sickly and gray. His beard's highlights shone not in gold or red, but in white.

"Please, we need you," Lago implored.

Banook wiped the sweat from his brow. "I've strayed too far beyond bearkind. I am weakening, losing myself."

"But you could still make it to—"

"No, cub, I cannot."

"What if we use Urnaadisilv? Won't you follow its call?"

"Stop," Ockam said, walking between them. "I will not force our friend toward his death. He has helped us, saved us, welcomed us, and trusted in us. I too am sorry to say farewell, but we must go before it's too late."

They all surrounded the man, the bear, and embraced him.

Banook opened his eyes and with his vanishing strength said, "I want you to take what you can. Jiara, the rope will be better in your capable hands. The shield, for Ockam, the protector. The helm for you, Alaia, to safeguard that beautiful nub of yours."

Alaia let escape a sad smile. Banook smiled in return, but his smile felt grimly forced.

"We'll miss you so much," Alaia said, then hugged him tighter.

"You've been a blessing," Jiara said, wiping away tears. "I hope we can come back soon and explore the rest of your back yard."

Ockam leaned in close and whispered in his ear, "I will take care of him no matter what. Be strong. He will come back to you someday."

The three of them walked away to give Lago and Banook a bit of space, unable to hear their parting words due to the roaring of the creek.

Lago clung tightly to Banook's neck, feeling the gentle arms wrapped around him. "I love you. I'm sorry I tried to push you… I was being selfish. I wish you could come."

"Me too, cub. Maybe one day in the future, the bears will once again venture south. Until that day comes, I will be here, waiting for your return. I love you, more than I've loved anyone else in my long life. You've shown me joy, you've brought me youth, you lit my mind with curiosity and my heart with passion. I will be with you wherever you go, for as long as you can hear the mountain song. Go now, follow your heart, and let it one day lead you back to me."

Lago kissed him, breathing in the fresh scent of lemongrass one last time, and held the kiss with eyes so tightly closed that he saw lines and shapes in his vision, like the threads that connected them and would keep them bound for life.

Banook let go of his embrace. Lago took a step back and stared at the tears filling his bear's honey-colored eyes. The big man was smiling, that same wide smile he had shared the first day he'd seen him in the cabin—that same loving, selfless, and kind smile.

Lago slowly stepped backward, holding Banook's tender hands. He let go of them, then turned away, marching solemnly toward the untrodden path ahead of him.

End of Book 1

THE NOSS SAGA
CONTINUES
ON BOOK 2

MASKS OF THE MISCAM

LEARN MORE AT
JoaquinBaldwin.com/book2/buy

APPENDICES

All the materials found in these appendices can also be found online with much cleaner formatting and with additional goodies, such as a complete Miscamish dictionary, full-resolution maps, and updated illustrations. They are included here for your convenience, but I recommend you check them out on the official website.

Scan this QR code or type in the following URL to access the extras:

JoaquinBaldwin.com/book1/extras

To keep updated on new book releases and to gain access to unreleased illustrations, deleted chapters, tutorials, and lots more, sign up to my mailing list in the following link:

JoaquinBaldwin.com/list

THE MISCAM TONGUE

Excerpts from *The Miscam Tongue and Runic System* by Artificer Griteo Amberzeva, first published in 1387 A.D.

————————— ☾ —————————

STRESSED SYLLABLES

Miscamish words are stressed on their first syllable, with the following exceptions:

- Words with long vowels (AA, OO, UU) are stressed on the syllables with the long vowels.
- A diaeresis to indicate a vowel is pronounced in a separate syllable also indicates that that syllable and vowel are the stressed ones.
- An acute accent mark (´) always carries the stress, ignoring all previous rules.

Shisendinn (west): SHI-sen-dinn - standard usage
Quanódinn (Harvestlight): qua-NO-dinn - accent mark carries the stress
Mahumaalt (wonderful): ma-hu-MAALT - long vowel carries the stress
Galassuë (beauty): ga-la-ssu-E - diaeresis splits diphthong and indicates stress
Úrproo (autumn): UR-proo - accent mark supersedes the long vowel rule

Some words (mostly names) are compounded with hyphens (-) and have two stressed syllables. To find the stresses, these words can be considered as two separate words with a space in the middle.

Salish-Hathúr: SA-lish ha-THUR
Menegoi-Halaari: ME-ne-goi ha-LAA-ri
Gwolléno-Kúbraan: gwo-LLE-no KU-braan
Halva-Shindull: HAL-va SHINdull

Do not confuse glottal stops (') with hyphens (-). Glottal stops have a particular phonetic compound, while hyphens do not. Glottal stops do not change the stressing rules mentioned above.

Tulé'i (broad): tu–LE–'i
Tule'iclëi (broadsword): tu–le–'i–CLE–i
Ongu'ur (onguday): ON–gu–'ur
Ca'éli (pilgrim): ca–'E–li

PLURALIZATION

Miscamish nouns are pluralized by adding the phoneme SH at the end if the word ends in a vowel, or ESH if the word ends in a consonant.

Octopus: umult
Octopuses: umultesh
Mother: ukhaada
Mothers: ukhaadash

If the word ends in an S, the S phoneme is replaced by SH.

Apple: stules
Apples: stulesh
Dagger: ildes
Daggers: ildesh

Words ending in long (double) consonants do not need suffixes to be pluralized, though it is sometimes customary to add ESH at the end when clarification is essential.

Light: dinn
Lights: dinn (or dinnesh)
Army: khambarr
Armies: khambarr (or khambarresh)

Phonemes

Although Miscamish originally assigned strict phonetics for each rune, the language has adapted to a more Common-like pronunciation when the flow makes it feel more natural. The five vowel sounds are consistent, even when shortened in diphthongs and the rare triphthongs.

- **KH**: Though written using two runes in Common, the KH phoneme is singular, and represents a hard H sound, a voiceless uvular fricative rougher than the voiceless glottal fricative of an H.
- **C&K**: The voiceless velar plosive can be represented with either C or K. The letter C seems to be more standardized in southern territories, while the K is more common in northern ones. There is only one Miscamish rune to represent the single phoneme, as the phonetic language sees no distinction.
- **R**: There are three possible pronunciations of the R: a tapping sound when the R is at the beginning or end of a word; an approximant R when it is found at the end, that softens the sound; or a trilling sound in the case of a double R.

Doubled Letters

Doubled letters stretch the phonemes without changing their sounds. This applies to vowels as well (please note that OO sounds like a longer O, not U). There are a few exceptions:

- **RR**: carries a rolling trill, usually with two to three rolls.
- **SC**: when at the beginning of a word it acts as SS, as exemplified in *Sceres*, extending the S sound by a small fraction.
- **PP, TT, KK**, and **BB**: since the plosive phonemes cannot be stretched, they are simply emphasized with a pause during the air blockage, and a stronger strike on the release, similar to the effect of a glottal stop between vowels.

Glossary of Commonly Used Miscamish Words

Parts of speech:

adj. adjective	*adv.* adverb	*art.* article
conj. conjunction	*det.* determiner	*interj.* interjection
nan. animate noun	*nina.* inanimate noun	*num.* numeral
prep. preposition	*pron.* pronoun	*v.* verb

Animate nouns, pronouns, and determiners come in six levels, indicated by the numbers 1-6. An *s* is for singular, *p* for plural.

Key

spelling - *approx. pronunciation* /IPA/ (part of speech)
definition(s)

Agnargfröa - *ag-narg-FRO-ah* /ˌagnargˈfro.a/ (nan5)
voice of the canids

Agnargsilv - *AG-narg-silv* /ˈagnargsɪlv/ (nan5)
mask of canids

ash - *ash* /aʃ/ (adj)
white, blank

baakiag - *BAA-key-ag* /ˈbaːkɪag/ (adv)
please

bir - *beer* /bɪr/ (nina)
home

ca'éli - *kah-'EH-lee* /kaʔˈɛlɪ/ (nan3)
pilgrim

dinn - *dihn* /dɪnn/ (nan1)
light

drolom - *DROH-lom* /ˈdrolom/ (nan5)
dome

ëovad - *EH-oh-vahd* /'ɛ.ovad/ (nan1)
fire

esht - *esht* /ɛʃt/ (adj)
blue

far - *far* /faɾ/ (nan3)
pine, conifer

fel - *fell* /fɛl/ (nina)
island

fröa - *FRO-ah* /'fɾo.a/ (nan6)
voice

gralv - *grah-lv* /gɾalv/ (adj)
purple

idash - *EE-dash* /'ɪdaʃ/ (adj)
clear, transparent

isdinn - *IS-dihn* /'ɪsdɪnn/ (nan1)
sea

Iskimesh - *IS-key-mesh* /'ɪskɪmɛʃ/ (nan6)
Enchantress, the third planet from Sunnokh

jall - *jahl* /dʒall/ (nan2)
heart

keldris - *KEHL-dris* /'kɛldɾɪs/ (nina)
bay, harbor, cove, port

Khumen - *KHOO-men* /'χumɛn/ (nan6)
Dawn Pilgrim, the first planet from Sunnokh

klad - *clad* /klad/ (nan1)
lake

laaja - *LAH-jah* /'laːdʒa/ (nan1)
volcano

lerr - *LEH-rr* /lɛɾɾ/ (nan3)
liege (allgender honorific)

lorr - *lore* /loɾɾ/ (nan3)
lord, sir, mister

lurr - *LOO-rr* /luɾɾ/ (nan3)
lady, madam, miss

maarg - *mah-arg* /maːɾg/ (adj)
red

malpa - *MAHL-pah* /ˈmalpa/ (adj)
great

minnéllo - *mih-NEH-loh* /mɪˈnnɛllo/ (nan1)
waterfall

Miscamish - *MISS-kah-mih-sh* /ˈmɪskamɪʃ/ (nina)
Miscamish

ninn - *nihn* /nɪnn/ (nina)
pass

nokh - *noh-kh* /noχ/ (nan1)
sky

nu'irg - *NOO-'ee-rg* /ˈnuʔɪɾg/ (nan5)
ghost, spirit, soul

ommo - *OH-moh* /ˈommo/ (nina)
temple, church

Ongumar - *ON-goo-mar* /ˈongumaɾ/ (nan6)
Amberlight, the fifth planet from Sunnokh

quaar - *kwaar* /ˈkwaːɾ/ (nina)
soot (crystalline, durable form)

sajal - *SAH-jahl* /ˈsajal/ (adj)
foreboding

Sceres - *SEH-rehs* /ˈssɛɾɛs/ (nan6)
moon (the moon)

senstregalv - *SENS-treh-gal-v* /ˈsɛnstɾɛgalv/ (nina)
obsidian (special)

Senstrell - *SENS-trell* /ˈsɛnstɾɛll/ (nan6)
obsidian, the fourth planet from Sunnokh

shodog - *SHO-dog* /ˈʃodog/ (nina)
jacket (open-chested)

Silv - *silv* /sɪlv/ (nan5)
mask

Silvfröa - *silv-FRO-ah* /sɪlv'fro.a/ (nan5)
voice of the mask

stelm - *stelm* /stɛlm/ (nina)
mountain

ster - *stare* /stɛɾ/ (nan6)
star

stiss - *stiss* /stɪss/ (nan1)
river

sulf - *soo-lf* /sulf/ (nina)
land

sun - *soon* /sun/ (nan1)
flame

Sunnokh - *SOO-noh-kh* /'sunnoχ/ (nan6)
sun (sky-flame)

tago - *TAH-goh* /'tago/ (adj)
gray

telm - *telm* /tɛlm/ (nina)
valley

trell - *trell* /tɾɛll/ (adj)
black

trod - *troh-d* /tɾod/ (nina)
peak

urgei - *OOr-gay* /'uɾgɛɪ/ (nan3)
elk

ust - *oo-st* /ust/ (prep)
of, of the

ustlas - *OO-st-lahs* /'ustlas/ (nan1)
soot

wujann - *WOO-jan* /'wudʒann/ (adj)
icy

Characters, Gods, Items, Tribes

Acoapóshi - *ah-kowa-POH-shee*
The original Miscam tribe.

Alaia *(F) ah-LAY-uh*
Lago's best friend. Worker at the Withervale coal mines.

Alvis Hallow *(M) AHL-vis HAL-low*
General of the Second Legion of the Negian Empire.

Aness *(F) AH-niss*
One of Aurélien's magpie heralds.

Ansko Loregem *(M) ANS-koh LORE-gem*
Writer of the Barlum Saga and the Chronicles of Aubellekh.

Ardof Zaom-Zinemog *(M) ARD-of ZAH-om ZEE-neh-mog*
A ranger informant who frequents Brimstowne to gather information.

Aurélien Knivlar *(F) aw-REH-lee-en knee-VLAR*
Shaman in Fjorna's arbalister squad. Commands two magpie heralds,
Aness and Islav.

Aurgushem *(M) OUR-goo-shem*
Vicar at the Harrowdale Temple in Withervale.

Bahimir *(M) bah-he-MERE*
Alaia's supervisor at the Withervale coal mines.

Baldo of Barsubia *(M) BAHl-doh of bar-SOO-bee-ah*
Negian survivor inside the Heartpine Dome.

Balstei Woodslav *(M) BAHLL-stay WOOD-slav*
An artificer who studies the aetheric elements.

Banook *(M) bah-NOOK*
A mountain of a man who lives alone in the mountains.

Bear *(M) bear*
Lago's mostly mutt, barely shepherd dog.

Behler Broadleaf *(M) BEH-lehr BROAD-leaf*
General of the Fifth Legion of the Negian Empire. Snub-nosed.

Bonmei *(M) BON-may*
Heir to Agnargsilv. Son of Mawua, grandson of Sontai. Ockam's adoptive son.

Borris *(M) BOH-rrihs*
Lago's classmate. Portly bully.

Brahm *(M) braam*
Silvan guard at Thornridge.

Corben Holt *(M) CORE-ben holt*
Crysta's youngest son. Works at the shipyard and sails a catamaran.

Crescu Valaran *(M) KREHS-coo VAH-lah-ran*
Armsmaster in Fjorna's arbalister squad.

Crysta Holt *(F) CHRIS-tuh holt*
Lago's professor. Works at the Mesa Observatory. Secretly works for the Zovarian military.

Deon *(M) DEE-on*
Fat kid who goes to Lago's school. Dated Lago on and off.

Dooncam *(M) DUNE-cam*
Alaia's friend from the Withervale coal mines. Ebaja's brother.

Dravéll *(M) drah-VEHLL*
Character in the Barlum Saga. Main hero.

Ebaja *(F) eh-BAH-ja*
Alaia's friend from the Withervale coal mines. Dooncam's sister.

Edmar Helm *(M)*
General of the First Legion of the Negian Empire.

Esum *(F) EH-soom*
Havengall monk who works with the sunnograph.

Fjorna Daro *(F) FYOR-nah DAHR-oh*
Chief Arbalister from a specialist squad of the Negian Empire.

Frud *(M) frood*
Bear from the Stelm Wujann. Sabikh's cub. Also a Barlum Saga character.

Gaönir-Bijeor - *gah-OH-neer BEE-jeh-or*
"Shield of Creation." Takhísh's legendary shield.

Gino Baneras *(M) GEE-no bah-NEH-rahs*
General of the Fourth Legion of the Negian Empire. Longbowman.

Grunnel - *GRUN-el*
Square-shaped coins from the Graalman Horde.

Gweshkamir *(M) WESH-kah-mere*
Prophet. Writer of the Takh Codex.

Gwil *(M) gwill*
Chaplain at the Withervale chapter of the Havengall Congregation.

Gwoli *(M) WOH-lee*
"Younger brother" in Oldrin. Pet name Alaia has for Lago.

Hanno Uzenzo *(M) HA-noh OO-zen-zoh*
Consul. Trade representative for the Negian Empire in Withervale.

Hefra Boarmane *(F) HEH-fruh BOAR-main*
Naturalist who specializes in ornithology and entomology.

Holfster *(A) HOLEf-str*
Botanist from Bauram. Has a nursery in Withervale.

Ilaadrid Shard - *ee-LAH-drihd shard*
The beacon that shines on Sceres's face twice a month.

Ishkembor *(M) ISH-kehm-bore*
Character in the Barlum Saga. Dravéll's best friend.

Iskimesh *(F) IS-key-mesh*
Enchantress. Third planet from Sunnokh.

Islav *(M) IZ-lahv*
One of Aurélien's magpie heralds.

Jaxon Remon *(M) JACK-son REE-mon*
General of the Third Legion of the Negian Empire. Missing his left arm.

Jiara Ascura *(F) gee-AH-rah as-COO-rah*
Platoon commander in the Free Tribelands.

Jilpi *(M) JILL-pee*
Old miner from Brimstowne who likes to soak in the hot springs.

Kedra *(F) KEH-drah*
Zovarian scout who works for Crysta.

Khaambe *(M) KHAAM-beh*
Banook's first human lover. Nifréne's brother. Arlu's son.

Khopto *(M) KHOP-toh*
Havengall monk who works with soot and specializes in "seeing the threads."

Khumen *(M) KHOO-men*
Dawn Pilgrim. First planet from Sunnokh.

Krujel - *CROO-jill*
Sixteen-sided coins from the Negian Empire.

Lago Vaari *(M) LAH-goh VAH-ree*
Young man from Withervale who by chance inherits Agnargsilv.

Lai-Nu *(F) lie noo*
Professor at the Yenmai Institute. Cosmologist, focuses on quaar and soot.

Leif - *LAY-f*
"Fang." Lago's dagger.

Maree Oda *(F) ma-REE OH-dah*
Seneschal of Withervale.

Mawua *(F) MAH-wah*
Bonmei's mother. Sontai's daughter. Tundra fox half-form.

Muriel Clawwick *(F) MEW-ree-el CLAW-wick*
Arbalister in Fjorna's squad. Waldomar's sister.

Noss *(A) noss*
Second planet from Sunnokh.

Ockam Radiartis *(M) OCK-uhm ra-dee-AR-tiss*
Sylvan Scout in the Free Tribelands. Bonmei's stepfather.

Ofréia-Nifréne *(F) oh-FRAY-ya nee-FREH-neh*
Urnaadifröa. Spectacled bear half-form. Arlu's daughter. Khaambe's sister.

Ongumar *(M) ON-goo-mar*
Amberlight. Fifth planet from Sunnokh.

Osef Windscar *(M) OW-sehf WIND-scar*
Arbalister in Fjorna's squad.

Pellámbri *(F) peh-LUHM-bree*
The Lodestar. A pink nebula at the heart of the Sword of Zeiheim.

Penli *(M) PEN-lee*
Lago's Jabrak–Tsing classmate.

Pian–Thi *(F) pee-an TEA*
Empress of the Tsing Empire.

Pliwe *(F) PLEA-weh*
Oldrin deity with three horns.

Quggon - *KYOO-gone*
A cube made of 9 chips that add up to a value of one hundred Qupi.

Qupi - *KYOO-pee*
Chevron-shaped chips used as currency units.

Red Stag *(M) red stag*
Negian monarch.

Rowan Holt *(M) ROW-uhn holt*
Crysta's husband.

Sabikh *(F) sah-BEE-kh*
Bear from the Stelm Wujann. Frud's mother. Barlum Saga character.

Sceres *(F) SEH-rehs*
Noss's moon.

Senstrell *(F) SENS-trell*
"Obsidian." Fourth planet from Sunnokh.

Shea Lu *(F) SHEH-ah loo*
Arbalister in Fjorna's squad.

Sontai *(F) SON-tie*
Bonmei's grandmother. Gives Agnargsilv to Lago. Gray fox half-form.

Sterjall *(M) STARE-jahl*
Translates to "star-heart" in Miscamish.

Sunnokh *(M) SOO-noh-kh*
"Sky-flame." The sun.

Sword of Zeiheim - *ZEI-hime*
Legendary weapon crafted of lightning. Also a constellation.

Takhamún *(M) ta-kha-MOON*
The Unmaker, god of destruction from the Takh Codex.

Takhísh *(M) ta-KHEE-sh*
The Demiurge, god of creation from the Takh Codex.

Tor-Reveo - *tore REH-vee-oh*
"Spear of Undoing." Takhamún's legendary spear.

Trevin Gobbar *(M) TREH-vinn GOH-bar*
Arbalister in Fjorna's squad. Long nose.

Umbaarlis *(M) oom-BAR-lihs*
Shaman from the Barlum Saga with a staff that holds the universe in place.

Urcai *(M) OOR-ky*
Crafty artificer from the Negian Empire.

Uvon dus Grei *(M) OO-von doos gray*
Young emperor of the Negian Empire. Son of Grei dus Gauno.

Wailen *(M) WAY-lehn*
Lago's classmate. Bully.

Waldomar Clawwick *(M) WAHL-doh-mar CLAW-wick*
Arbalister in Fjorna's squad. Muriel's brother.

Yaumenn *(A) YAW-men*
Demigod whose red hands absorb life.

Yza *(F) IT-suh*
Demigoddess whose shade blesses all it touches.

Locations

Afhora, Kingdom of - *ah-FOR-uh*
One of the sixteen realms. Its capital is Sundhollow.

Agnargdrolom - *AG-narg-droh-lom*
Heartpine Dome. Located between the Free Tribelands and the Negian Empire.

Allathanathar - *ala-THA-na-thar*
Capital of the Kingdom of Bauram.

Anglass - *AN-glass*
Negian fortress on the south-east perimeter of the Anglass Dome.

Anglass Dome - *AN-glass*
Urgdrolom. Dome in the Negian Empire, wrapped by the Stiss Malpa.

Archstone Dome
Almeldrolom. Dome located between Dorhond Tribes and Graalman Horde.

Ash Sea
"White Sea." Northern sea teeming with icebergs.

Ashen Dome
Trommodrolom. Dome located in the southern Tsing Empire, with a top that constantly smokes.

Azash - *ah-ZAH-sh*
Capital of the Elmaren Queendom.

Azurean Dome - *ah-ZUR-ean*
Quajudrolom. Dome located in the blue sands of the Kingdom of Bauram.

Bauram, Kingdom of - *bau-RAHM*
One of the sixteen realms. Its capital is Allathanathar.

Bayanhong Tribes - *BAH-jann-hong*
One of the sixteen realms. Its capital is On Khurderen.

Baysea Beyenaar - *BAY-eh-nahr*
Often frozen bay in the Khaar Du territories.

Bergsulf - *BERG-sulf*
Land of independent colonies in the Unclaimed Territories, north of the Fractured Range.

Bighorn Dome
Rilgdrolom. Dome located between the peaks of the Stelm Rilgéreo and Stelm Rilganesh.

Brasha'in Scablands - *brah-sha-'EEN*
Volcanic wasteland in the western Zovarian Union.

Brimstowne - *BRIMs-town*
Mining frontier town in an independent Bergsulfi colony by the Stelm Wujann.

Cairngorm Strait
Narrow passage of the Ophidian Sea between the Loorian Continent and the Yenwu Peninsula.

Capricious Ocean
Southernmost of the four oceans, known for its unpredictable waters.

Cobalt Desert
Expansive desert of blue, black, and purple sands in Fel Baubór.

Corundum Monolith
Enormous crystal worshipped by the Khaar Du.

Da'áju Caldera - *da-'AH-joo*
Vast, static cirque glacier in the Stelm Wujann.

Dathereol Princedom - *dah-THEE-ree-ol*
One of the sixteen realms. Its capital is Therimark.

Dimbali - *dim-BAH-lee*
Negian city on the Topaz Beck.

Doralghon - *DOH-ralg-hone*
Capital of the Graalman Horde.

Dorhond Tribes - *DOOR-hund*
One of the sixteen realms. Its capital is Oskirin.

Dormendal - *DOOR-mend-al*
Negian city west of the Anglass Dome, with a port on the Stiss Minn.

Drann Trodesh - *drahn TROH-desh*
Sawtoothed mountains wrapping around Unemar Lake.

Druhal - *droo-HAL*
Capital of the Wastyr Triumvirate. One of three.

Elanúbril - *ella-NOO-breel*
Capital of the Khaar Du Tribes.

Elmaren Queendom - *EL-ma-ren*
One of the sixteen realms. Its capital is Azash.

Emen Ruins - *EH-men*
Dorvauros ruins with hot springs resting within a lava tube.

Esduss Sea - *ES-doos*
Sea separating Fel Baubór from the Loorian mainland.

Eyes of the Great Spider
Range of craters west of Baysea Beyenaar worshipped by the Khaar Du.

Falbagrish Range - *FAHL-bah-grish*
Prominent sierras in the Dathereol Princedom.

Farjall - *FAR-jall*
Negian fortress on the south-east perimeter of the Heartpine Dome.

Farkhalum - *far-KHA-loom*
Capital of the Wastyr Triumvirate. One of three.

Farsúksuwikh - *far-SOOK-soo-wee-kh*
Free Tribelands city on the eastern shores of the Klad Senet.

Farsulf Forest - *far-SOOLF*
"Pine Land." Forest north of the Heartpine Dome, south of the Stelm Ca'éli.

Fel Baubór - *fell bau-BORE*
Continent-sized island of blue sands, mostly of the Kingdom of Bauram.

Fel Varanus - *fell VAH-rah-noose*
Zovarian island on which the Varanus Dome spreads its tendrils.

Firefalls
"Minnelvad." Steaming waterfalls in the Stelm Wujann, northwest of Brimstowne.

Fjarmallen Peninsula - *fee-ar-MAH-lehn*
Loosely inhabited lands on the fast southwest of the Dathereol Princedom.

Fjordlands Dome
Nagradrolom. Located between the Zovarian Union and Khaar Du Tribes.

Fjordsulf - *FJORD-soolf*
Cold land of fjords and icebergs of the Khaar Du Tribes.

Flasketh Mesa - *FLASK-eth*
Lookout mesa south of Thornridge, at the edges of the Heartpine Dome.

Fractured Range
Old lakebed that crackled into massive slot canyons as it dried out, east of the Stelm Khull.

Free Tribelands
One of the sixteen realms. Its capital is Klemes.

Graalman Horde - *GROWL-mahn*
One of the sixteen realms. Its capital is Doralghon.

Gulf of Erjilm - *ERR-juhlm*
Circular gulf at the split between the two great continents.

Hashan - *ha-SHUN*
Capital of the Tsing Empire. Also called the "City of Bridges."

Heartpine Dome
Agnargdrolom. Dome located between the Free Tribelands and Negian Empire.

Hestfell - *HEST-fell*
Capital of the Negian Empire.

Illenev - *EE-leh-nehv*
Capital of the Wastyr Triumvirate. One of three.

Isdinnklad - *IS-dihn-clad*
"Sea Lake." Long, tapering sea splitting the Loorian Continent.

Jerjan Continent - *JER-jann*
Named after Laaja Jerja, tallest peak at 38,264 feet.

Karst Forest
Forest south of the Moordusk Dome.

Khaar Du Tribes - *khar doo*
One of the sixteen realms. Its capital is Elanúbril.

Khaar Du Wastes - *khar doo*
Icy wastelands of the north.

Khaarkadesh - *KHAR-cah-desh*
"Stone Road" in the Khaar Du tongue. Glacier valley in the northern Stelm Wujann.

Kilkarag Peninsula - *KILL-cah-rahg*
Southwestern peninsula of the Jerjan Continent, by the Ashen Dome.

Kingroot Woods
Wild woods east of the Heartpine Dome.

Klad Mahujann - *clad MA-hoo-jann*
"Very Icy Lake." Perpetually frozen lake between the Stelm Nedross and Stelm Wujann.

Klad Senet - *clad senate*
Largest lake in the Loorian Continent, at the heart of the Free Tribelands.

Klemes - *CLEM-uhs*
Capital of the Free Tribelands, west of the Klad Senet.

Knife Point
Sharp peak cutting through the northwest walls of the Heartpine Dome.

Laaja Jerja - *LA-AH-jah JIR-jah*
Volcano. Tallest peak of the Jerjan Continent at 38,264 feet.

Laaja Khem - *LA-AH-jah khem*
Volcano northwest of the Da'áju Caldera with old Dorvauros mines tunneling through it.

Laaja Khenukh - *LA-AH-jah KHEH-nookh*
Volcano on the eastern edge of the Brasha'in Scablands.

Lamanni - *la-MA-nee*
Negian City. Main Negian road also named after it.

Lequa Dome - *LEH-kwa*
Krostdrolom. Dome located in the eastern Negian Empire, by Bayanhong settlements.

Lequa Sea - *LEH-kwa*
Northeastern sea that funnels into the Ophidian. Dome is named after it.

Lerev, Republic of - *luh-REHV*
One of the sixteen realms. Its capital is Normouth.

Loompool - *LOOM-pool*
Bayanhong settlement east of the Lequa Dome.

Loorian Continent - *LOO-ree-anne*
Named after Mount Loor, tallest peak at 35,167 feet.

Lurr's Abyss - *LOO-rr*
Wasteland in the Stelm Khull, north of the Anglass Dome.

Maankel - *MA-an-kel*
Free Tribelands city in the Mugwort Forest. Has a prison.

Minnelvad - *ME-nell-vahd*
"Firefalls." Steaming waterfalls in the Stelm Wujann, northwest of Brimstowne.

Mireinfield - *ME-reign-field*
Bayanhong settlement southeast of the Lequa Dome.

Moonrise Dome
Gwonledrolom. Dome located in the far east, in the Elmaren Queendom.

Moordusk Dome
Mindreldrolom. Dome located in the Zovarian Union, near Zovaria.

Mount Loor - *lure*
Tallest peak of the Loorian Continent at 35,167 feet.

Mugwort Forest
Largest forest in the Free Tribelands.

Needlecove
Small Zovarian town close to the Northlock Strait. Known for its chalk promontories.

Negian Empire - *NEE-jann*
One of the sixteen realms. Its capital is Hestfell.

New Karst
Zovarian city on the Old Pilgrim's Road.

Ninn Tago - *nihn TAH-goh*
"Gray Pass." Old road cutting over the Stelm Ca'éli, connecting Withervale to Knife Point.

Nisos Dome - *NY-sus*
Okridrolom. Dome located in the Republic of Lerev, in Fel Nisos.

Nool - *nool*
Negian city close to Withervale.

Normouth - *NOR-muth*
Capital of the Republic of Lerev.

Northlock Strait
Narrow passage separating the Isdinnklad Sea from the Isdinnklad Lake.

Old Karst
Zovarian city on the Old Pilgrim's Road.

Old Pilgrim's Road
Longest road in the Loorian Continent. Runs from Umarion to Wyrmwash.

On Khurderen - *on khur-DEH-rehn*
Capital of the Bayanhong Tribes.

Ophidian Sea
Snaking sea separating the Loorian and Jerjan continents.

Oskirin - *OSS-kih-ruhn*
Capital of the Dorhond Tribes.

Quiescent Ocean
Westernmost of the four oceans, known for its calm waters.

Sajal Crater - *SAH-jall*
Round crater in the volcanic Stelm Sajal. Known for its warm waters.

Scoria Dome
Balastdrolom. Dome between Afhoran, Tharman, and Graalman lands.

Seafaring Dome
Amá'adrolom. Dome located in the Capricious Ocean, locked to an atoll.

Shaderift Aqueduct
Conduit built to carry water from the Klad Enturg to Shaderift.

Sharr Helm - *shahr helm*
Capital of the Tharma Federation.

Silverkeep
Silver mines near Brimstowne.

Silverkeep Road
Road that runs from Nool, to Brimstowne, continuing north into the Silverkeep mines.

Snoring Mountain
Peak in the Stelm Wujann that tends to tremble unpredictably.

Stelm Bir - *stelm beer*
"Home Mountain." Central peak inside the Heartpine Dome.

Stelm Ca'éli - *stelm cah-'EH-lee*
"Pilgrim Sierras." Range that separates the Zovarian Union and Free Tribelands.

Stelm Khull - *stelm khool*
"Graveyard Mountains." Range extending east from the Stelm Wujann.

Stelm Sajal - *stelm SAH-jall*
"Foreboding Mountains." Volcanic range east of the Brasha'in Scablands.

Stelm Tai-Du - *stelm tai-DOO*
"Night-Snow Mountains." Range north of the Tarpits Dome.

Stelm Wujann - *stelm WOO-jann*
"Icy Mountains." Vast sierras in the northern Loorian Continent.

Steps of Odrásmunn - *oh-DRAS-moon*
Columnar basalt formation on the northern edge of the Brasha'in Scablands.

Stiss Khull - *stiss khool*
"Graveyard River." Glacier-fed river extending east from the Stelm Wujann.

Stiss Malpa - *stiss MAHL-pah*
River that empties into the tip of the Isdinnklad Lake, right at Withervale.

Stiss Minn - *stiss mihn*
Tributary of the Stiss Malpa that starts at the Firefalls.

Sulphur Pit
Sulphur mines west of Brimstowne.

Sundhollow - *SUHND-hollow*
Capital of the Kingdom of Afhora.

Tarpits Dome
Hoombudrolom. Dome located in the Tsing Empire, by the Khonn Tar Pits.

Telm Klannath - *telm CLAH-nuth*
"Northern Valley." Valley with many rivers that feed the Stiss Khull.

Teslurkath - *TESS-lure-cath*
Iceberg-covered shores on the frigid, northwestern frontiers of Noss.

Tharma Federation - *THAHR-mah*
One of the sixteen realms. Its capital is Sharr Helm.

Therimark - *THEH-ree-mark*
Capital of the Dathereol Princedom.

Thornridge Lookout
Free Tribelands fortress protecting the perimeter road of the Heartpine Dome.

Topaz Beck
Wide river that enters the Heartpine Dome on the north and exits again on the south.

Tsing Empire - *zing*
One of the sixteen realms. Its capital is Hashan.

Tumultuous Ocean
Easternmost of the four oceans, known for its rough waters.

Udarbans Forest - *OO-dar-bans*
Uninhabited forest southwest of the Brasha'in Scablands.

Umarion - *oo-MA-ree-on*
Far western Zovarian city at the end of the Old Pilgrim's Road.

Unclaimed Territories
Areas not claimed by any of the sixteen realms.

Unemar Lake - *OO-neh-mar*
Placid lake surrounded by the five peaks of Drann Trodesh.

Unthawing Ocean
Northernmost of the four oceans, known for its icesheets and icebergs.

Varanus Dome - *VAH-rah-noose*
Kruwendrolom. Dome located in Fel Varanus, a far western island of the Zovarian Union.

Wastyr Triumvirate - *was-TIER*
One of the sixteen realms. Its capital is Illenev.

White Desert
Expansive desert of white sands speckled with Dorhond temples.

Withervale
Easternmost Zovarian city, on the border with the Negian Empire.

Wyrmwash
Negian port city at the mouth of the Stiss Negii.

Yenmai - *YEN-my*
Capital of the Yenwu State.

Yenwu Dome - *YEN-woo*
Kroowindrolom. Dome located in the Yenwu Peninsula.

Yenwu State - *YEN-woo*
One of the sixteen realms. Its capital is Yenmai.

Zovaria - *zoh-VEH-ree-uh*
Capital of the Zovarian Union.

Zovarian Union - *zoh-VEH-ree-uhn*
One of the sixteen realms. Its capital is Zovaria.

Calendar, Seasons, Months, Epochs, Holidays

In Noss's calendar, the year has 360 days, with one leap day added every 8 years at the beginning of the new year, called the *Day of the Lost.*

Months

1	Frostburn	7	Highsun
2	Mudfront	8	Harvestlight
3	Cloudpour	9	Fireleaf
4	Lustbloom	10	Dewrest
5	Pondsong	11	Fogdawn
6	Dustwind	12	Hoartide

Seasons

Winter - Tourmaline - Pink
Thawing - Pearl - White
Spring - Obsidian - Black
Summer - Sulphur - Yellow
Autumn - Amethyst - Purple
Umbra - Jade – Green

Days of the Week

1 - **Moonday** (for the moon, Sceres)
2 - **Khuday** (for the Dawn Pilgrim, Khumen)
3 - **Nossday** (for Noss)
4 - **Iskimday** (for the Enchantress, Iskimesh)
5 - **Onguday** (for Amberlight, Ongumar)
6 - **Sunnday** (for the sun, Sunnokh - pronounced SOON-day)

Epochs

Gestation	before -100,000 B.D.
Expansion	-100,000 B.D. to -10,000 B.D.
Revelation	-10,000 B.D. to -8003 B.D.
Unification	-8003 B.D. to -5177 B.D.
Equilibrium	-5177 B.D. to -556 B.D.
Segregation	-556 B.D. to 0
Downfall	1 A.D. to 200 A.D.
Reconstitution	200 A.D. to 1135 A.D.
Conquest	1135 A.D. to current

Holidays

(0/0) Leap day between Hoartide and Frostburn. Happens every 8 years.
Day of the Lost (most realms)
Forgotten Hours (Puqua)
Season of Promise or "Stammarg ust Baaf" (Laatu)

1/1 - First of Frostburn
Day of Renewal

3/15 - Fifteenth of Cloudpour
Thawing Equinox

6/15 - Fifteenth of Dustwind
Summer Solstice

8/1 - First of Harvestlight
Feast of Plenitude

8/2 - Second of Harvestlight
Vigil of the Famished

9/15 - Fifteenth of Fireleaf
Autumn Equinox

12/15 - Fifteenth of Hoartide
Winter Solstice

Units of Measurement

Units in the world of Noss are similar to those we are used to, but not exactly the same. Here is a list of the most common units used.

Time
Heartbeat, or beat = about 1 second
Breath = 8 heartbeats
Moment = 8 breaths = 64 heartbeats (about 1 minute)
Wick = 16 moments (a quarter hour)
Hour = 4 wicks = 64 moments
Day = 32 hours
Week = 6 days
Month = 30 days
Lunar cycle = 36 days
Year = 360 days

Distance
Hairbreadth = to measure something very tiny
Fingerbreadth = 64 hairbreadths (about 1 inch)
Handbreadth = 4 fingerbreadths (width of knuckles, pinky to index)
Handspan = 2 handbreadths = 8 fingerbreadths (from wrist to tips)
Foot = 16 fingerbreadths (about 12 inches)
Stride = 5 feet
Mile = 1,000 strides = 5,000 feet
League = 3 miles (nautical use only)
Orbit = average distance from Sunnokh to Noss (about one AU)
Starmile = distance from Sunnokh to Metheglin, the nearest star
(about one lightyear)

WEIGHT

Bit = weight of one Lode (about 5 grams)
Chip = 4 bits (weight of a Qupi chip, about 20 grams)
Cube = 10 chips (weight of a Quggon, about 200 grams)
Ingot = 25 cubes (weight of a magnium-steel ingot, about 5 kilograms)
Barrel = 20 ingots = 500 cubes (weight of a barrel of flour, about 100 kg)
Ton = 10 barrels (about 1,000 kilograms)

VOLUME

Thimble = about 32 milliliters or 1 fluid ounce
Mug = 16 thimbles (about half a liter)
Tankard = 2 mugs = 32 thimbles
Gallon = 8 tankards = 16 mugs (equivalent to our gallons)
Hogshead = 64 gallons (about a barrel)
Cask = 4 hogsheads = 256 gallons

CURRENCY

Lode = 0.1 (lead)
Qupi = 1 (steel)
Hand = 5 (chromium)
Cup = 10 (copper)
Horn = 20 (brass)
Hex = 60 (cobalt)
Quggon = 100 (1 Hex, 1 Horn, 1 Cup, 1 Hand, and 5 Qupis assembled into a cube)

VANITY CURRENCY (NOT IN COMMON CIRCULATION)

Diadem = 150 (silver)
Anvil = 300 (titanium)
Bolt = 600 (platinum)
Crown = 2,000 (gold)
Gauntlet = 5,000 (palladium)
Qubex = 10,000 (1 Gauntlet, 1 Crown, 1 Bolt, 1 Anvil, and 5 Diadems assembled into a cube)

The complex alloys in vanity currencies imbue the chips with marbled or striped patterns, unlike the solid colors of regular Qupi chips.

Acknowledgments

I find it strange to write an acknowledgments section for Book 1 of a six-book series, knowing that it should also stand for the next five books I wrote simultaneously. Some names (such as those of my generous beta readers) will change from book to book, but most of the thanks I want to give are to the same people and groups. So let the core of these acknowledgments stand sixfold, for each of the volumes of the *Noss Saga*.

I was spoiled by my parents, Angélica Delgado and Juan Carlos Baldwin. They would let me buy any book I wanted, encouraging me to devour Bradbury, Sagan, Tolkien, Allende, Márquez, Vasconcelos, Gaiman, Asimov, Borges, and so much more. All my passions sprout from their unrelenting support—it is all their fault. Gracias, a él y ella.

Writing can be a lonesome endeavor, but I had my husband, Timothy, always here beside me, to whom I could blabber incoherent thoughts at random intervals, like a bouncing board for spittle and nonsense. Too many of the best ideas for this saga came from me spouting something massively stupid, only to hear him correct me or point out a different route I had not the foresight to envision.

Awfully prematurely, when I was merely in the planning stages of the first book, I had begun to envision the covers. Since the very start I knew I wanted Ilse Gort to lend her skillful hands for the illustrations. I was terrified to ask for her help. I was so happy when she said yes, and happier still when she proposed ideas that were much better than my own.

My editor, Andrew Corvin, was instrumental in fixing up my messes with a barrage of thoughtful suggestions. His notes were not just simple grammar and typo corrections, but offered insights on the characters' motivations, flow of sentences, word choice, and even broader story notes that truly helped focus the work and keep the voice consistent.

I had the luck to count with a thoughtful and diverse group of beta readers, who gave me a ton of notes to work with. Thank you for believing in me and for offering your help—this book is far better thanks to you, Abs M Rice, Alejandro Renteria, Alex Mui, Amanda Leigh, Angie Lee Camp, Arthur Huang, BirdsongChoir, Blackquill, Brian Jackson, Carlos A. Luna Aranguré, Charlie McGrew, Conor Davitt, Cosmo, David "Professor Jefe" Jones, Edwin Herrell, Elliot D. Brown, Fana', FFAT, Franz Anthony, Jack Sanderson, Jul, Louis D.S, Marián Sulák, Markus Lundberg, Marston Jones, Matthew Green, Max Sjöblom, Miguel Ángel García García, Nora Rogers, North, Reverie Benedetto, Rosalea Barker, Ross Blocher, Rourkie, Sandra Malpica, Santi Rowe, Sean Wenzel, Shadow Worfu, Skiriki, Streuhund, Ted Sawyer, Tiberius Rings, Timothy Dahlum, Victor Hugo Guadagnin, and a couple of anons.

One thing I never lacked during this process was encouragement. As an introvert, having a community I can count on online has been a true blessing. I truly appreciate everyone in social media who has been hitting little heart icons to trigger tiny releases of dopamine in my brain. In particular, thank you to my fervent furry following, who taught me to be courageous enough to be myself, to write a story that speaks my truth. You inspire me.

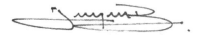

ABOUT THE AUTHOR

Joaquín Baldwin was born in Paraguay, where he first found his love of books by picking up every volume by Ray Bradbury he could get his hands on, and then by submerging himself into a single-bound copy of the Lord of the Rings trilogy—but it wasn't until much later that he'd acquire a taste for writing.

At age 19, he moved to the US to study film and animation, where he received a BFA from CCAD and an MFA from UCLA. He was the recipient of a full scholarship from the Jack Kent Cooke Foundation.

His short films have won over 100 awards and honors at festivals and competitions such as Cannes, the Student Academy Awards, Cinequest, and USA Film Festival. Soon after receiving his masters, he began working at the Walt Disney Animation Studios as a CG Layout Artist, and later as a Director of Cinematography, working on films such as Zootopia, Encanto, Wreck-It Ralph, Frozen, Raya, and Moana.

Never content with sticking to his lane, Joaquín has experience as a professional photographer, illustrator, comic artist, web designer, and 3D designer. His varied skillset came in handy when developing his fantasy saga, allowing him to create his own illustrations, maps, 3D models, book covers, website, and even his own language (phonetics, runes, and all).

Since the 2020 pandemic hit, he's been spending every second of his free time forging the complex world of Noss.

Sign up to Joaquín's mailing list:
JoaquinBaldwin.com/list

Connect with Joaquín on social media:
Search for @joabaldwin to find him on most sites, such as Bluesky, Mastodon, Facebook, Twitter, and Instagram.

Printed in the USA
CPSIA information can be obtained
at www.ICGtesting.com
LVHW090745091023
760559LV00015B/42/J